"POWERBORN"

Book One of the Zarryiostrom

A Novel by Nene Tina Thomas

and

Steven Christian Plagman

POWERBORN

Book One of the Zarryiostrom
First U.S. Paperback Edition

Nene Thomas Incorporated / July 2013

Published by
Nene Thomas Incorporated

First Hardback Edition Published 2011
First Paperback Edition Published 2013

Printed in the United States of America

Story by Nene Tina Thomas and Steven Christian Plagman
Cover Art and Interior Illustrations by Nene Thomas

ISBN 978-0-9851204-3-6

Please visit our website at
nenethomas.com

For Tina Antoinette Thomas
Both the 17-year-old girl sitting at the back of her school bus,
dreaming of *The Key to War*;
And the extraordinarily beautiful and talented woman
she grew up to become.
A labor of love is no labor at all.

~and~

For David and Sharon Weber
Your friendship and encouragement mean the world to us.

BOOKS OF THE ZARRYIOSTROM

Powerborn
Usurper
Marionette (Coming Soon)
Warlord (Coming Soon)

Introduction

Greetings, reader! What you are holding in your hand right now is the revised edition of "Powerborn: Book One of the Zarryiostrom." The first limited edition hardback was released in August 2011, and we quickly learned there were some problems with it. Despite endless hours of reading, rewriting, and editing, several errors made it through to the finished product. So, we're taking the opportunity to fix a few of the problems, as well as adding a couple scenes that weren't in the original version. Nevertheless, the story remains the same, despite our tinkering.

One of the primary criticisms Nene and I receive about this series is that some of the characters' names are extremely hard to pronounce. This was a deliberate choice on our part, and I thought I should take a moment to explain the reasoning behind the confusing names.

In "The Zarryiostrom", we deal with two races that enjoy extremely long lifespans, and in two cases, outright immortality: the Fae, and the Dragon Witches. Characters from these races are the source of all of the weird names, because many of them were born in an earlier era than the main storyline takes place. Most of them have survived for thousands of years, and to them, their names are not weird or unpronounceable at all. Zarryiosiad is the perfect example. The name looks confusing in print, and you may wonder why I would want to give her such a strange name, but it's no stranger than, say, Hammurabi, Methuselah, Nebuchadnezzar, or Gilgamesh would have been. 3,000 years ago, hearing names like those would most likely have been the same as hearing "Harry, Matt, Chad, and Gilbert".

Seasons change, and naming trends change with them, and let's face it, who really wants to spell out Nebuchadnezzar every day at school? But what if you are immortal? Do you change your name every few hundred years to keep up with current trends? Or do you keep the name you were born with, as a reminder of who and what you are?

The primary setting of "The Zarryiostrom" is a fantasy version of an early Renaissance period, but characters like Zarryiosiad would have been born in an alternate version of Babylon or ancient Egypt, or in the case of Severius and Severeielle, early Rome. They have survived for thousands of years, and would still bear the names they were born with. Younger characters would have names more appropriate to the time, such as Prudence or Deirdre, of course, but the immortal characters would not.

Luckily, in our story there are only a few characters with impossible names, and for the most part they are Dragon Witches. Draconic names have a long history in fiction of being nearly impossible to pronounce. For every "Smaug" or "Fafnir", there is an "Ingeloakastimizilian" (from R.A. Salvatore's "the Crystal Shard"—my personal favorite name!), "Ancalagon the Black" (from Tolkien—another favorite!), "Vermithrax Pejorative" (from the movie "Dragonslayer"), or Jormungandr (from Norse mythology). I could have named Astranaithes something like "Astra", or Furionchires "Fury", but dragons are supposed to be proud creatures with proud names. "Cass" is a great nickname, but would a dragon named "Cassiramaithris" settle for hearing that? Or would she consider such a pale name to be insulting?

Nevertheless, that leaves me with something of a dilemma. I can't ignore the fact that people find the names almost impossible to pronounce, nor will I change the names to make them less confusing. So, I decided on a third path. If the names of the characters are giving you trouble, I made a video of me reading the names from the glossary aloud, so you can see how they are spelled, and hear how they are pronounced. I hope that helps to alleviate the confusion, and I'm confident that once you hear the names, you will find them to be very pleasant to the ear.

You can find the video on the Zarryiostrom fan page on Facebook, at
www.facebook.com/Zarryiostrom

or on Youtube, at
http://www.youtube.com/watch?v=7m8DK1UNwPA

We do have a favor to ask of you. Nene and I decided to take a non-traditional path when we self-published this novel, and because of that, we desperately need your help. If you enjoy this book, tell someone about it! The only way the Zarryiostrom will ever truly become successful, is if you, the fans, spread the word about it. When the series is complete there will be nine books in total, and at the time I am writing this note, the second book in the series, *Usurper,* has already been printed, the third, *Marionette,* is waiting to be printed, and I'm 33% of the way done with *Warlord,* book four. So, please, if you enjoyed reading this book, tell your friends about it. Every fan we add along the way makes it easier for us to get the rest of the books finished. And if you have a question for either Nene or me about this series, join us on the Zarryiostrom Fan Page on Facebook. I go there every day, and I answer every question I'm asked. Thank you, and enjoy the story!

Steven C. Plagman
26 June 2013

The Song of the Two

Black as to white, or many to none,
One as the moon, the other the sun.
Command of all things in nature enjoy
But one to defend, the other destroy.
Two names will be written in blood and in bone,
Two lives will be entwined in power and throne
By fire and water, by mountain and storm
Creation itself will be theirs to reform
But paradise one in its image will make,
The other the world in its vengeance will break
Light as to dark, or master to slave
Life as to death, or cradle to grave

Dakkadia
D'arhak
Khad'deia
D'arhak
Laha' Knohs
Gray River
Fae and Elf
Lands
Palantine
Rohm
Fishing Village
Saerce
Teeth of Amhar
Illymar
Ithram
Illymaine
Skye
Badlands
To the
Grave of the Lyx
Silk Road
Shahalizaar
Zarus River
Ferralin

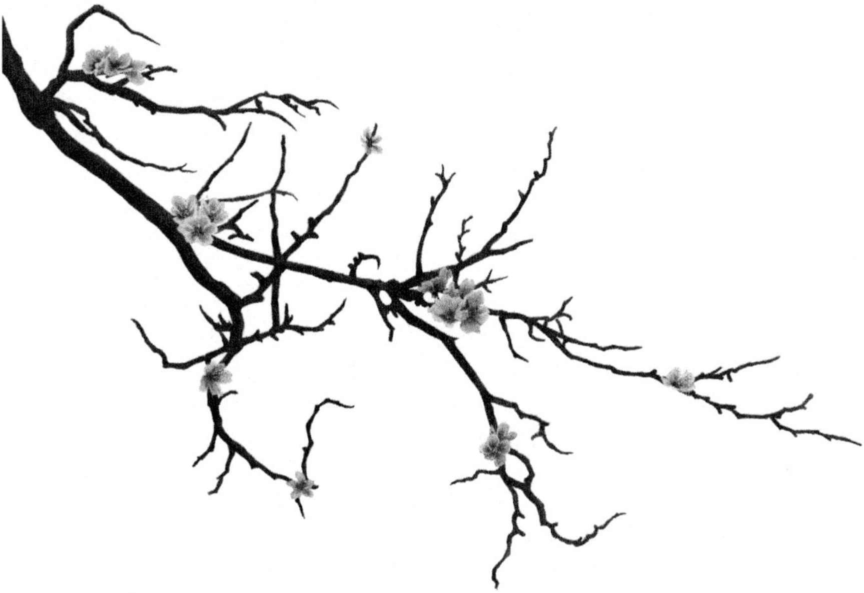

PROLOGUE

"Sacrifice"

On a hill overlooking a narrow valley, a woman watched a battle being fought below her. From her elevated vantage point, she could see hundreds of thousands of soldiers fighting and dying, in a futile attempt to break a stalemate which had lasted for days. Despite the obvious desperation of everyone involved, the fighting showed no signs of abating. Amidst the wreckage of war machines and splintered chariots, the battlefield was littered with the bodies of the dead and dying. Each and every victim of the war lay where he or she had fallen, for there had been no truce, no abatement, no pause to give the living time to help the wounded or to mourn the dead. The soldiers on both sides had long since fought past the point of exhaustion, and now, only pure hatred and rage kept them moving at all.

A gust of wind blew her waist-length brown hair off of her shoulders, and swirled it wildly in front of her for a few moments, before it died away as suddenly as it had arisen. The movement of her hair revealed that the woman was not truly alone, for upon her shoulder stood a tiny dragon with scales the color of an emerald. The dragon's tail draped protectively around the woman's neck, though the comforting gesture seemed lost upon its companion.

Behind her, a shadow grew from the ground, rising up and coalescing into a doorway of nothingness. For a moment, the hilltop became bitterly cold as a second woman stepped out of the shadowgate, and it folded behind her like leathery wings, becoming more and more insubstantial, until fading completely away. The newcomer walked forward, a black dragon draped across her shoulders in much the same way the green dragon graced its companion's shoulder. After taking a step, the new arrivals stood unmoving, awaiting a signal that their presence was welcome on the lonely hilltop.

The green dragon turned to look at its guest, bowing its sinuous head in welcome, before returning its gaze to the battle. After a brief silence, the newcomer spoke.

"I have been observing the fighting for a while, and though I am no warrior, it is clear to me that the battle is turning against Zarryiosiad. It won't be long now, Astranaithes."

The auburn-haired woman nodded in agreement, though she didn't take her gaze from the battle. Instead, she raised a graceful hand and pointed at a spot on the battlefield.

"There. After nearly 400 years of warfare, the end is in sight. This will be the last battle between Zarryiosiad and the Lyx, and that is where our fates will be decided." Severeielle stepped forward to join Astranaithes, looking at the spot to which the woman had pointed: a seemingly random point in the swirling melee. To the dragon's sharp eyes, every detail of the battle could be seen even from such a great distance. Here and there, she could see a bloodstained banner fall to the ground, only to be trampled underfoot by the uncaring soldiers struggling to gain an advantage in the press of battle. At first, Severeielle couldn't see the importance of the spot to which Astranaithes had pointed, but a small clearing opened up in the battle lines—a brief respite in which a single figure stood out from the rest. Severeielle gasped in recognition, for she knew that figure well. Severius, her beloved twin brother, wearing heavy black armor and holding the immense black spear named *Death's Mistress*, stood defiantly in the middle of the battle line. She could see that both the spear he carried, and the black armor encasing him, were drenched in blood. The dragon around his shoulders roared a challenge at the lines of opposing soldiers and then the respite ended, and the press of bodies obscured him once again.

"What is he doing here, Astranaithes?" Severeielle demanded. "We agreed to have no part in this!"

The auburn-haired woman turned and looked at her companion. For a split second, as Astranaithes met her gaze, Severeielle glimpsed a sorrow so vast that it threatened to swallow her whole. But the sorrow was covered instantly, replaced by a stern, almost arrogant look that bespoke a wisdom Severeielle had yet to match.

"He is here because it is his duty; a duty he willingly embraced. He knows the world lies in balance, and that his actions today will either deliver us, or destroy us. With him, the world has a chance. Without him, all is lost. He made his choice."

"Why is he fighting with the Lyx? If he is so important to this battle, shouldn't he be fighting for Zarryiosiad? The Lyx are monsters!"

"Severius does not fight for either side, Severeielle," replied Astranaithes patiently. "He fights for life itself." At Severeielle's confused look, Astranaithes continued. "Zarryiosiad's army will lose this battle. She underestimated the desperation of the Lyx. All of them are here, from the greatest of their nobles, to the weakest of their Mages. Fear of Zarryiosiad has united them as they have never been united before." She shook her head in admiration. "It seems that despite their madness, even the Lyx can recognize destruction when they are faced with it. Now, they act against their nature in the name of self-preservation." Astranaithes reached up and stroked the green dragon's head. "If Severius had fought for Zarryiosiad, he would have simply been one more spear." She gestured at the battlefield. "As you can see, there are plenty here. One more spear fighting for her would make no difference."

"But how is his fighting for the Lyx any different? He's still just one more spear!"

"Watch and see."

"Will he survive?" Severeielle asked fearfully.

Astranaithes gave her companion a disapproving look.

"You know as well as I that such things are beyond our ability to predict. I do know this: *if* he survives, he will prevent calamity, but he will also pay a heavy price for his heroism. I told him as much long ago, and, even knowing this, Severius chose to come."

"A *heavy price*? Severius is a historian, not a warrior! He should be standing here with us, chronicling this battle, not *participating* in it! If anything happens to him, it will be on your head!" Her voice lowered to a deadly whisper. "If my brother falls, you will have made an enemy of me. You will learn why I am called the Queen of Shadows."

"I am sorry that we will be enemies, Severeielle, but that is unavoidable. If it brings you comfort, know that I do not believe your brother will fall in this battle. His fate is much, much worse than to merely die. And while it breaks my heart that the very best of our number must suffer so the rest of us might live, if he doesn't, the world will end today in fire and ash." Astranaithes met

Severeielle's gaze unflinchingly, challenging her to dispute her words, and in the end, it was Severeielle who turned away. Astranaithes returned to her quiet contemplation of the battle, and Severeielle reluctantly joined her.

The silence between the two women deepened, until several hours passed without a single word spoken by either of them. The bright light of the afternoon sun faded into the dimmer light of early evening, when suddenly, Astranaithes' eyes narrowed in anticipation. The movement, slight as it was, caught the attention of Severeielle immediately. The Queen of Shadows leaned forward and saw that the desperate soldiers of Il'Amhar, against whom Severius fought, had finally broken. Zarryiosiad's men threw down their weapons, too exhausted to either beg for mercy or flee, and as the center of their army collapsed, Severius' triumphant soldiers rapidly filled the gap and began rolling up the battle line. The stalemate had finally ended, and the rout had begun. Zarryiosiad's soldiers were being slaughtered, and they knew it.

Almost as suddenly as the battle line faltered, however, the army of Il'Amhar reacted. A gleaming spearhead of heavy cavalry charged into the breach, led by two glorious figures in shimmering armor; one male, and one female. At first, Severeielle thought Zarryiosiad herself was joining the battle, but a closer look quickly dispelled that belief as she suddenly recognized the Dragon Witch known as Furionchires, the Queen of Battles, charging into the fray. The warrior was a legend even amongst her own kind, for she was drawn to war as a moth to flame, and was always victorious in battle. The bright red of the tiny dragon riding upon her host's shoulder looked like a firebolt as she charged into the melee, and the unexpected reinforcements cut down the Lyxan slave-soldiers as if they were made of straw. The soldiers who had broken through the lines reeled back in shock and confusion at the fresh assault, and threatened to break completely at the furious counterattack, when a single figure stepped forward and bellowed out a challenge to the Queen of Battles. Severeielle knew without a doubt who had issued that challenge, and she hissed in pain as her fingernails dug deep furrows into the flesh of her arms, as fear for her brother's life overcame her cool reserve.

Furionchires, black hair flowing like a banner, turned in her saddle to see who had dared to challenge her. When she recognized her opponent, she eagerly turned her blood mare toward him. The horse reacted to its mistress' command, and the beast charged toward the lone figure at full gallop. The Queen of Battles held her slender sword straight in front of her like a lance, but Severius stood his ground. As the warhorse bore down upon him, Severeielle covered her mouth to stifle a scream of anguish.

The Queen of Shadows expected her brother to be overrun, but instead, the horse fell to the side screaming. It crashed to the ground, transfixed upon Severius' spear like a wild boar. The Queen of Battles fell forward off of her horse as her dragon took flight to protect itself. She tucked into a graceful ball that robbed the impact of its power, and rolled out of the crash without injury. As the woman stood once again, the dragon landed lightly on her shoulder, and both of them turned to face their opponent. Severius wrenched the spear from the still-screaming horse and readied himself for her charge. Both of their dragons hissed at each other as they circled, prepared to fight to the death.

Severius struck first, thrusting his spear forward in a powerful blow that Furionchires narrowly avoided by pirouetting to the side like a dancer. Halfway through the pirouette, her sword shot out in a move meant to decapitate him, but he ducked the strike easily, and turned his spear's momentum into an arc meant to disembowel her. She saw the strike coming, and had to divert her swing into a block that just barely deflected his cunning stroke. They backed away from each other, slowly looking weaknesses in their opponent's defenses. Severius kept his spear loose in his hands and the tip pointed directly at Furionchires' heart. The Queen of Battles charged again, and again Severius drove her back, but neither of them could find an opening in the other's guard.

Severeielle could tell that her brother was totally focused on this fight: he knew better than anyone who he faced, just as he knew of her reputation for victory, but he also knew he had no choice but to win. In contrast, Furionchires seemed almost distracted, for every so often she took her eyes off of her opponent and glanced at the battle around her. From the grim set of her mouth, Severeielle could see the Queen of Battles had realized that the glorious charge of the heavy cavalry had been stopped by their opponent's own reserves, and the reversal had been averted. If she didn't end her fight soon, and somehow rally her forces, it would be too late to affect the battle even if she killed Severius.

With desperate energy, Furionchires and her human host charged the Lord of Time, swinging her sword in a flurry of crushing blows meant to overwhelm his defenses. The ferocity of her attack was incredible, and Severius knew better than to try and stand up to it. He retreated slowly from her assault, giving ground reluctantly, but still never letting her find an opening in his defenses. And then disaster struck: while retreating from her desperate charge, he tripped upon the legs of a dead soldier and fell to the ground, defense forgotten in his surprise. With a cry of victory, Furionchires swung her sword in a killing blow that Severius could not avoid.

Before the sword landed, however, the black dragon on Severius' shoulders raised his head and released a jet of white-hot flame that struck her full in the face. The surprise was total, and as she flinched from the unexpected attack, her deadly blow stopped short as she reflexively covered her face with her forearms. The flames had no effect upon Furionchires, for one of the protections afforded a host by their dragons was a virtual immunity to dragonfire, but the break in her concentration was all the opportunity Severius needed: he brought his spear around and in front of him, just in time to meet her interrupted charge. The heavy blade of Lyxan steel, willed into existence by an Earthborn, and hardened with dragonfire, parted her armor like parchment before stabbing her through the heart. As the blade emerged from her back, the Queen of Battles had a final moment to realize what had happened, before the sword fell from her nerveless fingers, and her body fell limp as it slid down the shaft of the spear until her knees hit the ground. The dragon on her shoulders cried out in agony as she suffered through her host's death, and then disappeared in a flash of light and flame. Severeielle knew that while the Queen of Battle's human body was dead, Furionchires herself would survive. The dragon was sorely wounded, but the loss of a host wasn't fatal—just agonizingly painful. It would take years for Furionchires to recover, and years longer for her to find a new host. And even then, she would remember only fragments of the time before her "death". Severeielle felt a great sorrow welling up for the pain she knew the Queen of Battles would go through, but with that sorrow came a pride she had never felt before: her brother had triumphed against a legend.

The soldiers of Zarryiosiad's army knew it as well: the loss of morale the death of their champion brought them shook the army to its core. Furionchires' companion in the charge moved quickly to rally his troops, and to somehow turn despair into hope. Severeielle couldn't make out his words, but his efforts did seem to have some effect on the soldiers. Slowly, they began reforming their line, and once again, a rout was averted. Whoever he was, he wasn't a Dragon Lord, and Severeielle didn't recognize him. Before she could ask about him, however, Astranaithes spoke.

"That is Kalindral, Zarryiosiad's consort. He is Faeish." As she spoke, the air around Kalindral wavered and began to glow. Great shimmering butterfly wings emerged from his back and he rose above the battlefield with a single mighty stroke. The glow around him intensified, and Zarryiosiad's soldiers somehow found the strength to rally one last time, as Kalindral unlimbered a bow from a golden case on his back, and began firing arrows into the opposing army. Everywhere his arrows struck soldiers died, and as the relentless tide of warriors began to fall back from the assault, Severeielle again saw her brother.

Severius stood up and pulled the spear from the fallen body of Furionchires' host, and stepped forward to confront the shining figure slaughtering his soldiers. Kalindral saw him and reacted by firing a burning arrow at him faster than the eye could follow. Severius didn't even slow down. He contemptuously batted aside the arrow with a sweep of his spear, and as Kalindral fired a second time, then a third, Severius deflected the arrows again and again while moving ever closer to the spot where the Faeish general hovered. Kalindral intensified his efforts, firing faster and faster, until the arrows seemed to be a golden line with no breaks to mark individual arrows. Time and again, Severius turned aside the arrows; with his hands, his armor, or his spear, it didn't matter. Nothing could turn him aside from his purpose.

Kalindral's face changed from a look of concentration and fury, to one of concern as his arrows, time and again, failed to reach their mark. Too late, he realized his mistake: he had allowed the Lord of Time to get too close. In desperation, Kalindral beat his wings to gain altitude to avoid the attack he knew was coming, but too late; a lifetime too late. Severius didn't hesitate. He launched his spear with a mighty throw that tore almost completely through Kalindral's body, knocking him from the sky and killing him instantly. The Lord of Time walked to the body of his downed foe and pulled the spear from his chest as the dragon on his shoulder bellowed victory. A great cheer erupted from the lines of men to either side of Severius, and the rout that both Furionchires and Kalindral had died attempting to prevent finally began in earnest. Everywhere on the battlefield Zarryiosiad's soldiers threw down their weapons and tried to flee, only to be cut down by the thousands, and each soldier who died brought the conclusion of the battle ever closer.

Suddenly, the cheers of victory were silenced by a single inhuman cry that shook the very ground. Zarryiosiad, the strongest Powerborn in the world, had watched her lover die, and her grief at his death devastated her. The Archon of Il'Amhar was the most powerful Mage in the world, but the combined might of the Lyx has stymied her throughout the battle. Now, in her rage, she struck out with a fury that no one, save the Queen of Fate, had ever witnessed. It was widely believed that no Mage could touch more than three of the four elemental powers, but Zarryiosiad could. Great pillars of flame erupted from jagged mounds of earth that shot up from the ground with lethal force. Lightning crashed down from the heavens, striking soldiers of both armies indiscriminately and killing men and horses by the hundreds. Scalding steam poured through rents in the ground, boiling men alive or pulling them to a watery death, and all of these powers were amplified by the blood pouring from her hands. Severeielle knew the Archon had just touched the forbidden power of Blood Magic, using her own life force to augment her powers, and the combination was indescribable.

As Zarryiosiad drew more and more power from both the earth around her and the blood within her, she began to change. The transformation was subtle at first, but before long she began to swell in size, her features elongating and becoming distinctively reptilian. In a matter of moments, the beautiful silver-haired woman was gone, replaced by an immense dragon of the purest silver, hundreds of feet high. The dragon spread its enormous wings and a hurricane of wind knocked men and horses to the ground as it took to the sky. In an instant, the battle was over. Soldiers from both sides of the conflict fled in terror from the monster Zarryiosiad had become, but there was nowhere for them to run. The dragon inhaled deeply, and the five powers blended together until a single blast of white-hot dragonfire exploded from the beast's mouth, instantly incinerating *both* of the armies on the field of battle.

Amidst the inferno, only a single man remained alive: the one man immune to dragonfire. Severius charged through the flames towards the dragon as fast as he could, with his enchanted spear clutched tightly in his hands. All about him, the earth exploded and pillars of flame erupted, water flooded and lightning crashed, but none of that could stop his mad charge. It didn't take long for the dragon to notice him, and it landed in front of him, clearly intending to finish off the last surviving threat on the battlefield. The silver dragon reared back to strike at Severius, and in that instant, the Lord of Time struck. Without even slowing his run, he threw the spear unerringly towards its target, and for the third time that day, *Death's Mistress* struck true. The weapon hit the dragon squarely in the chest, and the ensorcelled blade parted the metallic scales with ease. It buried itself deeply in the dragon's heart, and Severeielle knew that Zarryiosiad had just been fatally wounded. The dragon bellowed once with surprise and agony, then collapsed, falling to the ground with a deafening crash.

Slowly, the earth returned to normal as the power radiating from Zarryiosiad dissipated. As the life slowly bled from the dragon, it began to transform once again, shrinking in size, and changing back to the silver-haired woman. When the transformation was complete, she beckoned to him weakly. Severius approached her, and knelt down beside the dying woman. Zarryiosiad raised her hand to touch him lightly on the chest. He took her hand in his, and she turned her head to speak to him. At that moment, Severeielle would have given everything she possessed to know what was said between the victor and the vanquished, but whatever passed between them died with her. After the life had faded from her, Severius gently lowered her hand to the ground, and then tenderly brushed her silver hair back with his bloodstained fingertips as he closed her unseeing eyes. Finally, he stood up and pulled his spear from her unmoving corpse, before summoning a Shadowgate to carry him away. When he was gone, Astranaithes spoke.

"And so the Lyx and their armies are no more. Humanity is free, and a new age has begun." She smiled, but sadness touched her eyes. "The Lyx were simply too powerful for Zarryiosiad, just as their army was too strong for hers. In order to defeat them, she had to become something greater. She had to become the Harbinger, but only desperation and loss can trigger its' emergence. The deaths of Kalindral and Furionchires were tragic, but necessary. They caused Zarryiosiad to lose control of her magic, and in her grief, the Archon touched a power greater than even she could contain. When she became the Harbinger, she had the power to accomplish what the Archon could not, but the world lay in the balance. Had your brother not been here to stop her, she would have continued on to burn the world to ash in her grief, long after the Lyx had been destroyed." She hesitated, and then added, "It is a difficult thing for me—to see the rise and fall of another Harbinger. But I am proud of Zarryiosiad for having the strength to see this through to the end. And I am prouder still of your brother, for having the courage to face her."

Severeielle frowned in confusion and turned to look at the Queen of Fate. To her surprise, tears began to stream down Astranaithes' face.

"I don't understand," said Severeielle. "My brother yet lives. I thought you said that he would suffer a fate worse than death."

Astranaithes looked at her again, and the tears didn't abate.

"He has. With her dying breath, Zarryiosiad cursed your brother to suffer a living death. With the powers she had left, and the power of Blood Magic besides, the consequences are inevitable and unavoidable. Your brother will suffer untold agony for his heroism this day." She smiled proudly toward the spot in which Severius had disappeared.

"He will suffer as no other before him . . . but the world will live."

SEVERIUS, THE LORD OF TIME

ZARRYIOSIAD, THE ARCHON

CHAPTER ONE

"Obsessions"

Standing in the main chamber of the Grand Cathedral of the Zarryiostrom, an Elven Archimagus contemplated a mural painted on the wall directly behind the altar. Enaria Wintersong had been coming here for decades, and had seen the mural countless times before, but she had always been drawn to this particular image. Until recently, the magnificent painting had faded with age, but in preparation for the Convocation, a religious ceremony that took place once a century to celebrate the Ascension of the Archon, the mural had been meticulously restored to its former glory. When the Patriarch of the Zarryiostrom had announced the restoration, Enaria had had serious reservations, for the mural had been created by a master of her craft, and Enaria feared that lesser hands would ruin it. But, to her vast relief, the task had been perfectly executed. This was her first viewing of the mural since the artisans had completed their labor, and try as she might, she couldn't find any fault with their work. Officially, the Zarryiostrom wouldn't unveil it until the Convocation began, but as a personal favor, the Patriarch had invited her to view it in a private session long before the public would have a chance to see it. Now, she couldn't help but stare, for it was as if she was rediscovering the image altogether. The exquisitely detailed painting depicted Zarryiosiad after her

Ascension, transformed from mortal flesh into the form of a mighty dragon. The majestic silver dragon, with wings outstretched, towered above the mortal armies who had fought against each other in the Valley of Fire, and had just single-handedly destroyed the united armies of the Lyx with a white-hot blast of dragonfire. The flames of the painting had been so well rendered that Enaria could almost feel heat rising off of the mural, and the silver scales of the dragon seemed to reflect the light of the fires, turning the dragon into a beacon. The effect was entrancing, and Enaria never grew tired of experiencing it.

It had been at this battle that the one-time masters of the world, the corrupted Fae known as the Lyx, had been forever destroyed, and the rise of human civilization had begun. Enaria often wondered how different history would have been had Zarryiosiad never been born. Would the Lyx still be in power, forever dominating the lesser races with their immortality and their mastery of Earth Magic? Or would another hero have risen up to challenge the Lyx's power? She would have given much for the clairvoyance needed to see the answer.

Out of courtesy for her exalted rank, the priests always left her alone with her thoughts, believing that she was finding inspiration from the iconic imagery. In a way, she supposed she *was* finding inspiration, though it was very unlikely that any of the priests would approve of the direction of her thoughts. Most people came to this hallowed spot to honor the memory of Zarryiosiad, and to remember the sacrifices the Archon and her family had made for the good of the world, but Enaria came here for different reasons. While others gained inspiration and comfort from the thought of Zarryiosiad sacrificing herself to rid the world of evil, the only thing Enaria cared about—the singular focus of her life—was to learn how the Archon had accomplished it. What power had Zarryiosiad touched that had allowed a single Powerborn to destroy all who stood against her in a single instant? Enaria did not believe in a divine being, the way the prattling fools of the priesthood did. The only thing she believed in—the only god she prayed to—was power, and no matter how much power she achieved, she always hungered for more. Zarryiosiad had become a symbol to her of what she could accomplish if only she desired it enough, and so she had devoted her life to studying the achievements of the Archon.

She hadn't always been so obsessed with obtaining power. When she had first developed her Powerborn ability, she had fought against her parents' insistence that she receive her training from the Mage Citadel of Ithram as her brother had done. The idea that a human institution could actually teach her something of worth had been laughable, and she had tried to convince her parents of that fact, but they had been adamant. They listened patiently to her arguments, and then explained to her that, while it was true that the short-lived humans might not be the best teachers, not all of the teachers in the Citadel were human. In fact, unlike the Zarryiostrom, the Mage Citadel accepted Powerborn from every race without restriction, and the experience she stood to gain from being a part of the Citadel could only benefit her. So, against her will, she had been sent away from her home city of Cyn'Carath to the island of Illymar, where she found her new home in the city-state of Ithram.

Enaria clearly remembered her first view of the twin cities of Ithram and Illymaine, situated as they were on opposite ends of the same large bay. Her home city of Cyn'Carath was large by Elven standards, but in the Elvish tradition, it was spread out over a very large area, at harmony with its surroundings. The humans who had built Ithram and Illymaine clearly didn't share the same view, and Enaria hadn't been prepared for how crowded human cities tended to be. She'd felt more than a little claustrophobic when she'd first encountered the narrow streets and winding roads. Fortunately, she had been young enough that it didn't take her long at all to become accustomed to the way humans built things, and she quickly became a creature of the city, able to find anything she wanted almost without effort. Eventually, she'd found that she actually preferred the vast human city to her own home, for in Ithram there was so much for her to see and do. Compared to the energy and diversity of Ithram, Cyn'Carath was . . . uninteresting.

Once she had embraced her new home and mastered her studies, her once-shy nature changed dramatically. The raw power she could command, first as a Fireborn and later as a Windborn, had assured her rapid advancement in the ranks of the Mage Citadel, and she had worked hard to advance her position. Now she sat as the third ranking member of the Mage High Council, and held the permanent title of Archimagus. Her confidence had grown in proportion to her advancement in rank, and as a consequence, there was very little left of the wide-eyed innocent child who had first sailed into Ithram almost 250 years ago.

It had been mere chance that she had become interested in studying the Archon. Shortly after taking her place as a member of the Mage High Council, Enaria had been asked to attend a meeting at the Cathedral of Zarryiosiad. Though the Mage Citadel and the Cathedral were two of the most important structures in the world, she had never felt a desire to visit the epicenter of the Church's worldly power. When Enaria had accepted the assignment to visit the Patriarch she had done so with disdain, for she had little use for priests and religion. The Mage Citadel wasn't a part of the Church, after all; it was a separate but equal part of Ithram, and co-equal in authority with the Zarryiostrom. Furthermore, the Citadel was located miles away from the Cathedral, in order to better emphasize the separation of the two great powers. She'd preferred the separation, staying as far from the Cathedral as possible, but it was there that she had first come face-to-face with the power of the Archon.

The Cathedral of Zarryiosiad was one of the grandest structures in the world, and a clear sign to everyone who viewed it that it was the spiritual home of the Archon. But no matter how impressive it might be, it was still just a building, made of stone blocks and mortar, and built by human hands over the course of decades. No, the true example of the power of the Archon was the White Wall surrounding the Cathedral. It was a perfectly smooth stone wall, twenty feet high and hundreds of feet in both directions, forming a perfect square around the Cathedral and its grounds. She had known from her studies that the Wall had been raised in an instant by Zarryiosiad herself, using her powers as an Earth Mage to create it in one piece from the very bones of the earth, and it was a white so intense that it seemed to glow. In fact, so perfect was the White Wall, that since its creation 2,900 years ago, it was still as smooth as glass. Not so much as a chip had broken loose, and not a single crack had formed in all that time.

Enaria had read about the Wall in her studies, but she'd deliberately chosen not to see it for herself, simply because the White Wall belonged to the Church. For all of its influence and power, the Zarryiostrom was a human institution; and while Elves and Fae were welcomed into its fold, they were prohibited from holding positions of power—a restriction that Enaria found deeply offensive. To their credit, the priesthood did not seem to hate the Elves or the Fae, but the pointed exclusion of other races from their decision making irritated Enaria to no end, and so she'd simply turned her back upon them and refused to even acknowledge their existence. That self-imposed arrangement had worked right up until she had taken a seat on the Mage High Council. Archimagus Se-ir Windwhisper, the First Seat of the Council and a fellow Elf, had personally ordered her to extend her help to the Patriarch of the time, and she couldn't refuse the order. So, she had set aside her resentment, and went to the Cathedral.

The first time she had laid her eyes on the White Wall it had taken her breath away. Her studies simply hadn't been able to convey the sheer majesty of the creation, and seeing it in person had been a humbling experience. Zarryiosiad had created the Wall long before her Ascension, to allow her father some privacy from the worship of the citizens of Il'Amhar, and to provide him some protection from the assassins of the Lyx. Tragically, the wall had provided neither.

As Third Seat of the Mage High Council, Enaria had always thought of herself as being quite skilled in the use of magic, and had always believed that as a fellow Powerborn, Zarryiosiad's achievements must have been on par with what she herself could accomplish. As far as Enaria was concerned, Zarryiosiad's "miracles" had simply been displays of power that had been exaggerated in the telling. The White Wall had put the lie to that belief in a heartbeat. Absolutely nothing Enaria could accomplish with her power could remain so perfect in its creation that time itself could not touch it. Once her interest had been piqued, she began studying the Archon's other surviving creations, such as the Teeth of Amhar, the most powerful defensive fortification ever conceived or built, and the Throne of Obsidian, a mysterious artifact thats purpose had yet to be solved. But all of her studies had stemmed from her first viewing of the Wall.

And then there was the Cathedral itself. The vaulted ceiling still looked the same today as it had the first time she had seen it almost 300 years ago. As soon as a person passed through the main doors, the story of Zarus the Liberator and his daughter, Zarryiosiad the Archon, played out on beautiful murals from the ornate gilded doors all the way to the Great Chamber itself. The very first mural showed the Lyx in all their glory, forcing countless generations of slaves to build colossal stone monuments to their greatness. The original artist had captured the cruelty of those insane beings perfectly; complete with mounds of dead and dying men and elves, piled up almost as high as the ziggurats they had died to build. A slave of even the least powerful of the Lyx would have been worked under the cruelest of conditions possible, until he or she died unnoticed and unmourned, only to be replaced by yet another unfortunate soul in an unending cycle of meaningless death. Meaningless, for like Zarryiosiad herself, the Lyx were Earthborn—and so powerful were they, that they could have raised the ziggurats in an instant, using only their magic, in much the same way as Zarryiosiad had created the White Wall surrounding the Cathedral. The Lyx chose to use slaves instead, forcing them to raise the structures one stone block at a time through endeavors that took many generations of slaves to complete. Raising the ziggurats wasn't the point, after all. The *true* point was to exercise absolute control.

The second mural showed the coming of the human Waterborn, Zarus, and his rise to power as a great leader among the human and Elven slaves. History claimed Zarus had been a powerful and charismatic man, but Enaria felt certain that the Mage could not have been as certain of his path as the artist who had painted the mural had portrayed him to be. The light of wisdom and compassion glowed in the heroic figure's eyes, but Enaria had a shrewd notion that during his lifetime, desperation more than wisdom had had a hand in Zarus's true expressions. Still, Zarus had promised his people freedom, and had ultimately made good upon his word, eventually finding refuge on the island of Amhar.

The third and fourth murals showed the building of Il'Amhar, as it had then been known, a relatively peaceful time for Zarus and the escaped slaves, for the successful escape had ignited a civil war among the Lyx. Lesser Lyx, long jealous of the power of the greatest of their number, sensed weakness at the failure of their betters to capture or destroy Zarus, and had moved quickly to increase their own domains. Entire families of the Lyx were wiped out as a covert struggle for power eventually turned into open warfare. Zarus used the respite the civil war gave him very well indeed. He organized the former slaves and used them to build a great city on their island home, and made every man, woman, and child learn at least the rudiments of warfare. With Zarus leading them, the once-hopeless slaves forged themselves into a nation, and that nation soon built an army. Il'Amhar became a bastion of defiance against the tyranny of the Lyx, and the name Zarus became a talisman for the slaves still under the yoke of oppression. As word of Il'Amhar's defiance against the Lyx spread, more and more slaves attempted to escape, risking death and worse on the faint hope of reaching Il'Amhar. Not all survived the attempt, but those who did found safe haven upon the island, and the tales those slaves brought of widespread dissention among the Lyx dramatically strengthened the will of the new nation. Humankind had finally learned the secret that the Lyx had struggled so long to keep hidden from their slaves: despite their long lives, they were not gods, and like any other mortal, they could be killed.

Unfortunately, the Lyx were not the only ones who could be killed. Sometime during the civil war, one of the Lyx sent an envoy to Il'Amhar to discuss a treaty. The Lyx's name had been lost to history, but his actions had not: the envoy had actually been an assassin, and he murdered Zarus in his own home, before taking his own life. The Lyx had probably believed that by killing Zarus the slave revolt would end, but they hadn't counted on Zarus' half-Fae daughter, Zarryiosiad.

Zarus had simply wanted his people to be left alone, and had been content to leave the Lyx in peace. After the murder of her father Zarryiosiad hadn't wanted peace; she had wanted revenge, and the morning after her father's burial she began a 400 year-long war to get it. That war had finally ended with her death . . . and the deaths of every single remaining Lyx. She'd personally executed many of them over the 400 years, but the vast majority of her victims had fallen during her final battle, a battle that had come to be known as the Valley of Fire. It was there that Zarryiosiad had channeled a power greater than mankind had ever witnessed, and had used that power to destroy almost every living thing on the battlefield in a single moment. Unfortunately, only the most rudimentary of information had survived the roughly 2,500 years since Zarryiosiad had existed. Contrary to popular belief, there had actually been a few survivors of the battle—

those who had sense enough to flee the carnage before Zarryiosiad had destroyed everything else—and all of the survivors had agreed on a single point: Zarryiosiad had transformed into an indescribably huge dragon and had ended the battle with a single, impossibly powerful blast of dragonfire, before dying at the hands of the greatest villain of the age—the vile Severius—now known as the Dragonslayer.

Enaria began to study Zarryiosiad, trying to discover how she had accomplished such a miracle. As a member of the Mage Council, she had access to all of the secret histories of the Mages throughout history, and she had discovered a very interesting fact: contrary to the teachings of the Mage Citadel, physical metamorphosis such as the one Zarryiosiad had undergone was indeed possible, but *only* through the use of Blood Magic, the use of which was considered by both the Citadel and the Church to be heresy, and an offense punishable by death. A few Blood Mages throughout history, who had been unconcerned with law or propriety, had eagerly delved into the practice of transfiguration hoping to emulate the Archon and, to Enaria's surprise, she'd discovered that some of those Mages had even found a modicum of success. But these successes had been minor at best, and had carried a very high mortality rate. *It could be a fable,* she thought to herself, but the thought lacked conviction, for standing where she was in the very heart of the Cathedral of Zarryiosiad, looking at the mural portraying the Archon's triumphal moment, she knew beyond the shadow of a doubt that it was true. *But* how *did she do it?*

A small sound brought her out of her reverie and she turned to look at the person who had interrupted her thoughts. For a full second, her unfocused gaze failed to recognize either of the two men standing next to her, smiling. But the moment passed and Enaria finally noticed both Archimagus Cedric DeVir, Eighth Seat of the Mage High Council, and Samuel Varic, the Patriarch of the Zarryiostrom. When they were certain she had mentally joined them, Patriarch Varic spoke.

"I knew that you, of all people, would appreciate the work that has been done to restore the murals. When I was a very young boy, just after my family gave me to the church to be raised in the faith, the Cathedral had a visitor. As an Initiate, I was often given the task of sweeping these halls and polishing the benches and railings, and one day we were pulled aside and told that on that day we would have a very important visitor. We were ordered by the Draconus in charge of the novices not to disturb this visitor, and to go about our tasks as quietly as possible to keep from distracting her." Patriarch Varic's eyes grew unfocused as he became caught up in his memories. "To my great surprise, the visitor turned out to be an exceedingly beautiful Elf Mage, who stood in that very spot, and stared up at that painting completely lost in thought. I remember sneaking glances at this visitor as I swept—as did many of the other Initiates—and wondering what it was that she saw when she contemplated the painting." His eyes refocused and he grinned at her like a street urchin causing mischief, a look that seemed to make the years fade from his features. "As an Initiate, I knew better than to go against the orders of a superior for any reason, no matter how curious I might have been. But as the *Patriarch*, I find that I am suddenly in a position to ask the very person I watched so long ago the question that I've wondered about since I was a boy, without fear of either a lecture or a switching. Archimagus Wintersong, when you stand in that spot and look up at the painting of Zarryiosiad Ascended—may she guide and protect us forever—what is it that you see?"

Enaria, momentarily taken aback by the question, remembered an earlier thought and it made her smile. *You would not approve of what I am thinking, old friend.* Instead, after pretending to think about it for a moment, she replied,

"Zarryiosiad has been an inspiration to me for as long as I can remember. Whenever my burdens threaten to overwhelm me or my responsibilities become too onerous, I have but to stand here and reflect upon the burdens and the responsibilities that Zarryiosiad herself undertook in her life. It gives me great comfort to know that no matter how great my duties may have become, or what obstacles may appear before me, they pale in comparison to the trials of the Archon. This mural reminds me of that simple fact. I find the image to be inspiring."

Varic beamed at her words, and Enaria had to fight to keep her eyes from rolling in disgust at his naivety.

"Just so," he said. "The lessons we have learned from Zarryiosiad's example are legion. But, foremost among them is, that as great as our burdens may become, our sacrifices are as nothing when compared to the trials of the Archon. I thank you for answering my question, and for fulfilling a lifelong ambition."

Enaria bowed graciously to the Patriarch, all the while thinking, *If only my own lifelong ambition was so easily realized.*

Archimagus Cedric DeVir let this go on for a few more moments and then said,

"If we could get back to business? Our burdens may not be as great as those of the Archon, but they also aren't getting any lighter with us just standing here."

Cedric DeVir had a well-known reputation for being very practical, and another for not being an overly enthusiastic patron of the arts. He could appreciate the skill involved in the creation of the mural, but Enaria knew that, to him, it was simply another painting on a slightly grander scale, and paintings had no practical value. *Dakkadians,* she snorted, *even those from Dakkadian Principalities, such as Palantine or Rohm, have no appreciation for the finer things in life.*

Both Enaria and the Patriarch turned their attention to him, and Enaria said,

"I suppose we should. But allow me to compliment you as well, on the restoration, Patriarch Varic. It has been masterfully accomplished."

At that, a voice sounded from behind them.

"Indeed it has, Your Holiness. I trust you were not charged too much for the effort?" Enaria, Cedric, and Patriarch Varic turned to face the new arrivals, and when they recognized Enaria's older brother, Archimagus Tavian Two-Blade, the Second Seat of the Mage High Council, and Archidraconus Ephraim Semarill, the right hand of the Patriarch of the Zarryiostrom, they offered bows and handshakes amongst them. After the proper greetings had been exchanged, Patriarch Varic responded,

"Not at all, not at all. The Archon teaches us to be thrifty, but even *we* know that sometimes you get what you pay for. The group responsible for the restoration boasted that the results would be astonishing, but I never expected *this*." Varic swept his hand upward to draw attention to the glistening silver dragon, forever poised in triumph over a burning wasteland. "But, as Cedric has rightly reminded us, there is work to be done this day. Will you follow me to my offices? Ephraim, please join us."

The Patriarch's offices were very large and luxuriously appointed, yet somehow still managed to feel warm and inviting rather than oppressive. There was a fair amount of ostentation in the décor, but that ostentation took the form of large oil paintings in ornate gilded frames and elaborately worked candleholders, though the furniture was designed to be comfortable as well as decorative. At the end of the room was a large oak desk belonging to the Patriarch, but instead of walking to his desk to conduct the meeting, he led the small group over to a comfortable sitting area with several high backed chairs arranged in a circle. As the three Mages and the two priests took their seats, a steward appeared next to the Patriarch and stood waiting to see to any needs the guests might have.

"Shall I have Bertrand bring refreshments? We may be here a while."

"That would be fine, Your Holiness. And you're right, this could take a while. There is much to discuss." Enaria replied immediately.

The steward bowed deeply, and disappeared as silently as he had appeared. Tavian took the opportunity to start the meeting.

"The reason I came here to speak with you was to inform you that we have had word from several of the delegations that will be attending the Convocation.

By fortuitous coincidence, many of the replies came within hours of each other. Specifically, we have had word from the Kingdom of Dakkadia that King Madari himself, along with his wife, two children, and several of his most important nobles will be attending. King Madari's wife, Queen Aveliad, will be bringing her son, Phaedron, the Earl of Daane, as well."

"It will be wonderful to see my half-sister, Aveliad, again. We were very close when I was a child. She practically raised me. However, if King Madari himself will be attending, his half-brother, Morvandis, will be sure to attend," Cedric replied with a frown.

The other two Mages looked unsurprised and not the least bit pleased by the news. Archidraconus Semarill noticed the Mages' reactions and asked,

"Will this be a problem? Morvandis has been here several times in the past, and it is well-known that he is the most powerful Mage in the world. I would think the Mage Citadel would be happy to have him here."

Tavian shook his head in polite disagreement.

"It is not that we dislike him, or do not wish to have him here." Tavian said. "Though he may have earned a reputation for ruthlessness, his ruthlessness is married to iron self-control. Morvandis is no threat. It is more that his overwhelming power will tend to overshadow any negotiations into which Dakkadia may enter. The Convocation itself is important, of course, but one of the more important benefits of attending it will be the chance for the three kingdoms to arrange marriages, cement alliances, and conclude trade agreements. No doubt King Madari is eager to attend, for he has a son of marrying age and a daughter who soon will be. Prince Valeriad is seventeen years old now, and Madari has to be thinking of arranging a marriage with one of King Orem of Illymar's three daughters. Or two daughters, rather, now that Orem's oldest daughter, Princess Tais, has dishonored herself and fallen out of favor. What interests me, however, isn't the possibility of an arranged marriage between the ruling houses of Dakkadia and Illymar; it's that King Madari's son and stepson are both Powerborn. Valeriad is a Fireborn, and from all reports, a quite gifted Mage, while Queen Aveliad's son from her previous marriage is a Waterborn, and supposedly the more powerful of the two. Speaking on behalf of the Mage High Council, we look forward to seeing both of them, to find out just what kind of Mages they are becoming. I just hope for their sakes Morvandis' influence hasn't left them permanently marked."

"From the perspective of the Zarryiostrom, we, too, look forward to meeting the aspiring Mages," said Ephraim, "though for a different reason, of course." Ephraim's words had particular weight, considering his position as the head of the Inquisition, for they all knew one of the duties the Zarryiostrom took upon itself was the search for anyone able to wield Earth Magic.

In the past, the Lyx had used their mastery of Earth Magic to enslave millions of people, and had caused countless deaths and limitless suffering, so as a result, the Church had issued a condemnation against anyone who could touch the forbidden power of the Lyx. Anyone found to have that ability was declared a heretic, and hunted down relentlessly by agents of the Church. The pursuit of these proscribed Mages was an important duty of the Zarryiostrom, and every Powerborn, no matter what country they might have come from, had to be brought before the Council to be Tested.

It had been a very long time since the Zarryiostrom had found an Earth Mage, and the priesthood considered that to be incontrovertible proof that their methods were working. The Mage Citadel, on the other hand, wasn't so sure: most of the High Councillors believed that Earth Mages had simply become better at hiding their true natures out of a sense of self-preservation.

The steward returned with a tray bearing different foods and drinks. Once Bertrand returned to his pantry, Ephraim continued the conversation.

"We have also had word from the Empire of Ferralin that Emperor Xan himself will be attending. For a while, it seemed he would send his son, the Crown Prince Lain, to attend in his stead, but apparently his health has recovered enough for him to make the journey." At 76, Xan was, by far, the oldest human ruler still in power, but he was by no means a figurehead. After fifty years of his rule, Ferralin had become second only to Illymar in wealth, and Xan had used that wealth very wisely indeed, building roads and cities and, more importantly, a vast military to protect his people.

"Xan must want to take this opportunity to personally arrange a marriage for his son. Lain is 23 years-old, and as Xan's only child, he stands to inherit the empire upon his father's death."

"You are forgetting something about the Emperor: Xan may in fact be looking for another wife for himself." Cedric DeVir said, shaking his head in disagreement. "Remember, despite his age, Xan's tastes run towards younger women."

"Younger women?" Patriarch Varic snorted in disgust. "Children, you mean! Xan is at best a pedophile, and at worst, a murderer. He has been married over a dozen times in his life, but has somehow managed to outlive all of his wives. His latest wife died less than a year after they were married, and she was only 14!"

Enaria waited for a moment to let the Patriarch's point sink in and said,

"I think we all know what kind of man Emperor Xan is. But he is still a vastly powerful ruler and must be afforded every courtesy. And, while his reputation for *unpleasantries* may indeed be true, the simple fact is, the other rulers may not care. He is 76, and by all accounts, his health has been marginal for years. That would make the prospect of a daughter's marriage to either Lain or Xan very attractive to either King Madari or King Orem. What's a year or two of unpleasantness for a mere daughter, compared to an alliance with the largest military in the region? Furthermore, Xan would have to be very careful in how he would treat a daughter of either Illymar or Dakkadia. Taking either an Illvanin or Dhaerhan daughter as a bride would be entirely different from marrying the daughter of a Ferraline noble, and allowing one or the other to come to harm would inevitably lead to war with a country that matches the Ferralin Empire in strength of arms."

Enaria's brother, Tavian, leaned forward slightly and everyone turned to him.

"That brings up something I've been studying. The more I look at the situation, the more I see a problem on the horizon. Right now, all three realms are stable and prospering, but any move by one house to secure an alliance with another may upset that stability. Ferralin has the largest army of the three great houses, but no navy to speak of, and their tactics are completely outdated. As such, Ferralin is not a threat to Illymar's dominance on the ocean. Illymar has the strongest navy, and is, of course, an island, making the threat of an invasion of Illymar practically non-existent. But they cannot project power to the mainland. Despite their aggressiveness, Dakkadia's army is smaller than Ferralin's, but they are far better equipped and trained, and as a warlike state, their soldiers are unparalleled on the field. Their navy is relatively small, but very powerful on a ship-for-ship basis, and the new weapons they've developed are supposed to be absolutely devastating. Their newest ships carry these new weapons, and Illymar in particular is very worried about what this will mean for them."

Tavian raised a hand and a burning map appeared in the middle of the circle and slowly started spinning. The glowing map showed the main continent and the island of Illymar, with fiery lines dividing the continent into political entities.

"The prize is obvious. Standing between the Empire of Ferralin and the Kingdom of Dakkadia are the city-states of the Badlands, and collectively, the Badlands control the only passable land route to the Eastern Markets. This makes it an incredible prize for both Ferralin and Dakkadia, and a serious threat to Illymar's economy. Should Ferralin or Dakkadia seize the Badlands, Illymar would have to move quickly to neutralize the threat to their markets. Worse, the other side would be sure to attack as well. Dakkadia can survive an attack by Ferralin, but they could be overwhelmed if Illymar and Ferralin were to combine forces. The same holds true with a Ferralin invasion of the Badlands. Dakkadia and Illymar would most likely combine forces against them to protect their own interests. Hence the stalemate."

"It would seem that Illymar has already decided who they would rather be allied with then, as King Orem has already betrothed his eldest daughter, the Princess Tais, to Xan's son, Lain," Archidraconus Semarill said. "Though Tais' reckless actions have all but eliminated the betrothal, Xan must be coming to try and salvage the situation."

"Indeed," said Cedric DeVir. "And he may be able to accomplish just that. King Madari must believe it as well, for I have received reports that the Dakkadian army is increasing their numbers in anticipation of the threat of an alliance between Illymar and Ferralin."

"Despite what King Madari or anyone else might believe, repairing the damage Tais has already done to her country's future alliance with Ferralin by defying her parents, may very well prove to be impossible. You know how touchy Xan is about honor, despite his own lack of it. A younger daughter may not be lofty enough for his only son. At the very least, Orem will have to make some concessions to repair the damage. We shall have to see what form the concessions will take."

"Orem may decide not to make reparations at all," Patriarch Varic said, "and instead choose to ally himself with Dakkadia. Remember that the royal family of Illymar has not had a Powerborn in several generations. Madari has two sons, or rather a son and a step-son, and both of them are Powerborn. An intermingling of the bloodlines has to be attractive to Orem. Frankly, Dakkadia would stand to gain much more from an alliance with Illymar than Ferralin would, but the Illymari royal family stands to gain at least as much—if not more—from an alliance. The chance to inject fresh Mage blood into the family will be a high priority." He rose and spread his hands towards his assembled guests.

"There is no doubt that tensions will be very high at the Convocation. It will be up to us to monitor the situation and diffuse the tensions whenever possible, using the utmost diplomacy. Unfortunately, this task won't be easy to achieve, and should we fail in this duty, there is a good chance that open warfare will be the result."

No one disagreed.

King Orem Illvanin, third of his name and the absolute ruler of the island kingdom of Illymar, leaned back into his comfortable chair and rubbed his tired eyes before laying down the scroll he had been pretending to read. He closed his eyes, still rubbing at them, and when he opened them again, he instantly regretted his moment of weakness. He realized that he had somehow lost track of that particular paper amongst the piles of identical scrolls that had taken over his desk. He searched in vain for it, but as he sifted through the papers he suddenly realized that he had no idea what he had been reading and had no idea what he was looking for. He chuckled ruefully and stood up, more than ready to leave the mound of work behind him. When he rose, a virtual army of servants and courtiers rose with him and bowed respectfully, awaiting his orders. Orem rolled his eyes in exasperation as he saw that many of them were carrying yet more scrolls for his perusal.

"I'm going for a walk," he said.

He managed only two steps away from the desk before his wife stepped forward and held out her hand expectantly, an amused glint reflecting in her brown eyes. Orem chuckled again as he handed over the Royal Seal.

"Try not to give away any more of the kingdom, Althea. I'd like there to be something left to give to Ethan when I die."

Queen Althea took the seal from him, kissing him on the cheek.

"I'll try, my love, but no promises. At least half of the papers on your desk are petitions asking for grants or loans. Illymar is the wealthiest nation in the world, and we do have appearances to keep up."

"At *least* half," Orem said grudgingly. "Everyone seems to think that the treasury is bottomless." *Even you, Althea,* he added to himself silently.

"The well is far from dry, dear husband. Enjoy your walk. I'll try to have this sorted out before you return. You really should leave these matters to me more often, you know. You haven't the temperament to care for them yourself."

Orem ignored her gentle rebuke and left his office with only his three personal guardsmen in tow. As he closed the door behind him, he instantly felt his energy returning, along with his good humor.

He chose a direction at random and began to walk, and after a few steps, he glanced at the three guardsmen standing silently behind him and said,

"I believe the paperwork in that room is trying to kill me. You know, I can actually *feel* my energy being leeched away every time I look at that unholy mess?" He scratched his beard and asked, "Can you arrest a pile of paperwork for treason?"

The Captain of the Guard smiled politely and said,

"Unless and until that pile of scrolls somehow draws weapons and tries to attack you directly, I'm afraid there is little we can do. We are, however, keeping a very close eye on it."

Orem laughed at the image of the scrolls standing up and brandishing weapons.

KING OREM ILLVANIN OF ILLYMAR

"I hate to say it, but if that pile *was* to try and assassinate me, my last words would probably be 'I *knew* it.'"

"While I don't believe that you're in any true danger," The captain said with mock seriousness. "I have to admit I can't rule out the possibility completely. It might be a good idea to have a Fireborn nearby to protect you, just in case, of course. If anything, his very presence might be enough to keep the scrolls in line. Though, to be honest, I'm more afraid that it is going to tip over and crush you to death."

"Thank you for that, Captain. As if I didn't have more than enough to worry about already. Now, when I go to sleep tonight, I'll probably dream about being assassinated by a mountain of dagger-wielding paperwork."

Orem was still shaking his head at the image when he finally realized where he was and his good humor instantly evaporated. He had been wandering aimlessly, enjoying the simple act of walking rather than trying to get anywhere in particular, but somehow his feet had brought him unerringly to the Tower, the highest point in the Spire, and the place that the royal family sent their own to be punished. There was only one prisoner currently residing in the Spire's royal prison; Orem's eldest daughter, Tais.

He took a step toward the door, his hand already reaching for the handle, when he realized what he was doing and forced himself to stop. Tais had always been his favorite child, even more so than his son, Ethan, but she had to be punished for her disobedience. He deliberately turned his back on the heavy wooden door and looked his Captain of the Guard in the eyes.

"How is she doing?"

A flash of pity crossed the soldier's eyes.

"It is hard to tell, My Liege. By your order, she is allowed no visitors, but I do know that she is still alive and she eats the food she is given. Shall I check on her condition and report my findings to you?"

Orem started to say yes, but stopped himself.

"No. She is to remain locked up and isolated at least until the Convocation has ended. I do not want her presence at the ceremonies to be a reminder to Emperor Xan that our original arrangement has been altered. She's already caused enough damage as it is."

The Captain did not answer, so Orem took his silence for understanding. He turned away from the soldier and looked at the door one more time.

Tais, you are my daughter and I love you more than anything, but as harsh as your punishment may seem, the Archon knows you deserve much worse than you are getting for your betrayal. If you had been anyone else besides my daughter, it would have been the headsman for you.

With the dark thought still reverberating in his head, he began walking again, this time with a purpose.

"Where is Ethan?"

"In the courtyard, practicing his swordplay" replied the Captain.

"Then that's where we're going."

Prince Ethan Illvanin saw his father enter the practice salle out of the corner of his eye and barely suppressed a smirk of amusement.

Typical.

He knew that, at this particular moment, the King was supposed to be listening to petitions and taking care of matters of state, but more and more over the years, his father had simply grown tired of the business of governance and had sought ways to wash his hands of the entire mess. Ethan suspected that his father was seriously considering abdicating his throne and just tossing the Crown to him, but he hadn't said anything. *Yet.*

Instead, his father made surreptitious visits to watch him at the salle or in tournaments. The reason he gave for showing up unexpectedly was always the same; he found it "restful." But from the way Orem was watching him, Ethan could tell he was actually being evaluated. The Prince could have volunteered to help his father with his duties, and deep down he supposed that he should, but the truth was he didn't want the job either. He knew he would be a better king than his father, but doing so would mean that he would have to give up some of the luxuries in life . . . like fencing, drinking, and carousing.

Fortunately for Orem, Queen Althea had stepped forward to pick up her husband's dead weight, though not without causing some serious problems for the Crown, foremost of which had been the Queen singlehandedly creating a rift between Orem and his brother Ascham, the Duke of Saerce. *If I were to take my father's throne, most of the brothels in the city would go out of business, and that would have a devastating effect on the economy.* The thought made him chuckle.

When Queen Althea had first taken over her husband's governmental duties, Orem had watched her like a hawk to make certain that his policies were being followed to the letter. For her part, Althea had done a fine job of keeping the ship of state sailing on an even keel until she had finally earned Orem's complete trust.

Once she no longer had to worry about her husband's watchful eye, she had started using her position of authority to grant her family more and more power and influence. She started slowly enough, granting a favor here or a pardon there, but when she started giving out titles to her immediate family—all with the King's blessing, of course—the true nobles began to take notice.

It had finally come to a head when King Orem, at his wife's insistence, made her father, a mere commoner without a single drop of noble blood, the Duke of Skye. Ascham had exploded at the news that a *merchant* would be joining the highest levels of the government, and the heated argument that had ensued between King Orem and Duke Ascham had ended with the King banishing his brother to his domains in the north. The Queen had stridently insisted that Orem have his brother arrested and imprisoned for High Treason for the insult, but Orem had flatly refused.

Even in exile, Ascham had found ways to cause trouble for the Savonne family at every opportunity, and the Queen had responded to the Duke of Saerce's attacks by making every effort she could to gut his powerbase. Nobles who were loyal to Ascham invariably lost favor at court and had their lands and titles confiscated by the Crown, only to be replaced by members of the Savonne family. The dispossessed nobles usually found their way to Saerce, as Duke Ascham had made it known far and wide that he would gladly accept dispossessed nobles into his service.

Ethan realized that he had taken a bit too long to acknowledge his father's presence, and so he squared his shoulders and walked to where his father had taken a seat.

"Good morning, Your Majesty. Care to join us on the salle?"

Orem snorted.

"I'm a bit old to be fencing, son. But I do enjoy watching a good match. Reminds me of the old days."

"Well, the way the Weapons Masters tell it, you could have shown us a thing or two in the 'old days.' Luckily, I seem to have inherited your talent for the sword." He lifted the longer of his two blades up and showed it to his father. Predictably, Orem sneered at the weapons.

"In my day, we used longswords, not rapiers, and shields instead of the main gauche, but I almost wish we'd had your toys when I was young enough to learn their use. They always make for wonderfully entertaining duels at the tourneys, even if they would be useless in an actual battle."

Ethan saluted his father with his rapier.

"They work well enough for me. Why don't you sit back and prepare to be entertained, Father. Afterward, we can hoist a few flagons of ale while you tell us more about the old days."

As Ethan turned back to the salle, he rolled his eyes in disgust. He absolutely *hated* pandering to his father, but he didn't have a choice.

I want to be King someday, and that means I have to remain in his good graces. Otherwise, I could end up like Tais.

Duke Alessandro Savonne, and the father of the Queen of Illymar, finished reading the report he had received from his daughter and set it down on his desk to think about its contents. According to her, King Madari Dhaerhan would be attending the Convocation with his family and many of his nobles. Dhaerhan was rapidly becoming a very serious threat to Illymar, but Alessandro didn't particularly care about that.

What concerned him was the mounting threat Dakkadia posed to his own shipping. Savonne fleets were necessary to bring trade—and gold—into Illymar, and a greater and greater percentage of that wealth was being captured by Dakkadian pirates. *Privateers,* he corrected himself automatically, but no matter what name the practice went by, the end result was the same: Dakkadia was becoming richer and richer by stealing from Illymar . . . and from *him.* He took great pains to hide these losses from the Crown, but if something wasn't done soon, he would have to admit to his failures and accept the consequences. *Or, at least one of the other Savonnes will, that is.*

He picked up a snifter of brandy and then stood up to walk to a glass paneled doorway. It was early spring in Illymar and the trees were just starting to flower, and he smiled at the perfectly manicured grounds and the blossoming garden. He loved Skye in the springtime and, on impulse, he opened the door, stepping out onto his veranda to enjoy his drink in the warm sunlight. Below, he could see several of the gardeners working away, methodically weeding the grounds and trimming the bushes, and he sat down on a comfortable chair to idly watch them. Everywhere he looked, he could see signs of his immense wealth, from ornate marble statuary and fountains, to the vast expanses of the grounds of his home. He placed his snifter on his wide stomach and leaned back into his chair, basking in his good fortune.

In exchange for the King's favor, Alessandro had made the Illymari Royal Family rich beyond their wildest dreams, and it was because of his influence that people were calling this the Golden Age of Illymar. Art and wealth were everywhere, and the nobility enjoyed lifestyles that were the envy of the rest of the world. Lavish parties were a daily occurrence in Illymar, and before he had retired, Alessandro had thrown the best. Alas, he was too old to partake of such frivolities now, but he had already done his part for the family. Now, he felt he was entitled to his retirement.

With great wealth always came jealousy and avarice. Dakkadia, a country with a history of conquering their neighbors and adding their lands to its own, had set its hungry gaze upon Illymar. Fortunately, Illymar was an island and, as such, was relatively easy to defend—especially with the Teeth of Amhar surrounding it and providing an impenetrable defense—but Alessandro had seen the signs of Dakkadia's ambitions over 20 years ago and had taken steps to defend against it. The King had refused to employ the Illymari navy to attack Dakkadian shipping, because doing so would have been an aggressive act of war and would have invalidated their mutual defense treaty with the Mage Citadel of Ithram. But Alessandro had suggested the use of privateers to do the dirty work, and after much deliberation, the King had reluctantly agreed. For a time, Illymari privateers had been extremely successful against the Dakkadians, and everyone had breathed a sigh of relief that the developing threat had been dealt with. Unfortunately, five years ago, the Dakkadians had introduced a new weapon, and those weapons had changed the fortunes of the Illymari navy and merchant fleet almost overnight.

It had taken years for Illymar to realize what was happening, but eventually, repatriated survivors returned to Illymari shores to spread the word that Dakkadia was fighting back, and doing so very well. Fewer and fewer ships were available to venture out and attack Dakkadian shipping, and once Dakkadia had introduced their own privateers into the fight, the last of the Illymari privateers had vanished, never to be heard from again.

There were survivors from ships captured by the Dakkadian navy, much to Alessandro's surprise, for he had never expected Dakkadia to be reasonable where it came to prisoners. But Madari had followed the rules of war as laid down by the Zarryiostrom to the letter, and so far, at least, captured sailors had been released unharmed at the first opportunity in a neutral port. Usually, that port was in the Badlands, which was on the mainland, so it took time for sailors to find a way home. It soon became apparent as to why King Madari offered leniency to enemy sailors, for each surviving Illymari sailor had spread the word that the ocean was no longer a safe place for Illymari ships.

And, from a vast majority of those people who had survived encounters with the Dakkadian navy, they had learned the name of the person most responsible for the swath of destruction Dakkadia was cutting through the Illymari fleet: Lady Prudence Daemira. In fact, so good was she at finding and capturing prizes, she had earned herself a *nom de guerre*: The Corsair. Though she was quite young, both she and her ship, the *Sovereign*, had single-handedly captured a vast majority of the ships Illymar had lost. To date, no ship that had gone against the *Sovereign* had survived the experience, and it seemed that no matter how many ships they sent to sink her, she always prevailed. Illymari sailors viewed the ship and her captain with almost superstitious dread; dread made worse by the fact that the *Sovereign's* sails were black as night, with a single white stripe dividing it, representing Dakkadia. The rest of the Dakkadian navy was doing its part, of course, but she was the heart and soul of their fleet.

He took another pull of his brandy and stood up to return to his desk. As the sister of Prince Sethred Daemira of the Principality of Rohm, a Dakkadian vassal state, Lady Prudence Daemira was of royal blood, and thus had merited an invitation to the Convocation. No one expected her to accept of course, for despite her legal status as a privateer, she was still a wanted woman in Illymar, and the bounty on her head was exorbitant even by Savonne standards. Oh, the Zarryiostrom had issued the Peace of Zarryiosiad, which meant that anyone who accepted an invitation from the Church could enter and leave Illymar freely under the protection of Ithram for the entire length of the Convocation, but that didn't mean someone wouldn't be tempted to collect the bounty. It was so very much money, after all. But, where other people thought that she would be foolish to attend, Alessandro expected it of her. He had studied her history quite thoroughly, and he knew that she would not be afraid of a threat to her life. No, she would come here with the rest of the Dakkadians, and then she would dare anyone and everyone to try and collect the bounty they had placed upon her head.

Alessandro returned to his office, picked up a feather quill and a clean sheet of paper, and began to write. The coded letter was addressed to one of his factors in the Badlands, and in it, he asked his agent to find a group of people willing to take on a special assignment. There could be no ties to either the Savonnes or the Illymari government, and they had to be very, very good at what they did. Breaking the Peace of Zarryiosiad was considered blasphemy and could be punishable by death at the hands of the Zarryiostrom, so they also had to be discreet.

If the Corsair is foolish enough to accept the invitation that the Church is extending to her, then peace or no, I would be remiss in my duties as leader of this family if I didn't take the time to prepare a nice warm reception for her. I'd hate for her to think that we didn't care.

After he had signed and sealed the letter, he leaned back in his seat and picked up his snifter of brandy once again. He would have to inform his daughter of his plans, of course, but he knew that she would agree with him that this was the best course of action they could take under the circumstances. In fact, now that he had made his decision, the wisest course would be to leave the entire affair in her hands, for he had been away from the capital city of Illymaine for many years and had lost track of which Savonne held which position. The assassins would need help, and only a member of the family could be trusted enough to provide it. Just to be certain that he remained above suspicion, he would decline the invitation he had received from the Zarryiostrom to attend the Convocation . . . politely, of course, but firmly. He would cite bad health or some such as the reason he would not go, but he didn't think they would notice. There were too many other people attending the event to worry about one old man.

Alessandro stood up to return to his place in the sun, brandy in hand.

With any luck, in just a few weeks I will never have to hear the name 'Prudence Daemira' ever again.

CHAPTER TWO

"Powerborn"

Chesare Illvanna was sick and tired of beautiful clothing. As a Princess of Illymar, she understood the need to look her best for the Convocation, but after a full month of being forced to stand in one place day after day, as seamstresses measured, fitted, draped, wrapped, stuck, poked, and prodded, she'd found that she'd had more than enough. There were better things for her to be doing at the moment, or less *dull* things at least, but somehow she always ended up in this same spot, facing endless mounds of the finest silks and the stern expressions of an unending line of seamstresses with their pins and needles and shears. It made her want to scream in frustration.

At least the view is nice, she thought to herself, trying to find a silver lining to this particular dark cloud, for what seemed to be the millionth time. The fitting room was an open-faced terrace with a magnificent view of the ocean, and from the point she was standing, she could see both the Mage Citadel and the Grand Cathedral of Zarryiosiad across the bay. She had always loved the view of the Cathedral from the Spire, but after so many endless days of staring at it, even its grand design wasn't enough to dispel her boredom. Frustrated at her lack of distraction, she surreptitiously glanced over at her older sister. Lyrahe didn't seem to be bored at all, standing perfectly still while three different seamstresses marked her dress with chalk at a blinding pace.

At 17, Lyrahe was one of the most beautiful young women Chesare had ever seen, with porcelain skin and raven tresses that curled down her back in an elegant wave that she desperately wished her own hair could emulate. Chesare herself had just turned 16, and she self-consciously reached up to run her fingers through her unruly red ringlets, jealous of the perfection of her sister's coiffure. Lyrahe's hair was always perfect. As Chesare ran her fingers through her hair, one of the governesses clicked her tongue at her, a clear signal that she should stop behaving like a barbarian, and instead continue to emulate her perfect sister. Chesare couldn't help herself. She grimaced at the governess and stuck out her tongue, earning yet another disapproving look. The governess also crossed her arms over her chest and gave her a flat stare with one eyebrow arched that told her, quite clearly, she was very close to earning herself a harsh word or two, or worse, a lecture about maintaining one's *dignity*. Chesare sighed heavily, and then returned her gaze to the spectacular view, trying desperately to find something to occupy her mind. Once again, the view failed to provide a distraction and, once again, she found her eyes wandering to look at her sister.

Like always, Lyrahe had her nose stuck in a book even as the seamstresses worked, and without even looking at the title, Chesare knew that it was yet another romance. Lyrahe absolutely lived for the things, and as far as Chesare could tell, they were her sister's only vice. Lyrahe especially loved tales of tragic romances, with young lovers divided by fate only to end up dying in each other's arms or some other such silliness. Her favorite story was Zarryiosiad and Kalindral, of course. Chesare didn't particularly care for that story, as she much preferred stories with happy endings, but on more than one occasion she'd found Lyrahe dabbing at her eyes and sniffling, an open copy of *Love's Sacrifice* sitting next to her. Chesare let out an undignified snort of ridicule at the thought. When she realized what she had done, she glanced quickly at the governess but, thankfully, the humorless woman hadn't heard. Chesare barely suppressed a sigh of relief when she realized that she had somehow gotten away with it.

As the day slowly progressed, and the sun rose to its midday position, Chesare began to feel more than a bit warm. That was very strange, as it wasn't a particularly warm day, but even so, beads of sweat started forming at her forehead. There was a gentle breeze flowing from the ocean, and normally that would have been enough to cool her, but today it did little to help. One of the seamstresses noticed sweat dripping down towards the silk and quickly produced a kerchief to wipe it off.

It wouldn't do to stain the silk, would it? thought Chesare with a flash of ire.

She felt a surge of anger totally out of proportion to her irritation, and that anger in turn seemed to make her feel even hotter. She closed her eyes and started a relaxing exercise one of her tutors had taught her to try and calm herself. She had always had a temper, and this was the best way she'd found to control it. With her eyes closed, she started counting to one hundred, first in Illymari Standard, then in Elvish, then again in Faeish. She wasn't exactly fluent in either Elvish or Faeish, but she could read and write both languages very well and at least make herself be understood without too much embarrassment. Both of her older sisters were perfectly fluent in both languages, of course, with Tais being truly gifted. Unfortunately, Chesare was pretty sure that Tais had had little opportunity to practice her skills, now that she was imprisoned in the Tower.

Chesare couldn't understand why what Tais had done was so wrong, and why she had deserved such a harsh punishment. Over a year ago, Tais had fallen in love with an Earl from one of the country estates, and had run away with him despite her father's express order forbidding her to ever see him again. That was bad enough, Chesare supposed, but Tais had been promised to the Prince of Ferralin, a man she had never seen before, in order to cement an alliance between the two nations. Unfortunately, her secret marriage to the Earl had ended that betrothal quite handily, and their father, King Orem, had been enraged when he found out what Tais had done. He stripped the Earl of his lands and titles in absentia, and ordered their oldest brother, Crown Prince Ethan, to assemble an army to both retrieve Tais and punish the Earl. Lyrahe had thought the entire episode dreadfully romantic, of course, but that romantic viewpoint had been shattered forever when, weeks later, a nearly catatonic Tais had been unceremoniously returned to the castle by Ethan, who also delivered the Earl's head in a basket. Chesare couldn't be certain, but she honestly believed that King Orem had been very close to ordering Tais's execution for High Treason as well, and had only relented at the behest of their mother. Instead of facing the headsman, Tais was imprisoned in the Tower and not allowed to see anyone without the express permission of the King. A few weeks after Tais' imprisonment, Chesare and Lyrahe had timidly asked permission of their father to see her, but King Orem had told them coldly that they were never to mention their sister's name to him again, and neither of the girls had dared to defy that order. In fact, nearly a year later, so far as Chesare could tell no one had been allowed to see Tais at all.

PRINCESS CHESARE OF ILLYMAR

There were many rumors that had begun to spread, and one in particular Chesare found to be more disturbing than most. According to the rumor, Tais had been pregnant when she was brought back to the castle, and had given birth sometime during the past year. What had happened to the child after its birth was anyone's guess, but the most prominent rumor was that Orem had had the child executed. Chesare refused to believe that her father was capable of doing something so vile, but she couldn't help but remember the look on his face when he'd denied them permission to see Tais. She loved her father, but on that day his face had been that of a terrifying stranger.

"Your Highness, are you feeling well?" The totally unexpected question snapped Chesare out of her reverie and she looked around in a slight daze to find the speaker.

She noticed that Lyrahe had lowered her book and was staring at her in concern, and that the governess, who had given her the disapproving looks earlier, also had a worried expression on her face. Chesare opened her mouth to say that she felt fine, but noticed then that perspiration was pouring down her face, and the silk the seamstresses had fought to protect had been utterly ruined. She reached up to wipe the sweat from her eyes and again touched her hair. The sodden ringlets stuck to her forehead and neck, and the sweat began to pour through it to stream down the bare skin of her back.

The governess waved quickly towards a cupbearer and the servant sprang forward with a cool glass of water at the ready. Chesare took the cup and nodded her thanks, draining it as quickly as she could, but the cold water didn't help in the slightest, and Chesare began to feel faint. She couldn't remember ever feeling this hot before, not even when she had been feverish as a child, and she pressed the emptied glass to her forehead, clinging desperately to the cool glass as if it were filled with ice. Her knees buckled, and gentle hands quickly helped her to the floor while the governess frantically called for someone to fetch the physician.

The glass tumbled from her hands and shattered on the cold marble, but Chesare didn't notice. All she could feel was the roaring heat within her and she knew that if she didn't do something soon, it would consume her, devouring her completely and leaving nothing behind. She arched her back spasmodically and began thrashing on the floor as her eyes rolled back into her head. She could feel the seamstresses holding her hands and legs tightly, desperately trying to keep her from injuring herself, while the governess tried unsuccessfully to fit a leather belt between her clenched teeth. Chesare's head jerked from side to side uncontrollably, while tears streamed down her face until she felt the heat doubling, and then redoubling, again and again and *again.* In her mind she screamed in tormented agony as she burned alive, *Archon, please let this end!*

With a cry, the seamstresses and the governess leaped away from her, clutching their hands in pain. Anyone who had been touching the Princess's bare skin had been burned, and their cracked red skin blistered as it cooled. Lyrahe cried out in terror as her sister continued her uncontrollable thrashing, until suddenly, without warning, Chesare stopped moving. Her back arched one more time, almost to the breaking point, and then she collapsed like a rag doll and stopped moving altogether. For what seemed to be an eternity nothing happened . . . until Chesare's eyes snapped open.

Her green eyes were gone, replaced by two fiery red embers burning in her skull. Her eyes widened and blazed once, flaring from red embers to white-hot coals, and a wave of heat exploded from her body. Her clothes burned away, leaving her naked. The glass that she had dropped during her seizure instantly liquefied, bubbling and pooling where it had fallen beside the Princess's hand, while the piles of beautiful silk were reduced to ash as a sheet of fire reached hungrily towards the other people in the room. The attendants and seamstresses had already been backing away from the princess, but slowly, almost as if they were paralyzed. As the fires spread outward looking for new fuel to consume, blind terror overcame their paralysis, and everyone scrambled out of the room in panic, trying to escape the flames that reached so hungrily for them. Chesare didn't notice their frantic flight, as every ounce of concentration in her body was focused on a single goal: shedding the heat as quickly as possible.

Instinctively, she placed her hands on the marble floor, and somehow—she knew not how—began forcing the heat from her body into her hands and then from her hands into the marble itself. A white-hot flare exploded from her, and everywhere it struck, the stone itself blackened and charred. The furniture disappeared altogether in the blaze, and the heavily gilded oaken doors warped and twisted in their frames. She couldn't have described exactly how she was forcing the heat away from her, but all she knew is that whatever she was doing was working. The flames within her flared angrily one last time, then banked, before slowly abating. Eventually, the fire under her skin cooled and disappeared altogether, and a naked and exhausted Chesare weakly curled up into a ball on her side and fell into blissful unconsciousness.

Several minutes later, the Captain of the Guard and a handful of men-at-arms broke open the door expecting to see the worst. Instead, they found the Princess completely unharmed, sleeping like a newborn baby in the midst of what had obviously been an inferno.

"Your Majesty, Archimagus DeVir has arrived." King Orem III turned to his Captain of the Guard and nodded, then looked past him towards the new arrival. Archimagus DeVir had obviously hurried, but had taken the time to change into his formal robes before being presented to the King.

"Your Majesty. I apologize for taking so long to arrive. I was in a meeting at the Grand Cathedral when your messenger found me."

King Orem didn't waste time on small talk.

"We don't know what happened, Archimagus, though we have our suspicions. Chesare is still unconscious, but she seems to be fine. The Royal Physician can find nothing wrong with her, so we called upon the Citadel. Perhaps you can explain."

"Can you tell me exactly what happened before she collapsed?" Cedric asked. "The messenger would only say that there had been a fire and that several people had been injured."

The King shook his head.

"There was a fire, but that isn't what injured the others. Apparently, only the people who were physically restraining Chesare during a sudden seizure were injured. Their injuries consist of burns and blisters, but the physician has already seen to their wounds. One thing is clear: the people who actually touched Chesare were injured, but she herself seems to be completely unharmed."

"Before I look in on her, may I see the room she was in when this happened? It's important."

The King looked at the Captain. The Captain turned to the Archimagus.

"If you will follow me?"

Archimagus DeVir stepped aside and allowed the Captain to pass, quietly falling in behind him.

Orem could not hold back his concern.

"Do you have any idea of what could have caused this? If it was an assassination attempt, I need to know immediately so I can have the security increased."

"That may be a bit premature, Your Majesty. I do have an inkling of what may have happened, but I need to see the room to confirm it. Rest assured, I will know as soon as I see the room."

Orem looked as if he wished to say something else, but closed his mouth. After several minutes of walking, the procession reached an ornate door flanked by two guards. The guards braced to attention and the Captain turned to Cedric.

"This is the room, Archimagus. No one has been allowed to enter since we removed the Princess."

Cedric closed his eyes and concentrated on the interior of the room.

"I sense no residual flames. It is safe to enter."

The guardsmen opened the doors. It took some effort, as the heat had warped the gilded doors, but the guards were able to pull them apart.

Cedric stepped inside, taking careful note of the scorch marks. Only one side of the pillars was blackened, and he quickly discerned the pattern. He walked forward, unmindful of the charring and the ash, and stepped to the spot from which the flames had originated. On the floor was a small pool of glass, melted, blackened, and fused into the stone.

A crystal goblet or wineglass, he thought, *liquefied in the heat.* He whistled silently in appreciation for the power that had required.

"This was where she was lying, yes?" The Captain nodded, and Cedric smiled. "This wasn't an attack, Your Majesty. The flames came from the Princess herself. I believe congratulations are in order: your daughter is Fireborn," he gestured at the blackened marble, "and quite a powerful one at that. The heat necessary to cause this much damage—especially to stone—is considerable. When she is properly trained, she will become an exceptional Mage."

As he spoke, King Orem's face changed from one of concern to one of cautious pride.

"You're certain? There can be no mistake?"

Archimagus DeVir smiled.

"I'm positive, Your Majesty. If I might be allowed to examine the Princess, I will confirm it."

At that, the King's face split into a wide grin.

"Of course, of course! This is excellent news, Archimagus. Simply wonderful."

Cedric politely inclined his head. When he looked up, he caught a different expression on King Orem's face. The monarch covered the look in an instant, but for a split second, Cedric DeVir had seen something other than paternal pride. What he saw was one of pure, unadulterated avarice.

When Chesare opened her eyes again, she didn't know where she was. A few moments of panic set in, until she recognized the gauzy canopy above her. Somehow, she was in her own apartments, lying in her own bed. She started to sit up when a gentle hand pressed down upon her shoulder to hold her down. She turned to see who was with her, but didn't recognize the distinguished man. Black hair with two white streaks at the temples clearly marked him as Dakkadian, but he wore his hair short and neatly trimmed in the current Illymari fashion instead of long, as a Dakkadian would. She also noted that he was dressed in a black Mage's robe trimmed with gold rather than silver, so she knew that he was an Archimagus, rather than a common Mage. She obediently relaxed and waited for him to speak.

"You've been through quite an ordeal, Princess. A great many people are very worried about you." His baritone voice was surprisingly deep, and the clipped, precise accent confirmed his nationality. At those words, the memory of the events of that afternoon returned to her and Chesare's eyes widened in alarm. Despite the presence of his hand, she shot bolt upright.

"There were flames everywhere!"

She looked down at her hands, remembering what she had done to rid herself of the heat, and half expected to see them blackened and burned from the fire. Instead, she noted with relief, that her hands were perfectly fine.

"Other people were there, Archimagus. Were they injured? What of Lyrahe? I didn't hurt her, did I?"

The rising panic in her voice was accompanied by tears welling in her eyes, but a quelling gesture from the Mage calmed her and allayed her fears.

"Your sister is quite well, though others in the room were indeed injured, if not as badly as they might have been. Their injuries have already been treated and, according to the Royal Physician, they will be fine with time and bed rest. You needn't worry about them."

His voice sharpened and took on the same intonation she had come to expect from teachers and instructors.

"Attend my words." He raised his hand and a tiny flame sprang out of one finger and began to dance from fingertip to fingertip. When he was certain he had her complete attention, he spoke. "Watch the fire as it moves. See how it twists and turns, always in motion and yet somehow always in control? I want you to concentrate on it. Now, imagine it burning inside yourself, as if you are an iron furnace holding the heat at bay."

Chesare stared at the flame that was flickering in front of her. His words washed over her, and his voice melded with the brightness of the fire to produce a hypnotic effect.

"Now, imagine the flames pouring forth from the furnace within you, seeking to join the one you see before you. Meld the flames together, until they are one." The fire flickered mildly and then doubled in size, and he smiled in approval. "Very good. *Very* good! The flame is now yours to command, Princess. Take control of it, and make it move the way you want. Bend it to your will."

Chesare frowned in consternation. *Bend fire to my will? I can't do that.* Still, as the flame moved over his hand from fingertip to fingertip, left to right, she concentrated on it, willing the flame to change direction and move from right to left. The little fire continued merrily upon its original path, unconcerned with her attempts to control it.

"Fire is fickle, Princess. It can be a powerful ally and a steadfast companion, but it must always be subservient to you. If you fail to control it—if you fail to bend it to your will—it will eagerly consume you." At that, the fire flared brightly, instantly tripling in size. The sudden expansion startled her, and she flinched, raising her hands up to protect her face. The flame froze for a second, then flew away from her and struck a far wall, flaring again, and then dying away completely. For an instant, the Mage looked utterly startled. He frowned at her briefly, squared his shoulders, and then started the lesson anew. A flame once more appeared above his fingertips, beginning its journey from left to the right.

"Attend. To control a thing, you must first lose your fear of it. To fear something is to give it control. Surrender control, and you become a slave. Fire is *yours* to command. Make it your servant."

Chesare let her hands fall to her lap and concentrated again on the flame. She began to feel strangely drawn to the man seated next to her, as if they shared a connection, almost a resonance. He clearly felt the same thing.

"Excellent, Princess. I can feel you exerting your will. Concentrate on the flame, and make it yours."

Chesare took a deep breath, and for a third time, she concentrated on the flame. It took a few moments, but before long she could feel the same resonance that she felt with the Mage emanating from within the fire itself. She seized upon that resonance and used it to exert control. The movement from left to right slowed, stopped completely, and then changed direction. Abruptly, the flame disappeared altogether, and the Archimagus grinned at her.

"Congratulations, Novice. You've done very well indeed for your first day."

At that, he stood up and turned toward the doorway. For the first time, Chesare noticed her mother and father standing there, silently watching the exchange. Her mother looked worried, but her father looked proud.

"She will need to begin her training immediately, Your Majesties. As I said earlier, she is exceedingly powerful. To have an untrained Fireborn with as much raw talent as she possesses remain unsupervised could have unfortunate consequences to those around her. The Mage Citadel is where she needs to be for now."

Her father frowned.

"What of the Convocation? It's less than a month away. Will she be able to attend?"

The Mage crossed his arms.

"That is entirely up to her, of course. If she is mindful and attentive, a month will be more than sufficient to prepare her. If she's wicked and idle, a lifetime wouldn't be long enough. At the Citadel, we shall find out which it will be."

He turned to Chesare and raised a single eyebrow.

"I am Archimagus Cedric DeVir, Novice. I am the Eighth Seat of the Mage High Council and I will be one of your instructors at the Citadel. Try to get some sleep. You'll need as much as you can get before you begin your training." He paused. "I have high expectations for you, Novice, as do your parents, I'm sure. With the amount of raw talent you possess, you will rise very high among your peers. You are the first Powerborn in ten generations born to the Illvanin family, and much is riding on your shoulders. Do not disappoint."

He turned back to the King and Queen and bowed respectfully.

"By your leave, Your Majesties. The Citadel will expect her on the morrow."

The King nodded, and the Mage walked from the bedchamber.

The King smiled at his daughter, but the Queen placed a hand on his chest and gently pushed him from the room.

"She needs her rest. Tomorrow will be an important day." She turned to her daughter, "Try and sleep, Chesare. We love you."

She stepped back and Chesare caught sight of Lyrahe, who waved cheerfully at her from the hallway. She returned the wave, and with that, her mother closed the door, leaving her alone with her thoughts. Chesare found that she was afraid of what the morrow would bring, but then she remembered something the Mage had said. *To fear something is to give it control. Surrender control, and you become a slave.*

That thought provided an odd sense of comfort and, with that, she fell asleep, dreaming of dancing flames.

During the ride back to the Mage Citadel, Cedric DeVir couldn't help but think over the day's events. The emergence of a Powerborn in the royal family of Illymar would send shockwaves through all of the royal families who would attend the Convocation—a conclusion that King Orem had already reached, if that one veiled look had been any indication. The situation Patriarch Varic had described earlier—the possibility of an Illymari/Dakkadian alliance through an arranged marriage—was no longer as much of a possibility. Dakkadia's most powerful bargaining chip had just been nullified, and they didn't even know it. King Orem no longer needed fresh Mage blood injected into his family line, so a marriage between one of the princesses of Illymar and one of the sons of Dakkadia was most likely no longer a possibility.

On the other hand, the shrewdest thing for Orem to do now would be to negotiate a marriage between Princess Chesare and Queen Aveliad's son, Phaedron, and after the marriage grant him generous estates in Illymar. This would serve to create a new line of Mages, while keeping them firmly under Orem's control. It will be interesting to see if this thought occurs to him.

Before beginning the test for the Princess, he had taken steps to ensure his complete control of the situation, as an untrained Powerborn could be a danger to everyone around her if preventative measures were not taken. He had believed that he had the situation well in hand, but even so, she had somehow seized control of the flame and hurled it away from her with no conscious effort, a feat that should have been flatly impossible. His shock and surprise—brief as they were—had been genuine, and he knew he hadn't been able to cover it quickly enough. Shortly after that, when she had finally achieved resonance, the well of power he had felt within her had been incredible. It was galling to admit it even to himself, but self-deception had never been one of his flaws: one day she would dwarf his ability with fire magic. In fact, he strongly suspected only one other living person could match her potential.

The only Mage alive with her raw talent is Morvandis, and she is half his age. This is yet another interesting development in a day full of them.

A match between Princess Chesare and either Phaedron or Valeriad, the Powerborn sons of his half-sister, Aveliad, would make for very potent Mage offspring indeed, and Cedric firmly believed King Orem would be a fool if he didn't pursue that connection as aggressively as possible. Illymar had been too long without a Mage in the royal line, and Orem desperately needed to fan this potential spark into a flame. He wasn't sure exactly how strong the boys were, but all of the reports he had received concerning the two sons of Aveliad mentioned that they were exceedingly powerful, and that Morvandis had pushed them very hard during their training. That could be good or bad, he supposed, but it wasn't skill Morvandis lacked, it was humanity and morality.

For their sakes, I pray the boys have learned those virtues from their mother.

CHAPTER THREE

"Tensions"

"Always keep your guard up, Valeriad. You're dropping your left hand whenever you plan to attack." King Madari Dhaerhan followed his words with a quick swing that caught his son's left arm just above the elbow. He used the flat of his blade instead of the edge, but he knew the blow would still sting. *The sharpest lessons teach best.*

Valeriad leapt back and raised his rapier and main gauche back into a guard position, and this time Madari couldn't find fault with the way he held his weapons, so he raised his longsword over his head and grasped it in both hands. He normally fought with a greatsword, but without his armor, he knew his son could easily defeat the slow but powerful weapon. So, for practicing with his son, he settled for a lighter blade, one that could keep up with the speed of the rapier.

They clashed twice more, and Madari easily deflected his son's strikes, until without even noticing he'd done so, Valeriad dropped his arm. This time he didn't bother to warn him. Madari simply stepped to the side and swatted his son's arm again, a little harder than before.

"You can't say I didn't warn you," he said in a light tone.

"No, I can't, can I?" replied Valeriad with a chagrined smile.

A soldier signaled from the side, and the King of Dakkadia sheathed his sword.

"It looks like they're ready for us. Time for another day on the road."

"At least this will be the last one," said Valeriad, still rubbing his arm.

"True. Then we'll have ten days on the *Sovereign.* Plenty of time for your bruised arm to heal up."

"And plenty of time for me to think about how I received the bruise in the first place, as well as how to avoid receiving more in the future." He sheathed his own weapons and grinned at his father. "I don't suppose you want to try a bout with Phaedron? He'd be more of a challenge to you, and I could see how he does it."

"Ah, no thanks," Madari replied quickly. "At my age, bruises don't heal quite as quickly as they used to, and Phaedron would love the opportunity to give me as many of them as he could. It would look bad for morale for me to lose in front of the men."

"Too bad," said Valeriad with a grin. "I was hoping he could avenge me."

"Just remember to keep your guard up, and one day you'll be able to avenge yourself."

Madari ruffled his hand through his son's long white hair, then took the reins of his warhorse from a groom. At 17, Valeriad was getting a bit old for him to tease him that way, but the two of them were very close. Each morning, after breakfast, he and Valeriad practiced their swordplay, before beginning the day's journey. It helped to keep them both sharp, and provided a bit of fun to the day before the tedium of the day's ride set in.

As he mounted his horse, his legs and buttocks protested the strain, reminding him that he actually *did* have bruises, just ones that he wasn't willing to discuss. Five days on horseback used to mean nothing at all to him when he was on campaign, but that was when he was young. He was much older now, and the idea of another day in the saddle filled him with a vague sense of dread at the prospect of even more aches and pains at journey's end.

He could see his wife and daughter climbing into their carriage, and for the briefest of moments he actually considered joining them, but his pride won out. Besides, the luxuries of sitting on a padded seat and stretching out his sore legs were offset by the knowledge that he would have to sit with his wife, Aveliad. *I'd much rather have saddle-sores and stiff legs than have to put up with an entire day of her smug looks at my discomfort. In fact, I'd rather be dragged all the way to the* Sovereign *behind my horse than give her the satisfaction of seeing me show weakness.*

With that thought providing him all the motivation he needed, he pulled himself adroitly onto the horse's back and settled his foot into the stirrup. As soon as he was ready, he signaled the scouts, and they rode off in clouds of dust to check the road ahead as the rest of the procession began the day's march to the port city of D'arhak Laha'knohs.

The first thing Phaedron, the Earl of Daane, noticed was the smell. The sharp tang of salt water filled his nostrils, and he breathed deeply to take in as much of it as possible. As he enjoyed the scent, out of the corner of his eye he spotted his younger half-brother shaking his head in amusement. Phaedron turned his horse slightly towards his grinning sibling and gave him a mock-severe look.

"Something funny?"

An unrepentant Valeriad grinned even wider.

"You. I can always tell when we're getting close to the ocean. You get this look on your face of smug satisfaction, and then snort in as much air as you can. I don't understand why you do it: the air smells exactly the same here as it did fifty yards ago."

As Valeriad spoke, Phaedron began shaking his head in feigned sorrow.

"Spoken like a Fireborn. You spend so much time setting things ablaze it's probably affected your sense of smell. Too much sulfur or something. I almost feel sorry for you."

Valeriad laughed, his long white hair flowing with the movement.

"There's nothing wrong with my sense of smell at all, Phaedron. In fact, my keen nose has detected something distasteful nearby. *Very* nearby." He cocked his head to the side as if contemplating something, tapped the side of his nose with a gloved finger, and took three delicate sniffs. "I can't quite make out the stench. Pretty rotten though." He paused for effect, and then took a significant look toward Phaedron. "Say, are you sitting upwind?"

Phaedron laughed brightly.

"I wish I could disagree with you, but you're probably right. Six days on a horse will do that to you."

"Oh, I don't think six days in the saddle would be enough to account for a smell this bad."

Before Phaedron could phrase an adequate reply, a soft, melodic voice interrupted their conversation.

"Boys. That will be quite enough. Six days of your incessant bickering and one-upmanship is wearying."

Both of the young men turned to look at the speaker and answered as one.

"Yes, Mother."

QUEEN AVELIAD DHAERHAN OF DARKADIA

Queen Aveliad of Dakkadia shook her head in exasperation as the two young men launched right back into their never-ending exchange of witty repartee and mutual insults, as if she had never spoken. Sitting next to her in the open carriage was her youngest child, Princess Deirdre, who was listening to her brothers insult each other, and giggling whenever a particularly telling blow struck home. Any time one of them made her laugh, the boys would press home the point to elicit even greater laughter from the younger sister they both adored. Aveliad suspected that if walking barefoot on crushed glass or hot coals would have amused the golden-haired Princess, either one of her sons would have gladly done it just to please her.

She leaned back in her comfortable seat and half-closed her eyes behind her ornate porcelain mask, while surreptitiously studying her sons' profiles. Valeriad, her younger son, was an exceptionally handsome boy, with clear blue eyes, fair skin, and flowing white hair that almost reached his lower back. Among Dakkadians, that white hair marked him as an oddity, for although white hair was fairly common amongst the Fae, it was practically unheard of in a Dakkadian who tended toward blue-black hair. Valeriad was seventeen years old; just the right age for marriage, and the eligible daughters from every house in Dakkadia and the surrounding lands were finding reasons to visit the capital city of Blackstone. The fact that he stood next in line for the throne would have been more than enough reason for an endless stream of eligible young women to show interest in him. But once these young women set eyes upon him, they quickly found that doing their duty for their families, as their parents insisted, wouldn't be such an onerous chore after all, for even amongst the Fae he would be accounted as extraordinarily beautiful. For his part, he seemed to enjoy the attention, but so far, despite the temptation, he hadn't taken advantage of the situation. Instead, his attention had been diverted to other pursuits. As tradition dictated, Valeriad had just entered service in the Dakkadian military, and had taken to his duties with a will. He had always been a serious boy, and the military lifestyle suited his demeanor quite well. Aveliad had no doubt that Valeriad would make a wonderful soldier one day, though as a mother she had reservations about him putting himself in harm's way.

Her older son, Phaedron, was a marked contrast to his younger half-brother; for where Valeriad was exceptional for a Dakkadian, Phaedron was the very image of a traditional Dakkadian noble, with long blue-black hair marked with the white streak unique to the nobility. Aveliad loved both of her sons dearly, but it was Phaedron who held a special place in her heart, for he was the son of her first husband, Lord Phaedril Daane. Phaedril had died over twenty years ago in a tragic hunting accident, shortly before Phaedron was born, so Phaedron had grown up having never known his father. Despite that, Phaedron was every inch his father's son, for he had Phaedril's lighthearted demeanor and quick wit, and with every day that passed, he looked more and more like his father. In a way, it was heartbreaking for Aveliad to even look at him, for she had never fully recovered from the loss of her beloved Phaedril. But knowing that a part of him lived on gave her all the comfort she needed.

She glanced down at Phaedron's side and noticed the hilt of his rapier riding at the proper angle on his belt. Valeriad would no doubt make an excellent soldier someday, but Phaedron was a warrior born. No one in the kingdom could match his skill with a blade, and through sheer merit, he had already been appointed as one of the military leaders of Dakkadia. As Master of the Light Horse, he led a new formation known as the Dakkadian Pistoliers; lightly armored horsemen who were known for bold charges and lightning attacks. His courage and tactical brilliance were already the talk of Dakkadia, and almost as many women were coming to see him as they were his younger brother. The women coming to the capital to try and trap him in their webs were destined for disappointment, for Phaedron rarely spent time at the Blackstone. Instead, he spent his time at his own home or riding with his men around the periphery of Dakkadia keeping the borders secure. As the Earl of Daane, he owned a sizeable estate that he had inherited from his father, and when he wasn't in the field, that was where he spent the vast majority of his time.

The reason for his constant absence wasn't that he hated court life or the attentions of fawning young women, it was that he bitterly hated his stepfather, King Madari, a sentiment Aveliad shared. For his part, Madari had tried halfheartedly to win the boy's affections, but had finally given up his efforts as a lost cause, and had instead allowed his stepson as much freedom as he wanted away from the capital. Phaedron hadn't wanted to attend the Convocation, turning down invitation after invitation until Aveliad had personally asked him to come, as a favor to her. Despite his reluctance, Phaedron hadn't been able to refuse a direct request from his mother, so here he was, riding beside the carriage and trying to make the most of the situation by bonding with his siblings.

Her thoughts were interrupted when she caught sight of her husband riding towards them from the front of the column, and all happiness seemed to drain right out of her. She reached up unconsciously, as she had done countless times before, and checked to see that the white enameled mask that covered her eyes was in place. The mask was graceful and elegant, adorned with feathers and jewels, but it seemed out of place anywhere except a court ball or an opera. Despite this, she never removed the mask outside of her own bedchambers;

chambers she did *not* share with her husband, nor would she, as long as she remained Madari's wife. Phaedron had his own reasons for hating his stepfather, but what he didn't know was that Aveliad had strong suspicions that the "accident" which had stolen her husband from her, had in fact, been nothing of the sort. Though she couldn't prove it—*yet*—she knew who had most likely been behind the murder. *When I find the proof I seek, I'll have my revenge. And on the day that Phaedril's spirit is finally at rest, I'll remove this mask and try to forget that you ever existed, Madari.*

As King Madari Dhaerhan of Dakkadia rode to the middle of the column, he pretended he didn't see his wife checking her mask. He had long since stopped caring that she chose to hide her beauty as much as possible around him. What did that matter? Her beauty was legendary, and everyone already knew that she belonged to him: the mask simply made her more alluring, if indeed that was possible. Aveliad was half-Fae, but the exotic beauty of her Faeish blood had been leavened perfectly by her human blood. He had been smitten with her the day he had met her, and it didn't matter in the slightest that she had belonged to another. He had pursued her with single-minded determination, and when his advances had failed and she had married another, he had turned to . . . other devices. The end result was his marriage to the most beautiful woman in the world. What mattered then the means? Unfortunately, success, in this case, had its price. To others, she may have been the most exquisite woman in the world, but for him she was ice, as cold and lifeless in bed as the alabaster her skin so richly emulated.

The three children saw him approaching and their faces spoke volumes. Phaedron, Aveliad's child of her first marriage and the eldest at 20 years, closed his mouth and assumed a rigid posture that mirrored his mother's almost perfectly. That boy had learned his lessons well from his mother, and Madari fought down a killing rage. The ungrateful wretch didn't seem to realize that he was lucky he hadn't been killed at birth. Madari had considered it when he learned his future wife was with child from her first marriage, but women were always unpredictable about children. Had he killed the child he might have woken up one fine morning with a dagger in his heart—or worse—and wouldn't that have been fun? The other two children were different. Valeriad, Madari's only son and 17 years of age, smiled when he saw who was approaching and raised his hand in greeting. Deirdre smiled as well at the father who doted on her.

At 14 years old, Deirdre was at the age where she wasn't quite a woman, but was no longer a child, and she was becoming more beautiful by the day. Fair skinned and golden haired, she was going to be every bit as beautiful as her mother one day, if not more so, and Madari was looking forward to receiving offers of marriage for his daughter's hand. Indeed, people were already calling her the "Jewel of Dakkadia". She would make a fine wife for some royal, and a strong alliance for Dakkadia, and that was exactly what he wanted for her. In fact, Madari hoped he could arrange marriages for both of his children that would bring even greater power to Dakkadia than he had already achieved.

When he reached his children, he reined in his horse and said,

"We are nearing the port, and the outriders have informed me that Lady Prudence Daemira is awaiting us with the *Sovereign.* Do not get lost, do not wander off, and do not cause trouble. I do not want you to slow our departure by a single second. Am I clearly understood?"

Phaedron nodded solemnly, and Valeriad touched his heart with his right hand in the traditional Dakkadian salute.

Deirdre, clearly excited beyond measure, could hold silent no longer.

"Father, I can't believe we are going to sail with the Corsair herself! She's the most famous pirate in the entire world! I can't wait to meet her!"

The girlish excitement in Deirdre's voice made Valeriad laugh, before he covered his mouth with his hand, shining eyes and shaking chest giving away his silent laughter. Phaedron lost his stony gaze and covered his eyes, a wide grin visible under his hand while, he too, shook with suppressed mirth. Deirdre didn't notice her brother's reactions, for all of her attention was focused on her father.

Madari turned a stony gaze toward Valeriad, who instantly stopped laughing and assumed an admirably grave expression.

"It's 'privateer,' not 'pirate', sweetling. You would do well to remember the difference and mind your tongue around her. Despite what the Illymari may believe, Lady Prudence is not a pirate at all; she's a court-sponsored privateer. That means she sails under the flag of Dakkadia and is able to attack merchant vessels and capture prizes legally. Privateers are soldiers; pirates are criminals. Remember that, and remember as well that we are merely guests aboard her vessel. Lady Prudence has graciously allowed us to make use of her ship to ferry us to and from the Convocation, but no part of our arrangement says that she has to waste her time answering your questions. Make any trouble for her and she'll toss you overboard and let you swim home."

Deirdre nodded solemnly, wide eyes not changing in the slightest.

"Phaedron, Valeriad, you will comport yourselves with absolute dignity aboard the *Sovereign.* I'm not exactly on the best of terms with Captain Daemira, and I had to call in a great many personal favors to get her to agree to bring us to Illymar, especially since there is a price on her head in Illymar. I want nothing at all to jeopardize our arrangement. It is more important than you know for us to put our best foot forward, from now until we return home again. Appearances are everything." Valeriad nodded to his father, but Phaedron sat unmoving, his posture and expression still a mirror image of his mother's. Madari looked directly at Phaedron and asked in a harsh voice, "Am I understood?"

Phaedron, unfazed by the tone, merely inclined his head in the slightest of nods. Madari stared at him for a minute longer, then turned his black charger back toward the front of the line and urged it into a canter, quickly leaving his family behind.

Valeriad rounded on his half-brother, mouth twisted in an angry frown.

"Why can't you even try to get along with him? He's a great man and a great father, and you refuse to see that! Nothing he does is good enough for you!"

Phaedron turned a cold gaze upon his younger sibling, all traces of his former mirth gone.

"This is not an argument we should be having in public." When Valeriad refused to back down, he said, "To *you* he is a great man and a great father. To me, he is simply the man who married my mother after my own father died. Your devotion to him blinds you to his reality, Val. He's a tyrant, and many people hate and fear him. People who go against his wishes, or stand in the way of his ambition disappear, are found dead of 'explainable circumstances' and he remains untouched. His father and both of his brothers died to clear his way to the throne. He's conquered every one of the kingdoms surrounding Dakkadia, sometimes brutally and without justification, and he keeps the heel of his boot on their necks. I don't appreciate his tactics, I don't respect him as my king, and I absolutely refuse to acknowledge him as a 'father'. I had a father, and he's as dead as everyone else who gets in Madari's way."

Valeriad felt his anger flare up at the veiled accusation, and the air heated around him as he began summoning his power.

"What did you say? Are you accusing my father of something, Lord Daane?" At that, Valeriad's eyes began to glow red, and he curled his fingers into claws as a ball of fire materialized between his hands. In response to the threat, Phaedron's eyes turned a shimmering blue and a white aura of frigid air surrounded him. Though he was young, Valeriad Dhaerhan was already an extremely powerful Fire Mage, even if he hadn't yet undergone the Testing, but both of them knew that Phaedron was an even more powerful Water Mage. Furthermore, Valeriad knew that Phaedron's frost shield would easily stop even the most powerful fireball that he could generate. Once his defenses were in place, Phaedron made no attempt to attack. He simply waited until Valeriad calmed down enough to speak.

"That's my father you're talking about, Phaedron, and I'll thank you to keep your opinions to yourself where he's concerned. You don't like him? Fine. I can accept that. But, whether you like him or not, he's your king, and as his vassal, you owe him both your fealty and respect." He let the ball of fire dissipate as he finally released his hold on his power and allowed the flames to extinguish. "I know that you didn't want to be here, Phaedron, and that *my* father is the last person you want to see, but it's going to be a long trip, and the two of you are going to be on the same ship for the entire journey. So, I'm warning you now, keep your mouth shut and your opinions to yourself where he's concerned or the two of us are going to have a problem. A *serious* problem."

Phaedron hesitated for a few moments before releasing his own hold on his power. Once the frost shield had disappeared, he bowed in his saddle.

"I spoke out of turn, My Prince, and I apologize. I humbly beg your forgiveness for the insults and insinuations that I made about your father. I'll try not to let it happen again." The words were proper, but Valeriad could see a hint of defiance remaining in his eyes. Despite that, Valeriad decided to let it pass.

"Good."

Madari rode to the front of the column and slowed his charger when he reached the front. A slim figure mounted on a black stallion nodded to him, long black hair marked with a white Dakkadian stripe, perfectly arranged with not a single strand out of place, despite the six long days on the road. Dressed in a fine black velvet robe embroidered in thread-of-silver, Morvandis looked every inch the powerful Mage Madari knew him to be. To Madari's unrefined tastes, his half-brother seemed to be almost foppish, but he knew better than to make the mistake of judging the Mage's character by his clothing. Madari had seen the iron fist concealed by the velvet glove and knew never to underestimate its power, or its ruthlessness.

Morvandis was the Mage-Lord of House Dhaerhan, and wielded more power than any other three Mages in the world combined. It was hard to tell, actually, because no other Mage in the world had dared to challenge him directly since his time in the Mage Citadel of Ithram. Madari couldn't evoke at all, but Morvandis more than made up for it.

"We will be there shortly, Your Majesty."

Morvandis almost never wasted breath on pleasantries, or unnecessary conversation, and Madari admired that about him. He always went directly to the heart of any matter, with no evasion or prevarication which made him the perfect advisor. Madari himself was like that, but in action, not word. Plain spoken and direct, he had been accused, more than once, of being coarse. As the absolute ruler of Dakkadia he answered to no one, and if someone took umbrage to his words, it mattered less than nothing to him.

"I want your oath that there will be no trouble between you and Daemira's pet Mages, Morvandis. This is too important to risk on personal vendettas. The *Sovereign* is our most visible and successful privateer, and the Illymari fear and respect her reputation. Arriving aboard her sends exactly the message I want to convey to every noble at the gathering, and if that means you have to spend a few days in the presence of a man you hate, you'll just have to bear it." Madari turned a hard eye on his Mage, and Morvandis inclined his head.

"You have my oath that I will cause no trouble. The problems I have with Mage Rantrefal are philosophical in nature. It is true that we hold no love for each other, but I feel no need to escalate the conflict between us. Had I been so inclined, I could have killed him outright years ago. I think he knows this, and is willing to let the situation stand as is. For all his faults, he is not always a fool, and he certainly doesn't want to die . . . especially not at my hands."

Madari snorted in amusement. That was true enough. The "philosophical" problems the two Mages had were quite simple: Cahrick thought Morvandis a murderous bastard, and Morvandis thought of Cahrick as a weak-willed fool with a big mouth.

The problem was that many years ago, shortly after Madari took power, Cahrick had made a very drunken—and very public—speech implicating Morvandis for the murder of the former Crown Prince of Dakkadia, Madari's older brother. Morvandis had been a child at the time, and everyone who had heard the speech dismissed it as the ramblings of a man too far into his cups, but a few years later, Morvandis had heard the entire tale from one of his informants and had not been pleased. He had ordered Cahrick's immediate arrest, but the Water Mage had somehow gotten word of the warrant and fled the port before Morvandis' agents could reach him. After that, Cahrick had found powerful patrons to ward him, but more importantly, he had learned to keep his big mouth shut. Queen Aveliad herself had finally ordered the warrant revoked, and it was her patronage that had kept the Mage safe ever since.

To this day, Cahrick claimed that he couldn't remember what he had said to make an enemy of the most powerful Mage in the world, but Morvandis had never been known for his kind and forgiving nature. Madari knew his Mage very well indeed: Cahrick would pay for his transgression someday, for Morvandis never forgot an insult.

Cahrick Rantrefal wasn't a happy man. As he stared intently at the half-empty bottle of rum sitting next to him, he cursed his miserable lot in life for the thousandth time.

"I'm a dead man. Dead. Cold and dead. Might as well slit my own throat."

Even as he said it, he knew he didn't mean it. He would never give Morvandis the pleasure of seeing him dead at his own hand, and as he reached for the bottle to try once again to drown his misery, someone clapped him hard on the back.

"Time to go, old man. Cap'n wants you on board . . . ."

The speaker didn't have time to finish, as several things happened at once. Cahrick hadn't even heard the words at all, he simply reacted in shock and blind terror to the unexpected blow. He simultaneously screamed, cursed, and tried to stand up, and managed to send his stool, his bottle, and his glass flying away in different directions as if shot from a cannon. He spun around quickly, grabbing his heart and gasping, and several more things happened. The bottle and glass landed in the middle of a table populated by truly unsavory characters, and all of them leapt to their feet, grasping daggers, blackjacks, and suddenly-broken bottles. The stool landed in the middle of another group of miscreants—equally unsavory—with similar results. The two groups whirled around, looking for the poor, unfortunate, soon-to-be-dead soul stupid enough to provoke them, and caught sight of each other, weapons drawn. Both sides drew the appropriate conclusion, and with blood-curdling screams, battle was joined.

Cahrick didn't even notice. Still clutching his heart, he caught sight of his shipmate and best friend, Rory Sornin, staring at him in shock.

When Cahrick could finally speak he shouted.

"Are you trying to kill me?!"

Rory ducked a flying bottle and shouted back.

"No! Cap'n wants all hands on board immediately! I came to fetch you!" A barmaid wielding a cudgel fell against him and he pushed her back into the fray without a moment's pause.

Cahrick shot his friend a murderous look.

"I'm not going! I already told the Cap'n that! I've spent the last 20 years avoiding that blackguard, and now she wants me to be on the same ship as him? I'm no fool! I'm running as far away as I can! I don't want him within miles of me!"

"Too late for that!" Rory said, shaking his head. "The King and his entourage are entering the city even as we speak. If you really wanted to run away, you should have done it days ago! So now you have two choices: either you get back to the ship and trust the Cap'n, or you die like a dog! Which is it going to be?"

As Rory made his point, a hand clamped onto his shoulder and spun him around. A large sailor, covered in scars and tattoos, had a balled fist ready and had already begun to swing when Cahrick grabbed a bottle and broke it over the sailor's head. The suddenly boneless sailor dropped to the floor.

"Let's go."

Cahrick was no fool, or at least he was *no longer* a fool, and he'd known that running wasn't the answer days ago. If he left the Captain's protection now, he really would be as good as dead.

The two of them forced their way through the melee, finally making it to the unhinged door. The brawl had already spilled onto the street, and people were joining in left and right. The fight was rapidly turning into a full-scale riot, and they both wondered how in the hell they were supposed to get to the ship through this.

"Wonder what started the fight this time?" asked a bewildered Cahrick to an incredulous Rory.

Rory didn't bother to answer. He simply grabbed Cahrick's collar and dragged him bodily towards the docks.

CHAPTER FOUR

"Appearances"

Lady Prudence Daemira stood on the deck of the warship *Sovereign* and tried not to let her irritation show. She had sent Rory Sornin to collect Cahrick Rantrefal over an hour ago, and they had yet to return. Having both of her Mages go missing at the same time irritated her to no end, and if they didn't get back to the ship soon, she vowed that there would be hell to pay.

For the hundredth time she berated herself for not sending more men to look for the old Mage. Rory was a good man, but digging through the dives that Cahrick liked to frequent wouldn't be an easy job, especially now. On the other hand, if Cahrick didn't want to be found, he wouldn't be, no matter how many men she sent to find him. In the past twenty years he'd had a lot of practice hiding.

She absentmindedly ran a finger across a polished rail and inspected her white glove for dust. Not so much as a speck was visible and she smiled inwardly. She had always run a tight ship, but even the crew knew that this was a special occasion. Having the King of Dakkadia aboard would be a high honor and no one wanted to give him any reason to regret choosing the *Sovereign* to carry him to the Convocation. They had worked tirelessly for days on end to mend every hurt the ship had suffered in its enviable career, and the deck and rails gleamed in the bright sunlight. Even the white stripe dividing the black sails seemed to glow.

Prudence herself wasn't happy at all with the arrangement, despite the "honor." She had always been a loyal subject of Dakkadia, but that servitude had always been rocky when it came to the ruling family. The Dhaerhans were a vicious lot, dealing harshly with even the slightest transgression, real or imagined. They made enemies easily, and were almost single-handedly responsible for the isolation Dakkadia enjoyed today. All of the neighboring countries hated Dakkadia, but none were powerful enough to challenge the warlike house directly. Her own family ruled the Dakkadian protectorate of Rohm, one of the most important of the Dakkadian provinces. Her father had wanted her to marry into some noble house or another to cement an alliance, but she had had no desire to do anything of the sort and had told him so directly. They had argued about it for days until he'd finally given in.

It still surprised her that he had surrendered so easily. She wasn't stupid or blind; as the daughter of the Prince of Rohm, she knew how valuable she was as a potential bride, and any number of lords and nobles would have jumped at the chance to add her pedigree to their names. The fact that he *had* given in had made her deeply suspicious, and rather than allow him to blindside her with some new thought about her future, she had taken a chance and enlisted in the Dakkadian Navy without his permission.

When her father had found out, he'd been livid. The arguments they had had about her filial duty to the house of Daemira had paled in comparison to the all-out bloodletting they had achieved with her enlistment, but in the end he had had no choice but to let her go. He wasn't stupid or blind, either, and he knew very well that any marriage he arranged against her will would have ended with the two houses embroiled in a blood feud, not an alliance.

She'd been 17 when she had first arrived at the Naval Academy in the Dakkadian port city of D'arhak Laha'knohs. Her noble birth had entitled her to attend Officer's Candidate School, where she had excelled, easily graduating at the top of her class. After she had graduated, she had had her pick of assignments. Her first berth had been aboard the *Tiderunner*, a cutter used for coastal defense, and it was upon her deck that she had learned the finer points of seamanship. It only took a week at sea for her to decide that she would make the navy her life.

Her second berth had been aboard the Dakkadian frigate *Frenzy*, a blue water warship tasked with providing escort for the Dakkadian Merchant Marine. It was there she had had her first taste of battle, and had done surprisingly well. None of her crewmates had expected the beautiful, raven-haired young noble to be of any use in a real battle, no matter how well she had done at the academy, and so they had been caught completely by surprise by her fighting prowess. They shouldn't have been, for she was a Dakkadian noblewoman and had been trained from an early age in the ways of battle. As such, she was a better trained swordsperson than almost everyone else aboard ship. As a child, she'd had the finest tutors and, thanks in part to their efforts, her swordsmanship and marksmanship were both top-notch. The *Frenzy* had been outsized and outmanned by the privateer squadron which had attacked her charges, but despite the size difference, it had been the *Frenzy* that had pushed the battle. By the end of the day, two captured privateers and dozens of prisoners had ensured that no one would mistake Prudence Daemira for anything other than a professional warrior ever again.

She was now 25 years old, and the captain of one of the three most powerful ships in the Dakkadian fleet. Three masts, five decks, and thirty cannons made the *Sovereign* more than a match for anything currently sailing, no matter what flag the ship sailed under. Illymar had learned to fear and respect her reputation, and though the island kingdom still boasted the largest navy in the world, ship-to-ship the *Sovereign* could defeat anything the Illymari navy had afloat.

The secret to the rapid increase in Dakkadian power was simple: gunpowder. No other kingdom had it, and no one else had discovered the secret to producing it. While the Illymari navy relied on its Mages to provide firepower, the Dakkadian navy didn't need to. Every single ship in the Dakkadian fleet was a viable threat, and the *Sovereign,* with its two Mages in combination with its cannons, was even more so. Rory Sornin was an Air Mage, able to bend the weather to his will with ease, and Cahrick Rantrefal was a Water Mage, the most dangerous weapon in a ship's arsenal. A skilled Water Mage could sink ships effortlessly, capsizing them under relentless waves of incredible size, or trapping them in whirlpools hundreds of yards in diameter. In fact, the only counter for a Water Mage in a naval battle was another Water Mage, preferably one with more power and experience, and Cahrick had both in droves.

The *Sovereign* was a privateer, tasked to harass enemy shipping and capture Illymari prizes at will. So successful was the ship and her crew at doing this, Prudence had earned a nickname that other sailors used with awe and respect—the Corsair. The last serious attempt to sink or capture the *Sovereign* had cost the Kingdom of Illymar three of their newest warships and their crews. Prudence had forced their surrender with humiliating ease despite the numbers, and Illymar had lost three precious Water Mages along with the ships. It was from the captured sailors of that battle she had first heard her nickname used, and she had found, to her amusement, that she rather enjoyed the notoriety. The crew certainly had, taking an instant liking to her new nom de guerre.

A disturbance in the city caught her attention and she raised a spyglass to take a closer look. After a moment, she could see that a riot had broken out in one of the poorer sections of the city, and a few buildings had caught fire. That brought a smile to her face, for a riot could mean only one thing—Rory had found Rantrefal at last. Cahrick was a walking disaster, able to cause chaos and destruction anywhere he went without even realizing he had done so. She knew from prior experience that riot was most likely his handiwork, so she handed the spyglass to her first officer and pointed wordlessly towards the violence. With a quizzical glance, Mr. Frederick raised the glass to his eye and focused it on the spot she had pointed out. It took a single look for him to realize the implications.

"Either an open revolt has begun on the streets and alleys of D'arhak Laha'knohs, or Mr. Sornin has found our wayward Mage, Captain."

"So it seems, Mr. Frederick. Prepare the ship to raise anchor. We leave as soon as the royal party arrives. I want no delays."

Frederick walked to the railing and began passing orders.

The crew, who had been relaxing on the deck, burst into instant action, manning stations, tightening ropes, and generally looking sharp. *This is a good crew*, she mused. There was no room on her ship for slackers or layabouts, and she had ruthlessly weeded out the weak links a long time ago. The men and women who served with her knew exactly what was expected of them, and stepped to in an orderly fashion.

"What of Mr. Sornin and Mr. Rantrefal, Captain? When they return to the ship shall I have them keel-hauled, or will a flogging suffice?"

Prudence assumed a pose of deep reflection, left arm under her ample bosom, right hand on her chin. She tapped her cheek a couple times, pretending to give the question some thought.

"I think a simple flogging would be better. After all the work the crew has done scraping the barnacles off our ship, keel-hauling wouldn't have the desired effect, would it?"

Frederick nodded sagely.

"Flogging it is. Shall I have them suspended by their ankles first?"

"No. Not this time. That would take too long. Besides, it wouldn't do for the first sight His Royal Majesty has of the *Sovereign* marred by the spectacle of those two hanging from the rigging like rotten fruit. No, it would be better to flog them quickly, and then get them out of sight where they can't do any more damage to our reputations. In fact, beat them with clubs. That would be better. I wouldn't want the crew to think I had gone soft, no matter what ridiculous clothing I'm wearing."

At the mention of her attire, Frederick took in the sight of his Captain and quickly suppressed a smile. Instead of wearing her normal comfortable, well-worn clothing, she had dressed to the hilt in what (he supposed) was the latest court fashion. Her uniform had no practical application at all other than to be purely ornamental, and the only reason he could think of for her to be wearing it today was to look impressive. The snowy lace at her wrists and neck was tastefully embroidered, the heavy, long-tailed white coat had enough gold braid for a dozen admirals, and her normal plain leather baldric had been replaced for the day by a cream-colored silk sash gathered at her left hip in a bow. Her hat was also white, with an oversized brim making it seem larger than it actually was. An emerald and gold brooch pinned the left brim up in a dashing sweep and several large white plumes trailed from it as ornamentation. Her long black hair had always been wavy, and the ebon locks flowing down her back contrasted sharply with the white of her uniform. The only things he recognized on her at all were her weapons. Her silver rapier and main gauche hung from opposite sides of her hips, and two pistols were tucked into her belt, front and back. She also carried a rather large number of concealed weapons hidden in the various nooks and crannies of her clothing. She would have felt naked without them.

Corsair gave her first officer a flat stare, daring him to say anything—anything at all—about her ridiculous uniform. Unfortunately for her, he recognized the dangerous look and schooled his own face into an admirably grave expression, neatly avoiding the need for her to have him killed out of hand. The clothing had been a present from her brother, Sethred, the newly crowned Prince of Rohm, after the recent death of their father to illness. Now, her entire wardrobe was filled with these monstrosities, each one more decorative and impractical than the last. The sternly worded note that had accompanied the wardrobe made it very clear that she was to wear the gaudy clothing at all times in the presence of the King, and in the presence of the gathered nobility at the Convocation. She was a "representative of Dakkadia, after all, and had to look as impressive as possible in the eyes of our hosts," etc., etc. She could picture her brother's face as he penned the missive, snickering incessantly as he imagined the horror and consternation on her face when she saw the blighted rags for the first time.

Still, she had to admit, that the effect was impressive. When she'd first left her cabin wearing the white and gold uniform, her crewmen had stopped what they were doing to stare in awe at her, eyes widening and mouths dropping open. She hadn't said a word, but after the shock finally wore off, she had caught sight of several members of her crew surreptitiously straightening their own uniforms or smoothing their hair and dry washing their faces, as if her glowing garb had made them feel shabby and dirty. The thought brought up a thoroughly unprofessional giggle despite her dismay, and she raised her white-gloved hand to cover her mouth. She didn't want the crew to think she was laughing at them, after all.

Valeriad's first sight of the city wasn't exactly what he had remembered from his last visit. For one thing, there hadn't been quite as much smoke, or as many injured people wandering about in a daze. For another, the townspeople hadn't been fighting in the streets. He gave Phaedron a puzzled look, but Phaedron just raised an eyebrow and shrugged: he didn't know what was going on either. However, both of them knew that whatever it was, it was going to make King Madari very, very angry.

As flames shot out of the windows of a two-story building, emphasizing just how serious the situation was, both of them wondered if they should do something. Just as Phaedron had obviously resolved to act, Valeriad caught sight of Morvandis riding towards them on his black stallion. Valeriad reached out and caught Phaedron's arm, and Phaedron instantly aborted whatever it was he was about to attempt. Valeriad pointed towards the approaching Mage, and the two of them waited for their instructor to reach them. Morvandis rode quickly and with purpose, but with little urgency. When he reached them he said,

"As you can see, a section of the city is on fire. As such, it would seem that this would be an excellent time for a lesson. Your Highness, I would like for you to deal with this. First, tell me what you can sense of the fires."

Valeriad stared at the town and concentrated.

"There seem to be several fires, including three separate sources that have the potential to become serious problems. There are many other fires in the area, but some of them are so contained they may well be hearth fires or forges."

"Very good," Morvandis said. "Now tell me the most efficient way to deal with the flames."

"The best way I can think of is to simply seize control of the fires and dissipate them. I think I can do it, but I'm not positive. It would be much easier to do them one at a time."

"I am not interested in guiding you down the easier path," Morvandis said coldly. "You possess more than enough strength to deal with the problem, so deal with it you shall. All at once." Valeriad paled visibly at the command.

"By your leave?"

Morvandis inclined his head slightly.

LADY PRUDENCE DAEMIRA, THE CORSAIR

For the second time that day, Valeriad's eyes transformed from their normal cool blue to red-hot embers. He reached out a hand toward the burning buildings, frowning in concentration. Morvandis watched his pupil for a few moments, and then turned his attention towards the town. Valeriad slowly closed his hand and the fires shooting out of the second story building began to die down. Just as the flames finally seemed to be gone, Valeriad recoiled in his saddle as if he'd been struck, and the fires suddenly roared back to life. He shook his head as if to clear it, but before Morvandis could intervene, he raised his hand again.

After several moments of concentration, the fires receded, then disappeared altogether, leaving only blackened timber behind as a grim testament that the flames had even existed. Once he was certain that the fires were gone for good, Valeriad's eyes returned to their normal blue, and he lowered his hand. He was perspiring freely, as if he'd been standing right next to the fires he'd just extinguished, but he looked expectantly towards Morvandis.

"You did well, My Prince," said the older Mage, and then added, "On the second attempt."

Morvandis's tone hadn't changed at all, but both Valeriad and Phaedron had expected the barb. Valeriad didn't say anything, for Morvandis hated excuses, and anything Valeriad had said in his own defense would be considered just that. Phaedron, on the other hand, seemed to be feeling a bit more daring.

"A lot of people could have been injured or killed in that fire, Morvandis. Some may still have been. You could have extinguished those fires in an instant, yet you decided that it was more important to give Valeriad some practice than it was to save those lives."

Morvandis didn't bother to reply, he just looked at him indifferently. This angered Phaedron even further, but before he could say anything, King Madari rode up to the small group.

"Morvandis did not start the fire, nor did he begin the riot. As such, he had no obligation to save the lives of people stupid enough to do either. That he decided to intervene at all was lucky for the townspeople. I would have let them burn."

Phaedron glared at Madari.

"Of that I have no doubt. But you're wrong. You're the King, and these people are your subjects. As such, it is not only your duty to protect them, it is also your duty to protect their homes and livelihood. Or have you forgotten that?"

Madari narrowed his eyes and balled his fists, but Phaedron refused to back down, daring him to strike. Instead of hitting Phaedron, Madari sneered, and then spoke, his voice dripping with scorn.

"You dare to lecture me about the duties of a King? My duty is to govern—to make the laws and to see them enforced—not to coddle people who refuse to obey them! *My* subjects were rioting and, as such, they broke *my* law. Should I so wish, I could have all of them put to death for breaking *my* peace. If a few people have died, then let them serve as an example to the others: laws are put in place for a reason, and breaking them can mean death."

Phaedron's eyes were cold before, but now they blazed with anger. He opened his mouth to reply, but before he could speak, Queen Aveliad interrupted him, her delicate musical voice sharp as a razor.

"Phaedron, desist!"

Phaedron closed his mouth, instantly obeying his mother.

"While you are lecturing him on his duties, Phaedron, you seem to have forgotten your own. Remember that he is your King and, as such, your duty is to obey him, not to question him."

Shocked at her words and tone, Phaedron shot his mother an incredulous look, but she met his eyes unflinchingly.

Madari sneered again.

"You should listen to your mother. Some kings would believe your insults to be treasonous."

Queen Aveliad held Phaedron's gaze for a moment longer, and then turned to look Madari squarely in the eye. Though her words were meant for Phaedron, her eyes never lost their hold on Madari.

"Of course, you have other duties as well, Phaedron, and one of those duties is to make certain your own morality is never compromised by the immoral actions of another, even if that person is your teacher . . . or your King."

At his wife's scathing tone, Madari's sneer turned into a snarl, and blue eyes, hot with anger, met amber eyes, cool with scorn. Madari gave the reins of his horse a sharp pull, dragging its head around towards the front of the column.

"We're wasting time here. We have a ship to catch. Morvandis. Valeriad. Follow me."

After the King had spurred his horse forward, Morvandis turned to Aveliad and gave her the slightest of nods, as if conceding her the match. For her part, she simply looked at him as if contemplating a particularly loathsome species of insect. After a moment's pause, he rode forward, with Valeriad riding close behind, leaving Phaedron and Aveliad in sole possession of the battlefield.

Prudence Daemira felt uncharacteristically nervous when the royal column came into sight. At its head rode the King himself, his Mage Morvandis, and a boy with long white hair she assumed was Crown Prince Valeriad. At the sight of him, she briefly contemplated the young Prince, idly wondering what kind of man he was becoming. She didn't waste much time wondering about that however, for she knew that she would learn soon enough whether the boy had escaped the influence of his father and his uncle, or if he had been irrevocably damaged by it. Knowing King Madari as she did, however, she gave the young prince only a 50-50 chance of being at least salvageable.

It had been a long time since she had personally spoken to the King, but she remembered her last meeting with him very well indeed. After her exploits on the *Frenzy*, she had been presented to the King to be honored, and King Madari had taken the opportunity to leer openly at her. After that, his eyes had never left her chest, and she crossed her arms over her breasts and frowned at the memory. She had been to dockside taverns that had shown her more respect and courtesy than her own King had, but it hadn't ended there. No, it had finally come to a head during the celebratory party that had followed the formal dinner.

An inebriated Madari had approached her with a *very* inappropriate invitation, and when she had declined—politely, of course—he had gotten more aggressive, going so far as to paw at her like some kind of an animal. With anyone else, she would have put the animal down, but this was her King. She hadn't known how to respond to his crude advances, and his lewd behavior had frozen her just long enough for him to actually grab her breasts. It had taken every ounce of self-control that she had possessed to keep from punching him, or kneeing him in the groin as she would have done with any other drunken lout, but somehow she had kept herself in check.

Instead, she had pulled away from him as quickly and decorously as she could, and excused herself for the rest of the evening. The worst part was he had laughed at her as she had retreated. Laughed! Then he'd shouted at her six words she would never forget.

Your parents named you well, Prudence!

The heavy emphasis on the first syllable of her name had been one insult too many, and she'd whipped around to flay the King alive with her tongue, but the drunken Madari had already staggered back to the party. Even now, Prudence's face burned at the memory, and she could feel herself getting angrier and angrier by the second. Seeing him again brought back the entire humiliating episode, and she knew that she had better get herself under control again, and quickly. Letting her King know that she hated his guts wouldn't be the best way to begin the trip.

Frederick must have sensed something, because he cleared his throat next to her.

"Is something the matter, Captain? You look angry."

Prudence rounded on him and nearly snatched his head off to hand it to him, but somehow she restrained herself.

"What makes you think anything is wrong, Frederick?"

The evil glare that accompanied her words was more than enough of an answer for him, but he decided to risk death or dismemberment anyway, and leaned forward to speak quietly in her ear.

"Well, ma'am, when the King came into sight, your face turned bright red and a small vein on your forehead popped out and began to pulse. More than that, you were staring daggers at His Majesty. I'm surprised he didn't burst into flame, or drop dead on the spot."

She snorted once sharply, and he was relieved to see that his jest had clearly had the intended effect. She looked at him again, the evil glare changing to a mocking shadow of itself.

"Fortune does not love me so well, Frederick."

At that she began to chuckle, imagining the King bursting into flame or dropping dead right about . . . *now*. She glanced hopefully at the column of riders, but obviously Madari had refused to cooperate with her mental assassination attempt, for the column—and the King—continued to approach. She sighed regretfully, and then turned to her first officer.

"Prepare to receive our guests, Frederick. Full honors."

Frederick came to attention and saluted her formally, hand over heart, then turned to the crew.

"Crew, attention!"

The crew immediately formed up as a loud voice sounded from the dock.

"Permission to come aboard?"

Frederick turned formally to his Captain, and she responded just as formally.

"Permission granted."

Frederick instantly turned to the dock.

"Permission granted!" As the King of Dakkadia climbed the boarding plank, Frederick waited until the King was two steps from the deck of the ship before shouting, "Present arms!"

As one, the crew raised their right hands to touch their hearts, palms parallel to the ground in the Dakkadian military salute.

King Madari Dhaerhan stepped aboard, followed by his son and his Mage, and turned to Prudence. With parade-ground precision, she raised her hand in salute, and he returned the courtesy with one of his own. When he lowered his hand, her hand beat his to her side, and Frederick shouted again, "Order, arms!"

The crew snapped their arms to their sides as one.

"Welcome aboard the *Sovereign,* Your Majesty. Would you care to inspect the crew?" Prudence asked.

Madari followed her silently as she led him past the rows of sailors and marines standing at attention on the deck. Madari said nothing during the inspection, but Morvandis did stop briefly when the party approached Cahrick Rantrefal. He turned slightly towards the Mage, and Cahrick froze as if he were a field mouse staring at a cobra. The old Mage seemed to wilt without moving a single inch, as if he were trying desperately to hide behind himself.

"We meet again, Mage Rantrefal."

Cahrick swallowed heavily, but maintained his stance, beads of sweat appearing on his forehead. Morvandis's mouth twitched into a sardonic smile at the old Mage's obvious terror, but he didn't say anything else, simply turning to continue the inspection. Prudence gave Morvandis a sideways glance, but Morvandis hadn't done anything wrong at all, even if Cahrick did look as if he wanted to jump ship right then and there.

The inspection concluded shortly thereafter, and Madari turned to Prudence.

"A fine crew indeed, Lady Prudence, though I expected nothing less from the Corsair herself. And the *Sovereign's* unbroken string of victories tells me everything I need to know about their skill in battle. You have my appreciation for everything you have done for Dakkadia. You've made all of us proud."

Madari had pitched his voice to make sure every member of the crew could hear his words, and the crew swelled with pride at his praise. Prudence saluted him inwardly.

You may be a pig and a bastard, Your Majesty, but that was well done. Your words will mean the world to the crew.

Prudence shook her head slightly, and then smiled at her King.

"On behalf of myself and the crew of the *Sovereign,* I welcome you aboard. Should there be anything we can do to make your journey more pleasant, please do not hesitate to ask."

"Be careful what you offer, Captain, for be assured I will hold you to that."

Prudence grimaced slightly.

I'll bet you will, Your Majesty. I'll bet you will.

A bright voice interrupted her dark thoughts, and she turned quickly to the speaker though she hadn't been listening to what had been said.

"I apologize, My Prince, I did not hear you. Did you have a question?"

"I was just saying that my sister is dying to meet you, My Lady," Valeriad said. "She is a great admirer of your exploits, and she spent a great deal of time during our journey here talking about you. I can't wait to see how she reacts when she finally meets the person behind the legend."

Prudence took in the Prince's appearance and demeanor. All in all, she decided that she liked what she saw in him. He was an extremely pretty young man, she noted, with long white hair flowing down his back in luxurious waves that ended at his waist in the traditional Dakkadian style. His slightly tilted eyes and tall, slim build were obviously a gift from his mother, though his broad shoulders were most definitely his father's. Madari was built like the warrior he was, shorter and broader, and powerfully muscled. Valeriad, on the other hand, was lean and wiry. He was still a boy, but you could see traces of the man he would soon become.

If Madari is a warhorse—or, better yet, a plow horse—the Prince would be a stallion, and a fine one at that.

She grinned at the comparison.

"I look forward to meeting her, as well as the rest of the family. Now, if you will excuse me, I have to get the crew moving."

She turned to Frederick.

"Mr. Frederick, please dismiss the crew, and show His Majesty to his quarters."

"Aye, Captain." He turned to the crew and shouted, "Crew! Dismissed!" The crew instantly returned to their posts, and with that, the rest of the royal party began to board the ship. The boson dispatched some crew members to bring up their baggage, and the formality of the greeting disappeared completely as the well-trained crew went back to their jobs with a will.

As Frederick went below with the King, his son, and Morvandis, a vision in white silk boarded the ship. Corsair instantly recognized Queen Aveliad, and her face broke into an enormous smile. She looked exactly as Prudence had remembered, right down to the white enameled mask upon her face. Queen Aveliad looked around briefly until she saw Prudence, and then moved quickly and gracefully toward her, a matching smile on her face.

"Lady Prudence. It is wonderful to see you again. It has been far too long."

Prudence curtseyed appropriately to her Queen, but once the requirement had been accomplished, she held out her hands in greeting, her smile widening even further. Aveliad placed her impossibly delicate fingers in Prudence's gloved hands and squeezed them tightly. Prudence had always wondered how fingers that looked so frail and thin could contain such strength, but Prudence returned the squeeze gently lest she break them.

"My Queen, I welcome you aboard. It *has* been too long. And you look absolutely radiant, as always!"

"You flatter me. But I do thank you for the polite lie. Six days on the road is enough to make anyone look less than their best. But enough about that. Look at you!"

Aveliad took in the glowing clothing Prudence had tried so hard to forget about in obvious appreciation, and the reminder made Prudence's face turn scarlet with mortification. She dropped her gaze in embarrassment, evoking yet another laugh from Aveliad.

"The clothes were my brother's notion," Prudence explained quickly. "Sethred wanted to make certain I wouldn't embarrass the Dakkadian court with my normal garb, so he sent me dozens of these garish outfits, and each one is gaudier than the last." She looked up sheepishly and noted that Aveliad didn't look at all embarrassed for her. In fact, she had a pronounced look of approval in her eyes.

"If that is the case, you should send your brother a letter thanking him for his efforts. Trust me when I say that you are an absolute vision, and it is my prediction that you will turn many a head at the Convocation. With your beauty, as well as your reputation, men will be vying for your favor. Beware whom you speak to, lest jealous lordlings begin to duel each other, hoping to gain your attention. Mark me well: you could very well cause the untimely end for many a nobleman at the Convocation."

Corsair laughed again, her embarrassment forgotten.

"Now who is flattering whom?"

A serious expression came to Aveliad's face, though her eyes still twinkled with mirth.

"I speak but the unvarnished truth, Lady Prudence."

"I guess we'll soon find out. If the odd noble or two should end up dying for my attention, I'll be sure to lay the blame where blame is due . . . squarely on my brother's shoulders. As to thanks, now that I think on it, a letter will not be necessary. My brother, the Prince, will be attending the Convocation as well, which should give me ample opportunity to . . . *thank* him in person. That is, of course, assuming I can find him, or that his personal guard allows me within arm's reach. It would be too much to ask that he would allow me to carry weapons into his presence, but for an offense of this magnitude, bare hands should suffice. Perhaps I'll simply beat him to death with this hat."

Aveliad smiled in appreciation for Prudence's wry humor, but suddenly her face changed into one of concern.

"How was your meeting with my husband? I trust that he did nothing untoward?"

At the mention of the King, Corsair was again taken back to that horrible evening five years earlier when the monarch she had served so faithfully had treated her like a common whore, and her smile wilted visibly. But then another memory surfaced, and the remembrance of the events that had occurred after she had left the party, returned the smile to her face.

Queen Aveliad had come to see her in her apartments, a meeting Prudence had been dreading. She was terrified that the Queen would blame her for encouraging the King's advances, but nothing could have prepared her for what had actually happened when the Queen had finally sought her out. Prudence had been standing on her balcony, looking out over the Dakkadian capital city, contemplating the sudden catastrophic demise of her career and wondering how her family would react to her inevitable disgrace, when a soft voice from behind her had jerked her from her reverie and put an end to her dark thoughts.

"Though my husband has many flaws, drunkenness normally isn't one of them. But, it seems tonight is a special occasion. He is unconscious, too drunk to make it to his own bedchambers. He had to be carried."

Prudence hadn't recognized the biting tone at first, and she whirled around in surprise to look at her unexpected visitor. When she saw it was the Queen, she collapsed instantly into a deep curtsey, in a move so quick it almost seemed she had fainted. And all the while that she had held her curtsey, she had kept her eyes downcast, too ashamed of what had happened that evening to meet her Queen's gaze.

Aveliad had hurried forward and placed her hands on Prudence's shoulders, squeezing gently.

"Please rise, Lady Prudence. I saw what happened to you at the party, and I came to apologize for my husband's churlish behavior. When there is a beautiful woman about he is bad enough when sober, but when he gets too far into his cups, he becomes truly offensive. For his unforgivable insult to you and your honor, I humbly beg your forgiveness."

For the second time that evening, Prudence had been too shocked to respond. Her Queen was asking for *her* forgiveness? In her wildest imagination she hadn't even considered the possibility.

"I know what he did to you was reprehensible, but I hope you will remember that Dakkadia truly respects and honors you for everything you have done on its behalf. I pray you will continue to bring glory to yourself and your house, as well as to our kingdom, and if there is anything I can do to make amends, you have but to ask. In this, I am your servant." Queen Aveliad had curtseyed then, deeply, as a servant to a noble. Prudence had been mortified at the complete reversal of their positions, and had rushed to assure the Queen that there was nothing to forgive.

"When Madari is this deep into his cups, you can rest assured that he will have no memory of the night's events, which makes his behavior even more disgraceful, if that is indeed possible. Have no fear that you have incurred his wrath, Lady Prudence." She turned to leave then, but before stepping from the room, she turned to say one last thing. "Remember that you serve Dakkadia, and Dakkadia is more than just the man who wears the crown. You have a friend at court, and my offer is genuine. If there is anything—anything at all—I can do for you, you have but to ask. If it is within my power, it is yours."

The next morning Prudence had seen the King again. Despite the Queen's assurances, she hadn't believed she would be lucky enough that the King would actually forget what he had done, but Aveliad had been right: Madari *hadn't* remembered his behavior of the previous evening. Prudence had left the capital as quickly as she could to avoid any further confrontations, but she had decided then and there that for her, serving Dakkadia meant serving her Queen. Madari could hang for all Prudence cared, but Aveliad was a monarch who Prudence could serve with honor. She had never had reason to call upon the favor Aveliad had offered, but she knew that her current assignment to the *Sovereign,* the most powerful ship in the fleet, was the direct result of Queen Aveliad's influence.

She was also certain that Aveliad had also made sure that both Cahrick Rantrefal and Rory Sornin had found their way into her crew, and the addition of both a Water Mage and an Air Mage had turned the most powerful ship in the Dakkadian navy into the most feared ship on the entire ocean. In a very real sense, Aveliad had been responsible for Prudence earning the title Corsair.

With an effort, she pulled herself back to the present.

"No, My Queen. There were no difficulties with His Majesty." She paused a moment, then added with a sly smile, "My steward has orders to water down the wine at our meals to make certain that happy state of affairs continues. I would hate to make him walk the plank or some other such unpleasantness. It would also not do to let my guest fall overboard in a drunken stupor. Completely by accident, of course."

Aveliad laughed again, her worried expression gone in an instant.

"Please, Lady Prudence. It isn't kind of you to fill my head with such wonderful images. I simply can't bear the disappointment when they don't come to pass."

Corsair joined her Queen in laughter, when a second person joined them. Aveliad put her arm around her daughter's shoulder.

"Lady Prudence Daemira, please allow me to introduce to you my daughter, the Princess Deirdre. Deirdre, this is Lady Prudence Daemira, the Corsair herself."

Corsair took in the sight of Aveliad's youngest child and smiled openly. Deirdre was as beautiful as Valeriad, though her hair was a pale gold rather than her brother's shining silver. Her clear golden amber eyes were wide in awe, and she gasped sharply when Prudence gave her a deep bow.

"You'll have to excuse her, Lady Prudence," Aveliad said. "Normally, she is an extremely talkative child, but she has a slight case of hero worship where you are concerned. Although," she paused, "now that I think about it, you only have yourself to blame. You have been entirely too successful at what you do for your own good. Your legend is growing."

Princess Deirdre still seemed to be too overcome to say anything, so Prudence decided to have a bit of fun with her.

"Welcome aboard the *Sovereign,* Your Highness," Corsair said in her best Captain's voice. "While you are aboard we'll try to take care of you, but I make no promises! The sea is a dangerous place, and anything can happen. You'll have to keep a weather eye out, and mind the words of the sailors who are here to protect you, especially if we should happen upon some prey. Can you do that?"

Princess Deirdre nodded vigorously, eyes wider still, and still unable to say anything in the presence of a living legend. Beside her, Aveliad closed her eyes and shook her head in bemusement before asking,

"Captain, would your ship have someplace for us to wash ourselves? I must confess, I can no longer stand feeling this unclean, and I'm certain Deirdre feels the same way."

"But of course, My Queen. Quarters have been arranged for you, and the copper tubs in my room are available to you at need. Give me a moment and I'll have Mr. Cahrick join us. Water Mages are very useful for heating up water." She thought about it a moment and added, "Though I've always wondered about that. Wouldn't heating water be a Fire Mage's domain?"

She hadn't meant for the offhand question to be answered, but somehow Deirdre finally found her voice—and her voice sounded remarkably like her mother's.

"Phaedron says that heating water is a simple trick for Water Mages. He says while fire *can* heat water, Water Mages can simply command the water to agitate itself and force it to become heated on its own. He says it's faster as well. Of course, Val says that fire is *meant* to be used to heat water, and doing it any other way is unnatural, but Phaedron says the only thing fire is *meant* to do is roast meat. Then they roll their eyes at each other and call each other idiots. They do go on about it."

She must have realized then that she had actually spoken to her heroine because she silenced herself instantly in scarlet mortification, but Corsair merely nodded at the diminutive Princess.

"Cahrick said the same thing once, now that you mention it. Not about your erstwhile siblings being idiots, mind you, but about Water Mages agitating water. An excellent explanation, Your Highness, and I thank you for reminding me. But I've allowed myself to get distracted. My apologies. Let me get Cahrick and I'll have him heat your bath for you. Your trunks have already been brought aboard and stowed in your quarters. I promise you'll be up to your eyes in hot, soapy water in just a few moments."

She turned then to look at the deck of the ship, searching for her Water Mage, but her eyes were drawn instantly to one of the most handsome men she had ever seen. Her eyes widened and she inhaled sharply as tiny spots of color appeared high on her cheeks. At first, he looked like an older version of Valeriad, but the differences were telling. He was taller than Valeriad for one thing, and his athletic build fit his great height perfectly. He had long black hair that trailed down his back, with the thick white stripe that marked him as Dakkadian nobility contrasting sharply with his blue-black hair. On his waist, he wore a wire wrapped silver rapier and a matching main gauche that reminded her very much of her own weapons, and from the way he wore them, she could tell that he knew how to use them.

Apparently she had been staring a bit too long at the man, for she failed to notice the queen move up beside her to see what had caught her attention. Aveliad glanced coyly at the thunderstruck Prudence and said,

"The man speaking to Cahrick Rantrefal is my eldest son, Phaedron. I don't believe the two of you have met."

Prudence barely heard her, as if the Queen was speaking from a great distance, but one word did stand out to her, and she repeated it breathlessly. *Phaedron.*

"Phaedron."

The single breathless word contained many nuances, but above all Aveliad could hear the caress in the Captain's voice as she repeated his name softly to herself. Without a doubt, the Captain was smitten. Aveliad recognized the signs quite clearly, for she too had fallen in love with her first husband the moment she had set eyes upon him. Normally, that was a trait of the Fae, for Aveliad's people always *knew* when a person was right for them. She gave Prudence a knowing look, though the Captain didn't notice. She also gave her son a similar look, this one almost pitying, for Phaedron had no inkling of what had just happened, or how it would affect him. He still hadn't looked in their direction, too engrossed as he was in conversation with the Water Mage Aveliad had extended her protection to years earlier.

Aveliad knew Prudence well, and as much as she loved her son, she knew he was in trouble. When the Corsair set her eyes upon her prey, nothing short of death could stop her. She laughed in amusement at the thought of the pairing, for it would be a fine match, and exactly the one she had hoped to arrange for them years ago. It was too bad Prudence had fought so hard against it . . . but she was still young. She had yet to learn that fate had a way of forcing people to bend to its will, like it or not. She was happy for her son, and for the beautiful woman standing next to her, and she wished the future couple well.

Of course, there is still the little matter of the courtship. Knowing them both the way I do, I can say one thing with certainty: this will be an interesting journey indeed.

CHAPTER FIVE

"Weakness"

With trembling hands, Lain reached down to cover the child's eyes and tried desperately to hold back his tears. It took great effort and iron determination, but even then, he was only partially successful; his face and eyes did indeed remain dry, but within him his soul wept inconsolably. He gently touched the child's forehead—the flesh was already cooling—and said a brief prayer for the dead, entreating the Archon to show the child the mercy in death she hadn't found in life. Once he had finished his prayer, he stood up abruptly and nodded to the Grand Vizier who quickly pointed to the eunuch guards and snapped his fingers. Silently and obediently, the guards bent down and wrapped the body of the child in white linen, and just like that, the murder had never happened. As the eunuchs carried away the pathetically small bundle, Lain fervently wished his own memories could have been as easily removed. He knew that this child's face would haunt him to the grave, just as the faces of all the other children Xan had murdered over the years had tormented his dreams for as long as he could remember.

His father was spiraling out of control, and Lain knew it. A thought burned through his grief and horror like a lightning bolt: *Xan will never stop. Never.* The murders would come more and more frequently, and more and more children would die, strangled to death by a man who didn't even see his victims as human. "His pretties" he called them, never even bothering to learn their names, for they meant nothing to him as anything other than objects. Lain suspected that it had never even occurred to his father that they might have had names, or families, or hopes, before he took from them everything that they were and everything that they would ever be. He didn't understand what drove his father to do these horrific things, but in the end, it didn't matter. His father was untouchable, for he was simply too powerful to be called to account for his crimes. The nobles weren't fools—they knew exactly what kind of man Xan was, and the simple truth was they didn't care. Lain had no illusions about that: the provincial governors turned a blind eye to Xan's appetites because the stability and prosperity his long rule had brought kept them rich and powerful. They truly believed that the peace his long reign had brought the empire was worth far more than the lives of a few little children every now and again. Compared to the endless wars and the countless deaths that had preceded his rule, the lives of a few children didn't matter at all . . . they were an insignificant price to pay. So long as the palace continued to cover up his crimes—and as long as the wealth continued to flow into the coffers of the nobles—his father would never face justice for his heinous acts.

Lain hung his head in bitter shame. The nobles and the governors were wrong. Lain knew that as surely as he knew his own name: these children *had* mattered, and the price the Empire was paying for its prosperity was too high. The thought echoed and reechoed through his mind, and no matter how hard he tried to block it, he couldn't. A sudden madness overcame him, and tore through the clarity like a red wave, drowning him in his rage and pain and fury. *Too high! Too high! Let her be the last!*

The tears Lain had refused to shed fell then, pouring from his eyes like rain, and with a cry like a wounded animal, he whirled towards his father's cabin with murder in his eyes. Without realizing he had even drawn it, he found his scimitar in his hand. He would break down the door to his father's sleeping chamber and cut him down like a rabid animal. In his mind, he could see the event as clearly as if it had already happened, and once his father was dead, the souls of the countless children his father had murdered would at last find peace. He found a measure of comfort in that: at long last the children would have justice. His father was a dead man. That murdering his father could mean his own execution didn't matter to him in the slightest, for Lain already knew that he was damned for the horrors his father had committed. For him, death would be a welcome release. He took two unsteady steps toward the door separating him from his father, and violently threw his scabbard behind him. The sound of it striking the wall echoed hollowly through the wooden walls of the ship. Before he could take a third step, however, something caught his arm. He tugged at whatever it was trying to free himself, but it wouldn't budge. Still snarling, he looked down at his arm, and noticed for the first time that the Grand Vizier was holding it in a vice-like grip.

"The Emperor does not wish to be disturbed at this time, My Prince. It would be better if you returned later."

For several heartbeats, Lain could not comprehend the Grand Vizier's words. He tried to raise his sword, but something restrained him, refusing to budge no matter how hard he struggled. He thrashed then, tossing his head to and fro, trying desperately to regain his freedom. The harder he struggled, the less freedom he had. It was as if the air itself had congealed around him like a cocoon, as in fact it had.

The Grand Vizier waited for several moments more, and as suddenly as it had come, the Prince's killing rage ended. Lain's taut muscles strained one last time to the point of tearing, then slackened noticeably, and the Prince sagged until only the prison of air held him up at all. The madness had passed, but tears continued to flow unchecked down his face.

Once he was certain the Prince would do nothing . . . untoward, the Vizier lowered him gently to the floor and let the cocoon of air dissipate around him.

"Why, damn you?" Lain said, still weeping. "Why did you stop me? You above all others know what he is, what he does! *Why?*"

The question rose to a shout, and for a second the Vizier wondered if the madness had returned. He considered the Prince for a moment, but saw that rage, not madness, had spawned the shout. Once he was sure the Prince still had himself under control—as tenuous as that control was—he answered in a hard voice.

"I serve the Empire, as do you. You are the Crown Prince, and the Emperor's only son. It is my duty to protect both of you and to ensure the Empire and the succession remains safe. To protect His Majesty, I make certain no one finds evidence of his sickness. For you, it means I will prevent you from doing something irrevocable in a moment of temporary madness. If you kill your father, I will cover up his murder as I have done so many times in the past with so many of his victims. But secrets will out, My Prince, and the greater the secret, the faster it will be known and the wider it will be spread. Murder is a crime, but regicide is more terrible by far, especially for a ruler as universally loved as your father. If he dies of suspicious causes and you are implicated—if you are so much as suspected—the scandal would poison your reign. The nobles would have no choice but to have you assassinated, if only to quell the unrest in their own demesnes." He paused to let the point sink in, and then continued in a gentler voice. "Furthermore, I know what killing your father would cost you personally. You are not like your father, for yours is a gentle nature, My Prince. Murdering him would destroy you from within. I fear you would not long survive the Emperor if yours were to be the hand that slays him. Your noble nature simply wouldn't allow it, and you would destroy yourself in a vain attempt to atone for your perceived crimes. So hate me if you must, for I will continue to serve your father with absolute loyalty, and by doing so, I ensure the future will survive him."

Lain stared at the Vizier for several moments, then without saying a word, he slowly, leadenly, climbed to his feet. He reached down and picked up his scimitar, then silently looked around the room to find his scabbard. Once he had retrieved it, he sheathed the sword and returned it to its proper position at his waist. His tears were gone as if they had never existed, replaced instead by his usual veiled look, a look that gave no hint to the thoughts going on behind his eyes. He turned to the doorway leading out of the small parlor, and passed by the Vizier while walking towards it.

"What do you see when you find one of his victims?" Lain asked. "When you look in their dead eyes? What do you see when you are looking at another dead child, murdered for no reason other than to amuse your Emperor?"

"I see a necessary evil," the Vizier said with considerable sadness. "I see all the good your father has done, and I see the price that that good demands." The Prince waited for the Vizier to finish, and he turned to leave. Before he could take a step however, the Vizier asked him, "And what do you see when you look upon one of his victims? There must be a reason you insist on being notified whenever another one is found?"

Lain looked over his shoulder once again, his eyes shrouded in darkness.

"I see my mother's face." he said simply. With that he walked away, leaving the Vizier standing alone in a room that suddenly felt much colder.

Grand Vizier Shar thought about what the Prince had said for a long while, and many things he had only suspected about the young man suddenly became as clear as fine crystal. For one thing, Shar had never been certain if the Prince had even suspected his father had murdered his mother, for he had been very young indeed when it had happened. Now Shar knew the truth, and he decided that he would have to watch his future monarch very closely indeed. Had he not been there, Lain truly would have killed Xan, of that Shar had absolutely no doubt. For just a moment, Lain had been as mad as his father. *It is the close confines of this ship, and the proximity to his father that affects him so.*

Shar shook his head sadly. He had hoped that the madness that infected the Imperial line would die with Xan, but now he knew better. Shar had seen that look many times over the years on the face of his liege lord, and now he could recognize it instantly, no matter who wore it. Lain had no idea how very like his father he had looked when his dark mood had finally turned murderous. The Prince favored his mother in most things. His height, his coloring, his features—all of these traits he had received from his mother, but for just a moment, he had been his father's son.

He was certain Lain could not remember his mother as anything other than an impression, but she had been very beautiful indeed. She had been very young—as all of Xan's wives had been—and the daughter of a highly ranked noble of exceptional loyalty. Xan had been 57 years old at the time, and had already outlived several wives. Unlike the other wives, however, Tahani had had the good fortune to bear the Emperor an heir. Shar had believed that this fact alone would save her from the fate that had befallen Xan's other wives, mistresses, and concubines, but he'd been wrong. He could still remember Xan standing over her body 19 years past, panting like an animal with his fingers curled into claws and madness burning brightly in his eyes. Shar had been unable to act, so he simply watched and waited. It had taken some time, but eventually the madness had passed.

Slowly, oh so slowly, his panting had subsided, his fingers had uncurled, and his arms had dropped to his sides. Xan had then closed his eyes and hung his head, and his shoulders began to rise and fall gently with what Shar had assumed were sobs. A wave of pity had overtaken him, for he had believed that his Emperor had been overcome with remorse for his deed, but Xan shocked him. The Emperor tossed his head back and Shar was horrified to see that Xan's face had split into a ghastly smile, and that he hadn't been shaking with remorse—he'd been shaking with laughter.

Shar had thought the countless murders Xan had committed before Tahani had hardened him, but the beatific smile on Xan's face had turned Shar's very marrow to ice. Xan's head weaved slightly from side to side, as if he were listening to music only he could hear, and even in his horror, Shar had been fascinated. The Emperor listened for a little while longer, and then slowly opened his eyes . . . and only then had he seen the Grand Vizier. Shar hadn't known what Xan would do and had prepared to defend himself, but the Emperor merely nodded to his wizard as if nothing were out of the ordinary. He glanced down at the body of his wife and smiled again. Shar could still remember his Emperor's words as clearly now as if the Emperor was speaking them.

I can hear her voice, Vizier. She has joined the choir, my perfect choir, and her beautiful voice fills my heart with joy. They serenade me, you know. Every night, they sing me to sleep with their lullabies, and I treasure them for it. My pretties never leave my side, you see—I make sure of that. Now they sing their beautiful songs for me . . . only for me. I must find another, and soon.

Xan had gone to bed then, while the Vizier could only stare at him in disbelief. The second Xan's head had hit his pillow he had fallen into a sleep so deep and peaceful that Shar had almost believed that he had imagined the entire episode. Only the corpse of the former Empress at his feet convinced him of the reality of the event. In a daze, he had ordered the guards to summon the physician. Tahani had been too well connected, her family too important, to simply disappear the body as he had done with so many of the Emperor's other victims. So, at Shar's direction, the physician had proclaimed the death to be the result of a sudden sickness, and the Vizier had been left to tell the four-year-old Lain that his mother had passed away during the night.

Tahani's family hadn't believed the story of a mysterious sickness, of course, and had flatly refused to keep silent to preserve the peace. Shar had attempted to reason with them, and had later tried to bribe them, but neither had worked: they had simply taken the attempts as confirmation that their daughter had indeed been murdered. Threats—first veiled and later direct—had also failed, and their efforts to obtain justice for their daughter had begun to have an effect; the nobility had begun to stir.

In the end, the Vizier's hand had been forced. In the Emperor's name, he had reluctantly ordered the assassination of Tahani's family, and made certain that the manner of their deaths would send a very direct message to the other nobles. The bodies of Tahani's mother and father were found soon after, lying in their blood-drenched bed with their tongues cut out and nailed to their headboard.

After that, a new provincial governor had been appointed in their place. The newly appointed governor had been much more . . . accommodating, and had been amply and generously rewarded for his "loyalty." The murders, as distasteful as they had been, had gotten the point across, for the noble families of Ferralin had learned two valuable lessons. The first lesson was that no matter what your station or how just your cause, crossing the Imperial Family would invite swift—and fatal—retribution. The second lesson was that the Imperial Family could be very generous indeed to those who kept their tongues from wagging. In Ferralin, silence quite literally was golden.

So well had the lesson been learned, in fact, that Shar had never again heard even a whisper of dissent from the nobles. Perhaps fortunately for the empire, the nobles and provincial governors had learned not to offer their daughters to the Emperor. Instead, they would send young slaves of exceptional beauty or talent to the Imperial Court to "entertain" the Emperor, or they would send young concubines to be added to his majesty's harem. In the years following the murder of Tahani, it had become almost a game for the nobles to see who could find the most exotic "gift" for the Emperor. After all, everyone knew that the fastest way to curry favor with the Imperial Throne was to send the Emperor a sacrificial lamb. Unsurprisingly, the Emperor happily encouraged this competition, and he generously rewarded those whose gifts pleased him the most with riches or titles or lands.

Unfortunately, the nobility's tacit acceptance of the status quo had also emboldened Xan, for he had begun murdering children at a much faster rate. With a steady stream of victims constantly delivered to him by simpering nobles seeking to gain influence and favors, he never lacked for a victim, and as a result, the palace guard had had to become quite expert at disappearing the evidence of his insanity.

It has been said that with practice comes perfection. Had that only been the case, My Prince, you would have been spared much suffering.

The Emperor's bodyguard had been efficient at removing the bodies, but they hadn't been perfect. One evening ten years earlier, a 13-year-old Lain had come to his father's apartments to show his father a new trick he had taught his favorite puppy. He'd entered the Emperor's private garden to look for his father, and the playful puppy had squirmed out of his arms and gotten away from him. Lain had eventually found the dog gently licking the face of one of the Emperor's victims, lying next to a reflecting pool.

It had been a horrible mistake: the guards were away, dealing with the body of another victim. Unbeknownst to them, the Emperor had actually killed two girls within minutes of each other, for the girls had been twins. The guards, efficient as they were, had only known of a single victim and had moved quickly to remove the corpse. It had never occurred to them that there might actually have been two victims.

At first, Lain had believed the girl to be asleep and had pulled his puppy away from her unmoving form to keep the dog from waking her. Young as he was, however, he knew the instant he saw her face that the girl was not asleep. She had died a hard death indeed; her eyes bulged in horror, and her blackened and swollen tongue lolled out of her head. Shar himself had overseen the removal of the first body, and had just returned to the Emperor's garden to make certain no other evidence remained, when he heard Lain's terrified screams. He knew the Emperor was sleeping peacefully in his bedchamber, listening to the choir only he could hear, so Shar knew the screams couldn't be from another victim. He had responded instantly, hardening the air about him into an invisible shield and readying his best offensive spells. He followed the piteous sounds of the young boy's screams to the source, only to find that it hadn't been an attack after all. When he saw the body he understood instantly what had happened, and so he rushed to the Crown Prince's side to give him comfort . . . only to find the boy inconsolable.

It had taken a long time, but eventually Lain had calmed down enough to speak. Shar had pulled the young Prince away from the body and led him back to his room. A dazed Prince meekly followed the Grand Vizier without making a single sound, and only after the Prince was safely in his bed, had Shar quietly asked him what had happened. Lain told him the entire story, and after he had finished Shar had done the only thing he could for his Prince: he had looked Lain directly in the eye . . . and lied.

In his many years of service to the empire, Shar had lied countless times for countless reasons. Some of those reasons had been for political expedience, while others had been to cover up the Emperor's many crimes. Over the years, he had become more than adept at covering up inconvenient facts and he had accounted himself an excellent liar. He called upon all of the skills he possessed to weave a credible falsehood, to somehow convince the Prince that what he had seen had been a tragic accident. Lain had laid quietly in his bed listening to the story Shar had spun with such care, and when Shar finished, Lain had simply said,

"I don't believe you. Now tell me the truth."

As the Grand Vizier, Shar had been truly surprised only a few times, but this was one of them. All of his polish, all of his vaunted abilities at deception were undone in an instant by nine simple words spoken by a 13-year-old boy. He thought furiously, trying to come up with a lie that Lain might have believed, but in his shock, nothing came to him. All the while, Lain watched him without saying a word, demanding the truth with his eyes. After several moments of intense scrutiny from the boy, Shar had relented.

He told Lain everything . . . everything except for the fact that Lain's mother had been one of the Emperor's victims. Once the explanation was complete, he waited for a moment while the Prince coped with the truth.

"You must understand, My Prince, your father is ill. He has a sickness of the mind and of the spirit, and sometimes he does things that other people may see as evil. He does not intend harm, but he cannot control himself. When your father becomes ill, he hurts people. Sometimes he hurts them badly. But remember this: in all your years, your father has never harmed you or threatened you in any way. Your father loves you, Prince Lain, and he would never harm you. If you believe nothing else, believe that."

Lain didn't say a word. He simply rolled away from the Vizier and stared at the wall until his soft breathing convinced Shar that the boy had finally fallen asleep.

The next day, Lain had changed completely from the boy he had been. Gone was the boyish enthusiasm, the wonder and excitement of youth, burned away as if it had never been. It had been replaced instead by . . . intensity. No other word could accurately describe the change that had overcome the Prince. He had found the Grand Vizier the next day, and had given him the first command he had ever issued.

"Whenever my father is overcome by his illness, you are to send for me immediately."

Shar had protested, of course, for exposing the boy to the results of his father's acts of madness would be needlessly damaging, and Shar had no intention of helping to further destroy the child's innocence. Lain again surprised him, and spoke as if he had heard all of Shar's thoughts.

"I know now what my father is, Vizier, and what he does. The damage has been done. While I do blame him for what he does, he at least is not in control of his actions. You do not have his excuse. You conceal his crimes, and allow him to commit more. As such, the greater part of the blame is yours. For this you must be punished, and your punishment is to send for me whenever you find one of his victims. This is my decree."

The boy's tone had left no room for argument, and Shar knew that he would obey the order absolutely—obey it as absolutely as if it was the Emperor himself who had issued the decree. And it was in that moment that the Vizier knew Lain would make an exceptional leader one day, possibly the greatest that Ferralin had ever seen, so long as he survived his youth. He bowed low to the young Prince, and said simply,

"As you command, so shall it be." He hesitated, and then asked the Prince a question he would never have dared to ask the Emperor. "Why is it so important for you to view the bodies of the victims? What possible gain could there be for you to torture yourself over something that is not within your control?"

The Prince was silent for a moment.

"Your loyalty to our family is absolute, and you protect your Emperor well. But in doing so, you have forgotten something, Vizier, and I have no intention of making the same mistake as you. His victims were people once, and they deserve to be remembered. I will look upon their bodies, and I will say a prayer for their souls that they may find in death the peace they were denied in life." He paused, and then added simply, "One day I will rule Ferralin, Vizier, and I refuse to become my father. All life is precious and must be treated as such. If we forget this—no matter what the reason—we become no better than my father."

To this day, Shar had remembered his Prince's words, and he had obeyed his commands without question. Over the years, the Prince had proven, time and again, that the intelligence and insight he had shown as a boy had not been a fluke. In many ways, he had proven that he was wiser than the Vizier himself. Shar had never again attempted to lie or prevaricate to his Prince, and as the years passed, a bond of trust had developed between them. The two of them became . . . close. They were not truly friends, nor would they ever be, but what they had was stronger than mere friendship. It had taken time, but the Vizier had come to love his Prince. The Vizier served the Emperor out of loyalty to the Empire, but he served his Prince out of fanatical devotion to the man himself.

Shar's greatest fear, the one fear strong enough to bring him nightmares, was the thought that the Prince he loved so well might inherit his father's madness. Until now, Shar had seen no sign of the mental illness that so plagued the Emperor, but now that he had seen the first telltale sign of it, he would watch his Prince very carefully indeed. He loved his Prince . . . loved him well enough to know that Lain would rather die than ever become a monster like his father. Shar had vowed long ago that should the Prince ever be in danger of crossing that line, he would do whatever was necessary to either bring him back . . . or to end his pain. Shar did not believe in prayer, but for just this once, he bowed his own head as he had seen his Prince do countless times, and whispered a prayer he fervently hoped would be heard and answered.

"Archon, I beg you to let him find the strength he needs to resist the madness. Give him the power to be the man he is destined to become, and not the monster he has it within himself to be."

Ascham Illvanin, the Duke of Saerce and the younger brother of the King of Illymar, looked at his maps and smiled to himself. The stacks of vellum showed the island of Illymar divided in various ways, but the map that currently had his attention was split into political affiliations.

"It is clear to me that the monarchy has never been weaker than it is now," he said to his political advisor, Earl Vitaly Saxe. "So many nobles have been set aside by my brother and replaced by unpopular members of the Savonne family, that Orem is driving the remaining nobles into my arms." He gestured at the map. "Aside from the Southlands and a few regions clearly marked as Savonne holdings, the entire island stands beside me."

"Your allies are indeed many, Your Grace, but the Savonnes are wealthy almost beyond measure," the Earl said. "Should open warfare break out between you and King Orem, some of the nobles who are currently in your camp will undoubtedly succumb to bribe attempts. Human nature is uncompromising on that issue."

"While that may be true," Ascham said, "it really doesn't matter in the long run. I do not plan to go to war with my brother at all. I am building up the military not to overthrow the monarchy, but to prepare for the Dakkadian invasion I believe is inevitable. Orem knows Dakkadia is eyeing us as a potential conquest, but he believes that he can find a diplomatic solution to our troubles, and has no intention of preparing for the worst. In my opinion, that is not only shortsighted, it is also potentially deadly for our country. He bet heavily on an alliance with Ferralin to stave off Dakkadia, and with that arrangement nullified, we are more vulnerable than ever before."

Vitaly considered the point for a moment, and gave his Duke a slight shrug.

"Do you really think that Illymar itself is vulnerable? The true strength of our nation has always been our navy, coupled with the defense provided by the Teeth of Amhar, and our mutual defense pact with Ithram. The combination of the two gives us an unbeatable advantage. As long as our navy remains strong and concentrated at the single opening of the Teeth, Dakkadia has no chance whatsoever of successfully invading the island. And even if they did manage to make landfall, the Mages would destroy them out of hand. Attacking Illymar is a fool's errand, and Madari has to know that."

Ascham snorted at that and sifted through several piles of paper until he found a single piece of paper with a list of names. He skimmed it for a moment to make certain it was the one he was looking for, and handed it to his advisor for his inspection.

Vitaly looked at the paper and saw immediately it was a list of ship names, all part of the Royal Navy. There was no title on the page to indicate what the list meant, but a quick count showed him that the list contained the names of 27 ships, ranging from merchants to warships.

"These are ships of the Royal Navy, Your Grace. Does this list bear any particular significance?"

"Those are ships *late* of the Royal Navy, Lord Saxe. The significance of that list is simple: they are prizes captured by the Corsair and turned over to Dakkadian shipyards."

"Surely not! I recognize some of these names. Four of these ships are from the same squadron, and many of them had Water Mages assigned! A simple privateer should have had no chance against their combined might. No chance whatsoever!"

"That might have been true under the command of Lord High Admiral Arkady, but he has recently been forced into retirement, and the Queen, in her infinite wisdom, has placed her cousin, Lucas Savonne, in charge of the Admiralty." He waved a hand in a contemptuous manner and said in a dry voice, "Oh, I'm sure he's perfectly qualified for the post. His qualifications do include having worked for his father's textile business. As that business was centered in Illymaine, I'm positive he must have seen the ocean at least once in his life. After all, we do live on an island. Wouldn't you agree that that makes him uniquely qualified to command our ships in battle?"

Ascham's level look didn't change at all, and he handed a second piece of paper to his advisor.

"This is a report from one of my spies in Dakkadia. The ships on that list have already been repaired and are now flying Dakkadian colors. What's more, many of them are now equipped with the new weapons that we have heard so much about." Before Vitaly could ask, Ascham said, "No, my spies have been unable to find out what this new weapon is that gives them such an advantage. Whatever it is, it is apparently devastating, as attested by the crews who survive a Dakkadian attack. Surprisingly enough, Dakkadia has followed the rules of war to the letter and the surviving crewmembers of these ships have been returned to us unharmed, but that doesn't change the fact that nothing we currently have can stand up to the power of their new weapons. This list," he indicated the first list he had handed Vitaly, "includes only the ships the Corsair herself has captured. They have several other privateers at work in our waters, and while none of them have been as successful as the Corsair, they have been bad enough. The Dakkadian navy is bleeding us dry: we are hemorrhaging both hulls and gold, and with every ship we lose, we come that much closer to actual invasion. It is my estimate that, if these numbers remain constant, we face invasion in no more than two years."

"I respectfully disagree, Your Grace. You are still overlooking our pact with Ithram. Illymar has a long-standing agreement with the Mage Citadel for mutual defense. Should Dakkadia attempt invasion, we have but to invoke the treaty and Dakkadia will face not only our navy, but an army of Powerborn as well. I agree that Dakkadia is building up an invasion force, but I think the true target will be Ferralin or the Badlands. They won't risk annihilation by the combined forces of Illymar and Ithram. It would be pointless suicide."

"If it were pointless, my dear brother would not be so desperate to forge an alliance with Ferralin in the first place. No, he's not completely stupid: it is clear to me that he sees the same weaknesses I do and he's taking steps to repair them. Unfortunately, I believe strongly that he's taking the wrong steps, and unless someone does something soon, an invasion by Dakkadia is a very real and very deadly probability. He *must* be made to see this."

"What do you have in mind?" Vitaly asked. "Remember, your beliefs have made you extremely unpopular at court, especially among the Savonnes. King Orem has banished you to the northern reaches until he personally sends for you."

Ascham didn't respond immediately. Again he rifled through the papers until he found a cream colored envelope with his name written in elegant calligraphy on the front. The letter was unopened, but he turned it over and allowed his advisor to see the wax seal imprinted with the symbol of the Patriarch of the Zarryiostrom.

"My brother may have banished me from Court, but the Zarryiostrom still understands the importance of my position and title. I think it is time I returned to the capital, and have a little talk with my brother. If he sees reason, we will support him in every way possible. If he doesn't . . ." He trailed off, leaving the rest unspoken.

"I do hope the weather is agreeable in Illymaine," Vitaly said, smiling. "But then, with the Mages controlling it, I'm sure it will be."

Ascham laughed and clapped his friend on the back.

"That's the spirit! I'm sure my brother won't be at all pleased to see me, but then the ram is rarely pleased to see the black sheep. It doesn't matter. My duty is clear: I have to force Orem to understand how vulnerable we are, or I have to take other steps to ensure the security of our country, monarchy or no. We leave in the morning. I've already made all the arrangements."

CHAPTER SIX

"Resolve"

Tais Illvanna, oldest daughter of King Orem III of Illymar, stood silently in the tiny room that had been her prison for the past year and stared out of the single large window that she had been allowed in her imprisonment. A gentle breeze blew through the window and stirred her unruly golden hair, and she absentmindedly brushed away a few stray strands that covered her eyes with a sweep of her wrist. Her room was located at the top of the highest point in the Spire, known to everyone as the "Tower", and as the tallest structure on Illymar, it should have commanded a truly spectacular view—only there was nothing at all to see. The window was angled in such a way, that no matter which way she looked, all she could see was the ocean and the occasional sail of a ship.

That was a part of her punishment, she supposed, for Orem had decreed that she be allowed no distraction from the contemplation of her "treason." As such, even the very sight of the city she had so loved as a child had been denied to her lest she become "distracted." Moreover, she had been allowed absolutely no visitors. Other than a single servant who brought her food but wasn't allowed to speak to her, not a single person, aside from the Royal Physician, had come to visit her in the past year, and even he hadn't been to see her in months.

As the endless days of her confinement had turned to weeks, and the weeks had turned to months, she had moved well past the point of caring. She didn't know if her younger sisters, Lyrahe and Chesare, even knew she was still alive, but that meant nothing, for in her darkest moments she often found herself wondering if she actually *was* still alive. It was possible, she supposed, that she had in fact died and had been sentenced to some nameless hell, but she refused to believe that, just as she had so far refused the temptation to surrender to her despair and end her own life.

With no one to talk to, she had spent countless days lost in her memories, wondering what—if anything—she could have done differently. No answers had come to her during her imprisonment, and now she believed that none ever would. She looked down at the base of the Tower and smiled faintly at the waves crashing on the rocks far, far below. The waves and the rocks had become companions and friends of a sort since she began her sentence, and she felt keenly the seductive pull of their siren call. It would be so easy, she knew, to take a single step forward and end both her imprisonment and her pain forever. One tiny step would be all it would take for her to join her husband and child in death, and at long last, they would be together again.

She watched as a wave crashed against the rocks and turned into white spray, and for a moment the look of longing in her eyes intensified as she leaned forward, yearning for release, but then the momentary weakness passed. She closed her eyes, and with no little effort pulled herself away from the window and stepped back into the room. It was becoming harder and harder to turn away from that window and the surcease of pain it promised, but she still had many things to do before she died.

Now that she had made the decision to live another day, she walked to her simple cot and sat on the corner, once again returning to her memories. Tais had always had an outstanding memory, and a year of solitude hadn't dulled it in the slightest. Quite the opposite, actually, for her isolation had honed and sharpened it to a razor's edge, allowing her to recall with complete clarity anything she wished.

As a girl, her perfect memory had matched easily with her sharp intelligence and keen insight, and the combination had allowed her to learn history, politics, and languages at a much faster pace than any of her siblings. She had absorbed facts like cloth absorbed water, and had eagerly immersed herself in any subject she could get her hands on, no matter how advanced it may have seemed. King Orem—even in her mind she refused to ever again think of him as her father—hadn't approved. He believed that it would be very difficult to arrange a marriage for a woman who was more intelligent than the man she would marry.

But Tais had pointed out, quite reasonably, that the ability to speak intelligently on any topic a potential husband might find of interest, would serve to make her more attractive as a potential bride, not less.

Tais had always hoped that any husband Orem found for her would appreciate her for her intellect, but truthfully, she hadn't held out much hope. She was smart enough to know that of the many qualities noblemen sought in a wife, intelligence wasn't ranked nearly as highly as station, dowry, or the ability to bear children. The one redeeming quality that she possessed, as far as Orem had been concerned, was the ability to know when to keep silent. Tais had developed that ability very early in life, for she had discovered, quite by accident, that one learned a great deal more through careful listening than through talking.

Three years ago, her father had informed her that he had come to an arrangement with the Emperor of Ferralin for her to marry his son, Crown Prince Lain. She had been grateful, for Lain was very close to her in age, so she would at least be spared the indignity of being wed to someone far older. Knowing the identity of her future husband, she had begun to research Ferraline customs and political structure, and what she had learned had fascinated her. In Ferralin, a husband could have many concubines but only one wife, and the wife had much greater influence and freedom than an Illymari wife of equal station would have been allowed. As her studies had continued, she found herself looking forward to meeting the Prince, to see for herself just what kind of man she would be bound to.

Before that had happened, however, an event occurred that had altered the course of her entire life. Her brother, Ethan, the Crown Prince of Illymar, had entered into yet another one of his tournaments, and Orem had commanded her to attend. Tais despised tourneys, but the event had been part of the celebration for Ethan's 23rd birthday, and the entire family had attended in his honor. Her brother considered himself to be quite the swordsman, and normally he did quite well in the lists, but it wasn't Ethan who had prevailed that day. No, that honor belonged instead to one of Ethan's closest friends, a dashing young nobleman named Markus, the Earl of Danshire. With his brilliant swordsmanship Markus won the tournament—and the heart of one Tais Illvanna.

Tais closed her eyes in pain at the memory. He had been so very handsome! Markus had caught her eye early on in the tournament, and as he had advanced through the lists, she found herself sitting on the edge of her seat during every one of his matches, with her heart in her throat. In the finale, he had bested Ethan sword-to-sword, and with a brilliant smile on his face, he had presented her with the victory laurel, making her the Queen of the Tournament after he was declared its victor. At the celebration dance following the tournament, the two of them had shared the first dance, and she had felt as light as a feather in his arms.

In the weeks following the tournament, Markus had remained at court and had pursued her with single-minded determination. At first she resisted his advances, but despite her weak protests, she had been as eager to see him as he was to see her. Eventually, she had relented and the two of them had seen each other as often as they could, taking every possible opportunity to sneak away to dark corners and lonely corridors to be alone. At first, they were content to talk about their hopes and dreams, but soon enough talking turned to kissing, and their mutual infatuation had gradually changed to love. Then one day Markus asked her to marry him.

Even as he had asked she knew it was a fool's wish, for she was bound to another man, and that marriage would seal an alliance that would keep Illymar safe from the depredations of warlike Dakkadia—the only country that could challenge Illymar's dominance. She knew better than any other that it was her bounden duty to sacrifice her happiness for the good of her country, and until she had met Markus, it had been an obligation that she had willingly embraced. But those were arguments of the head, not the heart; and her heart had yearned desperately for the marriage that Markus had proposed.

With tears of joy in her eyes, she had accepted his proposal, but had warned him that King Orem would never allow the marriage to happen. Markus hadn't listened to her protests though, silencing her doubts by telling her that true love could make the impossible possible. He had been so sure—so convincing that she had been caught up in the moment, and Markus had taken her by the hand and the two of them had gone to see King Orem.

The meeting had not gone well.

In a speech both eloquent and impassioned, Markus had begged the King for his permission to marry her. He spoke of his family's lineage, his unswerving loyalty to the Crown, and of all of the myriad reasons he was worthy to wed her. She had been so proud of him in that moment, so filled with love that she was certain that his words would sway Orem into allowing the marriage to proceed.

The King had listened calmly until Markus had finished—and had then exploded in fury. Tais had never seen him like that, for his anger had never before been directed at her, and in the face of his elemental fury she shrank back in terror. But Markus absolutely refused to back down, and he shouted right back

PRINCESS TAIS ILLVANNA
--IN THE TOWER--

at the King, matching tone with tone and fury with fury. In the end there had been no argument, no exchange of reasoned positions . . . they had simply screamed at each other, and it wasn't long until Tais had been completely forgotten.

Finally, the King had had enough and ordered Markus's arrest for treason, and the young nobleman had been dragged away by the guard. When Markus had finally been removed from the King's presence, Orem had turned his wrath upon her and had held nothing back. After screaming at her for several minutes, without warning he silenced his own tirade and his demeanor changed completely.

The abrupt change caught her off guard, and when he spoke again, the chill in his tone and the lack of expression on his face convinced her that her very life—the life of his *daughter*—was hanging by a thread. He coldly asked her if she had dishonored herself with the Earl, and all she could do in the face of the frightening calm that had overcome him was to shake her head in denial, completely unable to speak. It was true, of course, for she had not dishonored herself with Markus, but she did not know what King Orem would do if he did not believe her. Something in her face must have convinced him, however, for once he had been reassured that her marriage with Lain could still proceed, he had ordered her to be confined to her apartments and had washed his hands of the matter. Queen Althea—just as with Orem, Tais refused to ever again think of the woman as her mother—who had been silent throughout the entire episode, grabbed her by the arm and marched her out of the audience chamber towards her rooms.

Tais was glad to be gone from the King's presence, for she desperately wanted to seek comfort in Althea's gentle arms as she had done so often as a child. She knew Althea would understand her heartbreak, and would know exactly what to say to make it all better, so she'd bravely held back the tears that threatened to drown her and meekly followed the Queen to her own apartments.

When they arrived at her rooms, the tears began to fall at last as Althea closed the doors behind them. When they were safely alone with no prying eyes, Althea turned to her abruptly, and with no warning whatsoever, slapped her. Tais had never been physically struck before and her bitter tears had dried up instantly in shock and disbelief, but Althea wasn't done. A second slap quickly followed the first, and then a third, and a fourth, until the slaps became blows that rained down on her without pause or mercy. She did not remember falling to the floor, but at some point during the beating she found herself lying there, desperately trying to ward off blows. Eventually, fists were replaced by a strap, and Tais's entire world had turned white in agony as Althea had beaten her relentlessly. And all the while she had beaten Tais, she had screamed at her that she was a stupid, stupid child and how dare she presume? How *dare* she!?

Eventually, Althea's arm had tired, and the blows had slowed and then stopped, but by then, Tais was nearly dead. She had curled up in a ball on the floor trying desperately to cover her head with battered arms too bruised to lift, bleeding from cuts that crossed her body from top to bottom. Althea let the strap fall to the floor and then reached down toward her daughter's face. Tais flinched at the movement, expecting yet more pain, and her mother had obliged. Althea knocked aside her arms and grabbed her by the hair, pulling her head back to look directly in her eyes. Tais was in shock and barely coherent, but the stranger who wore her mother's face didn't care.

In acid tones, Althea had told her,

"Your would-be lover will die for this, daughter. He will lose his head for daring to presume he was good enough to join this family. But you, daughter . . . *you* will marry Prince Lain, or you will join him in death." She let her daughter's head drop to the floor and turned to leave. As her hands touched the door handles, she turned back to look at Tais's crumpled form. "You are a Princess of Illymar and were raised to be better than this. Never disappoint me again. Ever."

With that, she left the apartments without so much as a backward glance at the broken girl who had once been her daughter.

In all her eighteen years, Tais had always been secure in the knowledge that her parents loved her. She had never had any reason to question that absolute belief, just as she had she never given them cause to be angry with her, but as she remembered Orem's voice and Althea's eyes, she had finally understood that she had never truly known them. The people who wore the faces of those she had thought had loved her were the faces of strangers, and those strangers were people to fear. To his daughters, Orem had always been a father first and a King second, but on that day Tais had finally seen the King in the man, and had learned to fear him.

Had the tragedy ended there, it would have been bad enough, but poor, sweet Markus had other ideas. When the guards had taken him to the dungeons beneath the castle, he had somehow seen an opportunity to escape and had taken it. The guards should have warded against the attempt, for it hadn't been a fluke that he had won the tournament. His swordsmanship was excellent, and sheer desperation gave him skills beyond those he already possessed. He disarmed a guard and took his weapon, then fought his way out of the prison through pure skill at arms. Somehow, he killed the last guard before the alarm could be raised and used the opportunity to sneak through the halls to her chambers.

Tais was still lying on the floor, unable to move, when she heard the sound of fighting in the hall. The sounds abruptly ceased, only to be replaced by the sound of a key turning in the lock and the gilded doors opening. At first, she had been terrified that her mother had returned, but when Markus stepped through the door her terror had been replaced by a relief so powerful all she could do was cry. He saw her lying on the floor and rushed to her side, and the love and concern in his eyes made her tears fall even harder.

"My love, what have they done to you? What have *I* done to you?"

He reached down to touch her forehead lightly, and tears streamed down his own face as she flinched from his hand like a terrified animal.

"Can you move, beloved? We don't have much time."

Tais had hovered on the brink of protesting, for she knew what would happen to the both of them if she defied her parents, but the memory of the vicious beating she had received at the hands of the Queen returned to her, and she found herself standing up, wanting desperately to somehow escape from the ruins of her former life. As much as the thought of running frightened her, she feared staying even more. They fled the castle with nothing more than the clothes on their backs, and Markus's friends smuggled them out of the city within the day.

The couple ran to his keep in Danshire, several days' ride north of the capital. Danshire was very small, and not terribly important, but neither one of them had anywhere else they could go. He mobilized his own militia, a mere handful of knights, 250 men-at-arms, and a large number of peasant archers, and then sent letters to his neighbors, asking for the aid of his fellow nobles.

King Orem's pursuit was inevitable and they both knew it. Markus told her that the key to their survival rested on the support of Duke Ascham. If Ascham could be convinced to extend his protection to them, the King would have no choice but to leave them alone or risk starting a civil war; but if Ascham *didn't* help them, they would have no choice but to leave Illymar and seek their fortunes elsewhere. Riders were dispatched to Saerce, and it didn't take long for them to receive a reply.

A year later, she still remembered the letter word-for-word.

To Markus, Lord Danshire;

I have received your urgent petition seeking the protection of Saerce and its allies in your challenge to the throne of Illymar. I regret to inform you that neither Saerce, nor any of its allies, will help you in this endeavor, for in so doing we too would risk being attainted of treason—something we absolutely will not do.

My sincere advice to you is that you end your foolish rebellion, surrender yourselves immediately to your King, and beg for his forgiveness. Perhaps he will be inclined to be merciful.

Ascham, Duke of Saerce

Markus had been devastated at the abandonment, for he had believed their cause was worthy enough that the other nobles would be willing to lend their support. Instead, he had been shunned, too insignificant for the others to risk their own titles to aid. Even worse, word came shortly after the arrival of the letter, that an army of 2,000 men, led by Prince Ethan himself, was on the way to Danshire to lay siege, and he had ordered the roads and ports watched. Escape was impossible. With no support and no avenues of flight left to him, Markus did the only thing he could: he prepared for the siege.

The two of them were married the day before the army arrived, in a small, private ceremony led by the Dracon of the county. They had tearfully exchanged rings and vows, and once the simple but beautiful ceremony had concluded, they had quickly retired to his rooms to consummate the marriage. She had been afraid, but he had proven to be a gentle lover, patiently and lovingly guiding her through her first time. Their lovemaking had been glorious, but it had also been underscored by a sense of urgency brought about by the approaching army. Neither one of them knew what the future held, but for one perfect evening, it didn't matter.

Tais did cry then, in remembrance of the man she had loved for so brief a moment in time. Within weeks of their wedding, Markus had been killed in battle, gallantly defending his wife and his unborn child with the aid of his few remaining men. His men-at-arms had held the keep much longer than they had expected, hoping that some noble or other would come to their aid, but ultimately, Ethan's numbers had prevailed and they had been overwhelmed. When it became clear that all was lost, Markus left the safety of the keep in order to challenge Ethan to single combat. Ethan was many things, chief among them a bully and a lout, but he wasn't a fool; he knew very well that Markus would kill him in single combat. So, he simply ignored Markus' challenge and ordered his men to shoot him to death with their crossbows.

Tais could still remember the horrible sound of the quarrels striking her husband's body, and the way he had jerked at the impacts again and again. His death had been mercifully quick, and when it was over Ethan had walked up to Marcus' body and, with a single stroke of his sword, had cut off his head. And just like that Tais was a widow, her unborn child fatherless.

Though Tais's memory was perfect in all other respects, she simply could not remember a single minute of the journey home to Illymaine. She had tried desperately to remember something—anything—about that time, but from the day she had been taken from Danshire, to their arrival in Illymaine, not a single image would form. Unfortunately, the same could not be said of her homecoming, for she remembered the meeting with her parents all too well. When she was brought before them she had thought that she would be executed on the spot, just as Althea had threatened. That was not to be, however, for Orem had a different punishment in mind for his wayward daughter.

To this day, she still did not know why he had ordered her imprisoned instead of executed, but after a year of solitary confinement, she had begun to think that the punishments were one and the same. In her early days in the Tower, she had drawn strength and courage from the child growing within her. At least one small part of Markus would survive, and she had taken great comfort in that simple fact.

The pregnancy had not been easy. The stress of the siege, the murder of her husband, and her confinement in the Tower had made a delicate condition even worse, and she had been sick for much of the time. The Royal Physician had been in to see her each week, but he was only allowed to ask questions directly related to her health or to the health of the child—no other communication was permitted. As the months progressed and the baby had developed, he had become more and more worried by her condition. The constant sickness and poor living conditions had been hard on her body, and the strain on her system was beginning to show.

When she finally went into labor, it was almost two months premature, and Tais had nearly died during the delivery. She did not remember the event, for she had fallen unconscious shortly after her water had broken. It was days after the baby had been delivered that she had finally awakened, to the concerned expression on the doctor's face. After checking her condition, the doctor told her quite firmly that she would live, and then had been taken away before he could say or do anything else at all.

After that there were no more visitors. Even her food was delivered once a day through a small hole in the door a foot from the floor. She had tried asking the servant who delivered her food about her child, but there was never an answer. She still didn't know if the child had lived or died, where it was, or if she would ever see it. It had been five months since the birth of her child, and those questions had yet to be answered. She didn't even know if her child was a girl or a boy.

Tais would have those answers if it took her the rest of her life. That was the reason she refused to jump to her death, the reason she refused to give in to despair. If the child was alive, she would take it back and raise it on her own, or if it had died, she would seek justice on its behalf. Orem, Althea, and Ethan . . . these people had all had a hand in what had been done to her, and she would have her revenge. She bowed her head, and for the first time since her punishment began, she prayed to the Archon.

Zarryiosiad, Mother of Justice, I beg you on behalf of my child to please allow me the opportunity to seek redress for my own sins, and grant me vengeance for the sins of others. If I must die for the harm I have caused, I will gladly die. But my child is an innocent. Grant me the opportunity to protect and nurture my child if he lives, or to seek justice on his behalf if he does not.

As if in answer to her prayer, Tais heard the sound of a key turning in the lock of the heavy oaken door guarding her cell. She shot to her feet in astonishment, too surprised at the unexpected event to do anything other than stare at the door, and when it swung open, her surprise turned to shock as she recognized Queen Althea and two of her handmaidens. The shock wore off quickly, however, and at the sight of Althea, Tais's eyes narrowed and she silently gave her heartfelt thanks to Zarryiosiad.

In your mercy, you have granted me the opportunity I have prayed for, Archon. I will not fail your trust; of this you have my word.

"You look both better and worse than I feared, daughter," Althea said, arms crossed, evaluating her from the doorway. "It looks as if we will have our work cut out for us if we are to make you presentable for the Convocation."

Tais knitted her brow in confusion at the statement. *The Convocation? After everything that has happened, you can't seriously be contemplating moving forward with my marriage to Lain.*

Even as the thought came to her she disregarded it, for she knew better than anyone that she was no longer an acceptable candidate to be the wife of the Prince of Ferralin. Several possibilities quickly crossed her mind, but she held her tongue and waited for Althea to continue.

The Queen stepped into the room and reached out with her right hand to touch Tais's unkempt hair. At the movement, Tais stepped back a full pace to keep Althea from touching her, never taking her hate-filled eyes off of the woman. Althea's expression widened in surprise at the completely unexpected defiance, and then hardened as the look on Tais's face registered.

"Leave us," Althea said to the handmaidens who had accompanied her. "My daughter and I must speak." The two servants curtseyed to their Queen, and then they silently and gracefully glided from the room. One of the young women closed the door behind her, but didn't lock it. When they were alone at last, Althea hissed, "You *dare* to defy me? *Again?*" Althea said in a low, dangerous voice. "Perhaps you blame *me* for what you have brought upon yourself? I *warned* you, daughter. I warned you that betraying your family and your country would have consequences. When we first discovered that you had fled with that fool, your father fully intended to have you executed as you so richly deserved. Fortunately for you, I cannot abide waste, and you may yet be useful." She paused for a moment, and then continued in a more normal tone. "While it is true that you are no longer fit to be Prince Lain's bride, with so many nobles attending the Convocation, I am sure I can find someone who will be willing to accept you as a wife . . . even as damaged as you are." She smiled joylessly. "Of course, the pool of men willing to entertain the thought of marrying a fallen woman will be quite shallow, but you should be grateful; any husband—no matter how repugnant he may be—is much better than you deserve."

It took Tais several painful moments to speak. For months, she hadn't spoken to anyone at all, and her unused voice protested at the unexpected exertion. She had to clear her throat several times, but eventually she was able to make herself be understood, though her normally melodic tone was very rough indeed and sounded harsh even to her own ears.

"What . . ." she cleared her throat again to make herself better understood "What happened to my child?"

Althea's eyes narrowed in anger at the question, but Tais didn't back down—she simply matched the Queen's icy gaze evenly and awaited her answer. Althea ignored the question.

"We have no time to waste. You are most certainly not presentable as you are, and the hairdressers and seamstresses will need to work miracles in the short time we have left."

As Althea reached for the door handle, Tais quickly stepped forward and grabbed her arm, turning her forcibly around to again face her. The anger and hatred welling up inside of Tais spilled forth, and she pressed forward, still holding the Queen's left arm in a tight grip. Her gravelly voice matched her words perfectly, and she glared down at the shorter woman, fury burning in her eyes.

"I asked you a question. What have you done with my child?"

For just a moment, Althea's eyes widened in fear, but that fear was covered in an instant by her anger at her daughter's presumption. Her full lips tightened into a line, and without saying a single word, she reached back with her right hand and prepared to swing an open palm at Tais's face in a vicious slap. For just an instant, Tais remembered the last time Althea had slapped her, but she was no longer the same person she had once been. This time there was no fear, and no hesitation. Before the blow could land, Tais released the Queen's left arm and reached up with her own right hand, intercepting Althea's slap in mid-swing. Althea's eyes widened in surprise at the interception, and the surprise changed to fear as she attempted to pull her arm out of Tais' vice-like grip and failed. Tais pushed Althea against the door, still clutching the older woman's wrist in her hand, and pressed her right forearm against Althea's throat hard enough to choke her.

"You will never lay your hands to me again, Althea. *Never.* You lost that right forever on the day I became a widow." She tightened her grip to the point that Althea whimpered slightly in pain, and pressed her forearm even harder against Althea's throat, choking her. "Now, answer my question, or by the Archon, I will have it from you . . . whatever it takes."

Althea couldn't believe this was happening to her. She had been so certain Tais's will had been broken by the months of solitude that she hadn't even bothered to bring along guards, for she had wanted as few witnesses as possible for this meeting. Now she cursed her foolishness, for she had believed that Tais would be so grateful for an opportunity to leave the Tower that she would be easy to control. She hadn't counted on the desperation, the fury, the *madness* that had overcome Tais, and she knew without a doubt, that her daughter could—and would—kill her.

At the realization that her life was actually in danger, Althea began to panic. The only people who could help her were on the other side of the door, and she would be dead long before they could summon help. As Tais increased the pressure on her throat yet again, it became increasingly difficult to breathe.

"Your child died within minutes of its birth," she said, her voice almost shrill with panic. "It was born too soon, Tais! Too soon! There was nothing we could do!" The last came out in a strangled shout, and the pressure on her throat increased for a second.

Althea's vision began to cloud, but then abruptly, the pressure was gone. Althea was relieved to see the fury in her daughter's eyes waning, and then dying altogether, and better still, the madness passed from her eyes. Tais released her and stepped away slowly, almost leadenly, and walked to the window of the cell to look at the waves crashing on the rocks far below. Althea rubbed her throat and wrist to relieve the pain, but she didn't take her eyes off of her daughter.

For several long seconds, neither of them spoke. Tais simply looked out the window at the sea, and Althea watched her warily. Tais broke the silence then, without taking her gaze from the water.

"Was . . . was it a boy or a girl?"

The look of longing in her eyes as she stared at the water touched Althea even as it frightened her, and she felt a momentary surge of panic at the thought of her daughter jumping to her death right in front of her.

"It was a boy. He was interred in the Savonne family crypt in secrecy."

A boy. At that, Tais began to weep softly, though her gaze never left the rocks far below. It would be so easy. One tiny step and the pain would end forever. *A son, Markus. We would have had a son.*

She felt Althea's hand upon her shoulder, and the soft tears became a flood.

"Come away from there, Tais. Let's go to your rooms and get you cleaned up. It's over now."

Tais snarled and pulled her shoulder away from Althea's touch. She scrubbed at her eyes furiously, wiping away her tears and hating herself for showing weakness in front of her enemy. When her eyes were dry once again, she said.

"It isn't over, Althea. Not by a far cry. Who did you give Markus's lands to? Which member of the Savonne family profited from his death?"

Althea jerked her hand back as if burned, and frowned in confusion at the sudden change of subject.

"A distant cousin—one you wouldn't know. How did you . . ."

"It matters more than you know, Althea," said Tais with a laugh of triumph. She turned to look at the Queen, and her tears were gone, replaced instead by a radiant smile of . . . *joy.* "You have already planted the seeds of your own destruction, and you don't even realize it. It's more than I could have hoped for."

Tais stepped towards the door, and when she realized that Althea hadn't followed, she turned again to the Queen.

"You needn't worry about my behavior ever again, Althea, for you can be assured that I have learned my lesson well. I will once again be the perfect Princess, though you should know I no longer think of you as family. I will obey your commands without question. Find a husband for me, if that is your wish. I will marry whomever you may choose without complaint, and I will make for him the perfect wife." Her smile changed then, and she could almost see the chill run down Althea's spine as the look registered. "I make you these promises, not because I fear imprisonment, or even death, but because I will do whatever it takes to be there to see the look upon your face as your entire world collapses around you, and you lose everything you hold dear. I warn you now: your own actions have already cost you this kingdom. The damage has been done. All I need do now is watch."

With that, she walked to the door and knocked, and it swung open slowly to reveal the two ladies-in-waiting. Despite her rags, her disheveled hair, and her tattered appearance, Tais looked every inch a Royal Princess.

"I believe you are here to take me to my quarters? Please lead on." The ladies looked past Tais to the Queen, obviously seeking her permission, and after a moment's hesitation, the Queen motioned them on, too shocked by her daughter's bold statement to say anything at all.

Queen Althea stayed alone in the tiny cell long after her daughter had been escorted away. Her reunion with Tais hadn't gone at all well, and she remained behind to think on what Tais had said to her.

You have planted the seeds of your own destruction, and you don't even realize it.

The words alone were disturbing enough, but it was the absolute certainty with which Tais had delivered them that had truly chilled her to the bone. She went over their brief conversation again and again, trying to fathom the meaning of the cryptic statement, but in the end she decided that Tais must have indeed lost her wits during her imprisonment. *If* that was true, her words could be disregarded as the ramblings of a madwoman, for a person touched by madness might be . . . unpredictable, but their words at least could be discounted.

Doubt plagued her though, for Tais hadn't *sounded* mad in the least. She'd been too certain, too *sure* about her pronouncement. No, it wasn't madness at all, of that Althea was positive. It couldn't have been. But her words were wrong—weren't they?

In the end, she gave up her speculation and left the room, quickly closing the door behind her as if to close off her doubts once and for all. It didn't work, however, for she was unable to shake her uneasiness, or the feeling that someone, somewhere, was walking over her grave.

QUEEN ALTHEA ILLVANNA OF ILLYMAR

CHAPTER SEVEN

"Swordplay"

It had been three days since the *Sovereign* left port, and Princess Deirdre of Dakkadia had had just about enough of her *beloved* half-brother Phaedron, Lady Prudence Daemira, and the never-ending stream of covert glances they directed at each other like love-struck idiots. The situation was completely intolerable, in her considered opinion, and she vowed that if one of them didn't break the impasse soon she would do it for them—whether they liked it or not. It was obvious to everyone around them that both the Captain and Phaedron were hopelessly attracted to each other, but neither one of them could see that the attraction was most definitely mutual. Worse yet, neither one of them seemed willing or able to overcome their nervousness and actually strike up a conversation that could end the impasse.

Nine . . . Ten.

She glanced at Phaedron once again and, right on schedule, he snuck yet another of his furtive glances at the captain and, right on schedule, the Corsair quickly averted her own eyes before he could see that she, too, had been secretly watching him. Deirdre desperately wanted to walk up to both of them and snatch them up by the ears like misbehaving children, or better yet, grab them by the scruff of their necks like puppies and shake some sense into them.

It might actually come to that. They're hopeless.

Of the two, she found that she had slightly more sympathy for Phaedron than for Lady Prudence. Phaedron's nervousness she could at least understand after all, for this was the *Corsair,* and as far as Deirdre was concerned, no mere mortal could possibly think himself worthy of her attention. On the other hand, she was quite disappointed in Lady Prudence's behavior. From all of the tales she had heard about the Corsair, she had thought the Captain would show more backbone than this. She again counted to ten, and right on cue, Phaedron snuck another look.

The crew had noticed the byplay as well, and had chosen to be amused by it. Deirdre had heard the whispers and the quiet chuckles—all where the Captain couldn't hear, of course—and had actually overheard a few snippets of conversation on the subject.

"Got it bad, the Captain does. Poor lass."

Poor lass? The 'poor lass' in question is a living legend, and it's about time she started acting like one. From what Deirdre could tell, the crew was unanimous in their happiness for the Corsair, but not a single one of them was willing to interfere. *Ten.* Another look, another quickly averted gaze . . . and Deirdre snapped. *That's it,* she thought with a snarl.

She whirled to the nearest crewmember and shot him a venomous look so severe that it made him drop a coiled rope he had been carrying and leap back like it had suddenly come to life.

"Where is the Master-at-Arms?" she demanded of the surprised sailor. He froze for a moment in complete shock, and then he raised his hands defensively and started stammering apologies, a look of terror in his eyes.

"I'm sorry, Your Highness! I didn't mean to stare at you! I'll stop, I promise! Please don't report me!" Deirdre's eyes rolled upward in disgust, and she sighed heavily. She put her hands on her hips and leaned toward him.

"I don't care about that. Just tell me where I can find the Master-at-Arms."

The sailor wilted at her acerbic tone and pointed to an older man wearing a sword and dagger on his belt, standing near the Captain.

"Thank you," she said, smiling brightly at the sailor. "Now go about your business."

The sailor didn't need to be told twice. The rope wound its way up his arm as if it actually *was* a living creature, and he disappeared without a second glance.

Deirdre rolled up her sleeves and marched up to the Master-at-Arms.

"Is there something I can do for you, Your Highness?"

"As a matter of fact, there is. I heard a story once, told by a person who claimed to have been aboard your ship. He said that any person at any time could challenge another crewmember to a swordfight. Is this true?"

The Master-at-Arms smiled and covered his chin in thought.

"Aye, Princess. 'Tis true. The Cap'n believes that all of her sailors should be ready to fight at any time, and all of their mates should be able to avoid getting killed. The rules are simple: one person can challenge another, or groups can challenge each other. The entire deck is fair play, and the duel continues until first blood is drawn, or until one person or one group is forced to yield. All of the other crewmembers are to continue working as if the duel was not taking place, and it is up to the duelists to avoid the obstacles, living or otherwise."

"It's been three days. Why have there been no duels?"

"Captain's orders. She doesn't want to disturb our guests—meaning you—any more than we have to."

Deirdre whirled to Lady Prudence, who had obviously been too distracted to hear any of the conversation that had just taken place.

"Captain Daemira? Might I ask a favor of you?"

The Corsair, who had been surreptitiously staring at Phaedron yet again, jumped slightly at Deirdre's voice, and turned quickly towards the diminutive girl as if she had been caught red-handed playing at some mischief. When she spoke, however, there was no trace of surprise in her voice.

"Of course. How may I be of assistance, Your Highness?"

"I was just speaking with your Master-at-Arms about your dueling policy, and I find it intriguing. Would it be too much trouble to ask for a demonstration?"

"I really shouldn't allow it, but for you I think we can make an exception," she said, pursing her lips in serious thought. "Very well. Mr. Salazar, the Princess would like a demonstration. You have my permission to accommodate her, providing you can find a volunteer."

The Princess smiled brightly and whirled back to the Master-at-Arms.

"Oh, I have just the volunteer in mind. You can 'accommodate' me by challenging my oldest brother to a duel. He should be easy to find: he's the one standing at the front of the ship trying desperately to pretend that he's watching the ocean."

The Master-at-Arms bellowed a loud, deep belly laugh that echoed over the ship like the report of a cannon. He turned and stalked towards his unsuspecting prey like a bear, sword in hand, as Deirdre settled down to watch the drama unfold with a self-satisfied smile on her face.

Phaedron spared a glance for Captain Daemira yet again, and found himself idly wondering what—if anything—she thought of him. It couldn't be much, he thought despondently, for as far as he could tell, in the three days since he had boarded the ship she had never even spared him a second glance. For his part, he had often found himself looking at her, and more than a few times he had actually resolved to speak with her. But for the life of him, he couldn't think of a single thing to say to her that wouldn't end in humiliation or disaster. Worse still, the very thought of speaking to the impossibly beautiful woman made him break out in a cold sweat.

During the six-day ride to the port he hadn't really thought about the Corsair except when Deirdre had mentioned her and he hadn't really formed much of a mental image of her. He'd dismissed the stories of her great beauty as the musings of court bards given to fanciful exaggeration. After all, she was the captain of a warship and, by extension, a soldier . . . and he knew a lot of female soldiers—none of whom could be considered particularly attractive. As such, he'd firmly believed that any expectations that the tales of her beauty would be even remotely close to the reality were utterly doomed, and since he *knew* that, he hadn't wasted time on speculation. He had never met her, and he wasn't sure what he had expected the Corsair to look like . . . but when he had first set eyes on her he knew that whatever it was he might have thought, he'd been completely and utterly wrong.

When he had first boarded the *Sovereign*, the presence of another Waterborn had distracted him. Curious to meet another Water Mage, he had introduced himself to Cahrick Rantrefal, and the two of them had just begun speaking to each other when his mother had called to him. He turned to see what his mother wanted, and his eyes had landed upon the most beautiful woman he'd ever seen. For just a moment they locked gazes, and Phaedron was overwhelmed by what he saw in the deep green pools. The moment was fleeting however, for she had broken their eye contact to give Cahrick an order. At the time, Phaedron had been thankful for the reprieve, for when his mother had finally introduced him to the raven-haired captain, he had somehow recovered at least some of his wits. Or so he had thought.

When he had tried to say something to her, those few remaining wits had deserted him. He'd tried desperately to think of something charming to say and had failed utterly. *No problem*, he'd thought. *Charming is out, so fall back to polite.* Unfortunately, polite words had also failed to form, so in desperation, he had said the first thing to come to mind.

"You don't look like a Captain."

He hadn't needed Deirdre's pained wince to know that he'd just made a complete ass of himself, and at that moment he would have given all he possessed and more to have those words back again. Lady Prudence had frowned slightly in bemusement, and with more than a bit of discomfort apparent in her voice she said,

"Ah, yes. Well, *ah*, I do hear that more often than you might imagine."

Even now, three days later, he wanted to throw himself overboard and drown himself in shame. *You don't look like a Captain? Idiot!* He heard a booming laugh far behind him, but didn't look back to see what might have elicited it. For all he knew the person was laughing at him, and why not? If it had been Valeriad in this situation, he'd be laughing just as hard. *Why is this so difficult? Think, Phaedron! You have to have at least* something *in common with her!*

Just then, something struck his rapier's scabbard with enough force to snap him out of his reverie, and he turned to see what had happened. To his surprise, the Master-at-Arms was standing directly behind him with his cutlass drawn and a grim expression on his face.

"Princess Deirdre says you need a good thrashing, so I volunteered, unless you're too busy making eyes at the Captain, of course." Phaedron glanced at the Master-at-Arm's cutlass, and then turned to look at his sister. Deirdre was sitting close by the Corsair with a cheerful grin on her face. She wiggled her fingers at him in a playful wave.

"I see. Any rules to this 'thrashing'?"

"Try not to kill the crewmen," the dark-skinned man replied. "Other than that, anything goes."

Phaedron nodded, for he'd expected as much. With a blinding move, he drew both his rapier and his main gauche and settled into a dueling stance. The Master-at-Arms withdrew two paces to give himself some room, and when he was sure Phaedron was ready, he struck. The first swing was rather slow and obvious, and Phaedron knew it was meant more as a test of his abilities than a serious attempt to break through his guard. Phaedron casually deflected the blow with a deft twist of his wrist. Salazar struck again, and again his blow was harmlessly diverted with barely a move by Phaedron. The third swing was followed immediately by a flurry of strikes, each of which was a serious attempt to penetrate his defenses. Phaedron blocked all of the blows with blades that seemed to be everywhere at once, and after the attacks had been defeated, his lightning-fast counterattack caught the sailor completely by surprise.

He smacked the Master-at-Arms lightly on the side of the head with the flat of his rapier and smiled.

"Quit holding back, Mr. Salazar. I think you'll find that I won't break."

Salazar dropped his guard in surprise at the blow, and when Phaedron finished speaking, he threw back his head and laughed uproariously for the second time that morning.

"So I see, Milord! So I see!" He reached behind his belt and unsheathed a cup hilted dagger that matched his cutlass perfectly, and then smiled at Phaedron. "Defend yourself!"

With that, the battle began in earnest.

Lady Prudence was flatly amazed at what she was seeing. Her Master-at-Arms had 30 years of experience with his weapons—ten more years than Phaedron had been alive—but it was clearly the much younger Phaedron who was pushing the pace in this fight. Salazar's expertise with weaponry was legendary in the Dakkadian navy, and she had had to fight hard to obtain his services for her crew. Even now, some of the other captains jokingly accused her of poaching him, but she didn't mind. He'd been more than worth the price of a little ribbing from the other captains. She had accounted herself an excellent swordsperson before she'd met him, but his training had made her even better. So much better in fact, that she was the only person aboard the ship who could force him to draw his dagger in a fight. Everyone knew that he considered using his dagger to be unfair in a friendly duel, so its presence here meant that he considered Phaedron to be a worthy opponent, and that he took this fight very seriously indeed.

A series of slashing attacks rained down upon Phaedron, and the young man gave ground reluctantly, concentrating completely on defense. Corsair knew what Salazar was setting him up for, because he'd used the same move on her a time or two. *Here it comes.*

With no warning whatsoever, Salazar threw a forward kick meant to take Phaedron full in the stomach, but Phaedron spun to the side like a top and avoided the kick altogether. When he completed the move his left arm shot under the weapon master's still-raised leg and lifted it skyward to overbalance him. The riposte worked perfectly.

Salazar fell to his back with an explosive grunt, and though he had obviously had the wind knocked out of him, somehow he was still able to deflect four lightning fast blows that came at him from above. He warded off the blows with some difficulty, and then took the opportunity to spin his legs like a windmill to gain enough momentum to turn over.

Phaedron pressed his attack, looking for an opening in the older man's defense, but Salazar continued to parry with his dagger and pulled himself to his feet with his sword arm. It took a supreme effort on the part of the Master-at-

Arms, but somehow he regained his footing and kept Phaedron from scoring on him.

Now it was Phaedron who again pressed the attack, forcing Salazar to give ground steadily. Not counting life or death battles, Salazar had only had to fight full out a few times in his life, but this was definitely one of them, and even so, it didn't look like it would be enough to stop the young noble.

"He's amazing. Where did he learn to fight like that?" Prudence asked herself.

"Phaedron has had a lot of really wonderful tutors," Deirdre unexpectedly answered her, "and Father says that he is one of the best natural swordsmen he has ever seen . . . even if he does get more than a bit grumpy when he admits it. He's much better than Valeriad, though Valeriad *is* improving. Phaedron has been working with him, you see." She paused for a moment, and a sly look crossed her cheerful face. She arched a single delicate eyebrow and said, "I couldn't help but notice that you wear the same kinds of weapons that Phaedron uses. I'm certain he would be happy to teach you a thing or two if you asked . . . you know, to help you improve your swordsmanship? I'm sure you could use the practice."

Corsair's eyebrows shot up almost to her hairline, her mouth dropped open, and her face turned snowy white as all the blood drained away from it in an instant at the deadly insult. *The nerve!* She couldn't *believe* that the Princess had actually said that. The implication that *her* swordsmanship needed improvement was bad enough, but to have this wretched little girl tell her that her *brother* would be happy to train her made the insult absolutely intolerable! The blood returned to her face with a vengeance, and her color went from ghastly white to a furious blood red in a heartbeat. She whipped her eyes around to glare in fury at the evil little Princess, but now the young girl was all sweetness and light, and the expression on her face was one of utmost innocence. Well! An insult of that magnitude couldn't go unanswered, and if she couldn't wring satisfaction out of the Princess, well, she would just have to find herself another target. In a fury, Prudence clawed at her weapons, eyes whirling back to where Phaedron was still battling the Master-at-Arms. Phaedron was clearly about to defeat the older man, but just as obviously, he didn't know what was about to descend upon him. As her green eyes attempted to bore holes right through him, she gritted her teeth and growled,

"We'll just see which one of us needs practice!"

At that, Corsair grinned maniacally with a malevolent glow shining in her eyes, and leaped down to join the fray. *Lord Daane, you're a dead man!*

The dead man in question was absolutely having the time of his life. The impromptu duel had ranged all over the deck, and for the first time in three days, Phaedron was able to forget about the Corsair and simply lose himself in the familiar swirl of combat. Mr. Salazar was an outstanding swordsman . . . probably one of the ten best he'd ever fought, but Phaedron had trained with the best swordsmen from three races and five countries. He'd successfully learned the elegant styles of the Fae and the Elves, and had blended their techniques into the more direct style favored by humans. The Fae were very long limbed, and their sword forms were designed to keep opponents from closing in . . . a technique that was working very well indeed against the short bladed cutlass and dagger used by Salazar. Elven techniques, on the other hand, were designed to take advantage of the Elves' greater reflexes. The unpredictable style that they had developed made for excellent close-in defense—as long as you could duplicate their speed. Phaedron was only a quarter-Fae and, as such, his reflexes were much better than a pure human's, but even with that advantage he had still lacked the speed an Elf could obtain with a sword.

The deficiency had plagued him for a while, but after careful study, he'd finally hit upon an answer. The long bladed main gauche he wielded in his left hand was much smaller and lighter than an Elven broadsword, and by using the lighter weapon, he was able to integrate their techniques into his own hybrid style. The few times Salazar had gotten past Phaedron's outer defense, he'd been stopped cold at Phaedron's inner defense, and the main gauche effortlessly turned aside blows that had been more than enough to defeat lesser men. When Salazar had finally learned that his speed couldn't match Phaedron's, he had tried to use his greater strength to batter through his defenses. Against an Elf or a Fae, that approach might have worked, but Phaedron was much stronger than he looked.

Human techniques emphasized strength and power over speed or finesse, and Phaedron had spent the majority of his training learning to take advantage of the greater power and strength his human side had granted him. He didn't look strong, for he wasn't as heavily muscled as King Madari, but his slender frame was rock hard and tight with muscle. After several abortive attempts, Salazar gave up trying to batter through Phaedron's defenses. Unfortunately, the Master-at-Arms was rapidly running out of options.

The close quarters of the ship's confines hadn't allowed Phaedron to truly unleash himself, but the techniques he *could* use were more than enough. Salazar's attacks were coming more and more slowly, and he was giving ground much more often to try and buy himself time to catch his breath. The older man's labored breathing and ruddy complexion showed clearly that he couldn't keep up with Phaedron, a man less than half his age, and his lifetime of experience wasn't enough to overcome the twin advantages of speed and youth. In contrast, the long hours Phaedron had spent in training were paying dividends as he was barely even breathing hard. As Phaedron blocked yet another series of attacks, he thought with more than a bit of regret, *I wish I could have fought you at your prime, Salazar. Your age is catching up with you.* In desperation, Salazar attempted one more combination and Phaedron quickly disarmed him, knocking away his cutlass with a deft counterstroke. *Two more moves and I have you.*

Before he could perform those two moves, however, his eye caught the movement of a shadow above him. The flash of sunlight on metal was all the warning he had, but somehow he was able to raise both of his weapons to parry the descending blades. He backed up quickly, not entirely sure what was happening, but the attacking blades came at him from every direction at once like a nest of vipers. Backing up very quickly turned to full-fledged retreat at the ferocity of the attacks and, in just a couple of seconds, all of the ground that he had gained against Salazar had been lost. He gritted his teeth and regained his equilibrium, and once he was able to center himself, he took stock of his situation. His eyes widened briefly when he recognized that Lady Prudence herself had attacked him, but after he got over his initial shock, he grinned at her and began fighting in earnest.

The Corsair's attacks were completely unpredictable, and she seemed to strike at every single opening in his defenses as if her blades were drawn to them by magic. Worse yet, it quickly became apparent that she knew every inch—every last detail—of her ship, and she ruthlessly and efficiently used that knowledge to her advantage. Several of his strikes were parried not by her weapons, but by ropes that seemed to come out of nowhere, and his footwork was often hindered by obstacles such as netting or barrels. Still, despite her advantages in knowing the terrain he was getting a feel for her style, and he knew that it was just a matter of time before he defeated her.

Damn, he's good! Prudence thought with heartfelt admiration. She'd used every trick she could think of, every possible advantage the terrain offered her, and she still hadn't managed to score on him. Worse yet, she knew he was getting used to her style, and it wouldn't be long until he regained the advantage. Almost as if he'd read her mind, he spun around and launched a series of attacks from an unexpected angle that caught her completely by surprise, and in desperation she tucked into a backward roll to buy herself some room. His pursuit was relentless, however, and just as she got back on her feet he renewed

LORD PHAEDRON DAANE OF DAKKADIA

his attacks, unfazed by her acrobatics. Now she was completely on the defensive, and he pressed his advantage to the utmost. She had to do something soon to break his rhythm or she would lose.

"I see you aren't just a pretty face, Lord Daane," she said.

"Funny . . . I was just thinking the same thing about you, Lady Prudence," he replied, grinning broadly even as he blocked yet another series of strikes from her, proving her attempt to distract him had failed. Once her attack had been stymied, he added, "Your footwork is exquisite, and you seem to know this ship like the back of your hand."

"I should: it's my ship. But you! You've been here three days and already you fight as if you know this ship nearly as well as I do." She punctuated her comment with a snaking move with her rapier that nearly penetrated his guard, but his main gauche trapped her sword and threw it to the side.

He took advantage of the opening she'd presented him by doing something completely unexpected. He leaped forward inside her sword's range and battered aside her main gauche through sheer power—the same move Salazar had tried on him earlier. Unfortunately for Prudence, she wasn't nearly as strong as Phaedron and the bold move worked flawlessly. She lost her grip on both her sword and dagger, and they flew away from her in opposite directions. As he angled his main gauche for the win, she turned quickly towards him and grabbed his shirt with both hands. She then fell backwards, using both her weight and his momentum to pull him down with her and, as she hit the deck, she interposed her boot between their bodies and threw him completely over her. As he came crashing to the deck, she followed up the move by using her own momentum to roll to her feet, and with a desperate dash, she reached for her dagger . . . just as Phaedron grabbed her boot from behind and tripped her. She, too, came crashing to the deck, but not before grabbing her main gauche and turning over, just in time to see Phaedron dive at her.

When he landed atop of her, she felt his main gauche touch her lightly on the throat and saw him smile in triumph. Unfortunately for him, however, as quick as he'd been, he hadn't quite been fast enough. She had had just enough time to get her own main gauche in position, and his smile disappeared completely when he felt it touching him lightly under the chin. Both of the duelists held their weapons to each other's throat, and neither of them was sure who had won. For several seconds they held their poses, and only the sound of their labored breathing could be heard on the deck.

The stalemate was broken when a pair of heavy boots appeared next to them, and as one they turned to look at the owner. King Madari was staring at the duo, a bemused look on his face and his weapon belt held lightly in one hand. He regarded them sternly for a moment, and then turned to the crew.

"A draw!"

The crew erupted in cheers, whistles, and more than a few groans, and money began changing hands as crewmembers, who had wagered on one combatant or the other, settled their bets. Amidst the cheering and the backslapping, Prudence and Phaedron remained unmoving. The two of them, still lying on the deck, took their weapons away from each other's throats slowly, almost lovingly. Prudence started to rise, but Phaedron was atop of her, and instead of letting her get up he leaned toward her, eyes shining. As his face came within inches of hers, she thought, *is he going to kiss me?* Her cheeks turned bright red with embarrassment, but she didn't turn away.

It wasn't to be, however, for instead of kissing her, he said in a low voice meant only for her, "You were magnificent . . . Prudence."

She could hear the tenderness in his voice as he said her name, and she realized in an instant that perhaps her infatuation wasn't one-sided after all.

In a flash the embarrassment was gone, and she gave him a smile so bright it took his breath away.

"So were you . . . Phaedron."

From the look in his eyes, he had realized the same thing.

Deirdre smiled in victory as the two combatants slowly came to their feet, eyes still locked on each other. She thought with more than a trace of smug satisfaction, *That was well done, if I do say so myself!*

King Madari left the pair and walked over to his daughter. She wiped the smile off her face as he approached, and replaced it with one of thoughtful calm, but he wasn't fooled.

"Somehow, you're to blame for this aren't you?"

As the sound of steel clashing against steel had made it below deck, Deirdre had seen her father and Morvandis come running to the deck with their weapons drawn. They had expected to find an attack, or worse, but it had taken only moments for them to recognize what was truly happening. Morvandis had simply turned around and walked back to the chart room, but Madari had remained behind to watch the duel. He hadn't actually taken part in the betting, but Deirdre had felt certain that that was because no one had been near enough.

"I have no idea what you are talking about, Father."

He gave her a stern look which she deftly countered with a look of supreme innocence, and after a few seconds he snorted.

"Of course, you don't. I have business below. Do try and keep them from killing one another. We still have several more days of travel left, and it wouldn't do for Lady Prudence or Phaedron to suffer a misfortune."

"I wouldn't worry about that if I were you, Father. I'd say they are working out their differences quite nicely."

She glanced at the couple, engaged in conversation punctuated by the odd hand movement. *Recreating their fight, I see.*

At a comment from Phaedron, Prudence laughed brightly and struck him lightly on the chest with the back of her hand. All of the awkwardness between them was as gone as if it had never been, and the way they acted now made it seem that they had known each other all their lives. Deirdre smiled in satisfaction, and caught the eye of the Master-at-Arms, who smiled back at her and winked.

Yes. Very well done, indeed.

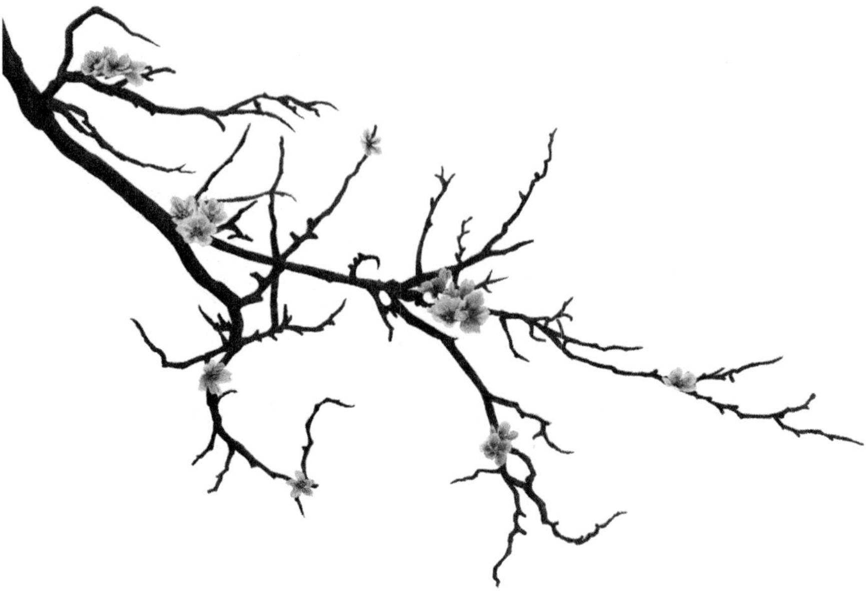

CHAPTER EIGHT

"Emerald"

Although Crown Prince Valeriad had very much been looking forward to this trip, he'd quickly found that he hadn't been at all prepared for the reality of sea travel. From the moment he had come aboard, he had been overtaken by a horrible case of seasickness that had eventually gotten bad enough to keep him confined to quarters. Unlike Phaedron, who loved to sail, he had never actually been aboard a ship before, and the experience had come as quite a shock to his system. His mind insisted that the ship was constantly moving, while his eyes told him otherwise, and his stomach hadn't been amused by the disagreement between the two.

Within an hour of setting sail, his stomach had made its displeasure known in the only way it knew how. After the third or fourth time he'd had to run to the railing, he had had enough and was more than ready to give up on sailing for good. Lady Prudence had been sympathetic to the plight of the landlubber, and out of courtesy—or pity—she had ordered both of her Mages to make the journey as smooth and gentle as they possibly could. Unfortunately for Valeriad, it hadn't made any difference. No matter how gentle the breeze was, or how smooth the sailing had been, he had been completely unable to hold down any food at all besides bread and weak broth, and the involuntary diet had been hard on him. He had always been thin, but now he looked absolutely gaunt. His eyes were shadowed, and his cheeks looked hollow and sunken. Even his clothes were noticeably looser.

On the morning of the eighth day, however, he woke up to find that the effect the constant swaying of the ship was having on him had lessened considerably. In fact, other than some lingering cramps in his stomach from the constant retching, he actually felt pretty good. Good enough, in fact, that it didn't take him long to decide that a trip to the deck was in order, so he climbed unsteadily out of bed and started looking for his clothes. For a moment, his weakened legs refused to support him, but he steadied himself on a bulkhead, and once he was sure he could manage, he staggered to the wardrobe to retrieve some clean clothes.

As he dressed himself, he found that the effort of moving around and doing something was helping him to feel even better. He stamped his feet into his boots, picked up his sword belt, and tried to fasten it around his waist. It quickly became apparent that he'd lost so much weight during his illness that it would no longer fit properly. More than a little irritated at this discovery, he marked the spot a hole would need to be added, and pulled off the belt.

His eyes flashed red for a second, and a tightly focused awl of white-hot fire extended from a fingertip and burned through the leather at the spot he had marked, making a neat hole exactly where he had wanted. The smell of burning leather briefly filled the small cabin, awakening an unpleasant rumbling in his stomach, but the smell—and the rumbling—quickly subsided. After checking the hole to make sure certain it was the proper size, he let the awl dissipate, and when he tried on the belt a second time, this time using the new hole, it fit perfectly. He tugged at it a few times to make sure it wouldn't slip, and once he was satisfied that it was indeed secure, he returned his sword, his dagger, and his pistol to their proper places on his waist. His father had taught him a long time ago that Dakkadian nobles were required to wear their weapons everywhere, and now, years later, Valeriad considered himself to be naked without them.

As he opened the door to his cabin, a startled sailor, who was reaching for the door handle while balancing a tray, jumped back in surprise, spilling a large amount of the broth he'd been bringing for Valeriad's breakfast. As the sailor started to apologize for his clumsiness, Valeriad interrupted him.

"It was my fault. I didn't mean to startle you." He glanced down at the weak broth and wrinkled his nose. "And don't worry about the broth; I wouldn't have eaten it anyway. Actually, I think I can stand something a little more substantial this morning. Do you know if there is anything other than soup left in the kitchen?"

"We call it a 'galley,' Your Highness," the sailor said, smiling good-naturedly, "and I'm sure Cook would be more than happy to provide you with anything you'd like. If you would like me to bring something for you, just name it and I'd be more than happy to oblige."

"Well, if it isn't too much trouble, anything at all, other than broth, would be just fine. If I have a choice, I'd really like some cheese and bacon, I think, but tell him not to go to any trouble. Just bring me whatever you have . . . and lots of it."

"That I will, Your Highness. Shall I bring it to your cabin?"

"Actually, I think I've had about as much of that cabin as I can stand for now. Please bring it to the deck. I think I need some fresh air, almost as much as I need food."

As Valeriad made his way toward the deck, several sailors stopped what they were doing and greeted him.

"I'm glad to see you up and about, Your Highness," a particularly jovial sailor said. "Took you awhile to get your sea legs, didn't it?" Other sailors laughed in agreement, and Valeriad joined in the general mirth.

"Well, I don't know about my legs, but my *stomach* at least feels much better." The sailors laughed with him. "Have you seen Lord Daane or my sister?"

"They're on the deck, Your Highness. Lord Daane and Princess Deirdre spend most of their time up there with the Cap'n."

Several of the sailors smiled at each other knowingly, but Valeriad didn't get the joke. Instead of asking, he simply nodded his thanks and turned to the stairs leading to the deck as the sailors returned to their duties.

When he reached the deck, the unexpectedly bright sunshine of mid-morning assaulted his sensitive eyes. He quickly closed them against the unexpected pain, and raised a hand to shield them even further until they could adjust to the brightness. With his eyes shut, he took the opportunity to listen to everything going on around him, and much to his surprise, he heard his sister's voice raised in song, accompanied by a violin playing a mournful tune. He opened his eyes cautiously, ready to close them again if they hadn't finished adjusting, but the bright sunlight no longer hurt him. Once he was sure that he could see clearly, he looked around for his sister and the musician playing for her. It didn't take him long to spot her, for she was standing at the very front of the ship singing for the crew. He didn't recognize the song, but every crewmember on the deck had their attention riveted to the Princess. In fact, Valeriad noticed that several sailors were openly weeping. The words of the song were as haunting as the tune, and he stopped to listen.

We honor friends we've lost at sea and comrades fallen past.
In memory we carve their names upon our hearts and mast.
And should I sink in waves of blue too far from port or shore,
Remember me a sailor true like those who sailed before.

As Deirdre sang the last refrain and the violin played its final note, the sailors didn't cheer or applaud the performance. Instead, one by one, they walked from where they had been listening and touched the mainmast with both sadness and reverence. Curious, Valeriad stepped away from the door and approached the mast, wondering what the crewmen were doing. As he got nearer, he noticed that it was covered with names, each one carved into the wood by different hands.

"It's a cenotaph," a voice from behind him said. "Sailors and marines who fall during a voyage or in battle are buried at sea, so there is never a grave or a headstone to visit when we reach shore. Instead, we carve their names into the wood of the mainmast, and in so doing they stay with us always, even in death." Valeriad turned to look at the speaker and smiled when he recognized Lady Prudence. "It's good to see you on your feet, Your Highness. We were all worried about you. I can't remember the last time I've seen a case of seasickness go on for so long."

"I feel much better now, Captain, no thanks to Lord Daane. During the first day of the journey, Phaedron spent quite a bit of time sitting by my bedside, gleefully telling me all about how the ship was rolling back and forth, back and forth, on the waves—to be helpful, I'm sure you understand. Once he stopped doing that and actually started looking worried, I knew things were pretty dire."

"A slanderous accusation, My Lady," Phaedron interrupted, false pain in his tone. "Base lies and calumny. You should never listen to anything that Valeriad says because it's certain to be untrue."

Valeriad snorted and said,

"Captain, did you know that Phaedron here is the finest swordsman in Dakkadia?" Valeriad asked. "He taught me everything I know. In fact, he is so skilled, that I have resigned myself to the fact that I can never hope to attain even a fraction of his artistry at swordplay and, as such, I am strongly considering trying out other weapons to see if I can find one that will allow me to be his equal." Corsair laughed brightly. "Furthermore, everyone at court loves and respects him, as do the soldiers and the commoners. He leads by example in all things, and the loyalty he inspires is truly awe-inspiring. He's a man among men, and one day his name will go down in Dakkadian history as one of the greatest heroes we've ever had."

“All true, Prudence. All true,” Phaedron said solemnly. “You should listen to Prince Valeriad. He shows wisdom beyond his years.”

Prudence raised an eyebrow at Phaedron.

“I thought you said I should never listen to anything the Prince says because it’s certain to be untrue. I believe the phrase you used was ‘base lies and calumny?’”

“Normally, that would be the case,” Phaedron said, nodding. “However, it seems Valeriad’s close brush with death during this journey has somehow turned his life around and changed him for the better.” He shot Valeriad an evil grin. “Although, now that I think on it, perhaps it would be more accurate to say that his life hasn’t so much turned around as its been turned inside out.” The group broke out in renewed laughter, and when it subsided, Valeriad said,

“Lady Prudence, you have my enthusiastic permission to toss this wretch overboard. In fact, the sooner you do it the better. You don’t want him contaminating the crew, after all.”

Corsair nodded gravely at that and turned to a large, heavily muscled man covered in scars, wearing a well-used cutlass and matching dagger, and carrying a violin.

“Mr. Salazar, we have a Royal Edict. Please toss Lord Daane over the side. There’s a good man.”

Salazar ran a calloused hand over his close-cropped black hair liberally threaded with silver, and gave her a sheepish look.

“Ah . . . as to that, Captain, well, you see, I’ve tried. He’s far too tough for me.”

“Next time, just shoot him,” Deidre said, joining in. “All that swordplay makes *me* tired, and all I do is watch.”

Valeriad gave Deirdre a quizzical look.

“You’ve been too sick to know this, but Phaedron and Lady Prudence have been dueling each other quite often over the past few days. So far, all of their fights have been too close to call, and neither of them has won a clear victory over the other.”

Valeriad’s eyes shot wide open in surprise at that, and he turned an incredulous gaze towards the Corsair.

“That’s quite an accomplishment, if you don’t mind me saying so, Lady Prudence. I was only half joking about Phaedron’s skill at swordplay. He’s the finest swordsman in Dakkadia, and even Father admits it. If you’re an even match for him, then I’d have to say that your reputation is very well deserved, indeed!” Valeriad meant every word, but Salazar, Phaedron and Deirdre laughed in response to his statement. “Did I say something funny?” he asked in confusion.

"Not at all, My Prince" said Corsair, with a sour look at the three. "If we were on dry land, I readily admit that he'd defeat me easily. But on my ship, I am, *ah*, able to control the conditions of the duel by utilizing whatever advantages I can find; advantages that might be considered, *ah*, less than honorable under certain circumstances."

The group looked at each other with flat expressions, waited three full seconds, and in a single voice, Deirdre, Salazar, and Phaedron said,

"She cheats."

As understanding dawned on Valeriad, the group broke out in laughter yet again, and this time he joined in.

"When you duel on my ship, anything goes. That's the rule." Corsair said defensively as she shot an evil look at Phaedron, daring him to argue.

"Who am I to judge?" Phaedron said with an elaborate shrug.

Salazar clapped Phaedron on the back and said,

"Just be glad that she likes you enough not to have kicked you in the crotch yet. She's been known to do that from time to time. And believe me when I say that 'anything goes' is small comfort when you're rolling around on the deck in agony."

Thanks to his prolonged illness, Valeriad hadn't had time to get an impression of the Captain, but now that he'd had the chance to speak with her, he decided he very much liked what he saw. It was obvious that both Phaedron and Deirdre admired her, and as far as he was concerned, that was good enough for him. What surprised him, though, was the complete ease with which she and Phaedron interacted. He'd have to ask Deirdre later if there was something going on between the two, but that was for later.

"That was a beautiful song you were playing," Valeriad said to Mr. Salazar, indicating the violin still in his hands. "I don't know that I've ever heard it before. Can you tell me about it?"

It was Deirdre who answered him.

"It's called the *'Sailor's Lament,'* and Mr. Salazar was kind enough to teach it to me today. I heard one of the sailors whistling it earlier, and I was curious. Mr. Salazar here has been very generously teaching me different naval tunes and sea shanties. You know how I love to learn new songs." She turned to Mr. Salazar and touched his forearm. "Thank you for playing for me. You're quite good."

"Your Highness, you've done us a great honor today by performing that song for the crew. It meant a lot to all of us."

"The 'Sailor's Lament' is usually played at funerals and memorial services at sea," Corsair said, "and normally Mr. Salazar plays it while the crew sings. Unfortunately, none of my crew—myself included—have what you would call a 'good' singing voice. It was wonderful to hear the song the way it was intended to be heard. In fact, I venture to say that you have the most beautiful singing voice I have ever heard, Your Highness."

Deirdre blushed and looked away in embarrassment.

"She is blessed with perfect pitch . . . a gift from our mother" Phaedron said. "But nobody knows where she developed her hunger to learn new songs. She can be quite annoying about it."

Deirdre stuck her tongue out at her half-brother, and he responded by patting her on the head like an adult humoring a very young, very precocious child. Deirdre rolled her eyes.

Valeriad was about to say something, but he spotted the sailor who had offered to bring him his breakfast approaching the group carrying a covered tray.

"I hope you don't mind, Captain, but one of your crewmembers offered to bring me something to eat, and I asked him if he would bring it to the deck so I could eat up here. It occurs to me now that I should have asked first. Will it be acceptable for me to take my meal here?"

"Of course, Prince Valeriad, of course. The only thing worse than a prolonged seasickness is a prolonged case of bulkhead fever. I don't blame you a bit for wanting to get some fresh air. In fact, if you don't mind some company, we'll adjourn to the aft. There are no proper seats, of course, but there are some crates that will do quite nicely."

"That will be perfectly acceptable, Lady Prudence."

Corsair turned to the approaching sailor and spoke a few soft words, and he quickly turned back the way he came.

"Shall we?"

At the rear of the ship, an unexpected person awaited the group. Morvandis stood looking out over the starboard railing toward a point on the horizon, and though a small feast was waiting for him, Valeriad found his curiosity overriding his hunger. He walked up to the railing next to his teacher and looked toward the spot that Morvandis was focusing on, but he couldn't see anything at all in the distance.

"What are you looking at, Morvandis?" he asked.

Morvandis didn't turn his head, but smiled faintly.

"Nothing yet, Prince Valeriad, but I can feel the approach of the Teeth of Amhar, and I very much look forward to viewing them again." He turned an inquisitive gaze towards his pupil. "I felt your channeling from my quarters. I was pleased to note that eight days of seasickness doesn't seem to have affected your control over your abilities at all."

"It was nothing special," Valeriad said, grimacing. "My belt didn't fit properly, so I had to burn a new hole in it to keep it from falling down around my ankles."

"Did you have any difficulties keeping your ability focused?'

"None."

"Excellent. Many Mages would have been unable to channel so much as a spark after an illness of that length and severity. Or worse, they might have lost their focus and let their ability run amok. That you were able to maintain your focus under less than ideal circumstances does you credit."

Valeriad waited for the barb that would accompany the compliment, but to his immense surprise, Morvandis simply turned his attention back to the horizon, dismissing Valeriad completely from his consideration. When he realized that Morvandis was going to leave it at that, Valeriad's eyes widened to the point that white could be seen all the way around his irises. Morvandis gave praise like a miser spending coin, but apparently even misers could be generous upon occasion. Not wanting to tempt his good fortune, he quietly retreated from the railing and walked to where the others awaited him with the food. As he sat down on a barrel, he decided not to mention the compliment. After all, no one would believe him. He prepared a roll with some bacon and cheese; the food now had his full attention.

"Did you ask what he's doing up here?" Phaedron asked. "We haven't seen much of him during this trip. Both he and King Madari have spent almost all of their time below deck with our ambassadors discussing plans and possible treaty terms for their dealings with Illymar and Ferralin."

Valeriad took a big bite of his roll, savoring the taste of the crispy bacon as it melted in his mouth. As he chewed his food, he raised a finger to Phaedron asking him to wait for a moment.

"Morvandis says he can sense the approach of the Teeth of Amhar," Valeriad said, after swallowing. "He doesn't want to miss the first sight of it."

Deirdre gave a squeak of excitement, jumped to her feet, and ran to the railing to stand next to the Mage, close enough to touch him. Deirdre herself wasn't a Mage and, as such, she had not learned to beware the Mage's displeasure or to respect his personal boundaries. The group watched as the excited Princess spoke to the Mage, and Morvandis quietly answered her. He pointed toward a spot that none of them could see, and Deirdre instantly silenced herself to look where he pointed.

"The Teeth of Amhar truly are a sight to behold," the Corsair said. "Although I didn't know Mages could actually sense them at this great a distance."

"I feel nothing," Phaedron said shrugging, "though I admit I haven't tried. Morvandis is much more powerful than we are, and his sensitivity is much greater as a result. I imagine that as we draw nearer, both Valeriad and I should be able to sense the Teeth as well. After all, they were created by Zarryiosiad herself, and it is said that anything she touched with her power still bears her resonance."

"To be truthful, if I were not just about to perish from hunger, I'd be standing on that railing right next to Deirdre," Valeriad said. "The Teeth are supposed to be incredible."

"That they are, Prince Valeriad," Corsair said. "As are many of the miracles created by Zarryiosiad. By the time you finish your food, we, too, should be able to catch the first glimpse of them."

Valeriad smiled at that, and attacked his meal with a will.

Morvandis gripped the wooden railing tightly and concentrated completely upon the feel of magic radiating from the horizon, totally oblivious to the world around him. Every sense he possessed strained with the effort of analyzing the power emanating from the tiny white spots in the distance, but as the ship slowly made its approach and the spots started growing into vertical lines, the Archon's magic came more clearly into focus. Even at this great a distance, he could just make out individual bands of energy, completely invisible to the naked eye, but as obvious to his magical senses as the grain of the wood under his fingertips.

He concentrated even harder on those individual bands, only to find that the cords themselves were interwoven with such subtlety and power that he could find no beginning or end to them. Moreover, they were so tightly knotted that pulling them apart would be the next best thing to impossible.

So caught up was he in his study, he didn't feel a slight tugging on the sleeve of his robe until the tugging became an insistent yanking. Irritated at the interruption of his study, he glanced down at the Princess and gave her a very stern look.

"It is very rude to attempt to gain someone's attention by pawing at their clothes like an animal, Your Highness."

"Oh?" said Deirdre, completely unfazed. "Is it as rude as, say, pointedly ignoring a person trying to ask you a simple question?"

"Much more so, I would say," Morvandis replied.

Deirdre rolled her eyes and shook her head, as if he was an imbecile.

"Ask me your question," Morvandis said, resignedly.

Deirdre looked for a moment as if she wanted to comment more upon his manners, but she thought better of it.

"What can you tell me about the Teeth? From here they don't look like teeth at all. They look more like unicorn horns."

"An apt description, Princess," he said, smiling. "Indeed, the Ferraline do call them the Horns of Amhar. We call them the 'Teeth' because of their design. They completely surround the island of Illymar, and each of the stones that you can see above the water is merely a small part of the whole. While you can see some of the fangs growing from the water, there are thousands more just beneath the waves that you cannot see. Think, if you will, of a dog's teeth. The longest teeth are the canines, the pairs of long, sharp fangs on the top and bottom. But a dog's jaws are lined with many smaller teeth, as well, which are just as sharp, though much less prominent than the canines. So it is with the Teeth of Amhar. The large spirals are meant as a warning to any who approach."

"A warning?"

"A warning from the Archon to any foolish sailors who would dare to approach her island that says, 'Any attempt to pass between the Teeth will result in the complete destruction of your vessel and the total annihilation of your crew.'" He glanced over at Phaedron and Valeriad, who were engrossed in conversation with the Captain and her Master-at-Arms. "Phaedron, Valeriad, please come here." Phaedron moved to join them, while Valeriad stuffed the remainder of his breakfast into his mouth as quickly as possible, before rising to join him. The Captain followed the pair to the railing.

"Captain, I would like to move the *Sovereign* closer to the Teeth to give my pupils a better view. Would this be permissible?" Morvandis asked.

"I'll steer us in closer," she said. "It shouldn't take more than a half-hour to get us close enough to touch them."

"No need, Captain. I'll take care of it."

Without awaiting her permission, he looked up at the sails and his black eyes changed to a brilliant white, a clear signal that he was using Air Magic. The sails filled instantly with a powerful breeze, and the *Sovereign* lurched in the water as it suddenly gained speed. After he finished intensifying the wind, Morvandis's eyes transformed, from the bright white they had become, to a brilliant azure, and the *Sovereign* suddenly began moving in a lateral direction as the water pushed the ship toward the Teeth. At the surprise movement, every crewmember on deck grabbed something to keep from falling overboard, but after the initial jolt the ride became very smooth indeed, and the *Sovereign* cut through the water much faster than before.

The evenly spaced white vertical lines that marked the boundary of the Teeth of Amhar began growing in size until their true magnitude became apparent to everyone. As the *Sovereign* moved closer and closer, the Teeth continued to grow, eventually towering hundreds of feet in the air. Morvandis chose the closest of the Teeth and angled the *Sovereign* toward it.

The gigantic stone was twisted evenly throughout its entire length like a horn, but it was also perfectly white and absolutely smooth. As more details became clear, the white stone was revealed to have an almost pearlescent sheen to it that made it positively glow in the sunlight. Even at the waterline the Teeth were perfectly smooth, for such was the power of Zarryiosiad that not even 2,500 years of exposure to the harsh sea elements had been able to damage them.

Only a few hundred yards away from the nearest monolithic tower, Morvandis allowed his control over the ship to subside. As the winds died down and the waves returned to normal, the *Sovereign* slowed to the point that it almost felt like it was standing still. Once he made sure the ship had regained its original course and heading, he glanced down at the golden-haired Princess to see if she had anything to say, but the normally loquacious Deirdre had been struck completely speechless by the awesome spectacle. She wasn't alone either, for many of the crewmembers, who should have been busy at their duties, were equally dumbstruck by the incredible sight.

He reached out with his right hand, his eyes turning azure once again, and the water level around the white stone began to lower, as if a giant glass was being pressed into the water. As the water moved away from the stone, dozens of smaller spikes began to break the surface. They had been hidden from view by the waterline, but as the water level steadily dropped and they were exposed to air, everyone could see exactly why they had earned the name of the Teeth of Amhar. The Fangs of Amhar would have been more appropriate, for the needle sharp tips looked as if they belonged in the maw of some deadly predator.

It didn't take Morvandis much effort to expose them, for they were hidden only by a few feet of water, but he wasn't finished. Even after the smaller teeth could be clearly seen, he continued to displace the water in front of the tower, exposing more and more of the stone, until it became apparent that the pillars extended for thousands of feet below the surface of the ocean. Several of the crewmembers backed away from the spectacle, for the *Sovereign* seemed to be on the very edge of falling into a nearly endless abyss, but the ship continued upon its course as if oblivious to the yawning chasm mere feet to the starboard side. It took a few minutes, but once the crew realized that they weren't about to fall to their doom, they began to edge back toward the railing to take a closer look. It was well they had, for the view they now had of the Teeth in all their glory was truly breathtaking. They stood in perfectly spaced rows, with the smaller spikes forming an unbroken line that led from one pillar to the next in either direction like a wooden fence. Despite the fact that they were much smaller than their colossal brethren, even the little spikes were magnificent to behold.

Without turning his head, Morvandis spoke to his pupils.

"Tell me what you sense about the spaces between the Teeth, if you will."

Phaedron spoke first.

"There's a latticework of Water Magic stretching from one of the great pillars to the next, and is interwoven through the smaller pillars as well. It's far too complex for me to decipher, but if I had to venture a guess, I'd say it's a trap. A tripwire set to activate if anything touches it."

"I can see the same thing, but to me it's a band of fire, not water," Valeriad said. "The scale of the lattice is incredible. It's an unbroken line miles long."

"I sense both of the streams that you sense, and an identical band of air besides," Morvandis said. "Zarryiosiad was known to be able to control three powers: Air, Earth, and Fire. The addition of a Water component in the spell tells us that she needed help in its creation, and the strength of the Water component tells us that she most likely enlisted the aid of her father, the Mage Zarus, in its construction. She would have needed his help to complete it."

Morvandis carefully released his magic, and the water began to rise up to its previous level very quickly. Once the ocean had returned to normal, he turned to his audience.

"Zarryiosiad's spell was perfectly conceived and executed, and it is because of her foresight that no other nation has ever been able to carry out a successful invasion of Illymar. Any ship—no matter how small it might be—that attempts to cross the barrier will touch one of the four invisible tripwires and will trigger a defensive spell thousands of years old. There have been reports of unimaginably vast bolts of lightning striking a ship and causing it to explode instantly. Other reports tell of pillars of flame incinerating ships outright, or whirlpools forming from nowhere to drag ships down onto the Teeth themselves. The records held by both the Mage Citadel and the Zarryiostrom, tell us that the Lyx attempted to invade Illymar only once: shortly after the assassination of Zarus by their ambassador. Their entire fleet was destroyed by the Teeth. There were no survivors."

"If the Teeth completely surround the island, how are ships able to reach Illymar, or to sail from it?" Deirdre asked, frowning. "Wouldn't they be destroyed before they could leave?"

"Zarryiosiad left a single passage through the Teeth on the far side of the island," Morvandis said. "The passage is relatively narrow, no more than three miles wide, but defending it is a simple matter for Illymar's navy. All they have to do is defend a single passage from assault, and they never have to worry about being flanked or attacked from the rear. With the ability to focus their entire navy onto a single point, they are able to magnify their power to a massive degree. In the entire history of Illymar, no invading force has ever been able to make it past them." Phaedron gave a small grunt. Morvandis turned his attention to him. "You have a question?"

"Not a question, Morvandis, just an observation. As you rightly pointed out, history tells us that the defenses that protect Illymar are impenetrable. But history also tells us that *no* defense, no matter how strong or how well-designed it may be, will remain impenetrable forever. Eventually, someone will find a way to break through the Teeth or through the passage, and when that happens, Illymar won't know how to react. If their entire navy is concentrated at a single point on the far side of the island, the rest of the island will be completely defenseless."

"I wasn't aware that your interests included the study of history, Lord Daane. You surprise me." He bowed slightly to Phaedron, and for the second time that day, Valeriad's eyes widened in shock as the Mage-Lord offered a compliment without an accompanying barb. "You are absolutely correct. History teaches us that *no* defense is perfect. However, I am sure that you would agree, that these defenses are a special case. After all, they were designed by the Archon herself, and very few mortals would dare to make the attempt to defeat them. You've seen the Teeth, and the spells warding them: and now you know what kind of effort and power it would take to negate them. The Lyx were unable to do it, and their power was unparalleled."

He paused, looking again at the white stone, and his voice became softer.

"There may come a day when someone will breech these defenses. But until that day comes, we should admire the Teeth of Amhar as one of Zarryiosiad's greatest creations."

As his attention was once again drawn fully into the study of the tower, Phaedron, Valeriad and the other people that had been listening to his explanation turned away, leaving him alone once again with his thoughts.

Cahrick Rantrefal stood at the front of the *Sovereign* and tried not to think about the sheer power that Morvandis had so casually demonstrated. Cahrick knew that he himself was one of the most powerful Waterborn alive, but Morvandis easily dwarfed his own abilities. Watching him displace that much water all the way to the bottom of the ocean, over a mile deep, had been beyond impressive, almost to the point of being truly miraculous. Had he been so inclined, Cahrick *might* have been able to do the same thing, but it would have taken him days to accomplish what Morvandis had done in moments.

He glanced toward the spot that Morvandis stood and shook his head in grudging admiration.

If you weren't a murdering bastard, you might have been someone to admire.

Cahrick furrowed his brow, wondering what exactly the younger Mage was thinking as he gazed out at the Teeth. He could just make out Morvandis's eyes changing color from white to red to blue, and for just a moment he felt a stab of jealousy. *So much power in the hands of one man. It just isn't right.*

As he turned away to resume his duties, he just missed a final flash from Morvandis's eyes. Before they returned to their normal color, for a single heartbeat, they flashed a brilliant emerald green.

CHAPTER NINE

"Prodigy"

Prodigy.

Everywhere that Chesare went in the Mage Citadel the word followed her like a shadow, and after hearing it so many times on so many tongues, she was heartily sick and tired of it. Even here, standing alone in a darkened hallway, she could feel the word upon her shoulders like a crushing weight. It had been a month since she had first been admitted to the Citadel, and to everyone's surprise—perhaps especially her own—there hadn't been a single aspect of her training that she hadn't been able to master with complete ease. Archimagus DeVir had told her on the day they had met that fire was fickle, and that she had to make it her servant or else it would consume her. But, after only a single month of study, she had not only made fire her servant, she had turned it into a willing slave.

It hadn't taken the Council long to recognize that she was an exceptional student, and after no more than a few lessons, they had decided to allow her to skip a few of the more basic classes to learn at a faster pace. And learn she had.

Within a very short span, she had outdistanced every single one of her classmates, and many of her teachers as well. She did not remember who first used the title "prodigy" when referring to her, but the name had stuck. Nor was it entirely inappropriate, if she was honest, for she readily devoured every lesson set before her like her fires consumed fuel.

Unfortunately, her rapid rise amongst the ranks of her classmates hadn't come without cost: several budding friendships had died before they had had a chance to blossom. She hadn't realized what was happening initially, for when she had first arrived the other students had welcomed her with open arms, and had celebrated her successes as their own. But as success piled upon success for her, the celebrations had slackened noticeably, and eventually, they had disappeared altogether. They seemed to believe the ease with which she learned new things cheapened their own achievements, and now, people who she had once thought of as friends treated her with cool politeness or even icy disdain.

Envy and friendship are a hard mix, she thought sadly, *even amongst Mages.*

It bothered her, she supposed, when she allowed herself to dwell upon it, but as a Royal Princess, loneliness was already a constant companion. All her life, the people who had been allowed to come close to her had been carefully screened, and only the most suitable companions were admitted. Sadly, very few of the people her parents had deemed "suitable" were actually worth knowing and, as such, she had never really had any true friends. In part, that was why she and her sisters were so close; even if they had no one else, they had each other.

Lost friendship opportunities aside, Chesare was enjoying her time in the Citadel immensely. After 16 years of nannies, governesses, and bodyguards watching every single move she made, even the relatively cloistered lifestyle of the Citadel represented an almost unheard of freedom for the sheltered Princess. When she had first arrived, her mother had tried to force the Citadel to allow the many people tasked with watching over her to accompany her everywhere she went, but Master DeVir had flatly denied the Queen's strident requests.

Chesare smiled at the memory of the conversation, for Archimagus DeVir had listened patiently to her mother rant for several minutes before speaking.

The Mage Citadel is a school, Your Majesty, and your daughter is here to learn. In order for her to do so effectively, she must be free of distraction. Remember that she is not here to learn politics or languages: she is here to learn how to keep herself from destroying everything—and everyone—around her.

He had gestured at the bandaged hands of several of the women surrounding the Queen.

Your servants were lucky that they were not burned alive yesterday. With Princess Chesare's strength, that could just as easily have happened.

Chesare's smile slipped a bit at that, for he hadn't been exaggerating, but within a second or two it returned, for the sheer joy of being allowed to walk unaccompanied through the halls of the Citadel, never failed to make her smile.

The truly remarkable thing was that the teachers treated her as they would any other student. Her lofty birth didn't impress them in the slightest, and she had found that she very much enjoyed being seen as an equal. Even being assigned chores and duties—simple tasks meant to fill her time productively—had been enjoyable.

A Princess never had to sweep floors or dust shelves. That's what servants were for, after all. Chesare laughed out loud at that. *Mother would die on the spot if she were to find out that I have to help wash sheets!* Well, technically she didn't *wash* them, but she did have to keep the water heated for the laundresses. Chesare stopped at a candleholder and concentrated briefly, and the candles obediently flared into life.

In fact, the reason she was standing alone in this hallway was because one of her duties was to walk this particular hall at sundown each day and channel the candles alight. Most of the other students hated this particular duty, for the hallway was very long and there were a great many candles to light, but Chesare absolutely loved it. Being allowed to practice using her abilities unsupervised was a high honor in the Citadel, and normally only more advanced students were ever allowed the opportunity. Being assigned the duty meant the instructors knew you could be trusted not to injure yourself, or others, with your abilities.

As Chesare channeled yet another candle ablaze, she caught a glimpse of movement out of the corner of her eye, and as she turned to see what it was, one of the heavy doors at the entrance to the hallway slowly opened and a head popped through to take a look around. When Chesare recognized her friend and fellow novice, the Lady Adrianna DeVir, she broke out in another smile, then waved at her friend. Adrianna grinned and returned the wave before stepping into the room and closing the door behind her. She started to walk towards Chesare, but after no more than two hurried steps, Adrianna's obvious excitement overcame her self-control and she broke into an all-out run. Only one thing in the world could make the black-haired girl hurry, and that was gossip.

When it came to the spreading of gossip Adrianna could never contain herself, and the bigger the news the faster she *had* to spread it. She was actually sprinting this time, clearly indicating that something monumental was happening. Her long black hair flew behind her pretty face like an ebony cloak, and as she ran toward her, Chesare braced herself. Adrianna DeVir had introduced herself to Chesare on the day she had arrived, and the two had quickly become close friends and confidants. Even her mother couldn't complain, for Adrianna was of impeccable birth. Not only was she an extremely powerful Airborn, she was the daughter of Prince Brendenn DeVir of Palantine, the largest of Dakkadia's provinces, and the niece of Archimagus Cedric DeVir. Unlike many of their classmates, neither Chesare's exalted birth nor her overwhelming skill with magic intimidated her in the slightest. Far from it, for she had the same practical view on power that Cedric DeVir did, as they both believed that one student's progression had nothing at all to do with another's, and that a true friend stood by you no matter what. When Chesare had first realized that the other students were starting to hate her, she had pulled Adrianna aside and told her, that for her own good, she should turn her back on her.

No one chooses my friends for me, Chesare, Adrianna had replied, angry that Chesare felt the need to suggest something so ridiculous. *No one. And if all it takes for them to stop being friends with me is for another person to be better than them at something, then they are fools and we were never friends to begin with.*

As a reward for her loyalty, Adrianna had lost some friends, but many others had learned from her example. Now, as the Dakkadian Novice barreled down upon her, Chesare realized two things in rapid succession: the first was that her friend was running very, very fast, and the second was that she was extremely close . . . and she hadn't started slowing down. Apparently, Adrianna realized the same thing, though a little late. The grin on her face changed to a look of concern, and when she tried to stop herself short of a collision, she failed. Adrianna smashed into Chesare with an extremely unladylike squeak, and as Chesare tried to redirect the force of the impact, they spun around twice, and then fell to the floor with Chesare falling beneath Adrianna and cushioning her fall.

"I'm so sorry! Are you all right?" Adrianna asked, horrified by the collision. "You aren't hurt, are you?"

Tears of mirth started rolling down Chesare's face as she laughed at the absurdity, and when she could speak, she said,

"This had better be good, Adrianna. That was excessive, even for you!"

"Oh, it is, Chesare, it is! The Dakkadian Royal Family just sailed into the harbor!" Chesare frowned at that, for she didn't understand what the big deal was, but Adrianna wasn't finished. "They came here aboard the *Sovereign*, and the Corsair herself is with them!"

The revelation struck Chesare like a thunderbolt: the most notorious pirate on the ocean had just sailed into her father's harbor, bearing the King of the most dangerous country in the world aboard her ship.

Everyone in Illymar had heard stories of Lady Prudence Daemira, the bloodthirsty pirate queen known as the Corsair, and the thought that she might actually get to see her filled her with instant excitement, for no matter what flag she fought under, she was an inspiration to young girls everywhere who chafed at the roles they were expected to play. Then a thought hit her.

"Aren't you related to the Corsair somehow?"

"As a matter of fact, I am!" Adrianna said, grinning. "Lady Prudence Daemira is my aunt!"

"Do you think we might get the opportunity to meet her?"

"I'm certainly going to ask! I'll beg if I have to. I can't believe it," she giggled excitedly, "The Corsair is here!"

With another squeak, she shot to her feet and grabbed Chesare's wrists to pull her up. As she jerked Chesare to her feet, she glanced around at the unlit candles still awaiting Chesare's ministrations and her face fell.

"There's still enough daylight that you can actually see the *Sovereign* from the east tower. Most of the other students are already there, but you're never going to get all these candles lit in time!"

Chesare glanced around the room at the candles and frowned in consternation, but then her mouth firmed into a line, she squared her shoulders, and her eyes flashed a brilliant red. She waved her left hand once, from right to left, and every candle in the hallway instantly flared into life.

As the darkened hall suddenly burst into brilliant light, a shadowy figure, standing motionless at the back of the hall, came into sight. The figure was an exotically beautiful, nearly naked woman whose arms and legs were covered in elaborate tattoos. She had long straight hair that at first seemed to be white, but a closer look showed that the white she could see was actually a long streak that fell from the center of her jet black hair, just like a Dakkadian. She had been well hidden by the shadows, but the sudden light had obviously caught her by surprise, and despite the distance separating them, Chesare could clearly see shock upon her face.

Chesare's heart leaped into her throat, for her first thought was that one of the teachers had just caught her misusing her abilities, but it quickly became apparent the stranger wasn't a teacher. The woman wore armor on her shoulders, hands and legs, but it seemed to be ornamental in design rather than functional because much of her arms, legs and midriff were left uncovered. The most astonishing thing about the woman though, was the tiny black and crimson dragon draped over her shoulder. At first, Chesare mistook the creature for a serpent, but as it raised its head and hissed silently, it spread a pair of bat-like wings as if it were going to take flight. The thin membrane of skin on the inside of the dragon's wings was the same deep crimson as the thick scales on its chest, but the rest of its scales were a black so deep they didn't even reflect the candlelight.

Chesare grabbed Adrianna's arm, her eyes widening in shock, but before she could turn Adrianna around to see the mysterious woman, the woman smiled slightly and stepped backward into a doorway of pure blackness. As the darkness enveloped her, Chesare had the distinct impression of a dragon's wings crossing in front of her like a cloak before she disappeared completely from sight. The last thing Chesare saw of the woman and her dragon was the malevolent glare in the dragon's glowing eyes.

Adrianna saw the look of fear in her friend's eyes and quickly turned to look at the spot where Chesare was staring, but there was nothing there.

"Is something wrong? You look as if you've seen a ghost."

Chesare opened her mouth to reply, but she quickly changed her mind, and decided not to tell her about the woman. She didn't know why, but somehow she knew Adrianna was better off not knowing about the apparition. It took a bit of effort, but somehow Chesare was able to pull her eyes away from the spot the woman had disappeared and force herself to meet Adrianna's worried gaze.

"It's nothing. I was just making sure that all of the candles are lit. The east tower, you said? We'd better hurry."

Her voice trailed off as she glanced one more time at the back of the hall, but there was no sign of the strange woman or her dragon. Adrianna grabbed her arm and turned her to the door, and together the pair left the hall and raced against the setting sun to catch a glimpse of the legendary *Sovereign.* As Chesare allowed herself to be led away, she couldn't get the image of the woman out of her head.

They did indeed make it to the east tower in time to see the *Sovereign*, and the last rays of the setting sun highlighted it beautifully. It was a majestic ship, even if the black and white sails made it seem menacing, but Chesare couldn't seem to shake the feeling that someone was still watching her. Chesare tried to listen to the gossip and speculation about what the Corsair might be like in person, but she couldn't get the image of the stranger out of her head. The mysterious woman had not tried to hurt her or attack her in any way, but Chesare was almost positive that she had indeed meant her harm.

The next morning, Chesare found herself in a section of the Citadel she had never been before. There was one person in the Citadel who might know exactly what she had seen, and before she had gone to sleep, Chesare resolved to go and see her as soon as possible. When the first glow of the morning sun could be faintly seen on the horizon, Chesare was already dressed, and she skipped breakfast to walk quickly and purposefully towards the library. When she reached the large wooden doors, she hesitated. She knew she needed help, but what if the librarian didn't believe her? She supposed that she *could* have imagined the entire thing, but the memory of the dragon's glowing eyes convinced her that what she saw had indeed been real, and with that assurance, she grasped the door handles and pulled the doors to the library open with a yank.

She had never been here before, and so she hadn't known what to expect, but the image that had come to mind had been one of dusty scrolls and piles of books spread chaotically throughout a dimly lit closet. The librarian herself would be a wizened old hag, probably toothless, whose entire existence was defined by the piles of books and scrolls that she never willingly left. When the doors opened, she was very pleasantly surprised, for perfectly aligned rows of shelves lined the walls and filled the open areas, and comfortable couches surrounded small tables to provide Mages with comfortable places to study. The entire room was very well lit, with large windows providing ready light during the day, and huge ornate chandeliers spaced throughout the room providing illumination during the evening. A large carpeted path led from the main door to the rear of the hall, and by the back wall there sat a huge ornate desk where she could see the librarian seated studying a book.

As she walked forward and thought about what she to say, the thousands of books housed on the shelves distracted her. History, Art, Literature, Magic; all of these were readily available, but to her immense surprise, she also saw a large section of books marked Romance. Unable to contain her curiosity, she veered off the path to look, and found hundreds of books dedicated to the very stories her sister, Lyrahe, adored. She felt a pang of sadness at the sight of *Love's Sacrifice*, for she hadn't seen her sister in a month, but then she remembered why she was here and started to turn back toward the desk.

"I do not often see Novices looking through the Romance section," said unexpected voice behind her. "Normally, they are too busy with other duties to consider reading books for their entertainment value rather than for their practical value, or for an assignment."

Chesare whirled around to look at the speaker and found herself staring eye to eye with a tiny golden dragon curled around the neck of an incredibly beautiful golden-haired woman. The dragon bowed its head to Chesare in obvious greeting, but then returned its attention to the books at which Chesare had been looking. The beautiful woman spoke to her again, saying "I noticed that your attention was drawn to *Love's Sacrifice* but that you didn't reach for it. Does this book hold any special significance for you?"

SEVEREIELLE, THE QUEEN OF SHADOWS

The dragon turned to look at her again and cocked its head to the side almost quizzically.

"It's my sister's favorite book. She reads it all the time." Chesare hesitated for a moment, and then continued. "I saw this section of books and it reminded me of her."

"I see now. You must be feeling a bit of homesickness. Time in the Citadel can be stressful, and Novices often find comfort in familiar things. You are more than welcome to borrow the book if you would like. I recommend the Elvish translation over the Faeish or the human. The Fae tend to be overly descriptive, and humans tend toward the vulgar."

"No, thank you," Chesare said, quickly. "Romance novels actually are not my favorite subject. I was just thinking about my sister. But I do thank you for the offer." She hesitated again, but a glance at the friendly face of the woman convinced her to dive right in with her dilemma. "What I really need is your help. I came here to see you."

At that, a puzzled look crossed the woman's face, mirrored by a quirking of the dragon's head in an unmistakably gesture of curiosity.

"In that case, shall we adjourn to a more comfortable setting? I'm not certain what help I can be for you, but whatever help I can offer is yours for the asking." The librarian led her to one of the many comfortable couches spaced throughout the library.

"Last night, I was attending to my chores in the hall leading to the laboratories, when I caught someone watching me," Chesare said, after taking a seat. "My duty was to light all the candles in the hall, but I got in a hurry and lit them all at the same time. It was when the candles came up that I saw her." She paused for a moment, unsure how to continue. "She was very beautiful, with black and white hair like a Dakkadian, but she had a black dragon on her shoulder that looked very much like your dragon. I think she had tattoos all over her body as well, but I couldn't tell what they were."

The librarian's eyes opened wide at the description and she stood up abruptly. Without saying a word, the woman left the couch and walked to her desk. She opened up a drawer and withdrew a large, leather-bound tome.

She returned to the couch, sat down next to Chesare and laid the book on the table in front of them. The cover of the tome contained no title, but the librarian opened the book, flipped through several pages, and stopped at a chapter entitled, "The Queen of Shadows." The book was written in Faeish, but Chesare's study of languages had included learning the Fae alphabet and symbols. Before she could read what was written about this Queen of Shadows, the librarian turned the page and revealed an unmistakable likeness of the woman she had seen.

"That's her! That's the woman I saw last night!" she exclaimed.

Taking a closer look at the tattoos covering the woman's arms and legs, Chesare realized they were stylized bones, like sharp ribs extending from a serpentine spine. The armor the figure wore was jagged and asymmetrical, but very beautiful.

"The chapter was entitled 'Queen of Shadows.' Who is she?"

"Odd that one so young can read Faeish," the librarian said, surprised. "It is a difficult language to learn. May I have your name, Novice?"

"I'm so sorry. I should have introduced myself to you right away. My name is Chesare Illvanna, and my parents are the King and Queen of Illymar."

Both the dragon and the blonde woman inclined their heads in identical bows.

"I'm honored to meet you, Your Highness. My name is Asiria, though most of the novices in the Citadel call me 'Halo.'" The dragon's wings stretched up behind her head until the tiny spines on top of the wings touched, creating the image of a golden halo above her head. The woman gave her a wry grin and said, "Although, for the life of me, I can't understand why anyone would have chosen that particular name for me." Despite her trepidation, Chesare giggled at the jest, and the dragon refolded its wings triumphantly. After a moment, a serious expression returned to the librarian's face. "The woman you saw last night is well known to me. Her name is Severeielle, and she is known to my people as the Queen of Shadows. If you saw her, you must have taken her completely by surprise, for she moves through shadow as easily as we move through air. Invisibility is her greatest weapon." She paused for a moment, and then gave Chesare an appraising look. "She must have underestimated you if you were able to take her so completely by surprise. She will not make that mistake again."

Chesare shrunk a little in her seat.

"Why is she watching me? What did I do to her?"

Asiria closed her eyes.

"For well over two thousand years, the Queen of Shadows has been seeking out Mages of exceptional power or talent, and watching them for reasons of her own. As far as I have been able to determine, she has never actually spoken to or harmed anyone, but then, only she knows why she feels compelled to watch these people."

Chesare's eyes widened.

"Over two thousand years? But you're human! An Elf or a Fae can live that long, but that's impossible for a human!"

"We are not human, little one," Asiria said, smiling politely. "Many people make the mistake of assuming that the dragon who sits upon my shoulder is an exceptionally clever pet, but that could not be further from the truth. The person you are speaking to now is not Asiria, the human. The 'person' you are speaking to now is Asiria, the dragon, and the woman you are looking at is my familiar. Dragons are highly intelligent, but we cannot communicate with humans, Fae, or Elves without a bridge. Our human bodies provide these bridges."

She opened the book and slowly flipped through the pages, allowing Chesare the chance to view the titles of several of the chapters. A few of the chapters had benign titles like Queen of Gardens or Lord of Snows, but others had very disturbing names such as the Queen of Assassins and the Lord of Death. She shuddered at the picture of a man wearing what seemed to be a porcelain mask, for the eyes of the mask were hollow, almost as if she were looking into a skull.

"There are many like me, and each of us has our own domain. I am known among my own kind as the Queen of Knowledge, and it is my purview to seek out knowledge in all of its forms to collect it. That is what drew me to the Mage Citadel, for in the Powerborn, I have found like minds. Mages seek knowledge in much the same way that I seek it, and we work together to obtain it. The same holds true for others of my kind." She opened the book to another chapter, and Chesare's eyes shot open in shock at the title.

"As you can see, I am not the only Dragon Witch to enjoy working with mortals. I am sure you recognize the name, but many people do not realize her true nature. This is Furionchires, the Queen of Battles, and she fought beside Zarryiosiad herself to end the reign of the Lyx. You see, Your Highness, each of the Dragon Witches has a purpose, and sometimes those purposes are at odds with each other. The Queen of Shadows seeks out Mages of great power. For what reason, I cannot guess. Should you see her again, try asking her. She may actually tell you." With that, Asiria closed the book and stood up. "You should run along now, Princess, while breakfast is still being served. Do not worry about Severeielle. I promise you that so long as the Queen of Shadows watches you, she will not harm you, for that is not her way. If she truly intended you harm, you would already be dead. No, she is looking for something specific, and so far she hasn't found it. When she does, she may reveal her motives. Until then, it is best not to worry."

Asiria watched as the young Novice left the library and considered what to do. Having the Queen of Shadows prowling around the Mage Citadel was bad enough, but having her watch a particular Powerborn made the problem much worse, for Asiria had lied to the Princess: she knew exactly what had brought Severeielle to the Citadel, and she knew exactly what she was searching for; but telling Chesare the truth would have brought her no peace. Quite the opposite, actually, for every Dragon Witch knew that for 2,500 years the Queen of Shadows had been searching for any Mage born with the potential to become a Harbinger—the creature that the Zarryiostrom knew as the Archon. Severeielle's hatred of the Harbinger was implacable, and Asiria knew, beyond the shadow of a doubt, that should Chesare—or any other Mage for that matter—ever show signs of becoming a Harbinger, Severeielle wouldn't hesitate to kill the Mage on the spot . . . or send her handmaiden, the Queen of Assassins, to do it for her.

That may actually be the best solution, in the end, she thought.

A Harbinger was a danger not only to those around it; it was a danger to the entire world. Severeielle had stood by as the last Harbinger had come to power, and it had cost her dearly. This time she would not make the same mistake.

Asiria made her decision.

Astranaithes must be warned. The Queen of Shadows has made a move.

She stood up and walked to a bowl of water that stood behind her desk. As she leaned over the bowl, the golden dragon's eyes flashed red yet again, and the surface of the water became a silver mirror. With the dragon's eyes blazing, the woman spoke a single word in a powerful voice.

"Astranaithes."

In a flash, the mirror-like reflection on the surface of the water changed to reveal a stone arch with an overcast sky behind it. Asiria didn't know exactly where the Queen of Fate made her home, but through the arch she could just make out mist-covered mountains in the distance. Abruptly, a face entered the view of the mirror, and when Asiria recognized the gorgeous auburn-haired woman's features, she smiled and bowed slightly.

"Asiria. It has been a while, my daughter. I trust things are well with you?"

"They are, Oracle. But, I have come across some disturbing news that you should be made aware of. Last night, a student caught the Queen of Shadows spying on her. Severeielle left without incident shortly after she was caught, but the girl was frightened enough to come to me for advice. I told her she has nothing to fear."

The last was more of a question than a statement, but Astranaithes frowned.

"Tell me of the student, Asiria."

"Her name is Chesare Illvanna, and she is the daughter of King Orem III and his wife, Althea. This is the first time I have met her, but I have heard her name being discussed by many of the Mages in the Citadel. She is considered to be a prodigy. Apparently, her strength as a Fireborn rivals that of Morvandis."

“Truly?” the Oracle’s eyes widened in surprise. “Then it is no wonder the Queen of Shadows is interested in her.” She narrowed her eyes in thought, and for several moments said nothing. Finally, she looked up and said, “She will have to be watched. Can you accomplish this, or should I send someone to assist you?”

Asiria frowned.

“Do you really think that will be necessary, Astranaithes? Severeielle did not attempt to harm the girl in any way. I would think that this would indicate the Queen of Shadows does not view the Princess as a threat. Providing a guardian would draw undue attention to her and may force Severeielle’s hand.”

“I did not say that she needs protection, Asiria; I said that she needs to be watched. All of the pieces are in place for the world to see the emergence of another Harbinger. Apparently, Severeielle realizes this as well.”

Asiria waited for Astranaithes to continue, but the Queen of Fate left it at that.

“If this is true, shouldn’t we allow Severeielle to eliminate the threat?” asked Asiria. “The Harbinger is a danger to everyone and everything. Surely killing a potential Harbinger before she has the opportunity to Ascend is the right thing to do? Sometimes a little evil can contain a greater one.”

Astranaithes smiled in amusement.

“And should Severeielle fail? What happens if it is a preemptive attack by her or one of her minions that triggers a transformation before the world is ready? No, Asiria. Allowing the Queen of Shadows to strike is not the correct path, for she is almost certain to fail. What Severeielle refuses to realize is that we will have only one opportunity to stop a Harbinger from fulfilling its *true* destiny, and that opportunity is granted to only one being. Until the Champion is revealed, the Harbinger must be allowed free rein. Without the Champion, the world is lost.” Her eyes changed suddenly, filling with regret and more than a hint of sadness. “You know as well as I that Severius will not be able to stand against the Harbinger a second time. We must allow events to play out as Fate wishes. Only then will the Champion be revealed.”

“I will do as you command,” Asiria said. “I will watch the girl for signs that she may be the new Harbinger, and I will report my findings to you. Do you have any further orders?”

“Not at this time, my daughter. If Severeielle strikes, do your best to protect the girl, and contact me as soon as possible. I will send aid, if and when it is needed. But remember this: if Severeielle chooses to act, she will most likely send Cassiramaithris. Beware the possibility, and ward against it.”

Asiria's eyes narrowed at the name. Cassiramaithris was the Queen of Shadow's most effective disciple. The Queen of Assassins was a relentless and deadly foe, and once she had been assigned a target, she never stopped—ever.

"I will remember, Astranaithes." She paused for a moment and closed her eyes, and then continued in a quiet voice. "I had hoped that Zarryiosiad was the last. It seems Fate has decided otherwise."

"Fate always does, my daughter, and it cares nothing for hope." With one last smile, the image of Astranaithes faded from view.

ASIRIA, THE QUEEN OF KNOWLEDGE.

CHAPTER TEN

"Promises"

The first thing I'm going to do when I become Emperor is to have formal court clothing redesigned to be more practical. "Traditional," indeed. The word "traditional" must be Elvish for "uncomfortable," or perhaps "sadistic." As one of his valets wrapped him in yet another confining layer of silk, Lain tried to remind himself that it was his duty to look his best during the official ceremony marking the formal commencement of the Convocation. *But why in the world does "looking my best" require so much silk?* The valet put the finishing touches on the current layer, and a second valet moved forward with yet another pile of silk. *They can't be serious.*

Unfortunately for the Prince, it seemed that they were, for the first valet bowed deeply and moved aside only to be instantly replaced by the next. Prince Lain would have returned the bow . . . had it been remotely possible for him to bend at the waist, but it wasn't, so he settled for nodding his head slightly in acknowledgment. Even that slight a movement was difficult, but it was still enough to earn him a frown of disapproval from the hairdresser tugging at his sleek black hair.

Most servants wouldn't have dared to give him a disapproving look, but this particular hairdresser had been with him for over twenty years. Unlike formal robes, which were thankfully only worn on formal occasions, the Ferraline queue was an indicator of rank and had to be worn daily. Lain's lofty birth guaranteed him at least an hour each day of the hairdresser's not-so-gentle ministrations, and after spending so much time with him—willing or not—the hairdresser had become a friend of sorts.

As the next layer of strata was added to the already overwhelming ensemble, Lain heard someone clear his throat behind him.

"I'd turn around to look at you, Vizier, but I'm being tied up at the moment."

He heard a laugh behind him and smiled at the knowledge that his jest had slipped past the Vizier's guard.

"I envy you, My Prince. For one day soon, your silken cocoon will burst open and you will float away on wings of gossamer. I am certain that you will become an impressive monarch."

Lain laughed, knowing Shar meant the butterfly and not the ruler, and earned yet another disapproving tug from his hairdresser. Shar moved around to face his Prince and took the opportunity to examine every aspect of his appearance.

"I'm sure you are very uncomfortable, Your Highness, but the overall effect is actually quite impressive. You look very distinguished, as befits your station."

Lain snorted at that, and without moving his head so much as a fraction of an inch, turned his eyes towards the Mage and gave him a disdainful look.

"I see now why you are such a fine Air Mage, Shar. Being filled with so much hot air must have made it inevitable that you would eventually wield it."

At first, Shar didn't respond, and for a moment Lain believed that Shar would let his insult pass unchallenged. However, before Lain could claim victory, Shar spoke.

"I'm sorry, My Prince. I was lost in thought for a moment." Lain gave him a suspicious look and Shar didn't disappoint him. "I was merely reflecting on the thought that we will be here for a full month, and each day will have many formal events," a malicious look crossed his face, "Formal events which, I am certain, will require a great, *great* many changes of clothing. Sadly, I am only a Vizier—a glorified servant—and, as such, I am not required to wear the formal robes your exalted birth entitles you to. But you! I can only imagine the wonderful confections of silk that will be heaped upon you over the next four weeks. Remember that today's event is important, but there are many other events that will require even more formal dress." Lain blanched, and at his look of abject horror, Shar couldn't help but laugh again. "In all seriousness, My Prince, you look very impressive. That is good, because you will be meeting many potential brides over the next month and it may be easier for your father to marry you off if you are polished up a bit."

"I'm not being polished up; I'm being wrapped like a gift." He pointed at the elaborately tied sash at his waist. "I even have a bow. Several of them, in fact."

The Vizier smiled politely, then his face became serious.

"I've come to inform you about what I've learned about the current political climate, and what it means for the Empire and for you personally. As I see you are a captive audience, it seems I've chosen a good time."

"I hope you're bringing me good news, Shar. I think bad news piled upon my extreme discomfort could mean unfortunate things for you."

"The news is not bad, though it could be better. The first item is that the youngest Illvanin Princess, Chesare, has been discovered to be a Fireborn and is currently studying at the Mage Citadel. It is unknown to me if she will be attending the functions of the Convocation, but it is my belief that she will. She is the first Powerborn in ten generations born into the Illvanin family, and King Orem will not part with her willingly. Most likely, she will be married to a noble of Illymar to keep the Mage blood on the island proper. With Princess Tais currently in disfavor for her actions, only one eligible princess remains. Her name is Lyrahe, and she will undoubtedly be pursued relentlessly by King Madari for his son, Valeriad." Shar paused for a moment, as if to collect his thoughts. "For that matter, King Madari has a young daughter, named Deirdre, who is approaching marrying age. She is only 14, but a potential alliance with Dakkadia would profit the Empire greatly."

Lain thought about that for a moment, and decided he agreed with the Vizier.

"Marrying Deirdre would most likely ensure that we maintain our peace with Dakkadia. Unfortunately, that would also encourage Dakkadia to invade Illymar instead. I must admit that the idea of Dakkadia going to war with Illymar was more acceptable to me before I set foot on this island. It is truly a paradise here."

The city of Illymaine was located at the termination point of at least three major rivers, and the city itself was an incredible creation. With so much water available, hundreds of ornate fountains dotted the city and there were more canals than streets. The royal castle, called the Spire of Illymaine, was built on a cliff overlooking the wide bay, and there was even a waterfall that sent sprays of water tumbling down jagged rocks to the bay below. The overall effect was awe-inspiring, and Lain had been humbled by the display.

"If there is a paradise, it would hold that the home of Zarryiosiad would be it. I still remember my time here with great fondness. Both the Mage Citadel and the Cathedral of Zarryiosiad are just as impressive as the Spire, and a single lifetime would not be enough to explore all of the wonders they contain. Should our attempts to arrange a marriage between you and the Princess Lyrahe bear fruit, you may be able to spend more time here to explore those wonders."

"A pleasant thought, Vizier." He gave his valet a disgusted look and said, "Of course, in order for me to meet this Lyrahe, I have to be allowed to leave this room. And until these people are finished, I cannot do that."

The valet gave him an abashed look and finished his fussing. After the last tassel was put into place, he stepped back and bowed silently. Lain checked his appearance in the giant mirror in his dressing apartment, and try as he might, he could not find fault in their work.

"Do I look presentable, Shar? It would not do for me to bring dishonor to my family or to my country."

"You look splendid, Your Highness. Now, if you will, follow me. Your father's entourage is waiting."

King Madari finished buckling his sword belt over his black leather tunic, and then adjusted the belt's buckle until it was perfectly centered. He was turning back and forth in front of his mirror to check his appearance, when the doors to his apartments opened and Queen Aveliad entered.

"It is almost time to leave."

He grunted in acknowledgment, and without his asking, she glided over to him to check his appearance for herself. In Dakkadia, manservants and valets were uncommon amongst male nobility, for the Dakkadians placed great value in self-reliance. Even the King dressed himself, though Aveliad had showed him over the years that the two of them had differing opinions on what constituted being dressed. She crossed behind him to check the line of his tunic, and tugged slightly on one side to straighten it. She then moved around him to look at him from the front and could not find any further fault in his appearance.

"Satisfied?" he asked, mildly amused by her fussing.

Aveliad brushed away some piece of imagined lint on his collar and then nodded. He grunted again and turned to his bed, where his sword and dagger lay waiting. Behind him, Aveliad frowned.

"Will those be absolutely necessary, Madari? We will be attending a religious ceremony, after all. Weapons would be inappropriate."

Madari snorted at that and glanced at his wife's reflection in his mirror.

"Zarryiosiad herself was one of humanity's greatest warriors, so I'm certain the Church is quite used to weaponry. But you need not be concerned, Aveliad. I made certain our ambassadors reminded the Zarryiostrom that Dakkadian nobility are required to wear their weapons at all times, especially during public functions. They assure me that the Zarryiostrom understands."

Aveliad shrugged ever so slightly at the explanation and turned to leave, but before she could take two steps, however, Madari grabbed her arm and turned her toward him.

"Your mask, on the other hand, could be construed by some as being inappropriate. This is a religious ceremony, after all, and not a masquerade." He lifted the delicate porcelain half-mask covering her eyes away from her face and up to her forehead so he could look at her. Her amber eyes flashed once with anger, then cooled instantly into chips of golden ice.

Because of the longevity her Faeish blood granted her, her perfectly smooth skin and delicate features hadn't changed in all the years they were married. She was still the most beautiful woman he had ever laid eyes upon, and despite the time constraints, he could feel a stir of desire at the sight of her uncovered face. Unfortunately for both Madari and his libido, however, Aveliad recognized the look on his face, and her eyes flashed with anger a second time.

"We do not have time to sate your lusts, Madari. The Convocation begins in less than an hour. We must depart immediately."

Madari snarled in anger at her rejection and violently thrust aside the arm he was holding.

"Why must you always be so cold to me, Aveliad? I've been a good husband to you and a good father for the children . . . even to Phaedron, who wants nothing to do with me. After all this time, what more must I do to earn your love and respect? Name it, and it's yours!" He yanked the mask off of her head and held it in front of her eyes like an accusation. "And this! What does this prove? For twenty-one years you've worn this mask to deny me even the sight of you! Why do you withhold what is mine by right of marriage? I'm your husband!"

Aveliad snatched the mask out of his hand and snarled right back at him.

"Why don't you ask one of your mistresses why I'm cold to you, *Your Majesty?* You have enough of them; I'm sure one of them can give you the answer you are looking for." She held up her mask and gave him a deadly stare. "And as for the reason I wear this? My family may have forced me to marry you after Phaedril's death, but make no mistake; I did it out of duty, not love. I had a love once, and he's dead, and I wear this mask in remembrance of him. For you, I will do what duty requires of me, but I will *never* love you."

She spun around, turning her back to him, and she crossed her arms under her breasts and hugged herself tightly. Madari glanced at the reflection of her face in the mirror and saw the tears falling silently from eyes closed tight with remembered pain. Madari glared at her reflection for another moment, and then turned back to his bed. Without saying a word, he picked up his sword and dagger and slid them into the proper places on his belt. Once the weapons were seated properly, he lowered his head, back still turned to his wife.

"I know now that it was a mistake to ask your family for your hand so soon after Phaedril's death. I didn't allow you time to mourn, and for that, I am deeply sorry. If I could undo that mistake, I would. My insistence stemmed from my love for you." He raised his head and turned around to look at her reflection. "As for my 'whores', I will not apologize. The Flower Court is an important and accepted part of Dakkadian life, and one for which I have the utmost respect. Even your husband utilized their services before you were married. But know this, Aveliad: I am not my father or my brothers. I do not feel the need to sleep with every woman who looks my way. Say the word. Remove your mask and consent to love me as I swear that I love you, and I will promise you that I will never attend the Flower Court again. Why would I need to? You are the most beautiful woman in the world, Aveliad. Love me as a wife should—as the wife you once were to Phaedril—and I will be more loyal to you than you could possibly imagine."

He placed both hands on her upper arms and squeezed gently, and she shuddered at the contact. Several moments passed in silence, and Madari began to believe that he was getting through to her. Eventually, however, Aveliad reached up and dried her tears on her white gloves. After she finished, she looked up at his reflection in the mirror and Madari's heart fell. The cool look had returned to her eyes, and her perfect features had schooled themselves back into the alabaster mask he knew so well, even when her face was uncovered.

"Do not speak to me of love, Madari. You claim to love me, but you don't, and what's more, you never did, for obsession is not love. You've never looked at me as a woman, or a lover, or a wife. You've always looked at me as a possession, a *thing* to be paraded in front of others to show them that *you* are important; that *you* are special. You constantly compliment me on my beauty as if that means something to me. It doesn't. It never did. My beauty only means something to *you*." Her cold voice turned acid. "You have your prize, *Your Majesty*. Parade me in front of the other monarchs, if you wish. Listen to them comment on how *beautiful* your wife is. Listen to them compliment you on how *fortunate* you are to be married to me." She held up the mask again, turning it slightly to give him a good look at it. "You should thank me for wearing this, for it only adds to my 'mystery' and your reputation. And after the ceremony—after everyone has seen your exotic, beautiful possession—we can leave. And tonight, despite the wishes of the woman that you claim to love, you can assert the *husbandly rights* that you are so quick to claim. In fact, the sooner we leave these apartments and attend the Convocation, the sooner we can return here so you can once again violate me."

At first, Madari reeled back in shock at her blunt words. They had had arguments before, but at the very least she had always managed to maintain some sense of decorum. This time she hadn't, and to his surprise, he found that she had wounded him deeply. Very deeply, in fact.

After twenty-one years of conflict, he had believed himself to be immune to her venom, but now he knew otherwise. She still possessed the ability to hurt him, and she could still cause him pain. He hadn't lied to her, for he had always hoped that one day she would come to at least appreciate him, if not love him, but now he knew that what he had hoped for would never be. She would never give him what he wanted, and she would never be what he wanted her to be. It wasn't easy to accept that truth, and he knew, that for the first time in his life, he had failed utterly at an endeavor. He stood there looking into the beautiful amber eyes staring back at him from the reflection in his mirror, and he finally accepted the truth: he hated her. He hated her for forcing him to waste his time on her and for allowing him to nurture the belief that one day he could make her love him. *Twenty-one precious years wasted on this ungrateful shrew.*

She had been nothing at all when they had first met: just the beautiful illegitimate daughter of the former Prince of DeVir. She was a half-breed slip of a girl no one knew what to do with, while he was just the third son of a worthless, pathetic excuse for a King. They should have been perfect for each other, should have found comfort and solace in each other's arms, but Aveliad hadn't agreed and had chosen another. He hadn't minded at first, for Phaedril was a good soldier and a loyal vassal, but as he spent more time with the happy couple, he had found that there was something about her, some indefinable *thing* that he desperately *needed*, and he only saw it when she was with Phaedril.

Eventually, his desire for her had turned to obsession, and that obsession had remained, even after his father had died and he had secured the throne for himself by walking over the broken bodies of his brothers. It remained, even after he had crushed the surrounding countries and added them to Dakkadia's domain, and it had remained even after he had finally succumbed to his obsession and had had Phaedril killed to make her his own. As he looked into her eyes, desperately searching for the thing he needed, he knew he would never find it. Not within her at least.

He wanted to hurt her, the way she had hurt him. For a moment, he hovered on the brink of the unthinkable. In all of their years of marriage he had never once raised a hand to her. He would never know where he found the willpower to keep his hands at his sides, but somehow he did. And as he had done so many times in the past, rather than fight a battle on her field and under her conditions, he simply withdrew.

Without saying a single word, he whirled around and walked towards the doors to his chambers, and as he passed his bureau, he snatched his golden circlet off of its pillow and set it carelessly upon his head. He walked to the doors and opened them without a backward glance, and when the doors closed behind him, they closed not only on his wife, but also on the smoldering ashes of a dream turned to dust.

Aveliad watched her husband storm out of the room and tried to feel pity for him. He was right: for all of his faults, he had always been a good husband and a better King. The Kingdom of Dakkadia had fallen into ruin under the mismanagement of his father, King Dhaegus, and his brothers, Dhaegus and Haddon. They had been the lowest sort of scum, interested only in adding more and more women to their list of conquests. The King also had several mistresses, each more avaricious and grasping than the last; and between them, they had drained the coffers of Dakkadia mercilessly. He hadn't cared that he was beggaring his nation, as long as his mistresses remained happy and compliant, and his two older sons were cut from the same cloth. Madari had grown up in a court of fools, and only he had had the wisdom and the foresight to know that eventually the trough would run out and Dakkadia would be left with nothing at all.

He was wrong about one thing: she did respect him—she respected him enough to fear him, for his rise to power had been swift and merciless. His father had died of mysterious causes; though Aveliad was positive those causes were not of Madari's making. However, he *had* taken advantage of his father's untimely death by eliminating his two older brothers to clear his own way to the throne. It had taken only days, but when the rubble had finally settled, Madari was the undisputed King of Dakkadia. From there, Madari had quickly assembled his armies and marched forth to crush the surrounding provinces and rebuild his country to its former glory. Generally, the rebuilding of Dakkadia went peacefully, as the leaders of the surrounding provinces came to realize that the new King of Dakkadia was cut from a far different cloth than the last. Some countries fought to the bitter end against Madari, but most realized that resistance would be futile and bowed to the inevitable. Generally, the reunification of Dakkadia had been bloodless, but Madari was particularly merciless towards those lands that had broken free from Dakkadia during his father's reign. It took years of campaigning, but when he finished, every land north of the Badlands belonged once again to Dakkadia, and with the country reunited under a strong leader, Madari settled down to rule. The coffers that had been so empty for so long filled themselves to bursting as taxes were collected,

KING MADARI DHAERHAN OF DAKKADIA
AND QUEEN AVELIAD

and Madari used his newfound wealth very well indeed. The navy, completely ignored by the previous king, was updated and modernized, the army was rebuilt into a force only Illymar or Ferralin could hope to stand against, and the country's infrastructure was repaired.

All of these things were admirable, and a man who could accomplish so much in so short a time was a force to be reckoned with, but the reason she refused to love him was simple: she strongly suspected that Madari had had her husband murdered. Oh, his hands were clean—he'd seen to that—but she believed that it had been his orders that had led to her husband's death. Unfortunately, all Aveliad had were her suspicions, for even after twenty years of searching, she still had found no proof. Madari had covered his tracks too well.

Over the years, she had developed a network of spies and contacts that was the rival of Morvandis's own spy network, but none of her sources had been able to find even a shred of evidence that he had killed Phaedril. Without that proof Aveliad refused to act, for if she was wrong and killed her husband, Valeriad would have no choice but to have her executed for treason and regicide. If it came to that, she would accept her fate, but Phaedril deserved better than blind vengeance. He deserved *justice,* and justice required proof. But one way or another, Madari wouldn't die a peaceful death in bed. She would see to that.

Aveliad squared her shoulders and raised her mask to her face, tying the cords tightly with practiced ease while her gaze never left the door. She would endure any pain, any humiliation as long as in the end, justice was served. She owed Phaedril that much.

Queen Althea walked briskly through the halls of the Spire, toward her husband's chambers, followed closely by her handmaidens. Her apartments were a considerable distance from her husband's, and it had taken much longer than usual to dress, so she walked a little faster than normal without actually seeming to rush.

With any luck, Orem will be ready to go and we can still be on time. It is very important that we arrive on schedule.

The thought galvanized her, and she increased her pace. As Althea turned the final corner, her heart sank. The doors to the dressing room were still closed, and the guards were still posted outside the door. That meant that Orem hadn't emerged, and therefore wasn't ready to leave yet. She tried in vain to suppress an annoyed sigh, but failed utterly. For a moment, she considered waiting outside of his apartments until he emerged, but her own impatience got the better of her and she turned to her handmaidens.

"Wait here. I will check on His Majesty."

The four handmaidens curtseyed low in response, and dutifully took their position against a side wall. Althea turned back to the doorway, smoothed her dress with her palms, and stepped forward to within five feet of the bodyguard. Instantly, the three members of the bodyguard reacted. The two soldiers on either side of the door crossed their pikes in front of the door to bar her way, and the third, standing in front and between the other guards, raised his right hand to grasp the hilt of his sword and lowered his stony gaze to the Queen.

"Who goes there?"

Normally, the ritual pleased Althea, for it provided visual proof of the importance of her husband. Today, however, she was irritated at the delay and wished she could just order the guard to step aside and let her pass. Unfortunately for her, she knew that the guardsman would continue to bar her way until she fulfilled her part of the ritual, and she closed her eyes in irritation as she spoke.

"Queen Althea, to see the King."

The guard took two steps backwards and knocked once upon the door. Two more heartbeats passed, and a muffled voice emerged from the closed doors. At the sound of the voice, the soldier took two steps forward to the same spot he had been standing at when she first arrived, and the guards on either side of the door returned their pikes to a vertical position. The captain then lowered his hand from his hilt and bowed to the Queen.

"You may enter."

As he spoke, he stepped smartly to the side as the doors opened slightly, and Queen Althea stepped forward and entered her husband's dressing room.

Orem was standing in the middle of a series of mirrors and was checking his appearance from every conceivable angle. Althea stepped forward quickly and began taking in his appearance. Despite herself, she was impressed. The heavily embroidered red coat with white ermine trim he wore fit him perfectly, and the broad shoulders gave him a powerful appearance. He wore spotless white hose over low black shoes, and the pantaloons he wore reached his mid-thigh showing off well-turned legs. The fringes of his clothing were also lined in ermine, and his silver hair and beard were immaculately trimmed. Althea took the opportunity to check her own appearance one more time, just to make sure their outfits matched. As she stood next to her shorter husband, she smiled at the image. The two of them made a very impressive pair, if she did say so herself.

"We have to leave, my love," she said. "We are going to be late as it is."

"I'm the King of Illymar, and the most important man on this island. I'm never late. Everyone else is simply early, as it should be."

"Tell that to King Madari and Emperor Xan."

Orem laughed sharply and turned slightly to look at her out of the corner of his eye.

"King Madari is a barbarian, unworthy of consideration. Under his rule, Dakkadia not only became even more warlike than it already was—if indeed that is possible—but it also it became expansionist as well. Emperor Xan is marginally better, but if our ambassador is correct about him, he, too, is a monster. As far as I'm concerned, both of their nations are less than nothing compared to Illymar, and if that means they have to wait an extra few minutes for me to arrive, then they will just have to live with that. Either that or they can go home. It's not like we want them here."

"With an attitude like that, we are going to have no friends whatsoever when Dakkadia's fleet sails into our harbors. I've seen the same reports you have, my husband: Dakkadia is growing in power, and we may not be able to match them in just a few years' time. If you've forgotten that, all you have to do is look out your window to see the very symbol of Dakkadia's naval power. You can't miss it: it's sitting in our harbor with its horrid black and white sails and the Dakkadian flag flying from the tallest mast. We both know that the only thing keeping their army in check is the army of Ferralin, and the only way we can keep the status quo is by buying an alliance with Ferralin, however we can."

"Don't remind me," Orem said, scowling. "I had that neatly taken care of until that unutterable fool Danshire ruined everything by stealing away Tais and making her unsuitable for marriage. Believe me, if I could kill him again for his treason, I would. In fact, I should have ordered Ethan to bring him back alive, just so I could kill him in front of Xan. As it is, I'll just have to settle for the knowledge that Tais is safely locked in the Tower where she can do no further harm to our negotiations with Ferralin. Xan does not need a reminder that we've already broken one arrangement with them. It could drive Ferralin straight into the welcoming arms of Dakkadia."

"Tais can still serve a role in this, Orem. Remember that Ferralin does not treat women the same way we do, or, for that matter, the way Dakkadia does. In Ferralin, they believe that a woman who does something as stupid as Tais did can be forgiven simply *because* she's a woman and therefore isn't expected to have known better."

"That's too much to hope for," Orem said. "Other than for her single, colossal mistake, Tais is the smartest person I've ever known, and if he was to meet her, it would take all of twenty seconds for Emperor Xan to realize the same thing.

They certainly would never believe that she didn't know *exactly* what she was doing when she unilaterally broke her betrothal and married another man against my express orders."

"That may be true, Orem, but everyone knows that even the most intelligent of women can be swayed by foolish romantic notions, especially if they believe that they are in love. Tais certainly did, and my own regrettable actions that day may have driven her into Danshire's arms. I lost control of myself, I'll admit, and I regret that, but what is past no longer matters. What truly matters is that we have to somehow repair the damage Tais has caused before Dakkadia invades our island and forces us to accept surrender terms at sword's point."

Orem turned back to the mirror and scowled.

"Which is why she remains locked away. Someday soon, I will have to decide what to do with her, but at the Convocation she will cause more harm than good."

Althea's brow furrowed in anger at that, and she crossed her arms over her bosom in irritation.

"You aren't thinking, Orem. The Ferraline will forgive a girl for foolish behavior, but only if she begs for forgiveness. That means the *only* person who can repair the damage is Tais herself. She *has* to convince Xan that her actions were those of a foolish, besotted child, and were not meant as a deliberate slap at Ferraline honor. We *need* her, Orem."

He considered her words for several moments and then shrugged.

"It doesn't matter. Even if—*if,* I say—I were inclined to agree with you, Tais would never obey my command. I am sure by now that she believes she hates us more than we could possibly imagine. What's more, I made certain that the conditions of her imprisonment were very harsh. If I hadn't, the nobles would have questioned her preferential treatment. There's no way she could be ready in time to meet with Xan."

"Which is why I had her freed from the Tower two weeks ago, my husband," Althea said calmly. "She's been confined to her apartments with no visitation allowed, but I've had the seamstresses and hairdressers working day and night to repair the damage her time in the Tower has caused."

Orem whirled on his wife, face turning blood red in anger.

"*What?* How dare you countermand my orders? She was to remain there until I commanded otherwise!"

Althea weathered the storm calmly, and when he paused for breath, she uncrossed her arms, put her hands on her hips, and leaned forward aggressively.

"We will have only one opportunity to repair the damage she has done, Orem. She has to apologize to him for her affront to his dignity, and she cannot do that from a cell! I knew you wouldn't even consider the possibility, so I circumvented the entire issue. After the Convocation concludes, we can marry her off to some unpleasant minor noble from one backwater province or another to secure their loyalty, but for now, I need her to be seen as the Princess she still is. I've made certain she understands the importance of this occasion, and she knows quite well that we will happily toss her back into the Tower and throw away the key if she crosses us. But I think we both know that—while she may despise us—she's still an Illymari. And as such, she doesn't want Dakkadian soldiers setting foot on Illymar any more than we do." As she spoke, the red began to fade from Orem's face and his color slowly returned to normal. "She will be waiting for us in the hall when we are ready to leave, Orem, so prepare yourself now for the sight of her. You do not have to forgive her for her betrayal, Orem. All you have to do is understand, that right now, we need her here more than we need her locked away in the Tower."

King Orem turned again to his wife and the level look he gave her spoke volumes. Still, he didn't speak, and Althea took that to be a good sign. After a few moments, she turned to the door.

"We're late. We must leave now, Orem. The streets are packed with citizens. The guards are keeping the streets as clear as possible, but that doesn't mean the trip there will be smooth or quick. And we already are on the defensive with Xan; it would not do to add further insult to his honor by arriving too late."

Tais barely recognized the woman staring back at her in her mirror, and somehow she resisted a compulsion to reach up and touch her face. *Could I have changed so very much in the last year?* Setting the question aside for a moment, she turned slightly to check the fit of her gown, and decided that she liked what she saw very much. The golden dress fit her perfectly—no small feat considering the time constraints her imprisonment had imposed upon the seamstresses—and it flattered her body wonderfully. The pale gold of the cloth was the exact shade of her hair, and the overall effect was radiant. Her hair was also perfectly coiffed, and just like the seamstresses, the hairdresser had worked miracles in the two weeks she had to work with. As a prisoner in the Tower, Tais hadn't had access to hair brushes or oils, and when the hairdresser had seen the condition Tais's hair was in after her ordeal, she had nearly run screaming from the room, for a Princess *never* looked like that. But the shock had worn off almost instantly, and the hairdresser had rolled up her sleeves and took to her work with a will.

After two weeks of constant care, her hair had finally returned to its normal golden sheen, and both Tais and the hairdresser had been more than pleased with the result. But the clothes and the hairstyle were simply part of the whole, and Tais dismissed them from consideration as she returned her attention to her face. It didn't seem possible, but the truth reflecting in the silvery glass was undeniable: gone were the soft features of the pampered Princess she had once been, replaced instead by the perfectly defined angles of a sharply carved beauty. She could still see traces of her old self in her reflection, but the few features she could recognize were completely outweighed by the changes.

Have I aged so much?

Unable to resist any longer, Tais reached up and touched a high, sharp cheekbone, and her reflection dutifully reached up and touched its own cheek. As she wrestled with the notion that the pretty girl she had once been had somehow survived her misspent youth, and had grown into a beautiful woman, her door opened slightly and one of Queen Althea's hand-picked guards looked in on her. When she saw Tais, she nodded politely.

"Your Highness, the procession is ready to leave. We must join them."

Tais took one last look at herself in the mirror and turned to the door.

"I'm ready." She faltered for a moment as a thought crossed her mind. "Are my siblings there already?"

The handmaiden nodded.

"Yes, Your Highness. The King and Queen have not joined the rest of your family, but a runner has sent word that they are on the way from his apartments. Queen Althea wishes you to be there before they arrive at the procession. Your sisters are already there, and they look simply stunning."

Tais stopped.

"And Ethan?"

A look of understanding crossed the handmaiden's face, followed instantly by one of sympathy.

Yes, Your Highness. He is there as well," she said softly.

For a moment Tais paused, unsure if she could face her husband's murderer, but the promise that she had made to Queen Althea came to her, and so she squared her shoulders and lifted her chin. Ethan *had* hurt her, but he had done so at the order of King Orem. *Why hate the hangman?*

As the pair left her chambers and walked to the main hall, Tais caught sight of dozens of servants and guards surreptitiously looking at her from every doorway and alcove. None of them said anything, but she could feel their eyes upon her from every angle, and as she passed, whispers quickly broke out behind her. As more and more people came to see her, she realized what was happening. Apparently, everyone wanted to see the "fallen" Princess with their own eyes. Everyone wanted to be the one that could tell his or her friends that they had seen the living example of a highborn brought low.

She wondered idly just how these people expected her to act. Should she be raving like a beast? Crying, wailing, or gnashing her teeth? Did they expect her shame to show on her face like some sort of a badge or a scar? Whatever it was they expected, she vowed not to give them the satisfaction. The silent stares became uncomfortable during the long walk from her chambers, but she never bothered to return their looks or listen to their whispers. Tais began to feel like a prisoner being escorted to the gallows, with crowds of people gathering to view the spectacle.

Before long, the crowds disappeared altogether, and Tais soon realized why. She had been so lost in thought that she hadn't been paying attention to her surroundings, and so she hadn't realized that they had arrived at the doors to the main hall. The guards came to attention for her and opened the door, and for the first time in a year, she saw her brothers and sisters. Their reactions varied, from pure joy on Lyrahe's and Chesare's faces, to shocked surprise on Ethan's, but Tais found herself fighting back tears at the sight of them. She hadn't realized just how much she had missed her sisters, and from their glistening eyes, they had missed her just as much.

She stood in the doorway for a moment as no one knew what to do, until Lyrahe broke the stillness and rushed to Tais, followed immediately by Chesare. Tears did find their way from her eyes then, as her sisters hugged her close. Her younger brother, Lorne, only five years old and painfully shy, hesitated for a moment as if he didn't recognize her, but when she smiled at him he finally overcame his fear. She bent down and scooped him into her arms, hugging him tightly as she remembered the child she had lost, but then she looked at Ethan, and her tears went away as if they had never been.

As his surprise faded away, Ethan gave her an arrogant look. She had always hated the smug look of superiority that he could so effortlessly achieve, and seeing it now reminded her of the last time she had seen him in this very room. The reminder was painful, but she weathered it well. As she set Lorne back down, Ethan spoke.

"I see you've been let out of the Tower, sister. I'm surprised you didn't take the easy way out a long time ago and jump to your death. It would have saved us all a lot of trouble."

"That was never a possibility," she said. "You see, unlike you, I am not a coward. I will face my fate—whatever it may be—on my feet."

"A coward, am I?" He laughed in derision. "Dare I ask how you came to that conclusion? Or have you gone mad from the isolation?"

"Markus challenged you to single combat, Ethan, or had you forgotten? Instead of accepting the challenge as a *man* would have, you had him shot down with crossbows. Crossbows you stood safely behind, I might add."

Ethan's face turned red at the insult and a furious expression crossed his face.

"I don't have to listen to that from you, *traitor*. Danshire got what he deserved, though his death was quicker than he had any right to expect. You, on the other hand, have yet to pay for your treachery. You think a single year in the Tower is enough punishment for all the harm you've caused? Think again." He turned his attention to Lyrahe and the sneer returned to his face threefold. "You rush to her arms like a good little sister, but it's obvious you haven't thought this through. Now that Tais has shown her true nature, like the slattern she is, you, sister dear, have to take her place. Father and Mother are going to make *you* marry Prince Lain, in order to buy us an ally against Dakkadia . . . assuming he'll even have a lesser daughter. He may not, you know." He pointed an accusing finger at Tais and said, "Tais seemed to be the perfect daughter, but she spread her legs *wide* for the first man who ever looked at her twice, and the Kingdom be damned. You don't think they are going to remember that when they look at you? Don't fool yourself: *every* time they look at you, they are going to be wondering if you are anything at all like Tais, and deciding whether or not you are worthy of one day becoming their Empress. You'd better hope that they see something worthwhile in you, because if they *do* decide you are like Tais, you'll be lucky if they let you become a concubine. Still, better that than a whore."

He turned to Tais as he said the word 'whore' to let her know exactly who he was referring to, and Tais gathered herself to renew her assault when, to her astonishment, Chesare spoke.

"You apologize right now, Ethan, or you will regret it. I promise you; you *will* regret it."

Ethan glanced down at Chesare, and to Tais' surprise, he swayed backward, as if he wanted to step away from his youngest sister but had managed to stop himself. Tais looked at Chesare's face, wondering what could have caused such a reaction in Ethan, when she saw that Chesare's eyes were glowing a bright, fiery red. *Chesare is a Powerborn? When did this happen?* After his initial panic, Ethan took control of himself and leaned toward Chesare in an intimidating manner.

"I will *not* apologize, you little snippet. Why should I? I've done nothing wrong!" Chesare's eyes seemed to flare as she gathered herself to attack him again when he suddenly whirled away from her and pointed at Tais. "If you don't believe me, then ask her! Just ask her if I'm right. You may not like what I'm saying, but every word that I've spoken is true, and Tais knows it. So you ask her, and if she disagrees with me, I'll give her the apology that you think I owe her."

He crossed his arms over his chest and tried to glare at all of his siblings simultaneously in a manner that was meant to be intimidating, but only served to make him look like a petulant child. Lyrahe and Chesare turned to look at her, waiting for her to deny Ethan's words. Before she could speak, however, a booming voice interrupted them.

"What in the name of the Archon is going on here?!"

All three of the girls jumped at the bellow, and Chesare's eyes flared once more before returning to their normal color. As one, they whirled around and saw that King Orem and Queen Althea were standing behind the group, and neither one of them looked pleased. King Orem gave Tais a single furious glance, and then turned his full attention upon Chesare.

"Is this what you are learning at the Mage Citadel? You are learning how to use your powers against your own family? If that is the case, we can end your time at the Citadel right now."

Chesare looked abashed and lowered her eyes in shame.

"I'm sorry, Father."

Orem glared at Chesare for several moments, and then nodded when he felt that the point had been driven home long enough. He then turned his attention back to Tais.

"Your mother just told me a few moments ago that she had you released from the Tower. I'm telling you right now that she did so against my express orders and I am not happy about it. As far as I am concerned, you can go right back to the Tower and stay there until you rot. Fortunately for you, your mother is a kinder soul, and she assures me that you will behave yourself from this point on. But I'll have that from you: do I have your word that you will behave yourself?"

Tais curtseyed formally.

"You have my word, Your Majesty. I will bring no further dishonor to the Royal Household."

The King considered his wayward daughter for a few seconds and seemed to decide that he could take her at her word.

"We are leaving. Remember that you will be meeting the heads of state for several countries, not the least of which will be our mortal enemies and our most important allies. You will all comport yourselves as befits your station at all times."

As the King turned to leave and the rest of his family fell in behind him, Ethan sidled up behind Chesare and grabbed her upper arm in a painful grip to hold her back. He waited until the rest of the family had left the room before bending down to speak quietly into his youngest sister's ear.

"The next time you point a weapon at me," he hissed, "you'd better use it. Threaten me again, sister dearest, and I promise you that you *won't* live long enough to regret it."

He squeezed her arm one last time to make his point, only to gasp aloud in pain and snatch his hand away from her as if he had been burned, as in fact, he had. A look of disbelief crossed his face as he realized that Chesare had actually dared to use her power upon him. As he cradled his hand tightly to his chest, Chesare rounded on him and clenched her fists, leaning forward slightly as if preparing to fight him physically.

"Father isn't here for you to hide behind right now, Ethan. So if you're ready for the lesson in humility that you so richly deserve, I'll be more than happy to provide it."

Ethan recoiled from her in shocked surprise, partly because of her display of power, but mostly because she wasn't backing down. She'd always been intimidated by him before, but it seemed those days were over. As if reading his mind, Chesare's lip curled in a spiteful sneer.

"I'm no longer a child, Ethan, and you do not frighten me." Her eyes flashed a bright red one last time to emphasize her point before she released her hold on her power. "Come on. We're going to be late." With that, she turned her back on her oldest sibling and hurried out of the main hall.

Ethan stared at her back for several moments, absentmindedly shaking his hand to ease the pain, and wondered just when his youngest sister had grown up. He had never bothered to get to know Chesare, mainly because of the difference in their ages, but the woman who had threatened him today was completely different from the young girl he'd bullied as a child. And then there was Tais. Ethan wasn't sure why his mother had allowed Tais to be released, but he hadn't been prepared to see her, especially like this. For just a brief moment when their eyes had met, he had seen a look of hatred so deep it had almost frightened him. She had covered the look quickly with one of icy disdain, but he wasn't fooled in the slightest. *No one hates like Tais. No one. She'll kill me if she has the chance.*

Ethan felt a surge of anger, not toward his sister, but toward his father for putting him in this position. *It should never have come to this.* Markus Danshire had been his best friend, and Ethan had been the one to introduce him to Tais. He had known when he'd made the introductions that Tais liked the dashing young nobleman, but if he had had even the slightest inkling of where that infatuation was going to lead, he never would have done it.

When Markus and Tais ran away together, Ethan had secretly wished them well. But then his father had called him into the Throne Room and had given him an ultimatum: lead an army to bring Tais home and execute Danshire for his treachery, or be locked away in the Tower himself for High Treason. At the time, he dismissed his father's threat as being nothing more than the bluster of an angry old man, but now he knew that Orem had meant every word, for Tais' fate had proven how serious the threat had been. *Father blamed me for introducing the two of them to each other, and if I had defied him, he would have followed through with his threat. I had no choice but to do what I did.*

Tais had accused him of cowardice for choosing not to face Markus in single combat, but the truth was, a duel between them would have been stupid and pointless. If they had fought and Ethan had won, things would still have ended the same way for Tais, whether she believed that or not. If Markus had won, the King would simply have sent someone else, or more likely, would have led another army himself, and things would have been even worse for Tais when she was finally brought home. And he? He would have died for nothing. So, out of respect for their friendship, he had chosen instead to be merciful. The traditional method of execution for traitors was castration, followed by being hanged, drawn, and quartered, with the body parts then divided to be spread to the far corners of the kingdom as a warning to anyone else foolish enough to defy the King. Crossbows, on the other hand, while messy weapons, at least offered a quick death, and Ethan had ordered his men to aim for the heart. Thankfully, the archers' aim had been true. Markus had died almost instantly, and Ethan had waited until his friend was truly dead before cutting off his head to appease the King's need for vengeance.

After it was all said and done, Tais had been locked in the Tower, and Ethan found that the experience had changed his view, both of his father and of his own worth to the family. Before Danshire's "rebellion" he had always tried to be a good Prince and a better son, but after Danshire's death all of that had changed. He had never consciously made a decision to rebel against his father, but he had done so just the same. Where he had once been a good son who always did what he was told, now he was infamous for his debauchery, his churlish behavior, and his contempt for authority . . . authority that very definitely included his father. He stopped taking his official duties so seriously and instead began drowning his sorrows in swordplay, wine and pleasant company. And if His Majesty didn't like it, well, that was just too bad. *Such are the perils of tyranny.*

Ethan glanced at the door that his family had walked through and shook his head, his thoughts turning once more to Tais. *I promised myself that if I ever got the chance, I would tell all of this to Tais and ask for her forgiveness. But now I can see*

PRINCESS TAIS ILLVANNA OF ILLYMAR

that it won't do any good. That one look held all I needed to know. Tais will never *forgive me for what I've done to her. It would be stupid of me to even try. And what's more, part of me thinks that I deserve her hatred.*

"So be it" he growled. *If she wants to be enemies, then that's what we'll be, apology be damned. One of these days I will be King, while she'll never be anything more than a useless widow who looks a little like someone who was once a Princess.*

CHAPTER ELEVEN

“Realizations”

“They’re late,” Archimagus Enaria Wintersong said in a disgusted tone. And beside her, Cedric DeVir smirked knowingly as he held out his hand.

“I did warn you this would happen. You chose not to heed my warning,” he said smugly. Enaria sighed heavily and reached into a pouch to pull out a single gold coin. She held it up for a moment as if regretting her actions, and then slapped it into his palm. “Easy money” Cedric said, smiling as he flipped the coin victoriously into the air.

Enaria grimaced and gave him a sideways glance.

“You would think that an occasion as important as the Convocation would be enough to import a sense of urgency to the aristocracy, no matter what nation they may hail from.”

“Ah, Enaria,” Cedric said, laughing loudly, “it must be nice to live in such a perfect world. You must allow me to visit someday. It would be such a wonderful break from reality.” She let out a disgusted sound at Cedric’s impertinence, but it only made him laugh once more. A movement caught his eye and he turned toward the front of the hall. “Tavian! Glad you could join us. Any sign of the Royals?”

"None," Tavian said, sighing. "The roads are fairly clear, considering the number of people who have lined up to catch a glimpse of them, but as far as I can tell, not a single carriage has even left the enclaves yet."

Cedric's smile turned into a grin, and he held out his hand once again, this time loudly clearing his throat. With an annoyed look at Cedric, Tavian reached into his belt pouch and fished out a gold coin, a twin to the one his sister had just handed Cedric.

"I am paying you under protest, Archimagus DeVir. There really is no excuse for their being this late. You must have bribed them."

"Ah, yes, if I am not mistaken, *that* is the sound of sour grapes slowly being trod underfoot to make a bitter vintage of whine," Cedric said, cupping his hand to his ear as he said it. "You know, it saddens me to think that our illustrious Second and Third Seats would be naïve enough to actually believe that Royals of any nation would feel any sense of urgency about schedules set by lesser beings. Luckily, I am not cursed with such appalling innocence. When you have spent as much time with royalty as I have, you quickly realize that punctuality is something Royals demand of others. It is not something they aspire to themselves."

Tavian snorted at Cedric's astringent tone, but before he could speak, Archidraconus Semarill stepped through a doorway hidden behind the main altar and joined the small group. Cedric turned to greet the newcomer, but Ephraim held up a hand to forestall him, then produced a third gold coin. As Cedric reached for the coin, he grinned yet again at Enaria and Tavian, but neither one of them would rise to the bait. Before he could claim his prize, however, Ephraim pulled the coin back slightly out of reach.

"Before I pay you your blood money, Cedric, Patriarch Varic asked me to remind you of the evils of gambling and the misfortune that will befall anyone who would sink so low as to take advantage of a humble servant of the Church. He wants you to know that, although he would never even consider reneging on a wager, he also believes that the devastating blow the Church's prestige has suffered today should be punishment enough. Paying you as well would be an unnecessary cruelty."

Cedric stayed his hand for a moment as if considering the point, and then without a word, his hand shot forward and took the coin right out of Archidraconus Semarill's fingers.

"We'll have to agree to disagree, Archidraconus. Unlike our esteemed Patriarch, *I* think this is just enough of a punishment." He flipped the coin into the air and caught it adroitly, and then began walking it from knuckle to knuckle as he smiled at the priest. "I could be wrong, of course, so I'll take some time to ponder the question later, as I am spending the Church's money on unsavory things like strong drink and women of negotiable virtue." He paused, as if deep in some serious thought. "And with all of the money I've made today, I should be able to consider his words for a good long while. Speaking of which," he pocketed the coin, raised his hand, and snapped twice in rapid succession at Ephraim, then opened his hand palm up. "Aren't you forgetting something? I seem to remember you mentioning something to me about 'a fool and his money' right before you placed the same wager as your illustrious Patriarch."

Ephraim Semarill sighed deeply and pulled out a second coin. As Cedric triumphantly reached for his fourth gold coin, Ephraim narrowed his eyes and said,

"Sinner." All four of them broke into laughter at that, and with a chagrined look on his face, Ephraim handed over the coin and looked at Enaria. "Remind me never to bet against him again, especially if the wager looks to be a sure thing. The unholy glee with which he rubs your face into your failure when you lose is not worth the possible gain."

As the general laughter died down, an acolyte came running from the front of the Cathedral, and Tavian turned to his companions.

"From the haste with which your acolyte is approaching," he said, "I would say that our guests have finally started to arrive. We should probably take our positions."

Cedric and Enaria agreed, but before they could walk toward the section reserved for members of the Mage High Council, Ephraim spoke.

"The first three people who will enter the Cathedral are the three great leaders, King Orem III, King Madari, and Emperor Xan, followed by their wives and their heirs. After that, entrance will be granted by precedence, but all seating has been prearranged. Cedric, I just wanted you to know that, although they won't be among the first groups to enter, your family will be seated near the front of the Dakkadian section, fairly close to King Madari."

"I appreciate your taking the time to tell me that, Ephraim," Cedric said. "I'll readily admit I have been looking forward to seeing everyone. The last time I saw my family was when I went to Dakkadia to bring back my niece for training."

"As to that, Novice Adrianna will be seated with her family for this occasion," Ephraim said. "It seems she misses her family very much because she was quite insistent about being seated near them during the Convocation."

"I would say that she is more interested in being seated next to Lady Prudence Daemira than actually setting eyes on her family again," Cedric replied, smiling slightly. "I understand that Lady Prudence will be seated with my family?" Ephraim nodded slightly, with a puzzled look on his face. "As with many young women, Adrianna has a slight case of hero worship when it comes to the illustrious Corsair," Cedric continued. "I fully expect her to make herself a nuisance to her heroine at every opportunity."

"Well, she won't be seated next to Lady Prudence, but she will be within two or three seats of her. Oddly, we had a last-minute request from Queen Aveliad concerning the seating arrangements for her son, Lord Daane. Apparently, Queen Aveliad wishes her son to be seated next to Lady Prudence. As an Earl, Lord Daane would normally be seated towards the rear of the Cathedral, but a request from the Queen of Dakkadia carries the weight of a command." He frowned slightly. "An odd pairing, that. Aren't Lady Prudence and Lord Daane related somehow?"

"Only through distant marriage," Cedric said. "Lady Prudence's older sister, Danae, is married to my brother—and Queen Aveliad's half-brother—Prince Brendenn DeVir. It's all very convoluted, but suffice to say, there is no blood relation between the two."

Ephraim turned his attention to the acolyte who had been running to the group. The young man was breathing hard from the exertion, and had to take a few breaths before he could speak.

"Your Eminence, the Royal Coaches have arrived and Their Majesties are ready to enter the Cathedral at your word."

"It would seem that our guests have finally arrived," the Archidraconus said. "Today will be a long day, my friends, as will tomorrow. I won't have a chance to speak with you again until after today's ceremonies are concluded, but I will be attending the gala King Orem will be throwing this evening. If I am not mistaken, Queen Althea has dinner parties and galas planned for the entire month of the Convocation, which should be very interesting indeed. Perhaps the knowledge that extravagant parties await the attendees after each day's services will motivate them to arrive on time in the future."

"Would any of you care to wager on that?" Cedric asked with a smile that somehow managed to mix pure innocence with a hungry, diabolical evil.

Ephraim Semarill, Enaria Wintersong, and Tavian Two-Blade looked at each other, and as one, turned and walked away, leaving Cedric where he stood.

As the massive bells of the Cathedral tolled to signal the beginning of the Convocation, a susurration passed through the crowd gathered outside the ornate doors. As he waited for the guards to allow them entry, Emperor Xan surreptitiously looked out of the corner of his eye at the men standing on either side of him without moving his head in the slightest. On his left stood the tall and broad shouldered King Madari of Dakkadia, wearing a perfectly tailored black uniform complete with a silver-chased long sword riding on his hip.

Dakkadian style did not include an overabundance of ornamentation, and King Madari was proof of this. Even the Dakkadian crown was a simple golden circlet, set with a single ruby diadem in the center. But what the broad shouldered, powerfully muscled man lacked in ornamentation, he more than made up for with sheer presence. He was extremely handsome, and the white streak in his long black hair made a shocking contrast to the rest of his dark appearance. He looked every inch the warrior king that he had proven himself to be over the last twenty-five years. Just by looking at him, Xan could tell that this was a man to be reckoned with, and one not to be taken lightly.

Xan moved his attention to the King of Illymar standing on his right. Orem's clothing couldn't have been more different from Madari's if he'd planned it. The rich red velvet he wore was covered in ornamentation, including ermine and gold braid. Several gold chains hung from his neck, and the crown of Illymar itself was a confection of gold and priceless sapphires. He did not wear a weapon, but he did carry a heavy golden scepter that matched the design of his crown perfectly. While Orem himself wasn't as impressive physically as Madari, he did project his own sense of power and confidence to everyone around him. Unlike Dakkadia, Illymar's strength lay in its tremendous wealth and influence, and not in its military. Orem's appearance reflected that very well indeed, for while he did not measure up to Madari's physical presence, his *power* was undeniable.

At some unseen signal from within the Cathedral itself, the formal guards standing at the door turned as one to face each other, and in a precisely timed sequence, reached up and opened the giant doors. When the doors had been opened fully, the guards took up positions to either side of the opening and resumed their position of attention. A priest stood in the doorway, and once the guards had completed their part of the ceremony, bowed low to the three monarchs.

"You are welcome in the House of the Archon," he said, voice booming. "You may enter." All three of the rulers had been instructed on what to do next, and they each bowed slightly to the priest, and then entered the Cathedral.

It had been a long time since Xan had last been in the Cathedral, and he marveled at all of the renovations that had taken place. Each and every aspect of the Cathedral glowed as if burnished, and the monolithic murals lining the vaulted ceiling looked as if they had been freshly painted. The overall effect was humbling, as it was meant to be, and Xan could tell that both King Orem and King Madari had been equally impressed at the display.

As the three monarchs moved through the halls, the families and dignitaries of all three realms and their allies were allowed to enter the Cathedral in a carefully choreographed procession. The first people to be allowed entrance behind the monarchs were their wives, and then their heirs. Xan didn't turn his head to look, but he knew that his son Lain was directly behind him. Xan hadn't had an opportunity to look at the children of Madari or Orem, but there would be plenty of time for that later. As far as Xan was concerned, Tais Illvanna had done a tremendous service for Ferralin by defying her parents and breaking her betrothal. Ferralin would profit either by extorting better terms from King Orem and Illymar, or by seeking a new alliance with Dakkadia.

Xan considered himself to be an excellent negotiator, and the size, wealth and stability of the Ferralin Empire stood as a testimony to his skills. He was not actually angry with Tais for her actions, for young women were known to do foolish things in the name of love, but Xan would be a fool if he didn't use the opportunity to make King Orem writhe. The thought brought a smile to Xan's face, and he looked forward to crossing swords with each of his adversaries in the coming days and weeks.

As the formal procession filed into the Cathedral and the dignitaries found their seats, Enaria Wintersong tried to look attentive. She was not an adherent to the teachings of the Zarryiostrom, but as a member of the Mage High Council she had no choice but to attend. In the end, it really didn't matter to her, but at least she would have yet another opportunity to view the magnificent murals looking down upon the assembled peerage. She settled back into her seat to get comfortable, but the presence of several Powerborn in the crowd caught her attention.

As a master of both Fire and Air Magic, Enaria could sense the resonance of Mages who shared either ability, and her attention was drawn to several people of exceptional power. The first was Princess Chesare Illvanna, of course, for her potential dwarfed that of anyone else in the chamber. But the power radiating off of the young Crown Prince of Dakkadia was exceptional as well, though not as great as that of Chesare.

Prince Valeriad was extremely handsome, and Enaria marked that down as the influence of his half-Fae mother. In the Ferralin contingent, she could see Grand Vizier Shar, and as she turned to look at him, she noticed that he was also looking at her. She remembered him quite fondly from his time at the Citadel, and she smiled and nodded a greeting at him. He had aged considerably in the last thirty years, but his sharp features and intelligent gaze had only intensified with time. He returned her smile and gave her a half-bow before finding his seat.

Enaria fully intended to return her attention to the murals, but suddenly she felt an overwhelming wave of power wash over her senses.

She grasped the arms of her chair, as if to steady herself against the sheer strength of the resonance, and once she had regained her equilibrium, she turned in shock to find the source of that power. It took only a moment, for it radiated from a single man standing at the front of the Dakkadian contingent, but it took her another moment to recognize him. *That can't be Morvandis, can it?* She narrowed her eyes and gave the man a closer look. *It* is *Morvandis!*

Enaria had met Morvandis before, of course, and she had been one of his teachers during his brief time at the Mage Citadel, but at that time he had been a very young, very serious boy. She had not seen him since then, but she could still see traces of the boy in the man standing by King Madari. As a youth, his magical potential had been incredible, but the power radiating from him now dwarfed even his early potential.

Enaria had always been drawn to men with strength and ability in magic, and she freely acknowledged to herself that it was her defining trait. Therefore, it was only natural that she be drawn to the strength she felt within him now, and it made her take a closer look at him. It seemed that the years had been generous to him. It was well known among the peerage that Morvandis was the illegitimate son of King Dhaegus of Dakkadia, but what was not commonly known was that his mother had been a member of the Flower Court . . . in effect, a glorified whore. Enaria wasn't familiar enough with Morvandis's parentage to remember what his mother's name had been, but she had been brought to Dakkadia from the Far East by one of the trading caravans to have made the crossing through the Badlands. She turned her attention to King Madari for a comparison, and saw many points of similarity between them, but while both he and Madari shared some features, the exotic touches Morvandis's mother had bestowed upon him gave him an incredible beauty that Madari would never match. Despite herself, Enaria was intrigued.

As Morvandis took his seat, Enaria couldn't help but wonder what other changes Morvandis might have undergone in the past twenty years. It always surprised her when she was confronted by mortality, especially when it concerned humans. Elves could live to be a thousand years old, and because of this, she did not feel the passing of time as keenly as humans did. Looking at Morvandis now reminded her that, for all his power, for all his strength, he was only mortal, and someday his power and strength would disappear as if it had never been. That was for the future, however. Today, Morvandis stood at the pinnacle of his power and everyone with the ability to sense it knew it.

Enaria turned her head to look at the First Chair of the Mage Citadel. Se-ir Windwhisper was much older than her, and more powerful as well, but even his attention was focused on Morvandis. Her brother, Tavian, sat between Enaria and Se-ir, and she saw Tavian turn slightly to the High Councillor and whisper something. Without taking his eyes from Morvandis, Se-ir nodded once, firmly. Curious, Enaria waited until Tavian returned his own attention to Morvandis before speaking.

"I see you've noticed that Morvandis seems to have grown in power." Tavian grunted once, neither confirming nor denying her statement. When Enaria realized he meant to leave it at that she pressed on. "Se-ir seems to have noticed him as well."

"Of course we noticed him—we aren't blind," Tavian snapped. "It's like having the sun sitting in the middle of the Cathedral. Look around you, Enaria: every Mage here has noticed him, though many try to hide it. No one wants to admit he's there, but he's impossible to ignore."

Enaria bristled.

"Why would anyone want to deny his power or try to ignore him?" she asked. "Think of the benefit to the Mage Citadel his presence would be if we could entice him to join us. He would be a tremendous asset."

"You haven't thought this through, Enaria," he said, disagreeing. "He's mortal. The lesson we've learned time and again from mortals is that the more powerful the Mage—the more promise he or she shows—the less willing they are to give up that power . . . especially to death. Morvandis is at the peak of his power now, but one day soon, he will age and decline. When his mortality becomes undeniable, what measures will he take to forestall his own death? We've both seen it before. He may very well turn to Blood Magic in an attempt to prolong his life. Would you enjoy facing him hundreds of years from now as a vampiri'i, or worse yet, a lich'esti? Somehow I doubt it." He shook his head again, firmly. "No, Enaria, that much power in the hands of a mortal is disturbing, to say the least." He paused then, as if something had just occurred to him. After a few moments of consideration he said quietly, "Two Mages of exceptional power, born in the same generation? I wonder if there is a pattern here?"

As his voice trailed off, Enaria suppressed a sigh of irritation. Tavian had a tendency to become lost in thought when a particularly intriguing problem surfaced. He could, quite literally, spend days unmoving, completely lost in contemplation. Normally, that was a trait of the Fae and not the Elves, but Tavian had never been particularly Elf-like. Unfortunately for him, Enaria wasn't prepared to indulge his eccentricities, and before he could fully enter his fugue state, she pinched his arm hard enough to make him wince. He frowned at her in irritation as his attention returned.

"What was that for?" he asked, growling.

"This is no time for you to become lost in thought," she said. "What did you say to Se-ir?"

"I told him that Morvandis would have to be watched. Closely."

Enaria settled back into her chair. Once again, her gaze found the severe-looking Mage radiating so much power, and she half closed her eyes in contemplation as she began carefully studying every aspect of his appearance and demeanor.

"Oh, I agree" she said in a quiet voice meant only for her ears. As her eyes lingered on his beautiful features and her magical senses basked in the glow of his resonance, she whispered again, hungrily, "I agree."

Patriarch Samuel Varic placed his formal headpiece on top of his head and let the wide tails trailing from it settle into place. Once he was certain that his appearance was perfect, he turned to a small group of high-level clergy. At this signal, the assembled priests bowed and began filing out of the anteroom toward the hidden doorway leading to the main chamber. As the priests slowly filed out of the room, Varic touched his friend and advisor, Ephraim Semarill, on the arm to gain his attention.

"A very important day, old friend. I have to admit a certain amount of trepidation, married to an eagerness to be about my work. I am very much looking forward to seeing the stewards of our flock assembled in one place. You saw the monarchs as they entered the Cathedral?"

Archidraconus Semarill nodded.

"Tell me quickly, what is your impression of them?" the Patriarch asked.

"Aside from my extreme annoyance at them for their tardiness, as well as for the loss of a perfectly good coin, I have to say that I am very impressed indeed. All three rulers are very strong, and they project that strength very well. To be honest, I expected them to make all sorts of unreasonable demands to show us how important they are, but to my surprise, none of them did."

"How did they react to each other when they finally stood face-to-face? Do you foresee any problems?"

"To put it delicately, I think we are in for an interesting time. The order the rulers entered the Cathedral was determined by lot, but it ended up mirroring life a little too closely for my tastes. Emperor Xan stood between King Orem and King Madari in much the same way that Ferralin stands between Dakkadia and Illymar. And from the pleased look upon Xan's face and the determined looks on both Madari and Orem's faces, the bidding for an alliance with Ferralin is going to be very steep indeed."

"When the services are over for the day, I want you to approach each ruler in turn," the Patriarch said. "Please remind them that the Church remains at their service should their delegations wish to meet upon neutral ground. If any of them accept our mediation, see to it that all of their needs are met, regardless of the cost. We must do everything in our power to ease the tension between the realms. If we don't, things will turn to bloodshed all too quickly. We must prevent that."

"It will be done," Ephraim said, bowing. "But for now, you're going to be late for your own sermon."

"Considering the fact that they themselves were late, I don't think they have a right to complain too bitterly if I'm a little late as well, old friend," Varic said with a wicked grin. "And if they do, I will simply tell them that their own procrastination has already cost the Church two golden coins. Let them make of that what they will!"

Laughing, the two leaders of the Church of Zarryiosiad left the antechamber to begin the service.

CHAPTER TWELVE

"Invitations"

I'll never get used to this, Lady Prudence Daemira thought, as she took in the opulence of the dining room and marveled at the sheer spectacle of it all. The sermon had adjourned shortly after the noon hour and the assembled peerage had left the Cathedral to prepare for a formal dinner hosted by the Illvanin Royal Family in the Spire. Their hosts had spared no expense, in either the setting or the food, and the hand-blown crystal made musical sounds as it touched the odd bit of delicate porcelain or golden flatware during the sumptuous meal. There were well over a hundred guests at this dinner, all seated at a single, enormous table custom made for the occasion. Dozens of stewards, dedicated to serving a single guest each, stood watch around the massive table looking for any opportunity to swoop down and fill a partially empty glass with more water or wine, or to whisk away used dishes or silverware.

Several different conversations were taking place around the table, some serious, some jovial, but Prudence didn't bother to join in on any of them. As the sister of a Prince, she had merited an invitation, but her relative lack of rank meant that she was seated very far down the table, which upon reflection, was exactly the way she wanted it. *My lack of rank may mean that I will not take part in any high level discussions like my dear brother, but I have to admit that I wouldn't have it any other way.* The reason for her good humor was simple: as an Earl, Phaedron was also too junior to be seated near the front. So the two of them sat side-by-side and made faces at each other whenever they thought no one was looking.

If someone had told her that she would fall head-over-heels in love with someone, especially a Dakkadian noble, she would have laughed in their face. But somehow it had happened, despite the long and sordid history between their two countries. The Principality of Rohm—her brother, Sethred's realm—was a vassal state of Dakkadia, but it retained much of the independence that they had enjoyed before the Kingdom of Dakkadia had turned expansionist five generations ago and had conquered it.

When Dakkadia had turned its avaricious gaze towards Rohm, her great, great, great grandfather had been offered a simple choice: swear allegiance to Dakkadia, or face invasion and subjugation. Many of his advisors had wanted him to fight Dakkadia to the death, but he had been a very wise man indeed. Instead of offering useless resistance to Dakkadia, he instead chose the harder path. The moral courage it had taken to bow his head to the King of Dakkadia must have been incredibly difficult for the proud sovereign to muster, but in the end, the "alliance" had worked out quite well for both countries.

Under the orders of her Prince, Rohm had offered absolutely no resistance to Dakkadia of any type, and Dakkadia had repaid Rohm's wisdom and foresight with a surprisingly generous amount of autonomy. Not only had the Prince been left in power, but the nobility had been left completely intact as well. Many other realms hadn't possessed the same amount of wisdom: they instead chose to resist, and Dakkadia had dealt with them very harshly indeed. For at least two countries, the Dakkadians had not only destroyed their army, they had also eradicated the nobility and replaced them with Dakkadian nobles before finally turning their attention on the peasantry. The names of both of those countries had been lost to history, but the stories of rape, plunder and cruelty that had been visited upon their people still remained. Afterward, the Dakkadian King had left the cruelest, most sadistic nobles he could find in charge of the conquests to break their spirits, and those despots had done their jobs very, very effectively.

None of that had happened in Rohm, however. Instead, in return for a small, but noticeable, tax and a modest levy for troops—mainly for the navy—Rohm enjoyed the complete protection of Dakkadia from all other would-be predators. The strategic positioning of Rohm was very important to the Kingdom, because it stood directly between Dakkadia and Ferralin and shared a common border with the Badlands. Any invasion by Ferralin into Dakkadia, or vice versa, would have to travel through either the Principality of Rohm or their inland neighbor to the east, the Principality of Palantine. So, all of the Kings of Dakkadia had done their utmost to ensure the loyalty of the citizens of both countries. After all, if war ever did break out between Ferralin and Dakkadia, Dakkadia would need the cooperation of both Palantine and Rohm to ensure that any battles that were fought would be fought away from Dakkadian soil.

Prudence raised her crystal goblet and took a sip of the strong burgundy the steward had poured for her. The rich flavor of the wine coated her tongue and she savored the superb taste for a few moments before swallowing. A thought crossed her mind, and before she could stop herself, her shoulders began shaking with laughter.

"And just what do you find so amusing?" Phaedron asked, leaning close. It was only after Prudence had stopped shaking from quiet laughter and was sure that she had regained control of herself that she dared to respond.

"I was just admiring the wine selection . . . and wondering how King Madari is handling his drink."

Phaedron frowned in confusion at her, and the look upon his face almost made her break out in another round of giggles.

"I had a . . . difference of opinion with the King some years ago. He had had too much to drink and made a complete lout of himself, so I ordered my steward to water down his wine over the course of our trip here. "

Phaedron thought about it for a moment, and then once again leaned in towards her.

"That must have been some occasion. I'm sorry I missed it. I have my own problems with His Majesty, but honesty compels me to admit that if he acted inappropriately toward you while drunk, it was probably because he is unpracticed at being inebriated. King Madari very rarely drinks to excess, and *never* when he's surrounded by enemies. As he's very definitely surrounded by enemies tonight, I honestly don't think there will be a problem." He lowered his voice conspiratorially. "And even if he was so inclined, Mother has a tight rein on him this evening. After all, it wouldn't do to have Dakkadia expelled from Illymar on the first night of the Convocation, would it?"

"I don't suppose it would. But King Orem, for one, would rejoice at the expulsion. It would clear the way quite handily for him to renegotiate another alliance with Ferralin."

Before Phaedron could answer her, a movement at the head of the table caught her attention and she batted Phaedron's chest lightly to draw his attention to it. King Orem stood holding his glass in a toast. As the dinner guests realized what was happening, everyone seated at the table raised their glasses in an answering salute.

"To the Archon!" King Orem said, in a voice loud enough for everyone to hear.

Every voice in the room sounded as one as the guests repeated the toast, and both Phaedron and Prudence took a sip of their wine in honor of Zarryiosiad.

"My friends, I thank you for attending this dinner marking the opening ceremonies of the Convocation," Orem said. "If you will follow me to the ballroom, we can continue our celebration in a more relaxed setting. Or, if you would prefer, the Spire of Illymaine is open for your exploration. You will find that the Spire houses untold wonders, some of which date back to the Archon herself. While you are here, I invite you to view these wonders at your leisure. The guards will be happy to answer any of your questions about the castle or the grounds, or even to take you on a formal tour, if that should be your desire. Remember that you are my honored guests, and my home is your home."

Orem nodded to King Madari and Emperor Xan and the three of them left the dinner table together and walked into the adjoining ballroom.

The other guests began following the monarchs, but before Prudence could get in line, a distinguished man in the uniform of an Illymari Admiral stepped in front of her and bowed slightly, clicking his heels together smartly. Curious despite herself, Prudence allowed him to pull her aside.

"May I be of service, Admiral?" Her voice trailed off as she let him know that she didn't recognize him.

"Savonne. Lucas Savonne, Lord High Admiral of His Majesty's Navy. May I have a word with you, in private?"

She glanced at Phaedron, and he shrugged indifferently, before stepping away and taking himself out of earshot. Once Savonne was certain that no other ears were listening, he spoke.

"I would like to extend an invitation to you to join me for lunch tomorrow at the Admiralty House. I would very much like the opportunity to speak with you concerning matters of grave import."

"An interesting invitation, Admiral," Prudence said, "and one I have to admit I find very intriguing, especially since we are both aware I am not exactly the Illymari Navy's favorite person. May I inquire as to what topic you wish to discuss with me?"

Admiral Savonne smiled slightly at her statement. *Not exactly the Illymari Navy's favorite person* was putting it mildly. The Corsair was the most wanted person in Illymar, and a king's ransom would be paid to the person who finally brought her down. Illymar recognized her Letter of Marque, and they did make a distinction between her privateer status and that of a mere pirate, but they still hated her with a vengeance and wanted her dead or permanently removed, whatever the means.

"You need not fear for your safety, Lady Prudence," the Admiral said, raising his hands in a gesture of openness. "Rest assured that we will honor our King's pledge of safe conduct. As for the topic for discussion, I would very much like to save that for the actual meeting. Assuming you accept my invitation, of course."

Prudence considered it for a moment, but she could see no harm in accepting the meeting. The Peace of Zarryiosiad would protect her for the entirety of the Convocation. *Only a fool would risk the wrath of the Zarryiostrom.* She glanced at Phaedron, who stood several paces away waiting for the conversation to conclude.

"If you will allow me to bring a guest, I will gladly accept your invitation."

Admiral Savonne looked at Phaedron and frowned slightly, clearly considering the request.

"Is he the guest you wish to bring?"

"He is."

"The matters I wish to discuss with you are of a private nature," the Admiral said. "If you are certain he can be trusted to maintain our confidentiality, I see no harm in allowing him to attend."

The last was phrased as a statement, but she could hear the question in it.

"I trust Lord Daane implicitly. He will not divulge any information you may wish kept private."

"Then I shall expect you for lunch tomorrow at the Admiralty, say, after the morning Mass is held? Will that be convenient for you?"

"Quite acceptable, Admiral Savonne. Will there be anything else?"

He smiled, but the expression did not reach his eyes.

"No, My Lady. Please enjoy yourself this evening. I look forward to speaking with you tomorrow."

He turned and walked through the doors to the ballroom. Phaedron watched him leave and stepped over to Prudence.

"What was that all about?"

Prudence frowned, looking at the doors through which the Admiral had passed.

"I just accepted an invitation from the Lord High Admiral of the Illymari Navy for lunch tomorrow, and you're coming with me."

"As a bodyguard?" he asked with a raised eyebrow.

"As a witness."

Princess Lyrahe Illvanna tried not to stare at Valeriad, the white-haired Prince of Dakkadia, but it was hard—very hard. Every time she looked at him, her heart began to race, her mouth went dry and her breathing quickened like a frightened doe. She had never seen such a beautiful man before, and she wanted desperately to meet him. Unfortunately, there hadn't been an opportunity. He was standing near his father and taking part in conversations with several nobles of the Dakkadian conclave, and his natural charm was apparent even from her distant vantage point. At the moment, he was listening intently to a story being told by a nobleman she didn't recognize, and when the group burst into sudden laughter, his easy smile made his face light up.

She found it strange that the Prince of warlike Dakkadia could smile so easily, for she had been taught to believe the worst about Dakkadia, but looking at Prince Valeriad now made it easy for her to discount the rumors as nothing more than idle gossip. In a word, he was dashing. In fact, he looked very much as she imagined one of her heroes would look if he stepped out of the pages of her books and came to life, and that made her want to meet him all the more. An orchestra was playing pastoral music in the background, but all of the guests were too busy mingling to dance, which, in her opinion, was a shame, for she dearly loved to dance. As she watched him, she wondered idly if the young Prince knew how to dance as well. He looked so slim and graceful that she knew he would make an excellent partner, but once again, the lessons she had been taught about Dakkadia came to mind: if her tutors were right, he would have been too busy learning how to make war to learn about the finer points of polite society.

Lyrahe turned away from the vision of masculine beauty to try to collect her thoughts, and her gaze settled involuntarily on her brother, Ethan. When she saw him, she remembered what he had said that morning, and she found herself looking around the room for the man to whom her father would no doubt try to barter her. It didn't take her long to spot him, for he was standing near his own father and listening to yet another group of fawning nobles vying for their attention. When she saw him, she wasn't sure what to think. The dusky-skinned Prince Lain looked very serious, and she wondered what kind of husband he would make. A good one, she hoped, assuming her father had his way, but if she had her choice . . . once again her eyes turned toward Prince Valeriad. He was still listening to the same noble, but for just a split second, she thought she had seen him looking at her. The thought that he might be watching her the way she was watching him made her blush.

As she began her careful study of Prince Valeriad once again, a pair of hands grabbed her upper arm and tugged. She glanced to her side, and saw Chesare standing beside her with an excited look on her face.

"I think I'm in love, Lyrahe. Can you believe him? He's gorgeous!"

Lyrahe turned toward her sister and giggled.

"I saw him first, Chesare. Go find your own Prince!"

A look of mock hurt crossed Chesare's face and she pretended to pout.

"But he's perfect for me! He's a Fireborn, like me, which means we have more in common. You *have* to let me have him."

"He's my age, which makes him far too old for you," Lyrahe said with a laugh, though only two years separated them. "No, *you* have to find someone else. He's mine." The two of them shared another laugh, and then they both turned their longing gazes back to the Prince, only to find him looking in their direction. No, not looking in their direction . . . he was looking *at* them. When Valeriad caught her attention, he smiled brightly at her, and Chesare tightened her grip on Lyrahe's arm, but the thunderstruck Princess didn't even notice. He broke their gaze by turning to his father to say something, and when he finished speaking, he gestured in their direction. King Madari turned to look at the spot his son had indicated, and when he saw them, he nodded curtly and returned to his own conversation. Valeriad excused himself and began walking toward them.

Lyrahe's tongue clove to the roof of her mouth when she realized he meant to speak to her, and the only thought in her head was a desperate prayer to Zarryiosiad.

Archon, give me strength!

A few moments later, Prince Valeriad stood in front of them and gave them both a formal bow. In a daze, Lyrahe raised her hand to him, and he reached out with long, slim fingers, took her hand in his, and kissed her knuckles. He repeated the formality with Chesare, and when he had finished, he spoke.

"Your Highnesses, please allow me to introduce myself. My name is Valeriad Dhaerhan, and I am the Prince of Dakkadia." As one, the princesses curtseyed appropriately to the introduction, and when they were finished he turned to Chesare. "In a few days, my half-brother, Phaedron, and I will be going to the Citadel for Testing. I've been given to understand that you are a student there?" Chesare nodded and Valeriad smiled. "Then I hope to see you there, in a less formal environment. Perhaps you could give Phaedron and me a tour of the Citadel?"

He raised his delicate eyebrows and turned his head slightly to the side in a hopeful look.

"I would like that very much, Prince Valeriad. Novices are kept very busy with their studies, but I'm certain something can be arranged."

From her tone, Lyrahe knew that Chesare would make sure something would be arranged or she would burn the Citadel to a cinder, and the thought made her grin. Valeriad glanced at her then and caught her smiling, and his own expression brightened in response.

"I shall look forward to it then, Princess Chesare."

With that, he turned his complete attention to Lyrahe, and once again her pulse quickened. Before he could speak, the musicians began playing a new song, this one a traditional Illymari waltz, and he cocked his head to the side when the first notes began to play.

"I believe I know this song. Will you dance with me, Princess Lyrahe? It seems a shame that people are wasting such a wonderful opportunity to improve relations with their neighbors."

Somehow, Lyrahe kept her mouth from falling open in shock, and she hesitantly placed her hand in his and allowed him to lead her to the floor.

Though her family considered her to be bookish and introverted, she truly loved to dance, and after no more than three steps, she knew Valeriad would be a perfect partner. The two of them moved together as if they had been dancing with each other all their lives and Lyrahe quickly found herself wishing that the music would never end. Midway through the song, other people began finding their way to the dance floor, and soon the couple found themselves amidst a sizable crowd. Valeriad looked around at the pairs with a pleased expression on his face.

"It has been my experience that most people will dance only if someone else starts first."

Lyrahe nodded, dipping into a complicated series of steps that Valeriad matched perfectly. Despite her own nervousness, she found herself responding to his words completely naturally, and as she spoke, her hesitation vanished as if it had never been.

"That's a shame, truly. The orchestra is the finest in Illymar, and it would be a terrible blow to their reputation if the guests didn't honor their performance with at least one dance. But you are correct: for some reason, no one wants to be the first on the dance floor."

"As royalty, it is our solemn duty to provide solid examples for the nobility to emulate," Valeriad said. "They look to us to lead, and we must always strive to present the best possible appearance for our subjects." He paused to allow her to cross in front of him in an intricate move that he executed flawlessly, and then continued in a quieter voice. "I noticed you from across the room, and I found myself wondering what kind of a dancer you would be, and now I know. You are grace personified."

Lyrahe smiled in remembrance of her own speculation about Valeriad's dancing skills.

"I must confess, I was wondering about your skills as well. Dakkadians aren't exactly known for their dancing, and I'll admit I wasn't even certain if you knew how to dance."

"Mother insisted that all three of her children learn, though honesty compels me to admit I strongly resisted the idea. Fortunately, my half-brother, Phaedron, explained to me that learning to dance would dramatically improve my swordsmanship, and that was all it took."

"How can dancing improve your swordplay?" Lyrahe asked, confused.

"Footwork is a vital component of swordsmanship. A strong arm and good reflexes are important, but the most important aspect of swordplay is making certain your footing is solid and your body is centered. Dancing hones those skills."

"I see. Your half-brother sounds like a very wise person indeed. Is he here? He didn't sit with your family during the dinner."

"Phaedron is here, but he was seated further down the table with his companion, Lady Prudence Daemira. They've been absolutely inseparable since we began the trip from Dakkadia."

Lyrahe missed a step at that, and only Valeriad's quick reactions kept her on her feet. He deftly maneuvered her to keep them moving in the right direction, and only a dance instructor would have seen that anything at all had been amiss.

"Your half-brother is with the *Corsair*?" Valeriad grinned and nodded again, and Lyrahe laughed out loud. "Now I can't wait to meet him."

"It would be an honor and a privilege to introduce you to them as soon as the dance ends, Princess Lyrahe, if you would like."

Lyrahe leaned closer to him than was entirely proper and gave him a coy look through long eyelashes.

"Later," was all she said.

Princess Tais stood by one of the open windows looking out over the perfectly manicured lawns, trying to ignore the fact that everyone was avoiding her. The party had been going on for well over an hour now, and not a single person had even spoken to her to introduce themselves. In fact, no one had even approached within fifteen feet of her. Even the servants holding trays of food or drink kept their distance. She began to wonder if they thought she had contracted a particularly virulent disease during her imprisonment, or perhaps

PRINCE VALERIAD DHAERHAN OF DAKKADIA
AND PRINCESS LYRAHE ILLVANNA OF ILLYMAR

they believed that being a social pariah was catching. Even her sisters hadn't spoken with her, though from the brilliant smiles coming from Lyrahe as she danced with the dashing Prince Valeriad, and the laughter of Chesare standing beside her Dakkadian classmate watching the pair, she knew that they, at least, weren't avoiding her the way everyone else was. They were simply busy with other endeavors.

Lyrahe looked radiant, dancing as she was with the Dakkadian Prince, and Tais found herself hoping that, somehow, the two could find a way to be together as they were so obviously meant to be. Tais was too intelligent to believe that could be a possibility, however, for she knew better than anyone what the political situation had been, even before she had been thrown into the Tower. An alliance between Dakkadia and Illymar sounded good in theory, but the truth was, any alliance between Dakkadia and Illymar would be temporary, at best. It would take Dakkadia years to conquer all of the Badlands and the Ferralin Empire, but it would eventually succeed. When it did, the Dakkadian army would eventually turn upon the only threat remaining to their new empire: Illymar. No, the only thing a marriage between Lyrahe and Valeriad would gain for Illymar would be time, and that wasn't nearly enough to offset the disadvantage of allowing Dakkadia a legitimate claim on the Illymari throne. She glanced at King Orem, standing among the assembled peerage of Illymar and frowned, wondering what he thought of Lyrahe dancing with the enemy, and more importantly, why he allowed it. The two had shared every dance with each other, ignoring all attempts to divide them, and truthfully, they should have known better. In this, the highest of societies, the scandal they were courting could destroy either one of them, in much the same way that Tais herself had been destroyed. Unfortunately, it seemed that both of them were too young and too naïve to understand that.

So why then did Orem allow the dancing to continue? He knew, as well as she, that what the younger Princess of Illymar was doing had to be stopped before it could be allowed to start. So, why did he allow it? She turned her intellect toward solving the question, turning it about in her mind and analyzing it from King Orem's perspective until she hit upon the answer. He was sending a message to Emperor Xan and the Ferralin delegation that they were not the only option available to Illymar. Yes, the advantages that allying with Ferralin offered Illymar were substantially greater for Illymar than tying themselves to Dakkadia would be, but that didn't necessarily mean that Orem wouldn't consider it if negotiations fell through with Xan. No, by allowing his daughter to dance with Prince Valeriad, he was in effect telling the Ferralin contingent that they would either have to come to acceptable terms with Illymar, or their worst fears would become reality.

Now that Tais understood why King Orem allowed the spectacle to continue, she turned her attention to the Emperor of Ferralin. One look at the Emperor was enough to convince Tais that Xan wasn't fooled by the drama playing out on the dance floor. Emperor Xan was standing to the side with his own nobles and advisors surrounding him, and he couldn't have looked more serene if he had tried. In fact, unless she was mistaken, he was *amused* by the display, and by Orem's pathetic attempt to intimidate and influence him. Tais smiled to herself, for the message Xan was sending to Orem was just as transparent as the one Orem was sending to him: *I know what you are doing, and it won't work. You need us more than we need you, and we know it.* And as Emperor Xan wasn't making a move to approach King Orem, it was clear he intended to make Orem come to him.

When Tais realized this, she knew instantly that she was standing at a crossroads. King Orem would never concede that much of an advantage to anyone, and that meant he would not be able to repair the damage she herself had created. He desperately needed a bridge to be built between the two delegations, one that would allow him to save face. Tais had not spoken to Queen Althea more than a few times in the last two weeks, but she knew Althea expected her to try and make amends for the damage that she had done to the alliance in any way that she could. Looking at the Emperor now, she knew the time was perfect for her to make a difference, but the question before her wasn't *could* she; it was *should* she?

As she turned away from the Ferralin contingent and looked out the window of the ballroom, for just a moment she was back in the tiny room at the top of the tallest Tower, looking out over the ocean. She hated the King and the Queen for what they had done to her, and part of her wanted their Kingdom to suffer for her pain. Why should she lift a finger to help them, when they had taken *everything* from her without a second thought? She closed her eyes and thought about the husband who had been taken from her, and the child she had lost, and she could feel the tears gathering in her eyes. Before they could fall, however, a harsh voice sounded in her mind, scolding her for her weakness at this most crucial of times. *No, Tais. This is not the time for your tears or your regrets. Decide! Decide now and live with your choice.*

She knew what she had to do, and despite her momentary weakness, she had known it all along. Tais gathered her grief and pain and despair and locked them away within her, in a tiny place that only she could find, and walked determinedly to the Ferralin contingent with dry eyes and her head held high. No, sabotaging King Orem's efforts to secure the safety of the Illymari people for so pathetic a reason as personal revenge wasn't justice at all, for the people of Illymar would be made to suffer for it. Dakkadia wanted Illymar for itself, and she would be damned if she would allow that to happen. The dire situation that Illymar faced now was entirely her fault, and she was honest enough to admit that. Ethan had been right all along. She glanced at the radiant figure of her sister, dancing in the arms of her handsome Prince and felt a moment of remorse. *For what I am about to do, I hope you can someday forgive me, my sister. But, first and foremost, we are daughters of Illymar. Our destinies are not our own.*

She looked at Emperor Xan and began to smile, and her beautiful smile intensified when she caught his eye. As she curtseyed low to the Emperor of Ferralin and awaited his permission to rise, Tais held her smile even as a part of her died inside, knowing what she was about to do to her beloved sister's chance at happiness.

Madari smiled to himself as his son shared yet another, in a seemingly endless string, of dances with Princess Lyrahe. He had long since lost count of the number of dances the couple had shared with each other, but from the quiet whispers coming from differing groups of nobles and the speculative looks on so many of their faces, people were beginning to notice that the Crown Prince of Dakkadia and the Princess of Illymar seemed to have eyes only for each other. Madari was happy for his son and had every intention of strongly encouraging the courtship, for not only was the stunningly beautiful, raven-haired Princess a good match for Valeriad, a marriage between the two would seal an alliance that would allow Dakkadia to bring the Badlands—and Ferralin—to their knees.

He knew that it was probably too much to ask, but Madari truly hoped that somehow he could find a way to allow his son to not only do his duty for Dakkadia, but marry a woman he could love and who could love him as well. He knew all too well the pain and heartache of being trapped in a loveless marriage, and while an alliance between Illymar and Dakkadia had to be his overriding concern, he wanted to avoid that fate for his own children if he could.

Thoughts of marriage brought to mind his argument with Aveliad, and almost against his will, he scanned the room looking for her. They hadn't spoken to each other since he had left his bedroom, and while he had no intention of seeking her out now, he did wonder where she had gone. It only took him a moment to locate her; she was standing with Deirdre and talking with two other tall, graceful Fae women. From their formal robes he could tell both of them were members of the Mage High Council, but he could only remember one of their names. Archimagus Kyaran, a willowy, blond-haired Fae, was speaking to Aveliad while looking at the dance floor.

"Who are the Mages speaking to Aveliad?" Madari asked Morvandis. "I believe one of them is named Kyaran, but who is the other?"

"They are Archimagus Kyaran, the Fourth Seat of the Mage Council, and Archimagus Lirielle, the Seventh Seat. They are the only Faeish representatives on the High Council."

Madari nodded at the reminder of their names and ranks and returned to watching his wife interact with the Faeish Powerborn.

If he hadn't been certain of what they were talking about before, the huge smile on Deirdre's face as she watched her brother would have been more than enough to confirm that the subject under discussion was Valeriad. For a moment, Madari was surprised that the two Fae would deign to speak with his wife, for even though she was a Queen to the humans, to the Fae, Aveliad was merely a half-breed and an object of disdain.

The Fae were known to be very adamant about the need to protect their heritage from contamination, and because Aveliad was a half-blood, many Fae—including many of her own family—refused to acknowledge her existence. Indeed, it was that very inability to accept "contamination" that had eventually driven Aveliad from her home among the Fae, and had forced her to seek out her human parent. When she finally found him, he had welcomed her with open arms, much to the consternation of his own family. To be sure, they had no problem with her mixed parentage . . . what they despised was her status as an elevated bastard.

From what Madari could tell, neither Kyaran nor Lirielle had any qualms whatsoever about speaking with Aveliad. At first he was surprised at this, but then he realized that members of the High Council of the Mage Citadel would be used to dealing with people of all races and creeds on a daily basis—including half-breeds—and, as such, they would have a much broader viewpoint than others of their race. Despite his smoldering anger with Aveliad, he was glad that she had found someone of her own race to whom she could talk. He toyed with the idea of joining the group and introducing himself, when a movement caught his eye. He turned to see what had captured his attention, and he frowned when he realized that the oldest daughter of King Orem, the disgraced Princess Tais, was moving toward the Ferralin group.

Tais awaited the permission of the aged Emperor of Ferralin to approach, and after receiving a curt nod, curtseyed low; not the polite curtsey of a noblewoman standing in her own home, but as a penitent seeking forgiveness. Madari's eyebrows climbed at that display of humility, for arrogance was the defining trait of the Illymari, and he glanced at Xan to see how he would react. A look of surprise crossed the old Emperor's face, and he gestured to her to rise. Madari was too far away from the group to hear what they were saying, but something about the way the Illymari Princess moved struck him as odd, and he couldn't quite put his finger on it. As if reading his thoughts, Morvandis spoke quietly into his ear.

"Her body language has altered, as have her movements. The differences are subtle, but quite clear, if you know what to look for. Princess Tais is emulating the movements and mannerisms of a Ferraline woman." He paused to watch her make a graceful gesture, and when she had completed it, Morvandis continued in tones of the deepest admiration. "Her representation is absolutely flawless."

Madari frowned in concentration, but try as he might, all he could see was that something about her was completely different than it had been just a few moments before. But one thing he did notice was the reaction she was receiving from the Ferralin contingent: they were responding to her almost against their will, and from the way their wary postures were beginning to relax, she had effortlessly put them completely at their ease. As Madari watched, the Emperor actually laughed at quiet words from the golden-haired Princess, and once the cool reserve had been breached amongst the delegation, other members began to surround her. After a few minutes of quiet conversation, punctuated with an occasional smile or laugh, Princess Tais curtseyed formally once again and gestured gracefully toward the place where her father was standing. Emperor Xan waited only a moment before allowing her to lead him to the Illymari contingent.

As the group moved towards King Orem, Princess Tais looked in Madari's direction and smiled at him when she caught his eye. It wasn't a mocking smile or one of triumph as he might have expected. Instead, it was a smile of acknowledgment, and Madari found himself returning it just as involuntarily as the Ferralin Emperor had. He raised a hand in salute, as he would have done to a particularly worthy adversary, and Tais closed her eyes and nodded elegantly in reply. After that, she returned her attention to the task at hand and provided an introduction between Emperor Xan and King Orem.

After formal introductions had been made, both monarchs began talking to each other in a very friendly manner, with Tais providing a clear bridge between them. Beside him, the second most powerful noble in the entire Kingdom of Dakkadia, Prince Brendenn DeVir of Palantine, whistled appreciatively.

"Now that is a formidable woman," he said. "The Emperor never stood a chance."

"This will be difficult to overcome," Morvandis said. "She may very well undo the damage she has already done to the alliance."

Madari watched the Emperor of Ferralin and the King of Illymar laugh perfectly naturally at a comment made by the Princess.

"She already has," Madari said thoughtfully.

As he watched Tais work her beguiling magic on everyone around her, he found himself wondering what she would be like in person. And as his eyes travelled down her body taking in every glorious curve, he also began wondering what she would be like in bed.

"She is indeed a formidable opponent," Madari continued, "and one I will not underestimate again." He turned to his Mage. "I want you to find out everything you can about her. *Everything.* I would like to know what I am up against."

Morvandis stepped away from the group silently, heading for the exit. As the Mage left to carry out his orders, Madari dismissed him from his consideration and turned once again toward the radiant Princess, now standing back from the two monarchs to allow them to speak. Though she wasn't looking, he saluted her one more time, and smiled.

Formidable indeed. I very much look forward to crossing swords with you again, Princess.

After leaving the party, Morvandis did not move toward the exit immediately. Instead, he remembered the invitation that King Orem had made to his guests, and his curiosity got the better of him. He approached a pair of guards in full dress regalia and said,

"I would like to view the Archon's artifacts."

One of the guards bowed formally.

"It would be my honor to escort you to the Hall of Zarryiosiad. If you will follow me?" Before Morvandis could follow the guard, however, a musical voice came from the doorway leading back to the party.

"That won't be necessary, guardsman. I would be delighted to escort Mage Morvandis to the Hall." Morvandis recognized the voice immediately, and he turned to see Archimagus Enaria Wintersong standing in the doorway, regarding him with a sultry smile on her face and a raised, questioning eyebrow. When he didn't reply immediately, she continued. "Unless you would prefer to be alone with your thoughts?" She turned slightly, as if to leave him alone, but Morvandis looked back at the guard.

"Thank you, guardsman, but it seems I have found an escort."

The guardsman returned to his duty station, and Morvandis turned his full attention back to his former teacher. A brief examination confirmed what he had already known would be the case; she hadn't changed at all in the 15 years since he had last seen her. He wondered briefly what she thought about the changes that he'd undergone in those years.

"Kyitsun a'djall elasora, Enaria N'jai. Yelsarya a'tellus kyalin."

Enaria's eyes widened at his words, and her smile widened noticeably as she returned his bow and answered his formal greeting in Elvish.

"Kyitsun a'djall telasora, Morvandis M'jai. Yelsaryan a'tellus kyalin syora." She switched back to Illymari Standard. "Your command of the Elven language does you great honor, Mage Morvandis." His greeting and his accent had been perfect, no small accomplishment for a human, especially because she knew that during his time as a student in Ithram he hadn't known how to speak a word of Elvish.

"I thank you for the compliment, but it seems now that I was wrong, for it is clear to me that time has left its mark upon you after all," he said, his tone uncharacteristically teasing. "I remember well that words of praise from you were few and far between, and were to be treasured all the more for their paucity."

"The Hall of Zarryiosiad is this way, Mage Morvandis. We can discuss the changes we have both undergone in the past 15 years along the way."

Despite her statement, Enaria was silent for the first part of the walk. Now that the pleasantries had been exchanged and compliments had been paid, she wasn't sure where she should lead the conversation next. She remembered how quiet and serious he had been as a boy, and decided that the direct approach was probably the way he would prefer things. "You caused quite a stir at the Convocation today, Morvandis. The Mage Council was awestruck by the sheer power you possess. Your resonance was overwhelming."

She waited for a reply, but Morvandis didn't answer. In fact, he acted as if she hadn't even spoken. She frowned slightly at his lack of response and decided to continue.

"With as much power as you hold, as well as your reputation for ambition, I must confess that I am surprised you are content to remain the advisor to the King of Dakkadia. I would have thought that you would aspire to greater power."

Morvandis did react to that. He turned his head slightly towards Enaria and gave her a disdainful look.

"What you truly wish to know is why I have not returned to Ithram and pressed a claim upon the Mage Citadel for a seat on the High Council."

Enaria was taken aback by his astringent tone, but she responded honestly.

"Yes, I do wonder about that. Why settle for being less than you are, Morvandis? You belong with us. In a few years, you could rule the Mage Council."

Morvandis returned his gaze to the hallway and shook his head in disagreement.

"I do not aspire to worldly power, Enaria, and I never did. You never understood that, even when I was your pupil. My loyalty lies with my King and my country, and I will never betray the trust they have shown me."

Enaria rounded on him and grabbed his arm.

"Why? Why do you continue to serve a lesser being when you could *rule*? You are so much more than he is, and you could be so much more than you are now."

Morvandis looked down at his former teacher and saw the naked ambition coursing through her eyes. He reached up with his right hand and touched her face in a gentle gesture, completely at odds with his flat expression, and her eyes widened at the intimacy of the touch. He leaned closer to her as if to kiss her, and as she looked into his eyes she felt herself being drawn in to their depths. Once he had ensnared her with his unblinking gaze, he spoke in a low voice meant only for her ears.

"You have forgotten your own lessons, teacher. 'True power does not have to be seen to be wielded.' You taught me that." He pointed back down the hall toward the Grand Ballroom and she reluctantly broke her gaze and followed the line of his finger. "You say I should aspire to greater power, that I could be more than I am. Tell me, Enaria N'Jai, who is the more powerful? The man trapped by his station, surrounded by sycophants and toadies, completely unable to act because all eyes are upon him watching his every move? Or the man who is content to serve, knowing that by doing so, he ensures his own freedom to act as he sees fit?" He lowered his arm and caught her gaze once again with his own tilted eyes. "I do exactly what I want to do, Enaria, when I want to do it. I know better than all of you how powerful I am, and I don't need a title or a crown to prove it, nor do I need you to remind me of it. You claim that in a few years I could rule the Mage Council. Why would I want that? What power do you hold that I should aspire to, Councillor? What can *any* of you offer me that I would actually want? I can think of nothing, and by that same token, I can think of nothing that any of you has left to teach me. Only one person has anything left for me to learn, and she has been dead for 2,500 years."

Enaria's eyes narrowed at the realization that Morvandis was studying the Archon and her works for the exactly the same reasons she herself was. Power.

Morvandis eyed her for a moment, awaiting her response, but when none came he simply turned back down the hall and began walking again, uncaring if his former teacher followed him or not. Enaria shook herself to regain her composure, and after the shock wore off, she rushed after him. When she caught up with him, he didn't look at her, he simply kept his attention focused at some spot down the hall.

"I had not thought of things in that way, Morvandis, and I thank you for enlightening me. But allow me to say this: while you are correct in saying that there are many kinds of power, with a crown—or a position as a High Councillor for that matter—you gain a different type of power: the power of prestige. This does not sound like much at first, but know this; I have been studying the Archon and her works for almost three hundred years, and as a High Councillor, I have a power that you do not: access. As just one example, I have been in this hall countless times before to view the artifacts of the Archon, and the King of Illymar welcomes me back every time. You have yet to see this hall, and that is because you have chosen not to avail yourself of the privileges rank can bring. That is your choice, of course, but if you truly wish to study the Archon, you need the access that respectability will bring you."

"The advantages of which you speak come with too high a price, Enaria. For every hour you spend studying these artifacts, countless days are wasted in useless councils and meetings, where important matters are discussed but nothing is ever decided. No, Archimagus, I prefer to do things my way."

Morvandis fell silent again, and this time Enaria respected his feelings. After a quiet walk through silent corridors, they came to a room protected by two guards standing to either side of an ornately carved door. At the sight of the two Mages, the guards turned as one and opened the doors, allowing Enaria and Morvandis to enter the Hall of Zarryiosiad.

From the first step into the room, Enaria knew that Morvandis was absolutely transfixed by the display. Dozens of artifacts lined the room, displayed in glass cases or sitting on marble pedestals, all with elaborate plaques explaining what they had been used for. Morvandis didn't even spare these minor items a glance, for his complete attention was drawn to the most impressive piece in the collection. At the back of the room sat an immense throne, created from a single piece of black obsidian and decorated with exquisitely rendered carvings of creatures of all shapes and sizes. The most prominent of these carvings were the armrests; designed to be two roaring lions looking down at anyone standing before the Throne. As if drawn to it, Morvandis began walking toward the monolithic stone seat.

When he stood before the artistic masterpiece he stopped, unsure if he was allowed to touch it.

"It is quite alright to sit upon the Throne of Obsidian, Morvandis," Enaria said. "Zarryiosiad herself created it, and like all of her creations, it cannot be damaged by mere mortals."

Morvandis didn't need to be told twice. He touched one of the armrests lovingly, before turning around and seating himself on the stone seat. As he placed his hands on the armrests, he closed his eyes in concentration. Enaria leaned forward anxiously, desperately wondering what Morvandis was feeling.

"The resonance echoing through this seat is incredible, and from the feel of it, it was created for a specific purpose, but the power rests. The Throne is asleep."

Enaria licked her lips as Morvandis spoke, hoping that with his greater ability he would be able to decipher that hidden purpose, but to her disappointment, he merely stood up and stepped away from the seat without elaborating any further. As he moved off the raised dais that the throne sat upon, he glanced at it one last time before returning his attention to the rest of the displays. Enaria frowned at him in consternation, but he didn't seem to notice as he walked around studying the other artifacts, one after the other. But, no matter how closely he scrutinized the artifacts, he didn't touch anything, and perhaps even more frustrating from Enaria's perspective, he didn't say a word.

Once he finished examining the last of the artifacts, he turned back to Enaria and nodded.

"I think I have seen enough for one evening, and I have an errand I must complete. The collection is exquisite, but I would have thought that there would have been more artifacts in the collection. After all, the Illvanin family can trace their lineage in an unbroken line all the way back to the Archon herself."

"Most of the artifacts once housed in the Spire have been donated to the Zarryiostrom over the last 2,500 years," Enaria said. "What you see here are many of Zarryiosiad's most private belongings. Their value to the Zarryiostrom is incalculable, but even the priesthood must admit that the collection is in excellent hands."

Morvandis simply nodded at the explanation and stepped toward the door, clearly intending to leave. Before he could reach it, however, Enaria stepped in front of him and crossed her arms over her chest.

"I account myself an expert on the Archon, and my research has led me to several interesting bits of information, one of which concerns the Throne of Obsidian. It is said, that when the Archon sat upon the Throne, her power could be felt throughout the land. Tell me, what did you feel when you sat in her place?"

Morvandis looked back at the Throne once again, and his eyes seemed to caress the perfectly smooth surfaces as he took in every detail.

"As I told you, I felt her resonance echoing through the Throne." He gave her a calculating look, as if judging whether or not he should say something else, before speaking again. "I felt exactly the same resonance from the Teeth of Amhar as we sailed here to Illymar."

"Do you think they are somehow connected?" Enaria asked, surprised at the possibility.

Morvandis gave her a level look, and much to her dismay, Enaria found that his expression was completely impossible for her to decipher.

"Who can say? If there is a secret to the Throne, it seems to have been lost to history. Perhaps you, with your access and your power of prestige, can discover that secret."

He reached for the door handle, and this time Enaria let him pass unhindered. As he opened the door, he stepped aside to allow her to pass through first. Lost in thought, she walked through the doorway and passed the guards, but a sudden thought occurred to her and she turned around to ask him another question, only to find him looking back at the Archon's seat of power.

As she watched him staring at the Throne, she saw a hunger in his eyes that somehow slipped past the mask he wore, and she knew then that he was hiding something from her. She whirled back around to keep him from noticing her watching him, but even as he closed the door and rejoined her, her mind fixated on a single thought.

He knows more than he's telling me. I must find out what he knows.

CHAPTER THIRTEEN

"Uninvited"

Princess Lyrahe Illvanna picked at her breakfast in a halfhearted fashion, but found that she didn't have an appetite. The food itself was perfectly prepared and presented, but she was far too miserable to appreciate the effort the cooks and servants had put into it. The reason for her depression was apparent every time she saw her father's face; for he was the happiest she had seen him in over a year. He cheerfully joked with the members of his family, and he had even asked—not commanded—his children to attend breakfast with him. And to everyone's surprise, that invitation had included Tais.

An interesting change, Lyrahe noted, for it seemed that her father had completely forgiven his oldest daughter for her crimes, and he genuinely seemed to want to make a fresh start of things with her. It wouldn't work, for Lyrahe knew her siblings very well. In fact, she had always been the best at reading her family's faces, and though Tais tried to hide it, Lyrahe could tell that she was merely going through the motions with their father. King Orem seemed oblivious, but Tais kept a carefully guarded expression on her face that Lyrahe could see right through, and because of this, she knew something her father didn't know: Tais had no intention of ever letting down her guard with him again. That was beside the point, however, and Lyrahe allowed herself to remember the previous evening's events . . . as well as the aftermath. For hours, she had danced with the man of her dreams, and time had seemed to fly by for them. Eventually, however, the hour became too late for dancing, and they had reluctantly stopped. At a signal from his father, Valeriad had told her that his family was retiring for the evening, and that he hoped to dance with her again at the ball following the second day of the Convocation. She had fallen all over herself agreeing to see him again, and she had been the happiest she could ever remember being, until she had seen her father.

King Orem hadn't been looking at her at all; he'd been speaking with Emperor Xan and his son, Lain, and seeing the two of them together brought Ethan's words back to her like a death sentence; *Now that Tais has shown her true nature, like the slattern she is, you, sister dear, have to take her place. Father and Mother are going to try and make you marry Prince Lain, in order to buy us an ally against Dakkadia . . . assuming he'll even have a lesser daughter.*

She had been too caught up enjoying herself with Prince Valeriad to notice what was happening around her, and she cursed herself for her stupidity. The look on her father's face had told her instantly that the discussion was going very well, but it was the look on Tais's face that had made her blood turn cold. Tais had looked up, and when she caught her eye, the one overriding emotion Lyrahe could see on her sister's face was *pity.*

Her father had looked up then, and he, too, caught Lyrahe's eyes. When he was sure that he had her attention, he smiled broadly and gestured to her to join the informal group. Lyrahe had instantly obeyed, her face automatically smoothing itself into a pleasant mask. She walked as gracefully as she could, all the while feeling as if she was a condemned woman walking to a gallows, and when she had joined the group, her traitor knees had nearly buckled during her formal curtsey. Thankfully, no one noticed, or if they had, the Ferraline were polite enough not to mention it to her. The conversation had been brief, but it was clear from the questions that Emperor Xan was trying to form an impression of her.

Again, Ethan's words came back to haunt her, *Don't fool yourself: every time they look at you they are going to be wondering if you are anything at all like Tais, and deciding whether or not you are worthy of one day becoming their Empress.* Lyrahe couldn't remember any part of the conversation with the Emperor, but she remembered quite clearly her introduction to Crown Prince Lain. He had been perfectly polite, and quite charming, she supposed, but almost immediately, she had begun making comparisons between Prince Lain and Prince Valeriad, and as far as she was concerned, compared to the gallant Prince of Dakkadia, the Prince of Ferralin would never measure up.

The two groups had remained together for a little longer, with Emperor Xan and King Orem parting on friendly terms and the two monarchs agreeing to begin formal talks in the near future, but Lyrahe wasn't listening. She turned back to look at where the Dakkadian entourage had assembled and saw her Prince smile at her. She desperately wanted to go to him, but standing next to both her father and the man she would most likely marry, she knew she couldn't. So she merely inclined her head slightly in polite acknowledgment, and returned her attention to her father . . . turning her back upon Prince Valeriad.

When the party ended, and the groups had returned to their own villas, a stern-faced King Orem had taken her aside and spoken to her.

"Emperor Xan is amenable to a marriage between you and his son, Lain, a marriage this kingdom needs very badly indeed. I allowed you to dance with Prince Valeriad to send a message to Xan, but now that formal negotiations are beginning, it is a message that is no longer needed or wanted. Therefore, I am forbidding you to socialize with Prince Valeriad, or to even speak with him again, without a chaperone present. Disobey me, and you will find that the prison cell that held your sister will hold you just as easily."

The threat of imprisonment was likely a hollow one, for her father had already admitted to her that the kingdom needed the marriage very badly, but again, Ethan's words returned to her with perfect clarity, *You'd better hope that they see something worthwhile in you, because if they do decide you are like Tais, you'll be lucky if they let you become a concubine.* She knew that the next few days were critical. Every aspect of her character would be scrutinized by Emperor Xan. If she failed to measure up to his standards in any respect whatsoever, the marriage would not take place. And the threat her father had made to her would most assuredly become all-too real. Lyrahe knew that she had no choice but to obey her father, and she would. Still, she found herself once again thinking about her perfect evening with Prince Valeriad, and hoping against hope that somehow they could one day find some way to be together.

Chesare watched Lyrahe pick at her food and tried hard to think of something that would raise her spirits. She didn't know exactly what was bothering her sister, but whatever it was, Chesare knew that it was bad. It was strange, for Lyrahe had been on top of the world the night before, but this morning she was acting as if she hadn't just met the man of her dreams. In fact, she was acting more and more like the world was about to end. As Lyrahe moved her food around her plate pretending to eat, Chesare decided to try and find something to lighten her mood.

"I think last night's ball was a tremendous success. It looked to me like everyone enjoyed themselves immensely." She gave Lyrahe a sideways look, hoping for a response, and then pressed on. "Lyrahe, you and Prince Valeriad were simply splendid on the dance floor. You moved so well together! And sharing every dance like that. You were the talk of the ball!"

She turned her head to look at Lyrahe directly, but to her surprise, Lyrahe didn't brighten up at the mention of Prince Valeriad. Quite the opposite actually, for Lyrahe's mood seemed to darken even further. Confused, she glanced around the table at her family to see what she had said wrong. Her first clue that she had made things worse was the look on Ethan's face. He was giving Lyrahe a smug smile, completely at odds with what Chesare had said. She glanced at Tais, and Tais shot her a quelling look. *What is going on?*

As if reading her mind, her father spoke,

"There will be no more talk of Prince Valeriad or last evening, Chesare. I have begun formal negotiations with Emperor Xan to arrange a marriage between Lyrahe and Lain, and I have forbidden Lyrahe from seeing or speaking with Prince Valeriad again."

Chesare gasped in surprise and turned to look at Lyrahe, who seemed ready to wilt in misery. That explained everything, from the pleased look on their parents' faces, to the triumph on Ethan's face . . . and most especially the misery on Lyrahe's. Chesare returned her attention to her own plate, desperately searching for something that would undo the damage she had just done, when a thought came to her. Suppressing a smile, she looked back up at Lyrahe.

"I'm so sorry to hear that, Lyrahe. I'm certain Prince Lain will make a fine husband, once you get to know him. But I'm also sure you are not ready to hear that just yet, so I have an idea. Next week, I will be returning to the Mage Citadel to resume my training. Why don't you come and visit me there? I'd love to give you a tour, and to let you meet my friends."

Lyrahe looked up from her plate and gave her a disinterested look.

"That sounds nice," she said in a deadened tone.

Lyrahe certainly can be dense sometimes! Chesare thought.

"Good, then!" She said aloud, "I'll arrange everything. I can't wait until you meet Halo—that's Asiria, our librarian—and all of the other students." She caught Lyrahe's eye and winked. "It's such an exciting place! Why, you never know who's going to show up there."

Lyrahe gave her a confused look at the non sequitur, and all at once her expression brightened as she obviously remembered what Valeriad had said the previous evening. *Next week, my half-brother, Phaedron, and I will be going to the Citadel for Testing.*

"Tonight you will be seen with Prince Lain," Orem said to Lyrahe, "so you are to look your best. Both the dinner and the gathering that follows it will be informal, but you will treat it as it is: a matter of State."

Lyrahe's smile wilted, but she inclined her head slightly in acquiescence and returned her attention to her breakfast. The dour expression remained on her face for only a few moments, however, as she began thinking about her upcoming visit to the Mage Citadel . . . and a possible clandestine meeting with a certain young Prince. Chesare smiled at Lyrahe one more time, and returned her attention to her own breakfast.

Madari had just finished applying lather to his face when a single knock at his door caught his attention. He picked up his razor and barked, "Enter!" before he began carefully scraping away the morning's stubble. He didn't even glance at the door to see who his visitor was, for only one person knocked on his door that way: Morvandis. Madari had been expecting him, for he knew Morvandis would come bearing the morning report.

"What have you found out?"

Morvandis's reflection stepped into the mirror where Madari could see him and bowed slightly. Before speaking, however, Morvandis's eyes turned a glowing azure, and suddenly the water in the basin before Madari began to steam.

"It seems that *Princess* Tais has had a very interesting year," Morvandis said, once the water had been properly heated. "We knew some of what happened when the negotiations ended between Ferralin and Illymar, but my spies have filled in the gaps to the story quite thoroughly. About a year-and-a-half ago, Tais and her family attended a tournament that Prince Ethan had entered, where apparently, she met and fell in love with a young Earl named Markus Danshire; a noble of very modest means but great skill with a sword. The Earl won the tournament, and spent the weeks following it wooing the Princess, who had already been betrothed to the Prince of Ferralin. Eventually, the two ran away together and her father sent Prince Ethan to retrieve her. This he did, and in the doing had Danshire killed, but not before the two were wed. And during this time, Tais apparently conceived a child."

At that, Madari whirled in surprise to look at Morvandis, but Morvandis met his gaze levelly.

"You're not serious?!"

Morvandis smiled very slightly, which for anyone else would have been the equivalent of peals of laughter.

"Of course, Your Majesty. The reports are quite clear. It would appear that the child did not survive, but I am seeking confirmation of this fact through my sources. The physician who treated the Princess during her pregnancy has disappeared, which indicates to me that her family had him eliminated to cover up the potential scandal. Upon her return to Illymaine, Tais was imprisoned in the Tower and kept in complete isolation for a year. She was released only two weeks ago, and not by King Orem's order. My spies are unclear about this, but it would seem that Queen Althea is the one responsible for her release."

"You emphasized her title when you began the report. Was there a reason for this?"

"Yes, Your Majesty. While King Orem had Earl Danshire killed and his daughter returned to the capital to be punished, it is very clear that the two were married legally, under the auspices of a Dracon of the Zarryiostrom. As such, from the moment she took her marital vows, she would have ceased being *Princess* Tais and instead become *Countess* Danshire."

Madari frowned at that and, after a moment's reflection, he shook his head in disagreement.

"The first thing King Orem would have done upon her return would have been to disavow the marriage. Danshire's execution as a traitor and the disbursement of his title to another would have ended her claim to the title of Countess anyway, but that doesn't matter, because as far as the monarchy is concerned, the marriage never happened."

"The Zarryiostrom does not recognize the power of a sitting monarch to end a marriage. That power belongs solely to the members of the Church, and to date, they have not been consulted on Princess Tais's current status."

Madari didn't respond, but he considered the implications of Tais's rank carefully. He knew Morvandis believed that he could use this issue to cause tension between Illymar and the Zarryiostrom, but Madari didn't necessarily agree, for the Zarryiostrom had never attempted to force an issue with a sitting ruler. The priesthood always took the long view, and whenever possible, they much preferred to acquiesce to preserve peace, hoping that the ruler—or his successor—would eventually come to see things from their perspective. Still, the idea did have some potential merit, for Madari knew that a successful invasion of Illymar would require not only the defeat of the army and the navy of Illymar, it would require that the Mage Citadel and the Zarryiostrom be kept out of the conflict . . . not an easy task considering their ironclad mutual defense treaties.

But that was for another day, for what truly interested Madari about Tais's nebulous status was much more personal. Following the party, the Dakkadian contingent had returned to their villa, and despite Aveliad's dire predictions of that morning, Madari had gone straight to his chambers without inviting his wife to join him. He knew that she had expected him to "force himself upon her," but he had been far too preoccupied with thoughts of the golden-haired Princess to care what Aveliad believed. Aveliad had made her position crystal clear, and one more night with her didn't appeal to him in the slightest. Once he had returned to his room, he had thought about Tais for a long time, but by the time he had gone to sleep, he had concluded that there was no way he could pursue her without causing a diplomatic incident. So, despite his growing infatuation, he had resolved to keep his eyes—and hands—off of her. After all, one simply did not do such things with a Royal Princess.

Morvandis's report changed that, however. True, attempting to bed Tais, the *Royal Princess,* was reprehensible. But, having an affair with *Lady Danshire,* the widow of the Earl of Danshire, was perfectly acceptable . . . so long as any affair between them remained discreet. Madari didn't care what his wife would think, but a potential scandal would be detrimental to the goals he hoped to achieve at the Convocation. Still, the more that he thought about it, the more he came to believe that she would actually welcome his attentions. Oh, he had no doubt that she would be a difficult conquest, but she was not only a widow, she had been imprisoned for a year besides. And even better, up until her actions to unite the Ferraline and Illymari contingents the night before, she had been a social pariah; someone too tainted to even speak to, let alone be associated with. He smiled to himself. Yes, she would probably welcome the company. And if pleasant company should lead to *more*, well, he would just have to see. He finished shaving and washed the remaining lather from his face.

"That is certainly interesting news, Morvandis, and I compliment you and your network for assembling such a complete report. Now, is there anything else I should know about?"

As he spoke, he reached for a tray containing the light breakfast he preferred, and picked up a mug of strong black tea. As he took a sip from the mug, he glanced up at Morvandis and saw something he wasn't accustomed to seeing on Morvandis's face: uncertainty. Madari took a second sip from his mug to allow Morvandis time to collect his thoughts.

"Last night I made a discovery that may allow us access to Illymar through any point in the Teeth of Amhar."

The sound of the mug shattering on the marble floor was deafening.

As King Orem took his seat in the Cathedral, he glanced over at Emperor Xan and nodded a friendly greeting, which the aged Emperor acknowledged with his own polite nod. Thanks in no small part to Tais' efforts, Orem had made incredible headway with the Ferraline delegation during the previous evening, and he couldn't wait for the second round of talks to begin. He turned his attention to the Dakkadian assemblage and regarded King Madari as well, and seeing him brought a self-satisfied smile to his face. Orem had yet to speak with Madari in anything other than polite formality, and that would be the way it would remain if he had his way.

As he stared at the barbarian masquerading as a king, he wondered what the man was thinking, for he had seemed distracted all morning.

Probably wondering how he can sabotage the talks, the warmonger. Well, it won't matter what he's thinking soon enough.

Orem hadn't mentioned his plans to anyone else, even Althea, but he intended to offer Lyrahe's hand to Lain the very second the negotiations concluded, and he would push to have the wedding ceremony concluded before the end of the Convocation. That wouldn't allow much time for planning, but that was a problem for other people to worry over. Xan might protest, but even he would have to agree that having the ceremony in front of the assembled royalty of three countries would be an auspicious beginning for the union. His eyes hardened as he considered the Dakkadian King. *And once we've set a date for the wedding, I'll write the invitation to Madari myself, may he choke on it.*

So caught up was he in pleasant daydreams of his daughter's impending nuptials, that he didn't notice when someone took the seat to his immediate left. He was still daydreaming when he heard a voice that shattered his pleasant reverie into oblivion.

"He looks more dangerous in person, doesn't he? No matter how well-tailored his clothing may be he can't disguise his true nature . . . or his ambition. Can he, Your Majesty?"

Orem's face turned purple in rage when he recognized his brother, Ascham's, voice, and he whipped around in anger to face him. It took all of his self-control to keep from screaming at the Duke of Saerce, but a quick look around him told him that this was neither the time nor the place to start a row; a fact that Orem knew Ascham was counting on when he decided to show up in the first place.

"You would know all about that, wouldn't you, *Your Grace*, for you and he have much in common," Orem said, his anger naked before Ascham. "Ambition is your defining trait."

Ascham returned his brother's heated glare with one of supreme indifference.

"Please. Do not lump me in with that barbarian. I am ambitious, I'll admit, but I have never been a threat to you, and I am most certainly not a threat to our neighbors."

Orem grunted at that and turned his attention to the dais, where Patriarch Varic had yet to appear.

"Not a threat to me or my kingdom, are you?" Orem said, never moving his eyes from the dais. "My informants tell a different story. You have quite an army ready to follow you should you so much as crook your finger. What enemy do you propose to unleash your horde upon, I wonder? I see no enemy around us." He involuntarily glanced at Madari's profile and amended himself. "Or rather, I see no enemy around us who requires a land-based army to fight."

Ascham's look of indifference didn't alter in the slightest at the revelation that Orem knew about his supporters and his military buildup.

"I am merely preparing for the inevitable war with Dakkadia," Ascham said. "Something you yourself should have been doing for years. Now that your negotiations with the Ferraline have fallen through, we are vulnerable. One of us has to take steps to defend Illymar, and since you refuse to do it, the duty falls to me."

Ascham clearly expected Orem to explode at that, but instead, the self-satisfied smile returned to Orem's face.

"Oh, that's right!" Orem said, clearly mocking Ascham. "You didn't attend the dinner last night, or the party afterwards, so you wouldn't know." His voice trailed off suggestively.

"Know what, exactly?" asked Ascham.

"You wouldn't know that last night, Emperor Xan and I were able to come to a preliminary agreement concerning a marriage between Crown Prince Lain and my daughter, Lyrahe."

Ascham's eyes opened wide and his eyebrows shot up almost to his hairline at the news, and Orem took great glee in the knowledge that he had just set his brother's ambitions on its ears. Orem pressed his advantage.

"Xan understands that Dakkadia poses a threat to both of our countries, and only by standing together, do we hope to keep Dakkadia at bay. Therefore, Xan has agreed, in theory, to allow his son to wed Lyrahe under the same terms that we had arranged for Tais. So you see, your self-imposed duty is neither needed nor wanted, and it makes me happier than you could possibly know that you decided to attend the Convocation uninvited so I could tell you that in person."

Ascham didn't speak for several moments, obviously struggling to come to grips with these unexpected revelations.

"When will the wedding take place?"

"That has yet to be determined. I'm confident that the two of us will set a date for the ceremony within a few days' time. You will, of course, be invited, and I believe that a suitable wedding gift from you would be the complete disbanding of your army. I think we can both agree that its existence will no longer be necessary."

Ascham snorted and crossed his arms over his chest before turning his own gaze toward the dais. The first of the Archidraconi had begun filing onto the dais to begin the services.

"That remains to be seen, Your Majesty. For myself, I will withhold judgment until they are safely married. After all, I would hate for another mishap to occur like that unfortunate business between Tais and Markus Danshire. I sincerely doubt Xan would be so forgiving a second time."

"Don't be so sure, Ascham. My youngest daughter is a Powerborn, which makes her worth more than both Tais and Lyrahe put together. If it comes to it, I would give up even as precious an advantage as my Powerborn daughter to secure this alliance." He dropped his arms to his sides and his voice filled with conviction. "It doesn't matter. This marriage will happen, as will the alliance." He glanced one final time at Madari and said quietly, "This is too important to Illymar for me to fail."

These Illymari do enjoy dining, thought the Corsair, *No wonder their ships are so easy to capture . . . they are probably too busy planning their next meal to put up a proper defense.* The thought brought a smile to her face, and she glanced at Phaedron and caught his eye. When she was sure that she had his attention, she rolled her eyes in an elaborate display of disgust directed at her host, and his eyes flashed a matching look, before they each returned their attention to the serious business of eating lunch.

It wasn't the food that they found amusing, for as with any meal in Illymar, it was perfectly prepared and presented. No, her disgust was centered firmly on their host, who had been adamant that any business they had to discuss with each other would have to wait until after they had dined. That had sounded fine to Prudence, until she had realized that lunch to the Admiral had meant a formal seven-course event. By the third setting, both she and Phaedron had begun politely declining any further servings . . . which hadn't bothered Admiral Savonne—or his appetite—in the slightest. As serving after serving disappeared from his plate, Prudence had begun wondering where in the world the food was disappearing to, for the Admiral wasn't fat.

Well, he isn't fat yet, but then he is very young for his rank. I have no doubt whatsoever, that if he continues to eat the way he is now, he will eventually become as large as a frigate.

As the minutes rolled by, the only sound in the room was the occasional crunch of some delicacy or another being consumed by the Admiral. Prudence's patience began to wear thin, and to combat her boredom, she took the opportunity Savonne's feasting presented her to study her surroundings.

The building that housed the Admiralty was a beautiful structure, with several defensive fortifications surrounding it to provide it with some measure of protection. She hadn't seen much of the interior, but what she had seen had been quite beautiful, with tasteful displays and decorations placed everywhere . . . all meant to impress guests with the importance of the people the building housed. Even the dining room in which they were sitting was filled with elaborate displays, including several oil paintings celebrating different victories won throughout the illustrious career of the Illymari navy. She took a sip of water to hide another smile as she thought about the unending series of drubbings she herself had handed to the Kingdom of Illymar, and wondered if there would be any paintings of her on the walls one day. *Probably not,* she thought. *They would have to defeat me first.*

Eventually the meal came to an end, and the Admiral waited for the dishes to be cleared before dismissing his stewards. When the room was empty save the Admiral, his adjutant, Phaedron, and herself, Admiral Savonne finally broke the silence.

"I suppose you are wondering why I asked you here today, Lady Prudence." The words were a statement, but he looked at her as if expecting an answer, so she obliged him.

"I will gladly admit to my curiosity, Admiral. We both know that lowly privateers, such as I, are rarely invited to dine with the Commander of an entire navy."

"Quite so, though your modesty does do you credit," Savonne said. "We are both well aware that you are more than just a 'lowly privateer'. Your successes against the Illymari navy have made you quite the heroine to the masses. Bards sing your praises everywhere they go, playing up your heroics as great victories . . . no matter how much less heroic the truth might actually be, or how exaggerated the tales may have grown in the telling."

Phaedron frowned at the insult but didn't speak, despite an obvious desire to defend her reputation from the assault.

"I have no control over the tales of bards, here or anywhere else," Prudence replied. "As you well know, I spend almost all of my time at sea capturing prizes.

But then, while there may be *some* exaggeration in those tales, no one doubts my skill as either a warrior . . . or a sailor."

The riposte hit home with a vengeance, for the untried Admiral had received his commission for his relation to the Queen, and not for any skill he possessed as either a warrior or a sailor. In fact, as far as Prudence had been able to learn, Savonne had never practiced actual command of a ship at sea, let alone a flotilla or armada. Her sailors had learned much at the taverns around Illymar, and many of them had brought back stories of the "Bathtub Admiral;" a nickname Lucas Savonne had earned because, supposedly, the only ships he had ever personally commanded were the toys that floated in his bathtub. She rather doubted that was the case, but then, his inexperience was as obvious to her as her competence was to him. "I do not believe you asked me here to trade barbs, Admiral. So what exactly can I do for you?"

"I asked you here to persuade you to cease your blatantly illegal attacks upon our shipping." He held up his hand in a placating manner before she could speak and said, "I am well aware you hold a Letter of Marque that gives you the shred of legitimacy under which you operate, but believe me when I say that that piece of paper is all that protects you from a hangman's noose. The Illymari navy, and His Majesty the King, take a dim view on piracy . . . even piracy that shelters behind specious legalisms."

"I find it very amusing that the Illymari navy and His Majesty the King would suddenly take such a dim view on privateering," Prudence said, "Especially since it is a practice the Illymari navy invented over four centuries ago, and continued to use until only three years ago, when I personally hunted down and sank the last privateer who dared to fly Illymari colors." She leaned back in her chair and crossed her fingers over her stomach in a very satisfied gesture. "I remember that engagement very well indeed. I was quite disappointed that the *Sea Lion* didn't put up more of a fight before I sent her to the bottom."

The Admiral's eyes flashed in anger at her words, but the anger in the Corsair's own green eyes easily matched his in intensity.

"The actions of the previous Admiralty have no bearing on the navy under my own command," Savonne said. "I have already recommended to His Majesty that we no longer recognize Letters of Marque as a legal document, and that we finally recognize privateers as exactly what they are: bloody-handed pirates. When he agrees with my proposal—as I am certain he will—the Age of the Privateer will be thrown into the dustbin of history as the unneeded relic it is."

Prudence laughed sharply at that, and the anger in her eyes instantly transformed into amusement.

"I wish both you and your King good fortune in that endeavor, Admiral, for I can guarantee that no other country will listen to your useless prattle. You see, too many countries have had problems with privateers in the past—especially privateers flying your colors and bearing your Letters of Marque—for anyone else to care what you or your King decides is legal or illegal. In fact, even if the Illymari navy unilaterally decides to outlaw privateering, Letters of Marque are filed with the Zarryiostrom as a neutral party, and they—not you—decide the status of a privateer. No, Admiral, you can't just take your toys home with you when you start to lose a game. That would be unsporting."

The not-so-veiled reference to his nickname turned his face bright red with anger, and he slammed both of his hands down on the table in fury.

"You think this is a game?" Savonne asked, shouting. "This is no joking matter, Lady Prudence! Your harassment of our shipping will stop, one way or another! How your career—and your life—ends is up to you." After his outburst, his anger visibly lowered and he settled back in his chair. His voice became silky smooth, and a sly look appeared on his face, which raised the hackles on the back of Prudence's neck. "I apologize for that unseemly outburst, Lady Prudence. I have something of a reputation for hotheadedness, as you can see. But we seem to have strayed from the subject at hand. The reason I asked you to meet with me is to convey an offer . . . one I would highly recommend you accept. His Majesty recognizes that you, Lady Prudence, are the single biggest threat our navy currently faces, and is prepared to be very generous to you should you agree to turn your sights on other prey. *Very* generous, indeed."

The Admiral's sudden change of tactics surprised her, but then, knowing the Admiral's background as a merchant, she had come to the meeting expecting a bribe attempt. Prudence assumed a look of avarice and leaned forward in her chair, placing her elbows on the table with her fingers entwined.

"Just how generous are we talking, Lord High Admiral? As you can no doubt tell, I have very expensive tastes."

Next to her she could almost hear Phaedron blink, but she didn't let any of her amusement show on her deadly serious expression. Admiral Savonne hesitated, obviously sensing a trap, but his eyes were involuntarily drawn to her elaborately tailored and embroidered clothing, whose expensive cut was readily apparent to his merchant's eye, as well as to the delicate lace falling from her neck and wrists. She could tell that he was trying to convince himself of her sincerity and of her *expensive tastes*, and it didn't take him long to come to the very conclusion she had wanted him to draw when she had selected her apparel, with malice aforethought, from the piles of useless clothing her brother had given her.

"I see that you do, Lady Prudence." He glanced at his adjutant before continuing. "You are no doubt aware that the Kingdom has a ready source of income, from which we bring in regular shipments of precious metals and gems. I know you are aware of this because you have succeeded in capturing two of these shipments: one aboard the *Kingsland*, and the other aboard the *Seraph*. The capture of these ships was very . . . *annoying* to the Kingdom, but believe me when I say that there is plenty more where that came from. Should you agree to seek your prey in different waters, we are prepared to offer you one out of every twenty of these shipments, to be delivered to the port of your choice. We would simply transship the cargo to you, with no risk to either you, or your crew, at all. All you would have to do is collect your prize with my thanks, and the thanks of the Kingdom of Illymar."

Prudence steepled her fingers in front of her and considered the offer Savonne had just made to her. The prizes aboard both the *Seraph* and the *Kingsland* had been beyond reason, and her cut of the prize money from just one of those ships had been more than enough to allow her to live out the rest of her days in luxury . . . had that indeed been her goal. She had always wondered about the source of that wealth, for the ships had sailed from the open seas, far beyond the normal boundaries that ships kept to, and as far as Prudence knew, nothing existed in that direction except an endless, unbroken expanse of ocean.

The captains and officers of both ships had died in the fighting, and none of the surviving crewmembers could or would tell her where the gold had come from. But from the absolute certainty in his voice, his estimation of the amount of wealth available in this secret location wasn't a mere exaggeration. But then if it wasn't, losing the occasional shipment shouldn't matter at all to them. As he himself had said, it was simply an annoyance. So why buy her off? Suddenly, one detail of the deal he had proposed came back to her. He had specifically mentioned that they would give her one out of every twenty *shipments*. He had made no mention whatsoever about the ships themselves.

"When these shipments arrive at the port of my choice, I assume that I would keep the ships as well as the shipments? It may look suspicious otherwise."

Savonne's aide stiffened at that, which told her exactly what she needed to know, but she didn't allow any trace of triumph to show on her face or in her body language. She kept her attention firmly on Savonne and awaited the answer she knew he would give. He didn't disappoint her.

"Of course not, Lady Prudence. The Royal Navy needs every ship it has, as well as every ship it can build. We are willing to sacrifice shipments to mitigate the damage you are doing to our fleet, but the ships themselves are out of the question."

Prudence smiled at that, for Lucas had just told her everything she needed to know. It wasn't the money they were afraid to lose: it was the ships. Savonne hadn't been bluffing about the ease of which the money could be obtained or replaced, but the loss of a ship would be felt keenly, for Illymar had only a limited number of trained shipwrights and building slips. It didn't matter how much money one had if they could only build a handful of ships at a time. And perhaps even worse for Illymar, the capture of a ship actively strengthened the one threat Illymar faced, for Dakkadia routinely bought every hull she captured, no matter how damaged, and refitted every single one with modern weapons before putting them into service against their former kingdom.

No wonder they are willing to bid so heavily for my complicity: they still don't have a counter to our new weapons, and they are hemorrhaging ships. So long as we continue to capture ships faster than they can replace them, we make the threat of a Dakkadian invasion that much more of a reality.

She pushed her seat back and stood up abruptly, and though she had surprised them, all three men rushed to stand with her.

"I think I have heard enough. If you would be so kind as to provide an escort, we will be departing immediately."

Savonne blinked in surprise at her words, completely at a loss to understand her intent. He didn't respond instantly, trying to buy himself time to think.

"Ah, of course, Lady Prudence," he said. "Ah, do we have an accord?"

"We do not have an accord, sir," Prudence said in an icy tone, "And the only thing keeping me from challenging you to a duel right here and now over your slight to my honor, is the Peace of Zarryiosiad that both of our kingdoms agreed to before we arrived for the Convocation. But nothing in that agreement entitles you to impugn my honor with threats or clumsy bribe attempts, nor does it require that I sit here and listen to them for one instant longer. You have made your position on privateers quite clear to me, Admiral, as well as how low you are willing to stoop to make us disappear. If you truly want to stop privateering as you say you do, the means are simple: put down your fork, pick up your cutlass, and come after me yourself. You claim I am hiding behind 'specious legalisms', but you are the one who seeks to end the practice of privateering with the pen and not the sword. I promise you this: the only way you will ever stop me will be to defeat me, and to do that, you will have to leave the safety of this compound and put yourself in harm's way."

She turned her back on the Admiral and began walking to the door, but before reaching for the latch she turned her head to glance at him over her shoulder.

"I'll look forward to the day that I can face you over a broadside, *Lord High Admiral* Savonne. Though, somehow, I don't believe that day will ever come. Thank you for the meal, and good day."

With that, she pulled open the door and walked out of the dining room with Phaedron close behind, leaving both Illymari officers standing dumbfounded in her wake.

As Phaedron and Prudence left the grounds of the Admiralty, Phaedron half expected the Lord High Admiral to come running out of his office screaming for the guards to seize them or some such, but Prudence seemed to be completely at ease walking amongst the enemy's soldiers. Despite her unconcerned attitude, Phaedron kept looking around them for awaiting soldiers or assassins, though none ever materialized. It wasn't long before the couple had reached the busy street and the relative safety of the crowd, and only after he was sure that they were safe, did he speak.

"That was informative. I'm not sure he realized just how much he gave away at the last. I half expected to be arrested or killed before we could leave the grounds."

"That was never a possibility. The Peace of Zarryiosiad is very specific about what will happen should a guest of the Zarryiostrom be murdered or detained by the Illymari Crown before the end of the Convocation. Savonne's life would be forfeit, and both the Church and the Mage Citadel would withdraw their support of Illymar for a great many years . . . more than long enough for King Madari to exact a suitable revenge."

"I'm not sure about you, but knowing I would eventually be avenged would be a very small comfort against the chill of the grave."

"Oh, I agree completely. But the point is, Savonne will never willingly risk his own neck by seeking our deaths. That would require far too much imagination. Tell me, what was your opinion of the good Admiral?" Prudence asked as they walked down the cobblestone streets. "And what did you think his reasons were for attempting to bribe me?"

"As to the Admiral, he's nothing; an empty uniform at best. If he is an example of the quality of soldier Illymar routinely employs, it is a given that Illymar will become a vassal state of Dakkadia within the next few years. What really interested me was how much information he gave away. Tell me about the *Kingsland* and the *Seraph*."

"Both of those ships were treasure galleons which were heavily laden with an extremely pure shipment of gold, and dozens of casks filled with absolutely flawless gems, any of which would be worth a king's ransom," she said. "I found the ships purely by luck: the Water Mages assigned to both of the ships knew their business. They were masking their ship's movements, with the Mages working to keep the ripples from spreading more than a few inches from the ship's wake. You are a Water Mage, so you know how difficult that would be; mainly because the Mage would be unable to rest, but if it is done right, the ship effectively becomes invisible to any other Water Mage who might be looking for them. Unfortunately for them, however, Cahrick quite literally caught their Mage napping and was able to track them. Once we ran them down, the end was a foregone conclusion." Prudence was quiet for a moment. "I say that now, but that wasn't true. Though I fought them at separate times, the crews of both of those ships fought *hard*. By the time the smoke cleared, the captains of both ships and all of their officers were dead, as were a majority of their crews. Normally, a captain who knows his ship is going to be captured will strike his colors and lay down his arms in order to save the lives of his crew. Neither one of the captains of these ships did that: they fought to the bitter end, and it cost them their lives."

"It sounds as if they chose fanatics to crew these ships," Phaedron said. "Either that, or they found a powerful motivation for them to complete their assignments."

"I hadn't thought of that," Prudence said, intrigued by the idea. "Illymar does not breed or utilize fanatics for the most part, so that leaves motivation. Do you have any ideas?"

"I can think of one," he said. "If I wanted to ensure that a ship's captain would not succumb to the temptation that so much wealth would undoubtedly bring, and I wanted him to do whatever it took to complete his given assignment, I would hold his family hostage as surety. In fact, to prevent the possibility of the captain losing his ship through mutiny, I would hold the entire crew's families hostage."

Prudence stopped dead in her tracks at that, and Phaedron saw her clench her fists in sudden fury.

"That makes sense," she growled, "Damn their black souls to hell. None of the sailors we captured would speak a word about the origin of the shipments, and they destroyed the charts before we could seize them, but their desperation tells me you may be right."

She whirled around to face in the direction of the Admiralty compound and took a single step towards it as if she were planning to return. Phaedron caught her arm.

"That won't help, Prudence. You have your duty and they have theirs. Fortune is fickle, and is unmoved by either righteousness or desperation. The captains of the *Kingsland* and the *Seraph* rolled the dice and lost, as simple as that. That isn't your fault; you simply did your duty better than they did theirs. That's all."

Prudence looked up at the man she was falling for and saw nothing but compassion and understanding in his eyes, and somehow that made it better. She glanced one more time in the direction of the Admiralty and swore a silent oath to the Bathtub Admiral.

I will break you for this, Admiral Savonne. I swear it.

With that, she allowed Phaedron to turn her away from her enemy, and once again, they resumed their walk. For a time they walked in silence, until suddenly, on impulse Prudence slid her hand into his. As their fingers intertwined, she squeezed once to thank him for his support and understanding, and he returned the squeeze, a radiant smile on his face.

CHAPTER FOURTEEN

“Seductions”

For the second evening in a row, music filled the great hall, but this time there was no dancing, for no one was brave enough to be the first onto the floor. Valeriad would have loved to ask Lyrahe to dance again, but he could sense that something was wrong. Immediately following dinner, the various political entities had once again coalesced into their familiar groups, and Valeriad had again found himself standing near his father and a collection of his political cronies. The conversation was brisk and the banter actually quite engaging, but Valeriad wasn’t in the mood for banter. Instead of joining in any of the conversations, he withdrew into his own thoughts and tried to hide his disappointment and mounting despair.

After the dance ended the previous evening, Valeriad had thought about the raven-haired Princess until he fell asleep, and she was the first thing on his mind when he woke up. He had desperately looked forward to seeing her again, but to his surprise, when they arrived at the Cathedral she refused to even look at him. He had tried to catch her eye several times during the sermon, but she had steadfastly refused to even look in his direction, and when her family left to prepare for the evening’s festivities, she left without saying goodbye. Dinner had been an ordeal, for while she had sat close enough for him to speak to her, she didn't even try to strike up a conversation, which confused him to no end. The thought that he might have offended her somehow kept echoing through his head, but try as he might, he could think of nothing that he had done to elicit such a severe change in her behavior towards him. Clearly, he had done *something* wrong for her to ignore him like this, and whatever it had been, must have been very bad indeed, but for the life of him he couldn't think of what it could have been. *This is maddening!* he thought.

After the dinner had ended and the parties had moved into the Grand Ballroom, there was a subtle difference in the group dynamics that even Valeriad could see. He noticed that though the three factions had split into their separate groups, there was actually quite a bit of movement between the lower level dignitaries of both the Ferraline and Illymari delegations. The members of both groups were intermingling and talking, something that they hadn't done the previous evening, though King Orem and Emperor Xan had yet to move toward each other. But the one thing in particular Valeriad noticed quite clearly was that Lyrahe hadn't left her father's side for an instant.

During the previous evening, Lyrahe had spent all of her time with her younger sister, Chesare, but the same wasn't true this evening. For a second, his heart skipped a beat as a thought occurred to him. *Did I somehow get her into trouble?*

As the thought worked its way through his mind, he began looking at their dancing in a different light. Instead of simply remembering it for the wonderful time it had been, he began looking at it in the harsh light of political reality, and what he saw was very bad indeed. In polite society, two dances were the most that two unmarried people were ever supposed to share with one another. Any more than two risked courting scandal, and they had done much worse than that, for they had danced every dance together. That wasn't merely courting scandal—that was rushing headlong into its waiting arms.

He closed his eyes and groaned as the severity of his blunder finally dawned upon him, and he glanced at her father and resolved to speak with him as soon as it would be proper, to apologize for his churlish behavior.

I'm a fool! I should have known better.

Deirdre must have seen the grim look on his face and recognized it for what it was.

"Cheer up, Val," she said. "I'm sure she would much prefer to be dancing with you than standing around with her father."

"I know. I'm worried that I might have gotten her into trouble. It just occurred to me that we shouldn't have danced every dance like that. It simply isn't done."

"You mean to tell me that you're only now realizing how wicked you were? Such scandalous behavior!" Deirdre said, teasingly. "The two of you were the talk of the party last night! Didn't your mother teach you any better than that?"

Valeriad grimaced at her and rolled his eyes in disgust.

"Apparently not. I should apologize to her father before she gets into any more trouble."

He turned to face King Orem and squared his shoulders, but before he could take a step, a powerful hand grabbed the back of his neck.

"You will do no such thing, Valeriad," his father said. "Orem is playing a game with Emperor Xan, and he's using his daughter as a pawn." Valeriad shot his father a puzzled look, but waited for his father's explanation. "Orem seeks to marry off Lyrahe to Prince Lain of Ferralin, to buy an alliance against us. The first attempt to arrange a marriage ended in scandal and ruin because of the actions of Tais, Orem's oldest daughter. Lyrahe's actions last evening could have come near to duplicating the experience, but her father allowed the two of you to remain with each other to send a message to Xan. Now that the message has been received and understood, Orem will not allow you to speak with his daughter again. Doing so would jeopardize any future arrangement between the two states, and speaking with Orem will change nothing."

As the situation became clear, a crestfallen Valeriad's face fell, and he became even more depressed. Deirdre gave him a commiserating look and tried once again to jolly Valeriad out of his black mood.

"It's not all bad, Val. At least you met someone worth knowing. Look at Prince Lain. He's been miserable for two days. No one is even speaking with him, let alone asking him to dance. Not that he even could dance in those ridiculous clothes."

Valeriad looked at Lain, who was dressed to the hilt in layer after layer of silk and standing quietly near his father, but try as he might, Valeriad could feel no sympathy for the Prince. After all, he was more than likely going to end up married to Lyrahe.

"Oh, yes. My cup runneth over in sympathy for poor Prince Lain," he growled. No sooner had he spoken than his breath left him in an explosive grunt as Deirdre elbowed him hard in the side.

"Don't be mean just because you're in a bad mood, Val," she said. "He's just as much a prisoner of duty as you are. You should introduce yourself to him; I'll wager the two of you have more in common than you might think. You might even like him. He looks as serious as you."

"Sorry, Deirdre. I really don't mean to be the black cloud at the party, but hearing that he is the man most likely to marry Lyrahe isn't exactly calculated to put me in a festive mood."

"Apology accepted," she said, smiling. "And even if *you* won't speak to him, I think I will. He could probably use a friend right about now. After all, he's about to be traded to a total stranger to seal an alliance."

Before she could make good on her word, however, the Illymari and Ferraline groups began to move. The two monarchs at the center of the delegations approached each other, son and daughter in tow. After an exchange of pleasantries, Prince Lain and Princess Lyrahe were formally introduced to each other and the rest of the delegations moved to the side to allow them room to speak with a modicum of privacy.

Valeriad couldn't hear anything being said, though from what he could tell the conversation seemed to be going fairly well. But one thing above all stood out clearly to him: there was a noticeable lack of enthusiasm from both Lyrahe and Lain. Surprisingly, Valeriad didn't feel any better about the lack of a spark between them. It took him a second to understand why, but the answer surprised him.

I want her to be happy. If we will not be allowed to be together, I pray that she can at least find some measure of happiness with the man whom she does *wed.*

After spending no more than an hour with his potential bride-to-be, Lain knew that should he and the fair Princess Lyrahe actually marry, it would be a long, *long* marriage, indeed. They had both tried very hard to find common ground, but all of their attempts had so far been for naught. Now the two of them were reduced to standing together in an uncomfortable silence that seemed to stretch on for an eternity. Lain looked at her from the corner of his eye and tried to form an opinion of her, and he decided that, for the most part, he liked what he saw. Lyrahe was very beautiful, with an expressive face and perfectly even features, but the two of them had absolutely nothing in common.

During the previous evening's festivities, she had been alive and excited, and watching her twirl around the dance floor had been wonderfully entertaining. And when she looked at Prince Valeriad, Lain had found himself hoping that one day someone would learn to look at him in the same way. Having met her, however, he now wished that she would look at him at all. Oh, he could not fault her perfectly proper behavior, but the wooden expression upon her face seemed completely out of place after seeing it awash with the glow of life. As he studied her, Lyrahe looked up at him again for what he guessed would be yet another attempt to start a conversation.

"Do you enjoy reading, Your Highness?" she asked in a mildly curious tone.

"I do enjoy reading, Princess Lyrahe, though I am afraid that my tastes run to history and philosophy. Very dry reading, I'm afraid." He bowed slightly to her to impart his curiosity. "And what of you?"

"I love to read, though I prefer historical romances and romantic poetry to such serious subjects as philosophy and history," she said, her smile becoming slightly more natural.

"Indeed? I must confess my complete ignorance on the subjects of historical romance and romantic poetry, though they sound fascinating. Can you recommend any good books with which I may educate myself?"

At that Lyrahe launched herself into a treatise on the best stories and writers that she could remember, at times quoting particular passages and verses from memory. He smiled as she spoke, but did not interrupt, thankful that he had at last found a subject that he could use to break through the wall standing between them. He wasn't actually familiar with any of the authors or the stories that she so breathlessly spoke about, but he quickly decided that he had better learn as much as he could about the subject, if only to avoid any more unpleasant silences.

Eventually, she slowed down enough for him to ask her a question in return.

"Do you enjoy music, Princess?"

"Oh, I do very much, though I myself am a terrible musician. My instructors tell me that I simply do not have the ear for it, unlike my sister, Tais, who is a very gifted musician. She can play any instrument that you can name, though her singing isn't quite as good."

At the mention of his former betrothed's name, Lain glanced to where she stood. Once again, the gloriously beautiful golden-haired princess stood by the windows as she had on the first day, looking out over the gardens completely lost in thought. She was standing perfectly still in exactly the same pose she had been in when he had watched her the night before, though he was certain she hadn't noticed him watching her.

She looks so sad, he thought, *as if she finds refuge only in her memories.*

He longed to see her the way she had been yesterday, for then she had been radiant, and in just a few minutes time, she had wrapped their entire delegation around her fingers so skillfully that they had found themselves completely under her spell. Even his father hadn't been immune to her charm, and that was saying much indeed.

Looking at her now, there was no sign of the woman who had won the admiration of everyone in the delegation. Once she had made the introductions—or rather, once she had built the bridge—between the two groups, she had been summarily dismissed by her father. Lain couldn't fault him for that, for though he had needed her to prepare the ground from which he had built his position, King Orem clearly did not want her to remain around to remind anyone of her mistakes. So, he had thanked her for making the introductions, and had sent her to mingle with the guests as soon as it was decorous. To her credit, she took the dismissal with a grace few women could match.

She is quite a woman, Xan had said to Orem as she left. *If she is any indication of the quality of women Illymar has to offer, we would be fools not to seek a closer relationship between our two countries.*

The satisfied smiles on both Orem and Xan's face told everyone that the difficulties Princess Tais had caused between the two countries had just been mended, and it was all thanks to the beautiful woman standing alone and ignored in a room full of people who tried their hardest to pretend she didn't exist at all.

It was then that Lain came to a decision. The one activity that he enjoyed above all others was playing the traditional Ferraline flute, an instrument he had mastered years earlier. For the next evening's activities, he would bring his flute and stand under her window to play her a song as thanks for her service to two lands. She deserved that much from him, at the very least.

Madari turned to Morvandis and caught his attention, before narrowing his eyes and looking briefly at the door. Morvandis understood the signal instantly, and bowed slightly before moving to carry out his orders. Madari wasn't sure if Morvandis would be able to complete his assignment, for Morvandis himself wasn't sure, but they had to take the chance. If Morvandis could indeed open a corridor through the Teeth of Amhar, the advantage that would confer to Dakkadia—even if they never used it—would be priceless.

If he can complete his assignment, the only thing standing between us and Illymar will be the Mage Citadel and their mutual defense treaty with Illymar. We will have to find a way to eliminate that threat before we can take action.

Morvandis might be the most powerful Mage alive, but the Mage Citadel had more than enough Powerborn within its walls to pull him down with sheer weight of numbers. That meant Madari had to find a wedge big enough to force Illymar and Ithram apart before he could even consider invading, but so far nothing had presented itself. He knew that he could force Archimagus DeVir to vote to allow an invasion, but that was only one vote out of eight. All it would take for Illymar to implement the defense provisions of the treaty would be a simple majority, and Madari had no way to exert pressure on the remaining members of the Council.

None of this had any bearing on Morvandis's assignment whatsoever, however. When Morvandis had broached the subject that morning, Madari had issued his orders after only a moment's hesitation, for if there was any way at all to take away the shield that Illymar relied upon so heavily for defense, Madari would have been criminally remiss in his duties as the King of Dakkadia not to pursue it. Personally, he didn't hold out much hope that Morvandis could do what he said, but by that same token, he would never bet against the Mage, for somehow Morvandis always found a way to make the impossible happen.

It doesn't seem possible that a mere mortal like Morvandis could find a way to defeat defenses that were put in place by the Archon herself—defenses that were more than enough to eradicate everything the Lyx could send against them—but then, the Lyx never tried to defeat them from within, did they?

Madari had no idea how long it would take Morvandis to accomplish the task, but he had no intention of sitting around and waiting for the Mage to return. No, he had other things to do.

He turned to look at Princess Tais—*No,* he corrected himself, *not 'Princess Tais' at all; I have to think of her as the former Countess Danshire*—and decided that it was time to satisfy his curiosity.

"If you will excuse me," he said to those surrounding him, "I feel the need to introduce myself to the architect of the recently reinvigorated alliance between Illymar and Ferralin."

His nobles and diplomats bowed formally to him, and he stepped away from the group. No sooner had he done so, when a tall, broad-shouldered, Illymari nobleman approached him. Madari didn't recognize him immediately, but he had the both the look of a veteran warrior as well as the fair coloring of an Illvanin. *This has to be Ascham Illvanin, the Duke of Saerce.*

"Good evening, Your Grace."

"And to you as well, Your Majesty." He cocked his head to the side. "How did you know who I am?"

"There's only one warrior in the Illvanin family. Your reputation precedes you." He held out his hand, and Ascham took it. "I'm a great admirer of your work in the Badlands. You did well, protecting Illymari interests in the region. Did you find the City-States to your liking?"

"The Doges can roast in the Archon's fires for all I care. But I found the timing of the attacks to be more than a little convenient for my tastes. Did you have something to do with them?"

Madari shook his head. Ascham was referring to a series of attacks by well-armed and well-trained mercenaries against Illymari holdings in the Badlands fifteen years ago. That had been around the time Dakkadia had finally began fighting back against the Illymari privateers who had plagued Dakkadian shipping unmolested for years.

"No, Your Grace. I was occupied at the time, and had nothing to do with their adventurism. As far as I can tell, they simply saw an opportunity, and took it."

Ascham stared at him for a long moment, but Madari had told him the simple truth. *Not all plots and schemes against Illymar are of my making, Your Grace.*

"I believe you, Your Majesty."

"Is that why you went to the Badlands personally? To see if I was involved?"

"If you had been, that would have been an act of war, and not simply an extension of our ongoing skirmishes on the high seas. I had no choice but to go there and see for myself."

"If I had known that you would go there personally, I would have hired my own mercenaries to draw you out, and then gone after you myself. I confess, I've always wanted to test myself against you."

"We may yet have the opportunity to cross swords, Your Majesty. If my King's negotiations fail and our nations *do* go to war, I promise you that you'll have your chance. I'll look for you on the field."

"While open warfare between our countries is not yet inevitable, it *is* long overdue. I look forward to testing Illymari steel against my own."

"Be careful what you wish for, Your Majesty. You may not like the result. Good evening."

As Ascham moved away, Madari did not move directly to the golden-haired Countess standing by the window. Instead, he looked for a servant carrying refreshments, and when he located one circulating through the party, he reached out and took two long-stemmed glasses from the tray. With drinks in hand, he put his meeting with Ascham Illvanin out of his mind and began walking toward her, all the while thinking about what he was going to say. She didn't notice his approach, for she was still staring out the window at something only she could see, so when he reached her, he cleared his throat softly to catch her attention.

As the sound registered to her, Madari saw her blink several times, clearly trying to pull herself back from wherever her mind had taken her, and only after her thoughts had caught up to the present, did she turn around to see who had interrupted her. When she recognized him, her eyes widened a bit, but that was her only indication of surprise. She smiled politely at the King, and curtseyed low, to which Madari bowed in return.

"This is a party, Countess. Someone as beautiful and capable as you should not be standing all alone when there are so many interesting people to meet."

Tais blinked again, this time in confusion, and asked,

"Countess?"

Madari assumed a look of innocent confusion and said,

"Ah, yes. You are a Countess, are you not? I was given to understand that you had married a noble; one Earl Danshire, I believe? Does that not make you a Countess?"

A look of intense pain entered Tais's eyes and for a second Madari worried that he had overplayed his hand, but instead of excusing herself to run and cry as he half expected her to do, Tais simply frowned, which only made her look more beautiful as far as Madari was concerned.

"I hadn't thought of it that way," she said, shrugging, "but I suppose you are right. Or rather, you would have been right if the Danshire title hadn't been awarded to someone else upon my husband's death."

"A nasty affair, that. Your father handled the situation badly, if you will pardon my frankness. He overreacted; a mistake that a father can make, but a King cannot. Regardless, please allow me to express my sincerest condolences on your loss. Or losses, if my information is correct."

Again, her eyes flashed with remembered pain, and this time Madari clearly noticed that her eyes were welling up, but again, she was able to suppress her grief . . . and the tears. Despite himself, he was impressed. *This one is steel. What a wife she would make. The Ferraline are fools.*

He allowed her a moment to blink away her unshed tears, and when she looked into his eyes again, he saw something that he hadn't expected in those amber depths: gratitude.

"I'm sorry for seeming to be so emotional, Your Majesty, but you're the very first person to ever express sympathy for me. Those words meant more to me than I could ever possibly express. I am profoundly grateful, Your Majesty."

She curtseyed again, and when she rose up he handed her one of the glasses he had taken from the servant.

"I have no idea what this is, but you look as if you could use a drink." He held up his own glass and smiled, before adding, "I hope you don't mind if I join you, Countess."

"Of course not, Your Majesty. I would be honored to share a drink with you."

He raised his glass to her in a salute, and she raised hers in a matching gesture, before they both took a drink at the same time.

"So, how do you find our country, Your Majesty?" Tais asked, as she lowered her glass. "From what I understand, it is quite different from your own."

"Indeed, it is. The city of Illymaine is much bigger than my own capital of Blackstone, though I must say, with no small modesty, that my castle is much bigger than the Spire. It looks more like a castle should as well."

"The man who designed the Spire of Illymaine is accounted by many to have been a genius: the greatest architect who ever lived. The Spire was designed to stand in harmony with the surrounding land, not in opposition to it. Its soaring towers and pointed turrets were painstakingly designed to maximize the visual effect, while still being functional in design. Weren't you in the least bit impressed?"

The last sentence she spoke ended in a teasing note, and Madari took that as a very good sign indeed.

"Oh, the Spire is quite breathtaking, but no matter how I look on it, it simply doesn't look like a proper castle. The Blackstone is also quite breathtaking, but where the Spire has low narrow walls built of white stone, the Blackstone has smooth black walls a hundred feet high . . . set with proper cylinders instead of delicate towers. Looking at your home, I almost believe that one strong gust of wind could knock over every wall in your castle."

"Do you think so?" she said almost playfully. "Then I probably should encourage that way of thinking, rather than remind you that the Spire has stood unbent and unbroken for hundreds of years, while the Blackstone was taken in a single day. You are the enemy, after all."

The look he gave her was perfect: pained innocence wrapped in just the right amount of boyish hurt. He grabbed his chest as if she had struck him with an arrow.

"You wound me to the heart, Countess, truly you do. Whatever gave you the idea that I wish ill upon any of my neighbors, especially my generous host . . . and his exquisitely lovely daughter?"

"Please, Your Majesty," Tais said laughing. "Despite what my family and my fellow countrymen believe, I am not a fool. Nor am I blind to the threat that your country poses to my own." She arched an eyebrow at him and continued, "Now that I've met you I'll admit that I find you to be completely different than what I had imagined, but that isn't saying much: in my imagination you had fangs and horns."

His face split into a devilish grin, and he gave her a very sinister look before saying,

"Oh, I assure you; I do indeed have fangs and horns, My Lady. I simply wear them on the inside."

Morvandis retraced the route to the Hall of Zarryiosiad Archimagus Enaria had led him on during the previous evening's festivities, all the while keeping a careful eye upon his surroundings. He wasn't trying to be stealthy at all, for he was an honored guest and the King had made it perfectly clear that his guests were free to roam about the Spire, but the last thing he needed right now was company or some helpful soul offering to guide him. No, he needed complete privacy for this particular mission. He wasn't sure how dangerous it would be, but the chances were good that Zarryiosiad had left some form of defense on the Throne of Obsidian. He would have to decipher that defense before he could test his theory on the true purpose of the Throne.

The guards at the door were not the same ones from the previous evening, but as with the other pair, these two did not challenge his right to be there at all. One of them nodded to him in polite greeting, and the other opened the door for him.

"I may be a while—several hours perhaps," he told the guards. "This may be my only opportunity to study these relics and I would very much like to take advantage of it. Will that be a problem?"

For some unknown reason, the two guards found what he had said to be highly amusing. They looked at each other and smirked knowingly before the guard who had opened the door for him returned his attention to Morvandis and shook his head.

"No, Magus. We are used to the . . . *needs* of the Mage Citadel, and we will allow you complete privacy, if you so wish it."

Morvandis nearly showed his surprise at the honorific and the hesitation in the man's words, but then his eyes narrowed as he subconsciously took in his formal silver-trimmed black robe, and he realized that they had mistaken his clothing for that of a Mage of the Citadel.

"That would be most helpful. Thank you for your understanding."

Both guards bowed to him and stepped aside to allow him access to the object of his mission.

"If there is anything you need that we can provide, you have but to ask," the guard said as he entered the room. "We will be happy to bring you anything that you require." They closed the doors behind him.

Too easy, he thought.

Again his eyes narrowed, and he moved to the center of the Hall, looking around suspiciously. The room appeared to be empty, but there was a faint smell that hadn't been present on his previous visit. *Copper. The air tastes of copper.* Suspicion warred with impatience, but he knew he had to make absolutely certain that there was nothing out of place. He simply could not afford to be observed while activating the throne, for the cost would be too high.

The first power he touched was Air, for Air was the most commonly used tool for spying, and as his eyes turned white, he slowly looked around the room searching for any scrying spells or wards. Seeing nothing, he switched to Fire. Fire magic wasn't commonly used for spying at all, but most defensive wards were created from it, and he did not want to set off a spell meant to foil would-be thieves. Again, he sensed nothing, and so he switched to Water, his eyes flashing from fiery red to cerulean blue. Satisfied that the room did not carry any of the most commonly used wards and that he was safe from prying eyes, his eyes flashed a brilliant emerald green as he touched his most secret of abilities: Earth Magic.

To Mages everywhere, it was a law of nature that no Mage could touch more than three of the four powers—or five, if one included the heretical Blood Magic—but Morvandis was living proof that, for 2,000 years, the Mages had been wrong. It was risky for him to use Earth Magic this close to the Mage Citadel—and the Zarryiostrom—but he rather doubted anyone would notice. After all, the last recorded Earth Mage had died several hundred years ago; hunted down and killed by the Zarryiostrom for daring to be born with the ability to touch the forbidden power of the Lyx. In all other respects, the Church was actually quite liberal, but in the pursuit of Earth Mages they were absolutely relentless. Anyone even *suspected* of using Earth Magic was arrested by the Zarryiostrom and put to the question. It was as simple as that.

It amused him that the erroneous belief that no Mage could touch more than three powers kept him absolutely safe from the one group who would like to see him dead more than any other. For it was a given that a Mage who could touch Air, Fire, and Water Magic could *not* touch Earth Magic as well, and therefore Morvandis was one of only a handful of Mages who could be trusted utterly by the Zarryiostrom. By the very nature of his powers he was above suspicion, a fact that he never took for granted.

As he scanned the room a final time using his Earth powers, he noticed nothing at all out of place. Satisfied that there were no traps or wards waiting to spring, he approached the Throne of Obsidian, but stopped himself in front of it. He reached out and touched it lightly, feeling the perfectly smooth contours of the carvings on the arms, and slowly ran his hand up the arm, across its back, and down the other arm like a man caressing his mistress. Once his fingertips had completed their journey, he turned and sat upon the Throne as if afraid it would disappear.

The first thing he noticed was that the seat was warm, as if someone had just left it and he could still feel the heat the person had left behind. It wasn't an unpleasant sensation in the slightest, but as he considered exactly whose seat this was, he became uncomfortable at the feeling. He placed his arms on the armrests, settling his fingers in the folds of the lion manes carved into the front of the armrests. Then he took a deep breath and prepared himself mentally for what he was about to attempt. Morvandis knew that like him, Zarryiosiad could touch all four powers, and he decided that that would be the best way for him to begin. As he slowly let out the breath and focused his mind, he summoned all four powers simultaneously and used them to give the Throne the lightest of touches. He wasn't prepared for what came next.

Instantly, the throne reacted by pulling his power into it as if trying to devour it all. He fought it at first, attempting to pull himself away from the chair, but try as he might, he could not disengage: the Throne of Obsidian held him firmly in place. As more and more of his power drained into it, Morvandis could feel something interesting occurring. The chair wasn't draining his power; it was absorbing it and using it to bring itself back to life. It had lain dormant for 2,500 years, and at his touch, it had awakened hungry. So, instead of fighting the Throne, Morvandis began cooperating with it. He poured every bit of power he could manage into the seat, and the Throne greedily accepted the tribute. He held nothing back, allowing all the power that the seat needed to pass through him and into it. Finally, just as Morvandis was starting to believe that he had made a terrible mistake, he felt the pull slacken and eventually fade, until the seat stopped pulling power from him at all and once again sat dormant and ready.

Morvandis knew then that there had indeed been a trap awaiting anyone without the power to give the seat what it wanted. The Throne of Obsidian was absolutely useless to anyone without the ability to touch all four powers, but it was absolutely *lethal* to anyone who *could* touch all four powers but didn't have the necessary strength to feed it. Had a lesser Mage attempted the same thing Morvandis had—even if he or she could touch all four powers—the seat would have continued to drain the unfortunate soul until every ounce of power was gone, and then it would continue to feed off of his life force until all that remained of the Mage was a desiccated husk left behind as a warning to others.

The knowledge that he possessed enough strength to awaken the Throne of Obsidian from its slumber was intoxicating, for it answered a question that he had wondered since he had first learned that he was a Powerborn: was he as powerful as the Archon? The trial he had just overcome told him, quite clearly, that his power was at least comparable to what Zarryiosiad had possessed before she had Ascended, but he had no way of knowing what she had been capable of at the height of her power.

All of that was unimportant, however, for he had work to do. He set aside his speculations about the Archon and began testing the Throne. He closed his eyes and sent a stream of Water Magic into the arm of the chair. Dutifully, the Throne absorbed the magic, and opened a vista before him, in shimmering water, floating several feet off the floor. He began to see things that were far away, as if he were looking at them through a window. It took him a moment to understand what he was seeing, but as he manipulated the scene, he learned he could move his vision with great speed over tremendous distances.

To form a reference point, he concentrated on the Spire, and the image obediently switched to a view of the castle from the front gate. From there, he moved his vision to the *Sovereign,* sitting at rest at the docks. It took no effort at all to focus in on the deck of the ship and the crew going about their duties. He smiled inwardly as he focused briefly on Cahrick Rantrefal, and he toyed briefly with the idea of striking him down where he stood. It was only a passing thought, however, and he decided to let Rantrefal live for another day. Morvandis quickly moved his vision on to other areas, some of them hundreds of miles away in the remotest parts of the island of Illymar. He then moved his vision out to sea, to learn how far his vision extended. He soon learned of the boundary to his enhanced vision, for try as he might, he could not extend his sight out of range of the Teeth.

I can see everything on the island, and anything approaching the Teeth of Amhar. This would be most useful for spying upon armies or watching for possible invaders.

The second thing he attempted was to manipulate the weather near one of the Teeth. Within a few moments it began to rain, exactly where he wanted.

Not just a scrying device, then. It can be used to project power as well. No wonder the Lyx never successfully invaded: she could have defended the entire island from this very seat.

Finally, he used his power to disrupt the flow of the energy between the Teeth of Amhar themselves. He had to be careful here, for he only wanted to disrupt the flow between the few dozen towers at the closest point between the Illymar and Dakkadia. Any more than that, and he risked warning every Mage in Illymar that something had happened to the Teeth. He had believed the task would be difficult, but in actuality, it was simplicity itself. Within moments, he had opened a back door to Dakkadia that Illymar would never suspect existed—and couldn't possibly close, even if they did.

He wanted to test the capabilities of the Throne even further, but he knew that doing so would be an unnecessary risk. He had already done what he had come here to do, and staying any longer than he had to could mean detection. Reluctantly, he pulled his hands away from the arm of the chair, and disengaged his power from it. At once, complete exhaustion crashed down upon him, and his knees threatened to buckle as he stood. The moment he stepped away from the seat, it reverted to its powerless state, once again becoming nothing more than a beautifully carved piece of stone. Without a single look back, he walked to the doors and opened them, stepping through them quietly and closing them behind him before thanking the guards for their help. Both of them gave him knowing smiles which Morvandis didn't care for, but he let it pass without comment. He turned down the hallway and began walking back to rejoin the party.

Enaria Wintersong stood in the corner of the Artifact Room, still draped in the cloak she had created, and thought about what she had just seen. When she had come to view the artifacts with Morvandis on the previous evening, she had hoped that he, with his greater abilities, would have some new insight into their uses. He had disappointed her then, but the more she had thought about their time together, the more she knew he was hiding something . . . something very important, indeed. She didn't know exactly what it would be, but she knew it was something that he wanted kept from her. So, she had set a trap for him, one that he had no possibility of detecting, no matter how powerful he was, for Enaria had a secret of her own: she was a Blood Mage.

Blood Mages were considered heretics, for they used the power of life to work their spells instead of the power of the elements. The reason it was considered heretical was simple: the life force used in Blood Magic spells didn't necessarily have to come from the person casting the spell. It also could be provided by another person, either willingly or unwillingly. Enaria was a master of Blood Magic—had been one for almost two centuries—and the spell she had used to cloak her presence had masked her from any form of detection, both physical and magical. The spell had worked flawlessly, for Morvandis had looked at her several times, both with his eyes and with his powers, and had seen absolutely nothing. She, on the other hand, had seen everything he had done, from the moment he had stepped through the doors to the moment he had left, and the discovery that he was an Earth Mage had shocked her to the core.

*For so many years we knew—*knew!*—that it was impossible to hold four powers. I have devoted my entire life to the study of Zarryiosiad, and even I never suspected the truth: the Archon could touch all four powers, and she isn't the only one. This discovery* *changes everything I've ever thought or believed about the Archon. It changes everything I've ever believed about magic!*

And not just the Archon either. Though Morvandis didn't know it, he had just become the center of her world . . . whether he liked it or not.

Enaria knew she was in more danger now than she had ever been in her life, for Morvandis would kill her in an instant if she approached him with this knowledge in the wrong way. But, she also knew that she *would* approach him, for she knew better than most that the greatest gains often entailed the greatest risks. If she could convince him not to kill her out of hand when she revealed to him that she knew his secret, she knew she would then be in a position to learn from him . . . and perhaps one day to manipulate him. She gave the Throne of Obsidian a long look, marveling at what he had accomplished while sitting in it. She had seen only a little of what he had done, and understood less, but from the tiny look of satisfaction upon his strained features, it had to have been important.

She released the power holding the cloak around her and suddenly returned to view before she stepped to the doorway and opened it. The two guards turned to look at her as she walked through the door, and one of them gave her a lecherous grin.

"The two of you were in there for a good long time. I trust you found something *interesting* to discuss?" He wagged his eyebrows at her in a knowing fashion, and Enaria fought down the urge to make the man spontaneously combust for his impertinence.

"Oh, we didn't say a word to each other," she said calmly, allowing her sudden, murderous rage at the man's vulgar temerity to dissipate. "There wasn't time to talk, you see. We were too busy doing . . . other things." She gave him a sultry look and the guard laughed and slapped his companion on the stomach with the back of his hand. Enaria smiled at them and handed over two small bags of gold, one for each man. "For your cooperation . . . and your discretion."

The men eagerly took the gold from her, and as the bulging coin pouches slid into hidden pockets, the lecherous guard said, "I would thank you for your generosity, but you were never here." At that, the two soldiers resumed their positions at the door and pointedly looked away from her.

The guards may have been pigs, but they had also given her an idea. Thanks to them, she knew exactly what she was going to do about Morvandis. It could still go wrong, she knew, but then it still gave her a better than even chance of living through the night, and getting her everything she had ever desired. She squared her shoulders and began walking down the hall. *There is much to do, and I have no time to waste.*

Despite herself, Tais found Madari to be extremely charming, and after overcoming her initial hesitation, she found herself relaxing in his company. The most common belief in Illymar was that Dakkadians were all barbarians, but the reality couldn't have been further from the truth. Madari was suave, debonair, and very, very handsome, and Tais was extremely attracted to him. He was around forty-five years old, with black hair just starting to turn grey, marked by the thick white stripe indicating Dakkadian noble blood. She had had a wonderful time speaking with him, and her disgrace coupled with his status as an unwanted intruder, meant no one had interfered in what had turned out to be a fascinating conversation. The hour was getting late, however, and the guests were beginning to leave, in singles and in small groups. Madari noticed as well.

"It seems that the party is coming to an end, though I am not sure where the time went." He frowned slightly and added, "I do apologize for monopolizing your time, Countess. But you are nothing at all like a typical Illymari."

"No apologies are necessary, Your Majesty. The evening would have been quite boring for me had you not sought me out." She swept a hand to indicate the other guests at the party. "It is not like anyone else wishes to be seen with me. I am out of favor, if you'll remember."

"Then they are fools, and their loss is my gain. I would like to speak with you again. Tomorrow, if that would be agreeable," he said. "Perhaps you could give me a tour of the grounds." He glanced at King Orem, who was still talking with Emperor Xan. "It's not like I will be busy either . . . your father seems interested in pursuing only a single goal during the Convocation." He clapped his hands together and said, "If I will not be allowed to discuss business with your father, the least I can do is enjoy his hospitality. Will you be free tomorrow?"

Tais blushed slightly at the knowledge that Madari wanted to see her again. She knew that she shouldn't, for he really was the enemy and no amount of charm or polish could hide that simple truth, but she found that she didn't care.

"Of course, Your Majesty. I would be delighted to speak with you again. And should you wish a tour of the grounds, I would be most happy to accommodate you."

She held out her hand to him and he raised it to his lips and kissed it. The formality concluded, he smiled one last time and said,

"Tomorrow then, Countess."

"I'll look forward to it."

As the Dakkadian royal party returned to their villa, Morvandis touched his monarch's arm to pull him aside.

"I was successful," he said without preamble.

Madari wanted to press for details, he knew better than to talk openly in a room Morvandis hadn't had time to properly ward. The news was too good for him to believe, however, and he bellowed a laugh as he slapped Morvandis on the back.

"Outstanding! But you can tell me about it in the morning. Tonight you deserve a rest!"

Morvandis bowed slightly, and gave his half-brother a tiny smile of chagrin.

"I'll admit that the experience took more out of me than I was prepared for. A rest would be most welcome."

"In the morning, then," Madari said. "I'll expect a full report."

Morvandis bowed deeper at the command from his King and then left for his chambers. He hadn't been exaggerating about his fatigue, for using the Throne of Obsidian had taken more out of him than he had realized. As he made his way to his room, he unconsciously began checking his wards and alarms. What he found banished his weariness instantly: someone had been there.

Morvandis knew that no one in the Dakkadian entourage would have been foolish enough to disturb his chambers. Even the servants had been warned not to approach without permission, and so far, they had obeyed the command absolutely. That didn't change the fact, however, that *someone* had breached his security, and had done so openly. He could sense no attempt whatsoever to bypass the wards or to deactivate them, so whoever had done so hadn't cared at all about being discovered. The knowledge that someone would be so brazen, combined with his recent use of Earth Magic, put his nerves on edge.

Through his weariness, he reached for three of the four powers at his command, and formed his four personal defensive circles. Anyone attempting to attack him would find their attacks rendered absolutely worthless, no matter what form the attack would take, magical or otherwise. Only after he was satisfied that his wards were in place, did he move to the doorway.

He did not bother to attempt to sneak into his own room. Instead, he pushed the door open and stepped in, looking around for the intruder, and he saw her instantly. She had her back to him and was looking out of one of his large arched windows, her long blond hair spilled down her back to below her waist. She wore a long silken robe that hung from her shoulders like an elegant cloak.

Morvandis's expression hardened at the sight of his uninvited guest, but she hadn't moved when he opened the door, and, as far as he could tell, she did not seem to be a threat. Whoever she was, he could sense no resonance emanating from her, so she couldn't be a Mage. But there was one other thing present. *Copper. The room smells of copper, just like the Hall of Zarryiosiad.* He was already touching his power, so it was a simple matter to scan her for hidden weapons or the like, but what he found stunned him: as far as his abilities were concerned, she didn't exist at all. He blinked in surprise at the revelation, and tried a second time to analyze her with his power, and again, nothing at all registered. It was as if he was looking at a ghost.

"That won't work, Morvandis. One of the more useful gifts granted to a skilled Blood Mage is the ability to mask yourself from view, to include any form of analysis, both magical and physical. As long as I channel this ability and limit my movements, I can remain completely shielded from magical detection. If I stand perfectly still, I can even render myself invisible. Had I so chosen, I could have been standing right in front of you and you would never have seen me, despite your power."

She turned her head to the side, and Morvandis received his second shock in as many minutes, for he recognized Archimagus Enaria Wintersong's profile instantly. She still hadn't turned around to face him, but she gave him a sultry smile over her shoulder, and her half-lidded eyes threatened to elicit an entirely inappropriate response from him. He was no fool, however, for he had more than enough experience with the fairer sex to know when one was trying to manipulate him.

"Am I to understand then, that a member of the Mage High Council is a Blood Mage? I find that very hard to believe. Almost as hard to believe, say, as you standing in my bedchambers admitting it openly would be." Still, he had no other explanation for what he was seeing. And now that he knew what she was, he knew he had been wrong about the smell of copper. *It was blood, not copper. Blood Magic requires the life energy of its user to work.* He continued to probe her with his magical senses, but they could find nothing at all in the spot in which she was standing. He moved into the room, prepared to defend against any trap, but he left the door open behind him.

"How can you not believe it? The evidence is standing right before you."

She gave him a playful look before turning her head back to the window, and reaching out with her hands to trace the window frame slowly with delicate fingertips. As her arms reached higher and higher on the frame, the sleeves of her robe slid down her forearms to reveal perfectly smooth, pale skin, unmarred by blemishes of any kind. Her hands came to rest on either side of the window, slightly higher than her head. He could see nothing past the silken robe, but her spread-eagled pose was extremely sensual, as was the unexpected revelation of her skin. He felt another stir of desire for her, but again her actions only served to warn him that something was amiss.

"What do you want, Enaria? This isn't like you at all. You've never shown any interest in me before for my somewhat dubious masculine charms."

Enaria again turned her head to look at him through half-lidded eyes.

"Masculine charms are interesting in their own way, I suppose, though I must admit that I have always found you to be more exotic than manly. No, Morvandis, what has always attracted me to a man—what I have always desired in a lover—is power. I make no secret of this to you, because I know you and I are the same. I have looked a long time for a kindred soul such as yours, and I believe that together we can go far." She hesitated for an instant and continued in a breathless voice, heavy with anticipation and what sounded like to him like fear. "I watched you as you sat upon the Throne of Obsidian tonight. What was it like, to feel the power that only the Archon herself has ever before touched? What did you learn today, Earth Mage, from your time on the Throne?"

Instantly, he seized his power and readied a strike which would incinerate her so completely no one would ever know what had happened to her, but she didn't move to defend herself at all. She simply looked at him over her shoulder as if expecting an answer.

"Everyone knows that it is impossible for a Mage to touch four powers, and I already touch three. What makes you think that I am an Earth Mage?"

She closed her eyes and her shoulders began to shake with silent mirth. When she again opened her eyes they were shining with amusement.

"Morvandis, I am not a fool. Please do not treat me as one."

She dropped her arms to her sides, and again looked out the window. Or rather, she looked at his reflection in the glass.

"Believe me when I say, that from the moment that I saw what you truly were, you became the single most important person in the world to me. Through you, I can finally realize my lifelong ambition; to learn everything there is to know about the Archon . . . and perhaps, one day, to touch divinity." She looked over her shoulder once again. "That is why I come to you now, laying bare my own secret in the hope, that by doing so, we can somehow find common ground. Your secret is safe with me, Morvandis, as I hope my secret is safe with you."

Morvandis narrowed his eyes in thought. On the surface, it seemed too good to be true. Enaria's revelations had placed her life in his hands, and he knew it very well indeed. The fact that she was standing alone, and apparently vulnerable, in his chambers when she could also have summoned the entire Mage Guard to arrest him as a heretic wasn't lost upon him either. Still, it would be safer by far for him to kill her now. If he did so, his secret would be completely safe. *But then, would it?*

He did not know what preparations she had made for the possibility that he would murder her to protect his secret. Chances were she had done nothing, but he wasn't prepared to risk his life to find out. Besides, she had other uses as well. Something Madari had said that morning returned to him.

Even if you somehow find a way to breech the Teeth of Amhar, there is still the threat of the Mage Citadel to deal with. We must find a way to eliminate that threat before we can deal with Illymar.

In a flash he made up his mind. He quirked an eyebrow at her and crossed his arms over his chest.

"Common ground, you say? How do you propose we find such a thing?"

The smile she gave him was brilliant, and he felt his mouth fall open as she turned around to face him for the first time since he had walked into the room. Other than the open robe hanging loosely from her shoulders, she wore not a stitch; and he let his control over his power slip as he took in every glorious curve of his former teacher. As she stepped toward him from the window, her eyes sparkled and her smile turned seductive.

"Oh, I am sure we can find a way . . . wouldn't you agree?"

Morvandis didn't bother to answer. Instead, without taking his eyes from her, he reached back, touched the door with his hand, and closed it firmly behind him even as she dropped her robe to the floor.

CHAPTER FIFTEEN

"Thorn"

It isn't like Morvandis to be this late. I think I'd better check on him.

Countess Thorn Demestira was Morvandis's most trusted spy, and she had accompanied him to the Convocation to act as his official spy mistress. Normally, he would have filled the position of spymaster himself, but this time he had known that he would be far too busy attending social functions with the King to do his job properly, so he had ordered Thorn to take his place. She didn't mind, for having been a member of the Flower Court from a very early age, spying was second nature to her.

Though officially the Flower Court was a glorified brothel, one of the secret functions of a Courtesan of the Court was to collect information of value and report it to the Master or Mistress of the Gardens. Morvandis had been the Master of the Gardens for sixteen years, which wasn't particularly notable for the length of his rule, but it was *definitely* remarkable considering the extremely young age that he had been when he had first taken control of the Court. Morvandis had only been nine years old when he had killed the previous Master and only fourteen when he had begun his rule. No one had mourned the death of the previous Master—a man who had earned the court name of Marigold—for he had been a useless pig who had turned the once-exalted Court into nothing more than the lowest sort of whore houses. When Morvandis killed Marigold and released the Court from his control, the Flower Court had eagerly repaid Morvandis by submitting to his rule. The decision to bend knee to Morvandis had been a simple one, for despite his current position, he had been raised as one of them.

That was a secret none of the members of the Court would ever reveal, for Morvandis had reached awe-inspiring heights of power and prestige, and had brought the Flower Court with him. Long before he was born, his mother had earned the court name of Orchid, one of the most prized and sought after titles of them all, but Orchid had richly deserved it. She had been brought to Dakkadia from the Eastlands as a prize, and in Dakkadia she had been treasured as a rare and exotic beauty.

King Dhaegus, the previous King of Dakkadia, had taken notice of her early on, and had quickly become her patron, showering her with gifts and money and eventually fathering Morvandis. Dhaegus had been informed of his son's birth, and had given Morvandis his name, but then had quickly dismissed him as 'just another bastard', of which he already had many. After Dhaegus' death, Madari officially recognized Morvandis' royal blood before raising him to the position of Court Mage and granting him the title of Duke. With his elevation, even at such a young age, the Flower Court quickly became again what it once had been, and their loyalty to the man who had made it all possible, was absolute.

Thorn had much in common with Morvandis, for her mother had also been considered an exotic beauty. Unlike his mother, however, who had the long black hair, yellow skin, and the tilted eyes of an Eastlander, Thorn's mother had come from the southernmost reaches of the Ferralin Empire. Her mother's skin had been as dark as night, and Thorn's own skin had inherited much of her coloring, though it was a rich mahogany rather than the near perfect black skin her mother boasted. Her mother's hair had been short and curly, but Thorn's own black hair was long, with an elegant wave that she could never quite rid herself of . . . a gift from her father, she supposed, whoever he was.

Though Morvandis had been trained to be an escort, he had never actually become one, for his connection to the royal family, as well as his Powerborn abilities, had made him too valuable to waste as an inamorato. Thorn, however, had actually been an active member of the Flower Court, and had spent many years as a courtesan. It was there that she had met her future husband, yet another bastard of the previous King. Thanarilliad Demestira was the illegitimate son of King Dhaegus and Countess Demestira, the widow of one of his nobles. When Madari had come to power and had slain or exiled all of the grasping mistresses his father had once collected, Countess Demestira had wisely sided with him. Her foresight had allowed her to not only to survive the various purges, but to prosper from them as well. And like Morvandis, Madari had repaid her loyalty by recognizing Thanarilliad's noble birth, and allowing him to inherit his mother's estates.

Thanarilliad had met Thorn at the Flower Court, and had quickly found in her a kindred soul, for both of them shared a love of inflicting and enduring pain as part of their lovemaking. Thanarilliad was quite ingenious at inventing new and unique ways of hurting people, and together they had plumbed the depths of human depravity in all its forms. In her, he had found a perfect match, and it had been inevitable that the two would marry.

That was how she found herself here in Illymar, for her positions in both the Dakkadian Court and the Flower Court had allowed her to enter society at any level, making her the perfect spy. Each morning, she was tasked with the duty of bringing to his attention any and all information that could be of interest to the kingdom, and she was extremely diligent in carrying it out. Two nights ago, Morvandis had asked her to find out all she could about Princess Tais, the oldest daughter of King Orem, and in only one night's time she had found out things that no one else had even suspected. Today she had nothing quite as juicy to report, but then Morvandis had given her a different assignment.

He never told her why he wanted her to do certain tasks, but then, she never cared to know. Last night he had asked her to watch the front gates of the Mage Citadel for any signs of agitation, and to come to the Spire and warn him if she saw trouble of any kind. The night had passed quietly, however, and so in the morning she had returned to the Dakkadian villa to make her morning report before heading to bed. Unfortunately, Morvandis seemed to be running more than a bit behind which automatically made warning bells ring in her head.

Morvandis was *never* late for anything, and the fact that for some reason, he had decided to choose today, of all days, to begin made her worry. As she approached his doors, she knew she was setting off all sorts of wards and alarms, but she didn't hear any sounds at all coming from his room. So, she knocked quietly at first, and then became more insistent when he didn't answer. She reached down and grasped the door handle, and with a firm twist of her hand opened the door . . . and saw Morvandis's nude body sprawling face down upon his bed, feet toward the headboard and one arm draped over the side of the bed with one hand resting on the floor. The sheets and blankets were a tangled mess, with bloodstains dotting it everywhere.

Her hand shot to her mouth in alarm, for his back was covered in blood, and she stopped herself from rushing forward to check him for signs of life.

Whatever had attacked him had been vicious, judging from the many scratches on his back, and she pulled a dagger out of a concealed sheath on her forearm and began looking for signs of the beast. Whoever had attacked him, he had evidently put up a fight, for the room was a shambles. The curtains hanging above the arched windows were askew, the furniture had been knocked aside, and the items that had been resting on them hadn't simply fallen to the floor, they'd been thrown. After a quick but thorough search of the room and its antechambers, and after she was satisfied that whatever had attacked Morvandis was no longer in the room, she took three steps toward the bed to examine his unmoving body. It was then that she heard a sound which filled her with relief, for though his back was not rising and falling, Morvandis was, quite clearly, snoring.

She laughed out loud at the realization that he hadn't been attacked after all, and slid the dagger back into its hidden sheath before walking to the bed to examine him. A closer look at the bloody scratches down his back told her that they had been made by a woman in the throes of passion, and from the sheer number of them, Morvandis had done the Flower Court quite proudly indeed. Feeling a sudden wash of affection toward her lord and master, Thorn brazenly slapped him on the buttocks to awaken him. The loud *crack* of flesh meeting flesh yanked him from his slumber with all the subtlety of a horsewhip, and his head shot up in surprise as he sleepily looked around the room for the source of the sound.

"Enaria?" was all he said, as he peered around the room with bleary eyes, and Thorn's eyebrows shot to her hairline as she recognized the name. *Archimagus Enaria Wintersong?* She gave Morvandis a low whistle of appreciation. *The Elven High Councillor of the Mage Citadel? Morvandis sets his sights high!*

As she gave the room a second look, she couldn't help but be impressed at the Councillor's handiwork.

"Time to wake up, sleepyhead," she said in a teasing tone. "You are late."

She again slapped his bare bottom and, at the unexpected blow, he came fully to his senses. He glanced back at Thorn through a curtain of unruly hair.

"What time is it?" he asked.

Thorn stood up and walked to his window, and set the curtains aright before drawing them open. The bright sunlight of midmorning fell across Morvandis's face, and he closed his eyes tightly to shield them from the sudden assault. With a small groan, he lifted his arm off of the floor and used it to push himself up from the mattress, and then he set first one foot and then the other on the floor. Thorn stepped from the window to the ornately carved armoire that contained all of Morvandis's clothing, and opened the door to rummage through the neatly arranged clothing to find something suitable for him to wear.

"I wouldn't have thought the prim and proper Enaria Wintersong would have been capable of doing this much damage, especially to the Master of the Gardens. But I guess sometimes the quiet ones can be the most surprising. You must be woefully out of practice, Morvandis. When we return to Dakkadia, I will have to schedule a few sessions with the Gardeners for you. They will prune you back into proper form in no time."

Morvandis groaned at the mention of the taskmasters of the Flower Court.

"That will not be necessary. It is not stamina or technique that I lack. She merely took me by surprise. Next time I will be ready for her."

Thorn laughed silently at that and selected a particularly severe outfit with very high collars. As she turned around to offer her selection, she saw that Morvandis was no longer in bed. He had reached a pitcher of clean water and lifted it up, before pouring its contents directly on the floor. She crossed her arms over her chest and took a nice long look at Morvandis's nude body. She definitely liked what she saw, for though he was a bit on the lean side for her tastes, he was covered with hard muscle. The scratches on his back were quite dramatic against his pale skin, and she smiled in admiration for the efforts of the Elven mage.

As she stood by with his clothing in hand, his eyes turned blue as he touched Water Magic, and the pool of water on the floor began to swirl around him, slowly at first, but quickly picking up speed. After a few seconds, the water rose up in a funnel and completely engulfed him. He lifted his arms up to shoulder height and allowed the water to wash over him, before the vortex died down and the water returned to the pitcher. A freshly bathed Morvandis returned the pitcher to its proper place and stepped to Thorn, reaching for his clothing.

"Not so fast, Morvandis. Turn around."

Morvandis frowned at the order, but complied nonetheless, and Thorn clicked her tongue at him in mock sympathy. The quick bath had broken open the scabs that had covered his back, and fresh droplets of blood were pooling.

"Lie down on the bed, face down."

Morvandis hesitated and gave her a suspicious look, but an irritated Thorn wasn't in the mood to waste time. Instead, she grabbed one of his shoulders, forcibly turned him around, and pushed him toward the bed. When it seemed like he was about to protest, she slapped him on the back and laughed at his elaborate wince. When he had recovered from the pain she showed him her hand, which was covered with more than a little blood.

“You look as if you have been mauled by a wild animal. I have an ointment that will deal with this problem, but you need to let me apply it.”

Morvandis allowed her to push him to his bed and dutifully lay down upon it, face down, while Thorn reached into her belt pouch and produced a small jar of ointment. She rubbed a generous amount of it on her hands and began applying it to his scratches. He groaned again, this time in relief, as the cool cream did its work.

“Was there any activity at the Mage Citadel?” he asked while she worked.

“None, whatsoever. I spent a quiet night outside of the Citadel. It was quite restful, unlike your evening, which was apparently spent in wanton debauchery appeasing your insatiable libido and animalistic lusts.” She rolled her eyes elaborately, and said with more than a hint of irritation, “And to think, people believe *my* tastes are deviant!

“Well, Thanarilliad and I may have earned our reputation for enjoying the darker side of loveplay, but the two of us have never actually destroyed a room during one of our sessions.” She looked around the room and nodded in admiration. “Well done. Very well done, indeed.”

“If you are finished, I have work to do,” he said, dryly.

She winked at him, but refrained from slapping his buttocks for a third time.

“The ointment will heal your scratches within just a few days and shouldn’t leave any scarring. Despite how bad the cuts looked at first, they actually weren’t that bad, after all. She was careful.”

As he stood up, she handed him the outfit that she had selected. As he took it from her and examined it, he raised an eyebrow and glanced at her.

“Why this one? The collars make it a bit uncomfortable.” She smiled at him and pointed at his mirror. He checked his reflection, and froze at the sight of the love marks Enaria had left upon his neck. The marks were huge and very noticeable, and when he saw them, he meekly began donning the outfit she had selected without another word of complaint. “High collars it is, then.” He turned back to Thorn and gave her a grateful look. “Thank you for your assistance this morning, Thorn. I really needed your help.”

Thorn nodded her acceptance of his thanks, and stood back to watch him don his clothing. She did not understand why he had cultivated such a severe personality among his peers, for the only facet of his personality that he ever allowed them to see was his cold professionalism. Thorn suspected that even King Madari had never seen this side of Morvandis before, and she rather doubted that he ever would, for Morvandis truly did not wish people to believe him to be human.

With the Flower Court, he was different, for he could occasionally let down his guard among the people who had raised and sheltered him, long before he had ascended to such rarified heights in the world; but even among those who knew him best, he was still reserved, if less so than around the nobility. The courtesans and housemistresses of the Court treated him like a favored son or a beloved sibling, and in exchange, he allowed them to see a side of him he would never willingly show any other . . . but only sometimes. Thorn bantered with him as she would a brother, and he allowed it, because to Morvandis, the Flower Court was, quite simply, his family.

When Morvandis finished dressing, he glanced into his mirror to judge his appearance. A brief flash of white in his eyes told Thorn that he was again accessing his magic, and his damp hair began to fly behind him as if he were facing into a strong wind. After only a few moments, the wind died down, and standing before her was the Morvandis that she recognized. With his appearance taken care of, he assumed his mask of cold disdain and turned for the door. Thorn beat him to it, bowed slightly without a trace of mockery, and turned the handle to open the door for him. He did not thank her for the courtesy; he simply walked through at a slightly brisk pace and immediately turned for the King's chamber. As Thorn caught up with him, he said,

"I have another assignment for you, once you've rested." He did not look at her at all, simply continuing in his normal cold tone. "You are to look for weaknesses in the Illymari monarchy. Find out everything you can about the King and his nobility, and look for the best ways to disrupt their kingdom."

"Shall I be looking for simple disruption or outright chaos?"

Morvandis looked at her then and gave her a small smile that did not reach his eyes.

"If King Madari is unable to make diplomatic progress with either Ferralin or Illymar, we will be forced to attack Illymar. If and when we do, I want their government to be weakened, and unable to oppose us in any meaningful manner. If it comes to war, we must defeat Illymar quickly: the longer it takes us to break Illymar, the more likely Ferralin will intervene and attack Dakkadia from the south."

"Chaos it is, Your Grace. Leave it to me."

She turned around and walked to her bedchambers to get a good day's sleep. She would need it, for she would have much to do that evening.

Madari had just closed the door to his room and had begun to walk to the foyer where the rest of the Dakkadian party awaited, when he saw Morvandis

COUNTESS THORN DEMESTIRA
OF DAKKADIA

striding toward him with Countess Demestira in tow. He had wondered where his Mage was, for it was not like him to be late for their morning strategy sessions, and he had waited as long as he could for Morvandis to come to him before deciding that he couldn't wait any longer. As he turned to face the Mage, the dark-skinned Countess turned away and walked back the way she had come, and Madari's gaze involuntarily fell to her shapely posterior as she sidled away. He had always found Countess Demestira's overtly sexual nature to be quite refreshing, though her well-deserved reputation for deviant tastes had assured her complete immunity from Madari's attentions. While he would be the first to admit to a certain weakness for attractive women, he definitely drew the line when the woman in question employed torture as foreplay. Still, as he watched her go, he wondered yet again if he should feel sorry for her husband, Thanarilliad, or jealous of him.

The approach of Morvandis distracted him from the sight of Thorn walking away, and he turned his attention to his Mage. He didn't bother with pleasantries.

"You're late."

"My apologies, Your Majesty," Morvandis said. "Last night's exertions took more out of me than I had expected. I overslept."

"You told me that you were successful," Madari said. "Tell me everything."

Morvandis summoned his powers to ensure the wards surrounding Madari's section of the villa were still intact before speaking.

"I was able to access the power of the Throne of Obsidian and use it to remove a small section of the barrier protecting Illymar from Dakkadia. I could have lowered the entire shield, but to keep from warning the Mage Citadel that something is amiss, I made certain that only a relatively small section was removed without disrupting the rest. The channel is 12 miles long, and is located at the closest point between Dakkadia and Illymar. As the barrier is invisible, only a Mage who is actively looking for a break in the barrier will find it, but even if they do somehow locate it, there is nothing they can do."

"Well done, Morvandis!" Madari smiled, pleased at his Mage's work. "I must admit that I didn't actually hold out much hope that you could accomplish it, but, as always, you continue to surprise me. I still don't want to invade Illymar, but I can't have them at my back when we press our claims in the Badlands. With Orem all but ignoring me, I can't pursue negotiations with him to eliminate Illymar as a potential ally against Ferralin. He's being rude to me—pointedly so—and it seems to be working."

"So it would seem, Your Majesty," Morvandis said, agreeing. "The time may come when patience and diplomacy are no longer the correct path. Illymar seeks this alliance with Ferralin because they fear us. It may be time to remind them of why they fear us in the first place."

Madari considered Morvandis's words carefully.

"Perhaps. But not yet. I will give him the chance to come to me on his own. If he avails himself of the opportunity, I will deal with him fairly and let bygones be bygones. But, if I am forced to go to him, things will be much different." He grinned suddenly, and the smile looked somehow wolfish on his handsome face. "Whatever Orem may decide, it's time to lay the foundation for our potential, but entirely legitimate, invasion of Illymar. It seems to me that an opportunity for you to begin that process has arisen. Valeriad and Phaedron are going to the Mage Citadel tomorrow to begin their Testing. I want you to accompany them, and use the opportunity to look for something we can use to divide the High Council in the event that we are forced to invade Illymar. Even with the Teeth no longer providing protection for them, Illymar is safe so long as Ithram stands ready to defend it. We must find a way to neutralize the threat the Council poses to our plans."

Morvandis acknowledged his orders, but refrained from mentioning his tryst the previous evening with Enaria. He knew that, while the affair might provide a wedge that Dakkadia could use against the Council, it was too early to tell for certain. His time at the Citadel would afford him the opportunity to judge whether or not her ambition could be used against Ithram.

"I don't expect to see you again for a week, unless you have something you feel you need to report," Madari said, unaware of Morvandis's thoughts. "Until you return, Countess Thorn will assume your duties. I'll take my reports from her while you're gone."

The pair arrived at their destination. Madari didn't waste words; he simply turned to the front door and walked out, while his family fell in step close behind him.

Before the opening ceremonies of the third day of the Convocation, Archimagus Cedric DeVir approached Princess Chesare. The Princess curtseyed at his approach.

"Good morning, Archimagus DeVir. May I help you?"

"I wonder if I might speak with you for a moment," he asked, glancing around them to see who was nearby. "Privately."

Chesare allowed Cedric to pull her aside.

"Tomorrow, Prince Valeriad and his half-brother, Lord Daane, will be moving to the Citadel for a week to undergo their Testing. While the Examination itself will take a relatively short amount of time to accomplish, neither of them will be allowed to leave the Citadel for the full week of their stay. As they are not students of the Citadel, and are simply here for the Testing, we normally assign novices to act as liaisons for our guests. I wondered if you might be available to act as the liaison for Lord Daane? As the next scheduled Church service is a week away, there shouldn't be a conflict."

Chesare smiled at the thought of spending time with Prince Valeriad, but then she remembered what her teacher had actually said.

"Um, you said that you want me to be the liaison for Lord Daane? Wouldn't it be better for me to be assigned to Prince Valeriad? We're both Fireborn, after all."

Cedric's expression lightened somewhat at her words, as if he found them somehow amusing, but despite his amusement, his answer was definitely not the one she had been hoping for.

"I'm sorry, Your Highness, but that duty has already been assigned to my niece, Adrianna. I felt it best not to expose you to any potential scandal by *officially* placing you in such close proximity to Prince Valeriad."

Chesare's face fell. Despite her disappointment, she knew he was absolutely right to be worried about courting scandal. Lyrahe had already proven the danger of being linked too closely to the Prince of Dakkadia.

"I understand, Archimagus DeVir, though I would be less than honest if I didn't admit to being more than a bit disappointed." She thought for a second, and added, "I'm afraid that I am not familiar with Lord Daane at all, except that he and Lady Prudence Daemira are involved with each other. Can you tell me about him?"

"Phaedron is slightly older than Prince Valeriad at 20 years of age," Cedric said. "Unlike Valeriad, who is a Fireborn, Phaedron is a Waterborn, and he is also my nephew. I have known him for years, though it has been some time since we have last spoken, but he is lively and intelligent and has a quick wit and a wicked sense of humor. You will enjoy your time with him immensely."

"Well, then, I would be happy to act as Lord Daane's liaison, Archimagus DeVir. I will return to the Citadel early tomorrow to be there to meet him."

"That would be perfectly acceptable, Your Highness. You will be excused from your regular classes to allow you the freedom to act as his guide." As Cedric turned to leave her, he stopped himself and turned back again as if suddenly remembering something. "Oh, I forgot to mention something. Prince Valeriad and Lord Daane are quite inseparable under normal circumstances. The constraints imposed upon them by the Convocation and the formal gatherings that accompany it, haven't afforded them much of an opportunity to spend time with each other, but I assure you that you will have plenty of time to get to know both Lord Daane and Prince Valeriad."

Walking away from her, Cedric did not see the smile of joyful glee now on the Princess's face. Leaving the Princess to her own thoughts, Cedric approached the other members of the Mage High Council. Tavian looked past the Archimagus to the young Princess beyond.

"What did you say to Novice Illvanna, Cedric? She's beaming."

"Oh, I merely informed the young Princess of a new assignment that I have for her when she returns to the Citadel tomorrow." He glanced at Chesare, who was still smiling, and said, "It would appear she views her new assignment to be somewhat less than onerous." He didn't explain further, and Tavian let the matter drop.

A few seconds passed between them in silence, when Cedric noticed an odd look on his friend's face.

"You seem concerned, Tavian. Is something amiss?"

"Enaria is late," Tavian said, clearly annoyed. "That is most unlike her."

Cedric glanced at the Mages around them. He realized that Tavian was correct, for Enaria was not among them. He turned his attention to the Cathedral in general to look for her, and within a matter of moments, he saw her graceful form moving toward them from the entrance, walking briskly past the Dakkadian contingent. He was just about to call attention to her approach when he saw something that made him doubt his eyes. As she had moved past the nobles filing in, she walked up to Morvandis from behind and surreptitiously ran her hand down his forearm, before putting her delicate hand into his to give his fingers an affectionate squeeze.

The movement had been so fast, that had he not been looking directly at her at that exact moment, he wouldn't have seen it at all, but then she followed up the brief hand clasp with a sultry look at Morvandis that made Cedric's mouth go dry. He blinked once, and then again, as if disbelieving what he had just seen, and when he looked again, she had moved past Morvandis as if nothing at all had happened between them. As he stood there trying to comprehend what he had just seen, Tavian's voice pulled him out of his shocked state.

"Is something amiss, Cedric? Your mouth is hanging open."

Cedric forcibly closed his mouth and shook his head quickly as if to clear it.

"No, Tavian. Everything is fine. I just thought I saw something, but it was nothing." He pointed a finger at Enaria and added, "There's your sister."

"Ah, excellent. I was beginning to worry. She disappeared from the party last night and I didn't see her again for the rest of the evening."

Cedric took another look at Enaria and noticed a self-satisfied smile upon her face, which disappeared completely when she noticed the two of them staring at her.

"Good of you to join us," Tavian said, once Enaria was close. "I was beginning to wonder if you were going to arrive in time for us to avoid another lecture on the importance of being punctual by Patriarch Varic."

"No chance of that! I want to avoid that fate as much as you do . . . though now that I think on it, I believe we have Cedric here to blame for that experience."

Cedric raised a hand to his chest in mock indignation and looked at her with guileless eyes.

"Me? I had nothing to do with the late arrival of the royalty on that first day. How can you hold me accountable for that excruciating lecture?"

"While it may be true that you weren't the cause for their tardiness," Enaria said, snorting, "you certainly were quick to profit from it . . . even from Patriarch Varic, if memory serves."

"Ah, good times," Cedric said in mock bliss. He gave her a sly look and took the opportunity to change the subject. "Tavian was just telling me that you left the party early last night and didn't return at all. Did you have an eventful evening?"

"Not particularly," she said. "I'm afraid that my tolerance for formal parties is a bit lower than yours."

"They are an acquired taste, of that there is no doubt." Cedric took in her appearance and added in a teasing tone, "You look quite radiant this morning. Very well-rested, indeed. You must have slept very well last night. Care to share your secret with us?"

Enaria frowned.

"What secret would that be?"

Cedric gave her a sly look.

"The secret for getting such a good night's sleep, of course. There is a secret, is there not? About last night?" He arched an eyebrow at her and gave her a knowing look, but she simply crossed her arms over her chest and gave him a severe look.

"There's no secret, Cedric. Simply retire early rather than stay up until all hours of the night."

Cedric shrugged noncommittally, and let the matter drop, but after a few moments of quiet he spoke again.

"Prince Valeriad and Lord Daane will be admitted to the Citadel in the morning to begin their observation period before the Testing begins." He paused and gave her another sly look. "It is my understanding that Mage Morvandis will be accompanying them to the Citadel and remaining throughout the entirety of their Examinations." He saw Enaria stiffen at the mention of Morvandis' name, and turned his attention to the Mage in question. As he took in Morvandis's appearance, he began to notice little things about his attire and his demeanor that seemed out of place.

"Morvandis seems tired this morning. Perhaps you should have a word with him, Enaria. As you are his former instructor, I am certain he would appreciate your insights as to how he may achieve a restful night's sleep. The two of you should have plenty of time to discuss the subject over the next week."

Cedric wagged his eyebrows at her in a knowing fashion before finally granting her a reprieve by taking his seat. As the other Mages followed suit, Cedric took the opportunity to analyze his own thoughts about a potential relationship between Enaria and Morvandis. He wasn't sure how that had come about, for she had never expressed an interest in the Dakkadian Mage-Lord before, but he had seen their byplay with his own eyes, so the evidence was undeniable.

He looked at Morvandis again, wondering what exactly Enaria saw in him, for Morvandis was now, and always had been, a cold, passionless man. Despite her willingness to participate in his playful banter, Enaria, too, was considered to be severe, even by Elven standards, and he found it difficult to believe that the two would have much in common . . . or much to talk about. The thought of them as lovers was almost laughable. Cedric had never heard even a rumor of Enaria seeing anyone on a romantic basis, and if she had decided to start now, why had she chosen Morvandis? He pondered the question for a while, but no answer presented itself, and after the Convocation began in earnest, he dropped the matter completely.

Shortly after the evening meal, the guests adjourned to the anteroom to continue the third in a seemingly never-ending series of parties. Deirdre normally enjoyed parties very much, but the Dakkadian contingent was systematically being ignored by the other groups. Given the Dakkadian reputation for warlike behavior, Deirdre wasn't at all surprised, but three nights in a row of being treated like a pariah was getting on her nerves. As she watched little groups of people mingling with each other, she began looking for something to do to alleviate her mounting boredom. She had thought about touring the castle, but had restrained herself, despite the appeal, for she firmly believed that it was up to her to find a way to bridge the divide between the groups. The warrior in her refused to leave the field of battle until she had found a way to break the stalemate.

Her gaze returned involuntarily to Prince Lain of Ferralin, who stood once again with Princess Lyrahe of Illymar. Both of them looked thoroughly miserable, and neither of them had spoken more than a few words to each other all evening. Deirdre felt truly sorry for both of them, for it was obvious that Lyrahe, at least, had somewhere else she would rather be.

Or rather, someone else she would rather be with, she corrected herself.

Lyrahe hid her disappointment well, but the fact that she hadn't even glanced at Valeriad in two days spoke volumes about the reasons for her misery. Deirdre understood the reason for Lyrahe's unhappiness, and she did sympathize, but the person she truly felt sorry for was Prince Lain.

No one wanted to be a second choice, especially for something as important as marriage, and it was obvious to everyone that that was exactly what Lyrahe considered him to be. Deirdre had watched him closely for three days looking for some way to speak to him, but the Prince had not left his father's side, even for an instant. He was handsome enough, after a fashion, with the dark reddish-brown skin and black hair common to the Ferralin Empire. But compared to her brother—*both* her brothers—he was actually quite plain. *Still, there's something about him underneath the surface. Almost a darkness,* she thought. *That, and the obvious intelligence behind his eyes makes him extremely interesting—a fact which seems to have escaped Princess Lyrahe's notice.*

Until she could catch him alone, there was no way she would risk being rebuffed by the courtiers and hangers-on surrounding him. Having watched him so closely, she had noticed one peculiar thing: he spent quite a bit of time looking at the quiet figure of Princess Tais, his former betrothed, who always stood unmoving in the same spot in the grand chamber staring out the window. She was there again this evening, silently gazing out the window, lost in her thoughts and ignored by the other guests. Lain never tried to speak to her or approach her at all, but every time he looked at her, Deirdre could see a look of concern cross his handsome features.

As she watched him watching Tais, a look of resolution crossed his face and he turned to speak with Lyrahe. After a few quiet words, she curtseyed deeply to him and he bowed to her, before he turned to a manservant standing behind him and held out a hand. The manservant bowed low to his Prince and extended a long, elaborately carved case, which the Prince took before leaving the group unaccompanied. Deirdre expected him to walk to Tais but, to her surprise, he instead moved toward the ornate doorway leading to the exit. In a flash, Deirdre moved, silently following the elegantly dressed Ferraline Prince. She had no idea where he was going or what was in the case, but she knew that she would never have a better chance to speak with him, and she *had* to seize the opportunity.

Like Prince Lain, Madari was watching Tais. His nobles and diplomats had each made attempts to draw him into conversations covering a variety of topics, but he hadn't allowed himself to be distracted. He had instead spent his time studying his quarry and looking for the opportune moment to approach her. A brief movement at the Ferralin and Illymar group caught his attention, and as he watched, the Crown Prince excused himself and left the room. A second later, Deirdre too moved toward the exit, and Madari decided that this was as good an opportunity as any to approach Tais.

"If you will excuse me," Madari said to his hangers on. Without acknowledging the bows or curtsies of his nobles, Madari moved away from the group and toward a steward carrying a tray of glasses, where he again procured two drinks. With the glasses in hand, he walked up behind Tais and cleared his throat to gain her attention. She gave a small start at the sound and turned to look at him, and when she recognized who it was, her face blossomed into a beautiful smile.

I could lose myself in that smile, thought Madari. Gazing into her amber eyes he thought, *I could drown in those depths.*

He stood there, not saying a word as their eyes held each other, until Tais broke the silence by glancing at the glass in his hand.

"Good evening, Your Majesty. Is that drink for me?"

He closed his eyes briefly and gave himself a slight shake to break the spell she had cast over him, and proffered one of the glasses to her before responding.

"Good evening to you as well, Countess. Indeed, it is. Are you well today?"

She took the glass from him, taking a sip.

"Quite well, indeed, Your Majesty. I'm glad to see you again. I must confess that I've been thinking about you quite a bit. I had a lovely time last evening, even if it may have been wrong of me to monopolize your time like that." She peered at him over the rim of the glass through long lashes before continuing. "I look forward to continuing where we left off."

Madari smiled.

"I believe that you offered to show me the Spire and its grounds yesterday, Countess. Would this be a convenient time to call upon you for a tour?"

Tais's smile widened, and a mischievous look crossed her face.

"Oh, I think I can somehow pull myself away from my busy social schedule for someone as important as you."

His smile matched hers and he extended a hand to her, palm up. She placed her fingertips into his hand and allowed herself to be drawn away from the window and toward the exit. As they walked side-by-side to the door, she turned to Madari.

"Where would you like to begin the tour, Your Majesty?"

"This is your home, so I leave the decision in your capable hands. We have all the time in the world," he said.

As the pair left the hall, another set of amber eyes watched them leave. Unlike Tais's eyes, however, Queen Aveliad's eyes held no amusement at all.

Prince Lain moved silently through the corridor until he came to the entrance to the closed veranda, directly beneath the open window Tais normally stood before, and he opened the hand carved case containing his most prized possession: his flute. The flute was four feet long and quite thick, a master's work that had been a gift from his father many years ago. His fingers found their proper places along its length, and he took a moment to consider which song to play for her. Once he had decided on an appropriate tune, he stepped forward and glanced into the window she had been standing before to make sure certain she was still there. Unfortunately, he found that she wasn't there. As he lowered the flute to his side in confusion, he began looking at the other windows, trying to see if she had perhaps moved, but it soon became apparent that she was no longer standing in front of any of the windows. His disappointment mounting, he lowered the flute to his side and began to chuckle at his atrocious luck.

I can't even do this one simple thing correctly.

The chuckles began to grow louder, and eventually, they turned into gales of laughter as the events of the last three days replayed in his head. Tears formed in his eyes from the hysterical laughter, and fell freely as he let the bitter humor of the moment wash over him. Soon enough, however, the amusement faded and he wiped his eyes and reached for his case. As his fingers felt for the latch, a small voice sounded from the doorway.

"Oh, please play something. It would be a shame to return so beautiful an instrument to rest without having played at least one song."

Lain whirled around in surprise to see who had spoken to him, mortified that someone had seen him in his moment of weakness. He recognized the diminutive Princess instantly, though he wondered just how Princess Deirdre had found him, and perhaps more importantly, just how long had she been standing there.

"I followed you, Your Highness. I've been watching you for the past few days looking for a way that I might speak with you."

Lain quirked an eyebrow at that and felt his familiar cloak of formality settle across his shoulders.

"Good evening, Princess Deirdre. I apologize for my unseemly display. I did not realize you were there."

Deirdre stepped into the veranda and curtseyed formally.

"I did not wish to interrupt you or embarrass you, but my curiosity got the better of me, I'm afraid. I love music, you see, and from the way you handled the flute I could tell that you share that same love."

"Oh? You can tell simply by the way an instrument is held whether a person has a passion for music?"

She flashed him a beautiful smile.

"Of course, for you hold it with reverence. I can tell quite easily that your flute is an important part of you."

Despite his wariness, he found himself warming up to her. In a flash, he made his decision.

"I would be happy to play for you, Princess. Is there something in particular you would like to hear?"

Deirdre thought about it for a moment before responding.

"Play whatever you wish, Your Highness. I enjoy all music equally."

Lain bowed formally to her and then raised the flute to his lips to begin his performance.

The song he chose to play was the same one he had chosen to play for Tais. It was a very sad tune, a lament to lost love quite popular in the Ferralin Empire. As the notes filled the quiet garden, he lost himself in the tranquility of the moment, enjoying the night air and the stillness of the veranda.

The Ferraline flute was famous for the mournful sounds that it could produce, not at all like the playful notes of a traditional flute. Deirdre was spellbound by the haunting tune, listening in absolute fascination to the performance, and as the song progressed, Lain thought he could see a glisten in her eyes that hadn't been there before. The song became deeper, with a dolorous melody that spoke of bitter loss and unending heartbreak. When the song finally ended, Deirdre didn't say a word; she simply reached up with a lace kerchief and dabbed forcefully at her eyes. Lain smiled at the quiet sniffles she was desperately trying to conceal, and when she finally regained her composure, she gave him a mock frown, the severity of which was belayed only by the gleam in her eye.

"I would say that that makes us even for my embarrassing you earlier, Prince Lain." She dabbed her eyes again and said, "That was beautiful. I can't believe I'm crying like this." She waited until her tears had dried before speaking again and, before she spoke, she gave him a radiant smile. "Your rendition of 'So Far, My Love' was exquisite. That is a difficult piece to play at the best of times, and yours was the best I've ever heard."

At that, it was Lain's turn to frown, for the title she had given the song was unfamiliar to him, and he hadn't been aware that the song had ever been played outside of the confines of the Ferralin Empire. Deirdre's smile faded a bit at his expression.

"Did I say something wrong?"

"Oh, no, Princess Deirdre. It's just that I've never heard that name before. In Ferralin, the song is called 'Regret'. I was not aware that anyone outside of Ferralin had even heard it."

"Of course I've heard it. It's my mother's favorite song. Does your version have words to accompany the music?" she asked with a smile.

Lain shook his head sorrowfully.

"I'm afraid not, Princess Deirdre. Or if it does, I've never heard them."

"Then, would you mind playing it again?"

Lain nodded gracefully, and raised the flute to his lips to play once again. As the first notes filled the garden, Deirdre's crystal clear voice joined in perfect harmony to the music. The words were haunting.

In spring our love seemed everlasting,
The sun shone high above.
We filled our days with dreams and passion,
And filled our nights with love.

In summer fair we drank of life,
And lived without regret,
We promised we would never leave
Our love we'd not forget

But autumn came and you fell ill,
And from my arms you've flown.
So, now, what once seemed without end,
Has left me all alone.

So far, my love, so far away,
Your love has gone from me,
And now I sit in winter's chill,
And dream of being with thee.

So far, my love, so far away,
Your love has flown from me,
And I pray that soon the wind will blow,
And fly me home to thee.

Lain reluctantly lowered the flute from his lips, wishing he could somehow prolong the moment, but the unexpected intensity of the song and the words would not allow him that luxury. The Princess's singing voice was like a delicate crystal, perfect in pitch and absolutely flawless, and was far and away the most beautiful he had ever heard. Lain looked at the young Princess, and felt connected to her in a way he hadn't felt with either Tais or Lyrahe, and for the first time he looked at Deirdre, not as a young Princess from a rival nation, but as a beautiful young woman of glorious talent and boundless grace in her own right. A thought blew through him like a thunderbolt, and before the flute had reached his side, he knew he had finally found someone he could learn to love.

As he gazed at her, trying to come to terms with this unexpected revelation, he realized she must have felt something similar: the connection he had felt with her was mirrored within her, but she, too, seemed to be unable to cope with the unexpected connection. For just an instant, he allowed himself to envision a life with Deirdre, raising a family together and standing side-by-side as the rulers of Ferralin, but the instant passed and reality returned with sickening suddenness. *That life can never be*, he thought in sadness. *I belong to another.*

Deirdre looked as if she wanted to say something, but he turned his back to her firmly, opened the case to his flute, and placed the instrument in the velvet confines before closing the case and re-latching it. Once the instrument was safely away, Lain spoke, his back still toward her.

"I must return to the party now, Your Highness. I have been too long away. My betrothed will be wondering where I am."

He hesitated before picking up the case, and he felt Deirdre's delicate hand touch his back in a comforting gesture.

"I understand, Prince Lain, and I will not keep you from your intended. But, I thank you for your indulgence in satisfying a childish whim. The memory of your perfect play will be something I will cherish until the end of my days."

Lain did turn to her then, the cloak of his formality once again firmly settled upon his shoulders. He started to say something proper, something vague and polite, but the words would not come. Instead, he spoke from the heart, something he had never done before.

"I am not certain if we will be afforded the opportunity to see each other in such an intimate setting again, but I will hope for it. Good evening."

He bowed to her in respect, but instead of curtseying as was proper, Deirdre impulsively stepped forward and embraced him, wrapping slim arms around him and squeezing gently. He hesitated in surprise at the unexpected contact, but despite his initial hesitation, he found himself returning the embrace. Together, the two stood in each other's arms for several moments before Deirdre broke the embrace and stepped back.

"The Convocation will last for a few more weeks, and who knows? There may be another opportunity for us to see each other," and without another word, she walked away, leaving him standing alone in the quiet veranda.

I hope so, Your Highness.

PRINCESS DEIRDRE DHAERHAN
--THE JEWEL OF DAKKADIA--

CHAPTER SIXTEEN

"Citadel"

Two liveried members of the Mage Guard allowed Phaedron and Valeriad entrance into the Citadel, but did not follow them in. They waited in the foyer for several minutes with no sign of a guide anywhere.

"I hope someone is going to meet us," Phaedron said. "I have no idea where we are supposed to go."

Valeriad grunted, and the two of them peered around at their surroundings wondering what exactly was expected of them. The entrance hall wasn't particularly large, for the Citadel was not designed for large gatherings the way the Cathedral of Zarryiosiad was. Instead, the outer doors led into a circular chamber with a vaulted ceiling and three sets of doors, all leading in different directions.

There was no sign of any arcane runes or mysterious symbols on any of the doors, and Phaedron actually felt a bit of disappointment, for he'd hoped to see something a bit more dramatic from the center of the Mage community in the world. Instead, the walls were paneled wood, stained a dark mahogany, and very tastefully designed. Phaedron had just about decided to try opening one of the sets of doors when the center doors opened silently on well-oiled hinges, and four people stepped through. Three of the figures were instantly recognizable to

Phaedron, as he knew Morvandis, Cedric DeVir, and Adrianna DeVir quite well, indeed. The fourth person was a mystery to him, however, and a casual glance at her novice robes told him that she had to be a student here at the Citadel. As if reading his mind, Valeriad struck him lightly on the stomach.

"The person you probably don't recognize is Princess Chesare Illvanna," he said. "She's King Orem's youngest daughter, and a Fireborn like me. I met her on the same evening that I met her sister, Lyrahe."

Phaedron smothered a smile, for Valeriad had spoken often about Lyrahe, and he had developed a tendency to put things in context as they related to the raven-haired Princess. Phaedron felt bad for Valeriad and his plight, and absolutely refused to tease him about her, but he still found Valeriad's obsession to be highly amusing. The quartet of Mages approached and Cedric spoke first.

"Welcome to the Citadel, Prince Valeriad, Lord Daane."

As he addressed them, he stepped forward and extended his hand for welcoming handshakes. After both Phaedron and Valeriad had greeted their uncle properly, Cedric stepped back.

"Because you are here for your Examinations, you will not be allowed to leave for the next week. However, you are by no means prisoners here. Rather, you are honored guests and you will be treated as such. The entirety of the Citadel is open for your exploration, and you are invited—even encouraged—to audit classes with the other students. The Citadel is a very large place, however, so I have taken the liberty of assigning escorts for each of you."

He gestured at the two girls standing behind him and said, "Adrianna will act as your escort, Prince Valeriad, while Princess Chesare will act as yours, Lord Daane. If you have any questions, feel free to ask your escorts, or any other Mage or servant you meet. Anyone here will be more than happy to provide you with an answer, or at least tell you where you can find one." He clapped his hands together once. "Now, if you will follow me, I will show you to the guest quarters." Cedric moved toward the set of doors to the right and Valeriad and Phaedron fell in behind him.

"This section houses the guest quarters, the Administration Offices, and much of the day-to-day operations. You will find the dining area here as well, though you are free to enjoy your meals in your own quarters or in any of the common areas."

As they walked through the exquisitely decorated hallway, a woman stepped through a doorway along their path and stopped to wait for them. As their group approached, Cedric nodded a greeting and said, "Good morning, Archimagus Wintersong."

The gorgeous Elf returned the courtesy absently and turned her attention to Morvandis.

"I wonder if I might have a word with Mage Morvandis, Cedric?"

Morvandis stepped away from the group.

"This may take some time," Morvandis said. "Please proceed without me." He then turned his attention to his two charges and said, "I will check on your progress later. Comport yourselves with the utmost dignity at all times. You represent Dakkadia."

With that, he and Archimagus Wintersong excused themselves and stepped through the doorway where she was standing.

Once the door had closed behind them, Phaedron turned to Valeriad and said, "Thank the Archon. I expected him to be watching us at every turn."

"We'd better find something to break or set on fire before he comes to his senses. We do represent Dakkadia, after all," Valeriad said. He stopped abruptly and turned to Chesare. "Where can we do the most damage in the least amount of time? We're on a schedule here: we need to make the most of our visit."

Both Chesare and Adrianna laughed at that, and Valeriad congratulated himself on his successful effort to draw out the Illymari Princess. Once she finished laughing, Chesare put her finger to her chin as if considering the question.

"I would have to say you should start with either the alchemy labs or the experimentation wing. Both of them have plenty of things that are already more than ready to explode all on their own. I should think that it wouldn't take much of an effort to push them over the edge into something truly catastrophic."

Phaedron laughed at that, but Valeriad assumed a look of excitement.

"Back that way?" he asked, pointing the way they had come.

At her nod of assent, Valeriad grabbed Phaedron's arm and began pulling him in that direction.

"We'd better hurry! With luck, we should have this place leveled by lunch!"

Phaedron, all-too-happy to play along, gave the girls a quick bow before whirling around and letting Valeriad pull him a couple of steps. Cedric, however, had other ideas, and cleared his throat to stop them in their tracks.

"I believe we were heading to the Guest Quarters? You can begin your careers as budding arsonists later." All four of the younger members began to laugh, and they fell back in behind the Archimagus when he again began to move. After no more than a few steps, Cedric added in an air of casual superiority, "Besides, the alchemy labs and the experimentation wing are the worst places to start. The rooms are ensorcelled to prevent just that sort of mischief. Believe me, I know." He raised his hand to his chin in a mirror of the pose Chesare had used when pretending to contemplate the problem of where to begin their mayhem. "If you really want to cause havoc, you should begin in the library. Plenty of tinder there to start with, and the carpets and heavy drapes will spread the blaze throughout the wing in moments."

For a moment, none of them could believe what the stern looking Archimagus had said, but the laughter in his eyes was more than enough proof to convince them that none of them had misheard him.

"That was a terrible thing to say, Archimagus DeVir," Chesare said. "What would Librarian Asiria say if she heard you threatening her library?" She pursed her lips in thought, "Though, now that you mention it, you're absolutely right: no one would ever expect it."

As laughter filled the hall yet again, Cedric joined in. Soon enough, however, the trip ended and Cedric opened a pair of doors, then stood aside to allow the guests entry. The apartments were sumptuously furnished, with a large canopy bed and elaborately carved furniture set around the room.

"Lord Daane, this is your room," Cedric said. "Prince Valeriad, your room is directly across the hall. The servants have already unpacked your things, so you will find everything you brought neatly arranged in the drawers or hanging in the armoire. You are allowed visitors, so feel free to invite whomever you wish."

"Yes, do please," Adrianna said quickly to Phaedron. "I would love to see the Corsair here in the Citadel. She never seems to attend the parties. Whenever I *do* see her, she's with you."

"Lady Prudence did mention that she might drop in to check on me a time or two," Phaedron said, smiling. "Something about 'keeping me out of trouble', or some such. I, of course, have no idea what she was could possibly mean."

"If you will excuse me, there are matters that I must attend to," Cedric said. "If you have any questions, Chesare and Adrianna will be more than happy to answer them." He paused for a moment before adding, "If you would truly like to test your skills and cause some mayhem, I would recommend spending some time in the training yard with the Mage Guard. I think it would be a good experience for both of you."

With that, he left the room, leaving the four of them alone for the first time. Valeriad spoke first.

"Princess Chesare, please allow me to say that it is wonderful to see you again. I'm glad you took me at my word when I asked if you would be willing to give us a tour of the Citadel. Please allow me to thank you in advance for taking on, what I'm sure will be, an onerous assignment."

"When Archimagus DeVir asked me if I would be willing to act as your liaison, I couldn't agree fast enough. I'm just sorry that Lyrahe isn't a Powerborn. She would have loved to have been here."

She glanced at Valeriad as if to gauge his reaction to the name, and he didn't disappoint her. A dark cloud seemed to pass before him, dampening his spirit somewhat from what it had been just a moment before.

"If I may ask, how is Lyrahe doing?" Valeriad said after a moment. "I didn't consider the consequences of my actions on that first evening when we were allowed to dance with each other. Did . . . did she get in any trouble for my foolishness?"

He glanced at her with more than a bit of trepidation, and she responded with a slight nod.

"She did, somewhat, though not through any fault of yours. My father favors a marriage between Lyrahe and Prince Lain, and he ordered her not to see you, or even speak with you again, without an escort." At Valeriad's crestfallen expression, she rushed forward and placed her hands on his forearm. "If it is any consolation, she regrets the restriction as much as you do. Given the choice, she would rather spend time with you than with Prince Lain."

Valeriad noticed a mischievous smile on her face. The gleam in her eye told him something was afoot, but he didn't press.

"*I* would very much like to see what Cedric was talking about when he mentioned the Mage Guard," Phaedron asked. "Would either of you be willing to show me the way?"

"That sounds just the thing I need right now," Valeriad said. "Ladies?"

The crash of weapons and the smells of sulfur and ozone filled the tremendous training compound, and both Phaedron and Valeriad instantly felt at home. Dozens of Mages, both male and female, were exercising or practicing weapon techniques, and Phaedron began looking around for someone to ask about participating. He didn't have to wait long, for a burly Mage with a bald head and huge arms stepped forward and examined him from head to toe. It was the appraising look of a purely military man, and Phaedron responded instantly by squaring his shoulders and placing his hands on the hilts of his weapons in a pose of casual readiness, the standard "at rest" stance of the Dakkadian army. Phaedron couldn't tell what the man thought of him, but after he concluded his examination, he stepped right up into Phaedron's face, until their noses were practically touching.

"I hear you two are supposed to be important people where you come from, but that don't mean nothin' here." he said, his voice more of a growl than anything else. "You want to wear the weapons of a warrior? Then you've got to prove yourself, Dakk Rat, same as everyone else."

The accent was instantly recognizable to all of them as that of a commoner from the Free Cities of the Badlands, and Phaedron responded instantly to the challenge.

"You certainly talk big for such a tiny man, Freebooter," Phaedron said, giving the shorter man a cocky look complete with sneer. He pointed to a large circle surrounded by narrowly spaced wooden posts and said, "I'll be over there waiting for you to screw up enough courage to come and face me. Dig deep—I don't have all day for you to find your manhood."

He stepped away from the man and arrogantly turned his back on him in a calculated insult. The guardsman watched him walk away from him toward the circle, before rounding on Valeriad and poking him in the chest with a hard finger.

"Stay right where you are, boy . . . I'll deal with you in a moment."

Valeriad yawned elaborately, before his right hand shot up unexpectedly and caught the man's finger in a vice-like grip. He slowly bent the finger backward while holding his gaze, and at the first flicker of pain in the guardsman's eye he smiled casually.

"The only thing that will be left of *you* in a moment will be a greasy, foul-smelling stain," Valeriad said, "and I'm sure even the stain will have bad manners."

He let go of the man's finger and stared at him until the man backed up, still glaring. The Mage walked to the half of the circle facing Phaedron and pulled a metal-bound cudgel from his belt. He swung the cudgel in an easy arc, first one way and then the other, obviously to loosen his wrist. Phaedron answered by drawing his rapier and main gauche, swinging them across his chest to loosen up his shoulders, before signaling his readiness. As one, both of the men's eyes transformed, Phaedron's into a brilliant blue and the Freebooter's into a fiery red. There was no formal signal to begin; instead the two extended their defenses outward until they overlapped, and then they began testing each other's strength.

Chesare had never been to the Mage Guard's compound before and she didn't know what it was she was seeing.

"I'm not familiar with this game," she asked Valeriad. "What are the rules?"

"The game is known by different names from place to place, but in Dakkadia we call it 'The Ring,'" he said. "The inside of the Ring is the battleground. Surrounding it are 60 wooden posts, randomly spaced and each of differing heights. Sitting on top of the posts are small clay pots or candles to act as targets, with one on each post. The Ring is divided into two halves, with 30 posts on one side and 30 on the other. The first Mage to break all thirty of his opponent's targets is declared the winner. You can use any means at your disposal to break them, be it weapon, power, or body. All that matters is the jar or candle must be destroyed."

He glanced at the man who had issued the challenge and continued.

"He made a mistake by challenging Phaedron first: Phaedron has been playing this game against Morvandis since before I developed my own ability. I've been watching him play for years, and he's quite good. Although, truth be told, he has never scored a point against Morvandis. Morvandis is just too powerful, and strength is an important part of this game. This will be fun to watch."

Chesare summoned her ability and began looking at the Ring with her power. The bald man had surrounded himself in a series of concentric circles of Fire Magic, with the circles extending far past the outermost ring of wooden posts. She knew from her training that when two Mages dueled, they always surrounded themselves with a variation of those circles. Their purpose was simple: attacks by one Mage against another could take many different forms, both aggressive and passive. The defensive constructs were used to detect an opponent's attacks, no matter what direction they came from or what form they took. Then, they acted as shields, protecting the Mage.

It was easier to defend when two Mages using the same power dueled, for you could always see where the threats were coming from. In fact, when two Mages of the same power dueled, it inevitably became a war of dominance, with one Mage trying to overpower the other through brute force. But, against an opponent who used a different power, it was much harder, for you could not see an opponent's weaves signaling an incoming attack. Until it crossed the boundary of one of your defensive circles, it was impossible to try and seize the other Mage's creation and turn it back upon him. You had to rely completely on your passive defenses and your reflexes.

The Mage Guard struck first, with a powerful blast of fire breaking through Phaedron's defenses and destroying a jug, but Phaedron immediately countered, summoning an icicle from the ground that split into three shards, each one finding a different target. He then darted to the left, swinging his cudgel in a backhand arc that Phaedron barely had time to deflect, but Phaedron countered by delivering a vicious kick to the Mage Guard's stomach that doubled him over in pain. As his opponent fell, Phaedron exploded in a whirlwind of action, his sword and dagger lashing out like serpent's tongues to knock over target after target. In just a few seconds, more than half of the Guard's clay pots were destroyed without a single answering strike.

The Guardsman recovered quickly and regained his breath, and reacted by sending a dozen balls of fire springing from his hands in twisting patterns toward targets all along Phaedron's hemisphere. The Dakkadian nobleman was ready for him, however, and a single wall of ice sprang into existence from one edge of his territory to the other, all along the circle's periphery. The fireballs struck the wall with a vengeance, but were unable to break through to their targets before being extinguished by Phaedron's shield.

The Mage Guard, clearly frustrated at his inability to score, turned his attention back to Phaedron and began a series of attacks with his cudgel that the younger man was forced to deflect. He was completely unable to penetrate Phaedron's guard, but the strength of his attacks did force Phaedron into a slow retreat. Even that worked to Phaedron's advantage, however, for he was able to control his retreat and angle himself toward a fresh section of the Mage Guard's territory. When Phaedron reached the periphery, he stopped his retreat and began parrying the cudgel using only his rapier. Without even looking, he reached behind himself with his main gauche and knocked over another candle. This went on again and again until only one target remained.

Chesare knew the combat wasn't as easy as Phaedron was making it look, because he was being sorely pressed on the magical front, but he was doing an outstanding job of negating the other Mage's magic. As she watched, the Mage Guard forgot about defense in an all-out bid to overwhelm Phaedron's defenses, only to crash to the ground an instant later. Chesare wondered how that could have happened, until she spotted a small patch of ice on the floor beneath his prone body that was the obvious culprit for his unexpected fall.

Without a moment's hesitation, Phaedron whirled around, swinging his rapier in a wide slash that seemed to miss the last candle altogether. As the sword finished its arc, he turned away from the target and sheathed his main gauche, then reached down with his empty hand and gave the Mage Guard a hand standing up. The man gratefully accepted the aid, and with Phaedron's help, he stood up quickly, careful to step around the patch of ice on the ground. He looked quizzically at the sole remaining candle on his side of the ring, and Phaedron answered his unspoken question by touching the top of the wax target with the tip of his rapier, and pushing gently. To everyone's amazement, only the top half of the candle fell away, cut so perfectly he hadn't even disturbed its rest. The Mage Guard immediately extended a hand to Phaedron in welcome, and Phaedron took it with a smile.

"Welcome to the Mage Citadel, My Lord. My name is Barrax. When we heard that two Dakkadian noblemen would be coming to the Citadel, all of us bid heavily to be the first to challenge you. When I won the right, Archimagus DeVir warned me that my reach had almost certainly exceeded my grasp." He raised a hand to his head and rubbed his bald pate twice in a chagrinned gesture. "It seems he was right; I haven't been manhandled like that in a very long time." He barked a laugh and clapped Phaedron on the back in a comradely manner. "If you are an example of what Dakkadian Warrior-Mages are like, Illymar is right to be worried."

To the side, Chesare heard the man's words and instantly stiffened in indignation. She rounded on the Mage Guard, who stepped back at the heated look she gave him. Chesare put her hands on her hips and in an icy voice asked,

"Is this a game that anyone can play?"

Two sets of eyebrows shot up in surprise at her tone, and the Guardsman hesitated.

"Anyone can play, Novice, but you have no weapon training," the Guardsman said. "Without a weapon, it might be a bit too dangerous for you."

Chesare didn't listen; she stepped forward and raised an eyebrow at Phaedron before gesturing toward a second Ring.

"We'll just see about that." She gave Phaedron a saucy look. "I'll be over here waiting for you to gather up enough courage to come and face me." She turned her back on him and walked a step toward the circle, before tossing her long hair and looking over her shoulder and adding, "Dig deep . . . I haven't got all day."

Everyone who heard her words broke out in whistles of approval at her audacity. Phaedron looked taken aback, but after a second or two, he shrugged and dutifully followed Chesare to the challenge circle. As he took his position, he glanced down at his weapons as if wondering what exactly he was supposed to do with them against an unarmed girl, but Chesare didn't give him long to ponder the question. Instead, she tapped into her power and began setting her defenses into a much more intricate pattern than Barrax had used. As layer after layer of defensive screens fell into place, Phaedron did the same, while simultaneously drawing his weapons.

She waited quietly until he was prepared.

"Begin."

Phaedron hesitated for a moment before launching himself at her, sword extended to disrupt her concentration, but he hadn't taken a single step before he shouted in surprise and dropped both of his weapons. The blades were smoking slightly where she had used her ability to heat the metal to the point that they were too painful for him to hold. She waited until he began circling her and testing her defenses magically before she acted. Chesare pointed a finger at one of Phaedron's targets.

"I will destroy that one first."

Phaedron stiffened at the challenge, and readied himself for her strike. A simple ball of fire shot from her hand, and he reacted to it by raising a shield of ice in front of the jug to block it. Just before the fireball struck the shield, it split into four parts, all of which moved around the shield as if they had a mind of their own. The sound of shattering crockery filled the room.

Every person in the room stopped what they were doing to watch the combat unfold. Phaedron released his hold on the shield and turned to attack, sending shards of ice like rain at her side of the floor. She didn't move at all, but every icicle he had summoned disappeared in flashes of light and heat before they could even come near their targets. Phaedron intensified the attack, seeking to batter his way through her shield, but Chesare paid that no mind. Instead, she pointed at a second jug.

"I will destroy that one next."

Phaedron reacted by encasing it in a cylinder of ice that was surrounded by a shimmering aura that would be more than sufficient to stop any lesser Mage's attacks. Chesare waited until Phaedron was prepared for her, and then unleashed her power in a single blazing line, almost too thin to see, that burned a neat hole right through both the aura and the sheath as if they weren't there. The icy cylinder exploded, and again the sound of breaking crockery filled the room.

This went on for some time, with Phaedron preparing a defense and Chesare defeating it with contemptuous ease, until only two of Phaedron's jugs were left. She turned to Barrax.

"Despite what you may believe, Illymar does not fear Dakkadia," Chesare said. "We simply feel that the loss of life which would occur, should the Kingdom of Dakkadia attempt some reckless and foolish action, would be a tragedy that we Illymari must seek to avoid. Should Dakkadia choose not to heed our warnings, we will be forced to chastise them." With no warning whatsoever, the next to last jug exploded into fragments.

Suddenly, all of the Fireborn in the room felt a massive presence emanating from the doorway. As they turned to see what had caused it, Morvandis stepped into the room from where he had been watching the display and walked into the Ring to stand beside Phaedron. He gave Chesare a polite bow, before saying,

"If you choose to ignore the threat Dakkadia poses to your nation, you are a fool," Morvandis said, "for the threat is very real, Princess. However, despite our reputation for warlike behavior, King Madari seeks a diplomatic solution with your Kingdom that would leave your island untouched by Dakkadian expansionism. For the last three days, King Madari has waited patiently for your father to speak with him, and for three days your father has repaid that patience with utter contempt." He gestured to the line of jugs on her side of the arena. "I will be destroying all of them at once."

Chesare responded to the challenge by drawing in every bit of power she could handle, and setting a shield she felt confident would be enough to stop any attack he could create. Her eyes blazed white from the sheer power she was drawing, and Morvandis waited until she was ready for him before igniting his own Fireborn magic. As he extended his own power toward the shield and felt her resonance, he said quietly,

"You have great strength, Princess, and I predict that one day soon you will be my equal in the use of Fire Magic." His eyes flared once, and Chesare screamed in fright, as he used his complete mastery of his ability to overwhelm her defenses at every point of her shield. Shards of crockery fell like rain as all thirty jugs exploded at the same time. When the dust settled, he gave Chesare a severe look and said, "Today is not that day." He turned and walked back toward the entrance, and as he reached the door, he turned back to her and said, "Illymari arrogance is not only foolish, it is dangerous. You would do well to shed that trait as soon as you are able. And if you have any influence with your father, I suggest that you use it. We could be great allies, if only he could look past his preconceptions."

Morvandis stepped through the door and disappeared.

The silence that filled the room after Morvandis's departure was deep. Phaedron was the first to move, having seen more than enough of Morvandis's power over the years to become accustomed to it, and he walked to where he had dropped his rapier and main gauche, reached down, and picked them up. To his obvious relief, they were cool to the touch, and he returned them to their scabbards with a flourish. As he turned back to her, she hung her head in shame. With a look of concern on his face he walked up to her.

"What's the matter, Princess? Did he injure you?"

She didn't meet his eyes.

"I'm fine," she said. "But you must hate me now, after what I did to you. I'll talk with Archimagus DeVir about finding you a replacement liaison." Still refusing to look at him, she turned away, but Phaedron caught her arm.

"What are you talking about? Why would I hate you?"

"I was showing off. It wasn't until Mage Morvandis defeated me that I understood how you must have felt. I'm ashamed of myself." She again lowered her eyes, finding some spot on the floor to focus on, so she didn't see Phaedron's face split into a wide grin as he began to laugh. He raised a hand and lifted her chin until she was looking into his eyes again.

"You obviously do not understand Dakkadians as well as you think. We respect strength above all else. The way you defeated me tells me that you are worth having both as a friend and an ally." He glanced at the doorway that Morvandis had passed through. "The fact that Morvandis himself came to deliver that message is a great honor. It shows that he considers you to be a potential threat, or a valuable ally."

Chesare's gaze followed his to the doorway.

"That was . . . humbling. I should thank him for the lesson, I think. It's obvious that I have been taking my own strength for granted. I'll have to work harder." She glanced up again at Phaedron's smiling face, and said, "I look forward to the rematch."

Phaedron laughed again and put his hand upon her back in a friendly gesture, then guided her to where Valeriad and Adrianna were standing, well away from the arena. As they approached, both of the spectators began to clap their hands in approval for her performance.

"That was an amazing display," Valeriad said. "Adrianna told me that you first learned about your power a month ago. The skill you have already achieved is incredible, especially considering how little time you have actually been studying. And, on a personal note, having been on the receiving end of an endless string of defeats by Phaedron here, all I can say is 'thank you' for putting this upstart in his place."

"Phaedron is a big bully," Adrianna said, agreeing with him. "He only picks on people weaker than him."

Valeriad made a strangled sound at that pronouncement.

"Besides Morvandis, I'm the only person he fights!"

Adrianna assumed a look of blissful innocence before she responded in a sweet tone.

"Like I said: weaker."

Valeriad gave her a mock glare and reached behind his back and patted it a few times. He then examined his hand as if looking for something.

"*Hmm.* No blood. As a character assassin your skills are unmatched. I barely felt the knife enter my back, traitor."

All four of them laughed as one, and Phaedron snapped a finger as if just remembering something. He took his arm from around Chesare's shoulder and moved back to the circle where they had fought their duel. As the other three wondered what exactly it was that he was doing, he walked to the sole remaining intact jug and picked it up. It fit easily into the palm of his hand and he hefted it once before walking back to the group. With a flourish and an easy smile, he proffered the jug to Chesare.

"A memento, Princess, from your humbled opponent. To the victor go the spoils."

Touched, she accepted the prize and in return she gave him a quick kiss on the cheek.

"Thank you," she said, blushing.

The group turned to leave when a boisterous voice stopped them in their tracks.

"Where do you think you're going? You and I have unfinished business."

With an elaborate groan, Valeriad turned to face Barrax, who was standing in a third circle waiting, cudgel in hand.

"Are you still here? I would have thought the drubbing you just received would have been more than your pride could handle."

Barrax simply grinned at that and pointed to the circle he and Phaedron had fought in.

"What, that? That was a good meal. Now it's time for dessert!"

"Don't go anywhere," he said to the group. "This won't take long."

He was already drawing his weapons as he walked away from the group and toward the Guardsman.

As Morvandis walked away from the Mage Guard's training area, he thought about his duel with the youngest daughter of King Orem, and the possible implications of her growing strength. When he had first set eyes upon her four days ago, he had been very impressed by her raw strength. None of the members of the Mage High Council could match her ability, and that alone made her of interest to him. Unfortunately, raw strength alone did not a Mage make. He could measure her potential power compared to his own, but until he actually tested himself against her, he could not be sure just how strong an opponent she would become.

Unfortunately, without challenging her, he had been unable to devise a way that he could test her to see how far she would rise. So, when he felt her drawing upon the vast reservoir of her power in her duel against Phaedron, he had sensed it from the other side of the Citadel and knew that he had to investigate. Enaria hadn't been happy he had felt compelled to leave her, but despite her charms, he was glad that he had. Chesare was much stronger—and much more gifted—than he had anticipated, given her relatively short training period, and seeing her actually use her abilities had been very educational.

Phaedron was an exceptionally talented Water Mage, but he had been totally outclassed when faced with the sheer power of the Illvanin girl. From Morvandis' unseen vantage point, he had watched her carefully as she displayed her ability, and he had been more than a little impressed.

The reasons he had intervened in the duel were two-fold. First, and foremost, he had wanted to test himself against the best the Citadel had to offer, and it was clear to him she truly was the best they had. Second, he had wanted to curb her arrogance before it ruined her as a Mage.

It was far too easy for Mages of such great strength to take their power for granted and refuse to push themselves to their limits and beyond, and a Mage of her budding talent was far too valuable to lose to mediocrity. It didn't matter to him that he was, in effect, aiding the enemy, for if she took the lesson to heart and became the Mage she had it in her to be, he firmly believed that one day he might learn a thing or two from her. Assuming she didn't kill him, that was. *That which does not destroy me empowers me,* he thought to himself.

He'd given her a taste of true power—power backed by years of experience, as well as raw strength—and hopefully, she would build upon that lesson and make herself even stronger. When he'd challenged her, he'd decided to restrict himself to using only Fire Magic, and when he'd begun his attack, he had put pressure against the entire length of her shield before beginning a rapid buildup of power. She had quickly matched him in that buildup, and it became clear to him that no matter how much pressure he applied, she could keep pace with him. So, he had done the unexpected; instead of continuing the gradual buildup as she had expected, he had suddenly trebled his power with absolutely no warning whatsoever.

It was the magical equivalent of a sudden sprint after a long leisurely walk, and she hadn't been prepared for it. She paid the price her for complacency, as he broke through her shield at every point and destroyed his targets before she could react. *A fine piece of work against a formidable opponent,* he thought, with more than a hint of self-satisfaction.

Enaria had asked him to join her in her private chambers after he had completed his investigation, and his stride was a little brisker than normal in anticipation of their meeting. It had been many years since he had last taken a lover: not because he wasn't interested in sex, but because he was very particular about his partners. As the Master of the Flower Court, he could have his pick of any of a thousand different women, but that was one line he had absolutely refused to cross.

The previous Master of the Flower Court, a man named Marigold, hadn't felt the same and the result was a complete loss of trust and respect from the very people he was supposed to lead. He had treated the Flowers as common whores, and they had so despised him for it, that they had celebrated his death. Morvandis had had his own private reasons for hating Marigold, but that particular account had been settled long ago.

As he turned the corner toward Enaria's personal chambers, he saw her waiting for him at the end of the hall, and what he saw made him grin in pleasant surprise. Enaria stood in front of the closed door to her chambers wearing absolutely nothing at all. Her flair for the dramatic appealed to his darker nature, and he began to slow his approach to delay his arrival, forcing her to stand nude and vulnerable for several seconds longer than absolutely necessary.

Though they were alone in the hallway, it was lined with doors, and the chances that a servant or another Mage would enter the hall and catch her in her exposed state, was a distinct possibility, but Enaria didn't seem to care in the slightest. Instead, when she saw him slowing his approach, she laughed quietly and gave him a smoldering look. She then reached up with one delicate hand and ran it down her soft curves in an incredibly sensual manner. She then followed up the caress with a look of abject desire that forced him to increase his pace, despite himself.

As he approached her, he expected her to open the door and step inside, but instead, she held out her arms in welcome. He stepped into her waiting arms and kissed her delicately parted lips, and then turned her to the side to press her back to the wall next to the door. Enaria hungrily returned his impassioned kiss, and reached up to run her fingers through his long black hair. When she finally broke the kiss, her fingers found the white streak in his hair at the center of his forehead and followed it all the way down to his waist. After her fingers finished their journey, she gave him a playful pout.

"What took you so long? I've been lonely."

He leaned forward while holding her eyes with his own, and with his left hand, he took hold of both of her wrists and lifted her arms above her head, pushing them gently against the wall. A small shudder of excitement passed through her at the aggressive contact, and she half-closed her eyes and looked at him through heavy lashes, awaiting his next move. He smirked at her in a mocking fashion, and then looked down at her perfect body, his eyes lingering on her flat stomach and firm breasts. He slowly ran his eyes over her body upon the same path she had caressed herself until he was once again looking into her eyes.

"I had to impart some instruction to young Novice Illvanna. She was, indeed, the source of the power we sensed."

Enaria, hands still held firmly above her head, smiled seductively.

"So *that* was what I felt. From the power level you achieved after you found her, the instruction must have been quite sharp." He chuckled, confirming her theory of the events, and she continued, "Now that you have finished playing with the children, perhaps we can move on to more pleasant matters?" She glanced at her door. "Shall we adjourn to my chambers? Or would you rather have me here in the hall?"

He expected her to somehow make her question a jest, but to Morvandis's immense surprise, the question had been a serious one. Had he so wished, she would have allowed him to have his way with her where anyone could witness them. For a second, he was tempted to take her up on her lascivious offer, but instead, he released her hands and stepped back.

"For now, I believe discretion to be the wiser course." She started to turn toward the door but he pushed her back against the wall one last time. "For now," he repeated in a deep voice.

He reached up with his free hand and ran it over her body in a caress, eliciting even more shudders from her desire-racked body. When he again stepped away from her, she pouted for a moment, and then reached for the latch of her door and allowed him to enter her private chambers.

Morvandis wasn't sure what he was expecting when he entered her room, but what he actually found definitely wasn't it. Her room was beyond messy, to the point of being truly slovenly, with articles of clothing scattered haphazardly in every conceivable direction, hanging from the corners of her furniture, or simply tossed into careless piles. Books were lying about in stacks, some obviously on the brink of tipping over. Scrolls and pieces of parchment were stuck to the walls in no apparent order, and bottles of different concoctions sat on every table. Thankfully, there were no trays of food anywhere to be seen, or that would have been more than sufficient to drive him from her chambers, no matter how unbelievably seductive she might have been. Enaria noticed his horrified scrutiny of the room and laughed brightly.

"I know the room is a disaster, but I absolutely never let servants into my chambers, unless I am here to supervise. Since the start of the Convocation, I have not had time to do a proper job of it, so I let it fall to ruin." She hesitated a moment before glancing at him shyly. "I hadn't expected to find anyone worth inviting to my bed. It has been a long time since I have taken a lover. A *very* long time."

The invitation in her eyes was obvious to Morvandis, but he didn't fall for it immediately. Instead, he reached out with one finger and delicately lifted a tiny scrap of lacy cloth that was obviously a finely made piece of ladies' undergarments, and raised an eyebrow at her mockingly.

"I can see why you would want to supervise the servants. It wouldn't do to allow the uninitiated access to what is obviously one of the Mage High Council's deepest, darkest secrets." As he inspected the underwear with a critical eye, clearly impressed by the daring nature of the scanty garment, Enaria shrieked in feigned outrage and tried to snatch the lace out of his hand. Morvandis turned to the side to keep the cloth out of her hands and grabbed her with his free hand, pulling her close. She kissed him again, and punctuated the kiss with a small nip to his lower lip. At the distraction, she again reached up and snatched the undergarment from his hand, and then tossed it to the side before grabbing his robe and pulling him to the bed. The bed, he was pleased to see, was neatly made and clear of clutter, a pleasant state that ended abruptly as she lay across it and pulled him to her.

Several hours later, Morvandis leaned casually against the headboard with a pillow behind him, and caressed Enaria's hair as she lay peacefully with her head nestled upon his lap. She wasn't sleeping; she was merely basking in the intimacy of the moment and enjoying the afterglow of their lovemaking.

"I first discovered that I was an Earthborn at the same time I discovered I was Fireborn," Morvandis said, breaking the silence. "I was nine years old, and an apprentice of the Flower Court. In the court, training begins almost as soon as you learn to walk, with lessons on history, art, dance, music—anything a client may find pleasing. Sex is the last thing an apprentice learns, and that training only begins when the apprentice is judged to be old enough by the Gardeners and the head of the household to which the apprentice belongs.

"The previous Master of the Gardens, a man named Marigold, considered me to be special and decreed that I was to undergo his personal tutelage. Training under the direct eye of the Master of the Flower Court is normally the greatest of honors, for the Master is supposed to be the epitome of everything the Flower Court teaches. Unfortunately, Marigold was . . . not. It was when I was with him that my power first developed.

"Something . . . happened to me to trigger the event, and I felt my body heat to the point that I thought I would die. At the same time, the ground began to shake; an earthquake centered upon me. As the power built inside of me, I did the only thing that I could: I released it. The explosion of fire and earth destroyed the center of the manor house where I was undergoing my . . . training. Luckily, only the Master of the Flower Court was injured—killed, actually—though the house was completely consumed in the fire. Marigold was the first man that I ever killed, and for freeing the Flower Court from his rule, I was hailed as a hero." He took a deep breath, letting it out in a ragged stream as his memory returned. "Everyone told me what I did was good. It wasn't my fault, it was less than he deserved; that sort of thing. But I was nine, and the memory of his body exploding from the tremors I began within him, before the few parts of him that remained intact caught fire and disintegrated into ash, still haunts me to this day." He hesitated. "I've never told anyone that before. I don't know why I'm telling you now."

His hand stopped caressing Enaria's hair, and she rolled slightly to look up at him, still lying peacefully across his lap.

"I chose to study Blood Magic two hundred years ago because the gifts it offers are another form of power, and another step toward the Archon. All my life, I have dreamed of the day I would learn how she accomplished the things she achieved. That much power in the hands of one person never seemed real to me; it never seemed *possible*. The more I studied, the more I despaired, for my own limitations were apparent: I would never be the woman she was." She turned away again and sighed at the memory. "That was a hard thing to learn; that no amount of knowledge or study or research or Testing would *ever* allow me to understand exactly what it means to be the Archon. I will always be a lesser being, an insect staring into the sun. I will always be cursed with insignificance, for none of my own achievements will ever match those of Zarryiosiad. My fate is obscurity." She looked into his eyes, searching for something, he knew not what. "But now I have you. You can succeed where I have failed. And through you, I can perhaps become more than I am, and one day, leave a true mark. The power you hold is never granted whimsically. *Never.* You have a destiny. I will do anything you require of me to be near you when you achieve whatever it is that you were born to do, and mark me well, you were born to do something great—or terrible." Her eyes hardened, and her mouth pressed into a line with determination. "I will teach you anything you want, reveal any secret should you wish it. I will serve you in any capacity you desire without reservation, no matter what others may think of me. And, perhaps most importantly of all, I will teach you the secrets of Blood Magic, if you wish to learn them."

Morvandis's hand stopped moving through her hair as he considered her offer. The idea of learning Blood Magic was appalling to him, for he knew well the dangers of immersing one's self into forbidden magic, but Enaria's display of her own mastery of Blood Magic in his bedchambers two nights previous had been eye-opening. The ability to mask his presence to other Powerborn, to stand in front of them without registering at all, and to become truly invisible, was far too useful to pass up lightly.

On the other hand, history was filled with the tales of Mages who had gone too far in their pursuit of forbidden power. Vampiri'i , Lich'esti , Lycani'i and necromancers could still be found to this day; men and women gone mad in their pursuit of everlasting life.

Morvandis did not answer immediately. He needed time to think about the decision, and its possible consequences, before choosing a path. Instead, he pulled gently on her arms to bring her face close to his, and when she was inches away, he leaned forward and kissed her tenderly.

She laid her head against his chest as he wrapped his arm protectively around her, and together, they fell into a deep, peaceful sleep.

CHAPTER SEVENTEEN

"Wager"

Lyrahe wrapped her shawl around her forearms and glanced down the hallway, looking for the footman she had sent to fetch her carriage. He had only been gone for a few minutes, but it seemed a lifetime, as she stood and waited in the foyer. There was no sign of him or the carriage, and she tapped an anxious foot underneath her elaborate dress in impatience, for she had hoped to be away from the Spire and in the Citadel by now.

Desperate to find something to calm her nerves, she glanced at her reflection in one of the giant mirrors standing in the hall and walked over to it to check her appearance. It had taken longer than expected to choose her dress, and she had driven her maid and hairdresser to distraction with her demands for perfection. She knew she was being a harridan, but then this was the first time she had ever even *considered* defying one of her father's commands, let alone gone through with it, and she was almost as frightened as she was excited.

The possibility that she would be caught was a serious one, but she knew she would probably never have another chance to speak with Valeriad again, and she desperately needed to tell him exactly why she had been acting as if he didn't exist for the past few days. Yes, the thought of being discovered was terrifying, but so was the thought that Valeriad might blame her for her father's order or, worse yet, come to hate her for it.

The doors opened behind her, making her jump in fright, but it was the doorman and not her father. He looked around the foyer until he spotted her.

"Your carriage awaits, Your Highness."

She gave her reflection one final look before turning around firmly and walking to the door.

As she stepped through the doors and into the morning's sun, she had to raise a hand to shield her eyes until they grew accustomed to the glare. When she finally became used to the brightness, she glanced around until she spotted her carriage and began walking toward it. The sound of horseshoes on the cobblestones of the courtyard made her hesitate, however, and she turned to see who was approaching.

One look was all she needed to make her hurry to the carriage, for the rider was none other than Ethan, her hated brother. She hoped desperately that he wouldn't notice her, or at least that he wouldn't care enough to investigate. Unfortunately, her luck went from bad to worse, for Ethan noticed her rush to the carriage and decided to investigate. As a footman opened the door for her, Ethan spurred his horse and rode up to the carriage to get a look at the occupant. When he saw who it was, his face broke out in a mocking smile.

"Why, little sister! What has you up and about at such a reasonable hour?" He took in her elegant blue dress and her perfectly coiffed hair and his eyes narrowed in suspicion. "And where could you be heading in such a hurry, so beautifully dressed and arranged?"

Lyrahe's heart raced in terror at being discovered, but she didn't allow her fear to show on her face or in her voice.

"If you must know, I have decided to take Chesare up on her offer of a tour of the Mage Citadel. Her description of the library sounded wonderful, and I must see it for myself. Our own selection of books is becoming quite limited, and I am hoping that the Citadel's librarian will allow me to borrow a few new ones for a while."

She followed up her words with a level, almost bored, look, and for a second, Ethan seemed to take her at her word. He started to turn his horse away from the carriage but, before the horse could respond to his commands, he glanced back at her, eyes once again narrowing in suspicion.

"You are quite well dressed for such a mundane reason to visit the Citadel. Is this a special occasion? Perhaps I should take time out of my own busy schedule to pay a visit to poor, lonely Chesare. I do have some free time, you see."

Lyrahe stiffened, but caught herself instantly and forced herself to loosen her shoulders to avert his suspicion.

"The reason I'm dressed this way is because I plan to stay at the Citadel for most of the day. I won't have time to change into anything else before tonight's festivities, so I am dressing up now to save time. As for you visiting Chesare, well, that is your right, of course. But if my memory serves, I seem to recall a conversation between the two of you from the other day . . . something about your owing Tais an apology? I'm sure Chesare would very much enjoy continuing that conversation where you can't hide behind Father for protection."

A look of profound satisfaction lit up her face when she saw his reaction to the barb, for he snarled in anger at the memory of that morning, several days ago, when Chesare had refused to back down from his bullying. Ethan would never admit to it, but Chesare had frightened him badly. Or, at the very least, he had avoided her as much as possible since the argument. Unfortunately for him, he had yet to offer Tais an apology, so he had very good reason to be afraid. Chesare would love an opportunity to make him pay for his behavior, and he seemed to know it.

Ethan yanked on his reins to turn the horse away from the carriage without another word, and spurred the poor beast once to speed it up.

"I'll give Chesare your love," Lyrahe said to his retreating back. "I'm sure she'll appreciate the fact that you're thinking of her."

Ethan gave her a rude gesture without even turning around, and when he was finally out of sight, Lyrahe breathed a heavy sigh of relief. She leaned her head out of the window and said to the driver, "The Mage Citadel, please. And hurry."

The sound of a whip cracking in front of the horses was the only warning she had before the carriage lurched forward and drove out of the gates. She settled back into her seat and tried to put her brother out of her mind. Instead, she thought about what she would say to the white-haired Prince of Dakkadia, and how she would mend the damage she had done to their budding friendship by following her father's orders.

He is a slave to duty, in much the same way that I am. He will understand why things must be this way. And if he doesn't, I will make *him understand.*

The carriage ride didn't take nearly as long as she thought it would, and her heart began to race as the carriage slowed. She tried to calm herself, but her pulse thundered in her ears and she began breathing harder in anticipation of the reunion. Dimly, she wondered if Valeriad would feel the same kind of terror that she did, but then how could he? He had no idea that she was coming to see him.

The footman opened the door and lowered the steps for her to walk down, but for a few moments she couldn't move. She wanted to, but her legs were shaking so badly that she knew that she would fall the moment she tried to stand, so she sat quietly and tried to force herself to calm down. The footman glanced into the carriage, a concerned look on his face.

"Your Highness? Is something the matter?"

Lyrahe said nothing, but shook her head to allay his fears. With a deep breath to sustain her, she stood up quickly and stepped out of the carriage, praying to the Archon that she didn't fall or faint. Happily, she did neither, and once she had forced her feet to move, she found that it became easier and easier to walk. After all, her decision had already been made. All that was left was to see it through.

Valeriad groaned as yet another hit from a practice sword edged past his guard and struck him on the arm. The guardsman who had scored against him stopped his attack at the hit and stood back, lowering his weapon. Valeriad lowered his as well, nodding to the guardsman in acknowledgment of the point. Beside him, one of the instructors was shaking his head.

"You hesitate before you strike, Prince Valeriad, and that hesitation costs you every time. When you commit to a strike, you must follow through. Half measures will see you dead and buried." He walked up to Valeriad and clapped him in the shoulder. "You are very, very good, Your Highness. Not as good as Lord Daane, perhaps, but still quite good. Unfortunately, being 'good' simply isn't enough. You must be perfect each time, every time, or you will quickly find that being 'good enough' is cold comfort when someone better is running you through. Treat each fight, practice or no, as if it was a life or death situation. If you hold back in training, where the worst you will suffer will be a bruise and a blow to your pride, you might do the same when it counts, and that will get you killed. Look at Lord Daane. He understands just how serious this business is."

Valeriad glanced at Phaedron who was standing in a ring some distance from his own, fighting four men simultaneously. As always, Phaedron was pure poetry in motion as his blades leapt and darted around him with unerring precision, not only keeping the men at bay, but also striking back at every opportunity. Valeriad envied his perfect technique, and it was obvious that the Mage Guard, too, was very impressed with him, but that didn't help Valeriad at this particular moment. Some of his frustration must have shown on his face, for the instructor who was working with him smiled and put a hand on his shoulder in sympathy.

"A swordsman of Lord Daane's skill comes about perhaps once in a generation; if, indeed, even that often. His movements are so fluid, so perfect, that he makes what he does look easy enough that anyone watching him can't understand why they can't do the same. Unfortunately for us mere mortals, where he can rely upon innate talent, we can only hope to emulate him through backbreaking toil." He stepped back to clear the ring for yet another round of combat. "You have the instincts you need to match him, but not the temperament or the decisiveness. Until you learn to trust yourself, you will never rise to the level that he will." The instructor raised his hand and said, "Begin."

Valeriad and his opponent attacked each other with a will, and this time Valeriad took the instructor's words to heart. His attacks came with more confidence, and before too long, he began to press his opponent, with more and more of his attacks nearly penetrating his foe's guard. He began to relax into the flow of the combat, and with the relaxation, came the confidence he had been lacking in the previous bout.

To the side, the instructor was nodding in approval, while his opponent was frowning in concentration, looking for a weakness or a break in his pattern that could be exploited. This time, however, Valeriad vowed to himself that there would be no weakness or break, and that he would be the one to score. He held tight to that vow until a movement, where his cousin Adrianna and Princess Chesare were sitting, caught his eye.

It took him a second to recognize the beautiful woman who had entered the room, but when he saw that it was Lyrahe, his eyes and his mouth shot open in surprise and he lowered his guard completely in shock. Unfortunately for him, his opponent didn't realize that he was no longer paying attention to the fight, and seized the opportunity to knock aside his weapons and deliver a painful hit to Valeriad's stomach that stole his breath from him and made him double over in pain. As he dropped his weapons and fell forward over the blow, the last thing he saw was three sets of eyes turning his way as they realized he had been injured.

A cool gust of air and a quick slap to his cheek was all it took to bring him back to his senses, and as his eyesight returned to him, he noticed five different people standing above him looking down at him in concern. The instructor waited until Valeriad began to move before reaching down and pressing his hand onto Valeriad's chest to hold him in place.

"You shouldn't move yet, Prince Valeriad. That was a nasty blow you took. Rest easy until you regain your breath."

Valeriad waved off the instructor.

"I'm alright. The padding held. I just had the wind knocked out of me. Help me up."

The instructor hesitated for a moment before removing his hand from Valeriad's chest and holding it out for the Prince to grab. The other people standing around him stepped back to give him room, and with more than a little bit of effort, he pulled himself upright onto slightly shaky legs. His opponent had a concerned look on his face.

"I'm terribly sorry, Your Highness," he said. "I didn't realize that you'd been distracted."

"It wasn't your fault. Morvandis always says, 'the sharpest lessons often teach best,'" Valeriad said. "The fault was mine for allowing myself to be distracted during a bout. Not," he glanced at Lyrahe who was standing to the side with a worried look on her face, "that I didn't have good reason to be surprised."

He turned to the instructor.

"I'm sorry, but would you please excuse me for a bit? It seems I have a visitor."

The instructor nodded his approval and turned back to the other students who were watching the byplay.

"All right, all right. Get back to work. Those weapons won't swing themselves."

"Princess Lyrahe," he said, as the room began to resume its normal activity, "this is a surprise. I hadn't thought that I would be allowed to speak with you again."

"I hope it was a pleasant surprise?" Lyrahe asked. "I wasn't quite certain my presence would be acceptable after the past few days."

Valeriad looked around at the people staring at the two of them and quickly took her arm in his hand. He turned her gently to one of the benches lining the training grounds and led her to an empty spot.

"'Pleasant' doesn't even begin to describe my feelings at seeing you again. The night after we danced with each other, I'll admit that I was more than a bit confused at your sudden change in attitude toward me, but my father told me what was happening and your sister confirmed it. For what it's worth, I'm sorry for what you are going through. It is your father's fear of my nation that is forcing him to push for the marriage between Prince Lain and you."

Lyrahe looked down in sudden misery.

"I don't know why my father fears you so. I'll admit that before I met you, I thought of Dakkadians only as warmongering barbarians who prey upon their neighbors, but now that I've met you, I can't believe I ever thought that way."

She glanced up at him, but he wasn't smiling at her words. Instead, a grim look came over his face as he looked back at her.

"I'll never lie to you, Lyrahe; even if that should mean you hate me for it." He pointed to where Phaedron was still dueling his four opponents. Phaedron was smiling and laughing, obviously having a grand time fighting against four of the best the Mage Guard had to offer, and winning. "Look at Phaedron. In many ways, he is the ideal Dakkadian warrior. You haven't met him, but trust me when I say, he is the nicest, most honorable person you'll ever meet. And yet, should my father ever order him to assemble his men to join the Dakkadian army in a war against Illymar, he will be in the vanguard." As Lyrahe watched, two of the men dueling Phaedron suddenly dropped their weapons and fell to the ground, signifying 'death' in their duel. "He won't be smiling and laughing when he fights, but he'll fight all the same, and you won't be able to stop him. That's what your father is trying to avoid."

Lyrahe turned back to Valeriad and caught his sky blue eyes with her own emerald green gaze.

"And you? Will you also willingly take up arms against my country should your father command it? Knowing that we pose no threat to your country, or to you?"

Valeriad didn't speak, but his silence was answer enough. For a moment, Lyrahe felt a shiver of fear as she looked into her Prince's eyes. Valeriad turned away in discomfort at her scrutiny and changed the subject.

"How did you convince your father to allow you to visit me? I would have thought that he would have forbidden you to see me again, now that your engagement to Prince Lain has all but been announced."

"I didn't ask for his permission," Lyrahe said, her head lowered and her voice small and hard to hear. "He doesn't even know I'm here." She glanced back up at him. "My official reason for being here at the Citadel is to visit Chesare and to see the library, but the truth is, I had to see you again, even if I risked being caught. If my father finds out I met you here, I will be in terrible trouble."

A sneering voice from behind her took her by surprise and made all of the blood drain from her face when she recognized it.

"I'm glad to know you understand just how much trouble you're in, little sister. It will make it all the sweeter when I tell Father just what you've been up to behind his back."

She whirled around in her seat and saw her brother, Prince Ethan, standing beside a marble pillar that had shielded his approach. He gave her a mocking grin.

"Father is going to be very displeased that you disobeyed him. If you're lucky, he will only lock you in the Tower for a year. But I suspect that he isn't going to take a second daughter's disobedience with quite as much calm and restraint as he did Tais's betrayal."

Lyrahe's hand shot up to her mouth at the realization Ethan had caught her red-handed defying their father, and even as she struggled to find some plausible explanation for her presence, she knew there was absolutely nothing she could say to Ethan to keep him from telling on her. Behind her, she felt Valeriad move.

"We haven't had the pleasure of meeting, Your Highness. I'm Valeriad."

Valeriad held out his hand in greeting for Ethan, but Ethan ignored it completely.

"I know who you are. And I wouldn't exactly say that meeting you is a pleasure. I would liken it more to meeting a rabid dog."

Valeriad let his hand drop to his side.

"Is that how it is to be, then? Well, your insults mean less than nothing to me. As one of the Mage Guard told me when I first arrived; 'Actions always speak louder than words'." He glanced at the weapons on Ethan's belt and gave him a sneer of his own. "You wear the weapons of a warrior, but that means nothing here. You have to prove yourself." He turned his back on Ethan and walked to the circle that he had just left a few moments before. "I've often wondered how skilled Illymari warriors are. I sincerely hope you don't disappoint me."

"This isn't over," Ethan said to Lyrahe. "I'll deal with you after I've dealt with your 'love.'"

He stalked over to the dueling circle and drew his weapons. Before he could begin, however, Valeriad offered another challenge.

"How do you feel about a little wager, Illymari? Something to make this a bit more interesting?"

Ethan agreed without a moment's hesitation.

"Absolutely, Dakkadian. It will be my pleasure to show you what a true noble can do."

Valeriad gave Ethan a half smile and called to the Master of the Field. He approached the pair, each of whom was poised for the duel.

"We have agreed to a wager for this duel," Valeriad said to the Master, "and I wish for a representative of the Citadel to witness the terms. Will you do this for us?"

"What are the terms of your wager?" the Master asked.

Valeriad turned to Ethan and said, "If I defeat you, you will hold your tongue about Princess Lyrahe's visit to the Citadel. As far as you would be concerned, it never happened."

Ethan had expected no less and nodded his ready agreement. The Master of the Field turned to Ethan.

"And what will you wager?"

Ethan thought about it for a moment, until he glanced down at Valeriad's own weapons and smiled.

"Everyone knows that a Dakkadian has to wear his weapons at all times as a symbol of his 'honor'. When I win, you'll surrender your sword and dagger to me as a prize, and you will not wear any others for the rest of your stay here on Illymar."

Ethan smiled triumphantly, for he expected Valeriad to refuse the terms. After all, a Dakkadian who could not wear his weapons in public had surrendered his honor, but Valeriad simply nodded his acceptance. The Master of the Field signaled his understanding of the terms and announced the duel to the assembled.

"A challenge has been declared and accepted between the Prince of Dakkadia and the Prince of Illymar. Let it be known that the Mage Citadel of Ithram stands as witness to the terms of the wager between the two parties. Violation of the terms will result in the Displeasure of the Citadel." He looked at the two Princes once again. "The duel will be to first blood, incapacitation, or capitulation. Prince Ethan is not a Mage, so magic will not be allowed in this duel. I will stand as judge to the duel. Am I clearly understood?" Both Princes saluted, and the Master of the Field stepped outside of the Ring before saying, "You may draw your weapons."

Ethan had already drawn his rapier and main gauche, so only Valeriad moved to obey the order, and as he drew his weapons, all movement in the room stopped as everyone turned to watch the unfolding drama. Valeriad spotted Phaedron standing next to Chesare, and when Phaedron saw that Valeriad was looking at him, he smiled and clenched a fist in front of him in an encouraging manner. Valeriad nodded back before turning his full attention to the task at hand. When both men signaled their readiness, the Master of the Field raised his hand.

"You may begin."

As he dropped his hand, Ethan burst into action.

The very first swing of the duel was almost enough for Ethan to win the match, as without warning, he flicked his sword's blade down toward Valeriad's foot. Valeriad hadn't been expecting the move, and it was only by the narrowest of margins that he avoided the quick strike. Ethan quickly raised his guard back to a level position before Valeriad could counter, and stamped his foot as he charged forward to try to break Valeriad's concentration. It quickly became apparent that the styles of the two Princes were completely different, for Prince Ethan was a tournament duelist, and had learned tricks that would score points in an arena. Prince Valeriad had been trained as a soldier, and his strikes were aimed at vital areas rather than extremities. In this sort of fight, Ethan clearly had the advantage, for all he had to do was score first blood and the match would be over.

His attacks came from extreme angles, as he sought to prick Valeriad's arms and legs, or any area that might be exposed. Valeriad had been trained by Phaedron, however, and Phaedron had taught him to be mindful of his defense and to be patient in the attack. Valeriad could tell from Ethan's style that the Illymari Prince was used to quick victories, gained by gimmicks and cheap shots, and the longer he could keep Ethan from scoring like that, the more frustrated he would become. Soon enough, an opening would occur. Until then, however, Valeriad had his hands full keeping himself from losing outright . . . and from accidentally killing the man.

After a particularly close strike nearly drew blood on Valeriad, Ethan stepped back and laughed.

"Is this the best you can do, Dakkadian? From your reputation, I expected much better than this. You should give me your weapons now. Why prolong the inevitable?"

"You should be thankful that this is a duel to first blood, and not to the death," Valeriad said, smiling. "You see, we Dakkadians do not play at war the way you do. Your skills may serve you in the tournament arena, but in a battle you'd be dead before you realized it."

Ethan scoffed.

"What know you of battles, boy? You've seen, what, sixteen? Seventeen years? I've *been* in battles. I've commanded men in combat, and I've taken lives. So, you tell me, *boy*, who is the one playing at war here?"

He followed up his mocking words with another blinding strike from his position at rest, but Valeriad was prepared for it. He had known, from the second Ethan had stepped back, that he was trying to trick him into lowering his guard. When the strike came, Valeriad reacted in a way that Ethan was completely unprepared for: he stepped forward into the other man's reach and swung a stiff-armed punch right at Ethan's face that caught him completely by surprise. The wire-wrapped guard of Valeriad's main gauche connected with Ethan's nose, and the older Prince went down with a sharp cry of agony as his nose seemed to explode in a spray of crimson. Uncaring of the injury he had just inflicted upon Ethan, Valeriad stepped forward and placed the tip of his rapier against his opponent's throat. Valeriad waited until Ethan met his gaze before speaking again.

"The victory is mine, Ethan, and by your word, your sister was never here." He pressed slightly with his rapier to force Ethan back until he lay completely prone, eyes more than a bit wide in both pain and fear. "Break your word to me and I'll meet you again. But next time, you won't survive the experience, Peace of Zarryiosiad or no."

He pulled his sword away from Ethan's throat and sheathed it, before stepping back to allow his foe the room to stand. Ethan stood slowly, calmly holding his nose to staunch the flow of blood. That calm was an illusion, however, which quickly shattered when one of the Mage Guard approached him with a towel and some ice. Ethan flew into a wild rage and knocked the items out of the guardsman's hands with a backhand blow.

"Get away from me!" he screamed, his voice wild with rage. "I don't need your help!" He whirled around to glare at everyone in the room before screaming again. "What are you looking at?" His eyes fell upon Phaedron, who was standing next to Chesare and giving him a half smile. "You think this is *funny*, Dakkadian?" He clutched at the spaces where his sword and dagger should have rested, but found only air. With a wild look in his eyes, he glanced around for his weapons and found them where they had fallen during his duel with Valeriad. With a cry, he dove for the weapons and snatched them up, whirling back toward Phaedron with murder in his eyes. But before he could take a step, he let out another cry of agony and dropped the weapons once again.

In disbelief, he looked down at his sword and dagger, only to see the blades were glowing red. Tendrils of black smoke wafted off of them where they had been heated to the point that he could no longer hold them. At first, he thought that either Valeriad or the other Dakkadian Mage had used their magic upon him, but when he looked back up from the weapon, it was his sister's eyes that were glowing bright red from magic. Chesare waited until she knew that she had his attention.

"You've lost, Ethan," she said. "If you can't be gracious in defeat, at least show a shred of dignity. Your actions today have shamed our family and Illymar, in the eyes of both our deadliest enemies and our most important allies. Leave now, Ethan, before you further damage Illymar's reputation with both Dakkadia and Ithram."

Ethan clenched his fists as if deciding whether to launch himself at her, but Phaedron stepped forward slightly to place himself bodily between Ethan and his youngest sister. The invitation in Phaedron's eyes was obvious, and the half smile his face had worn earlier had been replaced by a look of hungry anticipation. Phaedron made no move to draw his weapons, but even through his blind rage, Ethan could tell that the Dakkadian was ready for anything. From his stance and the level look the black haired Dakkadian was giving him, Ethan knew, instantly, that this was not a man to cross. So, instead of giving him the opening he so desperately sought, Ethan backed off. He wiped the blood away from his nose with his sleeve, before reaching down once again to pick up his weapons.

Chesare's eyes remained their flashing red as she glared at him, but he simply put the weapons back in their scabbards and turned toward the exit.

"This isn't over, Chesare," he said, fists clenched. He pointed at Lyrahe, still standing beside Valeriad. "And I'm not done with you either. Oh, you needn't fear that I will tell Father about your visit. I will keep my word: you were never here." He looked at Valeriad and noted the skeptical look upon his face. "Whatever else you may think, I will keep my word. The thing that makes us better than you, is that we honor our bargains, and we keep our promises. You see, unlike you, we have honor. It's all that separates us from the animals."

A glance at Valeriad told everyone who he meant when he said 'animal'. With that, he began walking straight toward Valeriad and Lyrahe, who were standing between him and the door, and using his shoulders and his elbows, he forced himself between them, none too gently, as he stormed out of the room.

When the door slammed behind him, Phaedron and Chesare walked up to Valeriad and Lyrahe, and Phaedron clapped his half-sibling on the back in a congratulatory manner.

"Please allow me to apologize for his actions and his words," Lyrahe said. "Ethan is, and always has been, the lowest form of lout. He does not represent the vast majority of the citizens of Illymar, who are good and decent people."

"There is nothing to apologize for, Lyrahe," Valeriad said. "His anger was my fault. While I did mean to strike him like that, I didn't pull my punch the way I had intended, and the hilt of my main gauche hurt him a little more than I'd expected." He looked at Phaedron. "I never understood the difference between tournament dueling and serious swordplay until my fight with him. He left his chest, his throat, and his face wide open in order to protect his arms and legs. I could have killed him a dozen times over in that fight. For that matter, Deirdre could have killed him!"

"And that's why I refuse to teach you that particular style of dueling," Phaedron said. "It teaches you some very bad habits which will most likely get you killed against a real opponent." Phaedron smiled at the two Princesses who were listening in rapt fascination. "A tournament-trained duelist wears a heavy mask that covers the throat, as well as a heavily padded breastplate. With blunted weapons, it is impossible to draw blood from those areas; but then that type of duel isn't to first blood, it's to touch. Simply striking a vital area is enough to win. Unfortunately for Ethan, this match wasn't to touch . . . it was to first blood. To make matters worse, they fought with live steel and no armor, which means they had to be careful not to kill each other. Ethan knew that a simple touch meant nothing in this match, so he concentrated on protecting his arms and legs, the places where blood is more likely to be drawn. What made it worse is that he fought as if he were wearing the armor that he's used to wearing during tournaments. He didn't realize just how open he was leaving himself, or how frustrating it would be for Valeriad. Valeriad could have struck those areas at any time, but not without killing Ethan outright. The trick was to not lose the match before finding a way to defeat him short of killing him, and that wasn't as easy as it looked: Valeriad has been trained to kill his opponents as quickly and efficiently as possible. Resisting the urge to take advantage of his opponent's weakness and run him through took true willpower."

The two girls gave Valeriad admiring looks, and his face turned an interesting shade of red in embarrassment.

"Ah, I think I've had just about enough swordplay for one day," Valeriad said to Lyrahe, changing the subject. "Is there something else you would like to do? You're a guest here as well."

"If you don't mind, I would really like to visit the library," she said. "I love to read, and Chesare says the library is second to none. I would really like to see it for myself."

"Would you mind showing us the way to the library?" Valeriad asked Chesare.

Chesare's face split into a beautiful smile and she pointed at the door.

"Follow me!"

As the group left the training area, Chesare began to laugh. Everyone turned to see what had amused her.

"I was just thinking about something Prince Valeriad said. 'Deirdre could have killed him!' Ethan would be mortified if he'd heard that!"

Lyrahe joined in with her laughter, but Phaedron, Valeriad, and Adrianna didn't. After a few seconds, the two Princesses stopped laughing.

"Did I say something wrong?" Chesare asked.

"He wasn't joking," Phaedron said. "Deirdre is actually a very accomplished swordswoman. She isn't a match for either Valeriad or me yet, but Ethan would have been in for a nasty surprise if he'd fought her instead of Valeriad. You see, she lacks our kind and gentle natures, as well as our sense of fair play, and she wouldn't have hesitated for an instant to gut him like a trout if he'd left himself that open against her."

At Valeriad and Adrianna's affirming nods, both of the Illymari Princess's mouths fell open in shock, which was more than enough to make all three Dakkadians burst into laughter.

Asiria stood in front of a shelf of books, frowning in consternation at what she was seeing. Someone had taken a book from the astromancy section and had carelessly put it back on the wrong shelf, which was a very great affront to the librarian's sense of order. After so many centuries of sitting amongst one of the greatest collections of knowledge in the world, Asiria knew where every single book and scroll was located, no matter how old or obscure it might have been. She pulled *Astromancy: The Collected Essays* out of the spot it had been placed, and began walking to the section it should have been resting, which was a shelf across the aisle from where she had found it. She made a mental note to have a little talk with Novice Stacy, the last person to touch the book, once the potential havoc such unrestrained chaos could wreak upon her precious library was averted.

Asiria didn't just remember where every single book rested after all, she also remembered every single person who had ever touched one. Some dragons hoarded gold or precious jewels. Others collected priceless art or statues. Asiria was the Queen of Knowledge, and she collected books.

The doors to her library opened and she turned to see who was entering her demesne. Asiria instantly recognized Novice Illvanna as she stepped into the room, though they hadn't spoken since the first time they had met, Asiria had been watching over her, nonetheless. It was harder to keep tabs on her when she was outside of the Citadel, but Asiria had followed Astranaithes' instructions to the letter. So far, other than her immense strength in Fire Magic, Asiria hadn't seen anything that could interest the Queen of Shadows in the young woman. She took a closer look at Princess Chesare's face and noted a lack of concern there. That probably meant that she'd had no further encounters with Severeielle, but then Severeielle wouldn't allow herself to be taken unawares that way again.

When a second person entered the room, Asiria smiled. *So, the Princess has brought friends this time!* Asiria loved to meet new people, for she almost never left the library. The large, but misplaced, volume she held in her hands was proof of what would happen to her collection if she were to ever leave it for an extended period, and she would never let *her* library fall into such a state of disorganization. The second person to enter the room was a tall, very handsome

Dakkadian. He had the long black hair marked with a white stripe that Dakkadians were famed for, and from his features, Asiria could tell he had a touch of Fae blood in him. *That would make my new guest Lord Phaedron Daane, the Earl of Daane, and the firstborn son of Queen Aveliad of Dakkadia,* she thought.

Asiria knew that the two Powerborn sons of Queen Aveliad would be coming to the Citadel for their observation period and their Examinations. She hadn't known exactly when they would arrive, however. The third person to enter the room was Novice DeVir, the niece of Archimagus Cedric DeVir. Asiria had had many conversations with the young lady, for Adrianna loved to gossip and Asiria was a most willing audience. Because Asiria rarely left the library, she gleaned most of her information from her various guests. Adrianna, who was gifted with a keen memory and a flair for storytelling, had spent many long hours in the library discussing a wide range of topics, such as who was romantically involved with whom, which important visitors were arriving or staying in the Citadel, and her current opinions on every member of the faculty and staff of the Citadel.

For the Queen of Knowledge, such trivial things should have been completely irrelevant, but she enjoyed her conversations with DeVir immensely, for they gave the Dragon Witch a keen insight into the everyday lives of the beings living and working in the Citadel.

The fourth person was unfamiliar to Asiria, but it took only a moment for her to realize who it must be, for her facial features shared many characteristics with those of Novice Illvanna. They were clearly related, and though this young woman had glossy black hair where Chesare's own curls were red, the similarities were unmistakable. Considering the first conversation Asiria had had with Chesare about the contents of the library, this newcomer could only be the second daughter of King Orem and Queen Althea, Princess Lyrahe.

Asiria's smile widened, and she moved toward the group to greet them properly, when a fifth person entered the room and Asiria recoiled in shock at the sight of him.

It can't be!

A loud *bang!* broke the silence in the room as Asiria's nerveless fingers lost their grip on the volume she was carrying and it fell to the floor. All five of the newcomers turned in surprise to locate the source of the sound. Asiria took a step back, as if frightened of what she was seeing, but there was no denying reality when it was staring her in the face.

"Severius?"

As soon as the name left her mouth, she wished fervently she could have it back again. Though the boy standing in front of her now was physically a perfect match for the man the Lord of Time had once been, he did not have a dragon draped around his shoulder, a clear sign that this was not the person she had believed him to be. The five young visitors looked at each other in confusion, and that was all the opportunity Asiria needed to regain her composure and her equilibrium.

With steady hands, she reached down and picked up the tome she had dropped and then stepped forward to meet her guests.

"Please come in, and allow me to welcome you to the library. I apologize if I startled you, but, for just a moment, I thought you were someone else." As the group entered the room and the door closed behind them, Asiria took in each of her guests. "It is a great honor to have so many illustrious guests in my library at once."

She turned to look at Lyrahe and smiled. "Princess Lyrahe, Novice Illvanna spoke to me about you during her first visit to the library. I believe she mentioned that you are interested in tales of romance and romantic poetry. I think you will find that the library houses many volumes on those very subjects. Feel free to borrow anything you like, and return as often as you wish for more."

The response Asiria received for the offer wasn't what she expected, for the raven-haired Princess glanced once at the boy, who looked so much like Severius, and then quickly turned away, her face turning bright red. Adrianna and Chesare raised their hands to cover their mouths, which were rapidly splitting into grins, while the two young men simply smiled in sympathy for the princess's apparent humiliation.

"Ah, thank you for your kind offer. I will be taking you up on that."

Asiria turned to the others.

"Lord Daane, I presume?" He nodded, and Asiria curtseyed in a formal greeting. "And that would make you Prince Valeriad?" At the younger man's confirming nod, Asiria curtseyed once again. "I am Asiria. If there is anything I can do to make your time at the Citadel more enjoyable, you have but to ask."

Phaedron nodded, but Valeriad's brow furled in confusion.

"When I stepped through the door, you dropped your book and called me 'Severius.' Why did you call me that? Did you mean the Severius who slew the Archon? The Dragonslayer?"

Asiria sighed slightly at the confirmation that the boy had heard her.

"Please join me over here." She pointed to a collection of comfortable couches nestled around a low table, and waited for the group to take seats before joining them. Once everyone was comfortably seated, she began her explanation.

"You may not believe what I am about to tell you, for it is never easy to set aside the things you *know* to be true to hear another side. All I ask of you is that you listen before you judge."

She looked deep into Valeriad's eyes and waited until he gave her a slight nod of agreement before she began speaking again.

"History has painted the man known as Severius as one of the blackest of villains ever to live. During the battle of the Valley of Fire, he singlehandedly killed three of the greatest heroes mankind has ever known—including Zarryiosiad herself. Perhaps worse, he committed these acts in the service of the Lyx, one of the greatest evils the world has ever seen. These are indisputable facts, and history has recorded them accurately. What history has forgotten, or perhaps ignored, are the reasons behind his actions. I will tell you now that I knew Severius very well, for he was one of my kind; a Dragon Lord."

At the shocked expressions on her audience's faces, Asiria nodded.

"This is a fact that the Zarryiostrom has known since its inception over two thousand years ago, but chooses to ignore for reasons of its own. Severius was known among our kind as the Lord of Time, and was revered as one of the wisest of our number. It was this very wisdom that led him to the battlefield that day, for he knew what would happen if events were allowed to unfold as destiny had intended. You see, the Lyx were not the only danger that day. The *true* danger was Zarryiosiad herself, the one now known as the Archon. Among our kind she is known by a different name, for we call her the *Harbinger,* and we knew her to be the greatest threat the world had ever seen. The Zarryiostrom teaches that in mankind's hour of need, Zarryiosiad was touched by the heavens and granted the strength and power to destroy all of the enemies of mankind in a single instant. To do so, she willingly sacrificed her own life and humanity, and in so doing, freed the world from the shackles of oppression that the Lyx had placed upon everyone. The Zarryiostrom also tells us that it was only after she had fulfilled her destiny to free the world from the Lyx that she was struck down by the vile Severius, who destroyed her before she could finish her blessed task to make the world a true paradise."

A sad look crossed Asiria's face and she hesitated a moment before continuing.

"Unfortunately, this simply isn't true. We Dragon Witches know the Harbinger as a terrible force of nature, a creature of chaos and destruction whose sole purpose is to destroy anything and everything it can, until the world has been reduced to what it was in the beginning: mist and ash. Zarryiosiad would not have created a paradise; she would have created a wasteland where nothing—absolutely nothing—could live, until the world could start anew."

Asiria crossed one leg over the other and continued.

"A Harbinger always has a purpose, for its emergence is never random. In their arrogance and madness, the Lyx nearly broke the delicate balance of the world by misusing their Earthborn abilities. Fate responded by unleashing the Harbinger to destroy them and restore balance to the world. Zarryiosiad's true purpose was to destroy the Lyx and remove their blight from this world forevermore. However, once she fulfilled that goal and completed her destiny, she had to be stopped before she could continue on and destroy everything else as well. That is where Severius came in."

She placed both hands on her raised knee and entwined her graceful fingers.

"Severius did not fight *for* the Lyx, for he was not part of their army. It is true that he did fight *alongside* their forces against those of the Archon, but not to support their cause. No, he had a different goal in mind. You see, Fate would never allow a creature such as the Harbinger to exist without a counter; something or someone capable of stopping it from destroying everything. The Dragon Witches call this counter the Champion, and for every Harbinger there has ever been—and there have been several throughout history—a single Champion is born. This Champion is the only person capable of stopping the Harbinger from destroying all of creation."

Asiria paused to make sure her guests understood her before continuing.

"In the Valley of Fire during Zarryiosiad's last battle, Severius was there to witness the rise of the Harbinger . . . and then to destroy it once it had fulfilled its purpose. That he was fighting on the side of the Lyx was irrelevant to him: he fought for mankind, just as Zarryiosiad herself had. And for this, he has been vilified; his name used as a focus for all the ills of the world." Asiria stopped herself and looked Valeriad right in the eye, and the young Prince found himself holding his breath in anticipation of her next words. "I called you 'Severius' because you look exactly like he did, more than 2,500 years ago. Your faces are identical, though you are perhaps a bit younger than he looked. A Dragon Witch is immortal in the same way a Fae is; that is, though we may be killed, time does not touch us the way it does the mortal races. I knew Severius for many years before the events of the Valley of Fire, and I tell you now; you do not just share a passing resemblance to him: you look exactly like him."

She held up a hand in a soothing gesture, as if to calm him from the shock of the revelation.

"I do not know what this means; nor do I know what—if anything—fate has in store for you, but the Lord of Time sacrificed absolutely everything he was to do what needed to be done. I truly hope that fate will be kinder to you than it was to him, but if it isn't, I hope that when the time comes for you to face your destiny, you, too, choose to do the right thing, no matter the personal cost."

CHAPTER EIGHTEEN

"Pretty"

Aveliad finished applying her cosmetics and checked her appearance in her mirror, before reaching for the delicate porcelain mask sitting on a velvet pillow to one side. With practiced ease, she brought the mask to her face and tied it securely into place without disturbing even a single lock of hair. Once it was comfortably positioned, she pulled on it slightly to confirm that it was, indeed, securely attached. Satisfied that everything was in order, she stood up and walked to the series of full-length mirrors standing to the side of her vanity to check her appearance once again.

The black dress with elegant white embroidery she had chosen to wear this evening looked magnificent, though it was a bit more revealing than the clothing she normally chose to wear. She turned slightly to the side to look at the dress from the rear, and nodded in satisfaction at what she saw. From the front, her dress seemed quite modest, though it lacked the normal bodice with hard boning that she normally favored. From the rear, however, the dress was quite daring, especially by Illymari standards, for the material gathered at her shoulders and plunged down in an elegant fall, completely revealing her alabaster skin from the top of her neck to the small of her back. It didn't—quite—cross the line from daring into indecent, but the difference was no more than a finger's width. She wasn't worried, however, for this dress was designed with her Fae heritage in mind.

Aveliad concentrated for a moment, and two elegant white butterfly wings with black markings extended from her back and settled into a position of rest. At first glance, Aveliad looked as if she were wearing a delicate cape, but a closer inspection would reveal the wings for what they were, and the color of the dress had been selected to match perfectly to her wings. She turned slightly to check her appearance from every angle, and when she was completely satisfied, she walked back to the vanity and began putting on her jewelry.

Normally, she didn't bother with elaborate jewelry or adornments, but this was a special occasion. Tonight, she had to look her absolute best; for if she didn't, Aveliad knew that the task she wished to accomplish this evening would be completely misconstrued, and she couldn't risk that. So, she slid delicate rings onto graceful fingers, and she fastened an elegant platinum choker with matching earrings into place.

Once she was satisfied with her selection of jewelry, she reached over to a small, hand-carved mahogany box and touched it reverently. Her fingers slid over the exquisite carvings of leaves and vines until they found a hidden latch, cunningly concealed behind a depression in the design, and she lifted the latch and opened the box. Nestled in among the satin-lined interior was a platinum bracelet of Fae design, her most prized possession. The bracelet had been a gift from her first husband, Phaedril, and she hadn't opened the box, even to look at it, since his death 21 years ago.

Memories long suppressed crashed down upon her, and her breath caught silently as her eyes filled suddenly with tears. With iron determination she somehow kept the tears from falling, and she reached into the box and removed it. A deft twist of another hidden latch opened the bracelet, and she slid it into place on her left forearm before snapping it securely closed upon her wrist.

The design of the bracelet was stunning: a thick band of platinum rested right next to her hand, and from it, long wires wound their way up her arm like delicate vines, each with a series of tiny leaves set with emeralds surrounding a topaz the exact color of her eyes. Its intricate weave covered her entire forearm, as well as the back of her hand, but so clever was the workmanship and so realistic were the vines and leaves, it looked as if the bracelet had not been placed on her wrist so much as it had grown there.

Aveliad closed the lid of the mahogany box and laid her hands flat on her dressing table before looking into her mirror and staring into her own eyes. She measured the resolve in their amber depths, and once she was satisfied that she was prepared to do what was necessary, she pressed down with her palms and stood up in one swift motion. She knew that she looked her absolute best—better, in fact, than she had looked in twenty years—but she didn't even glance at herself in the full-length mirrors as she left the room to attend the evening's festivities.

It is past time that you and I had a talk, Princess Tais, she thought, *and not as a jealous wife to her husband's potential lover. No, no matter what you may think, or what he may be telling you, you are a Princess of Illymar, and any affair that you may have with the King of Dakkadia will have repercussions that will cost people their lives. Perhaps even your own. You must be reminded of this, before it is too late.*

Tais raised her wineglass to her lips and took a tiny sip, wishing that the dinner would end so she could continue her ongoing conversation with King Madari. Over the past few days, he had gone from being someone to fear, to being a good friend, and perhaps one day soon, more than a friend. She blushed slightly at the thought of taking Madari as a lover, but the blush was not as deep as it once would have been, for Tais had never been one to lie to herself. She was falling for the handsome King, and falling very hard indeed. There was no doubt whatsoever that the attraction was mutual, and it was only a matter of time until they became lovers.

She lowered the wineglass to the table and idly ran a finger around the rim of the crystal, making it hum with a pleasant sound. Not for the first time, Tais wondered what Madari would be like as a lover. Powerful, certainly, but that was the only thing she was certain of. Markus had been a very gentle lover who always made certain that she was comfortable, and in his arms she had always felt safe. She knew Madari would be different, for not only was he an older man, he didn't just wear his power and authority like a cloak; it was the core of who he was.

Tais glanced at him from the corner of her eye and smiled inwardly at his chiseled features. He wasn't classically handsome, but she found him beautiful, nonetheless, for his weathered features seemed to be chipped from solid granite. There was nothing soft about him at all, from his square jaw and strong brow to his eyes. Those eyes spoke volumes about him, for they were the hardest thing about him. No, Madari would not care if she was comfortable or not, nor if she felt safe and protected. He would simply take from her everything she was willing to give and then demand more, and Tais found she wanted that. She wanted it desperately.

Tais glanced toward the head of the table, and her eyes narrowed as she took in King Orem's face, smiling happily as he joked with Queen Althea and some of the other nobles and guests seated near him. Her loathing of the royal couple—she still refused to think of them as her parents—had grown more and more intense since her release from the Tower. She lifted her glass to her lips once again and took a deeper sip of the wine, as she considered how she could hurt them the most. Against her will, her eyes darted back to Madari, and she winced internally when she realized that they had. Was that all there was to it? Was she enticing and beguiling the King of Dakkadia simply to punish Orem and Althea? She hoped not, for she did not want to use a friend in such a callous manner, but she would be lying to herself if she didn't admit the thought of King Orem's oldest daughter rutting with his greatest enemy pleased her immensely. *It would kill him to learn that I willingly gave myself to the man he most despises.* The thought brought her a moment's pleasure, but then she glanced at her brother's profile near the King. Ethan had been injured in a fall from his horse, and his nose and both eyes were blackened and swollen hideously. He refused to talk about his injury, but Tais didn't care about that. He was, and always had been, a bastard, and she was glad that he'd fallen off of his high horse . . . both literally and figuratively. The image made her giggle slightly, and she set her glass down lest she spill some wine on her dress. Her good humor slid away at another thought, however, and Ethan's words returned to her with perfect clarity.

Tais seemed to be the perfect daughter, but she spread her legs wide for the first man who ever looked at her twice, and the Kingdom be damned.

She didn't think of herself as a whore, as Ethan had proclaimed her, but then her actions with King Madari were telling. Here she was, considering taking to her bed a man her King hated and despised, for no better reason than to take petty revenge for yet another lover . . . and a dead one at that.

Abruptly, the dinner ended and the guests stood up, waiting yet again to move to the parlor to continue their simpering and toadying. Madari led the Dakkadian contingent into the room without glancing at her, and she was grateful for the thought that he, at least, understood that the proprieties must still be upheld. She waited until most of the other guests had entered into the room before stepping forward herself, but a gentle touch on her arm stopped her in her tracks and she turned to see who was trying to gain her attention. A single look told her who it was, and her eyes went wide at the knowledge that King Madari's wife, Queen Aveliad, had sought her out. Aveliad smiled slightly and pulled her hand back.

"Princess Tais. May I have a word with you? In private?"

Tais felt a moment of panicked shame, for she had been analyzing the potential gains and repercussions of having an affair with a man, without once thinking about the fact that the man in question was married. Madari had only spoken of Queen Aveliad once, and all he would say about her was that their marriage was not a good one. Because he had been reticent to talk about his marriage, Tais knew nothing at all about this mysterious woman standing in front of her.

"Would the veranda be agreeable? It offers considerable privacy." Aveliad inclined her head in the graceful fashion of the Fae, and turned slightly to the side to allow Tais the room to walk past her. Tais stepped forward, and Aveliad took a position next to her, close enough that they could speak without being overheard.

"You are most beautiful, Princess Tais. I can see why Madari fancies you."

Tais missed a step, but adroitly caught herself and continued on as if nothing had happened. *So, like most Dakkadians, Queen Aveliad is not one to waste time on pleasantries and small talk. That is very good to know, for it tells me how to proceed,* thought Tais. She decided that Aveliad's direct question deserved a direct answer, so she replied without a hint of apology in her voice.

"Your husband has been very kind to me, especially in light of my personal disgrace. He has spoken to me when my own family refuses to acknowledge my existence, and for that, I am profoundly grateful." She walked to a set of double doors leading to the veranda and opened them, before stepping aside to allow Aveliad entry. Once the doors were closed safely behind them, Tais continued. "I will be honest with you, Your Majesty: I am just as attracted to him as he is to me. Perhaps more so."

Tais expected an outburst, or a cutting remark . . . something that a jealous wife would say to a potential rival, but Aveliad surprised her. She smiled. Not a smile of spite or malice, but one of friendship and understanding. Instead of responding, Aveliad reached behind her head and untied the ribbons holding her mask in place. When the bow was untied, Aveliad removed the mask and allowed Tais to look upon her face, and Tais realized that the stories of Aveliad's legendary beauty were absolutely true.

She's the most beautiful woman I've ever seen. Madari is truly blessed.

Tais did not know why Aveliad wore the mask that disguised her beauty so effectively, but looking into the Queen of Dakkadia's eyes made her realize that the mask—or perhaps, what it represented—held great significance for her, and that showing her face to an outsider was a singular privilege. Aveliad sat down on a marble bench and placed it gently beside her before looking up at Tais and patting the seat next to her.

"As long as my mask is off, it would please me greatly if you would simply call me Aveliad. Aside from a few select servants and my immediate family, you are the first person in over 20 years to see my face without the mask to cover it; but I want there to be nothing but honesty between us this evening. No rank, no title, and no malice. I simply wish to speak to you as one woman to another. Will you do this for me?"

Tais hesitated, but only for a moment.

"As you wish . . . Aveliad. Please call me Tais. Although," she added, "as your husband rightly pointed out, I am no longer a Princess. I married an Earl, and that

makes me a Countess. Or a *former* Countess, now that he is dead and his lands and title have been seized by the Crown and given to someone else."

Aveliad smiled sadly and held out her hand in a simple handshake, a gesture that somehow put Tais at her ease.

"I, too, lost a husband far too soon. I grieve for your loss, and for the loss of your child. Believe me when I say that my sorrow for you is both sincere and heartfelt. What was done to you was wrong."

Tais felt her eyes welling up from the unexpected words of comfort, and she turned away to keep the wife of the man she was planning to seduce from seeing her momentary weakness. Aveliad put a gentle hand upon her shoulder and squeezed softly, offering yet another comforting gesture. At the touch of her hand, two tears found their way past Tais's control and trickled down her face. The tears were tiny and disappeared quickly, but Tais quickly reached up to wipe the moisture from her eyes and face before any more could fall. *Dakkadians despise weakness, but weakness is all I have shown.* Tais grabbed her emotions by the throat and forced herself back to calm, before turning once again to Aveliad.

"I thank you for your sympathy, but I assure you, I am dealing with my grief in my own fashion. You said that you wished to speak to me, woman to woman. Now, what is it you wish to speak about? King Madari? It must be."

Aveliad lowered her hand, unconcerned at Tais's harsh tone.

"It is. In both Dakkadia and Illymar, it is acceptable for a man to take a mistress, or a lover. Madari has had several over the last twenty years, though not as many as one might believe of a man of his station and stature. I have known about all of them, even the ones he has tried to keep from me, and I tell you now, I do not begrudge him his liaisons. So long as he remains discreet, and does nothing to disgrace the royal household, I will continue to turn a blind eye to his indiscretions. You see, Madari and I do not love each other."

She laughed once, though the laugh was tinged with more than a trace of bitterness.

PRINCESS TAIS ILLVANNA OF ILLYMAR

QUEEN AVELIAD OF DAKKADIA

"How could we? The man I loved has been dead for 21 years, and the woman Madari married loved another man. But, even though I do not love the man I am married to, I also do not wish to stand in the way of any happiness he might find in the arms of another." She stood up then and turned away from Tais to study the flowers blooming around the veranda. After a few moments, she crossed her arms in front of her and hugged herself, as if feeling a chill on the evening wind. "Madari's attraction to you is quickly becoming obsession. He will soon invite you to his bed, if he hasn't already." She turned around and looked Tais directly in the eye. "When he does, you must somehow find the strength to refuse him."

Tais frowned in confusion at the words. From what Aveliad had said just a moment ago, Tais had started to believe that Aveliad had taken her aside to tell her that she not only accepted the possibility of an affair between Madari and her, but that she actively approved of it. Why then would Aveliad reverse herself and ask her to refuse his invitation? She frowned at the Dakkadian Queen.

"I don't understand."

Aveliad smiled and sat back down beside the younger woman.

"If this were simply an affair between a man trapped in an unhappy marriage and a beautiful young widow, I would approve wholeheartedly in the hope that the two of you could find happiness and comfort in each other's arms. Unfortunately, he is not merely a man . . . he is a King. And as much as you may be trying to convince yourself otherwise, you are not just a widowed Countess, you are a Royal Princess of a rival nation." When Tais opened her mouth to protest, Aveliad raised her hand to interrupt her. "I know you want to believe you are a Countess, and that legally, you may even be right. But your father disavowed your marriage. As far as your family and your kingdom are concerned, your marriage never happened. I realize that your position at court is an uncomfortable one for you, but do not doubt for an instant that to your father, you are now, and always have been, a Royal Princess. And, as such, an affair between a Royal Princess of Illymar and the King of Dakkadia can only end in tragedy."

"I'm not certain I agree with you, Aveliad. I'm only one person, and a social pariah at that. My 'position' at court is that I *have* no position. King Orem," she spat out the name like an epithet, "saw to that when he took everything from me. I owe him nothing." It was her turn to laugh bitterly. "In a way, I should thank him. Because of him, I am a dishonored widow, utterly unsuitable for marriage. It doesn't matter who I choose to lie with."

Aveliad smiled sadly.

"It matters much more than you know. You are angry. You are in pain. I understand this better than you might think, and I truly empathize with you. I also understand, that somewhere in your anger and your pain, you feel the need to strike out at the one who hurt you, and to cause him as much pain as he has caused you. But, I tell you now, that this is not the way, for it will not be your father in Madari's bed—it will be you. Will you be able to respect yourself if you continue upon the path you are treading?" She held Tais's gaze with her own steady eyes, and it was Tais who looked away.

"And then there are the broader implications to consider. My husband wishes to take Illymar for himself. What he lacks is justification. Should you lie with my husband and become pregnant, he will use that as his pretext for invading this kingdom and conquering your island. Oh," she waved a hand airily, "I am certain he hasn't considered that yet. No, right now his goal is much simpler: my husband is a conqueror, and you are a potential conquest. He wants—more than anything—to bed you. He hungers for it. But, once he has had you, he will remember his ambitions, and you will become a means to an end. When that happens, thousands will die in a war between our nations. I do not think you want to be the cause of that."

Aveliad stood up and picked up her mask.

"I have said what I wished to say. When the time comes, I hope you will remember my warning. If you still choose to have an affair, even after my warning, I will not protest. In fact, I will be happy for you. But should the worst come to pass because of it, you will have chosen your fate for yourself." With that, she turned to leave the veranda. When she reached the door, she turned back to Tais. "One final word of caution, Tais: my husband is not the man you believe him to be. Look past the handsome, charming exterior, and try to see him for what he truly is. You may be surprised at what you find." Aveliad tilted the mask toward Tais to draw her attention to it, before raising it to her face and quickly tying it in place. "We all wear masks, Your Highness. Some are simply more obvious than others."

Princess Lyrahe looks to be much happier today than she was yesterday. Perhaps she is becoming more comfortable around me? Archon, I pray so.

Prince Lain studied his future bride from the corner of eye and decided that he may as well try, once again, to start a conversation with his betrothed.

"You look quite radiant this evening, Princess Lyrahe. And, if I may be so bold, much happier and more relaxed than you have the last few evenings. May I inquire as to the nature of your good mood?" Lyrahe started at the voice, quickly covering her happiness with a formal mask before looking at him. Before she even spoke, he sighed to himself. *I guess it was too much to hope I had something to do with her happiness. This isn't going to work.*

Lyrahe smiled at him, but the smile was merely friendly and not particularly warm.

"I'm sorry if my mind is wandering. I was thinking about a book that I just started reading. It's quite lovely."

"Speaking of which, I've started reading the book that you recommended to me," Lain said. "I have to say that *Love's Sacrifice* has quite an . . . *interesting* take on the story of Zarryiosiad and Kalindral. I did not realize that they were quite so . . . *passionate.*" That was an understatement. He had read the first four chapters out of sheer, painful determination before setting the book aside and dismissing it as nothing more than flowery tripe. Lain was a student of history, and the liberties the author had taken with the story of Zarryiosiad were more than enough to make the historian in him gnash his teeth in frustration. Before he had finally given up his vain attempt to read it, he had been only one more declaration of undying love away from setting it on fire, or ripping the pages out of the book and tearing them to shreds.

As he looked at his future wife, he knew he would have to make another attempt to read it, if only to avoid these uncomfortable silences, but it was going to be much harder than he thought to do his duty.

Her reaction to his words made his own sacrifice worthwhile, for she gave him a rare, unguarded smile, one of the first that he'd seen from her since they'd first met.

"That's wonderful, Prince Lain!"

She began to talk about the book, her favorite parts, her favorite characters, and just how romantic it all was. Lain tried to look interested, but it was much harder to do than normal, for he had heard much of this before. After a few minutes of listening to Lyrahe speak, Lain found his own attention beginning to wander. Luckily, Lyrahe didn't notice, for she was too caught up in her review of the romantic highlights of *Love's Sacrifice* to actually pay attention to him, and he used the opportunity to look for the person he really would have preferred to speak with. It didn't take him long to find her, for despite her relatively young age, Princess Deirdre tended to stand out in a crowd. He studied her for a moment as she spoke with a few of the nobles from one of Dakkadia's provinces. He smiled when he saw how energetically she spoke, and watched her face light up with pleasure at times and darken with anger at others.

As he watched the diminutive Princess, she turned surreptitiously and looked at him. When she saw him looking back at her, she smiled broadly and tilted her head at the door in invitation. Lain couldn't help himself; he smiled back, though he felt a moment of guilt for doing so. Thankfully, Lyrahe did not notice the exchange. Deirdre turned back to her group and said something, and the women she had been speaking to curtseyed to her and stepped back. Deirdre turned to the doors leading to the veranda and walked away. Before she left the room, however, she looked over her shoulder at him, narrowed her eyes slightly, and beckoned him toward the door. Lain glanced down at Lyrahe, who was still talking about true love and *Love's Sacrifice,* and came to a quick decision.

"I am sorry, Your Highness. Will you please excuse me?"

Her eyes widened in surprise at the interruption, but she curtseyed to him politely.

"Of course, Your Highness." She hesitated for a moment before asking, "Shall I accompany you?"

"That won't be necessary," Lain said, raising his hands to stop her. "These formal robes are very uncomfortable. I simply need a breath of fresh air. I will return in a short while."

Lyrahe curtseyed again, and Lain turned to the servant standing behind him and held out his hand. Obediently, the servant bowed and handed him the case containing his flute. Before he could leave, however, a firm hand took him by the shoulder.

"Where are you going, son?"

Lain turned around to look at his father.

"To the veranda. I need some fresh air."

Xan glanced down at the case Lain was holding.

"Perhaps you should take your intended with you and show her your mastery of the flute. Music is often enough to create common ground between a man and a woman where none existed before."

Lain shook his head in disagreement at that, and leaned closer to his father so his words would not carry.

"Creating common ground is not the problem, Father. I have already made strides in that direction. The problem is, I've had more than enough 'common ground' for one evening. I need some air."

Xan smiled sympathetically.

"I was listening to some of what she had to say," he said, just as quietly, "and I can't say I blame you. Enjoy yourself, but do not stay away too long. It is important that you at least make an effort to get along with your future bride."

Prince Lain bowed and stepped away from his father. As he walked away, carrying his instrument's case, he began thinking about the different songs he would play for Deirdre this evening. At the thought of another pleasant evening on the veranda with the gifted Princess, his pace—and his heart—began to quicken.

Over an hour later, Xan found himself becoming more than a bit angry at his son's all-too-obvious absence. Even worse, other people were beginning to notice his absence as well, especially his future bride, Lyrahe.

Where has that boy gotten himself to?

Xan turned to Grand Vizier Shar, his most trusted advisor.

"Lain has been gone for a long time."

"Shall I look for him?" Shar asked respectfully.

Xan started to nod his assent, but changed his mind abruptly.

"No. I think I will look for him myself. He told me that he was going to the veranda. Most likely, he is still there playing his flute, and a short walk will do me some good."

Shar bowed again and turned to the other diplomats and nobles to say a few quiet words. Xan did not pay attention to the deep bows and curtseys that followed his Vizier's words; instead he turned to King Orem.

"If you will excuse me, I would like to step outside. I won't be but a moment."

"Of course, Emperor Xan. But do hurry; I do not think I can hold off this pack of vultures on my own for very long!" He gestured grandly at the diplomats and courtiers surrounding them.

Xan chuckled and stepped away from the group with his Vizier right behind him.

"That boy has a lot of explaining to do," Xan growled, once they were out of earshot of the Illymari contingent. "His absence could be taken as a slight by the Illymari. And this is the second time he has disappeared from the gathering. Mark me, Shar, there won't be a third. Poor match or no, he needs to understand that this marriage is vital, and his duty to Ferralin overrides everything else. Everything!"

A perfectly pure note from an angelic voice stopped him short of the doors leading to the terrace. At first he doubted his own ears, but then a second perfect note followed the first, and Xan realized the sound was coming from the veranda. He held up a hand to stop Shar from approaching, and then stepped forward and pressed his ear to the wood. Through the door he heard singing so beautiful it took his breath away, and he stepped back from the door and frowned in confusion, wondering what divine being could be responsible for so pure a sound. He made no move to reach for the handles. Instead, he once again stepped close to the door and pressed his ear against it in order to hear the voice a little better without giving away his presence.

As the notes flowed through the door, muted but no less beautiful because of it, the choir in his head began to sing in accompaniment. The voices of his countless pretties blended and overlapped in his mind into a perfect harmony, and through the strains of the angelic choir thundering and resounding in his head, this newest, most perfect of voices shone like a beacon. The voices, which had sung him to sleep every day of his life, welcomed their newest member into their midst and wrapped themselves around it, as if all this time they had been waiting for this one perfect voice to lead them.

Xan wept at the realization he had finally found something he had never known he'd been looking for, and with this realization came the knowledge that one day soon, he could truly rest. He could not remember the names and the faces all of the countless pretties that he had strangled over the many decades of his life, but he knew now that only one more remained. Once this voice was added to the choir, it would be complete. Then he could sleep forever.

He waited for the song to conclude, and reluctantly stepped away from the entrance and wiped the tears from his eyes before quietly opening the doors to the veranda. There, in the walled garden sat his son, holding his precious flute close, but Xan barely spared him a glance. The veranda was lit by numerous lanterns, and it was in that soft light he finally laid eyes upon his prize. He did not recognize her, for he had been very busy over the past few days and hadn't had the time to acquaint himself with the different notables, but as he gazed upon her, his heart was gladdened to see the young girl was as beautiful as her voice.

A perfect angel, he thought, unable to take his eyes from her face.

He saw movement to the side, but he didn't bother to look, basking in this moment and reveling in the knowledge that his long journey was almost over. All he had to do now was step forward and wrap his hands around her neck, and her voice would join all the others in his choir, forever perfect. Then he would sleep, as the voices of his pretties wrapped themselves around him, warming him with their love and devotion. He raised his hands, fingers already curling, when someone stepped in front of him to block his view. It took Xan a moment for the voice and the words to register.

"Father, what are you doing . . . here?"

There was a slight hesitation in the word 'here', as if he had added it almost as an afterthought, but Xan didn't care. With great effort and determination, he pulled himself back from the precipice of his murderous intent, and looked into his son's eyes.

"You didn't come back to the party. I came to find you."

Lain looked around, noticing for the first time that the sun had set.

"I apologize, Father. I lost track of the time. We should go back."

He stepped forward and took Xan by the arm, but Xan shrugged his arm out of his son's grip and looked at the young girl standing before him. He gave her his most beatific smile.

"I heard you through the door, my child. The Archon has truly blessed you, for your voice is the most beautiful I have ever heard."

The golden-haired child started at that, but recovered quickly and curtseyed politely.

"I thank you for your kind words, Your Majesty, and I apologize for stealing your son away from the party. Prince Lain was kind enough to play his flute for me, and I think that we both lost track of time."

"We have not been introduced," Xan said. "Obviously, you know who I am, but who are you?"

"*Oh!* Please excuse my rudeness, Your Imperial Majesty. I am Deirdre, daughter of Madari Dhaerhan, King of Dakkadia."

At the name, Xan's eyes narrowed in recognition.

"You're the one they call the Jewel of Dakkadia?" She blushed prettily at the title and he chuckled. "I apologize for not recognizing you immediately. It seems my eyes are as old as the rest of me. Rest assured I will not make that mistake a second time." He paused and then raised an eyebrow in a questioning manner. "I would not have thought a Dakkadian would have such an interest in music, nor such a perfect voice."

"It's my mother's influence," she said, smiling. "She says, that even by Faeish standards, my voice is exceptional, but I think she is merely being polite."

Even before she finished speaking, Xan was shaking his head in disagreement.

"I have had the privilege of hearing the Fae sing many times in my life, and while I do agree that their voices are lovely, neither their songs nor their voices were ever truly meant for human ears." Behind him, Vizier Shar cleared his throat slightly to remind him that they were supposed to be at the party. "Yes, yes, Shar. I know everyone is waiting. Well, let them wait a little longer." He nodded at the diminutive Princess and clapped his hands together, almost the way a child would when pleased by some unexpected gift. "Please sing me a song, Princess; the sweetest song that you know. I promise you that I will be a most attentive and appreciative audience."

He sat down on a stone bench and smiled expectantly, and Deirdre pursed her lips together in thought for a moment before deciding upon an appropriate song. The decision made, she clasped her hands in front of her and began to sing without accompaniment.

From the very first note, Xan's attention—and imagination—were absolutely captured by the golden-haired Princess. He did not recognize the song, but it quickly became apparent to him that she had chosen to sing a traditional Dakkadian lullaby, and Xan thanked the Archon for such an obvious sign that she was meant to be his. Despite the simplicity of the words, the melody of the song was actually quite complex, but Deirdre's perfect pitch made it seem as if it had been written specifically for her voice alone. Xan was entranced by her, and the voices in his head turned silent to listen with him, as if they, too, had been caught in her spell.

When Lain recognized the tune, he began to raise his flute to accompany her, but without taking his eyes off of Deirdre, Xan raised his hand and touched Lain's arm, shaking his head slightly. Lain dutifully lowered the flute again to allow Xan the opportunity to hear her singing a cappella.

When the song ended, Xan clapped his hands in appreciation, his face beaming in radiant bliss. She curtseyed to him to acknowledge his applause, and he stood up quickly, giving her an ovation. Deirdre blushed in embarrassment at the over-enthusiastic praise and turned away slightly to hide her blushes. Her modesty sent a spike of white-hot desire through his veins, and he stepped toward her again, completely unable to resist the urge to touch her.

Out of the corner of his eye, he saw both his son and his Vizier stiffen as he raised his hands to Deirdre, but they needn't have worried. Xan wasn't stupid. Killing the Princess now would be a disaster for both him and his country, and it would almost certainly lead to his own death at the hands of her father, King Madari. No, he needed to find a way to bring her back to his capital in the heart of Ferralin, where he would be surrounded by his armies and vassals, safe from any possible repercussions. He placed his hands upon her shoulders and turned her to face him, looking her directly in the eye. When it became apparent to Lain and Shar that Xan had no intention of harming her they relaxed, and despite himself, Xan smiled.

"Your modesty is quite becoming, Princess. I should very much like to have you at the Ferralin Imperial Court, to perform for me in my own home. You see, my Imperial seat was designed in the manner of a concert hall, so my words can reach every ear without effort. You would be glorious there."

Standing so close to the object of his desire was maddening to him, but Xan fought desperately against the temptation her swanlike neck offered him.

It would be so easy, he thought to himself, *so easy to reach up and give her a little squeeze. A little squeeze and it would be over.*

So lost in his personal struggle was he, that he couldn't see the Princess wince in pain as his fingers tightened on her shoulders, leaving deep bruises where his wizened claws touched her youthful skin.

When Emperor Xan placed his hands upon her shoulders, Deirdre nearly jerked away from the unexpected and uninvited contact. As a Royal Princess, no one was allowed to touch her without her express permission, but Xan was quite definitely a special case, for not only was he an old man, he vastly outranked her as well. As his spidery fingers settled upon her flesh, she was startled by just how cold they were. The evening was quite warm and pleasant, but his hands felt like shards of ice upon her skin, almost as if he were draining the heat from her.

Xan smiled at her; a friendly gesture meant to reassure her that nothing was amiss, and she tried to return his smile, but she hadn't missed the reactions of either Lain or the Mage standing beside him as he had reached for her. They were frightened of something, and when Xan had touched her shoulders, their fear had intensified. At first, she had thought they were afraid of her, or of something she might do to the elderly Emperor, but then she noticed they weren't looking at her: they were looking at *him.* Lain spared a glance for her, completely unable to disguise the fear in his eyes, and with that single look, she realized something: they weren't worried about him . . . they were worried about *her.*

Deirdre looked deeply into Xan's eyes, trying to see what it was they were afraid of, and at first glance, she saw nothing out of the ordinary in the black pools. But, as she studied him closer, she began to realize that there was something amiss after all; the smile on his face didn't quite touch his eyes, and the eyes themselves were flat and without life, almost like those of a shark. The realization paralyzed her with fear, and she felt his grip tightening and tightening, until she let out a slight whimper of pain. Even with the unexpected pain, she couldn't tear her eyes away from his, and it didn't take her long to realize that there was no humanity reflecting in their depths . . . no humanity at all. There was only one thing she could clearly see behind his predator's eyes: hunger. He *hungered* for her.

Had she been any less of a Dakkadian, she might have fainted, for her heart was beating so fast she was more than a little surprised it hadn't burst apart in her chest. She had never felt such raw visceral terror before, and she wanted desperately to find a way to escape his grasp. But she couldn't even pull her eyes away from his, let alone pull herself away. Luckily, she didn't have to. Lain, perhaps sensing part of the byplay between his father and his friend, stepped forward and took his father's upper arms in his own hands and pulled him away bodily, breaking not only the physical contact between Xan and Deirdre, but the mental contact as well. Xan turned his head to the side to see who had dared to touch him, and whatever Lain saw in his eyes made him recoil in fear as well. Lain covered his own fear quickly and said,

"Father, we should leave. The Illymari are probably worrying about our absence."

For a moment Xan didn't answer, just held his son's eyes with his own, and Lain began to sweat under his father's scrutiny. It was just a little bit, but the perspiration dotted his forehead and upper lip, obvious signs of fear.

What is it about this man that inspires such dread? thought Deirdre. *He's just an old man. None of us should have a thing to fear from him.*

But even as she thought it, she knew she was underestimating the man, and that that kind of mistake could be fatal. Eventually, Xan's face underwent another change, and the kindly old man returned. The relief that crossed Lain's face at his father's transformation was dramatic, and he let go of the Emperor's arms and stepped away. Rather than following his son, however, Xan turned once again to Deirdre. When she saw him turning, she dropped into a curtsey as quickly as she could and lowered her eyes to the floor, not out of respect for the Emperor, but out of fear of meeting his hungry gaze again. She desperately did not want to become trapped in the glare of a madman again.

"I thank you for the serenade, Princess Deirdre," Xan said. "If at all possible, I would greatly enjoy hearing you sing for me again. I do not exaggerate when I say that you do your country great credit with your talent. Many people—including, I'm sorry to say, myself—consider Dakkadia as nothing more than a home for warmongers and mercenaries. I see now that I was an ignorant fool. I must atone for my ignorance." He turned to his son and his Vizier. "Come. We must return."

As they filed out, Xan stopped at the door and looked over at Deirdre one last time. His sudden turn caught her by surprise and she once again met his gaze, and saw a trace of the hunger return to his black eyes. He gave her a serpent's smile and licked his lips slightly.

"I hope to see you again, my *Pretty*. Soon."

With that, he left the room. The emphasis on the word "pretty" struck her as odd, but the words themselves were benign . . . or so she thought. But as Xan left the veranda, Lain looked back at her one last time, and she saw that his face was blanched in all-too-obvious terror.

As he looked at the empty spot that Princess Tais normally occupied, King Madari frowned in annoyance.

Where is she? he thought for the thousandth time. *She was at dinner. Why isn't she here now?*

He had been looking forward to taking another walk with her to "pass the time" in her pleasant company, but her absence had left him anxious and more than a bit concerned. He knew that she was almost ready to allow herself to be bedded by him, for their friendly banter had taken a decidedly sexual turn over the past two days. But, what had surprised him the most was that she had been the one to initiate it.

The first innuendo had been a mild jest concerning Dakkadian reputation for healthy libidos, but she had followed the remark with a seductive look, a raised eyebrow, and a tilt of her head that had made his palms sweat. He probably should have made a move when she had given him the opening, but it had been too abrupt a change in the tone of the evening. He had a reputation as a meticulous planner when it came to warfare and conquests, but that wasn't necessarily true; he simply knew when patience was the wiser course, and he always preferred to achieve a complete victory rather than a partial one. So instead, he had begun testing the waters, and had found them to be warm and inviting.

He had thought that with Illymar's reputation for prudishness he would have to work harder to seduce her, but it seemed that she had her own ideas about where their relationship should go and was taking steps to ensure that it got there. The signs were obvious, especially to someone with his experience with the opposite sex. She laughed at all of his jokes, and always answered in kind, even to off-color remarks and ribald jests. She touched him often, "accidentally" at first but with surprising frequency. And the touches were becoming longer and less casual. He knew that if he had tried to kiss her during the previous evening, she would have allowed it, but he had much more experience than she did at seduction. He left her that night without a kiss, knowing that it would make her want one all the more later. The looks she had given him at dinner were all the evidence he had needed to see that his patience was paying off spectacularly.

His pleasant recollections disappeared as suddenly as they came when he looked at the empty spot next to the window where she always stood. That was the one thing about their relationship she absolutely refused to change: she would gladly walk with him and spend a pleasant evening upon his arm, but he always had to come to *her* first.

"Are you enjoying yourself this evening, King Madari?"

The voice pulled him from his reverie and he turned to look at the speaker. To his surprise, it was King Orem, standing in front of his delegation and looking rather smug with one slightly raised eyebrow. Madari didn't answer at first, instead taking the opportunity to study the King of Illymar a little more closely. He could see where Tais had gotten her steady gaze and fine features, though Orem's own features had been ravaged by soft living and a lifetime of dissipation.

Still, she was her father's daughter and, under the surface, he could see the resemblance. But the smug look upon Orem's face rubbed at him the wrong way, as did the man's body language. Orem was spoiling for a fight. *This is going to get ugly*, he thought immediately. *Best to let him make the first move, and then cut him off at the knees.*

"Very much so, Your Majesty. You are a gracious host, and a generous one. The food and the entertainment have been quite extraordinary. And though our countries are rivals, it is my hope we can somehow set aside our differences and be friendly rivals rather than enemies."

"Somehow, I doubt that, Dhaerhan. Your ships have been preying on mine for twenty years now. It's hard to think of Dakkadia as a 'friendly' rival when your kingdom actively encourages and rewards piracy against *my* interests."

Madari's eyebrows rose involuntarily at the bare-knuckled attitude King Orem was showing. He hadn't thought Orem would have the backbone to provoke him in public this way but, apparently, he had been wrong. *No matter. The day I back down from a fight is the day I abdicate my throne.*

"I assure you that Dakkadia frowns upon piracy just as much as Illymar does, King Orem. In fact, my navy has standing orders to execute captured pirates on the spot. No trial, no clemency. A rope or a plank: pirate's choice."

Orem laughed loudly at that and looked around at his delegation, and though they had no idea what he had found so amusing, they laughed just as hard, like the sycophants they were. For his part, Madari refused to rise to the bait and allowed Orem his showmanship, while already planning his next riposte. Eventually, the laughter died away and Orem made a great show of wiping the tears of humor from his eyes.

"Oh, that was a clever jest, Dhaerhan! A clever jest, indeed! I would never have thought a Dakkadian would have such a bold sense of humor." His chuckles filled the room again, too loud to be genuine.

"There are many things people believe to be true about Dakkadia that are simply wrong. In point of fact, I have a very keen sense of humor, though, for some reason, I fail to see what you find to be so amusing."

Orem's false smile vanished at that, and he leaned forward aggressively.

"What I find amusing is that you would espouse your country's hatred of piracy, but choose to arrive here aboard the ship of the worst pirate the ocean has ever known. The *Corsair* and her foul ship are a blight upon the high seas. You say you offer pirates two choices: the plank or the rope, and yet, you continue to allow her to attack vessels as she pleases with, I might add, your generous support. Your own words prove you to be a liar."

Madari swallowed his outrage at the deadly insult, but only just. For a moment, he considered challenging Orem to a duel, but changed his mind abruptly. The Zarryiostrom would never allow it to take place, for they had invoked the Peace of Zarryiosiad before issuing the invitations to the Convocation. It was their holy duty to ensure the complete safety of all parties during the month of the Convocation. Issuing a challenge, only to have the Zarryiostrom interfere, would make him look weak. Worse, it would demonstrate to everyone present that Dakkadians settled all of their disputes with violence. So, he chose a different path.

"We choose to see things differently, then. You know, as well as I do, that *privateering* is not the same thing as piracy, and Lady Prudence is a registered and court-sponsored privateer. That you choose to view her otherwise does not make you right. In point of fact, it makes you look foolish and stupid. Should you wish it, I will have the Zarryiostrom remind you of her status in writing."

It was Madari's turn to smile, but inwardly he was preparing to weather another assault. Orem's response was predictable; his face turned purple with rage and he clenched his fists in anger.

"Call her what you want, cloak her in whatever protection you choose, but the fact remains that a pirate by any other name is still a pirate! She takes what isn't hers, and uses force to do it." His voice calmed a bit, and his color returned to its normal pale tone. "Much like you, I imagine. Your record of conquests is quite distinguished. During your time as King of Dakkadia, you have added so many lands to your banner that one would think you would be happy with what you have. But here you are, eyeing my country as a potential conquest." Madari opened his mouth to speak, but Orem raised his hands to interrupt him. "Don't bother to deny it, Dhaerhan: you've already proven yourself to be a liar. Anything you say to the contrary will be just that: another lie."

He crossed his arms over his chest, the smug look returning as if it had never left. Once again, Madari was forced to swallow the urge to issue a duel for the insult.

"Think what you will, King Orem, but my goal has never been to conquer Illymar. My goal is simply to press my claim upon the Badlands—a claim that you choose to regard as a threat to your country's sovereignty. How you could view my legitimate claim as a threat to your interests, I do not know—nor do I care to know—but your actions to forestall my liberation of the Badlands from the chaos that infests it have consequences. And may I remind you that *you* were the one who began attacking *my* ships twenty years ago, using the services of the very privateers you are so fond of denouncing? I simply responded in kind, years later. It is not my fault that your mercenaries are so much poorer than my own.

You knew my reputation when you decided to meddle in my affairs, so you only have yourself to blame for the position you are now in." Orem's face turned purple again and he tried to speak, but it was Madari's turn to interrupt the Illymari King.

"For reasons of your own, you have made it abundantly clear you choose to see a possible invasion of the Badlands as a threat to your own kingdom's interests, and you are prepared to resist us with force, if necessary. That alone makes you a threat to us, and you should know by now that we do not take threats lightly. I will say this plainly, so you understand the stakes: if you choose to interpose yourself between Dakkadia and the Badlands, you and your pathetic excuse for a kingdom will be ground underfoot. Illymar is not a credible threat to Dakkadia, and with every ship we take from you, you become even less of one. Press me again, and I will take your kingdom from you. And when I do, I will answer your unprovoked insults upon my person in the manner in which they deserve: I will kill you myself." He narrowed his eyes, and his voice lowered to a deadly hiss. "I trust that I have made my position perfectly clear?"

As King Orem gathered himself for a fresh assault, Emperor Xan stood in the doorway and quietly watched the entire exchange. Not a hint of what he was thinking crossed his face, but as he looked at Madari, his eyes began to gleam. He knew what he had to do.

The Pretty will be mine.

CHAPTER NINETEEN

"Depravity"

Earl Vitaly Saxe, the chief advisor and aide-de-camp of Duke Ascham Illvanin of Illymar, took a careful look at his surroundings to make certain he wasn't being watched. He didn't believe anyone was following him, but for clandestine meetings such as the one he was anticipating, it never hurt to be sure. And though he had been looking forward to this night ever since he had first learned that he would be returning to the capital, he couldn't afford to get caught here, of all places. *Here* was a quiet series of inns in an upscale section of town, with three-story buildings situated on a clean cobblestone avenue. The street was well lit, with oil lanterns placed at regular intervals, and above every doorway. Candlelight flickered in many of the windows, and he could hear faint music issuing from the common rooms of several of the inns. Satisfied that no one was following him, he walked to a certain establishment, and after glancing over his shoulder one last time, opened the door and quickly stepped inside, shutting the door behind him.

At first glance, it looked like any other inn in the city. A cozy fireplace with a few burning logs sat at one end of the room, with several tables arranged around it to take advantage of the heat. A handful of patrons sat at the tables, enjoying a quiet conversation or a cool drink, whichever the customer preferred, while a bar with dozens of bottles of alcohol and tapped barrels of ale and beer stood at the other end of the room, ready to cater to any need the patron desired. The bartender was cleanly shaven with a balding pate, who nodded a greeting while polishing the bar with a white cloth. Vitaly recognized the bartender instantly, and stepped forward to speak with him, but the man simply smiled and inclined his head toward a discreet staircase set behind the bar. Vitaly quietly stepped around the bar to the stairs.

The building had three stories, but the stairs he walked to led downward instead of upward. It had been a long time since he had last been here, and his hands were trembling with anticipation as he quietly knocked on a plain wooden door at the bottom of the stairs. On the third knock, a small knot opened at eye level, and a shadow passed across it briefly, as the person behind the door took his measure. But the scrutiny took only a moment, and the door was opened without a challenge.

As he stepped into the basement, an extremely beautiful and voluptuous woman wearing skin-tight leather walked up to him and kissed him deeply, before slapping him hard across the face. He grinned at the familiar greeting, happy to be back where he belonged.

"And where have you been, love? It's been ages."

The patrons of this establishment, known as "The Penitentiary", never used their own names as a form of protection, but he had utilized this particular mistress several times in the past and had thoroughly enjoyed each session. Seeing her again made his mouth water in anticipation, but he covered it with a smug look.

"Oh, I simply became dreadfully bored with this place and looked for another. Alas, I am sad to say, that this is the best I could find."

He had expected an instant response, and the mistress of the establishment didn't disappoint him. One minute he was standing smugly in the doorway, the next he found himself lying on the floor grasping his crotch in exquisite pain, with a stiletto heel pressed against his face.

"You'll pay for your infidelity, worm."

She grabbed him by the hair and pulled him to his feet, forcing him to work past the pain.

"I have a surprise for you this evening, my love. We have a guest. . . an incredibly talented guest. If you're properly submissive, she might even deign to notice you."

She turned his head by the hair to look at a dark corner of the room, and he caught sight of a beautiful, mahogany-skinned woman sitting in a chair dressed in black leather from neck to toe. Her dark hair fell in luxurious waves down her back, and though he wasn't usually one to go for exotically beautiful women—he preferred stouter, stronger women—the smoldering look in her eyes promised him pain and pleasure beyond his wildest dreams, and told him instantly that this one time he would make an exception. Decision made, he found himself looking forward to seeing what she could do. He desperately hoped that she wouldn't disappoint him.

Thorn Demestira marked her target at once, recognizing the Earl of Saxe from the Convocation. One of the skills her years of training with the Flower Court had provided for her was a preternatural sense of who would seek out the kind of services she could provide, and Vitaly Saxe had set off that sense the very first time she had ever laid eyes upon him. She knew that he would eventually seek out an establishment just like this one, and a little bit of research had provided her with the name of The Penitentiary as one of his favorite haunts.

Once she had the name of the establishment, she had come to the inn to speak with the mistress of the house looking for a temporary job. The mistress of the house had been very happy to have her, for as exotic as the newcomer was—and as skilled at her arts as she had proven to be—she knew Thorn would bring in customers by the droves, and Thorn hadn't disappointed her. She was very picky about her subjects, always looking for men or women with exceptional stamina or arrogance, before breaking them like twigs, one after the other. Her reputation grew with every "victim", but all the time she spent at The Penitentiary was to a purpose: she was waiting for a single mark to arrive. And here he was, ready to tell her everything she needed to know about Illymar . . . and even more importantly, how to break her. The best part about it was he would not only willingly betray his country; he would pay handsomely for the privilege.

When the house mistress dragged him before her, she didn't move. Instead, she took her time studying her prey, almost exactly the way a cat would study a mouse. She decided abruptly that she liked what she saw in him, for his arrogance was imbedded to the bone. He would make an excellent subject. She stretched luxuriously in her chair, openly displaying her charms and assets while promising him more to come, before she crossed her arms over her chest and gave him a severe look.

"When you entered the room you looked me in the eye, worm. Do it again and I will have one of them for my collection. Am I understood?"

He quickly lowered his eyes to the tip of her boot.

"Yes, madam."

She settled back in her chair.

"Mistress. You may call me Mistress Thorn. Shall we begin?"

"Yes, please, Mistress Thorn."

She rose from her chair and led him to a private room with stark walls covered in various instruments of torture, and closed the door behind them. It was only minutes later that his screams began.

Several hours later, Thorn walked out of The Penitentiary with a large bag of gold and a satisfied smile on her face. Vitaly had been quite forthcoming with information once she found his vulnerable spots, and she had mercilessly drained him dry of information. She'd made a game of it, telling him that by the end of the evening she would make him tell her everything there was to know about him, and promising him a reward if he could hold out even the slightest bit of information. He hadn't been able to hold anything back, but she rewarded him nonetheless, believing that it was only right that a traitor should be paid for his information. When they parted ways, he had to be carried up to a room that had been set aside for him on the second floor. She had done him no permanent harm—his bruises and cuts would heal in a matter of days—but she had also made certain that he would only remember bits and snatches of the evening's events. Torture—even torture of the sweetest sort—was like that: his memory would be a blur of pain and pleasure, and he would never know exactly what he had divulged and what he hadn't.

What she had learned from the Earl was very interesting, indeed. From the outside looking in, the Kingdom of Illymar seemed a towering pillar of strength. But, if what she had learned from the Earl was correct, that pillar of strength was being held together with weak mortar, and cracks already ran all the way through it. All it would take to destroy it utterly was a single blow, and that was exactly the kind of information King Madari had sent her to discover. She looked up and noticed that the sky was beginning to lighten, and quickened her pace to reach the Dakkadian enclave before the sun fully rose. She had a report to give, and eventually, a kingdom to bring to its knees.

Enaria woke just before dawn, as she always did, and looked over at her newest student, asleep in the bed next to her. She grimaced slightly at his sleeping form, and then smiled in memory of their previous evening together. Morvandis was an exceptional lover, far and away the best she'd ever had, but as a student of Blood Magic, his skills were sorely lacking. He struggled to grasp even the simplest of concepts or master the most basic of spells, and at first, she had been baffled and frustrated by his utter lack of progress. She simply couldn't understand how the greatest living Mage—perhaps another incarnation of the Archon herself—could be so incredibly dense when it came to Blood Magic.

The answer had turned out to be as simple as it was maddening, for Morvandis' mastery of the four types of Magic was based on utter control: control of himself, control of his environment, and above all, control of his power. Unfortunately, for the both of them, Blood Magic was different than mundane Magic, for it required a complete loss of control and an embracing of life and chaos that was alien to Morvandis's orderly nature. Intellectually, he understood that in order to master Blood Magic he had to give in to it, and let it have free rein, but there was a tremendous difference between knowing he had to relinquish control, and actually doing so. Morvandis always had to be in control, an odd trait in one so content to serve. But there it was: as long as Morvandis refused to free himself of his own restraint, he would never master the intricacies of the fifth power.

She was patient, though. She would wait as long as necessary to see that he learned everything she could teach him. And truth be told, things weren't *all* bad. Their days might have been filled with frustration and tension, but their nights had been filled with passion and wanton abandon. Had someone told her over twenty years ago that she would one day take the straight-laced and utterly serious boy he had once been to her bed, she would have laughed in their face. The very idea would have been absurd. But, as she looked at him now, sleeping soundly in the bed next to her, she knew she would have been wrong. There were depths to this man she hadn't known—hadn't even suspected—existed. When she had first decided to seduce him, she had come to the decision cold-bloodedly, as her best possible chance to control him. But, now that she had him, she was beginning to see other possibilities, other futures. She wanted power, and would do anything to obtain it, but Morvandis already had power. What he wanted, she couldn't even begin to guess, and he had been less than forthcoming about his reasons for accepting her offer. *Both* offers, actually, for Morvandis hadn't taken as much time as she had thought he would to decide to study Blood Magic. When she'd asked him why he had suddenly decided to accept her tutelage, his response was simple.

The Convocation will only last for three more weeks, and when it ends, I will return home with my King, as is my duty. Unless you plan to follow me to Dakkadia, that will put an end to both my training, and our relationship.

She looked down at his sleeping form again and wondered what she would decide to do. She could take a sabbatical and leave the confines of the Citadel, of course, but the Council wouldn't hold her seat indefinitely, and at the slow rate of progress Morvandis was making, it would take years to fully teach him the intricacies of Blood Magic. The years were not the problem, for she was an Elf and, as such, she had many centuries of life to look forward to, but the loss of her power base in Ithram would be drastic.

She thought back to the conversation the two of them had had concerning power and its uses. What would she truly be giving up if she were to resign from the Council and leave Ithram for cold Dakkadia? His words from that first evening came back to her.

For every hour you spend studying these artifacts, countless days are wasted in useless councils and meetings, where important matters are discussed but nothing is ever done.

He had been right, of course. The power of the Zarryiostrom and the Mage Citadel combined had ensured stability in the realms for well over two thousand years. But that stability had inevitably led to stagnation, and she knew now that the stagnation had been there even before she herself had been born. In the few council sessions she had attended since that first day, when Morvandis had made his pronouncement on the hollowness of the Mage Citadel, she had paid more attention to the matters brought before the Council than usual and had discovered something: none of those matters meant a thing. Oh, there was much discussion about what the Citadel's position would be on some trivial thing or another, but there was never a resolution. *Wait and see* was always the final decision to which the Council would arrive.

She gently pulled the covers away from her nude body and slid out from between the sheets, stepping silently to her bureau. She moved as stealthily as only an Elf could, but she needn't have bothered, for despite his claims to the contrary, Morvandis was a sound sleeper. Her room was clean, for a change, for Morvandis had made his discomfort with her slovenliness too apparent for her to ignore, and she had finally relented and allowed the servants to clean the room. Hanging neatly from a hook, next to a full-length mirror, sat her freshly pressed High Councillor robes, complete with her medallion of station. She reached up and touched the cloth of the robe, but made no move to take it down or don it, despite her nudity. *I've worked hard my entire life to achieve this; can I give it up so easily now?* She looked back at Morvandis and saw him looking at her. *Not such a sound sleeper after all,* she thought with more than a bit of bemusement.

He watched her silently for a while, making no move to get out of bed, and after a time she spoke.

"I've been trying to decide whether or not I will join you in Dakkadia permanently. To do so would eventually lead to my replacement on the High Council." She tugged lightly on the fabric of the robe. "I would have to give up this."

Morvandis closed his eyes in silent agreement.

"I would never ask that of you, Enaria. It is not within me to ask you to be less than you are, or to make you sacrifice your dreams and ambitions for mine. We share a common interest, to be sure, but both of us have different ideas of how to accomplish our goals. Who is to say which path is the right one?"

She smiled at him.

"Only time will tell, of that I am sure." She turned to face him, unmindful of her nudity and said, "I truly appreciate the fact that you will place no pressure upon me to choose one way or the other, but I would be less than honest if I didn't admit to you that I feel a certain amount of resentment I have to make this decision at all."

Morvandis shook his head slightly in answer to the question he knew was coming.

"You could stay, Morvandis. You would be welcome here." she said pleadingly. Enaria walked quickly to the bed and knelt beside it. "Would it be so very hard? Would it be so hard for you to give up your place as a mere advisor to a King in order to explore the mysteries of the Archon here beside me?"

Morvandis reached out and brushed her hair aside to cup her cheek with his palm. She reached up with both hands and held his hand tight against her skin.

"You would have to be Dakkadian to understand, Enaria. War is coming, and it is coming sooner rather than later. Dakkadia will be the cause of it; of this I have absolutely no doubt." He took his hand away from her cheek and pulled himself up in bed, letting the blanket slide down to his waist. "When Dakkadia marches to war, whether it is against the Badlands, Ferralin, or Illymar itself, I will be there. I will be there because it is my duty to my country, and to the man to whom I owe fealty." She tried to hide her disappointment but failed utterly, to Morvandis' amusement. "Illymar seems intent on standing in the path of King Madari's ambitions. It may be that we'll see each other much sooner than you might anticipate—especially if we are forced to conquer Illymar and march triumphantly into Illymaine at the head of the Dakkadian army."

Enaria snorted at the mild jest and stood up, pulling the blanket to the side and sliding back into bed next to him. He moved away from the edge of the bed to give her room, and she curled up next to him, wrapping a slim arm and a slender leg around him before snuggling her head into the crook of his neck.

"Somehow, I doubt that will ever happen, Morvandis. The Mage High Council would never allow Dakkadia to invade."

Morvandis reached up and stroked her hair.

"Would they truly interfere? I mean no offense, Enaria, but the Mage Citadel has never been an institution known for taking decisive action. Would they truly make an exception in the face of a Dakkadian invasion?"

Enaria started to respond sharply that *of course* they would take decisive action, but an earlier thought returned to her.

'Wait and see' is always the final decision to which the Council arrives. Perhaps, even in the event of a Dakkadian invasion.

"Truthfully, I don't know. The treaty between Illymar and Ithram is very specific when it comes to mutual defense. Simply put, an attack on one is an attack on the other, and we would have no choice but to respond to Dakkadian aggression by fighting beside the Illymari army. There might not even *be* a debate, should Dakkadia foolishly attempt to invade; we may just send an army of Mages to end the fighting as quickly as possible. On the other hand, that treaty has never been tested, and the policy of the Mage Council has always been to wait and see. For as long as I have been a member, we have been told, time and again, that taking reckless action will always lead to unpredictable or undesirable results. So, we prefer to gather as much information as possible in order to make the best decision we can. If Dakkadia can find a good enough reason to invade—one based upon a legitimate grievance, or better yet, a just cause, and not based simply upon naked ambition—the Council might decide to adopt a wait and see attitude. It would have to be a serious grievance or a particularly noteworthy cause: the Mage Citadel won't allow itself to be paralyzed by specious claims or bogus attempts to influence policy. It would make us appear to be weak."

Morvandis settled back into his pillow, though he did continue to stroke her hair. Enaria suddenly realized that his questions had been too pointed to have been merely a casual query, and the realization made her pull away from him and turn to look him in the eyes.

"Madari sent you here, didn't he? He wants you to look for weaknesses in the Mage Council he can exploit." It wasn't a question. Morvandis's expression didn't change, but Enaria thought she could see a hint of an apology in his eyes.

After a few moments, he sighed.

"Yes, he did. The mission he gave me was to look for a way to fracture the Council or paralyze it, should he be unable to broker an alliance with either Illymar or Ferralin." He hesitated for a moment, as if wondering how much he could tell her. "In the absence of such a treaty, our first objective will be Illymar."

Enaria gave him a level stare.

"You could have told me. I've sworn an oath of fealty to you, and when I did, I told you that I would obey any order, or betray any confidence to you. I meant what I said." Her eyes hardened. "If you want the Council divided, I will find a way to fracture it for you." She sat up and pulled away from him. "The only thing I ask in return is that you be honest with me. I am not stupid. Do not treat me as such."

Morvandis nodded, and Enaria held his eyes for a few moments more before lying down beside him once again. Morvandis was silent until her head was once again nestled in the space between his neck and shoulder.

"I am sorry, Enaria. My mission is not to subvert you. I am here simply to test the waters, as it were, and find out which way the Council will jump should we attack Illymar preemptively. I did not tell you because I am a spymaster. It is my nature to keep my personal motives and objectives a secret from everyone. Believe me when I say that I do not think you are stupid. I promise to be honest with you, in as much as I am able. Not all of the secrets I keep are mine to reveal."

Enaria thought about his words for a moment before sighing softly.

"Being with you is going to be more complicated than I thought," she growled. She lifted a closed hand and raised two graceful fingers. "If you were to invade now, I could guarantee you two votes in favor of allowing the invasion: my own, and Lirielle's. Like me, Lirielle is a Blood Mage, and one of my protégés; she will do as I ask. That would leave you with six votes against." She thought about it for a moment and added, "Cedric is a Dakkadian, but he would definitely vote against invasion. Despite the reputation that Dakkadians have for being warlike, he is a stalwart proponent of peace and order. He would vote against you."

Though she wasn't looking at Morvandis's face, she could feel him smile.

"King Madari will not allow Cedric to interfere in his plans. You can be assured of that. When the time comes for a vote, he will vote to allow invasion."

Enaria said nothing, not wanting to doubt his word but being skeptical nonetheless, but she continued on without commenting on his pronouncement.

"All of the other Council Members would vote to aid Illymar. Though Ithram is its own country with its own customs and laws, we are so tightly bound to Illymar that we might as well be Illymari. Worse, Madari has already made his true nature known to the other kingdoms. Any reason he could come up with to justify an invasion would be scrutinized for the slightest deception. He has no claim to the throne of Illymar, after all, and everyone knows it."

Morvandis said nothing.

They lay in silence for a while, until rays of sunlight began poking their way through her heavy curtains. Abruptly, she sat up.

"We have work to do today, Morvandis, and we should be about it as soon as possible." She stretched her arms up and thrust her bare chest out in a prodigious yawn, before turning quickly to see his reaction. Just as she had hoped, he was looking at her breasts with a tiny smile on his face. When he noticed that she had seen him staring, he grinned ruefully before reaching a hand out to try and cup one. Before he could touch her, however, she darted out of bed and said in a playful voice, "None of that now, Morvandis!" She pursed her lips in feigned thought and pretended to think out loud. "I seem to recall a certain Dakkadian Mage having a great deal of difficulty mastering a certain form of magic. I think it's time to try a different tactic." A wicked look crossed her face, and she crossed her arms over her bare breasts to block his view. She then turned away and looked at him over her shoulder in such a way as to make his mouth water in anticipation. "You are too easily distracted from important matters, Novice. So, no more love play for you until you show me some real progress."

His groan of despair made her laugh out loud, but he dutifully climbed out of bed to begin the day's instruction.

As the first rays of the morning's sunlight peeked through his window, Xan was already awake and climbing out of bed. He had slept poorly that night, with thoughts of Deirdre running through his head. Even worse, when he had finally quieted his mind enough to sleep, the choir had begun their serenade as they always had, but this time something was different. Something was wrong. Their beautiful voices hadn't changed at all, but this time the choir sounded hollow and empty. The voices had always soothed him, singing him to sleep with gentle melodies and lullabies, but this time, he found himself straining to hear the voice that wasn't there, and its absence was maddening. He knew he had to do something quickly, so he walked to the velvet curtains covering his window and threw them open before striding over to his nightstand and grabbing a crystal bell. He shook it once, and immediately the door opened to allow his personal servants to enter. Several of them bore trays with food or drink, or whatever else he might need, but he waved them away.

"I need my secretary. The rest of you may leave." The servants bowed low, and a single man, dressed in the livery of the Ferralin court, stepped forward, holding a folio and standing ready to obey his Emperor's command. When the doors closed behind the two of them, Xan gestured to his desk. "You may be seated. I need you to pen two messages for me."

The secretary took his seat, then removed a quill from a pot of ink and pulled out two sheets of crisp, heavy parchment embossed with the Ferralin coat of arms. When he was ready, Xan began to speak.

"To his Majesty, King Madari of Dakkadia: I wish to speak privately with you concerning a matter of mutual benefit to both of our kingdoms. I would like to meet with you at the offices of the Zarryiostrom, today at noon. If you are agreeable, please send your reply through the messenger who delivers this letter."

He watched the secretary write the letter in his elegant hand, waiting until the man signaled that he had completed it, before dripping a bit of melted wax on the letter and pressing his signet into it. The signet contained the coat of arms of the Ferralin Empire, an exact match for the watermark threading the parchment; a flying crane superimposed over a crescent moon. After the secretary had readied a clean sheet of parchment, Xan spoke again.

"To his Eminence, Patriarch Samuel Varic: It is my wish to use the services of your office to meet with King Madari Dhaerhan of Dakkadia this afternoon to discuss a matter of great import. As such, I wish to enlist the services of the Zarryiostrom to prepare a small meeting room, where it is my hope that King Madari and I will be able to discuss our concerns privately. I have asked His Majesty, King Madari, to meet me at noon today, and I expect a response in the affirmative shortly."

Again, he waited until the secretary indicated that he had completed the letter, and again, Xan sealed it with his signet.

"These letters are to be delivered by the Grand Vizier himself, immediately. See that he gets them."

The secretary bowed low and stepped away from the Emperor before leaving the room as quickly as possible. When the door closed behind him, Xan stepped to the window and looked out, seeing the Spire of Illymaine standing proudly in the distance. Despite his many years and his vast experience, he knew he was treading on new and potentially dangerous ground, but he no longer had a choice. He had to have his Pretty, and if Illymar had to pay the price, then so be it. He rang the bell again, and allowed his servants to prepare him for the day's events. As they bustled about him, he smiled inwardly. *How eventful they will be remains to be seen.*

Madari awoke to a foul mood and a fouler temper. His argument with King Orem had started badly, and had only gotten worse as the evening went on. As Orem had hurled insult after insult at him, secure in the knowledge that he could hide safely behind the protection of the Peace of Zarryiosiad, Madari could almost feel his priorities shifting. He had told Orem that his ultimate goal was the "liberation" of the Badlands—a polite way of saying that he wanted to conquer it outright—but, because of Orem's churlish behavior, that was no longer the case. The Badlands be damned: he wanted Illymar, and he wanted it over Orem's dead body.

Unfortunately, that was easier said than done. Illymar enjoyed the protection of the Mage Citadel, which already made invading the island impossible. But with Orem's daughter and Xan's son all but married already, attacking Illymar *or* Ferralin would turn the world against Dakkadia, and his armies would have no chance whatsoever against their coalition backed by the power of Ithram. He walked to his curtains and threw them open to allow the morning's light to enter the room, but instantly regretted doing so, for the Spire of Illymaine was the first thing he saw. He felt his teeth grinding in fury at the symbol of Orem's power and forced himself to relax his jaw. *There is a way. There is* always *a way. I just haven't found it yet.* He hoped Morvandis was making headway into his investigation of the Mage Council. If they could somehow find a way to keep the Mage Citadel from interfering, he would risk starting a two-front war with Illymar and Ferralin for a chance to sink his fangs into Orem's throat. Morvandis had already made that possible by opening a door for them through the Teeth of Amhar. *A lightning attack from an unexpected direction would see Illymar conquered within days or weeks. By the time word reached Ferralin that we have attacked their sovereign ally, it would be too late for them to interfere. The Dakkadian flag would already be flying over the capital, and I would be spitting on Orem's grave before taking his daughter to my bed.* Madari was not given to flights of fancy or pleasant daydreams, but the thought of taking Tais to his bed after destroying Illymar's army and killing her father lightened his mood considerably.

I might even take her while sitting on your throne, Orem. How would that make you feel, knowing that the man you hate most in this world is taking his pleasure from your oldest daughter on the very seat from which you used to rule?

Despite himself, he laughed at the thought.

A slight knock at his door took him away from his pleasant fantasies, and he barked an order to enter. The door opened up softly, and Thorn Demestira stepped through for the morning's reports. As always, his eyes followed the tight, glorious curves of her body so eloquently displayed through her skin-tight leather, and the sight of her, combined with his earlier thoughts of Tais, threatened to illicit an entirely inappropriate response from him. He quickly dragged his eyes away from her ample bosom and looked her in the eye.

"Good morning, Countess. What news do you have for me?"

Thorn grinned at him, impudently.

"Quite a bit, actually, Your Majesty. I had an eventful evening."

From the smile on her face he knew the news was good, so he offered her a chair before turning to his wardrobe to select his uniform for the day. Once he had made his selection, he stepped behind a privacy screen to undress.

"You have my undivided attention, Countess Demestira. Don't keep me waiting."

She chuckled at that but ignored the chair, preferring instead to stand in her King's presence.

"Last evening, I had the pleasure of meeting with one Vitaly Saxe, Earl of Saxe and chief advisor to Ascham Illvanin, the Duke of Saerce. He is a political insider of the first order, though he has been out of the city of Illymaine for some time in the service of Duke Ascham. According to Vitaly, it seems the Duke of Saerce and his brother, King Orem, have had an ongoing difference of opinion concerning a great many things, chief among them the sudden rise of the Savonne family—the Queen's relations—to prominence. This difference of opinion was serious enough for Orem to exile his brother to his estates in the far north to silence him. Furthermore, the rise of the Savonnes has come at great cost to the established nobility, and apparently, they aren't pleased with the Savonnes' good fortune either. He also let slip a second bit of information, that when taken with the first, makes the political situation in Illymar look quite a bit more interesting. According to Vitaly, Ascham has assembled a vast army to counter the depredations of a certain ambitious neighbor on the main continent."

Madari snorted at that, and Thorn continued in the same light tone.

"King Orem controls the country's wealth, filtered through the services of the Savonne family, but if Ascham were to make a play for the throne, he might just win it. The numbers are telling: Ascham's army numbers nearly 50,000 soldiers spread over the entire country to hide their true numbers. Perhaps even worse for Orem, Ascham also has a firm grip on the navy, despite the fact that a Savonne is ostensibly the Lord High Admiral. So far, Ascham has shown no inclination to move against his brother in any fashion. Apparently, his true purpose for assembling the army is exactly what he says it is: to combat Dakkadian aggression."

"He's a patriot then," Madari said. "That makes him dangerous."

He looked around the screen at Thorn.

"This is not good news that you are giving me, Thorn. I hope it gets better soon, or you may find yourself incurring your King's displeasure." The mock-severe look he gave her made her chuckle, and as he once again disappeared behind his screen, she continued.

"That's exactly what I thought, initially. So I posed a simple question to Vitaly. I asked him what he would do to throw the country into chaos. His answer surprised me. He believes the fastest way to sow the seeds of discord is to simply kill the King."

The sound of a chair or a footstool falling over, followed by a string of expletives, told her the information had caught Madari by surprise. He walked around the screen wearing only his breeches, holding a belt in one hand and a shirt in the other.

"That's absurd!" he bellowed, shaking the belt at her. "If Orem dies, Ascham will simply take the reins of the kingdom. From what you said a moment ago, he has the forces to do it."

Thorn nodded her agreement, and her acquiescence calmed him enough to allow her to continue.

"Again, exactly the conclusion I came to as well. Ascham, as the King of Illymar, *would* be a serious problem for us. But Vitaly reminded me that *Prince Ethan*, and not the Duke of Saerce, is the rightful heir. That gives him the legitimacy that Ascham lacks. Moreover, the Savonne family is fabulously wealthy and would use every bit of that wealth to ensure they remain in power. Furthermore, they hate Ascham. Saxe believes the Savonnes would move as quickly as possible after Orem's death to seize power and ensure Ethan succeeds his father—more than likely over Ascham's dead body."

Madari lowered his belt, and a speculative look crossed his face. As his thoughts turned inward, following her line of reasoning, he began to speak out loud.

"If Orem were to die suddenly—under mysterious conditions, of course—the first thing Queen Althea would have to do is have Ascham arrested and condemned for treason, in the belief that killing him would stop a rebellion before it could begin. Most likely, they would pin the blame for Orem's death on Ascham as the reason for his hasty execution, whether or not he was actually involved. With no leader, his army of supporters would melt away, hoping not to follow their leader to the headsman's block." He paused for a moment to think, and took the opportunity to pull his shirt over his head. As he absentmindedly yanked the garment into place, he continued. "If, however, they were to attempt to arrest or execute him, his supporters would have no choice but to act on his behalf. The result would almost certainly be open warfare. The monarchy may not have the sheer numbers that Ascham can call upon, but they aren't exactly helpless, either. Both sides would know that they are fighting for their lives, and that alone would rule out the possibility of a negotiated settlement." He grinned wolfishly. "Civil wars are always messy. I learned that the hard way during my own ascension to the throne of Dakkadia." He gave Thorn a sideways look. "This is good information to have, which naturally makes it suspect. Am I to understand that the good Earl of Saxe was kind enough to reveal all of his political secrets to you—a complete stranger—on a whim? Perhaps he betrayed his country over a bottle of wine and a lovely dinner somewhere? Somehow, I find that very difficult to believe."

His tone was astringent, but the cheerful grin didn't leave her face at his mockery.

"Oh no, Your Majesty; I had to beat the information out of him." The statement was made with a look of utter innocence, too real to be believed. Madari rolled his eyes and snorted at her 'jest' until he remembered exactly who it was he was speaking with. His eyes widened once in shocked surprise, before narrowing in speculation. She laughed at his expression and confirmed his suspicion. "Or more specifically, I had to beat, cut, burn, whip, and choke the information out of him slowly, over a period of several hours. The longest hours of his life, I'd imagine."

"You killed the Earl of Saxe?"

"Oh, no! There was no need. Vitaly Saxe enjoys exploring the darker side of his nature. I simply introduced him to the version of it we practice in the Flower Court. Our skills at using pain to induce pleasure are legendary, and I don't think he quite understood just what he was getting himself into. Believe me when I say that the information is genuine. He sang like a nightingale for me once I really got started." She reached for a heavy pouch tied to her belt, removed it, and tossed it to her King. He caught it and hefted the bag to judge its weight before opening it to look at the contents. At the glitter of gold coins he whistled appreciatively, then retied it and tossed it back to her. "As you can see, he enjoyed the experience immensely. In fact, he even begged me to meet him again . . . as soon as he recovers from the last session, of course."

Madari thanked Thorn for her report and dismissed her. She yawned once and stretched languorously, a move that made his eyes involuntarily follow her lithe form again, before she bowed and sidled out of the room. She had given him a lot to think about, and he needed to discuss the possibilities with Morvandis. The more he mulled it over in his head, however, the more convinced he became that the information was genuine and that the idea of killing King Orem had merit.

He couldn't quite shake himself of the notion that his anger with Orem was clouding his judgment, but he wasn't planning on killing Orem anytime soon. There was still hope—faint though it might be—that he could accomplish something useful here. Until the marriage ceremony actually took place, anything could happen.

After he finished dressing, he left his chambers and walked to the dining hall to break his fast. He had ordered the kitchens to serve only traditional Dakkadian fare during the few meals he took at home, for he had found that the rich Illymari foods didn't quite agree with his palate. Now that he had been exposed to the fine art of Illymari cooking, he found that he vastly preferred simpler foods. Unfortunately, with the number of events held each day serving Illymari confections and creations that he had to attend, sometimes a slice of ham or a rare steak was all he had to sustain himself. He nodded a greeting to his wife—the niceties had to be observed after all—before placing a napkin on his lap and nodding to a steward. The rich aroma of sizzling bacon permeated the air, and he found himself looking forward to his first bite.

A herald entered the room and hurried over to him as the steward placed the first slice of bacon on his plate.

"An emissary from the Ferralin delegation is here to speak with you. He awaits your pleasure in the main hall."

Madari frowned and stood up quickly, his food forgotten. He started for the door, but turned back to the others seated at the table.

"It would seem I have business to attend to. Don't wait for me; enjoy your breakfast." He turned again to the door and walked through, wondering what a Ferralin emissary could want with him.

I guess I'll find out soon enough, he thought.

Madari recognized the envoy instantly; after all, he'd spent the past several nights watching him stand next to Emperor Xan. He didn't know the man's name, but that would be remedied in just a few moments. From the way he dressed, he was obviously a Mage, though his formal black robe was shorter than the standard Mage robe and featured elaborate Ferralin embroidery. At the sight of Madari, the man bowed.

"Your Majesty, please forgive the interruption. I am Grand Vizier Shar, servant to His Imperial Majesty Xan. I bear a message that I have been entrusted to deliver to you."

Without rising from his low bow, he proffered a scroll sealed with turquoise wax and impressed with the coat of arms of the Ferralin Empire. Madari took the letter from the Vizier and signaled for the man to rise. He then opened it, and after scanning the contents briefly, frowned in confusion.

"Are you aware of the contents of this letter?"

"No. I was simply instructed to deliver it to you and await your answer."

The Vizier tried to hide his curiosity, but he kept glancing at the letter as if wanting to know what it contained. Madari handed him the missive and let him read it. The Vizier read quickly and his eyes widened in surprise at the contents.

"Do you have any idea what this proposed meeting is about?" Madari asked him.

"No, Your Majesty. I'm afraid his Imperial Majesty did not impart that information to me. What reply shall I return to him?"

Madari read the letter again.

"I'll be there. Please inform Emperor Xan that I'll also be bringing my Mage, Morvandis, with me."

"Of course, Your Majesty," the Vizier said, bowing once more. "I will deliver your reply immediately. Good day."

Madari watched the Mage leave, wondering what this could be about. Xan hadn't spoken to him at all since they had exchanged pleasantries on the first day, and he couldn't understand why the man would seek him out now. He walked back to the dining room and sat back down in his chair. A fresh plate was placed before him, and again the steward served him several strips of bacon. He absentmindedly picked one up with his fingers and bit into it, not even tasting the food as he chewed. After a few moments, a voice cut through his thoughts and he looked up to see who had spoken. Aveliad was looking at him through cool eyes, obviously expecting an answer, but he hadn't heard the question.

"I'm sorry, Aveliad. I was distracted, and I'm afraid I didn't hear your question. What did you say?"

"I asked if anything was the matter. Who did you meet with?"

Madari held out the note to the steward.

"Take that to Queen Aveliad."

The man bowed, took the note, and delivered it to the Queen sitting at the opposite side of the table. She read it quickly and set it to the side.

"So Emperor Xan wishes to meet with you today? Do you know what this is about?"

Madari started to answer his wife, when the sound of a glass dropping to the floor and shattering on the stone made them both look at the source. Deirdre had a stricken look on her face, and her normally pale complexion looked positively ashen. Madari started to ask her what the matter was, but Aveliad reacted faster.

"Deirdre? What's wrong?"

As a servant rushed over to clear away the broken shards and provide her with a new glass, Deirdre said nothing. Finally, when the servant moved away she looked up at her parents.

"May I speak with you? In private?"

Aveliad frowned at the unusual request, but Madari simply turned to the staff.

"Please leave the room. We'll call you when we need you."

The servants filed out of the room silently, leaving the three Dhaerhans alone. When the door closed behind the last of them, Madari turned back to Deirdre.

"Do you know something about this, Deirdre?"

She reached out a trembling hand and picked up her new glass, and took a drink before beginning.

"A few days ago, I snuck out of the party and approached Crown Prince Lain when he left to get some air. He had gone to the veranda adjacent to the dining hall to find a little privacy to play his flute, so I followed him outside and introduced myself to him, and we found that we both share an interest in music. He played his flute for me and I sang for him, and we had a lovely time. We didn't spend very long with each other, but when we parted, we parted as friends." She smiled at the remembrance, but then a dark cloud seemed to cross over her face. "Last evening, he signaled to me that he wanted to meet me again, and we went back to the veranda and resumed our musical interlude. I guess we lost track of time because his father came looking for us." She looked up, her face pale. "Emperor Xan heard me singing with Lain, and asked me to sing for him as well. I did, and he seemed to enjoy the song very much. When I finished, he applauded, and then invited me to come to Ferralin to sing for him at his home." She closed her eyes, and her voice lowered almost to a whisper. "I was so happy. Lain is a wonderful man and I really like him, but his father. . ." Her voice trailed off. Abruptly, she opened her eyes and continued in a stronger voice. "His father frightened me. He couldn't have been nicer to me, but there was something wrong. Even Lain was frightened of him. I couldn't understand why he would be afraid of his own father, but then I looked into Emperor Xan's eyes." She hugged herself tightly and closed her eyes again, but this time they opened quickly, almost as if she were afraid of what she had seen when she had closed them. Deirdre took a deep breath and blurted out, "Father, I think he's mad. He disguises it well, but I could *see* it. It's right there in his eyes. He put his hands on my shoulders and said kind things to me, but, Father, he hurt me. I've never been so terrified in all my life."

She reached up with her hands and lowered the neckline of her dress to reveal her shoulders, and two perfectly round bruises appeared, just below her collarbones. She turned around to show him her back, revealing eight more dark bruises, marks obviously left by hard fingertips pressing deeply into her flesh. She pulled her dress back into place and lowered her head.

"I think Emperor Xan wanted to hurt me, and I don't know what would have happened if Lain hadn't been there. Lain pulled his father away from me and told him that they should return to the party . . . that they would be missed."

Aveliad stood up and walked to her daughter, to brush a comforting hand through her daughter's hair, but Madari remained seated. Instead, he considered what his daughter had told him.

It was disturbing to see his daughter's reaction to the previous evening's events, for Deirdre was an outgoing and vivacious girl who didn't frighten easily, but she was obviously very afraid of Xan. Seeing the bruises on his daughter made him very angry with Emperor Xan for laying his hands upon her, but he could *feel* an opportunity presenting itself. From what Deirdre had said, both Xan and his son had been quite taken with her, and that information, coupled with the knowledge that Prince Lain obviously was not enthralled with his current betrothed, set the entire question of an Illymar/Ferralin marriage on its heels. He didn't want to speculate about Xan's motives for asking for this meeting, but opening a dialogue with the Ferralin delegation behind Orem's back would be an excellent first step in forcing a wedge between Ferralin and Illymar, even if nothing substantial came of it. Abruptly, he made up his mind.

"I will go to this meeting and see what Emperor Xan wants with me. To do otherwise would be a great offense to Xan, and would destroy any chance I have of negotiating a treaty or an alliance with him." He looked at his daughter and said, "I am sorry that he was a bit rough with you, Deirdre, but I really don't think that he intentionally hurt you. Even if he did, however, this is an opportunity that I must seize, even if it means turning a blind eye to his inappropriate treatment of you." His gaze sharpened and he looked his daughter in the eyes. "In the future, stay away from Xan unless I am present. Am I understood?"

She nodded quickly in response, but then a hopeful look crossed her face.

"What about Prince Lain? May I still talk with him?"

"Of course you may," Madari said, encouragingly. "Just stay away from his father. Am I understood?"

Deirdre smiled at her father and nodded happily, fear and misery forgotten in the face of her father's permission for her to continue to speak with Lain. Aveliad frowned slightly at him, but her budding displeasure at him couldn't dampen his good spirits. He smiled slightly at Aveliad, meeting her cold gaze with narrowed eyes.

Yes, Aveliad, I want her to meet with Lain, as often as she can. With a little luck, something good may come from it. But even if it doesn't, the simple fact that Xan is willing to meet with me behind Orem's back is important in and of itself.

He picked up a piece of bacon and bit into it, thoughts turning inward once again.

Today will be an interesting day. I wonder what Morvandis will make of it.

Prudence Daemira walked down the gangplank of the *Sovereign* and nodded absentmindedly at the harbormaster, before turning down a wide lane that led from the docks toward the city of Ithram. She was in high spirits, and there was a noticeable spring in her step as she thought about her upcoming meeting with Phaedron. A cheerful thought crossed her mind, and she smiled to herself.

I wonder if he's been as miserable as I've been.

She hoped so, because that would make this surprise visit that much better for the both of them. It wasn't like her to be irritable, especially to her crew, but ever since Phaedron had gone to the Citadel she had been restless. There were so many wonderful things to see in Illymar, so many interesting things to do; and without Phaedron there to enjoy them with her, all she had done was sit in her cabin and bark at anyone foolish enough to cross her path. The crew was on pins and needles, and eventually, Mr. Frederick had been forced to respectfully, but firmly, order her to get off the ship before her foul temper incited a mutiny. She tried to protest, but her half-hearted arguments had sounded hollow, even to her own ears.

Decision made, she had set to with a will. The outfit she had donned was yet another cloth monstrosity that her brother had sent to her, but she had wasted no time thinking evil thoughts about her wretched sibling as she put the garment on. When the last button was in place, and she could find nothing wrong with her appearance, she put on her rapier's baldric and tucked away a brace of pistols, and then left the ship behind without a backward glance. Mr. Frederick was one of the most capable officers she had ever met, and she knew that she could trust him to somehow keep the *Sovereign* afloat while she was away.

The walk to the Citadel was a considerable distance, but she didn't mind. Illymar truly was beautiful, and she enjoyed walking the streets to take in the sights and smells as often as possible. *I'll probably never get the chance to visit this city again during peacetime, so I'll have to enjoy it while I can.*

Truthfully, she was looking forward to seeing the Citadel, almost as much as she was looking forward to seeing Phaedron once again. While the Citadel lacked the grace and majesty of the Cathedral of Zarryiosiad, it was still one of the most impressive structures on the entire island, and she very much wanted to see it before she left.

The next time I come here, I'll probably be looking at this city over the muzzles of my cannons. If that happens, this country will very quickly become a lot less beautiful.

It was a sobering thought; that despite the majesty of this country and the hospitality of its people, they were still her sworn enemies, and one day she might be called upon to fight them. She didn't dwell on that for long, however, for she was a professional soldier and would fight both when and where she was directed. The Illymari would do the same.

But for now, they have nothing to fear from me and they know it.

Hawkers of every sort lined the crowded avenue, selling everything from cloth and textiles, to food or imported goods, and everyone seemed to be doing brisk business. The tantalizing aroma of cooking foods and exotic spices permeated the air, and her mouth began to water at the savory smells coming from the many small restaurants lining the avenue. A low growl from her stomach reminded her that she had skipped breakfast in her haste to leave the ship, and for a moment she was tempted to buy something to stave off her immediate hunger from one of the vendors. But, despite the temptation, she held herself firmly in check: a meal was infinitely more enjoyable with good company, and she could think of no better company than the Earl of Daane. She smiled at that, and then blushed slightly when she caught herself thinking about Phaedron yet again.

As she moved past the seller's market and into the city proper, she began to get the distinct impression that she was being watched. She had been so lost in pleasant daydreams that she almost hadn't recognized the signs, but the hairs on the back of her neck began to stand on end and she knew something was wrong. She didn't change her pace or show any outward signs that she suspected she was being stalked, but her right hand moved slowly underneath her heavy jacket to the handle of one of the pistols tucked into her belt. Prudence knew she might be imagining things, but then she also knew that, other than King Madari himself, she was the person the Illymari people would most like to see dead and buried.

Better, by far, to be wrong and alive, than right and dead.

She studied the layout of the street carefully and realized she was most likely walking into an ambush. The Citadel was too distant to be of any help, as was the Cathedral, but she *was* nearing the Illymari Admiralty building and grounds—the very place she and Phaedron had eaten lunch with Lord High Admiral Savonne a few days earlier. She wasn't certain who was following her, or how many of them there were, but the Peace of Zarryiosiad obviously wasn't enough to deter them from seeking her out.

In a flash she made up her mind. The Illymari would have no choice but to protect her from harm, or risk incurring the displeasure of both the Mage Citadel and the Zarryiostrom.

If I am attacked in defiance of the Peace, there will be hell to pay.

While she would most likely be too dead to appreciate their concern on her behalf, she could at least rest easy knowing that King Madari would quickly make his own displeasure with Illymar known by taking the country by force and burning it to the ground in her name . . . preferably while the priests and the Mages stood by cheering him on. The thought made her snicker, and to her relief, she found that the gallows humor calmed her down, considerably.

I'm glad I can find the humor even in a possible assassination attempt.

She stopped at an intersection and pretended to look at the street signs to get her bearings, while instead taking the opportunity to see what she was up against. Out of the corner of her eye, she saw at least one person stop as well, to watch her from where he thought he would be unobserved. After a moment, she deliberately turned down the wrong path and began walking toward the Admiralty, and away from the Cathedral and the Citadel. When the man began following her again, she knew it was time to act. She pulled a second pistol out of her belt and cocked both strikers without withdrawing her hands from her coat. She didn't think anyone had seen her pull out her weapons, but it probably didn't matter. The Illymari most likely wouldn't know what a pistol was capable of anyway.

After a short walk, the Admiralty compound came into view, with armed soldiers stationed at the entrance.

They have to realize where I'm going now. They'll strike soon.

The would-be assassins didn't disappoint her. She heard a quick movement behind her and whirled around, just in time, to see three men rushing at her with drawn daggers.

Only three of them? she thought in disgust. *I'm almost insulted that they would think so little of me!*

She jumped backward, pulling both pistols from beneath her coat and firing quickly without taking the time to properly aim. Nevertheless, both shots found their mark, and two bloodcurdling screams filled the air as her targets went down. The third one recoiled at the sudden carnage, and his mouth fell open in surprise as his fellow assassins dropped like puppets with cut strings, but his hesitation didn't last long. His face curled into an enraged snarl and he charged again, but the brief respite her initial shots had bought her was just enough of a distraction that she was able to drop both of her empty pistols and pull a third pistol from behind her back to fire again. The third shot also flew true, striking the assassin in the throat and dropping him backward in a spray of blood and gore. Unlike his friends, he didn't have time to scream, for death overtook him before his body had even hit the ground. She dropped the third pistol and pulled her rapier and main gauche from their scabbards, unsure if there were any more assassins left alive. Another sudden movement told her that there were.

A second group of three men rushed out of an alley, directly between her and the guards at the Illymari Admiralty building. Unlike the men who had been following her, these men carried cutlasses, not daggers, and from the looks of them they knew how to use them. Prudence looked past the new group toward the compound, hoping that the shots would have summoned help, but the soldiers posted at the gates remained where they were, weapons held at their ease. They were watching the fight with interest, but they clearly weren't going to interfere. With no hope of reinforcements, Prudence lowered herself into a fighting stance and gave the men a vicious smile.

"I hope that they paid you in advance, boys. Your families are going to need the coin to bury what's left of you."

None of the would-be assassins bothered to reply, and as one, they charged her. Even with her skill at swordplay, in a matter of moments she knew that she was in for the fight of her life. At first, it was all she could do to keep herself from being killed outright, but her skillful defensive footwork and brilliant swordsmanship kept her safe. Unfortunately, she couldn't strike back at any of the men without leaving herself open to an attack from the other two, but as they spread out and surrounded her, she abruptly changed tactics and charged the man standing between her and the Admiralty, yelling and swinging wildly. The man backed up quickly at the unexpected assault, allowing her to take several steps toward the compound as he recovered from his surprise.

The other two men rushed in to attack her from behind, hoping to strike her down as she retreated, but she suddenly stopped dead in her tracks and spun about to stab the closer of the two men directly through the heart in a single blinding thrust he didn't even see coming. As he fell forward over her blade, shocked eyes already beginning to glaze, she kicked up with her knee to turn his body enough to allow her to pull her rapier out of his chest. She moved quickly, but not quickly enough; the man who had stood between her and the compound slashed at her from behind, laying open her jacket and slashing the skin over her left shoulder blade. She felt the sting of the hit and grimaced at the pain, but without even looking at him, she knew he had left himself exposed to a counterattack. She stepped backward, directly into him, and spun around to her right, main gauche already reaching for his belly. The blade struck true, easily slicing through his stomach and up under his ribs to take his heart from beneath. When the wire-wrapped hilt struck him, she turned the weapon once to open the wound before pulling the weapon back out of his body.

As the second man fell, Prudence could tell that the third man had clearly had enough. He glanced at his two fallen comrades, and then at her, before dropping his cutlass and attempting to run away. She sneered at his cowardice.

This one needs to be taken alive. He'll gladly tell me everything he knows about whomever it was that hired him.

She expected him to run back into the alley in an attempt to escape, but to her surprise, he ran *toward* the compound instead of away from it. She turned to chase him, but he stopped on his own and raised his hands in surrender . . . not to her, but to the soldiers. Instead of arresting him, they took aim with their crossbows, and the man screamed,

"No! *NO!*"

The sound of several wet impacts striking flesh filled the air and his body jerked as quarrel after quarrel struck him. When he fell over backward, Corsair could see that the man was dead, and six Illymari crossbowmen were reloading their weapons as quickly as they could. Their marksmanship had been superb, for all of the quarrels had struck the would-be assassin in the torso.

I guess I won't be getting any information out of him after all, she thought, wryly.

She stopped where she was and sheathed her weapons, before realizing that the soldiers were now pointing their reloaded weapons at her. She raised her hands slowly to show them that she was no threat, but they still didn't lower their weapons. They didn't shoot, either, a fact for which she was profoundly grateful, but having six expert marksmen aiming their weapons at her was definitely making her feel very uneasy.

An earlier thought returned to her, adding fuel to her worry, *These people are my enemies.*

A shout came from within the compound, and the soldiers relaxed slightly, the tension in their faces eased by the understanding that someone in authority would soon tell them what to do. A second shout, closer this time, made the men lower their crossbows, but only after the last weapon was turned away from her chest did Prudence allow herself to relax. When Admiral Savonne himself rounded the corner, red-faced and breathing hard, she smiled. The men around him stiffened to attention, but he paid them no mind as he hurried to where she was standing, flanked by two men with halberds.

"Lady Prudence! Are you well? What happened?"

“Lord High Admiral,” Prudence said. “I was attacked by six men while on my way to the Mage Citadel. It was a planned ambush, and I have no doubt that they intended to assassinate me.” She gestured towards the three men lying around her. “As you can see, they failed.” She tried to cross her arms, but a sharp pain shot up from her left shoulder blade, as if to remind her she hadn’t emerged unscathed, and she turned slightly to show him her wound. “One of these bastards did this to me, but I’ve had worse.”

Admiral Savonne frowned in concern at the blood staining her coat.

“A nasty wound. Allow me to escort you to our physicians. They will see to your wound, while my men guarantee your safety. You have nothing to fear here: we hold to the Peace of Zarryiosiad.” Savonne gestured to his men and ordered them to collect the bodies. “We will see to the bodies of your attackers. If we can find anything out about them, I will personally inform you.” He shook his head slowly. “That anyone would think of breaking the Peace is unconscionable.”

Prudence frowned at that but said nothing, for something about the attack was bothering her. The last man, who had no longer posed a threat to her—or anyone—had been shot down like a dog while running *toward* the men who had killed him. Savonne’s mention of the Peace of Zarryiosiad was also interesting. He had been very quick to remind her that she had nothing to fear from the Illymari navy while under the protection of the Peace. That alone was enough to make her hackles rise up in suspicion.

“Thank you for your kind offer, Admiral Savonne, but I have business in the Citadel this morning and this attack has already made me late.” A soldier ran up to the Admiral after investigating the first group of men she had killed and presented a small bundle wrapped in cloth to him. The Admiral accepted the bundle and unwrapped it, revealing all three of her pistols. She smiled when she saw them. “Thank you for retrieving those for me. I had to drop them to deal with the second group of men.” She held out her hand for them expectantly, but Admiral Savonne didn’t give them to her right away. Instead, he picked one out at random and took it from the pile, to give it a thorough examination. Corsair narrowed her eyes in irritation as he carefully examined the weapon, even going so far as to cock the striker back.

“An interesting weapon you have here. Odd that something so small could so easily kill a man.”

He pointed the weapon at her and placed his finger on the trigger.

“I assume this is how you hold it?” Despite the pain in her shoulder, Prudence did cross her arms then, and gave him a level look, neither confirming nor denying his question. At her silence, he smiled. “I’ll take that as a ‘yes’. I don’t suppose you would care to tell me how it works? That kind of information would be very valuable to the right parties. Very valuable, indeed."

Corsair gave him a cocky grin that didn't reach her eyes.

"I don't suppose you would care to tell me why the last assassin ran toward your soldiers instead of away from them? Or why they only killed him after it was clear he was no longer a threat? It seems strange to me that he would seek shelter from the very men who killed him."

Savonne's eyes narrowed at the veiled accusation, but he didn't speak. Instead, he raised the weapon, holding it steadily at shoulder height and pointing it right between her eyes. As they tested each other's will, the soldiers surrounding the group began to fidget, unsure of what to do. As the long seconds dragged on, Corsair began to weigh her options, few as they were.

If they truly want me dead, then I'm dead.

Abruptly, Savonne lowered the weapon and extended the bundle to her, including the still-cocked weapon. He began to laugh as if it were all a big joke.

"I apologize for that unseemly display, Lady Prudence. But I had to try. As you may well imagine, His Majesty is very interested in that weapon, and how it works. We know it is the reason your ships have become such a threat to ours, but that's all we know. To have one actually in my hands is quite the coup."

Corsair accepted the bundle and pulled the cocked weapon out. Without changing expressions, she lifted the weapon to shoulder height with her right hand and pointed it right between Savonne's eyes. His face turned pale and he stiffened at the obvious threat from the unknown weapon, but she ignored his fear and gave him a predatory smile. Without warning, she pulled the trigger. The striker made a mechanical click as it struck a few sparks, but nothing else happened, except that Savonne jumped in shock, pale face turning positively ashen. The soldiers surrounding them didn't move a muscle. Satisfied at his reaction, Corsair lowered the weapon.

"This weapon has to be reloaded after it is fired, much like a crossbow. Once the weapon is discharged, it becomes nothing more than a pretty toy. That's why I dropped it in the first place; it was no longer useful to me."

She slipped the weapons back into their places on her belt without reloading them first. As she told Savonne, they were useless as they were, but she wasn't about to show him how to arm it. Admiral Savonne gave her a scowl when he realized she had gotten the best of him in yet another exchange, but his expression changed abruptly to one of feigned friendship as he spoke again.

"I see. That, too, is good information to know, I suppose, even if the demonstration was a bit disconcerting. But, enough of this. You're injured. Please allow me to escort you to our doctor. He'll patch you right up."

Prudence hesitated at the offer, for she knew she was losing a lot of blood, but the thought of willingly putting herself at the mercy of her enemies was a very bad idea. She looked around at the buildings surrounding the spot of the ambush. A large crowd had gathered, filled with curious bystanders wondering what had just transpired.

Savonne wouldn't try anything with this many witnesses, would he? Probably not, she thought, but the actions of the last assassin kept running through her mind. *He thought the Admiralty would offer him a safe haven, and Lucas, above all, wants me dead.*

With that thought foremost in her mind, she came to her decision.

"I thank you for your kind offer, but again, I must refuse. Your soldiers have my thanks for their assistance in this matter, belated as it was. I shall commend their accuracy in my report to His Majesty, King Madari."

The soldiers stiffened again at the veiled insult, but she paid them no mind.

"Good day, Admiral Savonne. I'm sorry to have pulled you away from what I am sure was an excellent meal."

She turned away from him and began walking the way she came without a backward glance. She didn't need to look at him to know she had scored a direct hit with her parting insult, and despite the rapidly spreading pain in her shoulder, she smiled. Behind her, she could hear the soldiers returning to their compound, and eventually, the sound of their footsteps disappeared altogether. Only after she rounded the corner to where she was sure the soldiers could no longer view her, did she stop to lean against a building. Now that the danger had passed, her back was sending scarlet fire through her body. It was by will alone that she kept herself standing.

I hope my brother doesn't see this coat. I'm pretty sure it's ruined.

Unsure of what to do next, she began to methodically reload her weapons. Conventional wisdom told her to return to the *Sovereign* as quickly as possible, but there might still be other assassins out there waiting for her to do just that. If there were—and they knew that she was wounded—they would most likely anticipate that she would return to the safety of her ship. Instead, she finished loading the last of her pistols and turned again to walk toward the Mage Citadel.

I hope I can make it. I'm bleeding pretty badly here.

If she could reach the Citadel, she was sure the physicians there would tend her wounds.

And Phaedron is there as well. I wonder what his bedside manner is like?

As she had before the ambush, she laughed, and again the humorous thought calmed her. Decision made, she stood up straight and began walking toward the Citadel, a pistol in each hand and a resolute smile on her face.

CHAPTER TWENTY

"Covenant"

Patriarch Varic lowered the letter that had been delivered to him by the Grand Vizier of Ferralin and frowned in thought. He had read the letter several times, trying to understand what exactly Emperor Xan was playing at, but no matter which way he approached the problem, no answer came to mind.

"Please inform His Imperial Majesty that we will be more than happy to accede to his wishes," Varic said to the Vizier. "We are honored that he would consider using our services to mediate between two such esteemed personages. We shall expect him at noon." The Vizier bowed and turned to leave, but Patriarch Varic stopped him. "Have you any idea what this meeting is about? With the impending marriage between Crown Prince Lain and Princess Lyrahe, as well as the birth of a formal alliance between Illymar and Ferralin, I hadn't thought Emperor Xan would have any desire to meet with King Madari, for any reason whatsoever."

The Vizier hesitated at that, and shrugged slightly.

"It is not my place to speculate on the motives of His Imperial Majesty. I have not been consulted concerning his reason for asking for this meeting, and it would be inappropriate for me to formulate my own opinions. I do as His Majesty bids and nothing further."

Varic frowned at that, but let it pass. Grand Vizier Shar stepped out of the room, and Archidraconus Ephraim Semarill entered in his wake.

"Please close the door," Varic said. "Something is happening between Ferralin and Dakkadia, and I could use your council."

Patriarch Varic handed the note to Semarill and gave him the opportunity to read it, and though the note was very short and to the point, Varic could see his friend frowning in confusion before reading it again. After his second time through the letter, Ephraim looked up.

"Emperor Xan wants to meet with King Madari? That makes no sense whatsoever! He has to know that at best, King Orem will be furious with him for meeting with King Madari behind his back. And at worst, this could throw the entire question of an Illymar/Ferralin alliance into disarray." He held up the letter and shook it once for emphasis. "This could lead to war."

"Your thoughts mirror my own. Emperor Xan makes no mention of King Orem being included in this summit, so I have to conclude that whatever it is he wishes to speak to King Madari about is something King Orem will not be pleased with. It is also interesting that he has chosen to meet with King Madari here rather than choosing the more informal setting of the nightly dinner parties. Has something happened that we should be aware of? I have heard of nothing that could jeopardize the alliance."

Semarill began to shake his head, but stopped himself abruptly. Varic narrowed his eyes when he realized that the Archidraconus had thought of something important.

"Last night, there was a public argument between King Madari and King Orem, instigated by King Orem. The argument was apparently extremely vicious, with deadly insults being hurled back and forth between the two. All of my sources agree that King Orem sought out King Madari for the express purpose of insulting him to his face, and that King Madari was uncharacteristically reasonable in his responses. If the report is accurate, King Orem took a terrible risk by trying to provoke King Madari, for both Dakkadia and Illymar recognize the Code Duello. Thankfully, King Madari refused to rise to the bait and challenge him to a duel."

Varic leaned back in his chair and frowned slightly.

"I would not have believed King Madari capable of showing such restraint. He has always been something of a blunt instrument, as it were, and from his reputation, it should have taken very little for King Orem to provoke him into issuing a challenge."

"It may be that he did not believe we would allow the duel to take place, no matter how grave the offense may have been. The Peace of Zarryiosiad is absolute and unyielding: no duels may be issued or accepted whilst the Peace is in effect. If King Madari had issued a challenge, Orem would have been well within his rights to decline the challenge and hide behind the Peace, all the while decrying the 'bloodthirsty' nature of the 'Barbarian of Dakkadia.' If that is the case, King Madari did well to see the possibility and take steps to avoid it."

"It sounds as if you are coming to admire King Madari," Varic said.

"Not admire, so much as appreciate his reasoned response. The insults Orem used were quite vicious, and the restraint Madari showed was quite unlike his reputation. That being said, the damage has been done. Madari will undoubtedly seek revenge for the very public insult to his honor, and Xan must see an opportunity in this."

Varic's brow wrinkled at the Archidraconus' conclusion.

"What do you mean?"

Semarill raised a hand to his chin in a thinking posture.

"We have had other reports that say the match between Crown Prince Lain and Princess Lyrahe isn't a good one. Apparently, there isn't even a hint of attraction between them, and that may very well be a factor in the Emperor's thinking. If he believes his son does not wish to marry Lyrahe, Xan may very well seek other options. One option would be for him to push Madari into doing exactly what he already wishes to do: attack Illymar. Though his response may have been quite reasonable at the party, Madari has to be seething right now. It wouldn't take much to convince Madari to set aside any claim to the Badlands and instead, attack Illymar directly. He may even be angry enough to give Ferralin concessions or assurances to secure his southern border before declaring war upon Illymar."

Varic leaned back in his chair and thought about the implications for a moment. It was at times like these that he most appreciated his friend's insight. The more he thought about the pieces of the puzzle, the more they seemed to fit the pattern his friend had laid out. He looked up and prepared to speak when a knock sounded from his chamber doors.

"Enter," he said, and Ephraim turned to look at the door. Another Archidraconus stepped through the door and bowed, awaiting permission to speak. Patriarch Semarill waited until the messenger looked up before saying, "What is it?"

"Lady Prudence Daemira was attacked on the streets of Illymaine this morning by a group of assassins."

Varic's eyes opened wide in shock, and his heavy chair seemed to fly away from him as he stood up abruptly.

"*What!?* Is she all right?"

"The details are still somewhat vague," the Archidraconus said, nodding, "but apparently, Lady Prudence left her ship a short while ago to visit the Mage Citadel, and was set upon by six armed men. She killed five of the assassins by herself, while a sixth was shot to death by Illymari soldiers as he attempted to escape. Lady Prudence was injured in the attack, but reports indicate that her injuries do not appear to be life threatening. I'm afraid that none of the assassins survived to be questioned."

Patriarch Varic's eyebrows furled in rage, and he slammed his hand down on his desk. The sound of it made the messenger jump, though Ephraim simply awaited the command he knew was coming.

"I want the Inquisition to investigate this attack *immediately.* I want to know everything about it down to the last detail, and I want to know the names of everyone who had a hand in it. Someone has willfully broken the Peace of Zarryiosiad, and by the Archon, *I will know who!*"

The Archidraconus bowed his understanding and left the room to see to the Patriarch's orders, and after the door closed behind him, Semarill spoke.

"The Inquisition will undoubtedly find nothing useful in their investigation. They will learn that the assassins were mercenaries—most likely from the Badlands—with no ties whatsoever to anyone or anything. If money is found amongst their possessions it will not have come from a specific country, nor will they have any connections that can be traced. It will be as if they never even existed."

Varic scowled, still furious that someone would defy the Zarryiostrom in such a blatant manner.

"Who do you think it was?"

Semarill's expression didn't change, but he obviously had been thinking very hard about the crime and the possible suspects for he answered without hesitation.

"It would almost certainly have to be the Savonnes, which means the order must have been handed down by the Queen of Illymar herself, or, perhaps, by her father."

Varic's eyes widened at the certainty in Semarill's voice, and he sat down again and indicated that the Archidraconus should continue.

"The Corsair has been a thorn in the side of the Illymari navy for years, and the Savonnes, in particular, have suffered greatly at her hands. Having the opportunity to end that threat, once and for all, must have been too hard to resist for them, and the Peace be damned."

"Why are you so certain that it was the Queen?" Varic asked. "Why would the order not come from Orem himself?"

"Simple: it would be the single worst thing he could possibly do, whether or not the assassination attempt succeeded. Until the marriage between Lyrahe and Lain officially takes place, and a formal treaty between Illymar and Ferralin is signed, the only things standing between Illymar and Dakkadia are the Zarryiostrom and the Mage Citadel. Breaking the Peace of Zarryiosiad is a High Crime, and should it be discovered that Orem is involved, we would most likely turn a blind eye to Dakkadian retaliation, even if that retaliation were to cost Orem his kingdom and his life. The Savonnes are a different matter altogether. They are merchants and, as such, they are not as concerned with the good of the kingdom as much as they are interested in lining their own pockets and protecting their investments. As long as the Corsair continues to prey upon their shipping, they will continue to lose money. Hiring assassins to murder her would make the most economic sense, but Queen Althea would have to take steps to insulate her husband from the slightest hint of blame. Therefore, it follows that she would have issued the assassination order herself without consulting him. That way, if the Queen is somehow caught and accused, she can simply say that she did what she did against her husband's wishes, and as such, should be the only one punished."

Varic nodded his understanding, but then a thought occurred to him.

"What is the likelihood that either Xan, or perhaps Madari himself was behind the assassination attempt? The timing was very interesting, after all. Xan might have ordered it to make Madari even angrier at Orem, and therefore, more likely to agree to a proposed treaty favoring Ferralin. Or Madari might have ordered her murder, hoping to cast blame on Illymar and force us to withdraw our protection."

As he finished speaking, Semarill shook his head in polite disagreement.

"Possible, but highly unlikely. As you so rightly said, King Madari is a blunt instrument. Assassinating his best and most prominent naval commander on the slim hope that we would set aside our alliance with Illymar is not something he would consider. Moreover, the Dakkadian navy still does not have enough ships to attack the Illymari navy head-on. They need more time to build or capture enough ships to absolutely guarantee a victory. If they attack too soon and suffer a defeat, or if the Illymari navy is able to sink even a few troop-laden ships before they can unload, it could set the Dakkadian invasion plans back by years.

"No, above all, Madari needs time to build up his navy. He won't do anything to upset the balance until he feels that he has exactly what he needs to destroy Illymar in a single blow. Xan is a trickier proposition. He *may* have decided to strike at the Corsair to get Madari to fixate on Orem, but Xan was present during the heated exchange between Orem and Madari. He knows that Madari doesn't need a push to fixate on Orem: he already has. Therefore, Xan will not risk incurring the wrath of the Zarryiostrom to achieve a goal which has already been accomplished. All he has to do is sit back and watch Orem and Madari beat each other to death. Figuratively, of course."

"Of course," Varic said, amused despite himself. "Well, I can't fault your logic. Until the Inquisition finishes its investigation and turns in a formal report, we won't know exactly what happened. That may take a while. The more immediate problem is what to do about the upcoming meeting between Madari and Xan. I want you to see to the arrangements personally. Use the formal meeting hall. We don't know how large their entourages will be, or what will be discussed, so be prepared for anything." Varic held Semarill's eyes for a moment. "And once the meeting is over, I want you to oversee the investigation of the attack on Lady Prudence personally. If Queen Althea *is* involved, I want to know. Mark me well, Ephraim: I will not allow this breach of the Peace to go unpunished, no matter who is behind it."

Phaedron tried not to break into a run in the hallway, but it was very difficult. Behind him he could hear the footsteps of his half-brother and their new friends, but he paid that no mind, for he had just been told that Prudence was in the Citadel and that she had been attacked and had suffered an injury. Phaedron hadn't waited for the details of the attack or a summary of her injuries in his rush to reach the hospital wing, but as his mind went over the different possibilities, he cursed his haste.

Damn it all, I should have asked about her condition! How bad is it? It must *be severe if she is in the hospital wing.*

By the time he had reached the entrance to the hospital, he had half-convinced himself she was lying on death's door, and that she only had moments to live. With her impending demise foremost in his mind, he rushed into the room, ignoring the warning of the nurse sitting at a desk by the entrance as he flew past her.

What he saw when he finally reached her room wasn't what he was expecting. In his mind, he had thought he would see Prudence lying in bed, moments from death. But what he actually saw was Prudence sitting on a stool, leaning slightly forward to allow a female physician to sew stitches into an ugly gash in her back. The wound wasn't the shocking part, however; more shocking by far was the fact that her bloody shirt lay on the bed beside her, and her naked flesh lay open to his incredulous gaze. His eyes moved on their own accord to take in soft, rounded curves, covered by surprisingly pale skin.

She looked up in surprise when he entered, and the pair each gave identical strangled yelps as they realized what was happening. Phaedron turned away quickly, his face burning with scarlet mortification, while Prudence reacted by grabbing her tattered shirt with one hand to cover her bare breasts, then snatching a pillow from a nearby bed with the other. Back turned, Phaedron started to apologize, but a well-aimed pillow struck him on the back of the head before he could get the words out.

"I'm sorry, I'm sorry!" he blurted to the outraged Prudence as the pillow fell to the floor, refusing to turn so much as an inch to look at her. "I thought you were dying!"

Before she could answer, another strangled yelp came from Prudence, and Phaedron had to restrain himself from turning back around to see what had happened.

"I *told* you to hold still, didn't I?" the physician said. "You only have yourself to blame for that one."

Prudence growled something under her breath about 'ham-fisted seamstresses using hemp rope and a gaffing hook instead of needle and thread', and he could almost feel the anger radiating off of her. That anger wasn't directed at the physician, however.

"How bad is it, Prudence?" he asked.

Corsair glanced at his back and laughed slightly.

"I've had worse. It's just a scratch, really."

The doctor chose that moment to stick the needle into her flesh yet again, and her easy laughter changed once more into a strangled yelp. The doctor laughed at her discomfort.

"Oh, hold still, you big baby. I thought Dakkadians were supposed to be tough! Look at you! A mere six-inch gash in your back—made worse by your refusal to accept immediate aid, I might add—and you let a little thing like a needle bother you? Grow a backbone!"

"I'm not a Dakkadian, you butcher! I'm Rohmian! And in Rohm, we use needles, not red-hot pokers!"

Phaedron sighed in relief. If the doctor were truly worried about her condition she wouldn't be joking with her, let alone poking fun at her.

"Are you covered yet, Prudence? I want to see your wound for myself."

"It's all right. You can turn around now."

Phaedron moved beside the doctor to get a better look. The slash was diagonal, starting from the upper left shoulder and moving in a straight line down and to the right, stopping just short of her spine. The doctor had almost finished with the stitches, but even so, the wound still looked terrible. Prudence glanced over her shoulder trying to see the wound.

"How does it look?"

Phaedron whistled softly in reply.

"I won't lie: it looks pretty bad. What makes it worse is that the doctor seems to be using a blunt knitting needle and wool yarn to sew it back together."

Corsair nodded sagely, as if he had just explained exactly why it was hurting so much, but the doctor merely snorted.

"Well, it's better than cauterizing it with a hot knife while she bites down on a leather belt, isn't it?" the doctor said. "Isn't that how Dakkadians normally deal with their wounds?"

"Oh, no, doctor. We eat our wounded," he replied.

Two disgusted groans sounded from behind the curtain separating the bed from the doorway, and Phaedron laughed. Valeriad, who had been hidden by the curtain, stepped into view and smiled at Prudence.

"Good to see you again, Lady Prudence, although I must say that you have looked better. Care to tell us what happened?"

"Someone foolishly decided to try and collect the bounty Illymar put on my head, Peace or no. I'm afraid that I had to kill them for their trouble."

"Better them than you," Valeriad said. "I'm sorry that you were wounded, though."

He glanced at the doctor.

"Will she lose any use of her arm?"

"No, she'll be fine with some hot food and bed rest. She's lost a lot of blood, but the cut was clean and it didn't hit anything important. You were lucky, young lady; three more inches to the right and the blade would have taken your spine." The physician glanced up at Phaedron and continued. "She just needs a little bit of time to recover." She patted Prudence gently on her uninjured shoulder and said, "Do try and get some rest. I'll send someone in with some food. Be sure to eat all of it, now. It will help you build up your strength and replace the lost blood."

As the doctor left, Prudence laid down in the bed face down, looking toward the entrance. Her back was still exposed to the air, but she didn't seem to mind. Phaedron sat down on the bed beside her, admiring her pale skin while trying not to look at the now-stitched wound. A number of scars crisscrossed her flesh from past battles, though none of the older wounds could match the newest one for sheer size. He didn't know what to say to her, so for a while he sat in silence and watched the rise and fall of her graceful back as she breathed.

After a few moments, the sound of someone clearing their throat broke him out of his reverie. He glanced around the curtain to see who had made the noise, and saw Chesare and Adrianna looking hopefully at him. It was obvious from the look on Chesare's face that she wanted to meet the legendary Corsair, but it was also obvious that neither she nor Adrianna wanted to intrude upon the couple if their presence wasn't welcome. Grateful for the distraction, Phaedron stood up and drew the curtain aside.

"Lady Prudence, please allow me to introduce you to Princess Chesare of Illymar. She is a Fireborn, as well as a student here at the Citadel, and she has been most helpful to Valeriad and me during our stay."

Chesare curtseyed at the introduction, and Prudence smiled at her.

"Pardon me for not standing and greeting you properly, Your Highness, but it is very nice to meet you. I'm sorry that you have been saddled with these two louts, but then you must have been particularly wicked to deserve such a cruel punishment."

"They are a trial, aren't they?" Chesare replied, enjoying the Corsair's sense of humor. "Are all Dakkadian men like these two? They've been nothing but trouble ever since they got here."

Corsair gave Chesare a knowing look.

"I can well imagine. But please don't let their bad examples color your opinion of all Dakkadians. Everyone knows the women run things in Dakkadia. We keep the men around because they are pretty. And someone has to do the heavy lifting."

"They are quite the decorative pair, almost too pretty to be believed." Chesare said with an impish smile. "But, seriously, please allow me to say that I have wanted to meet you for a very long time. I'm a great admirer of yours, even though your exploits have come at the expense of my own country."

"Can you tell us what happened today, Aunt Prudence?" Adrianna asked. "We'd love to hear about it."

Both of the girls sat down in chairs as if Prudence had already agreed to speak, and Phaedron laughed at the Corsair's obvious discomfort with her audience.

"They'll sit there all day waiting to hear the story, and I have to say, that I am very interested to hear it as well. You might as well get started, and leave nothing out."

Corsair sighed heavily, and began telling the story as well as she could remember it. When she was finished, instead of feeling proud of her for overcoming the ambush, Phaedron could feel himself getting angrier by the moment.

"Thank you for the retelling, Lady Prudence," Valeriad said, preempting Phaedron's forthcoming outburst, "but I think we'd better let you get some rest."

He gestured at Adrianna and Chesare.

"Ladies? After you." Obediently, the two young girls stood up and said their goodbyes and quietly left the room. Valeriad turned and looked back at Prudence. "I'll tell Morvandis what happened, so you don't have to repeat the story again. Do try and get some rest."

Prudence thanked the young Prince and climbed into bed face down, pulling a pillow under her chin. When Valeriad had left the room and closed the door behind him, Phaedron spoke.

"If I could kill those men again, I would." His mood lightened a bit as he remembered that they were already deceased, and he added, "I'm sorry you were injured, Prudence, but I'm still glad you came to see me."

"And what makes you so certain I came here to see you?" she asked with an arched eyebrow. "The Mage Citadel is one of the grandest structures on the entire island. Perhaps I was on my way here to see the sights. Really, you do have quite the inflated opinion of yourself, don't you? It's unseemly."

"Unseemly, is it? Well, I'll have you know, that upon further consideration, I feel nothing but gratitude toward those assassins for attacking you today."

Prudence looked up at him doubtfully, knowing that he was setting her up for something nasty.

"First of all, by taking such a vicious wound, your family will undoubtedly have to pay a much higher dowry to get rid of you, what with your hide being so damaged and all. If nothing better should happen along within the next few years, I may just allow them to bribe me to take you off of their hands. But only if the price is right, mind you! I mean," he indicated the stitches, "you are a bit worse for wear. And apparently I'm very *decorative*—'almost too pretty to be believed', if I heard Princess Chesare right." Prudence rolled her eyes elaborately, then narrowed her eyes as he gave her a lascivious look complete with wagging eyebrows. "And secondly, thanks to them, when I came into the room I got a *very* good look at you."

Corsair shrieked in mock outrage and threw another pillow at him that completely cut off what he was about to say.

The sound of a glass striking stone filled her antechamber, and Queen Althea watched the red wine the glass had contained trickle down the wall where she had thrown it in her fury. Admiral Savonne stood silently, his face more than a bit pale at being the target of his Queen's rage.

"You *idiot!* I asked you to accomplish one simple task, and you failed utterly! She was on foot, completely alone, and hopelessly outnumbered. A handful of children with rocks should have been able to kill her. And yet she lives. So, why don't you explain to me how the man I chose to command the entire Illymari navy could fail to kill one woman? I warn you now: your explanation had better be good. Family or no, your life depends on how well you answer."

What little color Lucas had possessed vanished in a heartbeat at the deadly threat, and he began to sweat in obvious terror.

"My Queen, I swear to you that their failure was not my fault. The Corsair was caught by surprise, as planned, but she carried several of those infernal Dakkadian weapons upon her person. If they'd all reached her, she would have been killed. Instead, she killed three of them before they could even come close to her. I've seen the corpses myself: one man had his head all but torn off, and the other two had holes as big as my fist ripped all the way through them. None of us knew their new weapons could be carried on a person. How could we? We've never seen one before."

The Queen narrowed her eyes at that, for what he said was true. The Dakkadian weapon was as much of a mystery to them now as it had been when it was first introduced years earlier. Dakkadian security had been brutally efficient in guarding the secret, and entire spy networks had been eliminated, root and stem, for trying to obtain information about it.

"I did learn something important though: much like a crossbow, the weapon can only be used once before it has to be reloaded. The Corsair demonstrated that for me after the ambush failed. The problem is the weapons are much smaller than crossbows. She carried three of them on her, and they were small enough to be easily concealed."

Althea crossed her arms over her chest.

"So she killed three of the assassins with her weapons. What of the other three?"

At that question, Lucas looked away in discomfort.

"As to that, the Corsair proved to be too good of a swordswoman for them to handle. She was injured in the attack, but she killed two of the men in a matter of seconds. The third man tried to run away, but I had crossbowmen ready to kill all of the assassins, whether they succeeded or not. Dead men tell no tales, after all. As I said, I have no doubt that had all six men been able to attack her, she would have been killed, but as it turned out, the three men who actually *did* manage to reach her just weren't enough."

Althea found herself nodding in unwilling agreement. Before she had summoned Lucas to this meeting, her spies had done some quiet investigating of their own, and everything he had just told her matched with what her spies had reported. Three men killed in as many seconds, even having taken her completely by surprise. That was more than a bit disconcerting on its own, for it told her that the weapons she carried were even more formidable than they had initially believed. But the brutally efficient way in which the Corsair had dealt with the second group of men told her that she had made the mistake of underestimating the woman. Althea closed her eyes and sighed heavily.

"You did well to kill the last man before he could be questioned. Now, go back to the Admiralty and await my orders. You will not make another attempt on the Corsair's life, even if the opportunity presents itself. We had our chance, and we failed."

Lucas bowed, clearly relieved that he would live to see another day.

"Ah, Your Majesty . . . the Zarryiostrom has sent over a group of Inquisitors to find out what has happened. What should I tell them?"

"Cooperate with them fully," the Queen said. "The only way we will survive this disaster is to appear to be completely forthcoming about everything we know. You are to speak only about the things you personally witnessed, however, so don't embellish or get fancy. You were informed of the assassination attempt, you ordered your men to assist her, and the assassins were dealt with. Keep to that story and we will be fine." He bowed to her, but before he could leave she grabbed his collar and pulled his face close to hers. "I hope I don't have to tell you what will happen if you fail me again. If the Inquisition asks questions you can't answer, you are to plead ignorance and refer them to the King. Do you understand me?"

He nodded quickly, face covered in sweat, but she held his collar for a few more seconds to drive home her point before letting him go.

"Get out of my sight."

As the door closed behind him, Althea turned to look at the third person in the room, who had remained completely silent during the entire conversation. Prince Ethan stood up, nose still bandaged from where it had been broken days earlier, and waited for his mother to speak.

"I should have him killed. He knows too much."

Ethan thought about it for a moment and shook his head in disagreement.

"It would look too suspicious to have the 'Bathtub Admiral' die so soon after the attempt on the Corsair's life. People will already be looking for conspiracies: all his death will accomplish now will be to confirm that one actually exists.

Better to let him live until the Inquisition finishes their investigation, and then find some other way to punish him for his failure."

Althea mulled it over for a second before nodding.

"Good point. The Admiral will live to see another day. Pity. The Savonne family tree could use some pruning to clear away the dead branches."

She walked to a window facing the main courtyard and pulled aside the heavy curtain to look out. She had hoped to see Lucas as he rode away, but there was no sign of the naval officer, so she let go of the curtain and stepped back into the room.

"You know, I still find it difficult to believe that the Corsair could overcome such overwhelming odds. These Dakkadians are much more formidable than I would have believed."

Ethan said nothing, but his hand moved on its own accord to touch his bandaged nose. When his fingers found the cloth of the bandage, he scowled. Althea frowned at that, but said nothing. No matter how many times she asked, he still refused to tell her how he had truly injured himself. She knew he was lying about falling off of a horse, but so far she hadn't been able to ferret out the truth. His reaction to her mention of the Dakkadians was interesting, though.

Could a Dakkadian have had something to do with his broken nose?

She thought about asking him yet again, but changed her mind. There were more important things to discuss at the moment.

"Tell me, what do you think our next course of action should be?"

"We should apologize to the Dakkadians for the assassination attempt," Ethan said, "and promise to help the Inquisition get to the bottom of it as quickly as possible. It's galling, I know, having to apologize for trying to put down a murderous pirate, but it can't be avoided. An apology will serve to allay suspicion. That's all we can hope for right now; that we somehow remain above suspicion."

"And if the Inquisition should find out the truth? That we *were* behind the attempt? What should we do then?"

"Why, then, we allow Lucas the opportunity to do what soldiers do best: fall upon his sword for King and Country, which, I might add, is yet another reason to allow him to live for the moment. We may still need to feed him to the wolves. That's the thing about pawns: sometimes they have to be sacrificed in order to achieve victory."

Althea smiled and walked to her oldest son. She patted him fondly on the cheek.

"Very good, Ethan, very good, indeed. I'll make a King out of you yet."

Madari was talking quietly with Archidraconus Semarill, who had offered to act as mediator for the proceedings, when Morvandis entered the room. Though normally he didn't want anyone besides Morvandis with him, this time he wanted an official witness to whatever was said, just in case the Emperor of Ferralin decided to play games.

"Glad you could join us, Morvandis, especially on such short notice. I know you are busy at the Citadel, but this is very important."

"I live to serve, Your Majesty," Morvandis said, bowing. "Can you tell me what this is about?"

"You know as much as I do. I will be meeting with Emperor Xan in just a few minutes, but I have no idea what he wishes to speak about. Neither does the Zarryiostrom, if Archidraconus Semarill here is to be believed. They were just as surprised as I was that he would extend an invitation." He turned his attention back to the priest. "Which reminds me; I want to thank you for preparing all of this on such short notice."

He indicated the room and the furnishings, as well as a small buffet sitting on a side table offering a variety of finger foods. Archidraconus Semarill bowed.

"It is our pleasure, Your Majesty. We are deeply honored that two such august personages would agree to use our humble services to mediate what I am certain will be an important meeting."

"Have you already heard about the attempt on Lady Prudence's life?" Morvandis asked.

"Archidraconus Semarill here is heading the investigation," Madari said. "They have already dispatched an Inquisitorial team to get to the bottom of it."

Morvandis started to ask something else, but the doors opened once again to reveal Emperor Xan and his Grand Vizier, both dressed in Ferralin formal robes, following behind another Archidraconus, who had obviously been assigned as his liaison. The ancient Emperor allowed the priest to guide him toward the small group, and when Xan was close enough, both he and the Vizier bowed in greeting. Madari, Morvandis, and Ephraim returned the formal bow, but afterward, Madari held out his hand for a more informal greeting. Xan looked at Madari's hand for a moment, as if unsure what was expected of him, but after no more than a moment's hesitation, he reached out delicately with wizened fingers and took Madari's hand in his own to give him a surprisingly firm handshake.

"You have a strong grip, Your Majesty," Madari said. "My daughter Deirdre said as much when she told me of your meeting."

He had deliberately mentioned his daughter straight away, wanting to judge the Emperor's reaction to her name, and the results were telling. Xan's breath caught, and a small smile crossed his lips. *So this is about Deirdre.*

He glanced at Morvandis and winked, though Morvandis would have had no idea what he was happy about.

"It is good that you brought up your daughter, for it is her I wish to speak to you about. I had thought to work up to the subject in some polite fashion, but that isn't the Dakkadian way, is it? You prefer to get straight to the heart of a matter. Am I correct?"

"While I do understand the need for niceties and polite conversation, I vastly prefer to, as you said, get straight to the heart of a matter. It tends to simplify things."

"That it does," Xan agreed. "Very well, I will be brief. I wish to discuss the possibility of a treaty between my country and yours, secured by a marriage to your daughter. Having had the distinct pleasure of meeting her, I feel that she will make both a fine wife and a better Empress."

Even though he had half-expected the words, Madari was still rocked back on his heels when they were spoken aloud. Moreover, he wasn't alone in his reaction. Everyone in the group had matching looks of stunned surprise, including the Grand Vizier. Even Morvandis looked as if he had been poleaxed, a reaction Madari had rarely seen from his advisor.

Madari looked at Archidraconus Semarill, and his eyes narrowed slightly. Before Morvandis had arrived, he had asked the priest to give him a general idea of what he could expect from Xan, as well of an overview of what he was like. Although Dakkadia and Ferralin were rival countries, Madari had only the most general knowledge of life in the Ferralin court, and in the limited amount of time they had, Semarill had filled him in as much as possible. One thing in particular stuck with him: the Emperor favored young wives . . . and the younger, the better. Yet, somehow, despite his advancing years, he always outlived them. As he thought back upon the words the Emperor had used in making his proposal, Madari suddenly realized that no mention at all was made of his daughter's marrying the *Crown Prince*.

He looked back at Xan and narrowed his eyes in thought. If he was to marry his daughter to Xan, she would be in a position to manipulate events throughout the Ferralin Empire almost immediately. Whether they were kings or commoners, newlywed husbands were all the same; they would do anything to please a new wife.

I could have it all: the Badlands, Illymar, even Ferralin itself, eventually. It's all there for the taking.

For just a moment, he imagined himself as the man responsible for reuniting the Archon's empire, a feat that had not been accomplished since the empire was divided between her children upon her death. But then his daughter's words from earlier that morning returned to him.

I think Emperor Xan wanted to hurt me.

As he remembered the look of fear and misery on his daughter's face, he could feel the vision of his reuniting the Empire of Zarryiosiad fading like mist before the rising sun. He couldn't do it. As a father, and as a man, he knew he couldn't give his only daughter over to a man who wanted to hurt her. Despite his ambition, despite his dreams, he found he loved her too much to do that to her. *Ah, Deirdre; if only you knew what I've just sacrificed for you.*

Decision made, he began to think furiously about how to salvage the situation. Allowing a marriage between Xan and his daughter was unthinkable, so how could he turn the proposal around? His breath caught as an idea occurred to him. The Emperor had been deliberately obtuse about *whom* he intended for Deirdre to marry. *Time to clarify things a bit.*

"I think a marriage between my daughter and *your son* would be a marvelous arrangement. From the way Deirdre has spoken about Prince Lain, I know she is already very fond of him. And, I think, he of her."

If he had had any doubt about who Xan had intended to marry to Deirdre, they disappeared completely at Xan's reaction. The smile faded instantly from Xan's face, and his eyes narrowed in anger at the deliberate emphasis Madari had placed on the words *your son.* He quickly regained his composure, but it had been enough for Madari to learn what he needed to know. *Semarill was right about you; you covet my daughter for yourself. Well, you can't have her, and it's time to drive that point home.*

"Should I agree to a marriage between *your son* and my daughter, what terms did you have in mind for the treaty between our countries?"

Again, he deliberately emphasized the words *your son,* but this time Xan didn't react to the words at all.

"That depends upon you, Your Majesty. What terms would you find acceptable?"

Madari smiled at that.

Let's see how badly you want her, shall we?

He crossed his arms over his chest.

"I want the Badlands. All of it."

Xan immediately shook his head.

"That is quite unacceptable, of course. It would profit the Ferralin Empire nothing to allow Dakkadia to seize control of those markets and the Eastern Road. No marriage—not even one to such an exquisite creature as your daughter—is worth that much of a loss. No, I have a different proposal in mind . .

. one I think you will find most intriguing. I will agree to turn a blind eye to any . . . *adventurism,* shall we say, that you may have in mind concerning our current host. We both know that Illymar is counting on an alliance with my country to keep them safe from you. Agree to this marriage, and I will withhold the protection of Ferralin from Illymar and allow you to do with her as you will."

For the second time that morning Madari felt himself rocked back on his heels. Again, from the stunned looks on everyone else's faces, he wasn't alone. Madari couldn't help himself. He had to ask.

"Why would you do that? Why would you be so willing to cold-bloodedly betray an ally?"

Xan smiled broadly at that, though his eyes remained as cold as winter.

"Despite what King Orem may believe, we are not yet allies. My reasons, such as they are, must remain my own. I will say this, however: one of the reasons I will stand aside and let you destroy Illymar, should you so choose, is because in Ferralin we understand honor. Orem publicly insulted your honor last night, a great offense by our standards and absolutely unforgivable in a host—especially one who is hiding behind a flag of truce. King Orem shamed himself and his entire country with that unseemly display at the reception. Then there is this morning's assassination attempt upon your subject, Lady Prudence. I think we both know who was behind that shameful attack, whether or not there is any proof to be found. They were fools to even *consider* striking at her, let alone to actually attempt it. It has already cost them their alliance with Ferralin, but it could cost them their alliance with Ithram as well. The fact that the attempt failed miserably simply illustrates the point that Ferralin is better off without them." He glanced at Ephraim Semarill and smirked. "Of course, it is not enough for me to stand aside. You still have to find a way to eliminate both the Zarryiostrom and the Mage Citadel before you can avenge your honor. I have a feeling they will not simply stand aside and let you have your way. Nevertheless, that is your concern and not mine. I will not help you in that particular endeavor." He returned his attention to Madari. "Do we have an accord?"

Grand Vizier Shar was still in a state of shock as they left the Cathedral to return to the Ferraline enclave. Though he had stood witness to the entire meeting, he still had trouble believing what had just happened. He turned slightly to look at the back of his Emperor's head, almost as if he were hoping that he could somehow see exactly what the man had been thinking simply by staring through his skull. Sadly, it was not to be, so he stopped staring and started thinking about the implications of the proposed marriage. King Madari had asked for time to consider his answer, but the damage had already been done. Lain's betrothal to Princess Lyrahe was over. All that was left to do now was to find out how bad the damage would be, and to try and limit it as much as possible.

As they climbed into the imperial carriage, Xan broke the silence.

"Do you think he will accept the terms?"

"It is too hard to say, Your Imperial Majesty. If I were to hazard a guess, I would say 'no', simply because it is not in his best interest for him to accept it. The smartest thing for him to do now would be to tell King Orem all about this meeting in an attempt to drive a wedge between Illymar and Ferralin, and then negotiate his own treaty with Illymar, possibly to include a marriage between his son Prince Valeriad, and Princess Lyrahe. Or if he's smart, he will demand the Powerborn daughter, Princess Chesare, as his son's bride. Either way, Dakkadia will attack the Badlands the moment the marriage is consummated. And as soon as he has conquered the Badlands, he will come for us."

Xan nodded in complete agreement, and Shar began to question his Emperor's already fragile hold on sanity.

Could it be that simple? Could he have lost his mind completely? If so, I may have to take action before the damage he has done to the Empire is irreversible.

He turned his gaze to the Emperor, looking for obvious signs of insanity, but he could find no traces of it at all in his Emperor's face. Xan looked out the window of the carriage and smiled slightly.

"Your insight does you credit, Shar. I congratulate you on so perfectly predicting how Madari will react, for you are absolutely correct: that is exactly what he will do. Madari will approach Orem—most likely tonight—and tell him everything that we have discussed, hoping to achieve all of the goals that you have so clearly laid out. He would be a fool not to, and Madari is no fool."

Xan's tone was light, and his smile became broader still. As Shar listened to his Emperor's words, all he could see was the impending disaster threatening to overtake Ferralin and engulf it completely. He desperately tried to think of a way to explain that to Xan, but the Emperor hadn't finished speaking. In a quiet voice, light with humor, he continued.

"The attempt will fail utterly, of course. Believe me when I say, that by the end of the night, Madari will agree to absolutely everything I have proposed. And when the opportunity presents itself, Dakkadia will fall upon Illymar like wolves upon sheep."

He did laugh then, but Shar didn't share in the laughter. Try as he might, he couldn't see how the Emperor's prediction could possibly come to pass, or how it would benefit Ferralin.

"How can you be so certain, My Emperor? Surely Orem understands how vulnerable his country is without an alliance. What makes you believe he won't accept Madari's proposal?"

Xan turned his head slightly and looked at his Vizier.

"I am certain because I have studied my adversaries, and I know them better than they know themselves. No matter how logical it might seem to be for Illymar and Dakkadia to ally with each other, the possibility of that actually happening is so minute as to be laughable. Mark me well, Shar: tonight Madari will agree to my proposal, and that will be the beginning of the end for Illymar."

Shar shook his head in disbelief at the certainty in his Emperor's voice.

"But then, Dakkadia will come for the Badlands. And ultimately, he will strike at the Empire itself."

Xan leaned back in his seat and closed his eyes, still smiling.

"Perhaps. And perhaps not. We shall see."

The formal garden of the estate the Dakkadians had appropriated for the Convocation was in full bloom and quite breathtaking, but Queen Aveliad didn't notice. Normally, the tranquility of the garden and its wonderful sights and smells was enough to erase her anxieties, but this time serenity escaped her completely. Madari had been gone for hours, but she had no idea what that meant. Her own spy network had been unable to discover the reason behind the surprise meeting between Madari and Emperor Xan, and their failure added fuel to her anxiousness.

This situation is intolerable. They could be discussing absolutely anything, and I am powerless to affect the outcome.

Despite the tension in their personal lives, Aveliad had worked very hard over the years to provide good advice to Madari. She knew that he had come to value her opinion greatly, and she had used her influence with him to curb many of his potential excesses. There were limits, of course, but she had learned, through painstaking trial and error, where he could be pushed or guided, and where she had to accept his command without complaint. It was odd to think this way of someone she detested, but he was an excellent leader, and a surprisingly good King. His willingness to see other sides of an argument and choose a moderate path was not something she would have believed him capable of when they had first met, but there it was: whatever his failings as a husband and a man might be, Dakkadia had seen worse kings by far, and few better.

She clung to that thought as if it were a piece of driftwood keeping her from drowning in a rough sea. The reason for her anxiety was the same as the reason he had excluded her from this meeting: when it came to her children, she couldn't set aside her personal feelings and look at a situation objectively. As a mother, this was acceptable . . . but as a Queen, it was inexcusable. When he had informed her that she would be remaining behind for this meeting she hadn't reacted well.

The one thing she knew never to do with Madari was to pick a public argument with him. She could argue as much as she wanted in private, but if he made his will known in front of others, he was as immovable as stone. Twenty years of marriage had reinforced that knowledge for her, but this time she had been completely unable to stop herself. When he had told her that she would not be accompanying him to the meeting, in front of both Deirdre and the various servants throughout the room, she had responded by telling him that there was no way that he would be going to the meeting without her. And this was the result: he was at the meeting, and she was waiting alone in the garden, exactly as he had commanded.

The sound of horseshoes on the cobblestone walk brought her to her feet in an instant. She rushed into the house in an undignified run, desperate to find out what had been discussed at the meeting, and she arrived in the main foyer in time to see Madari and Morvandis ride up to the main doors, where they were met by servants who took the reins of the horses and helped them to alight. She glanced at a mirror to check her appearance, and touched her hair lightly to tuck back a stray strand that had come loose during her brief run. It wouldn't do to let Madari know she'd been waiting anxiously for his arrival, after all.

"Welcome home," she said, her voice cold. As Morvandis entered behind him, she turned her attention to the Mage. "And welcome to you as well, Morvandis. I trust my sons are doing well?"

"They are, Your Majesty," Morvandis said. "Valeriad and Phaedron are very much enjoying their time at the Mage Citadel, and the Mage Citadel has been very impressed with both of them."

"Time for that later," Madari said. "Come to my office, both of you. There is much to discuss before dinner tonight."

Aveliad felt a wave of relief wash over her at the knowledge that he would be allowing her to participate in the discussion. She would once again be in position to influence events, and that was all she could ask in this situation.

"I take it the meeting went well?" she asked. "I must admit, I have been very curious about the subject of the meeting."

"In a nutshell, he wants Deirdre, and he is offering me Illymar to obtain her."

Aveliad almost missed a step at that, but caught herself before she could trip.

"Did you accept?"

Madari glanced at her with a bemused smile.

"Not yet, though I must admit that I am very tempted. I told him that I had to think about it."

He looked back at her and caught her sighing in relief, and a small smile crossed his face. He didn't say anything, however, and said nothing more until they reached his office. Once the door to the office was firmly shut, he sat down and gestured to the other seats.

"What are the specifics of the arrangement?" Aveliad asked.

Madari drummed his fingers on the arm of his chair for a moment before answering.

"The tentative agreement would be a marriage between Deirdre and Prince Lain to take place on Deirdre's seventeenth birthday. Xan wanted the marriage to take place immediately, but I told him Deirdre's a bit too young, and the Zarryiostrom agreed with me. In exchange for Deirdre's hand in marriage, Xan will set aside any potential alliance with Illymar and look the other way should I decide to attack. Furthermore, he will open Ferralin ports for our naval vessels to stage out of, effectively making him an ally against Illymar. They won't send troops, of course, and the non-aggression treaty between Dakkadia and Ferralin would be nullified instantly should I make a move towards the Badlands. He seems to believe that won't be a problem, however. I think he's convinced that conquering Illymar will be too much for me to handle."

Aveliad touched her mask.

"Will it?"

Madari leaned back in his chair and crossed his legs before answering.

"I hope it won't come to that. I intend to present the terms of this arrangement to King Orem and try to strike a separate deal with him. The truth is; while I want more than anything to repay Orem for his insults by crushing Illymar utterly, strategically, it would be a much smarter move for me to strike at the Badlands. The Badlands would be much more valuable to Dakkadia, both in terms of location and sheer monetary value, and conquering it would increase the size of my realm by over a third." He ran his fingers through his thick black hair and frowned in irritation. "I do want to conquer Illymar, eventually, but for strictly personal reasons. Illymar is very rich, it is true, but their isolation would make them much more difficult to control. And even if I were to somehow fight past their navy and destroy their army, it would still require far too many of my soldiers to hold it until it could be pacified. Therefore, I would rather not bother with them for now, and instead, concentrate on consolidating my hold on the mainland. Unfortunately, left alone, Illymar is a threat to my ambitions and so it must be dealt with before I can proceed." He leaned forward in his seat and fixed Aveliad with his raptor's gaze. "Xan seeks to play Dakkadia against Illymar, in the hopes that both of our countries will weaken each other to the point that Ferralin will no longer have to worry about either of us. But he has overplayed his hand: simply by offering to ally with us, he has already burned his bridges with Illymar. I must assume that he knew this before he made the offer, so he has to have something else in mind. For the life of me, though, I can't see what that goal could be."

"Isn't it obvious?" Aveliad said. "Emperor Xan does not believe that King Orem will agree to an alliance with you under any circumstance. He is counting on King Orem's loathing of you to poison any negotiation you attempt to enter into with him. That is why Xan was so willing to burn his bridges before having a treaty with you firmly in hand: he almost certainly believes that when—not if—your attempt at negotiation fails, you will immediately agree to his terms . . . and that you will be so incensed with King Orem you will forego your ambitions in the Badlands to strike at Illymar, strategically foolish or no." She looked directly into Madari's eyes. "Xan plays the long game. By pushing you into attacking Illymar, he ensures the safety of his realm for years to come. And should things go wrong for you in Illymar, his son's marriage to Deirdre would give him a thread of justification for conquering Dakkadia, especially if they have a child."

Morvandis nodded his agreement at Aveliad's analysis.

"I think Queen Aveliad is correct in her assessment of Emperor Xan's probable motive. If so, the question becomes whether or not you can overcome King Orem's ingrained prejudices and negotiate a treaty. If the answer is yes, the Badlands and Ferralin will be yours for the taking. If you are unable to do so, however, you will have to decide: should you take Illymar and risk becoming trapped in a potential quagmire? Or should you take the Badlands and hope that Orem will refuse to assist Xan out of spite?"

"I guess we will find out which one it will be this evening" said Madari. He gave Aveliad a speculative glance. "You surprise me. I half expected you to try and convince me I should give up my designs on both Ferralin and Illymar."

Aveliad stood up and moved toward the door.

"While I strongly believe that leaving our neighbors alone would be our best course of action, I long ago gave up trying to dissuade you from taking that which does not belong to you. My concern now is strictly for the children: I do not wish to see either Valeriad or Deirdre forced into a bad marriage in order to further your ambitions."

"Which would you rather see, Valeriad married to Lyrahe, or Deirdre married to Lain?"

She stopped at that and turned around. To Madari's surprise, she smiled.

"I would be happy with either arrangement, though I would prefer that they themselves be allowed to choose the one they will marry. There is more than one way to reunite an empire, after all, and having one of your children married to Illymar and the other to Ferralin achieves that goal. That being said, I do agree with you on this point: Deirdre is far too young to marry. So, when you speak with King Orem this evening, bartering away your children's futures, I will be praying that your negotiations go well. Not for your sake, or the sake of your ambitions . . . but for Valeriad's sake. You may not believe that love is important to a marriage, but I do. And I always have."

CHAPTER TWENTY-ONE

"Rage"

Lain raised his wineglass to his lips and took a drink, using the motion of lifting his glass to hide another furtive look at his new potential wife, Deirdre. The Vizier had told him of the morning's events shortly after both he and Xan had returned from the meeting, and even now, hours later, Lain still had trouble believing what his father had done—or more importantly, understanding why exactly he had done it. Lain wasn't certain what game the man was playing at, but as he scrutinized the young Princess from behind his glass, he found that just this one time, he didn't particularly care.

Oh, he could work out the sums well enough in his own head to guess what his father was most likely attempting, and though the end result *might* be a war between Ferralin on one side and Illymar and Dakkadia on the other, he really found it hard to believe that that would actually happen. He'd seen too much of Illymari arrogance to believe that Orem would ever bow to Madari, and after the high-handed way in which Orem had treated him the previous night, Madari would accept nothing less than Illymar's complete and utter submission. Therefore, what his father had done—while admittedly cold-blooded and risky—made perfect sense as a diplomatic ploy.

The entire purpose of an alliance between the two realms, after all, had been to present a united front to King Madari and thereby avert an invasion by Dakkadia against either of them, thus maintaining the status quo. But the events of this morning had destroyed that hope, for Madari would want revenge against Illymar for defying the Peace, and Lain didn't blame him one bit.

Attacking someone who is protected by a flag of truce is utterly barbaric, and such barbarism must *be punished. Even Madari understands that. In all of the wars that he has started throughout his life, not once has he violated a flag of truce, nor has he ever broken an agreement once made.*

If Illymar was going to be attacked by Dakkadia even *if* they allied with Ferralin, it followed that by allying with them anyway, Ferralin also risked falling under Dakkadia's sword. That would be the height of stupidity for Ferralin. Entering into a suicide pact with Illymar would gain them absolutely nothing. Emperor Xan could see that as clearly as he could, so what his father was attempting to do now was to openly invite Dakkadia to attack Orem first . . . to preserve peace in his own realm by sacrificing Illymar.

At least this way, we buy ourselves enough time to prepare. I really do not wish to sacrifice Illymar for our own security, but my father didn't bother to consult me. Therefore, it's out of my hands. He did feel some small amount of remorse for the Illymari, but not nearly as much as he could have. *By their own dishonorable actions, they have brought this upon themselves.*

He set down the glass and turned his thoughts away from politics and back to consideration of the beautiful Dakkadian Princess sitting across from him.

If all goes well tonight, in just under three years we'll be married. I wonder what she'll think about that. He smiled to himself suddenly, and raised a napkin to his lips to cover the smile. *I hope she'll be as happy at the prospect of marrying me as I am with marrying her.*

He glanced at his former fiancée, Lyrahe, and his smile disappeared.

I'm sorry it came to this, Lyrahe, but it is better this way . . . for both of us. As beautiful as you are, we both know that your heart belongs to someone else. I truly hope that you can find a way to be with him, for you deserve that much happiness at the very least, before the worst comes to pass.

He didn't see how that could happen, for just as it was in one of her fabled romance novels, her family and the family of the man she desired were mortal enemies.

And if you should find some way to be with your Valeriad, I pray, for both of your sakes, that your lives together will be long and uneventful, and not one of your storybook romances. For such stories, while powerful and compelling, rarely end well for anyone involved.

Tais checked her appearance in her mirror one last time to make absolutely certain that everything looked perfect. The golden evening gown she wore was much simpler than the dresses normally favored at court, but though it boasted very little in the way of embroidery and absolutely no lace, the elegance of the cut and the simplicity of the design allowed her natural beauty to shine through. As she studied her profile looking for flaws, she thought about the dress that Queen Aveliad had worn when they had spoken. Aveliad's daringly designed gown had been the inspiration for this one, and Tais had commissioned it from her seamstress this very morning. Aveliad had proven, quite convincingly, that while clothing *could* make the woman, sometimes it was the woman who made the clothes. The thought made her laugh.

I only hope I can do as much justice to this dress as Aveliad did to hers. That woman is a goddess.

As she ran her fingers down the front of the gown and thrilled to the feel of the gossamer silk as it pressed against her skin, it felt to her as if she was wearing nothing at all. The thin chemise she wore underneath the dress didn't help matters in the slightest, for it, too, was made of delicate silk, and conformed to her body with all the familiarity of a lover.

Lover.

Just thinking the word made her blush to her toes, but she had spent the previous night thinking about Aveliad's words, and despite the Dakkadian Queen's admonition of caution, she had ultimately made her decision: she would invite Madari into her bed and accept the consequences for her actions, whatever they may be. They would have to be careful, for King Orem would most likely have her executed for High Treason if he found out about them, but Tais found she didn't care about that either. She was done with being afraid of the man.

If Orem found out about them and had her executed, she would die happy, knowing that she had defied him to the bitter end. And if he chose to exile her instead, she would make her way to Dakkadia. Living out her life as Madari's concubine would be far preferable to the fate the Queen had in store for her. She had not forgotten Althea's promise to sell her to any country lord who would still have her, for whatever price she could bring once the Convocation ended.

Tais glanced at the clock on her mantle to check the time, and smiled again.

It's time to go. I hope you ate a good meal, Madari; you're going to need all of your strength tonight.

With a wicked grin, she stepped out of her room and moved quickly and purposefully toward the dining hall. When she reached the hall she didn't enter, instead standing just outside to watch the guests from the shadows as they finished their dinner. She had timed her approach perfectly, for after no more than a few seconds, the King stood up to adjourn to the ballroom and the guests emulated him. As King Madari stood up to follow Orem, Tais moved into the doorway and caught his eye. She flashed him a brilliant smile and laughed quietly at his response, for he had looked her up and down in obvious shock, and when he tried to set his napkin upon the table he missed it completely. As it fell to the floor, she turned her back to him and began walking away, but not before glancing over her shoulder to give him a final sultry look that had him moving toward her almost before the napkin had even touched the ground.

She stayed ahead of him, even when he increased his pace, until she reached a particular intersection and turned down it. As soon as she was out of his sight, she stepped to the nearer side of the hall and leaned against a side table to wait for him. She didn't have to wait for long, for he turned the corner and stopped when he saw her waiting for him.

"Did you miss me?" she asked huskily, her voice dripping with desire.

Letting his actions speak louder than words, Madari stepped forward and enfolded her in his arms, pressing her against the table before crushing his lips against hers in a violent, passionate kiss. Hunger overcame her and she returned his kiss tenfold, reaching up to hold his head with her hands as their tongues found each other. His hands moved on their own accord, down her chest to her waist, and then to her hips and legs, looking for the hem of her dress. As he lifted the dress up to reveal her bare legs, she broke off their kiss and pulled away.

"Not here. It isn't safe. Come with me: I know just the place."

She pushed him back and stepped away from the table before grabbing his hand and leading him down the hall. They walked for a long time, turning down several hallways, stopping every once in a while to embrace or kiss. As they turned again and again, the elegant trappings and fine tapestries gave way to plainer decorations, and eventually the decorations disappeared altogether. Finally she stopped at a heavy wooden door bound by iron. The window was blocked by iron bars, and when Madari tried the door, he found it to be locked. Tais smiled.

"It's all right. I have the key."

From a small pouch on her belt she pulled out a large iron key that fit perfectly into the lock, and with a single firm twist the door opened, hinges squeaking as if they were protesting the intrusion.

"This is the Tower: the highest spot in the castle. My family has used it as a prison for generations, but it is currently unoccupied. There aren't even any guards on duty here, so I guarantee you that no one will walk in on us. We will have complete privacy for as long as we need."

She pulled a lit torch from a sconce on the wall next to the door and stepped inside, waiting for Madari to follow her. Without another word, she began the long climb up the steps. After several minutes of climbing, she finally stopped at a windowless wooden door and turned to him once again.

"We're here," she said with a wicked grin, and pushed open the door to reveal a small cell and its narrow bed.

As she looked once more into the tiny room in which she had spent a year of her life, she had a fleeting instant to know she had just made a terrible, terrible mistake. The smell of the room was the first thing that she noticed, for the musty scent mixed with the salty tang of the ocean breeze took her mind back to where she had been only a few weeks before. The small bed that had been her only piece of furniture was still in its place, dirty rags still lying where she had left them. The large window overlooking the ocean beckoned to her as if she had never left, and its siren's pull drew her into the room despite her initial hesitation.

Her desire and passion disappeared as if they had never existed, buried alive by the more powerful emotions of raw pain and crippling fear. Old wounds that she had once thought healed were ripped open with a shocking suddenness she was utterly unprepared for, and singularly unable to cope with. A cold wind blew through her as she wrapped her arms around herself in a vain attempt to ward off the chill, and then without warning, she was once again trapped in the past.

When she had decided to seduce Madari, she had chosen to bring him to this room deliberately, as an act of defiance against King Orem. But she had made that decision in the comfort and safety of her apartments, not knowing just how badly she would be affected by simply seeing her prison cell again. Now, the powerful waves of emotion the room drew out of her threatened to drown her in their undertow. She shuddered again, as the cold seemed to pierce through her heart.

Warm hands touched her upper arms, and muscular arms wrapped around her from behind in a powerful embrace. She tried to find comfort in those arms, but there was no comfort to be had. Numb to everything but her memory, she felt herself turned around to face the man she had entered the room with. She didn't respond as he kissed her shoulders and neck, even when the cold air turned the cool marks that his lips left upon her skin into burning brands. She didn't move when he pulled the straps off of her shoulders and let her dress and chemise slide to the floor, leaving her standing naked and vulnerable in his arms. And she didn't resist at all as he laid her back on the bed, standing above her, eyes shining in triumph. It was only after he began to undress himself that she responded, as the profound sense of *wrongness* of the situation finally penetrated her thoughts. As he pulled his shirt over his head she found her voice.

"I can't do this," she said softly, not recognizing her own voice.

My voice is deeper, isn't it? Huskier? When was the last time I spoke aloud?

Madari stopped, shirt still pulled over his face. When she said nothing further he continued, raising his arms to pull them through his sleeves.

"I can't do this," she said again, firmer this time.

Madari didn't stop this time; he pulled his shirt off and tossed it to the side. He knelt by the bed slowly, and spoke to her gently, but for some reason she couldn't understand his words. He leaned forward as if to kiss her, one hand caressing her hair, the other hand sliding softly up her inner thigh, all the while he continued to speak those soothing words, as if she were a skittish filly he hoped to tame. As his fingers reached the top of her thigh, tears began pouring from her eyes and she raised her hands to cover her face.

"Please don't. I can't do this. Please don't. I can't do this." *Not here,* she tried to add, but the words wouldn't come.

Over and over she said the words, tears falling like rain down her face.

Markus, please forgive me! I love you! I love you!

Madari didn't know what to think or what to do. His amorous adventure with the woman of his dreams was clearly at an end, but he had absolutely no idea why.

Five minutes ago she couldn't wait to bed me. Now she won't even look at me! What happened? What went wrong?

As he stared down at the gloriously nude body of the woman who had haunted his dreams since the first day they had met, he found he didn't feel the slightest shred of desire for her at the moment. She was as perfect as he had imagined, and the sight of her naked and vulnerable should have been more than enough to drive him to distraction, but as she lay weeping on the tiny cot, all he could feel was shocked surprise; and his surprise was rapidly giving way to anger. He gave her a cold look, though her hands still covered her eyes and she couldn't see it.

"I don't appreciate being led here under false pretenses, Tais. Why bring me here if you never intended to bed me?" When she didn't respond, he pulled her hands away from her eyes and forced her to look at him. Tears were pouring from her red-rimmed eyes in torrents, and she seemed to be looking right through him. "Are you listening to me? You brought me here of your own volition! You want this as much as I do!" He pointed at her dress—the seductive garment was lying like a pool of molten gold on the stone floor. "You want this *more* than I do!" As he felt his anger overwhelming him, he let go of her arms and began unbuckling his belt. "No, I'll not be denied something that we both want. Things have gone too far for me to stop."

He threw his sword belt to the ground and began unfastening his breeches, angrily kicking off his boots to allow them to slide off. Dressed only in his smallclothes, he sat down on the tiny bed and grabbed her wrists. Tais reacted to his touch by thrashing in panic, kicking and screaming at him to stop. One hand came free of his grip, and she clawed wildly at his head, managing to scratch his face with her fingernails hard enough to draw blood. He reared back in surprise as the unexpected attack made him let go of her other hand, and by pure reflex, he slapped her cheek with the open palm of his right hand. At the last second he managed to pull the blow, for he didn't truly want to hurt her, but after the blow landed, her tears dried up completely and she stopped trying to struggle. Instead, she gave him a contemptuous look, filled with loathing, and her fingers curled into claws.

"Aveliad was right about you. You were never the man you pretended to be, were you? Everything you said to me . . . everything that I thought I loved about you was a lie. Well, I've seen through your mask now, *Dakkadian,* and I will *never* willingly give myself to you, *ever!*"

Madari stood up quickly, eyes widening in shock.

Aveliad? She spoke to Aveliad?

At the realization his wife was to blame for this situation his anger turned white hot, and he felt his own hands curling into fists.

You've done it to me again, haven't you, Aveliad: you've destroyed my one chance at happiness. But this time you've gone too far. This time there is a price to pay.

Tais glanced warily at his hands, obviously fearing another blow, but she refused to back down. Madari tightened his fists once, knuckles straining to the tearing point, before he suddenly released them. Without saying a word, he gathered up his clothing and began to dress, movements almost tired and leaden. When the last bit of clothing was in its proper place and his belt was securely buckled, he walked to the door and opened it. He looked down at the floor with his back still to her.

"I swear to the Archon that I never wanted it to be like this. I swear it, Tais. We could have been happy together. I know that you won't believe me—especially not after the way I just acted—but Aveliad was wrong about me, and so are you: with you, I never pretended to be anything other than what I am. I'm sorry that you couldn't see that, and I'm even sorrier that you chose to believe Aveliad's lies over the truth standing before you."

He did glance back at her then, and to her surprise, she saw unshed tears in his eyes. Abruptly, his sad expression changed to one of vicious hatred and his hand once again curled into a fist.

"But you've made your choice. You called me 'Dakkadian'. Fine. I promise you this: when next we meet, *Illymari,* you and I will be enemies. And after I've destroyed your country and burned this city to ash, I will show you just how Dakkadians treat their enemies."

He left without another word, and far behind him where he couldn't see, Tais collapsed onto the cot and once again broke down into unrelenting tears of anguish.

Orem looked around for a sign of his Dakkadian counterpart, but Madari had disappeared shortly after dinner and was still nowhere to be found. He was anxious to speak with him, for he had heard about the assassination attempt on the Corsair's life from Althea, and he wanted to express his concern about the attack, as well as show him his determination to see those responsible for it brought to justice. Unfortunately, he could do neither of those things until Madari showed up.

Where could he be?

The fact that he even had to speak with Madari yet again—and especially under such humiliating circumstances—had already put him in a bad mood, but there was something going on with the Ferralin delegation that he didn't understand . . . and definitely didn't like.

He had approached Xan the moment dinner had ended, as normal, but this time he had received a decidedly cool reception. Xan hadn't been rude, *per se,* but he also hadn't been exceptionally friendly either. All of his attempts to draw Xan into a conversation had failed, with Xan using either single word responses or, even worse, saying nothing at all. Eventually, Orem had given up completely, and had excused himself, ostensibly to speak with his wife. Xan hadn't even bothered to acknowledge his withdrawal.

All of this had him worried and on edge. He was beginning to wonder if the uncharacteristically cold reception he was receiving had anything to do with the unfortunate business this morning with the Corsair, but with Xan apparently not speaking with him, he had no way of knowing for certain. He truly hoped that Xan did not believe he had had anything to do with the attack, for the Ferralin code of Guest-Right was ironclad and completely uncompromising, but Orem was afraid that even if Xan *knew* he wasn't involved, it still wouldn't matter to him. As the one who had extended Guest-Right, he was bound by honor to protect everyone who chose to shelter under that promise of safe passage as if they were members of his own family. Now the Corsair had been attacked while under his protection, and as far as the Ferralin code of honor was concerned, that was all that mattered.

But we're not in Ferralin. Surely he can't be holding me to the Ferralin code of honor!

He looked around once more, wondering yet again where Madari had gone.

How can I begin repairing the damage that has been done if I can't even apologize?

As he glanced around, his eyes landed on Madari's wife, Queen Aveliad. Without consciously thinking about it, he began walking toward her.

Maybe she'll know where he went.

Orem had never spoken with her directly, so he didn't know what to expect. Her beauty was legendary, even in Illymar where it shouldn't have mattered, but the mask she wore spoke of eccentricity, and eccentric people could be unpredictable. As a rule, Orem didn't like unpredictability, still, he couldn't simply stand around hoping that Madari would show, so he walked straight to Aveliad and fixed a smile upon his face. When he reached her, Aveliad curtseyed appropriately, and he got his first good look at her. *'Legendary' doesn't even begin to describe her beauty.*

His smile became less formal and more natural as she waited for him to speak, and he could feel his foul mood easing a bit simply by being in her presence. He bowed slightly to acknowledge her curtsey.

"Have you any idea where King Madari has gone? I wish to express my concern at the cowardly attack upon Lady Prudence this morning. I hope she is recovering well?"

Aveliad returned his smile.

"I am not certain where Madari has gone, though considering how quickly he left the table after dinner, I would venture to say he has found amenable company and is entertaining her even as we speak."

Orem frowned, for she had spoken in a matter-of-fact voice that was completely at odds with her words. Any other woman he could think of, who even suspected that her husband was currently engaged in a tryst, would either be livid or heartbroken. But, Aveliad's tone hadn't changed in the slightest as she spoke, and her complete lack of concern made him frown in confusion.

"And you are fine with that? I had thought Dakkadia to be a bit more conservative."

Aveliad's smile turned into one of bemusement.

"I would not say that I am 'fine' with it, but I do not disapprove either. He does what he wishes, despite my feelings, and he always has. After twenty years of marriage, I find I couldn't care less who he dallies with so long as he sires no illegitimate children." Her smile became genuine again and she cocked her head to the side. "As for the attack upon Lady Prudence, I thank you for your concern on her behalf, and I assure you that she will be perfectly fine after a little bit of rest. Her injury was not that severe, but as is customary with all stubborn people, she made things worse by refusing to accept help when it was offered."

"It is my understanding that the Inquisition has been dispatched by the Zarryiostrom and is already investigating the attack," Orem said. "I have instructed my people to extend them every courtesy in their investigation. It is my hope . . ."

He trailed off as King Madari entered the ballroom and looked quickly around. As Madari's eyes landed first upon Aveliad and then upon him, they flashed with anger, and Orem took an involuntary step backward as the Dakkadian King squared his shoulders and marched toward them. Even from the distance they were standing, Orem could feel the menace radiating off of him, and he squared his own shoulders as if preparing to do battle. *This is going to get ugly.*

As Madari drew near, Orem was surprised to see four red scratches on his cheek, obviously made by a woman with long fingernails. He thought back to what Aveliad had said earlier, and a wave of amusement washed over him. *I guess the company wasn't as amenable* or *as entertaining as she thought. Well, at least she won't have to be concerned with illegitimate children! That should make her happy.* When Madari reached the pair, Orem spoke first to try and forestall another scene.

"King Madari! I was just asking your lovely wife where I might find you. Please allow me to express my concern about the attack on Lady Prudence. We are working with the Zarryiostrom to find the party responsible for ordering the assassination attempt, but I feel simply terrible . . ."

Madari cut him off with a savage snarl.

"Spare me your false words of sympathy, as well as your meaningless protestations of innocence. Everyone who matters knows exactly who was behind the attack, and if you haven't figured it out for yourself, then you are a bigger fool than even I believed. And though you don't know it yet, your treachery is going to cost you *everything*."

Aveliad tried to interpose herself between the two Kings, to try and calm her husband down, but Madari growled at her like an enraged animal and brushed her aside with a single sweep of his arm. Only Aveliad's fluid grace prevented her from falling unceremoniously to the floor, but it had been a very near thing, for Madari had used all of his strength. Orem began to sputter in shocked outrage at Madari's violent behavior, but the King of Dakkadia wasn't finished. He stabbed a powerful finger toward Orem and continued in a louder voice.

"This morning I met with Emperor Xan in the offices of the Zarryiostrom, where we came to a mutual understanding concerning your alliance with Ferralin. It's over: there will be no marriage between Crown Prince Lain and your daughter. Instead, Emperor Xan has proposed a marriage between his son and my daughter; a marriage I am very much in favor of."

When Madari had entered the room so full of fury, all conversation in the room had stopped as people turned to watch the unfolding drama. At his words, however, the entire room erupted with a collected gasp of shock, followed by hushed whispers of disbelief. Lyrahe in particular looked stunned. In a daze, she looked toward the Ferralin delegation and Emperor Xan for confirmation, and she wasn't the only one. Every single pair of eyes in the room turned to the Ferralin Emperor, who reacted by smiling apologetically at Lyrahe, before turning his attention to Orem.

"What he says is true. I was already having misgivings about the marriage, but today's attack upon Lady Prudence simply confirmed what I had already come to suspect: that tying our realms together would be a grave mistake." He looked at Lyrahe again. "I'm sorry you had to hear about my decision in this way, but it was painfully obvious to everyone here that you and my son were simply not meant to be together. This is in no way a reflection upon you, for you are truly a lovely child, and I would have been proud to have been your father-in-law. But my time here has shown me that as lovely as you are, your grace and beauty are simply not enough to outweigh the greater disadvantages of allying with a lesser power. And make no mistake, King Orem," he turned his attention back to the King, "*you* are the lesser power."

He folded his hands into his voluminous sleeves and looked toward Madari, ceding the stage for the enraged King to continue. Madari didn't keep him waiting for long. He gave a white-faced Orem a vicious smile.

"As I said, your attack on Lady Prudence has cost you everything. But, as much as I would love to sail my armada into your harbor and reduce this city to a smoking ruin as your treachery so richly deserves, I am a King, and I have a duty to put the good of my country above my own desires. Therefore, I have an offer for you. This offer will last until I walk out your door, so think carefully before you answer."

He raised his voice so everyone in the room could hear him.

"Surrender to me now and agree to become a vassal state of Dakkadia, and I'll let you keep your crown. You will pay tribute to me in the form of gold and ships, and your armies will fight when and where I tell them. Furthermore, my son will marry your daughter, Lyrahe, and your youngest daughter, Chesare, will marry Mage-Lord Morvandis. And finally, you . . . *you* will kneel before me right now and swear fealty to me as your liege lord. If you do not agree to these terms immediately, all of Illymar will suffer my wrath, and the wrath of Dakkadia!" He crossed his arms over his chest. "Now, what is your answer?"

Orem's shock was absolute. For several seconds all he could do was stare, first at Madari and then at Xan. Try as he might, he could not make his mind function; and though his mouth moved, no words came out. But then he looked back at Madari, and a thunderbolt of white-hot fury penetrated the fog that had clouded his mind, and his bloodless face flushed purple with rage.

"You *dare*? You *dare* to dictate terms to me in my own home? I tell you now, you may accuse me of striking at your pet pirate in defiance of my own pledge of safe conduct, but you'd better hope for your sake that you are wrong about me, for that pledge is the only thing that will allow you to walk out of my home tonight and sail off of my island alive! By all rights, I should have you killed where you stand for this baseless and unprovoked assault upon my honor!"

He whirled toward Xan, and froth formed at the corners of his mouth as he unleashed his rage upon the Ferralin Emperor. "And you! You were a welcome guest in my home! You ate my food and drank my wine, and all the time you pretended to be my friend and ally, you were planning to betray me! I expected treachery from this Dakkadian barbarian, but *you?* I wouldn't have believed that from you! And to think, just a while ago I was worried that I had somehow offended your honor. But then, how could I have when you've just proven that you have no honor to offend!"

He stopped himself to draw in a ragged breath, but before he could continue his tirade, Madari picked up right where he had left off.

"I'll take that as a 'no'. Very well, then. What comes next is on your head." He turned to leave, but stopped to look Xan. "We have an accord."

Xan acknowledged his words with a polite nod, and after he returned the nod, Madari turned toward the exit and left the room without looking back. The Dakkadian contingent filed out behind him, until not a single one was left in the room. When the last of them had left, Xan also turned to leave, a beatific smile of triumph on his face. The Ferralin diplomats fell in behind him, but Crown Prince Lain held back for a moment to speak with Lyrahe. He leaned forward and whispered quietly into her ear, before kissing her on the cheek and enfolding her in an embrace. As he pulled away from her, he gave her one last sad smile, and left the room without another look back.

For several minutes after the guests had left the ballroom, Orem didn't move. He simply stood where he was and stared at the door, shocked disbelief written all over his face. No one dared to move for fear of breaking the spell and inviting his wrath, but as the minutes stretched on with Orem staring at the door, one man finally did move. He walked up behind Orem and placed a hand on his shoulder. Orem spun around to see who had dared, but before he could explode in rage yet again, he recognized the face of his brother, Ascham. Instead of screaming at his brother, he swung his right arm up and knocked Ascham's hand off of his shoulder.

"I suppose you've come to gloat? To tell me that you were right and I was wrong? Tell me! Tell me what a fool I am!"

Ascham shook his head slowly before answering.

"What you did—what you tried to do—was for love of our country. You had to try; you had to make one final attempt to avert the bloodshed that is sure to come, and I respect you for that more than you could possibly know. I came to tell you that now, more than ever before, you have my complete and utter loyalty. Dakkadia will come for us as soon as they possibly can, and when they do, I will be standing right beside you defending what is ours . . . and so will my soldiers. We stand ready, My Liege, as we always have." He dropped to one knee, head bowed, and Orem stared at his brother, searching for any sign of triumph or mockery. Instead, to his relief, he saw only loyalty and devotion. A wave of gratitude came over him at the realization that his brother had meant every word he had said, and Orem reached out and squeezed Ascham's shoulder.

"Then perhaps some good has come of this disaster after all."

He raised his voice so that everyone could hear him.

"I hereby rescind my order of exile to the Duke of Saerce and his vassals, and invite them to once again return to Illymaine in full honor." He held out his hand, and Ascham took it without hesitation. "Welcome home, brother. It's good to have you back." He looked at the crowd, which was moving closer to hear their King's words. "Dark days are coming, and will soon be upon us. Illymar may have failed to gain an ally this day, but we cannot, and will not, dwell on what we have lost. Instead, we will look to the future and prepare ourselves for the storm to come." He turned to leave, pulling on Ascham's shoulder as he turned. "The two of us have much to discuss."

As Orem and Ascham left the room together, both engaged in quiet conversation, Queen Althea watched them go with a venomous look in her eyes. When the King and his brother finally disappeared from view, Althea turned to the kinsmen standing around her and said,

"We have a problem."

There was no conversation at all in the carriage as it pulled away from the Spire of Illymaine for the final time, and as the silence deepened, Aveliad began to worry. Deirdre was leaning against her, head nestled against her side, and Aveliad absentmindedly stroked her hair in a comforting gesture. She wasn't certain what Deirdre thought of the arrangement, but Aveliad wished that she had discussed the morning's surprise meeting with her to explain what it meant for her future. Instead, Deirdre had to find out about her betrothal with the rest of the guests, and from her silence, she knew her daughter was conflicted. She would speak with her in the morning, to tell her that the marriage would not take place for a few years and that she shouldn't worry.

Morvandis, too, was quiet, but from the look in his eyes she could see that the wheels in his mind were turning and turning, evaluating the situation from every conceivable angle and prioritizing the commands he would have to give. More than any of them, he had things to do before they left, but if he was to have any chance of completing them before the *Sovereign* set sail, he had to work quickly. She wasn't worried, for Morvandis was very, very good at what he did, and she knew she could trust him to make the best possible decisions under the circumstances; with or without orders. The two of them had an odd relationship; for while she disliked him personally, almost as much as she disliked Madari, she greatly admired both his competence and his absolute loyalty to the family. The unnatural silence that pervaded the carriage was no hindrance to Morvandis, for she knew that he, above all of them, needed no instructions.

But then there was Madari. This silence was completely unlike him, for after the evening's events, she knew he had much to do. Normally, he would have begun making plans with Morvandis even before they climbed into the carriage, for there were orders to give, plans to be made, and letters to be written. All of those things had to be accomplished quickly, for Illymar was no longer a safe place for a Dakkadian to be, and they had to leave as quickly as possible. Aveliad thought about saying something to that effect, but she knew he was already aware of the danger and still he chose to hold his silence, so she decided to allow him his privacy. There would be time enough to worry later.

Instead of speaking, Aveliad surreptitiously studied his profile and quietly contemplated the four fingernail scratches on his cheek. She frowned as she looked at them, for she had lied to Orem about not knowing where Madari had disappeared to that evening. She had seen Princess Tais appear in the doorway of the dining room wearing a revealing dress and a welcoming smile for Madari the moment the dinner had ended. When she saw the way Tais had looked at Madari, Aveliad had known the Illymari Princess had finally made her decision.

Disappointed as she was with Tais's choice, true to her word, she did not begrudge her the liaison.

I promised to be happy for her if she chose to be with my husband. But what could have gone wrong? I saw her face as Madari rushed to be with her. The look that she gave him was not one of someone uncertain of her actions. What made her change her mind?

Something else occurred to her. Madari had been enraged even before he had confronted Orem to demand his capitulation. That told her whatever had happened between the couple, it had been very bad indeed. She hoped that Madari hadn't hurt the young Princess, though she wasn't truly worried about that. Oh, intellectually, she knew that he was quite capable of hurting her, for Dakkadians had only one way of dealing with people they saw as enemies, but despite his reputation for enjoying violence, he had always confined his violent tendencies to the battlefield. In all the years of their marriage he had never raised his hand to her, no matter what provocation she had given him, and she was honest enough to admit she had given him plenty of provocation to strike her throughout the years.

The carriage stopped in front of their villa and the Dakkadian guards rushed forward to open the doors. Madari stood up silently and stepped outside, followed closely by Morvandis, and without looking back, the two of them went into the house. Aveliad watched him go in silence, still wondering about what had happened to him to affect him so, but she dismissed her concern as unimportant. If he wasn't going to do what was necessary, the duty fell upon her. She stopped stroking Deirdre's hair and kissed the crown of her head before saying,

"Go to bed, Deirdre. A lot has happened, I know, but there will be time enough to discuss what these things mean for you in the morning. Get some sleep."

Deirdre squeezed her mother tightly in an embrace, and then climbed out of the carriage to enter the villa as well. After Deirdre had disappeared into the doorway, Aveliad climbed out of the carriage and spoke to the captain of the guard.

"Things went very badly at the Spire this evening, and I am afraid we have overstayed our welcome here on Illymar. Therefore, we will most likely be departing as soon as Prince Valeriad and Lord Daane are allowed to leave the Citadel, so I want you and your men to be prepared to leave on a moment's notice."

The captain gave her a crisp salute.

"Do you think the compound may come under attack?"

Aveliad considered the question for a moment, then shrugged.

"I do not think so, for despite this evening's disastrous events, we are still under the protection of the Peace of Zarryiosiad. However, as the attack upon Lady Prudence proved this morning, the Peace alone may not be enough to keep our enemies at bay."

She nodded to herself as she came to a decision.

"Double the guard, and arm yourselves well. You are not to fight unless you or your men are attacked, but if you *are* attacked, I do not want you to hesitate to defend yourselves. In the morning I will send Morvandis to the Mage Citadel to have him ask for a detachment of the Mage Guard to support you, but until they arrive, keep a careful watch. Also, send two runners to the *Sovereign.* They are to inform Lady Prudence's first officer, Mr. Frederick, that they are to hereby consider this island and all of its inhabitants to be hostile. All crewmembers are to report aboard immediately, and they are to remain aboard with weapons to hand for the rest of our stay. I do not want any of them to risk being attacked the way Lady Prudence was. Also, no one is to be allowed anywhere near the ship that does not have a good reason to be there."

The captain saluted again and turned to his men to start issuing orders. Aveliad didn't wait to listen.

As she walked into the compound, she spotted Madari speaking quietly with Morvandis. Morvandis had his back to her and didn't see her enter, but when Madari spotted her, he closed his mouth and opened the door to his office. As Madari and Morvandis walked into the office, Aveliad moved to join them, but Madari deliberately closed the door in her face just as she reached it, and she heard the sound of the key being turned. The loud *click* of the oiled lock startled her, and she stopped where she was and stared at the door in surprise. The act of closing the door upon her told her everything she needed to know about his unusual silence on the ride back.

Madari is angry with me. Very *angry.*

She thought back to the evening's events and one thing stood out to her. When she had tried to interpose herself between Madari and Orem to calm him down, he had physically pushed her out of the way to continue his fight with Orem. *Could he be angry with me for speaking to his enemy, or for coming between them?*

In the end, she decided he would tell her soon enough what he was so angry with her about, so she turned away and walked to her chambers. As she opened the door, a thought occurred to her. *Madari was unable to consummate his relationship with Tais. I wonder if he will come crawling back to me to once again assert his 'husbandly rights'?*

Madari might be angry with her, but she knew there was a very good chance he would come to her that night. He hadn't been with a woman in weeks, after all, and for him that would seem like an eternity. And also, there was the situation with Tais to consider.

If she invited him to her quarters but changed her mind about sleeping with him, he will most likely be frustrated enough to come to me. She sighed inwardly. *I guess there is nothing to do then but to prepare myself. Perhaps he is angry enough with me to finish quickly and leave.*

Three lady's maids awaited her in her room, and without a word, they quietly and efficiently began helping her to undress. They untied the laces of her bodice and removed it, as well as the ribbons holding her mask in place. One of the ladies set the mask reverently upon its silk pillow, while another produced a silk nightgown for her to don that was conservative enough in its cut to seem almost prudish, while still being quite comfortable to wear. All of her nightgowns shared similar traits, for Aveliad had no interest whatsoever in attracting Madari's attentions. One of the ladies picked up a hairbrush and handed it to her before all three of them curtseyed and left the room. Aveliad sat down at her dresser and began to brush her own hair, silently counting out the 100 strokes in the same ritual she had performed every night for as long as she could remember.

It was on the 82nd stroke that Madari opened her door. He didn't bother to knock before he entered, and he didn't say anything as he closed the door behind him and locked it. Aveliad sighed at the confirmation she had guessed correctly about his amorous attentions, but she deliberately turned back to the mirror and continued brushing, silently counting out the strokes from 83 and ignoring him completely.

He still hasn't said anything. I'll make him wait until he does.

Unfortunately, so caught up was she in ignoring him, that she wasn't prepared for what came next. A sudden, horrifying pain from her scalp made her scream in fear and shock, and she dropped her hairbrush in surprise as something yanked her backward off of her footstool. She fell to the floor and reached up with her hands to find out what had happened, only to find Madari's fingers tangled in her hair. With a powerful tug that made her scream yet again, he dragged her to bed by her hair, and still gripping it in his fists, he lifted her up onto the bed and threw her unceremoniously onto the mattress. She fell onto her downy white coverlet with her scalp feeling as if it was on fire, but she tried to sit up, despite the agony. She had managed to get halfway up to look at him when a vicious backhanded blow to her face made her fall back to the cover, and this time she couldn't find the energy to get back up. He had struck her in the left eye with a balled fist, and it left her completely dazed and unable to defend herself for what came next. *All* of it.

When he was done, she knew not how much later, he stood up. Her lip was split and bloody, her eye swollen completely shut. Blood flowed freely from her nose, and her right wrist had been broken when she had tried to cover herself as he tore her clothes off like an animal. Practically every inch of her was badly bruised, and after he had finished beating her, he had raped her, again and again. As he forced himself onto her and into her, without regard to her pain, she knew, beyond any shadow of a doubt, that when he was finished, he was going to kill her. Somehow, she had pushed him too far, once too often; and now he was going to kill her . . . just the way he had killed her husband, Phaedril.

To her surprise, instead of feeling fear, she felt a peace that she had never experienced before. She surrendered to that peace, and it allowed her to endure what was happening to her tortured and abused body without protest.

Madari slowed his movements and eventually stopped, chest rising and falling with his exertions. He stood up and picked up a clean corner of her coverlet to wipe his hands . . . hands that were crimson with both his blood and hers, and when he had finished wiping away the blood, he inspected his fingers. Sometime during the beating he had torn his knuckles, and fresh blood welled up from the gashes and dripped silently onto her bed. As she lay there in her blood-soaked bed, looking up at him with her one good eye, she wondered when he would finish what he had started and kill her, but to her surprise, he instead turned his back to her and got dressed. She watched him pull on his shirt and buckle his belt, all the while waiting for him to turn back to her and slit her throat or stab her through the heart. It was only after he was finished dressing that he spoke, and after the terrifying silence that he had maintained throughout even the most vicious parts of his assaults, the quiet words seemed deafening.

"You're probably wondering why I did this to you; and what you could possibly have done to deserve it. This wasn't cruelty for cruelty's sake, *wife*: this was punishment. You've told me that you don't love me, and you never did. I understand that, and though I had at one time wished for more, I find now that I can live without your love. You also take great pleasure in mocking me, both in public and in private. That tells me that you have no respect for me. That, too, is fine; I can live without your respect as well. But tonight, Tais told me you *warned* her about me, and that—*that!*—I find I cannot abide. So, since you refuse to love me or respect me, then I swear to you now that instead, you will learn to *fear* me." He took a step toward her and she flinched, expecting another blow. Surprisingly, it didn't come. "I'll say this only once: if you *ever* interfere in my affairs again, I'll finish what I started tonight." He tilted his head forward and gave her a deadly glare. "Believe it."

With that, he turned and walked out of the room.

Immediately after he left her, women began filing into the room to help her, to clean her and bandage her wounds. Through a pain-induced haze, Aveliad wondered where they had come from and how they had come so quickly, but one of the women took her uninjured wrist into her hand and answered her unspoken question.

"His Majesty ordered us to be standing nearby ready to help, but he also told us that if anyone so much as touched your door before he himself came out, he would kill that person. I'm so sorry, Your Majesty. There was nothing we could do to help you. Please believe me."

As tears poured out of the servant's eyes, Aveliad tried to reassure the handmaiden that she was not to blame for what had happened, and to thank the woman for her kindness, but at long last, the blackness finally enveloped her and she drifted off into blissful unconsciousness, far, far away from her pain.

Madari walked to his room with his back as rigid as iron, fury still burning in his eyes. No one along his path would meet his gaze, and those people unlucky enough to cross his path quickly found other places to be. Madari found that that suited him just fine. When he reached his chambers, he shut the door behind him and leaned against it for a moment, tilting his head back to rest it against the cool wood. After a moment's respite, he stepped forward and pulled his pistol out of its holster and set it on the dresser next to the door. As he walked into the room, slowly unbuckling his sword belt, he caught his reflection in his full-length mirror, and suddenly his simmering rage boiled over. He screamed at his reflection in fury and self-loathing, and with a mighty heave, he hurled his belt, his sword and his dagger at the mirror and shattered it into a thousand pieces. Violence accomplished, he sat down on his bed and stared silently at his still-bloody hands.

What did I do, Aveliad? he thought bitterly. *What did you* make *me do?*

For the second time that day, he felt his eyes welling with tears, and this time was unable to stop them. So, instead of fighting back the tears, he let them have free rein, and as they rolled down his face, he put his head in his hands and hunched forward, back shaking with the force of his sobs.

I didn't want any of this to happen! Why did everything go so wrong?

Abruptly, he shot to his feet, snarling at himself in self-loathing.

You weak, pathetic fool . . . sniveling and whining will change nothing. Whether you wanted it or not, Dakkadia is now at war, and you are the King. So why don't you act like one instead of sobbing like a heartbroken child? You made promises today you have to keep, so you'd best be about it before you lose what little self-respect you have left. If you don't . . . if you give in to your despair now, Aveliad and Tais win.

He didn't bother undressing for bed; he didn't have the strength for it. Instead, he leaned back wearily and fell backwards onto the mattress, closed his eyes, and let sleep overtake him.

It was very late at night when Morvandis returned to Enaria's quarters. She was asleep when he opened the door, but as he closed it behind him, he saw her move, telling him he had awoken her.

"I'm sorry that I woke you, Enaria, but I'm glad you're awake. We have to talk. It's important."

"Come to bed and we'll talk."

Morvandis nodded and removed his robes, hanging them neatly on a wooden hanger next to hers. Enaria watched him undress, smiling all the while, and when he walked to the bed she pulled back the covers for him. As he slid himself between the sheets, she turned his head toward her and kissed him passionately, before settling herself back into her pillow.

"Now, what's so important?"

Morvandis placed a pillow behind him to lean against.

"We will be leaving Illymar tomorrow night. I've already spoken with Patriarch Varic and Archimagus Windwhisper about our expedited departure, so both the Zarryiostrom and the Citadel are already aware. Archimagus Windwhisper has graciously agreed to allow Prince Valeriad and Lord Daane to complete their Testing tomorrow, so as soon as it is completed, we will leave."

Enaria sat up in shocked surprise at his words, and Morvandis gave her the time she needed to process the information.

"You aren't supposed to leave for almost two more weeks! What happened? Why are you leaving now?"

Morvandis closed his eyes.

"It's complicated, but King Madari and Emperor Xan have agreed to an alliance that will be sealed by the marriage of Crown Prince Lain to Princess Deirdre. The marriage will not take place until she turns 17, but even with the wedding three years away, Xan has generously agreed to allow Madari to strike at Illymar whenever he wants, starting immediately. In effect, Ferralin has very publicly washed its hands of Illymar. Orem is aware of the arrangement, so, Illymar is no longer a safe place for us to be."

Enaria pulled aside her covers. As she climbed out of bed, Morvandis gave her a quizzical look.

“I have much to do before we leave. I suppose it would be too much to ask for Madari to delay your departure by a day so that I can prepare properly, but I’ll make do somehow.”

“As much as I wish it were otherwise,” he said, “you can’t come with me. I need you to stay here, at least for a little while, to tend to a few things for me. It’s important.”

She stopped where she was and turned back around.

“The Council. When Dakkadia invades, you need me here to break it.”

Morvandis shook his head and said,

“That is for the future. I have something a little more immediate in mind.” After he explained what he needed from her, she smiled.

“Very well, Morvandis, but I want something from you in return. When the time comes, I will do as you command. But, after it is done, I want your promise that you will allow me to accompany you to Dakkadia. Illymar can burn, and Ithram with it. All I care about is you. I want to make a new place for myself by your side, if you will have me. That is all I ask of you.”

“Agreed.”

ARCHIMAGUS ENARIA WINTERSONG
AND MAGE-LORD MORVANDIS

CHAPTER TWENTY-TWO

"Watchers"

A knock at the door woke Valeriad out of a sound sleep, and he rubbed his eyes wearily before answering.

"Come in! I'm awake!"

The door opened and Phaedron entered, fully dressed, but without his weapons. Valeriad frowned at that, for a Dakkadian nobleman without his weapons was considered to be naked, but Phaedron spoke before he could ask.

"We've been ordered to get dressed, but leave our weapons in our rooms. There was some sort of trouble at the Spire yesterday, and we're going to be leaving the island tonight. That means for our sins, we get to complete both our Observation period and our Testing early. So get dressed quickly, have some breakfast, and then go straight to the Grand Arena. I have to go there now, but Adrianna will stay behind to take you." A smiling Adrianna popped her head into the room and winked cheerfully, before disappearing back into the hall. "Good luck, Valeriad. You know how important this is, so pay attention to what you are doing for once in your life. Try not to embarrass yourself."

Valeriad yawned prodigiously.

"Refresh my memory here: which one of us let a 16-year-old girl humiliate us in front of the entire Mage Guard? Oh, that's right . . . that was you! Perhaps you should save your worry for yourself, Phaedron." As the barb struck home, Valeriad could hear both Chesare and Adrianna giggling, and in response to both the insult and the giggles, Phaedron widened his eyes in feigned shock, thumped a fist into his chest and staggered backward comically, as if Valeriad had just shot an arrow into his heart. Valeriad laughed at the display, but then his demeanor turned serious and he said, "Good luck, Phaedron. I know you'll do us proud."

"So will you. Remember to watch out for surprises. They'll try to break your concentration at every turn. Don't give them the satisfaction. And if you feel yourself weakening, just imagine the look of disappointment on Morvandis' face you'll see if you fail."

With that, Phaedron gave him a cocky grin and raised two fingers to his brow in a jaunty salute, before leaving the room. Valeriad climbed out of bed and began to dress himself as quickly as he could.

"Adrianna? What time do I have to be there?"

Adrianna answered him from the hallway as he pulled on his breeches, "They didn't say, but despite what Phaedron said, there isn't really any hurry. Only one person can be Tested at a time, and it can take several hours. Because there was no warning, Phaedron volunteered to take the first examination to allow you the time to eat breakfast and prepare yourself. He'll be taking the Test on an empty stomach."

Valeriad sighed heavily at the confirmation that Phaedron had, once again, taken the harder road to spare him any hardship, but this time he appreciated the gesture. The truth was, he was very nervous about the Test, for he had only been studying for two years, while Phaedron had studied for five. Valeriad knew that Phaedron would have no trouble passing the Test, empty stomach or no, but he himself would need the extra time to calm his nerves and prepare himself mentally.

He finished dressing and stepped out of his room, closing the door behind him. Adrianna gave his appearance a thorough examination.

"Shall we go to breakfast?"

"Before we left for Illymar," Valeriad said, "Morvandis taught both of us all of the forms that we will be expected to perform during the Testing, so I know I shouldn't be worried. But now that it's time to actually be Tested, I have to admit that I am more than a bit nervous."

Adrianna smiled at him encouragingly.

"That's to be expected. Practice is one thing, Valeriad. During practice, you can fail as many times as you have to before you get things right, but during the Testing, you have to get it exactly right the first time, or you'll be stuck here in Ithram until you *do* get it right. And even worse, you won't be allowed to try again for several months."

Valeriad gave her a flat look.

"Thanks for your words of encouragement, Adrianna. You always know exactly what to say to make me feel better."

"Oh, I think you'll find Ithram to be much more to your liking than you'd believe. Especially after what happened last night!"

"Phaedron mentioned that something happened, but he didn't have time to go into any details. Do you know what it was?"

"That's right! You haven't heard yet! Oh, you are going to love this!" She grabbed his forearm with both hands. "Apparently, last night your father announced at the party that Prince Lain won't be marrying Princess Lyrahe after all. Instead, Lain will be marrying your sister, Deirdre, and through the marriage Dakkadia and Ferralin will become allies! That's why you have to leave here tonight: King Orem was furious when he found out! Your father doesn't think Illymar is safe for you anymore, so he sent Morvandis here to make the arrangements to have your Tests expedited. But who cares about that? This means Princess Lyrahe is free again, and you can meet her if you want!"

Valeriad stopped in the middle of the hall in shock, and Adrianna stopped to wait for him.

"Lyrahe isn't going to marry Lain after all? That's . . . that's great!"

He whooped once in excitement, and Adrianna laughed and clapped her own hands in matching enthusiasm. But then, as the implications of the previous night's events occurred to him, his mood suddenly changed to one of anguish.

"We leave tonight? But that means I'll never see her again." He grabbed Adrianna's hand in a vice-like grip. "Don't you see what this means? If Father has made arrangements for Deirdre to marry Lain, then he must have declared war upon Illymar. That means, even if I do see Lyrahe again, when we meet we'll be enemies!" He let Adrianna's hand go and began pacing the hall, trying to think of something. "I know! I'll fail the Test! That way I'll be able to stay here for a few more months, and she can see me whenever she wants!"

Adrianna frowned at him in consternation.

"I guess I hadn't thought of it that way. You're right: this is worse than I thought. But the Test! Valeriad, you *can't* intentionally fail it! Your father wants you to leave immediately, and for very good reasons. If you are forced to stay after everyone else in your family leaves, your life would be in jeopardy. You're the heir to the Dakkadian throne! Don't you think that Illymar would do whatever it could to lay its hands on you? Or perhaps even kill you? That would mean that every time you take a drink or have a bite to eat, you risk being poisoned. You could never leave the confines of the Citadel for fear of being kidnapped. And no matter what you might think, Lyrahe would *still* never be allowed to see you. No, failing the Test is not an option."

Valeriad stopped pacing and clenched his fists in frustration.

"Then what do you think I should do?"

"Pass the Test and go home. Leave the rest to the Archon. If you're meant to be together, you will be."

Severeielle stepped through her Shadowgate and allowed it to close silently behind her, and quickly checked the area around her for wards and alarms. Sensing nothing, she moved cautiously forward to one of the large marble pillars surrounding the Grand Arena and settled back to watch the proceedings unfold. This was her first trip back to the Mage Citadel since that wretched little girl had taken her by surprise, and this time Severeielle was taking absolutely no chances. Spying on the Testing was very dangerous, for all eight of the members of the Mage High Council were in attendance, and if they spotted her, even the Queen of Shadows would have a hard time escaping from their collective power.

The Grand Arena was a magnificent structure, with a large open area surrounded by several floors, each divided by marble colonnades and stone arches for observers to sit. From past experience, Severeielle knew that there would be no observers allowed to view the Testing, and so she settled back to watch the drama unfold from a concealed alcove.

Below her, one of the two subjects she had come to observe was standing in the center of the arena, obviously preparing his defensive circles for his Test. She couldn't actually see the circles, for Dragon Witches weren't truly Mages and so couldn't actually touch or manipulate elemental magic, but she was quite capable of sensing the power emanating from him and judging his strength by the feel of it.

This one is quite powerful. Not as powerful as the girl, perhaps, but formidable nonetheless.

As she watched him, she began to sense something else about him . . . something that she couldn't quite put a finger on.

There is something familiar about him. It almost feels as if I know him somehow.

She frowned at the unusual feeling, but try as she might, she couldn't describe the feeling other than that he seemed somehow familiar to her.

Eventually, the young man bowed formally to the Mages sitting before him, signaling his readiness to begin. The first Mage to stand was the Eighth Seat; Archimagus DeVir, if she remembered correctly. Like the young man being tested, Archimagus DeVir, was a Dakkadian, and as such, they shared many similarities in both build and coloring. Their hair in particular was similar, for they both had the glossy black hair with white striping that marked Dakkadian nobility—coloring she herself shared—though DeVir had cut his hair short, while the Novice wore his extremely long. The Archimagus called out a series of commands to the younger Dakkadian and the younger man responded by casting a series of spells in sequence. First, a large plume of water burst into existence from the floor and instantly froze solid before evaporating into mist. The mist filled the room with banks of fog until DeVir called out another command, and the Novice forced the mist to coalesce until a large ball of water floating directly in front of him. The Archimagus' eyes flashed red, and a series of fiery hoops appeared at various intervals around the room. In an instant, the ball of water stretched once again into a plume, and it flew away from the Water Mage and directly toward the first hoop, where it flew right through the center without touching the ring and extinguishing the blaze. It immediately turned for a second hoop and repeated the feat, and then again at the third and fourth hoops. At the fifth hoop, the water changed its appearance, and suddenly the plume of water was a large, wingless, serpentine dragon, complete with scales. As the sinuous "dragon" completed the circuit with style and flair, Severeielle smiled in delight. She knew very well that that little display hadn't been part of the Test, and that meant the young man was showing off for the Council. She liked that; for it bespoke a confidence in his own abilities that most Novices lacked.

It seemed Archimagus DeVir also found the display to be highly amusing, for despite the solemnity of the proceedings, he laughed before shaking his head and cautioning the young Dakkadian against taking liberties during the Testing. The young Dakkadian shrugged elaborately in an obviously insincere apology, and Severeielle laughed quietly as the dragon, still floating next to the Novice, mirrored the shrug. Many of the other Councillors smiled at the humorous display, and the young man nodded his appreciation to his audience. DeVir let the rings disappear and without warning, launched a stream of fire directly at the young man. Smiling though he was, the younger Dakkadian was obviously prepared for the attack, for the dragon disappeared in an instant, transforming instead into a solid shield that dissipated the flames without trouble. A second ball of fire shot from the instructor's hands, and again it was deflected. Again and again, DeVir attacked the Novice, but each attack was turned aside almost effortlessly by the Waterborn, who had stopped smiling and was now concentrating fully on the task at hand.

The Testing went on for hours, with each Councillor using his or her own abilities to look for weaknesses in the Novice's training. Time and again he rose to their challenge, and from the satisfied looks upon the Councillors' faces, Severeielle knew that the Testing was going very well indeed for the young man. Several times he found ways to break the building tension using humorous tricks, and at the end of the Test Severeielle smiled and clapped her hands softly, silently applauding his performance. The High Councillors stood up and approached the exhausted boy, offering him their congratulations and words of encouragement. The Dakkadian Archimagus put his arm around the newly promoted Mage and led him through the main doors, followed closely by the other seven Councillors. As the doors closed behind them, Severeielle relaxed her guard a fraction. She knew they would be back in a short time to test the second novice, but for now she had a respite.

"Quite the display, wouldn't you agree? The boy has a flair for the theatric."

The voice, coming from directly behind her, made her start in surprise, and she whirled around in shock as she recognized the speaker's voice.

"Astranaithes!" Severeielle hissed the name in surprise and shock, and then instinctively crouched low, fingers curling into talons as she prepared to do battle. The black dragon on her shoulders flared its wings and hissed as well, also preparing itself for a fight.

Astranaithes didn't react to the aggressive move, however; she simply nodded in greeting and stepped beside her to look down into the arena. Behind her stood Asiria, the Queen of Knowledge, watching silently from the side to see how events transpired.

"There is no need for that, Severeielle. I am not here to fight you. I merely wish to speak with you, if you will allow it."

Severeielle stood up slowly, fingers uncurling slightly, and with one last spiteful glance for her hated enemy, she stepped forward to stand beside her at the railing.

"It has been a long time since last we spoke, Severeielle. Not since the Valley of Fire have we stood together like this watching events unfold. You look well."

Severeielle decided to play along.

"As do you. The centuries have been good to you—which incidentally proves something that I've suspected all along: the world does not exactly abound with justice."

"No, it doesn't," she agreed readily, "and it never has. How is your brother?"

"What do you care?" Severeielle asked, venom dripping in her voice. "We both know that as he is now, he can no longer be of use to you. Why even bother to pretend otherwise?"

Astranaithes gave Severeielle an angry look.

"I care more than you know, Severeielle. Severius is a good man and a better friend, and though I continue to honor his request for solitude, I still cannot help but worry about him."

Severeielle tossed her hair back and laughed, the bitterness echoing in her voice.

"He is as well as can be expected, considering his condition. As I said before, the world does not exactly abound with justice."

"When you see him again, please convey my wish to speak with him when he is ready. We have things to discuss, he and I."

Severeielle whipped her head to the side in anger, giving Astranaithes a harsh glare.

"You tell him yourself. I am not one of your servants." She glanced at Asiria, still standing quietly behind the pair. "Perhaps you can ask your pet bookwyrm back there to pass on your request. I'm sure she's quite used to doing your bidding."

Asiria didn't respond to the jibe, but Astranaithes answered for her.

"Has your bitterness buried itself so deeply within you that you strike out at everyone and everything? Asiria is a friend and an associate, not a servant, and if you must strike out at someone for how you feel you've been wronged, make certain your target deserves your venom. You belittle yourself otherwise."

Severeielle felt herself growing angry at Astranaithes's condescending tone. She returned her attention to her rival and crossed her arms over her breasts.

"Why are you here, Astranaithes? We haven't spoken to each other in 2,500 years. Why show yourself now?"

Astranaithes looked back down at the arena.

"I should think that would be obvious, Severeielle; you're here, which means you know what is coming. As such, I felt it was past time for us to speak again."

Severeielle sneered, and then looked into the arena as well.

"You are supposed to be the wisest of our number. You tell me why you think I'm here."

Astranaithes didn't hesitate.

"Your motives are transparent to me, but I thought I should be polite. You seek the Harbinger. You ceaselessly prowl the shadows of this Citadel, watching young Mages for any sign of its reemergence. And if ever you should see such a sign, I believe you will attempt to kill the Mage before their power can manifest itself."

Severeielle's head whipped back around to look at Astranaithes.

"The Harbinger is an abomination! Its very existence is an affront to nature, and my greatest regret—my *only* regret!—is that I was young enough, *naïve* enough, to listen to you all those years ago when I had Zarryiosiad at my mercy! I could have killed her when she was nothing but the daughter of a powerful Waterborn. Any of us could have done the same! You, above all, knew that I wanted to! But Severius made me stay my hand, and he paid the price for his mercy. And such a price it was! *He did not deserve what was done to him!* And I, *I* am the one to blame. If I had kept my own council and had not listened to your useless prattling, Severius would never have been harmed." She laughed bitterly, a harsh expression on her face. "I was a fool then . . . but you won't trick me the same way twice, Queen of Fate! Pray that you find the Harbinger before I do, for this I vow: if I find the Harbinger before you do . . . if I even *suspect* I have found it, I will destroy it where it stands. I will kill it, or I will die trying."

Astranaithes's expression didn't change, but she shook her head in disappointment.

"So you would arrogate to yourself a role that only destiny can assign, would you? Have you learned nothing in all these years? Do you still refuse to understand? The Harbinger is a force of nature with *purpose*. It exists for a singular reason, just as the Champion does. Your brother understood this all too well! You are correct: he, too, could have tried to kill Zarryiosiad at any time during her life, and yet he didn't. He understood the potential consequences of making such an attempt and wisely chose to let destiny run its course."

Severeielle slashed her arm down in a savage quelling motion.

"You dare speak to me of *destiny*? Don't make me laugh, Astranaithes! He chose not to strike at her because you *told* him not to! If we had known what Zarryiosiad was to become, and how dangerous she would be, either one of us would gladly have put her down like a rabid dog!"

"And if you had failed?" Astranaithes asked. "If your actions had triggered the Harbinger's emergence before Fate needed her? Think of the consequences. If you had made the attempt on her life in the middle of Il'Amhar and had triggered her transformation then, tens of thousands of innocent people would have died *to absolutely no purpose!*"

Severeielle laughed again, and the bitter sound of it echoed through the empty arena.

"Tens of thousands of innocent people *did* die, or had you forgotten that?"

Astranaithes closed her eyes and bowed her head.

"I forget nothing, Severeielle. You are right: tens of thousands of innocent people did die in the fires of the Harbinger. But with them went the Lyx . . . every last one of them. Their threat was eliminated from this world."

The Queen of Shadows glared at her rival but said nothing, for there could be no agreement between them, even about something as self-evident as the complete annihilation of the Lyx. For her part, Astranaithes seemed content to let the matter rest, so rather than begin the old argument anew, Severeielle smiled slyly and said,

"I've noticed that Dakkadia seems to have made great strides in military innovation recently. *Very* recently. Is this your doing?"

"Yes."

The simple answer surprised Severeielle, who had obviously expected a denial or an evasion, and she narrowed her eyes in suspicion, wondering why Astranaithes would be so willing to admit her role in Dakkadia's rapid advancement in military might.

"A bold admission. Does the Lord of Snows know you stole the designs of his newest weapons and gave them to another country halfway across the world?"

"I *stole* nothing. Kaizenerimakagi *entrusted* me with the designs for both his weapons, and his newest ships of war, with the full knowledge I would, in turn, give the designs to someone who would understand their value and use them accordingly."

"He *allowed* you to take them? I find that very hard to believe! His artificers and alchemists have been working on those weapons for centuries, as a bulwark against the armies of Myerasalomé. It is death by slow torture to allow a black powder weapon to cross the Wall without an Imperial writ."

"Even so, the Lord of Snows allowed it. He, too, understands what is coming, and he, too, knows steps must be taken to prevent the world from ending."

Severeielle was too intrigued by the thought that the Lord of Snows himself might be a willing accomplice in the spread of his most important weapons to rise to the bait.

"But why give the weapons only to Dakkadia? Why not give them to all of the Western countries? It seems somehow . . . unfair."

"As you yourself pointed out to me, the world does not exactly abound with justice. The world is at stake, Severeielle, and fairness is a luxury we cannot afford. I gave the weapons to Dakkadia because I knew Dakkadia would understand their value. But more importantly, I gave them to Dakkadia because I knew that they would *use* them." Severeielle opened her mouth to answer, but Astranaithes held up a hand to forestall her. "I must tell you something, and there is little time left before the High Council returns. Though it pains me to tell you this I have no choice, for I, too, am but a servant of Fate. The Harbinger is returning. A chain of events has begun in which even we Dragon Witches will play a part. In a few moments you will see incontrovertible proof that what I say is true." She looked into Severeielle's eyes and held them with the intensity of her gaze. "Before those doors open, you must know this: the return of the Harbinger also heralds the rise of the Champion, but I caution you: do not let appearances deceive you! It would be the height of foolishness to make assumptions based solely off of what lies upon the surface."

Severeielle's expression changed to one of wariness, for she had no idea what Astranaithes's game was. It was clear that the Queen of Fate was trying to prepare her for some sort of a shock, but though her enemy's warnings were meant to calm and prepare, they were actually having the opposite effect upon her, for now she felt a trepidation that hadn't been present before.

Before she could respond, however, the great doors opened once again and the High Council returned to their seats. Both Severeielle and Astranaithes backed away from the observation point in order to remain unseen, but they needn't have worried, for the High Council did not bother to check the alcoves for observers. Once they were all seated, the First Chair, Se-ir Windwhisper, briefly touched his power, and a gust of wind opened a second set of doors. A young boy with white hair stepped through and walked into the middle of the arena, and one look at him was all it took to make Severeielle stagger backward in shock.

It can't *be!*

She rounded on Astranaithes, suspecting an illusion or a trap of some kind, but the look of profound sympathy upon Astranaithes's face told her that the Queen of Fate had had nothing to do with what she had just seen.

If it wasn't her, then how could this be?

Severeielle's shock wore off enough for her to regain her composure and step forward to observe the Testing. Astranaithes turned to the arena as well, and together they watched the boy who looked so much like Severius prepare himself for his test. *There is at least one difference between this young man and my brother: Severius is not a Mage.* She watched in silence as the young Powerborn summoned his magic and prepared his defensive circles, and as he moved, Severeielle felt herself once again being overwhelmed by emotion. *Mage or no, the way he moves—the way he carries himself—he is a mirror image of Severius the way he once was! How can this be?*

After a few moments of consideration, the boy turned to look at the assembled High Councillors and signaled his readiness. Once again, the Dakkadian Archimagus stood up and moved forward to begin the Testing.

Rancor forgotten in her shock, Severeielle turned to Astranaithes.

"Who is he?"

"He is Prince Valeriad Dhaerhan, the Crown Prince of Dakkadia. The man who was Tested before him is his half-brother, Lord Phaedron Daane. They were both raised in the Dakkadian court, and they were both taught to use their magic by Morvandis, the Mage-Lord of Dakkadia."

Severeielle returned her gaze to the arena.

"Morvandis," she hissed. "There was a time when I thought that he could be the Harbinger. I watched him closely for years, until it became too dangerous for me to spy upon him any longer. He nearly caught me on a number of occasions."

"As you were caught by the young Illymari Princess? That must have been mortifying."

Severeielle tried to ignore the mild jibe, but embarrassment colored her cheeks and an indignant expression crossed her face.

"It was merely poor luck on my part, or good fortune on hers. Either way, it will not happen again." The color faded from her cheeks and she glanced once again at Astranaithes, giving her a sly look. "The girl bears watching as well. She has the potential to be another Morvandis. And, I must say, I find the timing to be quite interesting. You say the Harbinger is returning, and by fortuitous coincidence, we now have a new Powerborn with the potential to perhaps one day rival the ability of the greatest living Mage? Coincidence?" She gestured at Valeriad, still displaying his mastery of Fire Magic. "And then we have Valeriad, who is so much like the former Champion that even I, Severius' twin sister, would have difficulty distinguishing them if I had seen them standing together." Suddenly the rancor was back. "Or rather, I would have had difficulty distinguishing them had I seen them standing together before you forced Severius to take up arms against Zarryiosiad."

Astranaithes's lips tightened in anger, and Severeielle laughed quietly as the Queen of Fate fought to regain her serenity.

"Do you know who will become the Harbinger? If you do, you could spare me much trouble and avoid many unnecessary deaths by telling me now. Although I am not averse to killing anyone that I think could have the potential to be the Harbinger, I absolutely despise waste. And with so many candidates to choose from there would be a lot of waste."

Astranaithes shook her head.

"I do not know who will become the Harbinger, nor do I know when it will appear; but I do know that it will come soon . . . most likely within no more than a handful of years."

Severeielle gave Astranaithes a look of disbelief.

"Surely it won't be that soon! Zarryiosiad lived for four hundred years as the Archon of Il'Amhar, and she bore seven children before she became the Harbinger. You expect me to believe that so much power can be created in such a short amount of time?"

"The Harbinger is, and always has been, a creature of destiny. It comes when and where it is needed, and when it arrives, has nothing whatsoever to do with how long it lives or how much power it has amassed before it transforms."

"I see your point. So then, Norn Queen, why are you telling me all of this, especially after the argument we just had over how we will deal with it? You know what I will do with this information."

"As I said, it pained me to tell you, for I knew how you would react. You will strike blindly at anyone and anything you can reach, hoping that by sheer luck you will kill the Harbinger. I gave you this information freely, but although you consider us to be enemies, I would ask of you one favor."

Severeielle narrowed her eyes, suspecting a trap.

"Name your favor. I will decide if I will honor it."

"That is all I ask. My favor is this: stay your hand until such time as you are absolutely certain of who is to become the Harbinger. If you begin killing people you merely suspect to be the one, you may inadvertently kill the Champion, or perhaps someone else who may be crucial to either the creation or the destruction of the Harbinger." She gave Severeielle a serious look. "If you refuse to show mercy, at least show restraint."

Severeielle turned away from the testing and walked deeper into the alcove.

"I've seen enough. Come, Cassiramaithris. We have no further business here."

Asiria, who had been completely silent during the entire exchange, leapt up in surprise as a long, dull dagger passed in front of her eyes, removed from where it had been resting right beneath her throat. She whirled in open-mouthed astonishment to look into the golden eyes of Cassiramaithris, the Queen of Assassins, who was standing directly behind her, so close she could feel her breath. The red dragon sitting upon her shoulder watched Asiria closely as the white-haired, pale-skinned killer stepped back a pace and settled her dagger back into its sheath, before moving silently to where Severeielle was standing. In a panic, Asiria reflexively reached up to touch her neck checking for wounds, but to her relief she found nothing. Cassiramaithris' expression didn't change, but Severeielle gave her a cruel smile.

"Had I wanted you dead, bookwyrm, you would be dead . . . and you wouldn't have felt a thing. Cassiramaithris has been here for days, scouting out your wards and preparing the way for me to return."

She turned her cruel smile to Astranaithes.

"You see? Despite what you think, I *am* capable of showing restraint when the situation warrants it." She raised a mocking eyebrow and said, "I thank you for your information, and I promise you I will consider your request."

Black wings made of purest shadow emerged from behind her and settled in front of the two Dragon Witches, closing in front of them like a cloak.

"And how will I know your answer?" Astranaithes asked.

The shadows enveloped the women until only two pairs of glowing red eyes could be seen at all. From the blackness, Severeielle's voice emerged.

"Should you begin finding the bodies of promising young Mages littering these halls, you will have your answer. If not, restraint. You and I shall not speak again." Her voice began to fade slightly, as if she were moving away from them. "As I am feeling generous, I will pass on your message to Severius. If he wishes to speak with you, he will contact you himself."

With that, the darkness faded, leaving nothing behind to show that the Queen of Shadows and the Queen of Assassins had ever been there.

Asiria, still touching her neck, moved to stand next to Astranaithes.

"That was absolutely terrifying. I had no inkling Cassiramaithris was even here, let alone standing close enough to place a dagger to my throat. She could have killed me without warning." She gave Astranaithes a slight frown. "You choose your enemies well, it seems."

"And my allies as well, my daughter." Astranaithes arched an eyebrow, before looking at someone over Asiria's shoulder. "They are gone. You may come out, Furionchires."

Another movement from the supposedly empty alcove made Asiria jump yet again, and a brown-haired woman with a red dragon on her shoulders stepped forward, thin sword held in a gauntleted grip. The Queen of Battles sheathed her sword, before moving up to stand beside them. She gave the stricken Asiria a grin and clapped her soundly on the back.

"I could not have prevented her from killing you, perhaps, but I promise you that she would have joined you in death. Had that little backstabber struck you down, her body would now be lying atop of yours."

"Thank you for your assurances," Asiria said. "I'm sure I would rest easier knowing that you had so quickly and efficiently dealt with my murderer. Of course," and she shot Astranaithes another very level glare, "I would have rested even easier had I known you were there in the first place."

Furionchires' brown eyes flashed with humor and she clapped Asiria on the back yet again.

"I am sorry that I did not inform you beforehand of my precautions," Astranaithes said in apology, "but I needed Furionchires to stay hidden—just as I needed you to be completely unaware I had even brought her. Severeielle would not have spoken with me had she not believed that somehow she held an advantage, and your reaction to Cassiramaithris' appearance was convincing enough to confirm to her that she caught me off-guard. If it is any consolation, I do not believe that your life was ever in any danger: so long as I presented no threat to the Queen of Shadows, she had no reason to strike at you. Or me."

Asiria remained obviously unconvinced but was willing to give her the benefit of the doubt.

"Do you think she will stay her hand?"

Astranaithes closed her eyes.

"I cannot be certain, of course, but I believe she will. Not because I asked it of her, for her hatred of me runs too deeply for her to consider anything I say with objectivity. No, the only person she will listen to on this matter is Severius himself. That is why I insisted that she 'pass on a message' for me. Severius already knows what is transpiring, but I want *Severeielle* to speak with him, for the Lord of Time may be able to convince her where I could not."

"How can you be so sure? Severius has changed. The Lord of *Death* is not the man he once was."

She emphasized his new title, trying to judge Astranaithes's response, and to her surprise the Queen of Fate smiled in amusement.

"The warning I gave Severeielle also applies to you, Asiria: Do not let appearances deceive you. It would be the height of foolishness to make assumptions based solely upon what lies on the surface. Although Severeielle and Cassiramaithris have both become embittered by his condition, Severius himself has not changed from the man he once was."

Asiria frowned skeptically.

"How can you possibly know that? You said yourself that you have not spoken with him. How can you be so certain that the Lord of Death hasn't changed?"

"Because, I lied to Severeielle. The truth is, I have spoken to Severius a number of times since the Valley of Fire, and he has adjusted to his new reality surprisingly well. He chooses to view his situation with grace and humor, and without the slightest hint of doubt or regret. Anyone who truly knew him could have expected nothing less."

She nodded at Furionchires and stepped away from the railing.

"It is time for us to leave. If I am wrong about Severeielle and she does decide to start killing people at random, do not try to stop her yourself. Either

FURIONCHIRES, THE QUEEN OF BATTLES

Severeielle or Cassiramaithris would kill you in an instant. Contact me instead, and I will find some way to deal with the problem."

Astranaithes held Asiria's gaze until the golden-haired woman nodded her agreement. Suddenly, a green line appeared in the air and stretched into a circle that became a portal into darkness. Furionchires stepped through first, then Astranaithes stepped through behind her, but before fading into the darkness, she turned once again to Asiria.

"I thank you for your help today, daughter. This may not have seemed like an important event, but I assure you that it was. Sometimes, the greatest of triumphs or the most terrible of tragedies can begin with a seemingly insignificant event. Goodbye, for now. You know how to contact me."

With that, the doorway faded from existence, leaving the Queen of Knowledge alone on the alcove. As Asiria returned to her library, she thought about the things she had just witnessed, and could not help but wonder which way it would end; in triumph, or tragedy?

Valeriad wiped the sweat from his eyes and tried not to show his triumph. He had weathered everything the High Council could throw at him and was still standing, albeit a bit unsteadily. The Testing had gone on for hours, and now that they were nearing the end, he felt as if he had been forced to swim from Dakkadia to Illymar in the middle of a hurricane. He thought about Phaedron briefly, vowing to thank him for his generosity in taking the first Test.

I don't think I could have passed the Test if I hadn't eaten. This took every bit of energy I had, and some I didn't know was there.

He also vowed to thank Morvandis for his training, for the time he had spent preparing both Phaedron and him for the Testing had been time well spent. From what he could tell, the High Council seemed to agree with the sentiment, for they had each indicated their approval of his skills, and as far as he was concerned, that could only be a good thing.

The First Chair stood up, and Valeriad prepared himself for anything. Phaedron had warned him about being wary of surprises earlier that day, and he'd been absolutely right. Any time he had seemed to be losing concentration or tiring, whichever Mage was evaluating him at the time would strike at him without warning, and never the same way twice. He'd been singed a few times from close calls, but to his credit, nothing had actually reached him. *As Morvandis says, "'close' is simply a polite way of saying that you failed."* He grinned cockily at the Council despite his weariness. *Morvandis was right: you might have come* close *to reaching me, Councillors, but you didn't. That means you failed.*

He tensed himself for another attack, but the First Chair merely nodded.

"You may release the power and lower your defenses. The Testing is over."

Valeriad's shoulders slumped at the words, and what little energy he had left slowly left him. He released his hold on his magic, and the defensive wards he had placed around himself disappeared as if they had never existed. He wanted to sit down and catch his breath, but the Dakkadian in him would not allow him to show that much weakness in front of others, so despite his exhaustion, he stood up straight to hear their pronouncement.

"Congratulations, Prince Valeriad," the First Chair said. "After careful consideration of your worthiness to be awarded the title of Mage, the Council has decided unanimously to grant you the title without reservation. Congratulations, Mage. Your name will be entered into the records, and you will be allowed all of the rights and privileges associated with your title, as well as citizenship to Ithram."

As soon as the High Councillor finished speaking, Cedric DeVir smiled and began clapping. All eight members of the council joined him in the accolade and, as one, the Councillors stood up and moved around the table to shake his hand and congratulate him personally. Valeriad couldn't stop smiling as he shook each of their hands, and when they were done, they began filing out of the room through the door they had entered. Cedric stayed behind and placed a hand on his shoulder.

"That was very well done, Prince Valeriad, very well done, indeed. Some of the Council Members were a bit harder on you than they would have been with a regular Novice, not because of who you are or where you come from, but because you were not trained here. They considered it to be their 'duty' to prove that training outside of the confines of the Citadel is inherently inferior to the training you would have received here. But, between you and Phaedron, I believe they will have to rethink their positions in the future. You were both brilliant."

Valeriad took a deep breath.

"I'm just glad the Testing ended when it did. I don't think I had much left in me."

"That part is deliberate. We have to push you to your limits and beyond, to see exactly what you are made of. If you can be broken, it is better by far to learn it here where no one can be hurt than somewhere else where innocent people could die." He squeezed Valeriad's shoulder. "A Fireborn is a dangerous weapon! Always remember that. But, as with any weapon, in the right hands it becomes a tool of surpassing usefulness." He turned Valeriad toward the second set of doors and pointed. "Now go and get something to eat, and rest for a while. In an hour or so, I will collect you to escort you to the docks. Lord Phaedron and Lady

Prudence have already left for the *Sovereign,* so, for now, you are my responsibility—at least until you leave the island for good."

Valeriad opened the doors and stepped through alone, and was happy to see his friends waiting for him. Adrianna and Chesare stood to one side, while a third member in a hooded cloak stood talking to them with her back turned to him. He noticed that the third person was holding his belt, his sword and dagger, and his pistol, and he cleared his throat to gain her attention. As the girl turned around, his smile slipped and he stood dumbstruck as he instantly recognized Princess Lyrahe. Lyrahe's face brightened in glorious welcome when she saw him, and he stepped toward her quickly, holding out his arms for an embrace. She lowered his belt to her side and rushed to him, jumping into his arms and allowing him to squeeze her tightly. As they spun around and around, holding each other, Valeriad noticed Adrianna reach out and tug on Chesare's arm, and together they left the hall, giving Valeriad and Lyrahe their privacy. When they were alone, he let his hands travel to her waist, and stepped back still holding her.

"What are you doing here? You shouldn't be here!"

Lyrahe raised an eyebrow at him, a mischievous look in her eye.

"Oh? Should I leave then? I think my carriage is still out in front."

Valeriad frowned in mock disappointment.

"That won't be necessary, though I am more than a bit disappointed."

She raised her chin slightly and pretended to pout.

"Disappointed?"

He nodded soberly.

"Disappointed. You see, I had just about decided upon this elaborate plan to sneak out of the Citadel, scale the walls of the Spire, and climb in through your bedroom window to speak with you before we left, but you've put an end to that plan, it seems. Pity—it seemed like such a wonderful idea as I was imagining it."

"And in your fevered imagination did you also imagine the guards would simply allow you to scale the walls unimpeded? Or that they would let you climb to my window in broad daylight?"

"I'll admit that part did seem to escape my planning."

"I'm glad I came to you, then. Seeing your body lying beneath my window, feathered with dozens of arrows, would probably have been a little distressing."

He gave her a mock hurt look, and she rewarded him by leaning up and kissing his cheek.

"It's the thought that counts, I guess," he said with a smile.

She held up his sword belt.

"I held these for you. Adrianna said you would need them as soon as the Testing was completed."

He nodded thankfully and held up his arms, and with a playful smile she stepped behind him and reached around his waist while holding both ends of the belt. To his surprise, she pressed herself into his back and molded her own body to his, as she manipulated the sword belt without looking. She took her time, slender arms tightening around his waist, and he could feel the quick pace of her heartbeat against his back as she fastened the silver buckle in place.

Once she was done, she let go of his buckle and reluctantly stepped away, but he caught her hands before they could drop away from his waist. He turned around slowly, still holding her arms in his hands, and when they were finally face-to-face, he leaned forward and waited. He didn't have to wait for long, for she rose up on her toes and kissed him; tenderly at first, then with mounting passion. He returned her kiss with matching ardor, and with lips still pressed against each other, they backed up until they found a bench and sat down together. After several minutes she pulled herself away, face flushed with rapture.

"I never understood before. I never understood why Tais would throw away absolutely everything she had to be with the man she loved. But now I know. I would have done the same."

She punctuated her words with another passionate kiss, and then it was Valeriad's turn to pull away.

"Lain was a fool. I would take you with me if I could. I would take you away to Dakkadia, and marry you in an instant."

She gave him a pleading look that tore at his heart.

"Then do it! I'll willingly go with you! Take me away from here. I want to be with you!"

Even before she had finished speaking Valeriad started shaking his head.

"I would never do that, Lyrahe, not to you. I'll not steal you away in the night like some sort of brigand. No, my love, *when* we marry, I promise you that it will be in the open with all to see."

She shook her head in misery.

"My father will never allow it."

He gripped his sword's hilt.

"Then I won't give him a choice. My family leaves for Dakkadia tonight, but I swear to you now that I will be back for you. When the Dakkadian army returns, I will be with it. Nothing will keep us apart. If I have to defeat every army your father sets in front of me to get to you, I will. And when I have, when at last we are together, I promise you that I'll never leave your side again."

An hour later, Valeriad and Lyrahe stood together in the courtyard. Nearby, Cedric sat in the saddle of a spotted palfrey, holding the reins of a white stallion for the Prince. Lyrahe held his hand, refusing to let go even though they both knew he couldn't possibly stay. Cedric allowed them a little time, but eventually he cleared his throat to gain their attention.

"We have to leave. The tide is coming in and *Sovereign* awaits you."

Valeriad nodded to the older Mage and turned to Lyrahe.

"This is goodbye then, my love. Remember what I said in the hall. I will be back for you." She closed her eyes and nodded, fighting bravely against the tears threatening to fall from her emerald eyes. Valeriad's own sky blue eyes were moist as well, and he laughed at the absurdity of the situation. "Don't be sad, Lyrahe. This is simply the beginning. We'll see each other again, and when we do, we'll never be apart again."

With that, she threw herself into his arms and embraced him.

"Have a safe journey, my love. I'll be counting the days until you come for me again."

Unmindful of the people standing in the courtyard, he threw propriety to the wind and leaned forward to kiss her soundly. She melted into his arms, returning his kiss with equal passion, and then he pulled away from her, climbed into his saddle, and rode away. As they rode through the main gate, he looked back one last time; just in time to see her wave goodbye.

PRINCESS LYRAHE ILLVANNA OF ILLYMAR

CHAPTER TWENTY-THREE

“Schism”

Cedric guided Valeriad through the streets of Illymaine and to the docks, where the *Sovereign* was ready to depart. Crowds of people were standing nearby, watching the ship with expressions ranging from anger and rage, to awe and almost superstitious dread. He smiled at the last, for the black sails of Prudence’s ship with the single white stripe of Dakkadia, were a stark contrast to the white canvas sails of the Illymari fleet, several ships, of which, could be seen prowling nearby. Cedric knew that in the darker tales of the Corsair, the distinctive sails were described as a portent of great evil.

Despite those old wives’ tales, Cedric wasn’t worried that the crowd would try anything, for a full battalion of the Mage Guard was on hand to enforce the Peace of Zarryiosiad. The attack upon Lady Prudence had been an affront the Zarryiostrom, one the Mage Council refused to let happen again, so they had dispatched the soldiers to guard the ship as it sat vulnerable in the dock. By the terms of the agreement all three rulers had signed before the Convocation had convened, the Peace would hold until both the Ferralin and the Dakkadian contingents were safely docked in their respective harbors. After that, Cedric knew that Madari would declare open warfare between Illymar and Dakkadia. But, until then, the truce remained in effect.

As the Mages approached the back of the crowd, it parted for them without protest, although several people did strain their necks to catch a glimpse of the riders. Some of the citizens recognized his robe and bowed or knuckled their foreheads in respect before stepping aside, but most people didn't bother. Instead, they waited for the riders to pass and then returned their attention to the far more important matter of watching the Corsair's ship preparing to depart.

When they reached the warship, Valeriad dismounted and handed the reins to a sailor before yelling up to the deck.

"Permission to come aboard?"

The Master-at-arms stepped forward and looked down the gangplank.

"Permission granted!"

He didn't walk up immediately, however. Instead, he waited for Cedric to dismount and join him. Cedric handed his reins to the same sailor and held out his arm, indicating Valeriad should go first. Valeriad stepped onto the gangplank and walked quickly up to the deck, with Cedric following a pace behind him. When they reached the top, each of them could immediately sense that something was terribly wrong.

The crew was going about its business as usual, but quietly, almost as if they were afraid to draw attention to themselves. Valeriad frowned at Cedric, almost asking if he knew what was going on, but Cedric shrugged his own ignorance, for he knew as much as Valeriad did. Instead of talking to one of the crew members, Valeriad gripped his sword's hilt and walked purposefully toward the doorway leading below deck, Cedric again staying one step behind.

At the bottom of the stairs they heard someone shouting, and both he and Valeriad increased their pace to find out what was happening. When they reached the room that the shouts were emanating from, they found King Madari and Phaedron standing toe-to-toe with each other, obviously in the middle of a very heated exchange. Neither of them would break eye contact with the other, even when the two newcomers entered the room, and Cedric had no idea what to say. Valeriad did, however.

"What is going on here? Why are you fighting?"

Phaedron pointed a finger at Madari.

"This *man* beat our mother to within an inch of her life last night. Her eye is swollen shut, her wrist is broken, and she can't even sit up without help! She had to be carried aboard ship on a stretcher like an invalid!"

Cedric reeled back in shock, for if the accusation was true, it marked a tremendous change in the way Madari had decided to treat Aveliad. He knew that there was no love lost between Madari and Aveliad, but as far as he knew, Madari had never raised a hand to her before. Something serious must have happened between them to push him over the edge. Valeriad turned to his father.

"Father? Is this true?"

Madari nodded savagely, still refusing to take his eyes off of Phaedron.

"It's true," he growled. "What Phaedron here refuses to understand is that I've had just about all of the disrespect that I intend to take from either her *or* her son *ever* again!"

"Respect isn't given, it's *earned!*" growled Phaedron. "What you did last night was beneath contempt! By all rights, I should kill you right now for raising your hand to her!"

He reached for the hilt of his sword, but Madari spoke before he could touch it.

"Morvandis, if that blade leaves its scabbard, kill him where he stands!"

Cedric glanced to the side, where Morvandis had been standing so silently he'd been almost invisible. But as Phaedron's hand touched the hilt of his weapon, Morvandis's eyes seemed to ignite with white-hot fire. A single look at the Mage was enough to tell Cedric that if Phaedron was foolish enough to actually draw his weapon, Morvandis wouldn't hesitate to follow Madari's order. Luckily, Valeriad stopped Phaedron before he could finish committing suicide. He jumped forward and placed his hand atop of Phaedron's, preventing him from drawing his rapier.

"That's enough, Phaedron! You know what happened last night after the dinner! I'm sure Father didn't mean to hurt Mother, but after all the things that happened yesterday, including his fight with King Orem, I'm sure he just wasn't himself! He was angry, that's all! *I'm* angry, and I wasn't even there! So just forget about it. I'm sure Mother will be just fine. It's a long trip home, and she'll have plenty of time to rest and recover. Come on, leave it be."

He pulled Phaedron's hand away from his weapon and Cedric breathed a sigh of relief. Madari didn't look relieved, however, he looked contemptuous.

"Is that it, then? Is that all you have to say?" When Phaedron didn't reply, he said, "Good! Now *you* will listen to what *I* have to say, or by the Archon, I'll have Morvandis kill you anyway, you ungrateful little bastard! All these years I've tried to be good to you out of respect for your father's memory, but for some reason you decided you didn't want that from me. You continuously throw my generosity and compassion in my face, and then you hide behind my love for your mother to avoid the consequences! All your life you have treated me with the same contempt and disrespect your mother has shown me, so today you get your wish! Today I become your King, and *nothing* else! And as your King, I command you to stay away from me and *my* family for the rest of the journey home. You will not be allowed to speak to me, and you will not speak with anyone *about* me. I do not want to hear your name spoken by *anyone!* And when we make it home to Dakkadia, you will not continue on with us to the capital. You will go to your estates at Daane, and you will stay away from the capital until I personally send for you again. I have put up with your insolence and disrespect long enough! If you were anyone else but Aveliad's son, I would have killed you myself a long time ago! Now, *get out of my sight!*"

Phaedron glared at Madari for several seconds, then raised his hand in the Dakkadian salute, hand touching heart. Without saying another word, he spun on his heels and left the room, knocking Valeriad out of his way with his shoulder.

Valeriad turned to follow him, but Madari bellowed,

"Let him go! You are not to speak with him either, Valeriad!" The young Prince stopped in the doorway, hovering on the brink of defying his father, but he didn't. Instead, he turned back to his father and gave him a disapproving look.

"Despite what I said to Phaedron, whatever the provocation might have been, you were wrong to hit Mother. It was inexcusable. I hope you see that."

Madari's face tightened with anger, but instead of lashing out at Valeriad as Cedric expected, he seemed to let go of his rage as he looked down at his gloved hands, refusing to meet his son's gaze.

"I know it. And as shameful as it is for me to admit it, I knew it was wrong even as I was doing it. She has been cruel and spiteful to me throughout our entire marriage, but even she did not deserve what I did to her." He took a deep breath. "But done is done. I will not apologize either to her or to Phaedron for my actions . . . not that either one of them would ever accept any apology from me, no matter how sincere." He gritted his teeth and tightened his hand into a fist, then looked up at Valeriad. "A man or a husband can make mistakes, but a King cannot afford to. A country draws its strength from its leader. Therefore, to ensure a country stays strong, a King must make even his worst mistakes seem as if they were all part of a greater design. That is your first lesson in kingship, Valeriad."

Cedric cleared his throat to gain Madari's attention.

"If you don't mind, I will check on Queen Aveliad and say my farewells."

"You have my permission, but when you have finished speaking with her, I want you to come back here. You and I have something to discuss before we leave. Something important."

Cedric frowned slightly at Madari's tone, but said nothing

He didn't know exactly where to find her, so he stuck his head into several different rooms until he spotted her. She was lying asleep in her bed, a porcelain bowl on a stand next to her. He winced when he saw the bowl, for a moist cloth spotted with blood sat on the rim, and the water was noticeably pink. He moved to stand next to her, and when he saw the condition she was in, he felt his blood start to boil.

One look at her face was enough to send the normally mild Archimagus into a fury, and he had to suppress his murderous rage before he confronted Madari as Phaedron had done. Aveliad's face was red and raw, with large blackened bruises spotting her cheeks and eyes, and though she did not wear her mask, even he, her half-brother, could hardly recognize her. He reached down and touched her hair softly, and her one good eye fluttered open. For a moment he saw terror in her amber eye, but when she recognized his face, the fear slowly left her and she managed a tremulous smile through swollen lips. Her normally melodious voice was weaker than normal, but she still managed to make her words clear enough to be understood.

"Cedric. It is good to see you."

He reached down to take her hand, but then he noticed that the hand he was reaching for was wrapped in a tight bandage. He instead reached for her other hand, and held it gently in both of his.

"It's good to see you, too, Aveliad, though I have to say that you have looked better."

"I've looked better, it is true, but the physicians say that I will be fine with time and rest. I suppose I should be thankful; Madari was selectively brutal. What was done to me was deliberately calculated to hurt me without crippling or permanently scarring me." Her eye filled with tears and she squeezed his hand. "I thought he was going to kill me."

Cedric pulled up a chair next to her and sat down without letting go of her hand.

"Can you tell me what happened? Why did he do this to you?"

She looked away, closing her eye and shuddering as the memory of the vicious beating returned to her.

"He believes that I came between him and Princess Tais. He tried to seduce her, and I warned her against him. When he found out what I had done, he . . . he lost control of himself. Afterward, he called it 'punishment' and told me that if I would not love him, and I would not respect him, then I would fear him." She turned to look at him again, and he saw misery within her eye. "I do, Cedric. I fear him."

Cedric didn't know what to say to the abused woman, so he held her hand and let her cry herself out. Eventually though, her tears dried up and she gave his hand a grateful squeeze.

"Thank you for listening to me. I can't tell my children what happened or why, and no one else cares. It feels good to get it off of my chest."

Cedric was happy that he could be of some service at least.

"Speaking of your children, you would have been proud today. With no warning and no time to prepare, they still received top marks during the Testing. As of today, both of them have been awarded the title of Mage. You should be delighted that you have raised two fine young men such as Phaedron and Valeriad."

She smiled at the news, happy that Cedric had changed topics.

"I wish I could have seen them during the Test."

Cedric laughed.

"Phaedron, in particular, was quite entertaining." He leaned back in his chair and smiled in memory. "I swear to you, Aveliad, he looks more and more like his father every day. He has his father's keen sense of humor, his outgoing personality, and his finely honed charisma. Everyone at the Citadel liked him, and the Mage Guard in particular was sorry to see him go. I know for a fact that the Commandant of the Mage Guard was prepared to offer him a commission."

"Madari hates Phaedron, too, you know, and he always has. It's because he looks like so much like Phaedril that Madari hates him."

Cedric's smile disappeared.

"There is something you should know, Aveliad. I saw the two of them arguing just a few minutes ago. Phaedron wanted to kill Madari for what he did to you, but Madari ordered Morvandis to kill him if he tried anything. Phaedron desisted, but Madari has ordered him to stay away from all of the members of the royal family for the length of the voyage: including you. Furthermore, when you return to Dakkadia, Phaedron has been ordered to return to the Daane estates, and to stay away from the capital until Madari personally sends for him."

"So, he has taken my son away from me as well. Phaedron's reaction was predictable, and Madari undoubtedly counted on it to provide him with all the justification he needed to send him away." She looked back at Cedric and all self-pity was gone from her amber eye. "There will come a day when the bad blood between Phaedron and Madari will come to a head, and when that day comes, I want you to promise me that you will be there for Phaedron if he needs you. I have asked nothing of our family, not even when Phaedril died and our brother Brendenn sold me to Madari to secure his own titles and power. I ask this of you now: when the time comes, protect Phaedron from Madari's vengeance."

Cedric gave her hand one final squeeze.

"You have my word." He looked at the door and said, "I have to go. The *Sovereign* is ready to depart, and Madari wishes to speak with me before you sail. Be well, Aveliad. You have always been my favorite sibling."

She smiled at him in thanks, and he lowered her hand to her side and stood up. As he left the room to return to Madari's cabin, he felt his anger returning. He didn't want to speak with anyone capable of doing something so heinous, but he could not simply ignore the summons, so he set his anger aside and walked to where Madari was waiting. As he stepped into the doorway, he saw Madari sitting behind a large map table, studying some papers. Cedric knocked once on the doorframe and Madari looked up. As was customary with the Dakkadian King, he didn't waste time with small talk.

"We leave the instant your boots hit the dock, Archimagus. Before we go, however, I want to warn you that we *will* be back, and probably much sooner than Illymar would wish."

Cedric gave Madari a level look.

"So, you intend invasion. I wish you luck with that particular endeavor, Your Majesty, for I can assure you now that the High Council will not allow it."

"So certain are you? I think you may be surprised."

Cedric laughed harshly at that, letting some of his anger at Aveliad's condition show.

"As I said, I wish you luck with that. I, for one, will vote against allowing you to set foot upon this island again, especially if you are at the head of your army." He glanced at Morvandis and suddenly the image of Enaria touching Morvandis's hand at the Cathedral returned to him. His eyes narrowed as he suddenly realized the serious implications of that simple act. "You've been planning to invade all along, haven't you? And you needed to find a way to neutralize the Council as a threat. At least, I assume that's why Morvandis spent so much of his time at the Citadel attempting to seduce Archimagus Wintersong. You need her vote."

Madari frowned in confusion at the accusation, which surprised Cedric, but Morvandis smiled slightly.

"Though I will concede that a relationship does exist between Archimagus Wintersong and myself, you have drawn the wrong conclusions about the relationship's origins, for I did not approach her. Enaria came to me for reasons of her own; though I'll readily admit that after my initial hesitation, I welcomed the company. She is a remarkable woman, after all."

Cedric frowned at the admission, for as far-fetched as it might have sounded, he found he believed Morvandis's words.

He has no reason to lie to me, but in the end, does it matter if he approached Enaria or Enaria approached him? Either way, I have to assume that because there is a relationship, she will vote to allow a Dakkadian invasion.

Madari returned his attention to Cedric.

"Despite what you may think, I came to Illymar in good faith, hoping to negotiate a treaty between King Orem and myself. Unfortunately, I see now that I never had a realistic chance of accomplishing that one simple goal. When we first arrived, Orem ignored me completely, choosing to snub me in favor of toadying up to Emperor Xan instead of attempting to find common ground between our two realms. Later, when he felt that the alliance between his kingdom and the Empire of Ferralin was a matter of record, Orem publicly insulted me without provocation. He then attempted to have your own kinswoman, Lady Prudence, murdered despite the Peace of Zarryiosiad—a peace that both the Zarryiostrom and the Mage High Council were honor-bound to uphold. And finally, after Xan approached me to register his displeasure with the attack on Lady Prudence, and he and I came to an agreement that excluded Illymar, Orem lashed out at Emperor Xan, thereby impugning the honor of a sovereign ally of Dakkadia. These are all serious offenses that demand redress, so, you are right: I intend invasion. But you are wrong when you say that I have been planning to invade all along, for I did not want any of this to happen. By his own arrogance, Orem has forced my hand." He stood up and walked around the table to stand before Cedric. "When the time comes, and I do return here with the Dakkadian army, I hope you will consider what I've said to you today when the Council is forced to vote." Without warning, he reached out and pushed Cedric against the doorframe, holding him in place with a powerful hand. "And should you decide to vote against me anyway, I advise you to think about the example that I have made of Aveliad, and remember what happens to people who stand between me and the things that I want. If you bear any love at all for your sister, or her son, you will think twice before you cross me."

Phaedron sat upon his favorite spot on the *Sovereign* and watched Illymari ships pass by in the distance. There were more sails in the bay than normal, and he frowned as he realized that many of the ships were military vessels—several squadrons worth at least. They were all sailing in a complicated formation that had them interweaving with each other at relatively high speeds.

They're on maneuvers. Orem is already preparing his navy for war.

He studied the elaborate formations a bit closer, and laughed when he realized what the complicated pattern was meant to do.

It seems they've prepared a special 'good-bye' for us. That should make for an interesting departure.

He heard soft footsteps behind him and turned to see Prudence approach, also watching the ships. Her left arm was resting in a sling, but from what Phaedron could tell, she did not seem to be in any pain.

"Do you recognize the pattern? Do you know what they are planning to do?" she asked.

"Yes. They plan to entertain us with a pretty ballet, meant to impress us with their superior seamanship. Do you have a response prepared?"

She shrugged stiffly, minimizing the movement of her left arm.

"I was planning to ignore them. Let them posture. Their proud maneuvers will do them no good on the high seas when I have them in my sights. Although, I have to admit, that their movements are flawless. Say what you will about the Bathtub Admiral, but his navy is well-trained."

Phaedron went back to studying the sails. After a few quiet moments, Corsair sat next to him on the railing.

"I heard about your quarrel with . . ."

Phaedron raised his hand to stop her.

"I have been ordered by my King not to discuss that particular subject with anyone, nor am I allowed to see *his* family for the entirety of this journey."

Prudence frowned at his acerbic tone.

"The *Sovereign* is not *that* large. How are you supposed to avoid him for two weeks?"

"It doesn't matter. I did a good job of avoiding him on the way here. I'll simply continue to take my meals with the crew." He looked back at the men and women going about their business, preparing the ship for departure. "You have a fine crew, Prudence. I am proud to spend my time among them."

"You could join us, you know. There is a place for you aboard the *Sovereign* if you wish it."

Phaedron's eyebrows rose up in surprise at the offer, for it was one that he hadn't considered, but just as quickly, he knew that it was an offer that he couldn't readily accept.

"It is kind of you to extend the invitation, Prudence, but we both know that I shouldn't accept."

"Why shouldn't you?"

Phaedron leaned forward and took her hand.

"Because I could never be content to simply be one of your crewmembers, Lady Prudence." He gestured toward the crew they had just been contemplating. "The Dakkadian navy allows mixed crews, but does not allow those same crews to establish relationships aboard ship, and for good reason. What your crew does in port is their own business, but aboard ship they are not allowed to express their feelings physically, for a ship is too small a world to allow jealousy to rear its ugly head. If I was to come aboard as a crewmember, I tell you now I would not be able to keep my hands off of you, and that could only damage your ability to lead the crew."

Prudence smiled at him briefly, but then she closed her eyes, raised her chin, and tossed her hair back in a haughty gesture.

"I think you would be surprised at what behavior the crew is prepared to accept from their Captain. From the not-so-subtle talk I've overheard, and comments that have been made by Mr. Salazar and my officers, they seem to think that you are good for me. But that is beside the point. You seem pretty sure of yourself, Lord Daane. What makes you so certain I would allow you to 'express your feelings physically' with me? Perhaps I simply want to add another Waterborn to my stable of Mages."

Phaedron chuckled at that and let go of her hand.

"I guess there is only one way to be sure."

She opened her eyes just in time to see him lean forward to kiss her, and she responded to him by leaning forward to meet him halfway. As their lips touched each other for the first time, he enfolded her in his arms, turning her slightly to the side so that she rested gently in his powerful arms where he could control the intensity of the kiss. They remained like that for a while, lips moving against each other with rising passion. Eventually he tried to pull away from her, but her fingers had somehow found their way to the back of his head and she held him in place, not wanting the moment to end.

When they finally did part, they sat back and glanced at the crew, who had all stopped what they were doing to watch their Captain, broad grins on every single one of their faces. When they saw her look at them, they immediately turned back to their duties, ostentatiously pretending for her benefit that they hadn't seen a thing. The absurdity of the crew's actions made her laugh out loud, and at her side she could hear Phaedron join her in laughter. When she looked back at Phaedron, however, his smile had been replaced by a serious look.

"I've wanted to do that for weeks, Prudence, but there never seemed to be a right time. Call it cowardice if you wish, but I simply could not muster up the nerve to do what I now know we both wanted all along."

"I was wondering what you were waiting for," she said. "While I hesitate to admit that I desperately wanted you to be more forward with me, the truth is I've been looking forward to that kiss from the day I first set eyes on you. And at the risk of adversely affecting the discipline of my command, I want you to know that from now on I won't be waiting for you to make the first move. Two weeks isn't nearly as long as you might think." She reached out to grab the front of his shirt, pulling him toward her to deliver another powerful kiss. "From now on, I'll take what I want. I have a reputation to protect, you know."

His brilliant smile at her words filled her heart with joy.

Movement from the back of the warship forced them to part, and Cedric came to the deck followed by Madari and Morvandis. Cedric left the vessel without ceremony, and seconds after the Archimagus had departed Madari looked at Prudence.

"Take us away from this accursed isle."

Without waiting for her response, he spun on his heels and went back below the deck, followed closely by Morvandis. Corsair didn't hesitate. She gave Phaedron one last smile, before standing up and walking away from him, shouting orders to her crew that were instantly obeyed. Within moments, the *Sovereign* was moving away from the docks and toward open water.

As they pulled away from the harbor, Phaedron turned his attention back to the maneuvers the Illymari fleet was currently performing in the bay. Several squadrons, made up of dozens of ships, were sailing in a figure "8" pattern that had ships passing each other with only feet to spare at the center of the formation. It was an impressive showing of seamanship, meant not only to intimidate the Dakkadian sailors, but to block their passage, for attempting to sail through the figure "8" would be impossible to accomplish without at least one ship or another physically colliding with the *Sovereign.* What they were trying to accomplish with the maneuver was to force the *Sovereign* to back down and sail around them rather than risk collision. Unfortunately for the Illymari, the Corsair obviously had other ideas. She set her course toward the very heart of their formation, clearly intending to pass right through the center of it. Phaedron grinned in anticipation of the event, and felt two sets of boots approach him from behind. He glanced over his shoulder, already knowing who would be there, and he nodded a greeting to Rory Sornin and Cahrick Rantrefal as they moved to either side of him at the forward railing.

"Good evening, Your Lordship. The Cap'n sends her compliments, and asks if you would be willing to help us clear a bit o' rubbish from our path."

"I would be delighted," Phaedron said. "I'll take the right side if you'll take the left."

"The left side it is," Cahrick said with a laugh.

As the *Sovereign* neared the center point, Phaedron felt Cahrick summon his Water Magic next to him, and he responded by doing the same. As one, they unleashed their power, and two massive waves suddenly sprung up in a direct line from the front of the Sovereign, cutting the figure "8" directly in two at the narrowest point. With the parallel waves established, both of the Waterborn sent them in opposite directions to sweep aside the Illymari ships like twin brooms. Phaedron felt Illymari Mages trying to regain control of the situation, but it was already far too late. Rory Sornin filled their sails with a strong gust of wind, and the *Sovereign* sprinted forward like a charger through the breech they'd created. As the *Sovereign* passed through the formation, every crewmember aboard ship jeered or made rude gestures toward the nearest Illymari vessel on either side of the ship. The insults were returned by outraged Illymari sailors, but both sides knew exactly who had gotten the better end of the brief exchange.

"A shame their Mages were caught so unprepared," Phaedron said. "Our response to their formation should have been obvious. There is no excuse for allowing us to push them aside so easily."

"Well, I for one will spend the night shedding bitter tears of regret for the Illymari navy."

Phaedron laughed in response, and Cahrick grinned one more time before stepping away and returning to his duties, followed closely by Rory Sornin. Phaedron looked up to where the Corsair was standing and saw her looking at him. When he caught her eye, she smiled brightly and took off her oversized hat in an exaggerated bow. He laughed again and saluted her smartly, before turning away once again to watch the open sea.

Archidraconus Ephraim Semarill followed an Illymari Royal Guardsman closely, as the man led him through the wide halls of the Spire of Illymaine to where he knew King Orem was waiting for him. Ephraim had intended to wait for a few days before requesting an audience with the King, but Orem had taken the matter out of his hands by sending the Zarryiostrom a formal note, asking to speak with the person in charge of investigating the Corsair's assassination attempt.

With the complete failure of his attempt to ally himself with the Ferralin Empire, he must be desperate to make certain the Mage High Council does not blame him personally for the attack that caused the schism in the first place. He knows that if we turn our backs on him now, Illymar will fall to Dakkadia.

The guard led him to a set of ornate double doors guarded by two more members of the Royal Guard, who opened the doors for him without announcing his entry. Ephraim entered the room, and as the doors closed behind him, he stepped forward to give King Orem a formal bow. Aside from the King, only his brother, Ascham Illvanin, was in the room. King Orem nodded a greeting of his own and extended a hand, which Ephraim took without hesitation.

"I would like to know if you have found anything in your investigation," Orem said, without preamble. "I realize that the attack only occurred yesterday, but I have just learned that your investigators have already left the scene of the attack and are asking no more questions. That tells me that you must have learned something."

"No more investigation is necessary," Semarill said. "We do indeed know who was behind the attack."

Orem's eyes widened at the news that the Inquisition had somehow already discovered the culprits.

"Don't keep me in suspense, Archidraconus! Who was behind it?"

Ephraim crossed his arms.

"It was an Illymari plot from start to finish. The person who carried out the order to attempt the assassination was Lord High Admiral Lucas Savonne, though we strongly suspect he was simply following orders which originated here in the palace."

Orem rocked back upon his heels at the pronouncement, and for several seconds he couldn't speak.

"You think *I* was responsible for the attack?" Orem asked, finally finding his voice. "That's absolutely preposterous! What would I have gained?"

"I did not say that you, personally, were responsible for the attack. I merely stated that the orders sanctioning the assassination attempt originated within these walls. Admiral Savonne is, at best, a pawn, and he would not undertake something so potentially ruinous to your kingdom without higher authorization." At the King's stunned look Semarill explained. "The plot itself was fairly straightforward. We learned nothing from the assassins themselves, other than that they were hired killers from the Badlands, imported specifically to kill Lady Prudence if the opportunity arose. Until yesterday, Lady Prudence had been either aboard her ship, or escorted by Lord Phaedron Daane, so there was no such opportunity."

Orem frowned in confusion.

"If you learned nothing from the assassins, what makes you so sure that Illymar was behind the attempt?"

Semarill smiled tightly, eyes narrowing.

"After Lady Prudence killed five of her attackers, six soldiers armed with crossbows killed the sole remaining assassin. Through our investigation, we learned that your guards are only armed with pikes and swords; crossbows are never carried. Instead, they are always kept in the armory, which is located at the back of the compound. There was no time for Savonne's archers to reach the armory, procure their weapons, and return to the engagement in time to affect the outcome, and yet somehow they did. If that was not suspicious enough, the number of crossbowmen was the key, for there just happened to be six archers standing by . . . one for each assassin."

He uncrossed his arms and gave Orem a level look.

"The Inquisition believes, and I agree, that the archers had already been hidden nearby watching the attack. They had their weapons loaded and ready, with orders to either kill the assassins once they had finished their job, or to kill any survivors to prevent them from talking if captured."

Orem's face paled at the explanation and he took a step backward in disbelief. Ascham stepped forward.

"I will probably regret asking this, but you said that you do not believe the orders originated with His Majesty. Who, then, do you suspect?"

"We believe the attack was planned and executed by members of the Savonne family," Semarill said. "With that in mind, only two people in the family would have had the authority to issue such an order, and I think we both know who they are."

Orem closed his eyes in shame, realizing that the priest was undoubtedly correct about everything. For a few seconds he said nothing at all, but when he opened his eyes and spoke, he asked the question that Ephraim had expected to hear.

"Does . . . does Ithram hold me or my kingdom responsible for my wife's stupidity? Will you still support us if—*when*—Dakkadia attacks?"

Ephraim didn't respond immediately. He watched the King of Illymar with stern eyes, and as the seconds stretched on, the King slowly wilted under his gaze. When he felt his point had been made, Ephraim answered.

"No, we do not blame you for, as you so rightly put it, the Queen's 'stupidity', but *only* because Lady Prudence survived the attempt upon her life, and she herself dealt with her attackers. As a courtesy to an ally, the Patriarch has decided to turn a blind eye to the Queen's transgressions with the understanding that you yourself will assign a suitable punishment for the parties involved. In particular, Admiral Savonne must be severely chastised. Once we are satisfied that the guilty parties have been punished for breaking the Peace of Zarryiosiad, we will once again support you fully against Dakkadia should they attempt invasion." Ephraim allowed a hint of compassion to cross his features. "No one wants a war, Your Majesty, and we are not prepared to allow your citizens, or ours, to suffer for the ambitions of a single family, no matter how important that family might be. That being said, the blow to our own prestige has been severe, for we stood surety against just such an attack. Deal with the situation, and we will not speak of it again."

After the Archidraconus left the chamber, Orem shouted for a guard.

"I want Admiral Lucas Savonne brought before me within half an hour. I don't care where he is or what he is doing! Find him and bring him here; in chains, if you must."

The guard saluted and ran out the door, calling for several soldiers to follow him.

Orem signaled to a second guard and said, "After I've spoken to the Admiral, I want you to find the Queen and bring her to me as well." The guard saluted and returned to his post.

Ascham walked over to a cabinet stocked with alcohol and poured two snifters of fine brandy. Once the drinks were poured, he set aside the decanter and picked up the snifters, walking back to where his brother was standing. He offered the King a glass.

"I think we could each use one of these."

Orem accepted the glass gratefully and took a long sip, letting the alcohol slide down his throat to settle his nerves.

"We were incredibly lucky that the Zarryiostrom was in such a generous mood," Orem said. "They would have been well within their rights to withdraw their support from us and allow Dakkadia access to the island. I fully expected them to, you know. Breaking the Peace was the worst possible thing we could have done from their perspective." He closed his eyes, and the hand holding his drink started shaking. "If they had decided not to support us, I don't know what I would have done."

"We would have fought them," Ascham said, "with or without the priests or the Mages. It would have been difficult, I'll admit, but remember that Illymar has never been successfully invaded. So long as the Teeth of Amhar hold, Illymar is a bastion of invulnerable strength."

Orem opened his eyes and nodded tiredly, not completely convinced, but obviously trying to put as good a face to the situation as he could.

"Until the Archidraconus told me who was behind the attack, I would never have believed Althea capable of doing something so foolish and reckless. But I believe every single word that he said." He tossed back the rest of his liquor. "Which begs the question, what am I to do with them now?"

"About the Queen, I do not know," Ascham said, "for you must be careful not to damage the Monarchy when you assign her punishment. But as for the 'Bathtub Admiral', I think I have the perfect solution."

Queen Althea walked briskly down the carpeted hallway toward the meeting room to which she had been summoned. The guard who had brought the summons had been unable to tell her what the King wanted, but now that the Dakkadian and Ferralin dignitaries had left Illymar's shores, she assumed the meeting would be a strategy session where they would decide upon the best course of action to take to weather the storm they all knew was coming.

If it is a strategy session, Ascham will no doubt be in attendance, damn him.

The Duke of Saerce's sudden return to power and prominence after so many years in exile had the entire Savonne family up in arms, and there had been quite a bit of pressure brought to bear upon her to somehow deal with the problem.

Deal with the problem, shall I? How exactly am I to deal with the problem when Orem hangs on his every word?

When she saw two members of the Royal Guard standing before a doorway, she stopped well short to check her appearance in a large, ornate mirror. Satisfied that everything was in place, she turned back to the doors and nodded her readiness to the guards, and without a word, they opened the doors to allow her entrance. She grimaced slightly when she saw that her guess had been right on the mark, for Ascham stood next to Orem as he had since the previous evening.

As they both turned to watch her enter, she took a brief moment to study her enemy. Ascham and Orem were of a height, though Ascham had the powerful build of a warrior while Orem had the softer look of a scholar. And though they shared the same piercing blue eyes, there were worry lines etched around Orem's eyes that were absent around Ascham's eyes. Part of that was age, of course, for Orem was 61 years old while Ascham was still in his middle forties, but for the first time Althea could remember, Orem looked *old.*

She frowned in concern when she noticed that, for his burdens had not been the easiest to bear, and she had tried to shoulder as many of them as he would allow, but the strain of the past week was obviously wearing on him.

"You sent for me, husband?"

Orem held her gaze with eyes of blue ice.

"Now that we're all here, I would like some answers. And I warn you now, I will not tolerate even the slightest lie or prevarication." His voice was as flat as his expression, and she felt a wave of ice pass through her, shocked he would speak to her in such a manner. But Orem wasn't finished. "I would like to know just what in the name of the Archon you were thinking when you tried to have the Corsair assassinated!"

Althea rocked back on her heels at the accusation and tried to formulate a response. She hadn't even considered the possibility he might suspect she was involved in the attempt on the pirate's life, and she wasn't ready to answer any questions about it. So, she decided to stall.

"My husband; who has accused me of doing such a thing?" She looked at Ascham, who was smiling grimly at her. "Him? Need I remind you, that until last night, he had been in exile? He would say anything to get back in your good graces! He's hated me for years!" Ascham's smile broadened, and his chest shook with silent laughter. His response made her angry. "You find this amusing? This is a serious charge that you have laid at my feet! Making such an accusation against the Crown with no proof could be considered treason!"

Her anger seemed to amuse him even further, and before she could peel the flesh from his bones with her tongue, he pointed over her shoulder. Confused, she looked behind her, only to see her kinsman, Lord High Admiral Lucas Savonne standing silently to the side. His skin was ashen, and sweat poured freely down his face and stained his immaculately tailored uniform.

One look at his terrified face was all it took for her to realize that the spineless fool had told Orem and Ascham everything he knew, and she sighed once as she closed her eyes in defeat. After a moment, she opened her eyes and turned back to her husband, mentally preparing herself to weather the storm she knew was coming.

"No more useless denials? No more protestations of innocence, or attempts to redirect blame? Then shall we return to my question?" he asked. He leaned forward, face turning purple in rage. "*What in the Archon's name were you thinking?!*"

While his scream of fury washed over her, Althea jumped, as for the first time in their marriage Orem unleashed his rage upon her. Oh, he had been angry with her several times in the past, and they had argued about a great many things throughout their marriage, but he had never been so elementally enraged at her before, and she felt her forehead dotting with perspiration as she realized that this time she had overstepped herself.

"Orem, I did what I thought best for the country. You know that the Corsair is our single greatest threat! With every ship that she takes from us and gives to the Dhaerhans, we come that much closer to invasion by Dakkadia. *Someone* had to do something to protect us. We both know that she has to die!"

Orem stepped forward and screamed into her face.

"But not during the Convocation! Not when she was protected by the Peace of Zarryiosiad!" His voice lowered to a deadly whisper, which turned the perspiration into drops of cold sweat streaking down her face. "Do you realize what you have cost us? Do you realize what you *could* have cost us?!"

He spun around and walked back to where Ascham was standing, passively observing the confrontation. He turned back around, and though he still looked furious, his color slowly turned from purple to red. As Orem stared at her, waiting for a response, she gave Ascham a deadly look.

Orem saw the look.

"I know what you are thinking, but it wasn't Ascham who revealed your involvement to me. Oh, no. You are not that lucky. It was the Inquisition. *The Inquisition*!"

As he screamed the name at her, she almost fainted, for she finally understood that her life was in the balance.

If the Inquisition knows that I am involved, I could hang.

Orem smiled grimly as he watched her face, and he knew that she finally understood the possible consequences of her mistake. She swallowed visibly, and though her hands were shaking and her voice was quavering, she managed to speak.

"How much do they know?"

"They know all of it, Althea—every last detail. Fortunately," he pointed at Lucas, "that fool didn't manage to kill her after all. If he had, we would now be completely open to invasion by Dakkadia, because not only did your actions cost us our alliance with Ferralin, you would also have cost us the support of Ithram. Fortunately, the Zarryiostrom and the High Council have decided to be merciful. They have left your punishment up to me. When they are satisfied that you have been sufficiently punished for your actions, they may consider supporting us when Dakkadia finally comes for us." He smiled, though the smile didn't touch his eyes. "Which begs the question: how am I to punish you for your stupidity?" He crossed his arms over his chest and the smile slipped from his face. "What do you think I should do?"

Althea swallowed again, though there was no moisture in her mouth at all.

"I throw myself upon your mercy, Your Majesty. I only beg you to consider that what I did—what I *tried* to do—I did for the good of the country."

Orem didn't move at all as he considered what to do, and Althea looked at the floor in front of his feet waiting for him to pass judgment. Eventually, he leaned back against a table.

"I see only one possible course of action. If we can somehow convince the priests and the Mages that your ill-advised attack upon the Corsair was not meant as an attack against Dakkadia at all, but rather a strike against a single pirate—a wanted criminal—they may be inclined to be a little more lenient in the way they judge our penitence." He nodded. "The Corsair is a privateer. That means no matter what flag she flies under, her first loyalty has to be to money. Therefore, I believe that the best apology we can offer to her would be money—a very *large* amount of money considering the severity of the crime." He paused for a second to think, and then nodded in determination. "I think the cargo of a single Black Ship should be enough, even for her." He looked at Admiral Savonne. "In two weeks' time, I want you to personally sail to our outpost at the Hidden Lands and prepare a Black Ship with a standard cargo. Then, you are to take command of this ship and sail it to the Badlands, where you will deliver the cargo to our factors. We know from our spies that the Corsair maintains her personal accounts in the Badlands, so it should be a simple matter to contact her agent and come to favorable terms. Once I have been informed that the cargo has been safely delivered, I will contact the Corsair and offer her the gold, as well as our sincerest apologies, and that should be the end of it." He fixed Admiral Savonne with a level glare. "You have this one opportunity to correct your mistakes and make things right. Should you fail to deliver the Black Ship to the Badlands, your life is forfeit. Am I clearly understood?"

Admiral Savonne jerked in terror at his King's question and saluted shakily, almost sagging in relief that he wasn't going to be summarily executed.

"Get out of my sight."

Lucas saluted again and almost fell over himself in a rush to leave the room.

Althea watched her kinsman leave, steeling herself to hear her own punishment. Orem glanced at her for a moment before walking to a bar and pouring himself a glass of brandy. He took a sip, watching her from over the rim of his glass, saying nothing. As the minutes stretched on with Orem remaining silent, Althea found herself in the uncomfortable position of waiting for her husband's pronouncement. Finally, she could take the waiting no longer.

"And what of me, husband? Am I to sail with Lucas to deliver the bribe? Or did you have something else in mind?"

Orem's eyes narrowed with amusement and he set his drink aside.

"I do indeed have something else in mind, Althea. But before I tell you what that is, let me tell you something that I have come to suspect about the attack. You say you did what you did for the good of the country. But that isn't true at all, is it? The best thing for the country would have been for you to do nothing at all, and let the marriage and the treaty take place. No, I think you struck at the Corsair for a different reason. I think you wanted her dead because your family was losing money to her, and *they* demanded that you do something about her."

She said nothing, but try as she might, she could not keep a measure of guilt from showing on her face. Orem nodded again as he saw the confirmation that she couldn't quite hide.

"You put your loyalty to the Savonnes ahead of the wishes of your husband and the needs of your country, and by doing so, you and your family have provoked the very war that I have been trying so desperately to avoid. And for what? *Money?!*" He threw his glass against a wall where it shattered loudly enough to make her jump. He glowered at her in rage, hands clenching and unclenching as if he wanted to throttle her.

"Here is what I have decided. Because your family is the cause of this war, your family will bear the entire cost of it. As of now, any pensions, entitlements, or warrants that the Savonne family currently holds are *abolished.* The Royal Exchequer—*not* Savonnes—will be auditing your family's holdings and assigning a war tax that your family will pay, or they will suffer the Crown's displeasure. Your own estates are *not* exempt, and your own entitlements will be just as heavily taxed as the rest of your family's." Her face drained of color, and she raised a hand to her mouth when she realized what that would mean for her. "That's right, Althea. You chose your family over me, and there is a price to pay for that betrayal. The price I choose is the only thing that seems to matter to you and your family: money. Let *them* pay for your fine jewelry, your many servants, and your creature comforts," He crossed his arms. "Or not." He gave her a vicious smile. "I suspect that the Savonne family is going to be hemorrhaging gold before the end of the month, and they are going to be looking hard for someone to blame. You may find yourself suddenly without means." She held out her hand to protest, to somehow convince him that she didn't deserve his wrath, but she couldn't find the words. He watched her for a moment, then said coldly, in exactly the same tone he had used with Lucas.

"Get out of my sight."

CHAPTER TWENTY-FOUR

“Remedy”

“Is he asleep yet?” Lain asked without even looking to see who is visitor was.

Only two people aboard the Imperial Barge would dare to enter his room without announcing themselves first, and one of the two was currently lying in bed, battling a serious and ongoing case of insomnia. Shar moved around where Lain could see him and shook his head.

“He is attempting to rest, but sleep continues to elude him, and the Imperial Physician is at a loss as to explain his condition. I fear that it may be time to resort to other measures, though at your father’s advanced age, I will have to be very cautious in calculating the proper dosage, for too much could cause him serious harm. If he does not rest soon, however, I fear the effects on his already unstable mental condition will be even worse. The human body requires sleep to maintain proper health, and ever since our last night in Illymar, he has slept no more than a few fitful hours.”

“It was the night before, actually,” Lain said. “My spies amongst his staff have informed me he did not sleep at all the night before the confrontation at King Orem’s party. That means it’s been almost four days since he’s had a good night’s rest. If it was anyone else who was having this problem, I’d say they probably had a guilty conscience keeping them awake. Considering exactly whom we are speaking of, however, I don't believe that to be the case. After all of the crimes he's committed throughout his life, I don't believe he actually has a conscience left to bother him."

Shar chuckled at the black humor and poured himself a cup of strong tea from a steaming teapot sitting on the table. He poured four teaspoons of sugar into the drink and stirred it, before taking a seat across from the Prince.

"How many cups of tea is that for you tonight, Shar?" Lain asked, as the Mage took his first sip.

"Who knows?" replied Shar, shrugging elaborately. "So long as his Imperial Majesty remains awake, I, too, must be ready to serve him at a moment's notice. Although I require less sleep than most, your father's insomnia is keeping many of his servants up as well. I understand that the secretaries and undersecretaries have taken to sleeping in their uniforms in case he calls upon them. One very unpleasant side effect of your father's condition is that he is constantly in a foul mood, and none of his servants wants to be the one who isn't there the instant he calls for them. Who knows what he would do to the poor unfortunate soul. No one wants to be the first to find out."

"I don't blame them in the slightest." He paused, giving the Vizier an almost guilty look. "He hasn't murdered a child in over a week after killing one or two a week for the better part of his entire life. Do you think it's a coincidence?"

Shar grimaced, and he took a sip of his tea before answering.

"That could very well be the case, Your Highness. I do not know what has made your father decide to stop murdering innocents after so long, but I for one am grateful for the respite. Perhaps you are right that he does not have a conscience, but somehow, *I* still retain one, even after all of these years concealing his crimes. However, if this insomnia goes on for much longer, I may find myself strangling one of them on his behalf, just to be sure." Despite himself, Lain barked a laugh, and Shar smiled over the rim of his cup.

"A poor jest to be sure, Shar, though I must admit that the thought—as black as it may be—actually crossed my mind as well." Lain leaned back in his seat and sighed. "What did you think of Princess Deirdre? My betrothed now, I suppose."

Shar set his cup aside.

"She will be a fine match for you, Your Highness. Your father did very well by you at the Convocation; though it may have come at too high a price for Ferralin to pay."

"Again, the thought had crossed my mind as well. My father is gambling with the future of *my* realm, and I find that, as grateful as I am to be betrothed to such an exceptional young woman, I do not appreciate the risk. If Father had truly been interested in brokering a peace with Dakkadia, he would have given King Madari the Badlands. What he has done instead, is pitted Dakkadia against Illymar, betting that the two nations will destroy each other, leaving us untouched, and the Badlands open for us to take for ourselves. Deirdre, for all her incredible beauty and talent, is simply a pretty bow to put on top of the gift he is making himself of the Badlands. I should be grateful, I suppose, that he asked for Deirdre's hand on my behalf instead of his own. He could have done that, you know. Considering his history, I half expected it."

Shar stiffened in his seat, and Lain's stomach fell at the Vizier's reaction to his words. The Mage quickly recovered his composure and picked up his cup again to cover his slip, but it was far too late. Lain narrowed his eyes.

"Tell me all of it, Shar."

Shar closed his eyes and sighed, setting aside his cup. He took a deep breath and then looked his Prince directly in the eyes.

"Princess Deirdre's betrothal to you was not your father's idea: it was *her* father who set the terms. When your father met with King Madari, his exact words were, 'I wish to discuss the possibility of a treaty between my country and yours, secured by a marriage to your daughter. Having had the distinct pleasure of meeting her, I feel she will make both a fine wife and a better Empress.' There was no mention of the marriage being between Deirdre and you. In fact, from the wording he used, I actually assumed that he wanted her for himself. King Madari, however, shrewdly chose to interpret the meaning of your father's proposal in an entirely different way. His response to the inquiry was, 'I think a marriage between my daughter and *your son* would be a marvelous arrangement. Deirdre thinks very highly of Prince Lain, and from the way she has spoken about him, I know that she is already very fond of him.'" Shar smiled at the memory of seeing the Emperor so effortlessly outmaneuvered. "Your father's reaction was . . . not good, but he did not argue the point."

Lain said nothing at all about the revelation. Instead, he tried desperately to remember every detail about his father's meeting with Deirdre. One detail in particular came crashing through his mind: the terrible look of hunger upon his father's face as he placed his hands upon Deirdre's shoulders and slowly began squeezing. Stunned, he leaned back in his seat.

"It all makes sense, Shar. Father has not stopped murdering children because of a guilty conscience. He has simply set his sights on higher prey, and is unable to obtain her!"

He worked his way through the possible implications quickly in his mind. If Madari had agreed to allow Deirdre to marry Xan, and Xan in turn murdered his new bride, Dakkadia would instantly set aside its quarrel with Illymar to seek retribution for the death of their Princess. But Xan had to know that, so why do it?

Because he is insane, you fool! He does not care about what will happen to his realm should he murder Deirdre and invite invasion. Considering his advanced years, he may believe that he will die before he can face Dakkadian justice, leaving me—and my realm—to suffer for his *sins.*

He thanked the Archon Deirdre's father had shown such remarkable foresight and had taken steps to avoid it, even if he had no idea he had done so. Lain knew that the smartest thing for him to do now would be to send a message to King Madari breaking the engagement, even if he had to confess the reasons behind the sudden change of plans. *But if I do so, I will not be able to marry Deirdre after all.*

He closed his eyes in sudden pain, and realized instantly he was not strong enough to deny himself the opportunity to marry the beautiful Dakkadian Princess . . . the one person he desperately wanted to spend the rest of his life with. He clenched his fists, gritted his teeth, and came to a decision. *I should kill you for what I know you are planning to do, but I can't. For all your sins, for all your insanity, you are still my father, and killing you would damn me for an eternity. But I can't let you destroy the Empire either, so it is time to take other measures.* He turned to Shar and spoke very, very formally.

"Grand Vizier, I am very worried about my father's deteriorating health. I think it is time you saw to it that he gets some rest, even if you must resort to your 'other measures.'" Shar's eyes narrowed at the order, but he bowed his acquiescence. At his Vizier's acknowledgement of the order, Lain continued. "When he is asleep, tell the servants to get some rest as well."

Shar reached across the table to pull a clean teacup from the serving tray, and poured a fresh cup of tea. He then reached beneath his robe and pulled out a small pouch, opened it, and pulled out two tiny roots. His eyes flashed white as he summoned his power, and the roots floated out of his hands and began to hover, before instantly being crushed flat by what seemed to be an invisible mortar and pestle. Fascinated, Lain watched the Vizier at work as he used his mastery of Air Magic to grind the roots into a fine powder. Job completed, the powder fell into the cup of tea, and once the powder had dissolved into the tea, he released his magic, picked up the cup, and stood up to leave the room.

"Shar, I am charging you with the duty to ensure that my father remains well-rested for the entirety of the journey. In fact, when we finally return to Ferraldazaar, I want you to ensure he remains that way for the rest of his natural life." As the Vizier moved away to complete his task, Lain unclenched his fists.

I may not be a cold-blooded murderer the way you are, Father, but thanks to you, I've just learned something important about myself. In my own way I can be just as ruthless and terrible as you when the situation warrants it.

The sound of footsteps next to his bed brought Valeriad back to consciousness, and the first coherent thought that crossed his mind was, *this time I am going to die.* The seasickness he had suffered from during the journey to Illymar had resurfaced on the return trip, and he found that the second time around the effects of his illness seemed to be even worse, if, indeed, that could even be possible. For three days he had laid in his bed, once again unable to keep down anything but lukewarm broth, and he found himself vomiting constantly whether or not there was food within him.

He drifted in and out of sleep, too weak and exhausted to even sit up, and though he knew he was once again worrying everyone aboard the *Sovereign,* there was nothing at all he could do about it. Earlier that day his mother had stepped into the room to check on him, and despite his illness, he was very glad to see her up and about. She still winced in pain with every movement, but her bruises were starting to heal, and perhaps even more importantly, her spirit seemed to be returning. He'd tried to ask her about the beating, but she simply smiled and refused to discuss it with him. "*You needn't concern yourself with my problems, Valeriad,*" she had said. "*What passed between your father and me will stay between us, and I will deal with it in my own way. You need to concentrate on your own recovery, and not waste your strength worrying about me. I'm stronger than I look.*"

She hadn't needed to remind him of her strength, for his mother was the strongest person he knew. Though his father was the absolute ruler of Dakkadia, and everyone abided by the laws he set, somehow the entire Dakkadian court had molded itself to its Queen like a leather glove, and that glove hid a fist of tempered steel. He had asked Morvandis about it once, and Morvandis had surprised him with a rare showing of admiration.

Your father is a great King, for he knows exactly what he wishes to accomplish and is not afraid to take risks to achieve those goals. Unfortunately, he sometimes forgets that he not only has to worry about the larger governance issues, he must also take care of the everyday events at court as well. He considers these things to be inconsequential, and unworthy of his time and attention, but as with many things, small problems that do not seem to be important upon first glance, sometimes have the potential to become catastrophic if left unattended. Therefore, it is vital to have an administrator who understands the importance of the smaller details and can take care of these problems without having to worry about incurring the King's displeasure. The Queen is perfect for the role; for she understands that, in order for the Kingdom to continue to run smoothly and efficiently, someone has to deal with the problems that the King has no interest in handling personally. Over the years, Queen Aveliad has made a name for herself among her subjects as a fair and level-headed ruler who plays no favorites; who can be trusted to see solutions to problems that do not occur to others, but are obvious to everyone as the wisest possible course, once suggested. Without her deft hand holding the reins, the court would have fallen into chaos long ago.

Valeriad wasn't sure if his father's assault on his mother would change things between them once they returned to court, but somehow he doubted it, especially now that he had seen her up and about. His mother was a Dakkadian, after all, and she would bear her wounds without complaint. So he took his mother at her word and changed the subject to more pleasant matters, and for her part, Aveliad settled herself down to listen to him speak.

He talked about his three meetings with Lyrahe, and the friendship they had developed that had somehow turned to love, and she smiled and listened to him as he described the beautiful Princess and his hope that one day they would be together. Eventually, however, his exhaustion overcame him, and despite his efforts to the contrary, his eyelids slowly closed. As he drifted off to sleep, he felt her fingers gently brush his hair and her lips touch his forehead the way she had done every night before he fell asleep as a child.

He didn't know how long he had slept, but however long it might have been it, hadn't been long enough. With no little effort, he turned his head to the side to see who had awakened him, and the first thing he noticed was that it was a woman. From where she was sitting he couldn't see her face, but, to his immense surprise, the second thing he noticed was that she was only partially clothed, with ornate armor that covered some of her body but left the vast majority of her pale, flawless skin exposed. A series of black lines crossing her body caught his attention, and he saw that the black lines were actually elaborate tattoos meant to be a stylized skeleton of some type of serpent wrapping itself around her arms, legs and torso. She turned to him, noticed him looking at her, and smiled. Shock overcame his weakness when he saw her face, for looking into her eyes was like looking into his own eyes in a mirror. *She looks exactly like me,* he thought, once his mind started working again.

A closer look told him that there were some differences between them, and as he took in her appearance, those differences seemed to leap out at him. For example, while his hair was pure white, her hair was black, with a large white streak in the middle. That distinctive streak marked her as a Dakkadian, but he knew he had never seen her before, just as he knew she wasn't a member of the crew.

Before he could ask who she was, however, she leaned forward and lifted his head from his pillow, and placed a steaming cup of tea to his lips.

"Drink this, Prince Valeriad. It will help you with your seasickness." He looked at the cup with suspicion, for he had no idea who she was or how she had gotten aboard the *Sovereign*, and for all he knew, the drink was poison. As if reading his mind, she laughed. "It is not poison, Prince Valeriad. It is simply ginger tea, with a few extra ingredients that I have added to help you recover from your seasickness. Believe me, had I meant you harm I would not need to resort to poison. In your current condition I could do anything I want to you, and you would be helpless to resist."

He hesitated for a moment before shrugging slightly to concede the point, and he allowed her to tip the cup forward to pour the liquid into his mouth. The tea was slightly bitter, but not unpleasantly so, and he drained the entire cup in a single pull. As the last of the liquid disappeared, she took the cup away from him and set it on the nightstand next to his bed, and then set a small pouch next to the cup.

"The tea should take effect momentarily." She patted the pouch she had set on the table. "Should you feel the sickness return, simply brew another cup using these herbs, and that should take care of it."

He tried to sit up in his bed, but after a few moments' struggle he gave up.

"I thank you for your assistance, but if you don't mind my asking, who are you? And more importantly, why do you look like me?" She turned her chair a bit more to better face him, and for the first time he saw the black dragon sitting on her shoulder. When he saw the dragon he blurted out in surprise, "You're a Dragon Witch!"

"So, you are familiar with my kind," she said. "That is good. It will save time. I take it then, that you met Asiria in the Mage Citadel? Or did Astranaithes herself approach you?" She raised a curious eyebrow, watching for his response, but though he had met Asiria in the library, he did not recognize the second name. "So, Astranaithes has chosen not to reveal herself to you for now. Even better."

She leaned forward in her seat to give him a formal bow. "My name is Severeielle, and I am known amongst my own kind as the Queen of Shadows. Did the Queen of Knowledge mention my name to you, perchance?" He shook his head in response, and she said, "Pity. What did Asiria tell you about Dragon Witches?"

He thought back to the conversation he had had with the librarian during their first meeting.

"She told me that Severius the Dragonslayer, the man who slew Zarryiosiad herself, was a Dragon Lord, and that Furionchires, the servant of the Archon, was one as well."

"These are facts that are not widely known. Because of the myths perpetuated by the Zarryiostrom, fewer still believe them. Tell me, young Prince, did you believe any of the things that Asiria told you?"

"I don't know," he said, a frown crossing his brow. "As you said, the Zarryiostrom teaches us differently, but my mother once told me that human memory is almost as short as a human lifespan. The Fae remember things differently, for many of them were alive during the time of the Archon. Is it true that you are as immortal as the Fae?"

"My brother and I have seen well over 3,000 years of life. Asiria, the Queen of Knowledge, is younger than we are, though she herself was alive when the Lyx walked among us. Astranaithes, the Queen of Fate as we call her, is much, much older than I am, but to answer your question, 'yes' we are as immortal as the Fae."

"Then I find I cannot dispute your version of the events," he said. He hesitated for a moment before asking another question. "Did you know Zarryiosiad and Furionchires?"

"I knew them both. Zarryiosiad was a great leader, though absolutely ruthless in the pursuit of her goals. She hated the Lyx so completely that she would have sacrificed anything or anyone to destroy them utterly. In the end, her blind hatred consumed even her, for she willingly threw away her humanity for one last chance to sink her teeth into the throats of the Lyx. The romantic version of the tale of Zarryiosiad has it that she sacrificed her life to avenge her lover, Kalindral . . . the one great love of her life. But the truth is, while she did love him after her fashion, Kalindral was merely one man in a long line of lovers. I do not say this to defame her or to insult her memory, but to again remind you of the blessing—and the curse—of immortality. Zarryiosiad ruled Il'Amhar for over four hundred years after the death of her human father, Zarus, and during that time she had many husbands and took many lovers, a vast majority of which were human. As for Furionchires?" She smiled broadly and crossed one leg over the other. "Furionchires is a legend among our kind. She is known to us as the Queen of Battles, and she is older than my brother and I. It may surprise you to learn that she still lives, young Prince, although she does not look the same as she did when she served Zarryiosiad. In the Valley of Fire my brother struck her down, though he merely killed her host. And though it took her many decades to recover from the shock and select a new host, she did eventually recover."

Fascinated at the explanation, it took Valeriad a moment to understand what she had told him, but when he realized what she had so casually mentioned, his eyes shot open.

"Your brother is *Severius the Dragonslayer?*"

"He is indeed. We are—*were*—twins, and you look exactly as he did so very many years ago. That is why I sought you out, Prince Valeriad, for although Astranaithes told me not to read too much into your appearance, for appearances can indeed be deceiving, considering just who you resemble, how could I *not* seek you out? My brother was the Champion: the one preordained by fate to slay the Harbinger and keep the world from falling victim to her flames. Did Asiria tell you that?" Valeriad nodded. "In the Valley of Fire, Zarryiosiad willingly sacrificed her lover, her army, and her very humanity to become the Harbinger, the greatest evil the world will ever know. She sacrificed everything she possessed to strike down the Lyx, not caring what that 'sacrifice' would ultimately mean for the rest of the world. My brother knew the cost, however, for once the Harbinger begins its bloody work, it absolutely will not stop until *all* life is destroyed . . . even its own. Severius willingly stood against it, in defense of all living things."

She uncrossed her legs and gave him an intense look.

"I do not believe in coincidences, nor do I believe that your resemblance to my brother is an accident. It is my belief that you are the new Champion, the one man capable of standing between the Harbinger and life itself. Battle lines are already forming, for many of our number know that the Harbinger is returning, and when it does, I firmly believe that you must be there to stop it. That is why I have sought you out, young Champion; I want you to know that I will always be near you, watching over you from the shadows, ready to intervene should you need my assistance. I will be here to teach you, to guide you, and to help you when you are ready to accept your destiny, and should the worst come to pass and the Harbinger returns, I will make certain that you are able to fulfill your destiny and destroy it."

"How will I know when I am ready?" he asked.

She smiled and patted his sword belt, draped over the back of the chair on which she was sitting.

"The sword was never meant to be your weapon, young Champion. I do not know how it will come about, or why, but the day will come when you will choose to set aside this weapon and choose another. When that day comes I will return to you, and on that day your lessons will truly begin."

He stared at her for a few moments, wondering how much of what she had told him he could believe. Asiria had mentioned that he looked exactly like the

Dragonslayer, but he hadn't really thought about it, or what it might mean for him. Severeielle, on the other hand, was convinced that because he looked like her brother, he was somehow destined to become this "Champion" that both Dragon Witches had mentioned. One thing was certain: he didn't feel like a champion. Furthermore, he couldn't imagine a day would ever come when he would choose to set aside his sword, for after so many years of it resting against his hip, it felt like a part of him now. He didn't know what to say to her, so they sat together in silence for a while as he tried to work things out in his own mind.

"How do you feel?" she asked. "Is your illness still affecting you?"

To his surprise, he realized that during their conversation he had actually forgotten he was sick. But now that she had called his attention to it, he realized that the effects of the seasickness were abating. Though he was still feeling queasy and a little lightheaded, he did indeed feel much better.

"I feel fine, thank you. I have to admit that I was so interested in our conversation that I didn't even notice your tea taking effect."

She laughed softly and closed her eyes.

"Such is the nature of good conversation, young Prince. It can serve to inform and enlighten, but it can also serve to distract."

He joined her in laughter, but as she looked into his face he saw her smile turn sad.

"Severeielle, may I ask you something?"

She smiled again, and bowed her head.

"What happened to Severius after the Valley of Fire? Asiria wouldn't say."

The Queen of Shadow's smile faded slowly, and a look of sorrow crossed her face. But before she could answer his question, the shadows in the darkened room lengthened and deepened, and the temperature suddenly turned bitterly cold. As the shadows along the floor and wall seemed to come alive, a wave of visceral terror washed over him and the hairs on his arms and neck seemed to stand on end. A disembodied voice, as hollow and cold as the grave, echoed throughout the room, and he jumped at the sound of it.

"He willingly suffered the gravest of injuries so that others might live. A lesson every potential Champion should take to heart."

The shadows filling the room seemed to stretch, and a figure stepped into the room through a doorway of blackness so deep it seemed to fall into forever. As the darkness retreated, Valeriad saw a man standing before him, and knew instantly he was looking upon Severius the Dragonslayer himself. His curiosity overcame his terror, and Valeriad took a good look at the legendary villain.

The first thing he noticed was that the Dragonslayer was very tall, with long, straight white hair that seemed translucent and almost insubstantial. His features were covered by a porcelain mask sculpted to resemble a beautiful human face, white enameled and trimmed with gold leaf. The mask reminded Valeriad very much of the one his mother wore, but where Aveliad's covered only her eyes, the Dragonslayer's covered his entire face.

Valeriad peered into the eyeholes of the mask trying to see into Severius's eyes, but he could see nothing there but a profound blackness. The emptiness of the mask's eyes was very disconcerting, so he looked instead at the dragon sitting on Severius's shoulder. At first glance, the dragon seemed to be identical to the one riding on Severeielle's shoulder, but a closer look showed him that where Severeielle's dragon was covered in a sinuous pattern of glossy black scales, Severius's own dragon was as insubstantial as smoke, and when it moved, Valeriad could clearly see white bone through the black shadows.

Severius spoke again, this time addressing Severeielle. With each word came a wisp of coldness that had nothing to do with the weather.

"You should not be here, sister. You are interfering in matters of which you know nothing about. Leave now before you do lasting harm."

Severeielle stiffened at his words and her mouth tightened in anger.

"I will not, brother. Look at his face, Severius! Destiny has never been as clear as it is now! He must be prepared for what is to come."

The enameled mask turned to regard him, and though Valeriad tried to put on a brave front, he still found himself swallowing with fear. A soft rasping sound filled the room, but it took Valeriad a moment to understand that Severius was laughing, and the sound of it chilled his blood.

"Perhaps he is the Champion, or perhaps not. Who can say? Not you, sister, as much as you might believe otherwise. The very idea belies your arrogance. Even I cannot tell who the Champion will be, though I myself was once one. The simple truth you refuse to hear or believe is that fate, and fate alone, shall determine who will become the Harbinger, and who will become the Champion." He turned his head to the side and looked toward the closed door. *"Someone approaches. We must leave before we are discovered."*

Severeielle shot to her feet and walked quickly to where Severius was standing. She pulled her brother in close to her before crossing her arms in front of her and summoning a pair of black wings that seemed to enfold them both, but before anything else could happen, Severius held up a hand to stop her.

"Hold, sister. Indulge my curiosity, if you will. I wish to meet the person who can sense my presence."

Morvandis moved quickly down the narrow hallway, gathering every scrap of power he could hold and preparing his defensive circles on the move. He had been alone in the map room reading some papers when he felt a disturbance from somewhere within the ship a few moments earlier, and even now he could feel a dark presence nearby. He had never felt its like before, and it had taken him a moment to understand that somehow Blood Magic was involved.

A simple locating spell told him that whatever it was that carried so much taint, it was coming from within Valeriad's room. Fearing that an attack was imminent on the young Prince's life, Morvandis burst into action. As he reached Valeriad's room, he used a powerful ram of air to push open the door, before summoning a flare of white fire to light the room. The first thing he saw was a man and a woman, standing together at the foot of Valeriad's bed, literally cloaked in darkness.

Without conscious thought, he summoned a shield of air to surround the two figures, one more than sufficient to hold them both in place.

I have to find out who they are, and how they came to be aboard this ship before I destroy them, he thought.

He took a closer look at the figures, and saw that the woman was most likely a Dakkadian, though one he didn't recognize; but to his surprise she seemed somehow familiar to him. The man he had never seen before, for while he wore a porcelain mask that covered his face completely, Morvandis would have remembered someone radiating so much cold and death. Neither of the figures struggled against the shield, but Morvandis heard a tangibly cold and empty voice that had to be coming from the masked male.

"Ah, Morvandis, what have you done to yourself? Have you, too, become corrupted as have so many others before you? You must not allow your thirst for power to lead you any further astray. Believe me when I say that you meddle now with forces that are beyond your comprehension or control. The path of Blood can only lead to ruin, so I beg you, please: stop now, before you truly become one of the fallen."

Morvandis blinked in surprise at the words, for somehow this man he had never laid eyes on before had guessed that he had been studying the secrets of Blood Magic, but before he could demand answers, the masked man gestured calmly and the light that Morvandis had summoned was abruptly extinguished. He channeled a second flare, but too late, for during that brief moment of darkness, the man and the woman slipped through his shield and disappeared. He summoned his power and scanned the room to make certain that they had not left behind any traps, before turning to Valeriad.

"Are you injured? Did they harm you?" Valeriad shook his head, but Morvandis scanned him anyway, looking for any possible enchantments. He saw nothing, and caught himself before he could breathe a sigh of relief. "I can sense no trace of them. I think you are safe now."

"I was never in any danger, Morvandis. They simply wanted to talk to me."

"Who were they? I have never seen the man before, but the woman seemed strangely familiar to me."

Valeriad propped himself up in bed.

"The woman called herself Severeielle, the Queen of Shadows. The man was . . . well, you may not believe me, but the man was Severius, the Dragonslayer."

Morvandis hissed softly at the name, but quickly regained control of himself.

"What did they want with you?"

"Again, you may not believe this, but Severeielle brought me a cure for my seasickness. She gave me a cup of tea."

Before Morvandis could say anything, Valeriad pointed at a small pouch sitting next to an empty teacup on his nightstand. Morvandis picked up the pouch, opened it slightly, and sniffed at the contents.

Ginger, I would guess. With a few other herbs mixed in.

He set the bag back onto the table and crossed his arms over his chest.

"I trust you realize how very foolish it was to accept anything at all from someone you don't know, who just happened to appear in your room? A room on a ship in the middle of the ocean, no less."

"She could easily have killed me in my sleep, Morvandis. When I woke up, she was already sitting next to me in that chair, brewing a cup of tea and waiting for me to wake up. Honestly, once I got past the shock of her appearance, I very much enjoyed her company. She was quite friendly, and the tea really has made me feel much better. Severius didn't come into the room until much later, and I feel no shame in admitting to you that he absolutely terrified me. There was something wrong with him."

Morvandis sat down in the chair Valeriad had indicated that Severeielle had used.

"How long did you speak with this 'Severeielle' before the man claiming to be Severius entered the room?"

"Quite a while, actually. Severius came only a few moments before you yourself did, but Severeielle was here much longer. I think he was angry at her for coming to speak with me, but he only had time to say a few things to us before he told her you were coming. They could easily have escaped before you entered the room, but Severius wouldn't allow her to take them away until he saw who was coming. I think he was curious about you. What did he mean when he said, 'the path of Blood leads only to ruin?' And who—or what—are the Fallen?"

Morvandis grimaced at the question, for these were subjects he had never wanted associated with himself, but now that Valeriad had asked his questions, he knew that he had no choice but to answer. He thought carefully about his reply, for if he said too much, he risked exposing himself to the Prince as a novice Blood Mage, but if he said too little, Valeriad would become suspicious and would continue to ask questions that he could not afford to answer.

“The Fallen are Mages who have dedicated their lives to the study and pursuit of the darker arts, especially Blood Magic. No one knows how many of them there are, but one theory says that they started appearing shortly after the death of Zarryiosiad. Each Fallen is different, and has his or her own agenda, but the common thread uniting them is that they willingly seek forbidden power and are willing to do anything to obtain it. Power is seductive, Valeriad, and the pursuit of it has led countless Mages—and Kings—to ruin and destruction throughout history. Unfortunately, not all of the Mages who lose themselves in this pursuit die. Some of them are forever changed, and become twisted shadows of their former selves. Many of the monsters of legend were actually Fallen: including Vampir’i, Lich’esti, Lycani’i, and Necromancers.”

He leaned back in his seat and crossed his arms over his chest.

“As to why he warned me of the path of Blood, who can say? I assume he was warning me about not falling victim to the lust for power—a very real concern for one of my ability—but I cannot be certain. If that is what he intended, he needn’t have worried, for I understand all-too-well the struggle to resist temptation. As you seem to be feeling better, we shall now have a talk about your two visitors. I want to know every detail of your conversation, as well as your impression of everything you saw or felt about the two of them, no matter how inconsequential. You say that she seemed ‘friendly’, but the fact that they could reach you here where it should have been utterly impossible, means that they are a serious threat, no matter how they may have tried to disguise their intentions. I must know who they are, and what they want from you.”

Valeriad frowned slightly and grabbed his stomach, and a look of concern crossed Morvandis’s face.

“Is something the matter?”

“I just realized that I haven’t eaten for days. I don’t suppose you have any food on you? If this is going to take as long as I think it is, I’m going to need something to eat first."

Hours later, the sun was starting to peek through the cabin’s windows and Morvandis finally stood to leave. As he quietly closed the door behind him, he could hear soft snoring coming from the Prince that told him Valeriad had already fallen into a deep sleep before he had even left the room. Morvandis walked silently back to the map room that Madari had appropriated as his study, and again took his seat to be alone with his thoughts. What Valeriad had told him was troubling, for while fate might argue otherwise, Morvandis believed that the world had no need for another Archon. Perhaps worse, Enaria believed that he himself had the potential to *become* the Archon, which meant that if both Severeielle *and* Enaria were correct, his relationship with the Prince—the *Champion*—he corrected himself, would eventually become quite interesting indeed. He hoped that both of the women were wrong, but he refused to discount their words out of hand.

If Enaria is right, and I have it within me to one day become an Archon, that means the Prince may well be the one who will strike me down. Not a pleasant thought. He set aside those concerns and turned his mind to the problem of the mysterious visitors. In particular, he found himself thinking more and more about the woman who had seemed so very familiar to him. *I know that I have seen her before, but where?* Morvandis prided himself on his almost perfect memory, but even with his ability to recall facts and images, it still took him a while to dredge up the memory. *It was during my Testing, when I was a student at the Mage Citadel. I was seventeen years old, and I saw her standing in an alcove, watching my performance. I looked away to deal with a sudden attack, and when I looked up again, she was gone.*

Once the memory had finally returned to him, there was no doubt in his mind that she had been the one he had seen hiding in the shadows.

That in and of itself is not proof of what she says, although it tells me she has been searching for this supposed Harbinger for a very long time without revealing herself at all. If she is willing to show herself now, after so many years of spying from the shadows, she must be absolutely certain that she has found the Champion.

With that mystery solved, he turned his thoughts back to the masked man.

That was Severius the Dragonslayer himself, if Valeriad can be believed. To think that such a man actually existed! I would give much to have a chance to question him.

As he thought about the mysterious stranger, he remembered other things about the encounter he hadn't noticed at the time. The room had been very cold when he entered, as if all the warmth the room had contained had somehow been removed, leaving behind an almost palpable aura of chill. Morvandis was not one to put stock in childish horror stories, but he now understood the meaning of the term "the chill of the grave." Valeriad told him that he had been terrified when Severius entered the room, and that there was "something wrong with him." The Prince had been right, for he had felt the same thing.

It went far beyond simple Blood Magic to something even worse, but somehow Blood Magic was involved. He closed his eyes and thought about the Lexicon of Purifying Flame, the holy book containing the story of Zarryiosiad. He knew the book by heart, though he hadn't memorized it for its religious value. Rather, he had memorized it in the course of his study of the Archon's life and works. He closed his eyes and mentally searched the passages of the Lexicon for references to Severius the Dragonslayer. There were many to be found, but in the end he found them to be absolutely worthless as a source for information. The Lexicon had spent entire pages describing his treachery and evil, but said nothing at all about his history, or his eventual fate, save that Zarryiosiad had cursed him with her dying breath. *The Archon cursed him with her dying breath.*

That seemed somehow significant to him, for he had always believed the Lexicon had been enjoying a bit of hyperbole at the Dragonslayer's expense. But what if it hadn't? What if she actually *had* cursed Severius, and had somehow found a way to make the curse take hold? The Mage within him cried out in protest at the very thought. He had always been taught that curses, jinxes, and hexes were the stuff of fables told to small children to make them stop misbehaving and eat their vegetables, but Zarryiosiad had been an absolute genius in the use of magic. The Throne of Obsidian, the White Wall, and the Teeth of Amhar were three perfect examples of her ability to use magic in unique ways. *Why not Severius as well?*

Each of her creations were miraculous in and of themselves, but when you considered that all of them were created by a single person well over 2,500 years ago, and that they retained their power even today, he was not prepared to say that a simple thing like a curse was beyond her power. Thanks to his time sitting in the Throne of Obsidian, Morvandis knew that he could at least come close to matching the Archon in raw power, especially with his mastery of Earth Magic. But the very existence of the Throne also told him he was a child fumbling in the dark when it came to the subtle uses in which she had devised to use that power. *I will have to rectify that if I am to one day match her achievements. If Enaria is correct, and I am to one day become an Archon, I refuse to be the lesser of the two.*

He laughed to himself at the hubris behind the thought, and stood up to go to his cabin. It had been a very long night, and he needed a little rest before beginning the rest of his day.

Astranaithes was tending to a small garden, sitting beside a tiny waterfall in her hidden grotto, when she felt the telltale surge of power signifying a doorway being opened nearby. A wave of chill radiated from it, telling her instantly who her guest was, and she turned toward the doorway with a smile.

"You are most welcome here, Severius."

At the welcoming words, Severius stepped through the doorway and allowed it to close behind him, before bowing to her politely.

"It is good to see you again, Astranaithes, and I thank you for your welcome." He replied in an inhuman voice; one that sounded hollow and distant, and yet menacing all the same. *"It has been far too long since our last visit."* She held her hands towards him

in greeting, and he held out his gloved hands to allow her to slip her fingertips between his. He squeezed briefly, mindful not to hurt her, and then stepped back. *"You look well . . . better than I expected, considering you recently met with my sister. I must admit that I thought she would have tried to kill you on sight, especially since you caught her off guard."*

Astranaithes laughed musically at the comment and indicated a stone bench sitting by the pool.

"Severeielle is not so hard to understand or predict as all that, Severius. The Queen of Shadows was never one to confront her enemies directly, as both you and Furionchires prefer. That is why she keeps Cassiramaithris so close at hand. No, I chose to meet her in a location where I knew she would believe she held an advantage, and I approached her openly. Added to the surprise of seeing your apparent reincarnation in the form of the Prince of Dakkadia, I knew she would be more forthcoming than normal." Astranaithes gave him a considering look. "Have you seen your young mirror?"

"I have, indeed. When Severeielle told me she had found a boy who looked exactly the way I once looked, I was skeptical to say the least. I thought she was merely seeing what she wanted to see, but I was wrong. The resemblance is uncanny. I actually find his visage to be more than a bit uncomfortable, if truth be told. It is not easy to look upon a stranger and see yourself as you once were. Severeielle is absolutely convinced he is the one . . . the new Champion destined to destroy the next incarnation of the Harbinger, but I myself am not so easily convinced. It almost seems too easy. I am not used to Fate being as accommodating as that."

"Too easy, indeed. You should know by now, old friend; Fate is never so straightforward. It may be that he will become the new Champion, but until the Harbinger emerges, we cannot be certain." Again Severius nodded, but a look of concern crossed her features and she put her hand on his forearm. "You say that his features made you more than a bit uncomfortable. How do you feel?"

Severius laughed, his throat making the soft rasp that was all that Zarryiosiad had left him.

"I feel like death warmed over."

Astranaithes laughed slightly at the jest, and shook her head in mock irritation, but after the sound of his hollow laughter had faded he continued in a more serious tone.

"In the Valley of Fire, I did all that was required of me and more; and even knowing the price I would have to pay for doing my duty, I would gladly do it again. But, seeing the way young Valeriad looked today reminded me of everything I sacrificed when I did as Fate required of me. I truly believe I have not changed from the man I once was, no matter what I may look like today. But then that doesn't matter, for even if I haven't changed, everyone else has because of me. I lost a lover to her bitterness at my altered state. Do you remember Cassiramaithris as she once was?"

Astranaithes nodded sadly and squeezed his arm, though she knew he would not feel it.

"There is nothing left between us anymore. Not even ashes remain. Even more than my sister, she could not accept the changes I underwent after Zarryiosiad laid her curse upon me, and like my sister, she blames you. Watch out for her, Astranaithes; she'll kill you without a moment's hesitation if she has the chance, and even I would not be able to stop her, no matter what we once meant to each other. Severeielle, too, has changed from the woman she once was. You remember how close we once were? She refuses to even look at me now, and until today I had not spoken to her in some time—by her choice, not mine. I know the reason for the distance she keeps from me, even if she herself refuses to admit it. She blames herself for what was done to me, almost as much as she blames you. She, too, will kill you if she has the chance, so be on your guard."

He hesitated a moment, wanting to say something difficult but afraid to speak the words.

"If—when—either one of them comes for you, do what you must to protect yourself, even if that means killing them. If you don't, they will surely kill you."

He patted the hand she had resting on his forearm to reassure her that he would understand, though the gesture was completely unnecessary. They both knew she would do what she had to do.

"That was not the reason I came here today, though I am glad I had the opportunity to express my concern for your well-being. No, my actual reason for this visit was to tell you about something disturbing that I learned today. Morvandis has turned to the path of Blood. I could feel the slightest hint of corruption upon him."

Astranaithes gasped in shock and pulled her hand away from him as if it had been burned, but he did not look away.

"I spoke with him briefly, to warn him not to allow his thirst for power to lead him any further astray, but I do not believe my words will have any effect. How could they? I am nothing to him but a name in a book, and Morvandis has already tasted the power that Blood Magic offers. It is now up to him to somehow resist the temptation."

"This is terrible news indeed, Severius. I had thought Morvandis would be a valuable tool to use against Myerasalomé and her legions of Fallen, when the Queen of Havoc chooses to unleash her armies upon the world. But, if the most powerful Mage in the world has succumbed to corruption as well, Morvandis may very well become our most dangerous opponent . . . perhaps even more dangerous than Myerasalomé herself."

"If Morvandis should indeed join the legions of the Queen of Havoc, only one course of action will be left to us. Kaizenerimakagi must be warned. Only the Lord of Snows himself will have an army capable of matching Myerasalomé's army in sheer numbers."

"Simple numbers will not be enough. Look at the current situation in Zarryiosiad's empire: Dakkadia does not have the numbers that Ferralin boasts, and yet their army is the most feared among the four realms."

Severius touched his mask's chin, assuming a considering pose.

"While it is true that numbers alone do not a victory guarantee, they will always mean something on the field of battle," he said. *"I have watched Dakkadia's obsession with finding newer and more efficient ways to kill their fellow man with some degree of concern, but if Valeriad truly is the*

Champion, he will have more of a chance to fulfill his destiny with an army at his back. Especially when the army is as fine as the one that Dakkadia boasts. And if I am to be completely honest, I am afraid of what Myerasalomé will accomplish if there is no one to oppose her. It is for that reason I hope King Madari of Dakkadia is able to fulfill his own ambition and conquer Illymar, the Badlands, and Ferralin. Zarryiosiad's empire, reunited and under the banner of a single strong leader, would have the strength to resist the Fallen, even if Morvandis were to join them. Remember that Kaizenerimakagi and his own armies are too far away to easily intervene. It would take months for his army to assemble and cross the Grave of the Lyx to reach the lands of the Archon."

"I will send word to the Lord of Snows that the Queen of Havoc is growing in power," she said. "However, until we have definite proof that she is on the move, there will be nothing he can do to help. Therefore, I believe we need to be patient and watch events unfold."

"Then I will take my leave of you. It was good to see you again, Astranaithes. Please feel free to visit me whenever you wish. I have an eternity of time to myself, and no one to share it with but my books." He looked around and noticed for the first time that his presence had had an effect upon the area around them. The tiny garden she had been tending with such care was dying; plants lay withered and brown where they had succumbed to his aura of death, and several fish were floating dead in the pool as well. He opened his doorway of darkness and stepped through with one leg before turning back to her one last time.

"I never hated Zarryiosiad for what she did to me, even as I slowly became what you see before you. But when she cursed me, she unleashed a power that should never have existed. If there is any bitterness within me now, it is there because my reward for destroying one evil was to become an even greater one myself."

He gestured at the dead and dying plants and fish.

"I am sorry about your garden, Queen of Fate, but I fear that your flowers and your fish are not the only things that will die."

As he stepped through and closed the doorway behind him, Astranaithes bowed her head in agreement with his prayer.

I, too, hope that the future is not painted with the blood of the innocent. And, I hope as well, that should someone be called upon to pay such a terrible price to save us from this evil, he or she will bear the cost with as much grace and dignity as you have, my friend.

ASTRANAITHES, THE QUEEN OF FATE

CHAPTER TWENTY-FIVE

"Confidences"

Deirdre knocked quietly upon the door to the Corsair's cabin, but there was no answer. So, she tried again a bit harder, and this time she thought she heard a faint reply. Deirdre couldn't make out the muffled words, so she chose to interpret the sound as Lady Prudence's permission to enter. She opened the door, stepped inside, and closed the door behind her. Though the morning sun was peeking in through the shuttered windows, Prudence was still lying face down in her bed, with one leg poking out through her covers and her bare skin showing. Deirdre stepped quietly to the side of the bed and looked at the Corsair's back, wanting to see how well the wound she had sustained in Illymar was healing. To her relief, the wound seemed to be mending quite well, and there was no sign at all of the redness that would denote the presence of an infection.

Despite apparently waking long enough to grant her permission to enter, Prudence had quite clearly fallen back to sleep, and now that she was here, Deirdre found herself to be a little hesitant to wake her again. Instead, she looked around the room at the mementos and tools that Lady Prudence had collected and smiled mischievously. She had been in the room a few times before to bathe, but she had never taken the time to study the room's contents. *No time like the present,* she thought cheerfully.

Lady Prudence's cabin was quite large compared to the other cabins aboard the *Sovereign*, as befit her lofty status as the Captain, but it was also sparsely furnished, making it seem even larger than it actually was. Other than the bed, upon which the Corsair was currently sprawled, and a large leather-bound chest at its base, there was a small table with four sturdy chairs around it, a wardrobe, and a pair of copper bathtubs with a privacy screen set in front of them. She stepped past the bathtubs, which were still filled with water, and looked at Prudence's weapon belt, hanging from a peg on the large wardrobe. Three finely wrought pistols hung from special loops spaced about the belt, along with a few daggers and her sword and main gauche. Her silver and pewter belt buckle featured a grinning skull and crossed bones, the very image of something a blood-thirsty pirate would wear. She had asked Lady Prudence about the buckle once, and the Corsair had laughed and said that an associate of hers in the Badlands had had it crafted for her as a gift on the day she had brought in her first prize. The man had apparently intended it as a jest, but she had absolutely loved it, and proudly wore it even today. The scabbards of her rapier and main gauche were finely tooled leather, and featured the stylized seagull upon a striped sail - the symbol of the Daemira family.

The armoire that the weapons belt hung from was closed, but despite her curiosity, Deirdre made no move to open it. She knew that it would be wrong to pry into the personal belongings of her friend—unless they were being openly displayed, of course—and she had no intention of ever betraying that trust. So, with her curiosity temporarily abated, she walked back over to where Prudence was sleeping and cleared her throat. Prudence didn't even stir at the sound, and Deirdre found herself beginning to get irritated with the Corsair's persistent hold on sleep. So, deciding that direct action was called for, she threw open the shutters to let in the morning's sunlight, and then reached out and shook Prudence's good shoulder.

"Lady Prudence? Are you awake?"

Prudence mumbled sleepily, and then jerked instantly awake, as if Deirdre had jabbed her with a white hot poker when the sunlight hit her eyes. The Corsair spat out a particularly virulent oath and spun around to see who had dared to awaken her. Her reddish-black hair tumbled down her face in an unruly tangle, though the untamed locks did nothing at all to lessen her beauty, and when she finally realized who had interrupted her sleep, she let out a another string of bitter oaths and curses worthy of a pirate. The tirade went on for several moments, but Deirdre ignored them, until Prudence finally regained control of her tongue and glared at Deirdre through sleep bleary eyes.

"Does your evil know no bounds? What are you doing in my room?"

Evil? thought Deirdre, with a huff. *Why, I'm the very portrait of sweetness and light.*

"I knocked—twice—and you yourself invited me in, Lady Prudence. It's not *my* fault that you immediately fell asleep again."

Prudence frowned and gave her a doubtful look.

"Are you sure I invited you in? I don't remember hearing you knock." She peered at Deirdre suspiciously, but then her eyes narrowed in remembrance. "Although, I *was* having a particularly disturbing dream about a castle siege. If I remember correctly, the main gate was being assaulted by a battering ram, and if memory serves, the ram was being swung by a large group of very unsavory characters, all with long blond hair and amber eyes."

Deirdre lifted her chin and gave Prudence her most regal look.

"I'm certain that I have no idea what you are talking about. Are you always this disagreeable when you wake up in the morning?"

Prudence gave her a flat look and waited for two heartbeats before saying in a deadpan voice,

"Yes." Deirdre rolled her eyes in annoyance, but Prudence ignored her. "In fact, it's customary aboard the *Sovereign* for me to execute the unfortunate soul who wakes me in the morning. That's why no one in the crew will do it. They value their lives far too much."

Deirdre crossed her arms over her chest.

"I'd imagine your relationship with Phaedron is going to be very short and extremely grisly then, because he's an early riser. And just like me, he has a bright and sunny disposition when he wakes up, unlike *some* people I could name." Prudence's mouth flew open at the casually cutting remark, but before she could formulate a scathing response, Deirdre sighed miserably. "How is Phaedron doing? I want so badly to speak with him, but Father absolutely forbids it. Normally, I can assume a sad look and get Father to change his mind and do as I wish, but this time it's different. He's too angry to budge."

Corsair's annoyance faded instantly as she regarded the diminutive Princess, for she recognized the genuine concern that Deirdre was displaying, and she smiled in sympathy.

"Phaedron is doing quite well. We're taking our meals together, and last night he and I shared a bottle of wine—or two—which is why I slept in this morning. Normally I don't drink to excess, but considering the quality of the company, I made an exception."

"I'm glad the two of you are together, even if you aren't compatible as a couple and will probably make each other's lives miserable." Prudence goggled at her in disbelief, but Deirdre waved her hand and smiled. "That was a jest, Lady Prudence. Any fool can see the two of you were meant to be together." That seemed to calm Prudence down, but Deirdre's smile faded. "While I'm upset that Father won't allow any of us to speak with him for the remainder of the trip, I can at least rest easy knowing that he's in good hands. Unfortunately, his 'exile' has put me in a bit of a spot, which is why I came to speak with you. You don't mind, do you?"

"Not at all. You talk while I get dressed, and afterward, I'll have my steward bring us some breakfast." She pulled aside her sheets and climbed out of bed, and Deirdre blushed fiercely as she suddenly realized Prudence had been sleeping without a stitch of clothing. Prudence herself seemed unconcerned about her state of undress, but Deirdre turned her gaze away uncomfortably as Prudence looked about for her clothing. As she dressed herself, the Corsair asked, "Is something the matter, Your Highness?"

"Not at all. I just didn't realize that you slept without clothing."

Prudence grinned.

"Actually, I normally do wear clothing. Quite a bit of it, in fact. You see the *Sovereign* can get quite cold in the evenings, even during this time of year. But I guess that the bottle of wine your brother and I shared last night was a bit stronger than I had prepared for, as I was more than a bit tipsy when I staggered to bed last night. I'm afraid that I didn't bother to take the time to dress myself the way I normally do." She glanced back at Deirdre and arched a delicate eyebrow. "Does seeing me in my skin bother you? I have a sister, and because of that, I am used being nude around other women."

"No, you simply surprised me. I will say, however, that Phaedron is going to be a very lucky man when the two of you are decently wed." Prudence nearly choked at the word 'wed', but Deirdre didn't take notice. Overcoming her own shyness, Deirdre looked at Prudence's rounded chest, and then glanced down at her own flat chest and sighed heavily. "A *very* lucky man. I wish my own breasts would start to develop. I'm almost fifteen years old. Shouldn't they have started to grow by now?"

Prudence started to laugh, but caught herself at the miserable look on Deirdre's face and changed the laugh to a slight cough.

"I wouldn't worry about that, Princess. You're simply a late bloomer. If you want to see what you have to look forward to, just look to your mother. Queen Aveliad has quite a fine bosom, and one day you will as well. Trust me when I say that your future husband will have nothing to complain about." Despite the encouraging words the look of misery didn't leave the Princess's face. "Why don't you have a seat and tell me what's on your mind."

Deirdre dutifully sat down on one of the chairs by the small table and started talking.

"I'm glad you mentioned my future husband. Normally, I would talk with Phaedron about something like this, but Father won't allow me to. I've tried talking to Valeriad as well, but he doesn't listen at all . . . he just goes on and on about how wonderful Princess Lyrahe is and doesn't hear a word that I say. Mother is still recuperating, and I really don't want to remind her of that evening, so you're the only one I have left I can speak with." She sighed heavily and entwined her fingers on her lap.

"I've listened to Father talk about what is going to happen in the near future, and it's no secret he is making plans to conquer Illymar at the first possible opportunity. I like Lain very much, and I spent quite a bit of time with him during the parties—enough to know that he is a wonderful man, not at all like his father. I even think I could be very happy with him when we are finally married. But I don't want to be the cause of a war, and I don't want my happiness to come at Illymar's expense. Unfortunately, the way events are shaping themselves to be, that is exactly what is going to happen. My betrothal to Lain neatly clears the way for Father to have his way with Illymar, and it's my fault."

Corsair finished binding her breasts with a long cloth and pulled a loose, flowing shirt over her head.

"That's a bit melodramatic, wouldn't you say?"

"What do you mean?"

Prudence pulled on tight breeches that showed off her perfectly formed legs to great advantage.

"You forget your history. The road to war began over twenty years ago, when Illymar first chose to hire privateers to seek out and destroy Dakkadian naval vessels, shortly after your father took power. They did not attempt to find a diplomatic solution to combat what they perceived as Dakkadian aggression, nor did they seek an alliance that could have been beneficial to both countries. Instead, without cause or provocation, they began attacking and sinking Dakkadian ships, and continued to do so for fifteen years . . . until your father grew tired of their antics and organized his own privateer squadrons to combat them.

"Now that they have lost the advantage, Illymar cries 'foul' and claims that Dakkadia unfairly targets their shipping and has always coveted their lands and their wealth, but no one at all listens to them. The truth is too obvious to everyone else involved, and Orem's ham-fisted attempts to rewrite history fall upon deaf ears." She stamped her boots on and took a seat next to Deirdre, putting a hand on her leg.

"Your future marriage to Prince Lain has nothing whatsoever to do with what will happen. Whether or not you marry him, your father is going to crush Illymar, and I am going to help him do it. You see, I have my own score to settle with Illymar now, and I always pay my debts." She gave Deirdre's leg a friendly pat. "Be happy that at least one good thing came out of the Convocation. If you have found a man you can willingly marry and spend the rest of your life with, then you should concentrate on that to the exclusion of everything else, and let the chips fall where they may."

Deirdre was visibly cheered by this.

"Two good things came from this trip then. Despite your continuing lack of courage where my brother is concerned, I find that the thought of having you as a sister-in-law very definitely counts as a 'good thing' as well." She tilted her head to the side and gave Prudence an impudent look. "If you want, I'll find a way to speak with Phaedron to tell him that as a good Dakkadian man, it is his duty to ask you to marry him as soon as humanly possible, and take you away from this scandalous life. It's the least I can do for you."

Prudence reacted to the words by calmly picking up a pillow, and swatting the golden-haired Princess with it. Deirdre's laugh turned to a shriek as the blows continued to rain down, and after two or three more hits, Prudence finally set aside the pillow and grinned.

"Just when I think I'm starting to like you, you remind me that, deep down under that seemingly innocent exterior, beats a heart of the blackest evil. I'm genuinely surprised that you didn't burst into flame the first time you walked into the Cathedral of Zarryiosiad."

Deirdre again assumed her most regal pose.

"Once again, I'm certain I have no idea what you are talking about, Lady Prudence." She then gave the Corsair a genuine smile and asked impishly, "Now, about that breakfast?"

"Your Highness, pardon the interruption, but Princess Lyrahe is here to see you."

Tais nodded politely to the maid who had spoken and lowered her teacup to its saucer.

"Thank you, Bettina. Please show her in."

The maid curtseyed and left the room, and Tais smiled at her guest apologetically.

"I'm sorry, Mistress Sophia, but it looks as though we'll have to postpone our meal until later in the day. Perhaps an early dinner?"

Despite the fact that Sophia was an older woman with a severe face and stern demeanor, she smiled at the invitation.

"That would be quite acceptable, Your Highness. I will have the cooks prepare something special for you."

"That won't be necessary, Sophia," Tais said. "The cooks are far too busy as it is. I do not want to add to their burdens. Whatever they are preparing will be fine."

As the Head Housekeeper curtseyed gracefully, Tais stopped her by putting a hand on her arm. She placed a small pouch in Sophia's hand.

"This is for Wilhelm the stableman's mother. I've just learned that the woman is in poor health and is in dire need of help. See to it she receives these coins, but give them to her directly, mind you. If you give them to Wilhelm, I'm afraid he will be more inclined to drink to his mother's health than to actually see to it."

"He would at that," Sophia said with a rueful shake of her head. The purse disappeared beneath her apron. "I'll look forward to dining with you this evening, Your Highness."

With that, she swept out of the room, but left the door open behind her. Tais sighed and sat back in her chair, before reaching out and pushing her teacup away from her. She had been having a lot of these meetings recently, taking the time to send invitations to the more powerful or influential members of the household for breakfast or afternoon tea. The reason for the meetings was ostensibly because she was a social pariah and was simply starving for human contact, but her real reasons were more analytical than that. Tais was attempting to build a network of spies and informants within her family's household, and this was simply the quickest and easiest way that she had found to achieve her goals. Luckily, King Orem had helped her cause immensely by cutting Althea's household budget to an absolute minimum, which served to limit the Queen's influence dramatically.

No one knew exactly why he was punishing the Queen and her relatives, but where he once lavished her with money and gifts, he now refused even to speak with her. Tais knew, from meetings just like this one, that the entire Savonne family had somehow incurred the wrath of the King, and as such, her relatives were facing some fairly hard times of their own. Tais had a sneaking suspicion that she was partly to blame for the problems the Savonnes currently faced, but she couldn't be certain, and she wasn't about to ask. Fortunately for her, King Orem hadn't extended his wrath to his children, and he had even gone so far as to reinstate her income. The return of her personal wealth had made it child's play for her to begin building her own network of spies, and she found herself very much enjoying the challenge of gathering secrets and influence.

Before she could get too lost in her thoughts, a swirl of blue cloth caught her eye and she turned in her seat to watch her younger sister glide in. A genuine smile of welcome lit up Tais's face, and she slid her chair back to stand up and give Lyrahe a hug. Lyrahe returned the hug firmly before looking at the table.

"Is that tea?" Tais smiled, offered her sister a chair, and poured her a cup. Lyrahe took a sip and settled back in her seat. "I'm sorry to come into your rooms without advance notice, Tais, but I simply have to speak with someone. Do you have time to talk?"

Tais laughed once, trying to keep the bitterness out of her voice, but failing.

"I have nothing *but* time. It seems that whatever terrible social disease I contracted during my brief marriage and much longer incarceration did not leave with the Dakkadians. I'm sorry to say that none of my former 'friends' will have anything to do with me for fear of being tainted by my proximity. As you may have seen on your way in, I've taken to dining with the Head Housekeeper upon occasion simply to have someone to talk to."

"I see," Lyrahe said, sympathetically. "I'm sorry that I haven't come to visit you before this. I've been . . . distracted."

Tais's ears sharpened at the wistful tone of her sister's words and she leaned back in her chair. *This should be interesting.*

Lyrahe took a sip of her tea.

"Are you aware of what is happening throughout the Spire?"

Tais nodded slowly. Her blossoming network of paid informants was keeping her well-informed, but there were a great many happenings going on in the Spire, and Tais wasn't certain exactly which one Lyrahe was speaking of.

"I do not leave my apartments, I fear, but some word has reached me. It seems Althea has run afoul of King Orem's temper and is suffering his wrath . . . along with our extended family. Is that what you are speaking of?"

"Father has cut off all of Mother's funds, and has instituted a 'tax' upon the Savonnes which could ruin them completely. He says that the upcoming war is their fault, and therefore they will be the ones who must finance it."

Tais nodded and absently ran a fingertip upon the rim of her teacup. She knew about Althea's sudden money troubles, but had no idea what had caused the break between the King and the Savonnes, for none of her informants had been able to discover the cause. One of her informants was the Captain of the Guard himself. She was certain he knew exactly what was going on, but he had flatly refused to talk about that particular subject, and even his obvious and ongoing attraction to her wasn't enough to make him loosen his tongue. She crossed her legs in irritation.

"It was my impression that the reversal of fortune King Orem suffered during the Convocation was *my* fault. How, pray tell, could the Savonnes have been responsible for the failure of the alliance?"

Lyrahe looked at the table.

"That's what I don't understand: I thought it was *my* fault. I tried to be what Prince Lain wanted, but the harder I tried, the more he seemed to pull away from me. It was obvious to both of us that we had very little in common, but I swear I made an honest effort to try and make things work between us. He just didn't want me. By the end of the Convocation, he had even taken to disappearing for hours on end rather than stand with me." She reached out and toyed with the handle of her teacup. "I wasn't good enough for him," she said, her voice small. "That's why the alliance failed."

"I forget sometimes you are still young, and have not been raised the way I was, to be whomever or whatever the man who married me wanted me to be. Let me explain something to you that you may not understand, Lyrahe: arranged marriages—especially between nations seeking to ally with each other—are *never* about love, attraction, or any of your other storybook virtues. They are about breeding, wealth, and power. Lain had no choice in the arrangement made between his father and King Orem, just as you had no choice. Whether or not he was attracted to you had nothing whatsoever to do with the political aspect of the alliance. Had Emperor Xan wanted the alliance to happen, your marriage would have followed. It's as simple as that." Lyrahe looked as if she wanted to argue the point, so Tais raised a hand to forestall her.

"Your marriage to Lain would simply have been the physical representation of that alliance, whether or not the two of you were in love. No, something else happened to change the dynamic between our two nations . . . something that made Xan rethink the wisdom of allying with Illymar. I don't know what that something was, but *that* is what made King Orem angry with the Queen. I suspect that it had something to do with the assassination attempt upon the Corsair's life. I don't *think* Queen Althea would have been foolish enough to make the attempt, but I cannot be certain. The fact that her family is also suffering the King's displeasure is telling, however." She lowered her hand and leaned forward in her seat.

"If Althea *is* the one who plotted and organized the assassination attempt, then she is the one who made the alliance fail and so deserves whatever punishment the King decides to hand out. But the point is, this has nothing whatsoever to do with you. *You* did exactly what you were supposed to do: you made yourself as beautiful as possible each evening, and you dutifully stood beside your intended each night for all to see. That was all that was expected of you."

"I see," said Lyrahe with a sigh. "Well, enough about that." Her voice dropped to a whisper, and she said, "I secretly met with Prince Valeriad of Dakkadia on more than one occasion. On their last day here, I went to see him at the Cathedral. We talked . . . and we kissed." She laughed at Tais's stunned expression. "I know! Can you believe it? By then, the alliance had already been dissolved, of course, but, Tais, I think I'm in love with him!"

Tais's expression changed, and Lyrahe's good humor faded somewhat, as the look of anger registered.

"Stay away from him, Lyrahe. The Dhaerhans are a dangerous lot, and you should avoid them as much as possible. Doing otherwise will get you hurt."

Lyrahe sank back in her chair, obviously confused.

"I thought you, of all people, would be happy for me. You caused quite a stir in the court by spending so much time on King Madari's arm. I thought you liked him."

Tais closed her eyes and remembered the terrible scene in the High Tower.

"So did I. But he was not the man he pretended to be, and that is why you should stay away from Valeriad. The Dhaerhans are conquerors, through and through, and to Valeriad, that's exactly what you would be: a conquest."

Lyrahe frowned at her older sibling and crossed her arms over her chest, obviously upset.

"That's not true at all, Tais. I got to know Valeriad very well during his time here, and he is a perfect gentleman. I even offered to run away with him if he would take me, and he said, 'I'll not steal you away in the night like some sort of brigand.'"

Tais snorted her disbelief at Lyrahe's obvious blindness.

"Lyrahe, the only way the two of you will be together is if the Dakkadian army conquers Illymar and topples the monarchy. If that happens, you will be of no further use to either Valeriad or his father. They'll already have what they want, and you will be discarded. At that point, assuming he still wants you, the best you can hope for is to be his doxy. Remember what I said about political marriages? What use would it be for King Madari to marry off his only son to the daughter of a deposed monarch? No, if Dakkadia conquers Illymar, he will seek to marry Valeriad into one of the noble houses of the City-States of the Badlands to cement another alliance."

Lyrahe gave her a flat look and turned her head to the side in annoyance. Tais simply smiled and took a sip of her rapidly cooling tea and let Lyrahe think about what she had said.

"It's obvious to me that your own terrible experiences have given you a very different perspective on matters of the heart," Lyrahe said, not even trying to keep the bitterness from her voice. "Valeriad would never let his father do anything of the sort. And if Dakkadia does conquer Illymar—which I very much doubt—I would still have value as a figurehead, if nothing else. The citizens of Illymar would not accept a Dakkadian on the throne unless he had some sort of justification for being there. By allowing me to marry Valeriad, Madari would have exactly that sort of justification."

Tais somehow kept her mouth from dropping open in shock at her sister's words.

"And you would accept that? You would sell Illymar to Dakkadia for nothing more than your own personal happiness? Lyrahe, I am truly stunned to hear you say that. But let me warn you now: never say anything of the sort to King Orem, for he would call those words treason, and in the mood he is in now, you would be risking *my* fate—or worse."

"I *said,* I very much doubt Dakkadia will conquer Illymar," Lyrahe said, her voice snippy. "It isn't treason to talk of what can never be."

"Then tell me, what do you believe to be the more likely outcome of our troubles with Dakkadia? And where exactly do you fit in?"

Lyrahe leaned back in her chair.

"Dakkadia will attack us; of this I have no doubt. But I expect our navy to defeat them at the Teeth, and drive them away. I think this will go on for a while until Madari tires of the game and sues for peace, and at that time I expect him to offer to allow the two of us to marry. I think by then, Father will be more open to the idea of an alliance between Dakkadia and Illymar, and will agree rather than continue in a pointless war."

Tais closed her eyes and groaned at her sister's obvious ignorance to the reality of the situation.

"Lyrahe, King Orem and King Madari hate each other with a vengeance. When the two kingdoms *do* go to war with each other, the war will continue until one kingdom or the other is completely defeated. There will be no negotiated settlement or possibility of alliance; it will be until one kingdom is standing atop the ashes of the other. Given the military power the Dakkadians currently possess, the most likely outcome will be the destruction and surrender of our own country. Illymar is wealthy beyond its wildest dreams of avarice, but with great wealth comes great complacency. Our soldiers and sailors have forgotten how to fight. That's why Dakkadia destroys or captures our ships with such ease: we no longer have the will to defend ourselves." She held up her hands and indicated the room they were sitting in. "Look around you. Do the decorations in this castle indicate that the people who live here are willing to fight to the death to defend their country? We've become fat and lazy, and above all, complacent. That's why King Orem needed the alliance with Ferralin! Ferralin, for all its wealth, hasn't lost the will to defend itself. Their army is just that: an army. An army trained to fight and to kill, and to defend to the last breath anything they consider to be theirs. By comparison, our army is filled with second sons and minor nobles, each hoping to gain enough patronage to one day become rich enough to be named to the gentry or the nobility in their own right. They do not train to fight: they train to intrigue."

"The Savonnes have made things worse by hoarding away the vast majority of all the money that the kingdom takes in, and using it for other things besides defense. Our navy used to be the strongest in the world. That changed very dramatically just within the last fifteen years—not because of the Dakkadian weapons that we've heard so much about, but because the Savonnes haven't been building warships! Every last copper the Treasury pulls in is diverted to merchant shipping and merchant programs designed to make money. Not to make money for the *kingdom,* mind you, but to make money for the *Savonnes.* That is why King Orem is striking out at them right now. He is going to have to find the money to prepare us from *somewhere,* and the only people who have money right now are the Savonnes. If they *were* behind the Corsair's assassination attempt, then they provoked the very conflict he has been attempting to avert all along, and don't fool yourself, Lyrahe: this is a war that we aren't prepared for! It takes time to build warships, and to train and outfit a proper army. Dakkadia already has both, and what's more, they have the will to use them." Tais pressed her hands flat upon the table and leaned forward.

"Our *only* hope right now lies in the protection of Ithram and the Mage Council. As long as they support us, we will have the time we need to match Dakkadia's strength. But without Ithram's support, we would be attacked within a month or two at the outside, and after they conquered us, you would be able to spend your nights in the arms of your would-be lover. But not as his wife, Lyrahe. *Never* that. He wouldn't need you anymore, and Madari would never allow it."

Despite the vitriol of her own response, Lyrahe's reaction to her words still surprised her, for the younger Princess slammed her hands on the table and stood up, a look of wild fury on her face.

"I refuse to accept that, Tais! I absolutely refuse! It's clear to me now that your bitterness at the loss of your own true love has poisoned your heart. But I will not allow you to try and poison my heart as well! You air your opinions as if they are facts, and try to twist everything to suit your own callous purposes. Well, I will not sit here and listen to you malign Valeriad simply because you can't accept that anyone else could possibly love as 'deeply' as you!" Lyrahe placed her fists on the table and leaned forward to glare at Tais. "Valeriad is a good man, and despite what you may think, we love each other! You may believe that nothing good can come of this, but I will not accept that."

Tais found herself standing up, leaning over the table as well to hiss into her sister's face.

"We will see, Lyrahe! We will *see*! I tell you now, that sooner or later, Dakkadia *will* come for us, and when they do, I hope that you have the chance to prove me wrong. You claim that my opinions are based upon nothing but my own bitterness? Better that than basing my opinions on the silly, *useless* fables our nannies read to us when we were children! You should have grown out of believing those kinds of tales a long time ago, Lyrahe. You're smarter than that."

The two women stared daggers at each other for several moments, until Lyrahe turned and left the room without another word. Tais didn't try to stop her.

She stood there for a few minutes, replaying the conversation with her sister in her head.

Once upon a time, she thought bitterly to herself. *Once upon a time, I, too, believed in true love conquering all. It's hard to believe now that I was ever so foolish, or so naïve.*

In a sudden rage, she swept her hand across the table and threw the dishes to the floor. Despite the presence of a soft, finely woven carpet, the delicate porcelain tea service shattered upon the hard marble floor beneath it. She hissed in pain and looked at her hand, realizing that the edge of one of the teacups had cut her, perhaps in retaliation for its own sudden demise. The cut wasn't bad, but it was bleeding, so she reached down to the floor and picked up a napkin to press it against her hand. Two of her handmaidens ran to her side.

"Your Highness?" asked one of the handmaidens. "Is anything the matter?"

Tais allowed a rueful smile to cross her features. She had become very good at that recently; good at hiding what she truly felt or thought behind a pleasant façade, and only allowing people to see what she wanted them to see.

"I am quite well, thank you, Marissa."

She glanced down at the mess she had made on the floor.

"I apologize for that unseemly display, and for the mess as well. Would one of you be so kind as to clean this for me? I think I need some air."

Both maids curtseyed and began clearing away the porcelain shards, and Tais took the opportunity to walk outside to her open-aired balcony. She looked out at the bay, which seemed somehow emptier without the black and white sail of the *Sovereign* prominently displayed, and for the first time since the Dakkadian contingent had left, she allowed herself to think honestly about that night in the Tower with Madari.

It wasn't his fault, she admitted to herself. *None of it was his fault. He did not know about my history with that terrible place, nor did he know that simply being in that room would rekindle those memories within me. Every single word he said to me that evening was true, and everything he did to me was justified.* She closed her eyes in pain. *If only I had tried to tell him why I reacted the way I did, things might have been different between us. As it is, I am lucky he had the self-control and the common decency to stop himself from taking from me what, up until the moment we entered that room, I was so willing to give to him. He could have. He could have done anything he wanted to me, and I would have been powerless to stop him. But he didn't. Instead, he walked away from me, not understanding that none of what transpired was his fault, and though his wounded pride must have been screaming within him, he left me alone.*

The memory of him standing in the doorway, the unshed tears and the heartbreak written upon his face returned to her, and she reached up to dry her eyes before her own tears could fall. It was that single look that had told her that what he had felt for her had been true, and that her sudden and unexpected betrayal had cut him to the bone.

While it is true that Illymar and Dakkadia have long been rivals, it is I—I, and not the grasping Savonnes or the scheming Queen or the arrogant King of this corrupt kingdom—who truly succeeded in making an enemy of Madari Dhaerhan. I have no doubt that he will be back to extract his revenge, as he swore to me that evening, and when he does, I will bear all of it upon my shoulders as my punishment for repaying his kindness to a heartbroken and lonely little girl with nothing but humiliation and regret.

Prince Ethan watched his father and Uncle Ascham speaking with the Master Shipwright and frowned in irritation. His father had ordered him to the docks, and so here he was, though unwillingly. Ethan hated the docks and everything to do with them, for they always smelled of mildew and decaying fish, and he simply couldn't abide the stench.

But when your father is the King, you do as you are told and keep your mouth shut. Well, he thought with wry amusement, *at least there is something interesting to see for a change.*

What they were looking at was the Illymari answer to the *Sovereign;* a warship purpose-built to take on the Corsair and survive. It was one of over a dozen new ships being built simultaneously in the Illymari shipyards, but it would take months for it to be completed. The arrival of the *Sovereign* had been fortuitous for the Illymari navy, even if they hadn't been able to discover the secret of their new weapons. Instead, the Illymari shipwrights had gotten a very good look at the *Sovereign* and had been able to postulate on what the ship was capable of, and, perhaps more importantly, look for any weak spots in the design. From what Ethan had been able to tell, the shipwrights were very impressed with the *Sovereign*. They called it a 'frigate', whatever that was, and said that it was built for speed and maneuverability.

The most important discovery they had made about the *Sovereign,* however, was not the design of the ship itself: it was the number of Mages among its crew. The observers who had been watching the Corsair's ship had discovered that she had *two* Mages at her disposal. That would account for the failure of every attempt to capture her or sink her, for the Illymari navy was notoriously parsimonious in the deployment of their Mages.

Most ships had no Mages at all, while a particularly important warship might be assigned a single Airborn or Waterborn. With a two-to-one advantage in Mages, and the new weapons it carried besides, nothing that the Illymari navy currently had could stand against it. Now that they knew about the Mages, however, the next flotilla they sent out to destroy her would be better prepared.

The new ships currently being built were designed with an exaggerated forecastle and aftcastle set much higher than the deck of the *Sovereign,* though much lower than those found on a galleon. The purpose for these tall structures was so that crossbowmen could rain arrows down into the lower deck of the *Sovereign,* thereby negating the protection of its strong wooden walls. The crew compliment was much greater as well, with a large percentage of the crew being marines rather than regular navy.

The plan, as Ethan had come to understand, was to send out this ship, or others like it, with three Mages aboard each, to counter the *Sovereign's* two. The Mages would then force the *Sovereign* into a boarding action, where their superior number of marines would make short work of the Corsair and her crew.

Abruptly, the Master Shipwright bowed to the King and stepped away, and both Orem and his brother, Ascham, returned to where Ethan was standing with the horses. Orem nodded to him, but Ascham frowned when their eyes met. Ethan's irritation raised a notch at the look.

"Why are you frowning at me, Uncle?" he asked.

Ascham's lips pressed together at the question.

"You should have been over there with us, speaking to the shipwright. You need to know the details of what we are trying to accomplish in the defense of your future kingdom, in case something happens to your father."

Ethan gave his uncle an arrogant smile, marred somewhat by his slightly crooked nose.

"I understand quite well what you are doing, Uncle. You believe that these ships will be enough to destroy the *Sovereign.* As I know nothing about the design of ships of *any* type, it is better to let the professional shipwrights make the decisions and keep out of their way. Pretending you have something valuable to add to their design will simply add to cost of the ship, as well as the time it takes to build, without improving the design one bit."

Ascham's own irritation turned rapidly into anger, and he rounded on his nephew.

"Shipwrights are not soldiers. They do not understand concepts such as an unobstructed field of fire or protective bottlenecks. The design as they had it, would have made the forecastle and the aftcastle far too easy to storm. We need the archers to have as much time as possible to do their jobs should they ever run down the *Sovereign.*"

"It was my understanding that we are buying off the Corsair," Ethan said, doing nothing to conceal his contempt for his uncle. "Why bother to target her if she is amenable to bribes?"

Ascham said nothing for a moment, simply looked at him as if unable to believe what he had just heard. Finally, he took the reins of his charger and climbed into his saddle.

"Spoken like a true Savonne," Ascham said. "Sometimes I wonder about you, boy. When I look at you I see an Illvanin, but when you open your mouth all I hear are your mother's words. Which are you, then: a Prince, or a merchant?"

Ethan reached out and grabbed the bridle of Ascham's horse.

"Oh, I'm a Prince, Uncle." He tugged on the horse's bridle to emphasize his point. "I'm a Prince who doesn't have to put up with the insults of a mere Duke."

"If you don't like what I have to say, then I invite you to shut me up any time you like. Or *try* to shut me up, I should say. The day that a Savonne can defeat an Illvanin in battle is the day this country is truly in trouble."

Ethan tightened his hand on the horse's bridle and started to respond in kind, but Orem intervened.

"That's enough from the both of you. It is time to set aside our own differences and see to the defense of the country." He glared at them until they relented, and then he turned his gaze solely on Ascham. "And I'll thank you for keeping your insults about my wife's family to an absolute minimum. The last thing I need is for infighting between your two factions to hamper what I am trying to accomplish. Do I make myself clear?"

Ascham bowed his head to his older brother.

"Absolutely." He looked at Ethan and nodded slightly. "For my part, I am sorry about the harshness of my words. The Savonnes and I have had a long and unpleasant history with each other, but that does not involve you, no matter what I have said. As I said earlier, I look at you and I see an Illvanin. That's good enough for me."

Ethan glared for a moment longer, before nodding.

"Apology accepted, Uncle. What is next on the agenda?"

"The smithies," Orem said. "We have them working day and night on the weapons we are going to need, and I want to view their progress."

Ethan smiled at that, for that was something that he *was* interested in. As a tournament duelist, he had more than a passing familiarity with weaponry of all kinds, and he was looking forward to seeing what the blacksmiths were producing.

The rest of the day was spent viewing the preparations being made in every corner of the city. The citizens were concerned about the approaching war, but somehow their spirits were still high. It took him a while to understand, but he overheard a chance conversation that made everything clear to him. Two smiths had been talking where they had thought they were out of earshot, and one had said, "Now that the King is reining in the Savonnes, perhaps some of us will be able to make a living again." The other smith had added, "Every forge in the city has been relit. We're going to have more work than we can possibly handle trying to make up for the Savonne's short-sighted greed."

Ethan had been enraged at the comments, but had held his tongue . . . something which was completely uncharacteristic for him to do, for he knew their comments were not isolated. There was a groundswell of hatred against the Savonnes he hadn't known had existed, and now that they were no longer in the King's good graces, that hatred was starting to bubble to the surface. In effect, the Savonnes had used their position at court to tie up every valuable property in the country. Mineral rights, fishing rights, timber, farming futures . . . everything of value in the country somehow had to filter its way through Savonne hands. Anyone not willing to pay the exorbitant fees or outright bribes that the Savonnes required wouldn't be allowed to work . . . a fact that the blacksmith had just pointed out.

That had been fine while the Savonnes enjoyed the King's favor, for the Savonnes were very good about paying the King his due. That money had allowed for lavish decorations, extravagant parties, a never-ending stream of jewelry and fine dresses, and the finest of foods and alcohol available to be delivered in a constant stream to the Spire, and yet, somehow, there had never seemed to be enough money to equip the army or build a navy.

Orem blamed the Savonnes for all of these troubles, but the truth was even worse: the King himself had neglected the kingdom for years, and the Savonnes were simply a convenient scapegoat for him to blame his current troubles upon. Oh, certainly, the assassination attempt on the Corsair had gone wrong and had destroyed everything his father had been trying to achieve, but the desperation they felt now had more to do with his mismanagement of the kingdom than any actual threat. All it did was shine a light on just how threadbare the military's cupboard had become, and how far behind the Dakkadians they actually were. As expected, Orem accepted none of the blame for those problems himself.

No, the Savonnes are the actual *reason for the problems you are facing, aren't they, Father? Blame Mother for your own laziness and shortsightedness if it helps you sleep at night, but I know the truth.*

He narrowed his eyes as a thought crossed his mind . . . one that had made its way into his head more and more often as of late.

I would make a far better King than you, Father. A far better King. Only one real obstacle stands between me and absolute power should you suffer a mischief. He glanced at his uncle's profile and frowned. *Ascham's popularity has grown to the point he has become a serious threat to my eventual rule. If anyone deserves to suffer a mischief, it's that insufferable bastard. It's too bad we need him right now. He'd be so much more useful as a martyr.* He smiled. *Once we've repulsed the Dakkadians, I won't need you anymore, Uncle. When that day comes, watch your back.*

Vitaly Saxe made his way to the inn that housed The Penitentiary, carrying a bouquet of flowers, with a spring in his step and a smile on his face. He was meeting the fair Mistress Thorn for an early dinner, and afterward he had engaged her specialized services for the remainder of the evening.

Official business had prevented him from seeing her again after that first glorious evening, but now that he had some free time, he planned to make the most of it. She had haunted his dreams ever since he had met her, and he desperately wanted to see if she could outdo the performance she had given him on their first meeting. He could hardly remember any of the events of that evening, but the heights of pleasure and pain she had taken him to made him salivate for more, and so he had sent a note to The Penitentiary to ask her to clear her schedule for him. The reply had been tersely worded and to the point.

Be here at 7 o'clock sharp, and not one second later, or you will pay a heavy price for your lack of punctuality.

He looked up at the clock in the middle of the square, which showed the time as 7:01. He had planned his arrival perfectly, for he wanted to be defiant without actually being rude. It would make for a much more enjoyable evening on his part, and he desperately wanted to know what she meant when she said that he would pay "a heavy price." He tapped the bouquet of flowers that he was carrying against his hand in anticipation, idly wondering just how she would react to the colorful arrangement, for she definitely did not seem the type who would enjoy flowers. But both the bouquet and the lack of punctuality were calculated to bring out her best efforts this evening. After all, he had much to celebrate.

The reason he'd been so busy lately was that Ascham had finally capitalized upon all of the mistakes the Savonnes had made, and had used the opening they had given him to reverse his own misfortunes—as well as the misfortunes of a great number of his most loyal vassals. As his right hand man, Vitaly had constantly been tasked with delivering orders to his supporters, or even better, seeing that one Savonne or another was caught up in the whirlwind.

That was the best part for him, for he had found that he rather enjoyed kicking in doors to find secret stashes of contraband and wealth that all of the Savonnes seemed to have squirreled away for just such an event. Most of their information came from informers, of which there was no lack, for just as he and the Duke had scores to settle, so, too, did the commoners.

No one had been arrested yet, but several people had been detained for their failure to abide by the King's tax. Since the King felt that no Savonne could be trusted, it fell upon the Duke's men—namely, one Vitaly Saxe—to enforce the King's will upon the unwilling Savonnes.

Ah, life is good. Perhaps if I'm lucky, one of those merchant scum will be stupid enough to resist me. It would be nice to make an example of one or two of them. It might make the rest of them a bit more . . . pliable.

He set aside his pleasant thoughts and opened the door to The Penitentiary. As he entered the common room, he saw her sitting at a private table close to the fireplace. She saw him enter the room but didn't react, and he took a moment to scrutinize her appearance. She was wearing a white shirt with long, billowing sleeves, open to just below her perfect breasts, and a pair of tailored breeches that hugged her legs like a second skin. To complete the effect of a lady preparing to go for a pleasant ride in the country, she wore a pair of knee-high black leather riding boots, polished to a high sheen. She even had a riding crop sitting next to her on the table, and seeing it sitting there made him long to feel its touch. Careful not to meet her gaze, he approached the table.

"I'm sorry I'm late, Mistress Thorn, but I was unavoidably detained."

He proffered the flowers to her, which she took without a word. That vaguely disappointed him, for he had expected her to throw them in his face, or refuse them altogether.

"You were standing outside in the square, carefully watching the clock to make certain you were exactly one minute late. That little display of insolence tells me, quite clearly, that I failed to instill the proper amount of respect within you during our last meeting. If you still have enough defiance within you to disobey even the simplest of my commands, I will simply have to show you the error of your ways. Now, please have a seat. I suggest you eat very well tonight, my pet, for you are going to need your strength. *All* of it."

As he took the seat across from her, she raised an elegant foot from where it had been resting on the floor and placed it on the chair directly between his legs. When he saw it there, coiled like a polished black snake ready to strike at him, he began to sweat, both dreading and anticipating the blinding pain that he knew was coming, but again she surprised him, for she did nothing more than rest it there and smile an amused little smile. Before either of them could speak, a serving maid approached the table.

"My, what a beautiful bouquet! May I take those for you and put them in some water?"

"That won't be necessary," Thorn said, and tossed the flowers over her shoulder and into the fireplace without even looking. "I despise flowers, you see, a fact that my supplicant here should have known."

Momentarily distracted by the display of the bouquet catching fire, he was completely unprepared for the savage kick she delivered to his groin under the table. Doubled over in pain, and his face turned red in agony as she ground her heel between his legs, before she finally lessened the pressure enough to allow him to grasp at his crotch. Thorn laughed quietly as he tried to suffer in silence rather than disturb the other guests, and she waited a moment before turning back to the maid.

"I will have the baked cod," at the word *cod,* she ground the tip of her boot hard against his groin once again to prolong his agony, "with lemon and butter. He will have the veal—two servings, very rare. And just so he knows I'm thinking about him, he will also have a side of beets and turnips." Though he was hunched over and couldn't see it, she gave him a wicked smile. "The last time we saw each other, he told me that he simply *loves* beets and turnips. And to drink, I believe he will have a bottle of your finest red, and I will have a glass of white wine."

Completely unperturbed by their antics, the maid turned and went through a side door to the kitchen. After she left, Thorn leaned back in her chair.

"I hope you didn't mind that I took the liberty of ordering for you. You seemed to be distracted for some reason."

Though he hadn't quite recovered from the kick to his groin, he smiled at her, still careful not to meet her eyes.

"Not at all, Mistress Thorn. Although, I must admit, I did not realize that your cruelty extended so far as to making me eat vegetables I utterly despise. The kick was one thing, for I fully admit I deserved it. But no one deserves to be forced to eat turnips and beets. Have you no shred of pity?"

She surprised him by giving him a genuine laugh.

"So don't eat them. The kick—and the vegetables—were merely my way of greeting a friend, and I am not as cruel as you might think. Please look me in the eyes." He hesitated for a moment before complying, expecting her words to be yet another trick designed to catch him off guard, but she surprised him once again by removing her foot from between his legs and placing it firmly on the floor. She pointed at the door behind the bar. "Until we are safely behind those doors, you have nothing further to fear from me other than my healthy appetite, and my appreciation for fine wine. It would be very unprofessional of me to extend our activities to the main floor, and I am certain that the Mistress of the House would be displeased. Appearances must be kept, you understand. So, until we are behind those doors, I am simply 'Thorn', and you are a particularly handsome acquaintance with whom I have decided to share a pleasant dinner and scintillating conversation, with the understanding that dessert," she gave him a predatory look, "will come later. Can you accept that, or should we go ahead and adjourn to a more pleasant environment?"

"Thorn it is," he said. "If you have no objection, I find the idea of a pleasant dinner and scintillating conversation to be exactly what I am looking for. We can save dessert for after dinner, where it belongs."

"I know we are not supposed to share our names, but I have to call you something other than 'my pet' or 'worm,'-at least while we're in public. So what, then, shall I call you?"

He thought about it for a moment and saw no harm in telling her his real name.

"My name is Vitaly."

The maid returned at that moment and showed them a dusty bottle of wine, which Vitaly examined briefly before nodding his approval. After the maid had poured their drinks and had once again departed for the kitchen, he lifted his glass.

"To scintillating conversation."

She raised her own glass.

"To just desserts."

They clicked their glasses together, and then settled back to enjoy one another's company.

At the end of the dinner, Vitaly knew that he wanted to see more of this enchanting and talented woman.

"I would like to see you again, if you would permit it, Thorn, outside of the confines of this establishment."

"We haven't even gotten to dessert yet. How can you be certain that you want to see me again?"

He lifted his glass and swirled his wine for a brief moment before answering.

"I've had 'dessert' once before, and I already know that it suits me. What I am interested in is seeing more of you in a less formal capacity."

She batted her eyelashes at him playfully.

"Why, Vitaly . . . are you starting to fall for me?"

He laughed briefly and set down his wineglass.

"Let us simply say that I find you to be an extremely remarkable young woman, and I am intrigued enough by what I have learned about you so far to want to learn more. Who knows where it will lead?"

He glanced at the door leading to the basement of The Penitentiary.

"I can be very generous, you know. If you want, I can take you away from this place and allow you to live a life of luxury. Simply say the word, and I will make it so."

She smiled at him and reached across the table to pat his cheek.

"That is very sweet of you, Vitaly, but I am sorry to say that I must refuse. Your offer is very tempting, I'll admit, but I will be leaving the city very soon to meet with relatives on the other side of the island. I don't know how long I will be gone. In point of fact, I will be leaving shortly after our session this evening. I was planning on leaving tonight, but then I received your message and I just couldn't pass up the opportunity to see you again. You were such an . . . *enthusiastic* subject last time, that I simply jumped at the chance. There is so much left to try with you, you see . . . so many more delightful experiments I can perform upon you. I'm almost breathless with anticipation."

She said the last in a sultry voice that made his heart leap in his chest. Vitaly tried to hide his disappointment at her refusal of his offer, but failed utterly, and so he tried one more attempt.

"Thorn, I am a man of means and power, and when I say that I could keep you in a life of luxury for as long as you'll have me, I mean exactly what I say. You would be exclusive to me, and more importantly, you wouldn't have to work in establishments like this one."

"Again, that is a very generous—and tempting—offer, but I still must refuse. I do not do *this*," she tapped the riding crop sitting on the table beside her, "because I have to; I do this because I *want* to. It affords me the opportunity to meet new people and do cruel things to them, to see how far they—and I—are willing to go. If I were to accept your offer, I would lose that freedom to test my boundaries, and though you are infatuated with me now, one day you would learn all of my tricks and grow tired of me. And aside from all that, I simply refuse to be your pet. It would go against my nature."

She reached up with her right hand and touched her collarbone, and then ran her fingers across it to her right shoulder, subtly pulling aside her shirt to reveal more cleavage than she had shown all evening. His eyes were drawn to the seductive movement, and he set aside his napkin and slid his chair back to stand up.

"I suddenly feel the need to have dessert right now, Thorn. Shall we?"

Her throaty laugh sent shivers down his spine.

"I thought you would never ask, Vitaly."

The next morning, Thorn rode her horse from the stable with another large bag of gold tied to her belt and three remounts tied to her saddle. The Mistress of the House had bid her a reluctant farewell, but not before begging her to stay on. The Mistress had offered to pay her triple her regular fee to remain, but Thorn had other orders. Before he had left, Morvandis had summoned her to a meeting and had ordered her to wait for one week after the departure of the *Sovereign*, and then to ride all the way across the island to a small fishing village which sat upon the northern coast of Illymar. She was to come alone, but bring along enough supplies and remounts for herself and one other. She had no idea whom she was meeting, for Morvandis himself was gone and the Teeth of Amhar would stop any ships from approaching from that direction. But his orders had been explicit, and so she found herself riding out of the city at a gentle canter shortly before dawn.

The ride was going to be a very long one, and while he had indicated no particular hurry for her to arrive, she wanted to get the journey over and done with. By her estimation, the entire trip would take about six days, with only the occasional inn along the way, so the more daylight she used, the quicker the trip would go. She had not been lying to Vitaly when she told him she had been planning to leave the city before she received his invitation, but the opportunity to put him to the question once again was too good to pass up, and so she had delayed her departure for the hours it had required to complete her rendezvous with the Earl of Saxe. She was glad she had, for the information she had forced from him had been eye opening, and all of it was bad news for Dakkadia.

She didn't know how Madari would react to the word that after years of neglect, Illymar was getting its house in order. Or that Ascham had somehow regained Orem's favor, and was currently rebuilding their military into something that could possibly stand against Dakkadia, but she didn't expect his reaction to be a good one. Dakkadia was still not prepared to go to war with Illymar, and wouldn't be for some time, and with every day that passed, Illymar would become a much stronger opponent than they had planned on.

Once her mission was over, she hoped that she would be able to return home to Dakkadia to see her husband, Thanarilliad, again. They had been too long apart, and as much as she enjoyed breaking Illymari men and women to her will in the service of the Crown, she missed the truly ingenious and inventive ways her husband had devised to maximize both the pain and the pleasure for his own subjects. A vision of Vitaly flashed through her head, and she laughed in amusement.

It is too bad that you weren't able to meet my husband, Vitaly. If you think I *am good at what I do, you should try him. Thanarilliad would have you broken, saddled, and harnessed, before you even realized the bit had been placed between your teeth.*

It could still happen, she knew, but it would take a long time before the Dakkadian army was in the position to arrange a meeting between her spouse and her "lover." But before that day could come, she had a mission to perform and a job to do. So, she left the city, and turned her horse to the north to begin her journey.

CHAPTER TWENTY-SIX

"Cloak"

Phaedron dipped his quill into an inkwell and tapped it once against the opening to clear away the extra ink before signing his name to the letter he had just finished writing. He placed the quill back into its holder, and then sprinkled some sand onto the sheet to dry it. After tipping the letter to the side to let the sand fall to the floor, he melted some wax onto the sheet and pressed his signet into it. He folded up the message and poured more wax upon it to seal it shut, and then once again, pressed his signet into the hot wax to leave his mark. Once he was finished, he set the letter aside to sit among a growing pile of messages that he had written, and pulled out a fresh sheet to start the process over again.

The *Sovereign* was nearing the end of its journey, and he knew that at any time the word could come down that land was in sight, but before they made it to the port he had to finish writing out his orders for his factors and managers back home in Daane. If war was coming, and he knew it was, the citizens of his townships and counties had to be prepared to do their part to support the war effort, and his soldiers needed time to train and equip themselves. Normally, he would oversee the efforts himself, but he had decided upon a different path for himself, at least until winter came. That wouldn't matter to the citizens of Daane, however, for he had surrounded himself with very capable people and he trusted their decision-making abilities implicitly.

One thing his mother had always told him was; *one of the hallmarks of a good leader is to know when to delegate. Choose good people for your important posts, and leave them to do their jobs. Your vassals and subordinates will come to love you if you show them that you trust them and value their judgment.* That had been excellent advice, and he had used it well throughout his tenure as the Earl of Daane. He was not a figurehead by any means, but his people also knew that they should trust their own judgment, and that he would support their decisions.

Because he bunked with the crew he did not have his own room, but that didn't bother him in the slightest. Prudence believed the same way he did about surrounding herself with capable subordinates, and as such, she had gathered some of the finest people it had ever been his privilege to meet. Over the journey to and from Illymar, the men and women aboard the *Sovereign* had become good friends, and he was on a first-name basis with most of them. Not everyone would "presume," of course, but he was working on them. His hands, already calloused from years of swordplay, were growing new calluses in unfamiliar places, thanks to countless hours hauling on ropes or helping to clean the deck. That was what had cracked the reserve of many of the people he now considered friends, for it was hard to remain wary of a person willing to get on his hands and knees beside you to scrub the deck.

Someone knocked on a wooden beam by the door, and he turned his head to see who had come to see him. Prudence was standing behind him, leaning against the beam and smiling that beautiful smile he never grew tired of seeing.

"I certainly hope those aren't love letters, or we are going to have a serious problem, My Lord."

He glanced at the pile of letters and laughed, before giving her a cocky grin.

"I wouldn't exactly call them love letters, but I do want to keep in touch with my harem. You know how it is when you're young and good-looking. Women throw themselves at you everywhere you go. And then it becomes nothing but work to keep in touch with them."

"I know exactly what you mean," she said. "That's why I make sure to keep *my* harem divided among every port I stop in. That way I don't have to write to them. I can just stop in to see them any time I want, and I can mix business with pleasure."

He reached out and grabbed her hand to pull her into his lap. She let out an unladylike squeal as she fell backward onto his waiting legs, and when he finally had her at his mercy, he leaned forward and kissed her soundly. As they kissed, she reached up and ran her fingers through his long black hair, luxuriating at the feel of it between her fingertips. For his part, he slid a hand down the outside of her leg to touch her knee, and then slid it back up again until he was touching the side of her breast. Their kiss became more intense at the intimate contact, and her breathing became labored as her desire rose. Unfortunately, just as their passionate kiss was reaching a fevered pitch, a voice sounded from the hatch.

"Ah, Cap'n? Sorry to bother you, Ma'am, but the lookout has spotted land." With their lips still locked together, she groaned in frustration and reluctantly pulled her lips from Phaedron's.

"Fine. Tell Mr. Frederick to prepare to dock. I will be up to take charge in a few minutes." The sailor knuckled his forehead and left the two of them alone again. "It's always something, isn't it?" she said. "Just when things are getting good between you and me, someone reminds me that I actually have duties and responsibilities to attend to."

"Well, we should have plenty of time to rectify that over the next few months. I've decided to take you up on your offer to stay aboard the *Sovereign* for the rest of your hunting season, providing I can get permission from King Madari to join your crew. I've been banished to Daane, if you'll remember. It wouldn't be a permanent arrangement, even if he does allow me to stay aboard, because when winter comes, I will have to leave to oversee my lands. But for now, I would very much like to remain aboard, if you will have me."

She gave another unladylike squeal and hugged him, for all the world like he had just given her a particularly wonderful gift.

"You just leave His Majesty to me, My Lord. But tell me, what made you change your mind?"

"Well, the opportunity to study with Cahrick was the main factor, of course," he said, trying hard to sound casual. "He's one of the best Waterborn I've ever met, and I'm certain that under his tutelage I will really come into my own as a Water Mage."

She frowned again and crossed her arms under her breasts.

"Is he the only reason you decided to stay on?"

Phaedron pretended to think about it for a moment.

"That's the only reason that comes to mind at the moment. Why? Is there some other reason that you can think of for me to want to stay aboard?"

Still sitting on his lap, she rounded on him and grabbed his sides to tickle him.

"I hope you and Mr. Rantrefal will be happy together, My Lord. You should probably buy some warmer clothing before we depart, however. Something tells me the next few months are going to be very cold for you."

"Oh, I wouldn't worry too much about me if I were you. I have my sights set upon a particular wench aboard ship who I plan to use to ward off the cold. It shouldn't be too difficult to convince her to keep me warm at night. She already finds me irresistible, and she can't seem to keep her hands off of me." She halted her assault and gave him a haughty look, with one delicate eyebrow raised.

"Sounds like a real trollop. Anyone I know?"

He shrugged and shook his head sadly.

"Oh, who can remember their names? I never bother" Her mouth opened in outrage, but he wasn't finished. "It's not like it matters anyway. I'll probably just end up calling her 'sugar lips' or 'sweetling' or some other pet name. Women really love that sort of thing." She fisted him in the side hard enough to make him grunt.

"If you ever call me 'sugar lips', I'll have you keel-hauled. I can do that, because I'm the Captain."

"What has our once-proud navy come to that it would allow such a tyrant to command one of its finest ships?" He shook his head sadly. "I guess it's up to me to incite a mutiny the minute we leave port. Nothing personal, you understand, but it's for the good of Dakkadia."

She nodded her understanding, and then without warning her fingers leapt for his sides to continue her attempt to tickle him. He caught her hands in his and pulled her close once again, and she settled herself back to be thoroughly kissed one more time before duty separated them once again.

"Expertly handled, Captain," Madari said as the *Sovereign* settled into the port and dropped anchor. "Please allow me to extend my gratitude to you for the safe and pleasant journey. And if you don't mind, I would like to speak with the crew to thank them for their efforts before I leave. Would you be so kind as to assemble them for me?"

Corsair nodded once and turned to her first officer, and as the orders were passed among the crew and they assembled on deck, he ran his fingers over the well-worn hilt of his sword as he thought about what to say. Finally, the crew had lined themselves up in perfect rows, and Lady Prudence nodded to him again. Instead of speaking, he walked to where the wooden railing had been removed to allow a gangplank to be extended to the dock. He glanced down at the dock, where his soldiers and nobles were already beginning to assemble, ready to escort both he and his family to the Blackstone, and turned back to the crew.

"As soon as I leave this ship, the Peace of Zarryiosiad will be officially lifted and the temporary truce between our nation and the nation of Illymar will be abolished. For your exemplary service during the Convocation, as well as to thank you for honoring me by carrying my family and me into the lion's den and home again safely, I want you to be the first to know." He placed his hand upon the hilt of his sword, and in a much stronger voice he said,

"For their assault on the honor of Dakkadia, and for their treachery in plotting and carrying out the cowardly assassination attempt on your own Captain, I tell you now, I intend to demand an accounting from the King of Illymar, and the debt he owes us will be paid in blood. From the moment my feet touch Dakkadian soil, we will be at war with Illymar!" His voice lowered again, and he almost sounded wistful when he continued.

"I wish things could be different; I wish that I could reward you for your faithful service in the manner that you so richly deserve, but instead, I must now send you into harm's way to show our enemies what it means to choose to stand against the might of Dakkadia! Illymar chose the path to war, and once again, they did so under the banner of peace; and for that, we will drive them to their knees!"

To a person, the eyes of the crewmembers showed hard satisfaction at his words. Every single one of them already wanted revenge for the assault on the Corsair, which was why he had so pointedly reminded them of the attack in his speech. Just looking at their reactions, he could tell that the *Sovereign* by itself was about to tear a bloody swath through the Illymari navy. *As it should be.*

"You are the very tip of the Dakkadian sword and the vanguard of our retribution, and I am counting upon each and every one of you to do your duty to the utmost. Make them pay for their treachery! Take everything you can from them, and burn the rest! Leave them nothing but ashes for daring to raise their swords to us! And when you have done enough damage to their fleet, when the once-proud Illymari navy has been laid low, I promise you now, I will finish off what you are about to start." He gave them a Dakkadian salute, fist to chest, and the crew responded as one with a salute of their own. "All of Dakkadia will be watching you! So, good fortune, and good hunting! May the Archon guide your hands!"

The tight discipline of the crew broke completely as they let out a wild cheer and began slapping each other on the back and shaking hands with each other. He smiled at their reaction, and turned to Lady Prudence.

"Lady Prudence, it is imperative that you depart as soon as possible to attack the Illymari navy. I want you to take no unnecessary chances, but strike them as hard and as fast as you can. Capture prizes if you are able, but it is more important by far to sink or capture as many warships as possible. Because of the time it took us to sail home, Illymar already has a two-week head start on us.

That means you must assume that every ship in their fleet will be forewarned that we are coming for them. Moreover, I am positive that they will be searching for you personally to complete the task they failed to accomplish in Illymar. By your actions, you have become the very heart of the Dakkadian navy, and the one person they fear above all others. So, I want you to use that fear against them. Cripple as much of their fleet as you can before winter comes, but allow survivors to spread the tales of the destruction you are wreaking. All of the other ships of our fleet will be given the same orders as you, but you are the one the Illymari fear the most, so you are the one who must strike them the hardest."

Prudence pointed her chin toward Phaedron, who was standing at the prow of the ship, watching the crew celebrate their new orders.

"While I realize you are angry with Lord Daane and have effectively banished him to his estates for the time being, I have asked him to remain aboard as one of my crew, and he accepted my offer earlier today. If you want me to do as much damage as you're suggesting, having three Mages aboard will allow me to do exactly that."

He frowned as he realized she was informing him of her decision and not asking his permission, but he grunted his assent nonetheless.

"As you wish. We're going to need all the Mages we can get for this war, and he would be wasted sitting at home brooding. You can tell Lord Daane that he may say farewell to his mother and his siblings before we depart, and after we are gone, he has my permission to take his place among your crew until the winter." She smiled triumphantly and bounced up on her toes, but he gave her a level stare. "Remember though, that this is a warship and not a pleasure barge, and the Dakkadian navy does not allow liaisons between crewmembers of a warship. That especially holds true for the Captain. I have allowed you to carry on your relationship during this voyage because he is not a member of your crew, but now that he is, I expect you to comport yourself in a manner befitting both your rank and your station. Do I make myself perfectly clear?" He held her gaze for a long moment before she nodded her understanding, and even after she signaled her agreement, he continued to hold her gaze until he was sure that she understood the gravity of his orders.

Satisfied that the point had been made he said, "Very good, Captain. Thank you once again for everything you have done, and for everything you have suffered on my behalf. We will take our leave now, and let you begin your preparations. Try not to get into any trouble."

With that he turned and walked down the gangplank, leaving the *Sovereign* and the cheering crew in his wake.

Aveliad finished overseeing the packing of her chests and nodded to the crewman waiting in the doorway to collect them. With her permission, he signaled a group of men to enter, and in moments they had cleared the room of her possessions. When she was alone in her cabin at last, she looked around the room for anything she might have forgotten or left unpacked, but she didn't see anything at all. As her eyes passed over her mirror she hesitated, and then she found herself involuntarily walking forward to look into it. A quick glance at the doorway told her she was alone, so she reached behind her head and untied her mask, and then leaned forward to peer into the mirror.

Not a blemish or scar to be seen, and even the bruises have healed.

Her wrist was still tender, but it, too, was healing well, and she smiled in satisfaction to see there were no outward signs of what had been done to her. One of the many gifts that the Fae possessed was the inability to scar, no matter how grievous the wound might be, but until now, she hadn't been certain that the ability had been passed on to her, because she had never before been injured badly enough to test it. After only a moment, however, her smile faded.

If only my spirit would mend as quickly.

She had spent much of the journey home in her cabin, healing from the brutal beating Madari had given her, and to her vast relief, Madari had respected her privacy and had not come to see her a single time during her recuperation. She thanked the Archon for that, for she did not know how she would have reacted to his presence after what he had done to her, but now her respite was over and she would once again have to face him.

A knock at her open door made her jump in surprise, and she whirled around to see who it was with her mask still clutched in her hand. When she saw black hair with the distinctive white stripe her heart leapt into her throat, but after no more than a split second of unbridled terror, she recognized Phaedron's face and nearly sagged in relief. Phaedron must have recognized the look on her face for what it was because he looked away uncomfortably for a moment.

"I'm sorry I startled you, Mother, but the King gave me permission to speak with you before you leave for home." He looked at her again, clearly searching her face for signs of the beating she had received, but after a brief but thorough examination, he smiled. "You look wonderful."

Her pulse slowly returned to normal, and she gave him a smile of her own.

"He did no permanent damage, I'm thankful to say, and two weeks of enforced confinement and bed rest was more than enough time to heal." She touched her unmasked face and frowned. "Heal the physical wounds, at least."

Phaedron stepped forward and enfolded his mother in his arms.

"In time, the other wounds will heal as well. I'm certain of it."

She wrapped her arms around her much taller son and squeezed him once.

"I know. I just don't know how I am going to react when I see him again."

Phaedron pulled back and held her at arm's length, with a thoughtful expression on his face.

"I just remembered something I told a friend while Val and I were at the Mage Citadel, and I think that it applies here as well. We Dakkadians respect strength above all else. Nothing matters to us as much as knowing the people around us are just as strong and capable as we are. Even the King feels the same way. If you *think* you are a victim, then you *are*. Show him that you aren't, and he will never lay a finger on you again."

She thought about it for a moment and realized that there was some truth to what he was saying.

"Perhaps, but part of being strong means knowing when and where to fight your battles. Take you, for example. Picking a fight with Madari in front of witnesses, with Morvandis standing nearby, was perhaps not the best display of strength you could have shown. Or wisdom, for that matter."

He laughed and raised his hand to run it through his hair uncomfortably.

"True. Attacking from a position of weakness is never a smart idea. But then, I wasn't exactly thinking straight, was I? I've since had two weeks to think about the error of my ways and I see now where I went wrong."

She arched an eyebrow in suspicion.

"I shouldn't have spoken to him at all; I should have just gutted him like a trout right there before Morvandis could have lifted a finger. The look of surprise on his face alone would have been more than worth the hanging."

Despite the gruesome image, Aveliad laughed, and Phaedron grinned triumphantly, as he made his normally reserved mother laugh, despite the trauma she had undergone.

"Perhaps not the wisest course of action, I would think. You've already earned yourself an exile. If you had tried to 'gut him like a trout' and failed, I'm certain he would have been just a bit harsher."

"Ah, about my exile . . . Prudence asked me to remain aboard as a member of her crew, and King Madari agreed to let me go. According to her, he said that 'we are going to need all the Mages we can get for this war, and I would be wasted sitting at home'. So when the *Sovereign* sails again, I will be going with her."

This time, both of Aveliad's eyebrows rose in surprise, for she wouldn't have believed Madari capable of being so generous.

"That's wonderful news, Phaedron. I wish you could have joined her under better circumstances, but at this point, I will take what I can get. How are things between the two of you?"

"They couldn't be better. We spend pretty much every waking moment together, and exile aside, this trip was the best thing that's ever happened to me. I'm hoping that things will get even better when we go back to sea, but it seems His Majesty has other ideas about that. When he gave Prudence his permission to keep me aboard, he also reminded her that this is a warship, and so we can't be together as long as I am a crewmember. I understand that, and I promise I will honor his order, but just being near her is enough for me, and for her part, I think she is just as happy."

"I am glad for the both of you. If I am not mistaken, the sailing season will end with winter?" He nodded. "Good. When winter comes and you are home again, I will begin making arrangements for the two of you to wed . . . perhaps in the spring or early summer." She pursed her lips and thought out loud. "I will have to notify her family, of course, it wouldn't be polite otherwise. And we should hold the wedding at the capital: Daane is simply too small to house the number of guests that will have to attend. And I will want grandchildren immediately." She glanced over Phaedron's shoulder and said, "Several of them."

"Should the first one be a boy or a girl?" asked Lady Prudence, as she leaned casually against the doorframe, smiling at both of them.

"A boy, of course. The proprieties must be upheld, after all. But I will want a granddaughter immediately afterward. Perhaps twins, if you can manage them. I find the idea of my children bringing me many grandchildren to spoil brings me no end of satisfaction." Despite the levity of the moment, a wistful look crossed her face. "All joking aside, I am very glad for both of you. It makes me happy to know that at least one of my children will be able to be with the one that he loves, although from a few hints that Deirdre has let slip, I might have two happy children on my hands when she, too, is married."

"She will be. I think she already loves Prince Lain, but is frightened of his father for some reason. Still, I wouldn't be concerned about her eventual happiness." She glanced at Phaedron and smiled. "Or ours, for that matter."

Prudence stepped beside Phaedron and wrapped her hands around his forearm. Aveliad watched the affectionate gesture.

"I want you both to promise me that you will stay as safe as you can, especially considering the current political situation and what you are about to face. I understand you both want to put yourselves in harm's way, and I will honor your wishes, but while the Dakkadian within me is happy for you, the mother within me cannot help but be worried about you both. War is a terrible thing."

Both Phaedron and Prudence nodded solemnly. Aveliad leaned forward and hugged them both.

"I've put this off long enough. It is time for me to take my leave, and to face my own demon." She looked up at Phaedron. "And when I do, I will face him like a Dakkadian."

As the royal party began their preparations for the six-day return trip to the fortress of Blackstone, Morvandis began his preparations for an entirely different trip altogether. A quiet inquiry to the Harbormaster revealed a small sloop that was perfect for his needs, and he was quietly seeing to the provisioning of the vessel without ever leaving his King's side. He had given his agents a list of items he would need for his trip, and they had dutifully rushed off to carry out his orders. With his men occupied seeing to the tasks he had set for them, he kept near King Madari to answer any questions or to dispense any last minute advice the King might need.

King Madari was busy passing orders of his own and giving signed and sealed letters to the many messengers who had been waiting at port for his return. Morvandis had read several of the letters that had awaited their arrival, but from what he had seen, all was well within the kingdom, and there were no special priorities among the messages. The letters King Madari was mailing were entirely different, however, and within no more than two weeks, the entire kingdom would be on a war footing. Already, he could see signs of other ships of the fleet speeding up their preparations at their King's order. As King Madari was dealing with the messengers and speaking with his nobles, he looked up just in time to see Queen Aveliad appear on the deck.

From her elevated position, Aveliad looked down and met her husband's gaze, then walked down the gangplank with her customary grace and dignity. No matter what they were doing, everyone on the pier turned to watch her descend, and to his amusement, Morvandis found that he was no exception. He shook his head wryly, and turned to see what the King's reaction would be at seeing his wife again. To his surprise, the only reaction he showed at Queen Aveliad's appearance was a slight tightening of the eyes and a noticeable gritting of his teeth. For her part, after her initial look at her husband, Aveliad swept past him without a word or a second glance, and climbed into her carriage to sit next to Deirdre. Once she was seated, the spell she had cast upon everyone upon the docks was lifted, and work began anew.

King Madari clenched his fists once and scowled at the carriage, before turning back to his messengers and passing out the last of his missives. Once the final courier had departed, he turned his full attention to Morvandis.

"Let's take a walk."

Morvandis dutifully took his place at the King's right arm and waited for him to speak. They walked for a short distance where they had complete privacy before Madari finally broke the silence.

"Are you certain you can do this? If you can't, tell me now. I won't risk you for nothing, and I won't allow you to go on a suicide mission for me. You're too important, both to the kingdom, and to me personally."

Morvandis's expression didn't change at the compliment. He looked at the small boat that was being prepared for him across the pier.

"There are risks, of course, but none I am incapable of surmounting. Do not fear for me. I will complete my task, and I will return home safely once it is completed. All I need is for you to give me the command and I will discharge my duty."

Madari looked into his half-brother's eyes as if searching for something, and then he looked out over the water, as if he could see Illymar from where he was standing. A look of rage crossed Madari's face and anger burned in his eyes.

"Break them!"

With that, he turned away, and returned to where his family was waiting, leaving Morvandis standing alone behind him.

Hours later, under the cloak of night and long after the Royal Family had departed, Morvandis stepped onto the deck of the sloop he had commandeered and untied the rope holding it to the dock. He took a seat by the rudder and used his mastery of Air Magic to push the boat away from the jetty and toward the open sea. He was not an accomplished sailor, nor was he familiar with many of the functions of the small boat, but secrecy was absolutely vital for this mission, and so he would simply have to learn as he went. Fortunately for him, his mastery of all four Elemental Magics would ensure that storms would not be a problem, and the wind would always be favorable, but the task set before him would still be quite daunting.

As the sloop made it out of sight of land, he untied all of the ropes holding the mainsail in place and unfurled the canvas, then tied the boom securely, before again summoning his Air Magic and filling the sails with a powerful gust of wind. The sloop launched itself over the waves, as if it was sailing on a fast moving river instead of a calm ocean, and Morvandis sat down again and closed his eyes. Even with his abilities, it was going to take two days to make it to Illymar once again, and that was only if everything went well. To ensure there were no problems, he allowed himself to fall into a meditative trance and opened himself to all four of his abilities. The trance gave him two advantages: First, it would allow him to extend his senses outwards in all directions, to warn him of problems of all kinds, including hidden reefs or shallows, as well as other ships that might spot him and make a note of his passing. Second, it would allow him to remain awake and aware for the entire trip. It wouldn't be pleasant, and he would be exhausted at the end, but falling asleep in the middle of the ocean in a tiny sloop would be a fatal mistake.

After two days of uneventful sailing, Morvandis finally caught the first hint of the Archon's power emanating from the Teeth of Amhar. Exhausted as he was, he opened his eyes and smiled at the knowledge that he'd soon reach the protective barrier surrounding Illymar, and he had to restrain himself from pouring even more power into driving the winds. The strain of holding his power for two long days was taking its toll, and the need for it to be over ground at his patience like broken glass. He set aside his impatience and instead extended his senses to the Teeth. As he neared them, he discovered that his navigation had not been perfect, for the wall was completely unbroken in both directions. He pushed his senses as far as he could, but was met with an untouched wall of power as far as his senses could reach. *I have to sail around the perimeter until I find the break, but which way should I travel? North or south?* After no more than a moment's pause, he decided to sail south, retracing the route the *Sovereign* had used to sail to the island a few weeks ago. He did not approach the wall, for keeping his distance would allow him to sense more of the wall at the same time. But staying this far from the Teeth would increase his chances of detection by Illymari patrols, so he also began looking for ships that might also be approaching. In the time it had taken the Dakkadian Royal Family to return home, Illymar had undoubtedly made preparations to fight the oncoming war. They would have had plenty of time to set out a picket of lighter ships to scout for Dakkadian vessels. They wouldn't fear attack through the Teeth, of course, but the scouting vessels would provide advance warning to the main fleet and allow them time to prepare for any possible invasion. Morvandis smiled to himself at the thought, for Madari had no plans in place to invade immediately, so the ships would be watching for a threat that wasn't there, and wouldn't be coming anytime soon.

A few hours later, Morvandis opened his eyes and smiled in triumph as he sensed the break in the Teeth. The timing was poor, for the sun was high in the sky, and he had hoped to arrive at night, but he would have to make do. He reached out to confirm the break once again, and suddenly he felt another object in the water.

A ship, he realized. *One that will spot me before I can reach the break.*

Morvandis wasn't one to curse, but he did spare a moment or two for frustrated silence before making his decision. He angled the sloop away from the Teeth and moved to intercept the unlucky ship that had had the misfortune to cross his path. He might have been able to avoid the confrontation, but he couldn't take the chance that they would discover the gap and alert the Illymari navy.

It took a while to see them, for his extended senses allowed him to see for many miles in every direction, but now that he *had* seen them, he had work to do. He let go of his power, just in case there was a Mage aboard the other vessel. He did not want to run the risk of allowing them advanced warning that they might be facing a Mage as well, and thanks to Enaria's training, he could now mask his resonance from other Mages. However, he wouldn't be able to disguise himself if he actively channeled.

After a short time, it became clear that the other vessel had finally spotted him, for they changed direction and moved directly toward him. The flag of Illymar, a white lion on a field of sky blue, flew proudly from the light vessel's mast, and when Morvandis saw it, he didn't hesitate. Without warning, he seized all four of his powers and unleashed them at once in an overwhelming wave. He felt a brief spark of answering power that told him there was, indeed, a Mage aboard, albeit a very weak one, but it was far too late for the unfortunate Illymari Powerborn to do anything at all to stop him. An immense, razor-sharp blade of air cut the ship horizontally in two at the waterline, and then into quarters vertically. Simultaneously, he used his ability with Fire to instantly incinerate everything upon the deck of the ship, including sails and ropes—as well as the crewmen manning them—so quickly and completely that there wasn't even time for smoke to rise. Then, two massive waves rose up from either side of the ship, like watery hands reaching up from the briny depths, to grab the shards of the vessel and pull it completely under the water to its doom. And finally, he waited for the gutted hulk to reach the bottom of the sea before using his Earth Magic to pull the remains of the ship into the muddy ocean floor and beyond, making it disappear forever, not just beneath the waves, but beneath the ocean floor as well.

The "battle" had taken no more than a minute from start to finish, but Morvandis waited for much longer, looking for any signs of debris that could speak to the fate of the ship. To his relief, not even a single plank of wood was left behind to show that the ship had ever existed, and satisfied there were no witnesses to say that he had ever been there, Morvandis turned his boat back to face the break in the Teeth of Amhar.

When he finally reached the magnificent stone structures, he once again touched all four powers, and looked at the white stone pillars. To the right of the structure he could still feel the power and the fury of the Archon's magic jumping and crackling like energy, and yet tightly bound together like strands on a rope. But to the left of the tower, he felt nothing at all; not even the slightest hint of magic. He was suddenly glad that he had run into the Illymari picket, because if the captain of the vessel had been just a bit closer to the Teeth, his Mage might have been close enough to sense the break. It was vital that the opening remain a secret, or it could be used as a trap to draw in the Dakkadian fleet before attacking it in overwhelming numbers. He set that thought aside as he drew nearer to the white stone, and unable to contain his curiosity, he angled the boat even closer so he could physically touch the tower. As he reached out, he hesitated, unsure of what he would feel, but then he placed his hand upon the tower and felt the cool stone of the Archon's monolith beneath his own hand, the first person to do so in thousands of years. He slid his hand across the smooth, seamless rock with reverence, marveling at the perfection of the monolith and the artistry of its creation, and he stood that way for a while, simply touching the white stone, until he was ready. He summoned Air Magic and lifted himself from the deck of the sloop, until he was floating steadily just above the mast. Then he summoned his Fire Magic and used it to reduce the sloop to ashes, until nothing was left. Once even the ashes had disappeared beneath the waves, he let go of his control of Fire Magic and concentrated on moving himself on gusts of wind.

Flying was very difficult to achieve for even the best Air Mage, for it required both steady concentration and an enormous amount of control, but even after the better part of three days without sleep followed immediately by a battle, he propelled himself silently and quickly upward until he could see the coast of the island in the distance. Once he spotted land, he shifted the winds holding him aloft and flew forward, arcing himself toward a small area west of the fishing village he could just barely see. He kept himself high in the air so that the chances of someone actually seeing him were minute, but just to be certain, he summoned his Water Magic and created a rolling fog to disguise his approach. It took him a while to reach land, for he did not want to outrun the fogbanks, but eventually he set himself down adroitly, approximately where he had asked Thorn to meet him weeks earlier.

"I have to say that I find it unnatural to know you can actually fly, Your Grace," said a sultry voice. "Is that how you were able to cross over the Teeth of Amhar? I had thought that even flying over them would prove fatal to anyone foolish enough to try."

"Apparently not. I'm glad to see you, Thorn. Did you bring the supplies?"

"Of course. Your timing is excellent, by the by. I've been here less than a day."

"Were there any problems with your journey?"

"Not a one. I stayed at a few inns along the way, but when I did, I made sure to unlace my shirt a bit to uncover some cleavage." She indicated her spectacular chest. "I can almost guarantee that no one is going to remember my face." He smiled at her assurance, but before he could say anything, he yawned prodigiously. She frowned when she saw just how exhausted he was. "Did you fly all the way from Dakkadia?"

"No. Flying is useful for short distances, but it is tremendously draining. I commandeered a boat back home and sailed it to the Teeth, then flew from there. I've been awake for almost three days. Do you have a camp set up?"

"First thing I took care of. I wasn't sure what I was waiting for or how long I would actually be here, so I made camp a short distance from here in the tree line. Follow me."

He yawned again and fell in behind her as she led him from the beach to where a small tent had been set up. There was no campfire, but then he wasn't particularly hungry. Instead, he stripped off his robes until he was completely nude, and summoned a ball of fresh water he used to clean himself of the grit and the salt that his two-day journey had left upon him.

"Did you bring the bags that I left for you?" Thorn nodded and pointed at a few fat saddlebags sitting beside the tent. He indicated one of the larger bags. "There are a few changes of clothing in that one. Could you please hand me something to wear?"

She dutifully unbuckled the bag and pulled out a fresh set of robes and some smallclothes for him. As she handed the clean clothing over to him, he nodded his thanks and donned them, and then turned to look at his surroundings. After a careful scan of the area, he summoned his power and set up a series of wards around them that would provide warning should anyone come too close to the camp.

"I've secured the area, so try and get some sleep. I don't know how long I am going to be asleep, considering the exertions of the last three days, but we will be leaving as soon as I awaken." Without another word, he climbed into the tent and promptly fell asleep.

As soon as she was certain Morvandis was well and truly asleep, Thorn sat down cross-legged in front of the opening of the tent with her back to the Mage and pulled out a well-worn copy of her favorite book, *Love's Sacrifice.* Turning quickly to the page she had marked, she glanced over her shoulder to make absolutely certain that he wasn't secretly watching her at her favorite pastime, and began to read. Thorn had a much deserved reputation for her sexual proclivities and appetite, and she was very open about all aspects of her deviant behavior—all aspects that is, save one. The fact that she desperately loved to read "bodice ripper" novels was a secret she intended to take with her to the grave, because she knew that the careful persona she had crafted over the years of a cold-blooded, heartless wench would come crashing to the ground if ever someone was to come across her crying her eyes out over something so *feminine*. Even her own *husband* had no idea she had a weakness for overly dramatic tales of love and passion. So, to protect herself from scorn, she only read the contemptible things when and where she was absolutely positive that no one would discover her secret. And, if by chance, someone was to find out? Well, she would simply make the poor fool permanently disappear. No one would ever find the body.

After a few hours it became too dark to read, so she carefully put the book back into her saddlebag and left the camp to check on the horses. She trusted Morvandis's wards implicitly, but she wanted to make certain no one would stumble upon them by accident. Satisfied that they were safely secured for the night, she returned to the camp and climbed into the tent to lie down beside Morvandis. She, too, had had a long journey and needed her rest, and he didn't so much as stir as she settled herself next to him in the tent, and wrapped her arm around him as she pressed her body against his for warmth.

A gentle touch on her leg woke her from pleasant dreams, and when she opened her eyes, she had to quickly close them again as bright sunlight temporarily blinded her. A shadow passed in front of her to shield her from the light.

"It's time to go, Thorn."

Thorn crawled out of the tent. To her surprise, both of their horses were already saddled, and ready to go, and all of their bags were packed and buckled in place. A quick look around the camp told her that the only thing left to do was to pack the tent and her blankets and they could be on their way. She put her hands on her hips and turned to look at Morvandis.

"You should have woken me. I would have taken care of all of this for you. The Master of the Gardens does not need to sully his hands with such mundane tasks. Leave that to your servants."

"You are not a servant to me, Thorn, nor have you ever been. You are a friend. You are also a vital asset to the kingdom, and to the Flower Court. I promise you this: if I ever forget your loyalty, your friendship, and your exemplary service to both myself and our kingdom, and treat you as a mere menial, I will step down as the Master of the Gardens and appoint a successor. Now, help me disassemble the tent so we can be on our way."

Thorn found herself blinking back tears at the unexpected and heartfelt compliment. Morvandis was sparing in his praise at the best of times, which made a kind word from him even more precious when he offered one, but this was the first time he had ever told her that he thought of her as anything more than a glorified servant who happened to be good at gathering intelligence. She shook herself to break the spell of his praise, and without a word, stepped to one side of the tent to pull up the stakes. On the other side of the tent, Morvandis did the same. In a matter of moments, the tent had been disassembled and safely packed away, and once the task was completed, they mounted up and began their trip.

"Did you get enough sleep last night?" she asked. "You fell asleep the second your head hit your pillow."

"I have recovered well enough, though I perhaps pushed myself a bit hard at the end of my journey. The meditative trance we Mages are taught, allows us to rest without truly sleeping, and use our magic to sustain our bodies, but it is not the same as true sleep. When I reached the Teeth, I had to destroy an Illymari vessel to ensure there were no witnesses to my arrival. That was perhaps bad enough, but then I further strained my resources by destroying my own vessel and flying here." He gave her a steady look. "For what we are about, there can be no trace that we were ever in Illymar."

"I certainly hope you have some way to get us home after we're done doing whatever it is we're doing here," Thorn said. "I did not book us passage home, and if you sank the vessel you came here in, that means we're stuck. *You* might be able to fly home, but for me, it would be a long swim."

"Enaria has booked passage for the trip home aboard an Ithram flagged vessel. We will be returning to Dakkadia in a slightly more luxurious fashion than sailing aboard a one-man sloop."

"Thank the Archon for that. I've had about enough of Illymar. Thanarilliad has probably forgotten all about me by now and has taken up with some other woman."

Morvandis raised an eyebrow at her and said in a thoughtful tone,

"I would think that he would find your absence to be quite restful. He's probably sleeping peacefully, even now."

"And just what, pray tell, do you mean by that?" she asked suspiciously.

"Well, with your terrible snoring, as well as your tendency to thrash about in your sleep, I am certain he welcomes any opportunity for the kingdom to call upon your services as a chance to catch up on some much needed rest."

She squeaked in shocked outrage at his words, but after she had recovered from his deadly insult she gave him a withering glare.

"I do *not* snore. That's a base slander!"

"Think what you want, Thorn, if it makes you feel better. But you did not have to sleep next to yourself. Trust me, you snore. And you thrash about as well."

She pursed her lips and looked away from him, pretending to be upset. Eventually, however, she tired of the game and looked back at him.

"Before I left to meet you, I had another rendezvous with Vitaly Saxe. Did King Madari mention to you I had met with the Earl?" He nodded, and she continued. "The news isn't good for us. Apparently, the Inquisition has discovered that it was the Queen and her relatives who were behind the assassination attempt on the Corsair's life. The King is punishing her for her temerity by reining in her family, and the Duke of Saerce has taken the opportunity to begin preparations to resist invasion. From what Vitaly says, they have already made serious inroads into repairing the deficiencies left in the wake of the Savonne's rise to power." Morvandis frowned at the news, but Thorn wasn't finished. "There's more. Specifically, they have begun laying down hulls for a completely new and modernized navy, and every building slip in the country is busy making the ships as quickly as they can. They will continue building the ships throughout the winter as well, and they expect to have them ready by spring or early summer. With the Duke of Saerce no longer at odds with his brother, they now have access to enough trained soldiers to crew the vessels, and there is even a new Lord High Admiral of the fleet. Apparently, the Bathtub Admiral was a conspirator in the plot to kill Lady Prudence, and now he has been sent away from Illymar on some sort of a suicide mission to atone. Saxe did not know the details of the mission, unfortunately, but he did say that they never expected to see him again."

Morvandis nodded at the information but his expression didn't change.

"Are you going to tell me what our assignment is here in Illymar? Or is that still a secret?"

"I am here to undo everything they are trying to accomplish, in as direct a manner as possible."

CHAPTER TWENTY-SEVEN

"Daggers"

The gates of D'arhak Khad'deia, the fortress at the heart of the capital city of Dakkadia opened, and an honor guard of Dakkadian soldiers ran out and arranged themselves in perfectly even lines on either side of the drawbridge. The men were carrying either halberds or bayoneted muskets, and as the royal procession approached them, they braced themselves to attention for their King. Aveliad watched as Madari bowed his head in acknowledgement of the Guards' welcome, and then rode past them with Valeriad by his side. Her carriage followed soon after.

Even after six days, it still seemed odd to her not to see Morvandis riding at Madari's right hand, but she had learned Morvandis had been sent on an inspection of the various ports dotting the Dakkadian coasts. The ship builders were already building warships as quickly as possible, but Morvandis had been asked to find ways to speed up the building process. From what she could gather, Madari wanted to invade Illymar the moment the winter snows lifted next year. Aveliad herself thought that plan to be a bit over-ambitious, but then he hadn't asked her for her opinion, and she hadn't offered it. In point of fact, the two of them had said only a few words to each other over the last few weeks, and

Aveliad rather enjoyed things the way they were now. Unfortunately, now that they were home again, she would no longer be able to avoid him.

As the carriage in which she and Deirdre were riding slowed to a stop, Aveliad saw the serving staff of the Blackstone assembled in exactly the same ordered lines as the military, without the weapons, of course. No sooner had the carriage stopped, when two footmen ran forward and extended the stairs before opening the door and bowing to her. She stepped down from the carriage, happy to be able to stretch her legs. A tall, graceful Fae separated herself from the other servants and stepped forward to curtsey.

"Welcome home, Your Majesty."

"Thank you, Anahlian. It is good to be home. I trust all has been well during our absence?"

The Mistress of the Household inclined her head.

"All has been well."

Deirdre bounced out of the carriage and gave Anahlian a wide grin.

"Good day to you, Anahlian. Did you miss me?"

"I have indeed missed you, Your Highness. Did you enjoy your journey?" Deirdre nodded happily, but before she could say anything further, the Mistress smiled and said, "I am very glad to hear that, Your Highness, and I look forward to speaking with you about your adventures later. But first, now that you are home, I am certain that you will be most relieved to know that your tutors have all been anxiously awaiting your return. I should think that after spending so much of your valuable time attending lavish parties and other social events, you would be quite well-rested and most eager to return to your studies. So, I think that after a warm bath and a hot meal, you should be more than able to return to your lessons without delay. I will inform the tutors to be ready to resume your studies this very afternoon."

At the mention of her lessons Deirdre's cheerful grin wilted like a flower in summer heat, and Aveliad tried unsuccessfully to suppress a smile of her own at her daughter's sudden, manifest unhappiness. Deirdre had always been an excellent student and a quick study, but she was also a young teenager and, as such, she faced the prospect of endless hours of lectures and tutors like any teenager would in her place: very much like a condemned criminal facing a date with the gallows.

Deirdre's shoulders sagged dramatically and she gave Anahlian a dejected glance before allowing herself to be escorted back to her rooms by her own ladies-in-waiting. Aveliad watched her daughter leave, dragging her feet and sighing all the while, before stepping past the Mistress and walking briskly to her own apartments, the Mistress following closely beside her.

"We received word of your injuries only yesterday, My Queen. Are you well?"

"My injuries have already healed, Anahlian, but we have more important things to worry about now. Dismiss the staff as soon as they have arranged my apartments, and then join me there. We have much to discuss."

Anahlian curtseyed deeply and turned aside, speaking a few quick words to a nearby maid. Aveliad did not remain behind to watch, but instead continued on to her apartments without Anahlian. When she entered her parlor, she walked right past the laboring maids to her own open-aired balcony and waited for the Mistress of the Household to join her.

Anahlian had been sent to her by Aveliad's Faeish family on the day they had learned of Phaedril's death, and she had been by Aveliad's side since before Phaedron was born. Mistress of the Household was her official title, but to Aveliad and her Faeish family she was much, much more. The Faeish term was *Shasrathi'kithrin,* which translated loosely into "Family Honor Guard" or "Shield Bearer," but in effect, she was a bodyguard, a spy mistress, an investigator, and if need be, an assassin.

Aveliad had been very surprised, but deeply gratified, when her family had sent Anahlian to look into the death of Phaedril, for the Honor Guard was very, very good at what she did. Anahlian's family had been in the service of Aveliad's family for thousands of years, and she knew she could trust the woman absolutely, and that her "maid" would follow her commands without question.

Anahlian's search for the culprit responsible for Phaedril's death was an ongoing concern, but the investigation had stalled over the past decade or so for lack of evidence. Both Aveliad and Anahlian were absolutely convinced that his death was not an accident, but so far the *Shasrathi'kithrin* had been unable to find the evidence Aveliad required to act. The evidence they *had* collected pointed firmly to either Madari or Morvandis, or more probably the both of them working together, as the ones most likely involved with Phaedril's death. But, they had covered their tracks very well indeed. She also could not rule out the possibility that her own half-brother, Prince Brendenn DeVir, had ordered the murder, for he had profited greatly by arranging the marriage between his recently widowed sister and the new King. Either way, Aveliad refused to order anyone's death until she had hard evidence one way or the other. With evidence, her actions would be justice. Without it, it was murder. And if Aveliad had to have blood on her hands, it would be the right blood—no matter how long it took.

The investigation had now stretched to over two decades, but twenty years was no more than an eye blink for the Fae. To allay suspicion and to give Anahlian the freedom she needed to investigate, Aveliad had hired her first as a midwife, and later as the Mistress of the Household; the person responsible for overseeing the details of everyday life in the castle. Madari had been reluctant to assign an outsider such an important position, but his new bride had insisted, and he had relented. In a matter of days, Anahlian had proved her value to the King's complete satisfaction, and even better, she had done it without once raising his suspicions. Now, she ruled the household firmly but fairly, and over the years she had earned the trust and respect of the entire household staff. Once she had earned that trust, she had begun her investigation in earnest.

Only one person had ever shown any sign of distrust toward Anahlian, and that was Morvandis himself. The Mage had never uttered a single complaint about Anahlian, but Aveliad had seen how the Mage acted around her, and the only words she could use to describe his odd behavior toward her were suspicion and distrust. For her part, Anahlian viewed Morvandis as the single greatest obstacle to her job, and through her investigation, she had found his spies placed throughout the castle in a variety of positions.

Anahlian considered Morvandis to be a worthy adversary, despite his relative youth, and spent a considerable amount of time positioning her pawns to counter his. Aveliad did not know what the Mage thought of Anahlian's efforts, but so far, at least, he'd had absolutely no luck discovering Anahlian's true identity or what her true intentions were. Madari remained blissfully unaware of any byplay between the Mistress of the Household and the Mage-Lord, and neither Anahlian nor Aveliad wanted that situation to change.

The door to the balcony opened and Anahlian stepped through before closing it behind her.

"K'yitsunadjallelasora, Aveliad Ar'con. Yelsarya a'tellustkyalin."

The formal greeting was almost identical in Faeish as it was in Elvish, but the pronunciation sounded much more elegant than the Elves would have spoken it.

"K'yitsunadjallelasora, An'ahlian Sha. Kirsath zarafina, shasrathi'koi," Aveliad replied.

For security reasons, they always spoke in High Faeish when they met, for it was the language of nobility, and one that no one in the Blackstone other than Aveliad, Anahlian, and Aveliad's children could speak. She knew that Morvandis had a strong command of Elvish and could understand more than a considerable amount of Faeish, but the language of nobility was beyond him, and therefore it was safe to speak with each other openly, without fear of being overheard or understood. Anahlian spoke first.

"Shall I kill your husband for laying hands upon you in violence? Husband or no, he has the blood of the Faeborn upon his hands and must be made to suffer."

Aveliad removed her mask and lowered it so that Anahlian could see her face.

"No, Anahlian, the blame is mine. I was careless. I pushed him too far, and found to my own regret that there are limits to what defiance he will accept from me. I will deal with him myself, in my own way."

Anahlian changed the subject.

"Phaedron was not with the royal party. Has something happened?"

Aveliad smiled briefly and then frowned, for she had decidedly mixed feelings about his absence.

"It seems Phaedron has finally met his match in the person of Lady Prudence Daemira. He has decided to spend time with her aboard the *Sovereign*, at least until the winter snows come. I believe the two will marry, and soon."

"So, the marriage you intended to make all along has come to pass on its own." The Mistress of the Household looked extremely pleased at the news. "I am happy for both of them. They will be good for each other."

Aveliad gestured to a small table and the two chairs sitting opposite each other. Obediently, Anahlian took her seat and Aveliad took the other.

"Just so. You should have seen them together, Anahlian," she said wistfully. "They fit together more perfectly than I could have possibly imagined. I've already expressed my feelings about grandchildren to them. You may have your hands full again, and very soon."

"It would be my honor to usher in the next generation of your family, Queen Aveliad."

Aveliad's humor left her momentarily as she remembered something.

"Phaedron and Madari had a disagreement about what Madari did to me. Phaedron apparently threatened his life, but Madari ordered Morvandis to kill him if he made a move. Wisely, Phaedron desisted. Madari exiled him to his estates, but Lady Prudence made him change his mind, and allow her to take Phaedron to sea with her rather than face exile."

Anahlian's face went very still.

"Do you believe Phaedron's life is in danger? Madari is not one to allow threats to exist, and he has hated the boy since the day he was born. This could be the excuse he needs to see an end to the threat, once and for all."

"No. Madari will not strike at Phaedron, at least not for the foreseeable future. In the short term, he is safer aboard the *Sovereign*. In the long term, the conflict that we have been expecting and dreading has begun. Madari has declared war against Illymar, and has sent his fleet to engage theirs wherever they can be found."

Anahlian's mouth tightened in distaste, for the Fae viewed war as wasteful and foolish. They believed any problems or disagreements could be solved if given enough time, and they simply did not understand the human need to conquer or dominate everything they saw. There were times when one had to fight, of course, but to instigate a war instead of merely defending one's self from aggression was a terrible thing to the Fae. Aveliad considered that to be a bit simplistic herself, for the Fae's inexcusable lack of action concerning the Lyx had been a horrible mistake, and one they could have easily dealt with long before the Earthborn had seized power. Unfortunately, they hadn't, and humanity had suffered for it. The Faeish people did not view things that way, however.

"Perhaps he feels the Illymari will take care of his problem with Phaedron for him," Anahlian said.

"The thought had occurred to me, although you and I both know better than to try and dissuade Phaedron from doing something this important to him. If the worst should happen, and he should fall in battle, I will grieve for him as is proper. But I will also take comfort in the knowledge he was allowed to choose his own fate . . . a choice his father was denied."

"My Queen, no one chooses their fate. If fate was simply a matter of choice, we would all be kings and queens, and no one would ever die."

"Phaedron is a man grown, and it is time for him to find his own place in the world. Hopefully, fate has decreed that his place will be at Lady Prudence's side and there will be many grandchildren for me to dote upon, but I will settle for his remaining safe and unharmed."

"It is hard for me to think of him as anything other than a brilliant, precocious child with scraped knees and grass in his hair. It is his human blood. If he were a true Fae, he would still be a child. Twenty years is not so long a time for us." Anahlian sighed regretfully. "He grew up so very fast."

"I daresay that even if he had been a true Fae child, we would still be having this conversation 200 years after he was born. Children always grow up too fast for their parents' liking. Look at Deirdre: barely 14 years old and already betrothed to marry . . . and happy to be so."

"Who has King Madari chosen for her?" Anahlian asked in surprise.

"Prince Lain of Ferralin will be her husband when she comes of age. On our last night in Illymar, Madari arranged the marriage to seal a treaty with Ferralin. In exchange, when the time comes, Ferralin will stand aside as Dakkadia attempts to conquer Illymar, and the only thing it will cost Madari is his daughter. That has to be quite a bargain from his perspective." She hesitated, then sighed. "No. That is not fair to him. I have seen Prince Lain, and Deirdre herself met with him several times. She is very fond of him, and that is more than I could have hoped for her. I think she and Lain will make a fine couple and will be very happy together." Anahlian started to speak, but Aveliad held up her hand. "There is a potential problem, however. Deirdre also met with Emperor Xan, and the meeting frightened her tremendously. The reason I wanted to speak with you is that I want you to contact the Fae Court, and have them look into the Emperor's personal life, and see why he was so interested in Deirdre. More importantly, does she have good reason to fear him? Can you do this?"

"I can. The Fae have very good relations with Ferralin, and our delegates have been received many times in honor by the Emperor. I will send a message to Cyn'Rohmillyn and have our people begin an immediate investigation." She hesitated for a moment. "It will take time, however. When is the marriage to occur?"

"On Deirdre's seventeenth birthday. As the date draws nearer, we will make arrangements for the actual ceremony. I am certain Emperor Xan will want the wedding to take place within the Ferralin Imperial Palace, as is proper. But that is neither here nor there. The point is, you have time, but only if you begin immediately. Find out everything there is to know about both Emperor Xan and his son. If there is something that I need to know, I want to know about it before the wedding takes place."

"Understood. If there is nothing else, I will excuse myself to see to the messages I have to send. By your leave?" Aveliad nodded, and the Mistress curtseyed formally and turned to leave.

Before she could go, however, Aveliad said, "I will be seeing my husband this evening in his chambers. Please see to it that my things are prepared for me."

"As you wish, My Queen."

Madari rubbed his tired eyes and set aside yet another in a seemingly endless series of letters that were piled upon his desk. Normally, he had Morvandis read the messages and flag anything of particular importance for his attention, but Morvandis wasn't available at the moment. And so here he was, reading through messages from every part of his realm, and there was no way to tell if the message was important or not until after he had read it through. He reached out and picked up a wineglass and took a long pull on the rich burgundy wine that he favored.

When the glass was empty he set it down and picked up the bottle to pour himself another glass, but to his immense frustration, the bottle was already empty. He set it down again while frowning at it in irritation. He did not remember drinking quite that much, and yet, the bottle had been unopened when he had first sat down at his desk, shortly after returning home. He looked at the window and was surprised to see that the sun had already gone down, and judging from the position of the moon, it was already quite late at night. He looked down at the stack of papers and decided that he would start again in the morning.

Decision made, he stood up and picked up a candleholder, stopping to light it at one of the lanterns in the room. He opened his doors and the soldiers standing guard braced to attention. He closed the door behind him and began the long walk to his room. The Blackstone was huge, and his apartments were quite a distance from his private study, but he didn't mind the walk. He thought briefly about going to see Aveliad, but thought better of it. He did not want to deal with her this evening, not on top of the frustration of managing his kingdom at least. When he reached his apartments he opened the door, and the guards posted themselves at either side to resume their duty.

A pleasant fragrance, perhaps perfume, reached him first and served to clear his weariness somewhat. He glanced around the room to see where the smell could be coming from, but saw nothing out of the ordinary. The perfume, if that was indeed what he smelled, was quite lovely, and he found himself wondering who had been wearing it. Perhaps the perfume had been worn by one of the servants who had come to turn down the bed for him? He removed his pistol from its holster and set it on the nightstand near the doors and began to undress as he walked to his bedroom.

As he unbuckled his sword belt and opened the door to his bedchambers, a second, even stronger wave of the perfume washed over him. He glanced around the room, and to his surprise, he saw an unmasked Aveliad sitting on a cushioned footstool near his bed. She was wearing a silk nightdress with the conservative cut she preferred, but the material it had been made from was far thinner than she normally wore. He could quite clearly see her outline through the thin material, and against his will, his body began to respond to the seductive beauty of the woman sitting before him.

Though he was suspicious, he kept silent as she stood up and removed her nightgown, allowing him to see her in all her glorious beauty, almost against his will, he responded by stepping forward and dropping his sword belt to the floor. Aveliad pressed herself into his arms and wordlessly began to undress him. Despite his arousal, Madari felt another flash of suspicion at her actions, for in all of the years of their marriage, not once had she been this forward or this . . . *eager*, for his affections. One of the reasons he hated her so much was that she had always refused to give him what he so desperately craved, and part of him knew that this was too good to be true—especially after what he had done to her in Illymar. But despite his suspicion, his natural reaction to her forwardness clouded his judgment, and he allowed her to undress him and push him back onto the bed. She smiled seductively at him and sank to the floor in front of him, before rising back up and running her hand along his body from the tip of his foot all the way up to his shoulder. She laid herself beside him, still caressing him with her soft hand until she lay draped over him the way he had always dreamed of, and then she finally spoke, her face inches from his.

"In Illymar, you told me that if I refused to love you or respect you, I would learn to fear you. I came here to tell you that I have given your message very careful consideration." She punctuated her words with a soft caress that sent chills down his spine. "I thought about your words quite a bit during my recovery, and I have come to a decision." Her caressing hand moved down his stomach, and he felt himself straining to feel her touch. She smiled seductively once again and leaned forward to stare into his eyes, moist lips inches from his. "Do you want to know what my decision is, my husband?"

He nodded slightly, and her eyes suddenly hardened. The hand that had been so soft just moments before grabbed his manhood in a vice-like grip, but before he could move, he felt the cold steel of a razor-sharp blade resting against his neck, forcing his head back. She sat up suddenly, still gripping his manhood in one hand and holding the dagger tight against his throat.

"You underestimated me badly if you believe that a simple beating would be enough to break my will. You were wrong, and you of all people should know that that kind of mistake can be fatal." She punctuated her words by pressing the dagger against his throat even harder. "Now, it is time for me to correct some of your misconceptions. You may not believe me when I say this, but when I spoke with Princess Tais, it was to give her my *blessing* to bed you. I was foolish enough to think that she might find happiness in your arms. My *sole* concern was for the possibility of illegitimate children, and that is why I chose to speak with her. I do not know what happened between the two of you when you left the party together that last night, but I tell you now: whatever might have happened between you *it was not my fault.*" She hissed those four words to him, and to his surprise he found that he believed her. Her tone returned to normal, and she said, "But, that is in the past. Now we are home again, I expect things to go back to normal, in as much as they can, considering what we have done to each other." She smiled cruelly at him. "Despite our many differences, there is one thing about you I appreciate: you have provided me with exceptional children. Valeriad is a wonderful son; far, far better than I would have expected, considering just whom his father is, and there is no doubt in my mind that one day he will make a fine king for Dakkadia. Perhaps one of the finest Dakkadia has ever had."

Without warning, she lifted the dagger from his neck and in a single, move, raised it above his head and drove it to the hilt in the soft mattress right next to his head. The blade had missed him by a hair's breadth, and he could feel the cool steel against his flushed skin.

"If you *ever* lay your hands upon me again in violence, you had better kill me, for I promise you now—if you do and I survive, I will kill you in your sleep. And after I have done so, Dakkadia will learn for itself what kind of king Valeriad will make." She leaned back, taking her hand from the hilt of the dagger and leaving it in the mattress next to him as a warning. She gave him one last deadly look, and repeated his final words to her after he had beaten her.

"Believe it."

Madari said nothing at all as she dressed herself and left the room without looking at him, and once the door was closed behind her, he sat up and looked at the dagger sticking out of his mattress, wondering where she had hidden it. To his surprise, he saw that it was his own blade, and he looked down at the floor where he had dropped his sword belt. Sure enough, the blade was missing from its sheath, and he shook his head in admiration for how she had so completely controlled the situation from start to finish. She had known exactly how he would react to her presence, and had also known that he would be suspicious of her intentions. And yet, the hilt of the dagger protruding from his mattress was proof that had she wanted him dead, he would have been dead. It was as simple as that.

He would have to speak with her in the morning, to try and find some way to repair the damage that he had done to their marriage. He believed her when she said that she had encouraged Tais to be with him, and if so, whatever *had* happened that night had not been her fault after all. And if it hadn't, then the beating he had given her for her interference had been completely undeserved, and Aveliad had been right to react the way she had. He reached out and pulled the dagger from the mattress and slid it back into its sheath on his sword belt.

I will speak with her in the morning and somehow try and make amends. I do not expect to succeed, but I have to at least make the attempt. One thing is certain, however: I won't be raising my hands to her again, unless I intend to beat her to death. She meant exactly what she said, and I think I would find it very hard, indeed, to sleep with one eye open.

Enaria Wintersong felt a light touch on her arm, and when she looked over her shoulder, she saw one of the Mage Council's pages standing behind her. The young boy held out a sealed message for her and she nodded her thanks before taking it. After dismissing the page, she broke the seal and opened the letter, smothering a smile before the other High Council members could see it. It was the message she had been waiting for, and she leaned back in her seat to read the short note.

Archimagus Wintersong,

You have a package waiting for you on the docks—a special delivery you must sign for in person. If it is convenient for you, please meet the shipper this afternoon.

That was the only thing the note said, but she knew that the "shipper" in question was, in fact, Morvandis, and the delivery of the note told her he was waiting for her in a particular inn by the docks. She wasn't exactly sure what he intended to do during his clandestine stay, but whatever it turned out to be, she knew it would be very bad indeed for Illymar. The thought that Morvandis was here to harm the "allies" of the Mage Council bothered her not at all, and though some people might believe that by aiding him against a sovereign ally of Ithram she would be committing treason, she didn't care. *The sooner your King invades Illymar, the sooner the two of us can be together, Morvandis. And then let the world beware.*

She folded up the note and tucked it safely into her robe, then settled back to devote her full attention to the topic at hand. The Council was currently debating whether or not to allow a higher percentage of unaligned Mages to work aboard Illymari warships. A request had been made by the King of Illymar to the Mage Council to allow his kingdom to hire more Mages to aid in the defense of Illymar. Unfortunately for him, the request was not as simple as it seemed, for the treaty between Ithram and Illymar was one of mutual *defense.* What King Orem wanted to do was to place a greater number of Mages aboard his vessels in the name of self-defense, then use those warships to attack Dakkadian shipping directly.

She had laughed openly when she had first read the request, for he had chosen a decidedly loose interpretation of the term 'self-defense' if he wanted to attack Dakkadia openly. Enaria was completely against the idea, and would have been against it even if she hadn't taken a Dakkadian as a lover. The reason was simple: if they allowed Orem to use Ithram Mages to project force, instead of simply defending the home front as the treaty intended, he would effectively be turning Ithram from a neutral bystander into an active participant in the upcoming war. That could not be allowed, for Ithram had to remain above such conflicts or risk alienating other realms. At best, the other realms would view Ithram's tacit neutrality as a polite fiction, and deal with them in a belligerent basis. At worst, the realms would stop sending young Mages to them to be trained and Tested, for fear of them being used as weapons against their own people.

Fortunately, the other Councillors saw things the same way she did, and would not require convincing to keep their Mages out of the conflict. This debate was strictly *pro forma*, for no matter how ludicrous the request by King Orem might seem, his power and position meant that they had no choice but to give it serious consideration before dismissing it out of hand. Se-ir Windwhisper held up a hand to call for attention.

"I think we are in agreement not to release any additional Mages to Illymar at this time. Should Dakkadia indeed attempt invasion, we should convene again to reconsider the request, but for now, the request seems to be more than a bit premature."

Heads nodded around the circle, but to her surprise, Cedric DeVir raised his hand. Se-ir bowed his head to the Eighth Chair, and Cedric leaned forward.

"Illymar is currently in a state of flux, and King Orem is in a hard position. If we do not do something to show him that we understand the position he is in, he may turn his sights upon us and make his displeasure known in ways that we would not enjoy. I agree that giving him more Mages so that he might send them after Dakkadian ships is a very bad idea, but we have to do something."

"Do you have a recommendation?" Se-ir asked.

"Here is what I propose. There is a very high percentage of Illymari Mages on our lists who are currently citizens of Ithram, but still hold dual citizenship with Illymar. I propose that we allow these people to make the decision for themselves whether or not to take up arms for their birth country. I believe a fair percentage of them will, for nationalistic pride if nothing else. But to be fair, we should also extend the same courtesy toward Dakkadia. We have a decidedly smaller percentage of Dakkadian Mages here in Ithram, but by allowing them the freedom to decide for themselves, King Madari will have nothing to complain about for we will have dealt with him in exactly the same manner that we deal with Illymar. King Orem will be grateful for any extra assistance we can provide for him, and we would still maintain the position of neutrality that we currently hold."

"An elegant solution. Is there any debate?" Se-ir asked, clearly impressed by the idea.

Enaria immediately raised her hand and Se-ir ceded the floor to her.

"An interesting suggestion, Archimagus DeVir, though I have to wonder at your motive for making it in the first place. You, yourself, are Dakkadian by birth. Will you be taking up arms for the King of Dakkadia out of nationalistic pride?"

"You know quite well I am from Palantine, and therefore, I am not truly a Dakkadian. Furthermore, I emancipated from my family to become a citizen of Ithram as soon as I was legally able. My loyalty is to the Citadel and nowhere else, least of all King Madari. And to answer your question, 'no,' I will not be joining Dakkadia in a war of aggression, for I find that I am quite partial to the status quo. However, I also do not want to risk incurring Illymar's displeasure for standing aside when they needed us the most. This seems to me to be the best possible solution to a decidedly bad set of choices that have been presented to us."

"I meant no offense by my question, Cedric. I simply wished to know the reason for your suggestion. No matter how we phrase things, the end result will be that there are more Ithram Mages aboard Illymari vessels, a dangerous state of affairs for us no matter how you look at it. When every vessel that Illymar fields against Dakkadia suddenly has a Mage or Mages aboard, will Dakkadia understand that we are not actually acting against their interests in the defense of their allies?"

"I see your point. Unless we inform King Madari of the Council's decision, he may well draw the wrong conclusion." He glanced at Se-ir and said, "Consider my request withdrawn."

"No, his suggestion has great merit," Enaria said quickly. "As Archimagus DeVir says, we have a decidedly bad set of choices that have been presented to us. I believe that the best option open to us at this time, is to allow the Illymari Mages to make their own decisions about defending Illymar, and then send a representative to Dakkadia to explain to King Madari exactly why we did so."

Cedric stiffened in his chair slightly at the suggestion, but then nodded.

"I will, of course, be more than happy to convey the Council's decree to King Madari, should we all agree upon that course of action."

"No, your position as a *former* member of the Dakkadian nobility rules you out as a messenger," Enaria said. "King Madari will not like the news we will be delivering to him, and he may attempt to coerce you into attempting to change the Council's position on this matter by either appealing to your sense of nationalism, or by directly threatening your family or their interests." Cedric jerked as if struck at that, and Enaria's eyes narrowed in consideration. *Could Madari have already attempted to suborn Cedric?* "It would be better if I went. During the Convocation, I struck up a friendship with Mage Morvandis. I believe he would be willing to help me soften the blow, as it were."

Se-ir nodded and called for a vote, and not surprisingly, the measure passed without further debate.

With that final bit of business out of the way, the Council adjourned and Enaria stood up quickly. She had things to do before she left Ithram, and she fully intended on leaving this very night with Morvandis aboard the ship she had already arranged for him. Before she could leave, however, Cedric caught her arm.

"Could I speak with you for a moment, Enaria?" She waited for the other Councillors to leave before once again taking her seat. Cedric hesitated for a moment before taking a deep breath and saying, "King Madari has already threatened my family's welfare if I don't vote to allow Dakkadian invasion when the time comes." At her lack of reaction, he frowned and asked, "Did you know?"

"No, Cedric, I did not know, but I am not surprised. When I mentioned the possibility during the Council session you reacted very strongly. You covered yourself very well, but not well enough to fool me. I simply put two and two together to reach the proper sum."

"I don't know what to do," he said. "I don't want to see Illymar fall under Dakkadian rule. But by that same token, I have to think of my family. He wouldn't hesitate to kill them all if I attempt to thwart his ambitions."

She thought about it for a moment.

"Your suggestion today was your way of attempting to lend aid to Illymar despite the threat to your family?" He nodded, and she reached out to take his hand. "You are a good man, Cedric DeVir. What you should do now is continue upon your path of passive resistance, and pray that a formal vote to allow, or disallow, an actual invasion never takes place. If that day should come despite your best efforts, my advice to you would be to vote to allow invasion—no matter what your personal feelings are, and take comfort in what measures you have already put in place. Even good men can fall victim to the ruthless, and it would be wrong for you to put your family in jeopardy . . . even if by doing so you would be doing the honorable thing."

He nodded slowly, but then a miserable expression crossed his features.

"If the day comes when I do have to vote for or against invasion, whatever happens to Illymar will be on me." Enaria pressed her lips into a flat line and rapped him sharply on the crown of his head with her knuckles. "What was that for?" he asked with a frown.

"For your unmitigated arrogance, of course. There are eight of us on the High Council, and yet you believe that somehow, *your* vote will be the one which allows an invasion. Not everyone has family under King Madari's thumb."

He stopped rubbing his head and brightened visibly.

"That is true. Off-hand, I can think of no one, other than myself, who would vote to allow Madari to have his way with Illymar." He narrowed his eyes at her suspiciously. "Or two, now that I think on it."

"And just what is that supposed to mean?"

He gave her a level look.

"You were very quick to volunteer to go to Dakkadia to meet with your "friend," Mage Morvandis. And come to think of it, you spent quite an inordinate amount of time with him during his stay in the Citadel. *And*, I saw you slide your hand into his during the third day of the Convocation. That was more than mere friendship, if I were to hazard a guess. Is there something *you* wish to confide in *me*?"

She hesitated a moment, but knew that she had to say something to assuage his suspicion.

"It is none of your concern, but Morvandis and I became lovers during the Convocation. It happened quite by accident, but ever since we have been reacquainted with each other, I have been trying desperately to convince him to leave Dakkadian service and return here, where he belongs."

"He won't leave, you know. His loyalty to King Madari is absolute and unquestioning. In fact, I would not be surprised at all if Madari did not order Morvandis to seek a . . . *relationship* with you before he sent his son here to be Tested. Morvandis would do that for him."

"It was I who seduced him, Cedric," Enaria said, laughing. "He wanted nothing whatsoever to do with me before I snuck into his room to lie with him. I can be quite convincing when I want to be." She batted her eyelashes at him playfully, and laughed again when she saw him blush. "Why, Cedric, your face is turning red. Surely, you are not *embarrassed!* And I thought you to be a man of the world."

"Perhaps a *bit* embarrassed," he said. "It may surprise you to learn that I think of you as a sister." He squeezed her hand gently, before letting go. "If you have indeed sought out Morvandis for your own ends, I wish you well of it, but you should prepare yourself for failure if you believe that you can pry him away from Madari. You would not be the first person to try to manipulate Morvandis, after all."

"One of the virtues of a long lifespan is vast reservoirs of patience. Believe me, I will take as long as I must to overcome his resistance and bring him back to Ithram. Now, if there is nothing else, I plan to sail to Dakkadia on the first available vessel, and I need to prepare."

With that, she left Cedric alone with his thoughts. When the door closed safely behind her she smiled in triumph, for she had accomplished exactly what she had sought to do when she had stopped to speak with him. When the time came, he would vote as Morvandis wished, even knowing better. And it was all thanks to her. She patted the note she had placed in her pocket and thought, *Won't Morvandis be pleased? I guess I should go and ask him.*

Queen Althea had to restrain herself from trying to choke the life out of the man standing before her, but somehow she kept her rage from showing on her face as anything other than a tight grimace. The man in question was her father, Duke Alessandro Savonne, and he was the both the patriarch of the family and the man directly responsible for having found a way to make her Queen of Illymar. He hadn't been a Duke at the time, of course; he had merely been a powerful and influential merchant with an extremely beautiful daughter.

Alessandro was known throughout Illymar for his lavish parties, filled with excesses of every kind, and the King and his nobles had open invitations to attend the festivities. They didn't always attend, of course, but when they did, they had received the best treatment the Savonnes could offer, and with their wealth, that had been considerable, indeed. And on every occasion the King had deigned to attend, Alessandro had made certain Althea had been displayed as prominently as possible. With her great beauty and ample charms, she had quickly caught the King's eye, and she had ruthlessly used his interest in her first to seduce him, and later to marry him.

Oh, Orem still believed that he himself had been the one doing the seducing during their courtship, but the truth was Althea had played him like a violin. She had led him on for a full year with hints and promises of things to come, until he had finally reached the breaking point, and then she had willing given herself to him during a night of incredible passion. Once she had submitted to him sexually, she knew that he believed that he would have no further use for her, but he hadn't counted on her ambition. Even after he had taken her, she had discovered that the best way to keep his interest was quite a bit simpler than she could have ever imagined: she merely did absolutely anything and everything he asked in bed—and many things he had never dreamed possible—with no questions asked.

Orem himself was an unimaginative lover, but she had made up for his lack of inventiveness by providing the imagination for him, and so together they enjoyed a very lively and inventive love life. Her wicked behavior, coupled with her unparalleled beauty, meant that she never gave him a reason to stray. In fact, she saw to it that he never had the energy. For herself, she had never even been tempted to stray, for the slightest hint that she had betrayed him would have been ruinous to the Savonnes she had worked so hard to get elevated—Savonnes like her father, the Duke of Skye.

Unfortunately, she had now learned that there were other ways in which she could displease the King, that would also prove to be ruinous to the Savonnes. Now that they had lost the King's favor, the entire family had learned the hard way that the slide down was much faster than the climb up. Worse, some of the lesser merchant houses, and the people the Savonnes had ruined financially, were all too happy to help them on their path to the gutters.

Duke Ascham had been relentless in his pursuit of any Savonnes who foolishly tried to hold back anything at all from the Crown's Tax Collectors, and often, the people responsible for turning in one of the family was a "trusted" servant or a "loyal" vassal. The situation had become so dire that her father had returned to Illymaine from his semi-retirement on the Skye lands to speak to her. The problem was he still thought of her as nothing more than a possession that he could use to pry favors loose from the King by offering up the charms of his beautiful daughter. He did not come here to ask her advice or offer her his council; he had come to lecture her and berate her for her stupidity, as though he had had nothing whatsoever to do with the attempt on the Corsair's life. And for her own part, Althea had been Queen more than long enough to resent the intrusion of this useless parasite. When he finished speaking to her, she clenched her fists.

"Go back to your estates, old man, and let me handle this in my own way. I will let you know what I decide to do on my own schedule, not yours!"

Alessandro glared hotly back at her.

"You forget who you are talking to, *daughter.* I will not be spoken to as such by my own child!"

"And you forget who you are talking to, *Your Grace.* As your Queen, I command you to return to your own estates and leave the matter at hand to me. I will find a way to repair what has happened, and your presence here is neither needed nor desired. Go home."

He gritted his teeth and stepped forward to look down at her.

"Raise your voice to me one more time, and I will cut off your monthly stipend, starting immediately." She paled at the threat and shut her mouth with a click, for the threat was a very serious one indeed, and she knew he would follow through with it. Orem had made good on his threat, and had cut off all of her money except for just enough to pay one handmaiden. It had taken only a few days of this newly-perceived poverty for her to contact her father to beg for money. He had agreed to pay her a set amount; not exactly generous, but not particularly miserly either, in exchange for her promise to find a way to repair the damage that had been done. If her father cut her off as well, she would be in serious trouble and she knew it. He waited for a moment to let the threat sink in, and she said nothing. "Better," he said, after his point had been made. He turned from her and asked, "Have you tried to seduce him? Your charms have always done the trick in the past. I don't see why that would change now."

"I'm not fifteen anymore, Father. My charms no longer hold the same appeal to him as they once did."

He turned back and looked at her as if seeing her for the first time. There was a hint of grey in her hair now, and a few lines at the corners of her eyes. She was still quite beautiful, but she was heading—however gracefully—into her middle years. He looked at her for a moment and then nodded, and she sighed in relief.

"You are right. You have been married for over 25 years now. He has seen everything that you have to offer, and that means seduction won't work." He brought a hand to his face and rubbed his jaw. "Perhaps someone younger would be more successful in bringing the King around to see things in a different light. You have a number of younger cousins who are as beautiful as you once were. If I throw a party and arrange to have them paraded in front of him, perhaps he will take a liking to one and become more amenable."

If Althea had had a weapon she would have used it on the man, then and there.

"Try it and see what happens. I have too much to lose to allow some strumpet to try and take what belongs to me."

"Then what do you suggest, daughter?" he said, anger rising quickly. "How do you intend to put things aright?"

"I intend to do nothing for now. Despite the problems our family now faces, some of the changes Orem is making are actually good ones. As just one example, you let the navy become an absolute shambles in your single-minded pursuit of wealth. That neglect makes us vulnerable to invasion, and believe me when I say that if Dakkadia manages to conquer us, even the ruinous taxes we are facing now will seem nothing but a pleasant alternative to our outright ruin, and perhaps death, at the hands of the Dhaerhans. I propose that we allow events to run their course, and let Orem prepare the country to fight to defend *our* holdings. And once he has secured the island from any possible invasion, I will work on making things right for all of us." She lowered her voice and said, "There is no other option available to us, Father. Things have already gone too far for us to change his mind now. The gilding and fine tapestries could only cover the rot for so long, but now that the rot has been exposed, it is all-too-obvious for everyone to see."

"Perhaps you are right," he said. "But know this, Althea; my patience will not last forever. And just as there is a bottom to my indulgence, there is also a bottom to my largess. Find a way to fix this problem, or find a way to pay for your own comforts. Am I understood?"

When she returned to her chambers, she was surprised to find three Royal Guards at the door to her chambers. She nodded to them politely, knowing what their presence entailed. Orem was waiting for her in her room, and she had no idea what it was he wanted from her. She felt her heart pounding in her chest, and her palms turned cold and clammy. She rubbed her hands upon her dress to dry them and nodded to the middle guard. He responded by opening the door to her chambers and allowing her entrance. Orem was sitting at a side table waiting for her, and to her relief, she saw that Ascham was nowhere to be seen.

"How did your meeting with your father, the good Duke of Skye go, my wife?" he asked, a clearly-defined chill in his tone. "Did he give you his instructions on how you are to repair the damage between your family and the Crown?"

"He merely wished to express his concern at the direction our relationship had taken, and to impart upon me the urgency of making things right again."

"That couldn't have been pleasant for you. So tell me; do you perhaps have a younger sister I do not know about who he plans to offer to me as a bribe?"

Althea's shoulders slumped in defeat.

"No. He thought about offering you a younger cousin or two, but I convinced him that that wouldn't work, and that he would be stupid to even try."

To her surprise, Orem gave her a genuine laugh. She looked up a bit, hopefully, and found him smiling. It was a small thing, but the sight of it filled her with hope that perhaps things could be mended between them. She looked at the chair across from him.

"May I sit down? It has been a long day."

He waved his hand toward the chair, and she gratefully took a seat next to him.

"What did you tell him?" Orem asked.

"The truth. I told him that what you and your brother are doing now, while extremely painful in the short term for the family, is actually a good thing for the country. I fully admit I had no idea just how bad the problems—especially in our navy and army—had actually become. It was so easy to believe that nothing bad would ever happen to us; that no one would ever dare to attack us here in the very center of our power. But that belief was a lie, and I am happy that you discovered the problem before it became too late to undo the damage."

He looked down at his hands.

"I don't know if I *did* discover the problem in time. We are working as hard as we can to turn things around, but Dakkadia has become much more powerful in a much shorter time than we could have possibly imagined. The fact that I allowed our fleet to become so very weak was my biggest mistake. I trusted your father when he said it would be better for the kingdom to send privateers out to strike at the Dakkadian navy. 'Cat's paws' he called them. For a while it seemed to work too. It was much cheaper to hire a mercenary than it was to build a military vessel from the keel out and to pay someone to crew her. But now, the mercenaries are all gone, and we have been left to our own devices."

She reached out and covered his hand with hers.

"We will endure, Orem. We always do." She took a deep breath and said, "It isn't too late, you know. We could send an envoy to Dakkadia to sue for peace. The terms he gave you, while harsh, are better by far than being conquered outright."

Orem shook his head.

"You may not believe this, but I did consider it. It was shortly after my inspection of the docks when I realized how very bad the situation is. It will take months for the new ships to be built, and Dakkadia has undoubtedly unleashed its fleet upon us already. We have had no reports yet of fighting, but that does not mean that it hasn't happened. According to my military advisors, we have to hold out for one year. One year is all it will take to undo all the damage my negligence has caused. After that, our navy will be strong enough to hold the Teeth, with or without the Mage Council's help." He sighed heavily and said, "We have had word on that front, too. The Mage Council refuses to assign more Mages to our warships on the basis that I plan to actively attack Dakkadia with them. I knew that it was a long shot, but I had to at least try."

Althea squeezed his hands.

"I am so sorry that I caused all of this, Orem. I did not realize that this would happen. I was only trying to end the Corsair's reign of terror in the most economical method possible."

To her surprise, he patted her hands.

"There is a great deal of blame to go around, Althea. I came here to tell you I have reinstated your allowance, and to say that I am not as angry with you as I was. I have not completely forgiven you for choosing to obey your father over me, but I know now that I will. I love you too much for it to be any different. Things have changed somewhat between us, but as you said, we will endure. We always do."

She began to cry.

"Your understanding means a lot to me, my husband. Please tell me how I can make amends to you for my part in what is happening. I will do whatever you ask of me."

He stood up and walked to the door.

"I will think about it. Join me for breakfast tomorrow morning and we will discuss it."

He gave her one last smile and opened the door. Before he could shut it, however, she called after him.

"Tomorrow then, beloved. I will look forward to it."

As Orem left his wife to return to his study, the smile on his face refused to leave. It had been very hard for him over the last few weeks; for despite her flaws, he still loved her and it hurt him to have to punish her for her part in the Corsair fiasco. He had had many sleepless nights wondering if he had perhaps been too harsh on her, but the point had to be made that she was no longer a Savonne. Orem knew Alessandro still treated his daughter as if she were only that: his daughter, and not the Queen of Illymar. And he also knew that Althea hated him for it. That was good enough for now, as far as he was concerned.

She was still the Queen of Illymar and, as such, he could not afford to let her disgrace damage the Crown. He frowned when he thought about her father, but he set that problem aside for another time. The man's ambition had always been a concern, and this time he needed to be slapped down, but that, too, could wait. The truth was, it had been his own lack of attention that had brought the Kingdom to such dire straits, but at the time, the Savonnes had been a convenient target to vent his spleen upon. Now, he needed to rein in his people before they did lasting harm to the Savonne interests that were so vital to the Crown's welfare.

When Orem opened the door to his study, he spotted his brother sitting at one of the side tables reading a letter. Ascham looked up to see who had entered, and smiled when he realized that it was the King.

"Welcome back, Your Majesty. How did the meeting with the Queen go?"

Ascham's smile turned predatory at the anticipation of hearing about yet another well-deserved drubbing that the Queen had received, but this time Orem had to disappoint him.

"It went well . . . better than I'd hoped, actually. She didn't try to lie about the meeting or prevaricate in any way. I think that we can ease up on the Savonnes now that the shock of my failure at the Convocation has worn off, and we are making headway toward repairing the damage to the Kingdom."

"Ease up on them? We have them right where we want them! In a few more days I'll have them broken like twigs!"

"That is not what I want, and furthermore, it never was," Orem said. "I know that you hate them, but despite what you may believe, we will need them now more than ever. It is enough that they know that my patience with them has limits, and that if they break those limits, they can and will be punished like anyone else. If I let you break them, we will have to rebuild the economy from the ground up, and that would be the worst possible thing we could do right before a war. You are a warrior, and you always have been. What you fail to realize is, that in order to wage war effectively, you also need a strong economy . . . and that means merchants. The Savonnes make money better than any other group in the kingdom. We need that skill."

"They make that money by taking it from everyone else, using any means they deem necessary. Don't you see that what you are doing is bad for the kingdom? This 'strong' economy, as you call it, is anything but!"

He picked up a stack of papers from the desk and brandished them in front of Orem.

"Our auditors have determined that the state the Crown's finances are currently in is a direct result of usury and fraud knowingly perpetrated by the Savonnes! They've been robbing the kingdom blind for years, and you want to *reward* them for it? You should have the lot of them arrested and condemned for treason!"

Orem glanced briefly at the papers.

"And will you pay for the war? Will your estates pay for the ships we are building, the Mages we are hiring, or the soldiers we are training and equipping? Tell me, Ascham, if you have that kind of money, why are you holding it back?"

Ascham had no answer for that, and Orem nodded.

"I'm sure that most, if not all, of your accusations are correct. But I ask you, does that really matter? We need them . . . or more precisely, we need their money, or we lose it all."

"We're getting the money we need from them! If I have to, I will carve the last copper piece we need directly out of the Duke of Skye's fat hide myself!"

Orem grabbed the papers from Ascham and threw them back onto the desk.

"And what about next year? Or the year after? Once you've bled them dry, as you so plainly intend, our markets will collapse completely, and the Kingdom will fall into financial chaos. If we wring every single coin we can out of them, the way you want, you will learn what it means to kill the goose that lays the golden egg."

Ascham prepared himself to argue the point, but Orem waved his hand in a cutting-off gesture.

"Enough. I've made my decision, Ascham, and I ask you to abide by it. Tomorrow, we will begin to ease the pressure on the Savonnes, and turn our full attention to fighting this war. Am I understood?"

"Understood. But don't expect me to like it."

"I don't care if you like it or not. All you have to do is live with it." He pinched the bridge of his nose and squeezed his eyes shut.

"I have a splitting headache and I'm going to bed. If you want to argue about this some more tomorrow, it will have to wait until after breakfast. Tomorrow, I will be taking my breakfast with Althea, and hopefully, I will be able to find some way to salvage this situation short of the two of you killing each other."

Morvandis opened his eyes when he heard a knock at his door and nodded slowly to Thorn, even as he made certain the mask of Blood Magic hiding his power remained in place. He already knew who was at the door, for he could feel Enaria's resonance approaching the inn, but if he'd masked himself properly, she would have no idea who was in the room waiting for her. Thorn opened the door slightly and looked out, then grinned smugly and stepped back, allowing their guest to enter. When Enaria saw that it was Morvandis, she stepped past Thorn and kissed him soundly. Once they separated, Thorn cleared her throat.

"You two should get a room if you are going to be carrying on the way you are." She looked around at her surroundings. "Oh. I guess you *have* a room. I'll just leave the two of you to your privacy then."

"No, Thorn. Stay here for now. I do not want you wandering around where you might be seen or recognized."

"So, you are Thorn of the Flower Court?" Enaria asked. "I am pleased to make your acquaintance. Morvandis has told me absolutely nothing about you."

"Likewise, Archimagus Enaria," Thorn said. "Though Morvandis is notoriously tight-lipped, I have to say that I very much admired your handiwork upon Morvandis' back. That was expertly done."

"I always like to mark my possessions. That way if ever he should stray, everyone he meets will know exactly who he belongs to."

"I like her," Thorn said to Morvandis. "I think you can keep her."

Enaria smiled and sat down on a wooden chair before looking up at Morvandis.

"So, now that you have me here, what can I do to help you?"

Morvandis sat down next to her.

"Is the ship ready? We will have to leave in a hurry once my task is complete."

"The ship is ready to depart on a moment's notice. I have already taken the liberty of having my things brought aboard. I will be leaving with you." Morvandis started to protest, but she simply waved a hand and said, "This is official Mage Citadel business, and has nothing to do with you. I have been asked by the Mage Council to deliver a message to King Madari, and I will be taking the first ship out of Ithram. Lucky for me, that first ship happens to be the one that you will be sailing upon as well. In fact, it will serve to allay suspicion if I am aboard. A ship leaving in the night would normally be suspicious, but not if it is an official courier ship for the Mage High Council."

Morvandis thought about it for a second before relenting. Enaria smiled in triumph when she realized that she had won the argument without a single word of protest from him. Instead, he changed the subject.

"What is the message that you have been asked to deliver?"

Enaria leaned back, putting her weight onto her hands and then crossing her legs casually.

"I am to inform King Madari that King Orem has requested that the Mage Council allow him to hire a greater percentage of Mages to crew his vessels, as a counter to your new weapons. The Council rejected that request, but will quietly be allowing individual Mages to decide for themselves whether or not to fight on behalf of their respective nations. As you know, there are many more Mages of Illymari birth in Ithram than there are Dakkadian, so this will in effect provide Illymar with the reinforcements that they are asking for, without doing so officially."

"King Madari will not be pleased at the news. The first thing he will want to know is whether or not these *patriotic* Mages taking up arms against Dakkadia will be protected by the Ithram Accord or not."

At the mention of the Accord, Enaria sat upright and uncrossed her legs, a look of worry crossing her face. The subject of the Accord had never been broached during the Council's debates, and it should have, for the Accord set exacting guidelines for Citadel Mages in combat on behalf of a nation other than Ithram. In essence, the Accord said that Mages were to fight as best they could until their situation became untenable, and then surrender with no further struggle, never to take up arms against that enemy again. In return, the side that accepted the surrender would parole the Mage at the first possible opportunity to the Mage High Council, who would then ensure that the Mage would take no further part in the conflict.

This Accord existed for two reasons. First, a desperate Mage fighting for his life could cause unbelievable destruction, especially if he or she believed there was no hope, and second, to prevent the wholesale slaughter of Mages on both sides of a war. Mages were far too important to the world to be allowed to die for no reason, but by that same token, they were also far too powerful for an enemy not to target them. So to prevent the needless and senseless loss of life a Mage could inflict upon an enemy, the Accord allowed them to be captured rather than killed.

In the millennia since the institution of the Accord, every single kingdom had not only recognized the value of it, but had followed it to the letter. Even King Madari made his people abide by the rule, and the Corsair herself had captured many Ithram Waterborn on Illymari vessels over the past few years. Any Mage caught breaking the Accord would immediately be sentenced to death, and the sentence would be carried out by agents of the Mage Citadel. Mages still died in battle, and that was a tragedy, but that was also the price one paid for placing one's self in harm's way. All the Accord asked was that if at all possible, an army should endeavor to capture a Mage rather than kill him.

"To be honest, the subject never came up, but I believe that is because we automatically assumed they would still fall under the protection of the Accord. If you would like, I could return to the Citadel, and call the Council back into session. It would delay our departure, but you would have your answer."

"No. I will recommend to him that the Accords remain in effect, even for those Mages who willingly remove themselves from the protection that Ithram extends. But we will demand a concession, of course. We will want the Accord extended to our own Mages in exactly the same manner as it will be to the Ithram Mages fighting under the Illymari standard. Fair is fair after all."

Enaria hesitated a moment before nodding, because that was a very serious concession indeed. The Zarryiostrom dictated that any Powerborn had to be brought before the combined scrutiny of both the Church and the Mage Council before being allowed to practice their craft, but did not dictate that a Powerborn had to ultimately become a citizen of Ithram. During their stay the offer would be made, of course, but it was always a choice and not a command, and no pressure was ever brought to bear to affect the decision one way or the other.

A large percentage of Mages chose to accept the offer, for Ithram was a beautiful place and offered many advantages for its citizens, but many chose, instead, to return to their homes after their training to make their own way in the countries of their birth. The reason there were so few Dakkadian Mages living within the walls of the Citadel, was that a vast majority of them chose instead to return home and take up positions of honor in either the Dakkadian army or the navy. That had been the reason Orem had made his request of the Council in the first place, for the Dakkadian military boasted a nearly three-to-one ratio of Mages to what Illymar could field, even with Ithram located on the island of Illymar. That was not to say that there were more Dakkadian Mages than Illymari; it simply meant that more Illymari chose to accept Ithram's standing offer of citizenship, and the protection of the Mage Council than their Dakkadian counterparts. The tradeoff was, that a Mage who forsook the protection of Ithram to fight for his or her own country, also forsook the protection of the Accords. So called "rogue" Mages were expected to fight to the death just like any other soldier, and to take as many of the enemy with them as they could before they themselves were killed. If they were captured, they were expected to escape at the first possible opportunity and return to duty immediately, and since both sides knew that, captured Mages were never given the opportunity to escape. That also meant they were routinely targeted for assassination during wartime, for a dead Mage was no threat to either side. The reason so many Mages chose to go rogue was that even the weakest of rogue Mages could expect to be very, very rich by the end of a conflict.

"I think the Mage Council will agree to the condition. No one wants to see Mages routinely slaughtered during this conflict. It would be bad for everyone."

"We will talk more about this on the trip to Dakkadia. Now, I need you and Thorn to wait for me here while I complete my mission." He stood up. "When I return, we will leave immediately. Do not leave this room, and do not answer the door."

"What is your mission? Wouldn't it be better if I helped you?"

"No. I have to do this by myself. It may take some time, so be patient. As for what my mission is, I will tell you once we are safely at sea." He glanced at Thorn and said, "And don't bother trying to get the information out of Thorn; she doesn't know either."

He opened the door and stepped into the hall before closing the door quietly behind him.

He was wearing his customary black robes, but the soles of his boots were softer than normal to keep the sound of his steps to an absolute minimum. The sun had set hours ago, and the moon sat high in the sky, bathing everything in its silvery light, but it was more than dark enough for his purposes. Even so, he kept to side streets and back alleys, avoiding people whenever he could. Once he made it to the beach past the docks, he began walking briskly toward the Spire of Illymaine. As an added precaution, he used his rudimentary knowledge of Blood Magic to shield his own Powerborn aura, which would keep him from alerting any Mages who happened to wander near him. Mages could always sense the presence of another Powerborn with the same ability, and with his immense strength, he normally stood out like a beacon wherever he went. Thanks to Enaria's training, however, that particular problem was no longer a concern.

As he drew closer to the sheer cliff face below the Spire, he began angling himself away from the water and toward the massive cliff the Spire had been built upon. When he reached it, he looked up to get his bearings, then pulled the hood of his cloak over his head. He knew that there were no people nearby, but as an added precaution he closed his eyes to keep the emerald flash of light that signified the use of his Earthborn ability from being seen, and summoned his power. Even closing his eyes wasn't enough to fully suppress the green glow emanating from his eyes, but the hood of the cloak kept the glow contained. Even so, he worked quickly. He placed one hand on the solid rock and extended his power, and suddenly the cold stone became insubstantial to him. To an observer it wouldn't have changed at all, but to him it was as if the granite cliff had suddenly become air. The first part of his task complete, he walked into the stone and disappeared from the beach altogether.

Once inside the stone he was effectively blind, but he did not need to see where he was going. He simply needed to move upward. He could have used his Airborn abilities to fly up to the wall or to levitate upward through the stone; but using that ability would leave a residue that could be sensed, and perhaps traced. Using his Earth powers, his progress would be slower and much more difficult, but it would also be safer, for as far as he knew, there were no other Earthborn in existence. He selectively hardened the stone beneath him until a spiral staircase had been formed, and then he methodically began his climb up to the Spire through the not-so-solid rock. Once he reached the end of his climb, he stuck his head up through the ground to make sure he was where he wanted to be, and to watch for guards who could possibly see him. Not seeing anyone, he walked into the cellar of the Spire, passing directly through the stone floor.

The room he entered was a storeroom, filled with dusty old relics, and smelling of mold and decay, but he paid that no mind. Instead, he walked to the door and placed his hand on the wall, again summoning his Earthborn ability: this time to sense vibration in the rock. A quick but thorough scan of the area revealed no hidden servants; no random souls ready to destroy his plan by sounding an alarm, so he stepped out of the doorway and into the hall. He knew exactly where he was, for he had taken careful note of the Spire during their stay, and without thinking about it, he angled himself toward a tall fireplace that he knew rose up through the Royal Chambers . . . and directly into the King's own bedroom.

When Madari had sent him back to Illymar, it had been with strict orders. Kill King Orem.

It was late at night, but Morvandis had not been able to learn of the King's sleeping habits, so he had to be extremely careful. If he entered the room and the King was not asleep, he could conceivably sound an alarm before Morvandis could complete his mission. That could not be allowed, so he had taken precautions against it. Again summoning his Earthborn ability, he stepped into the fireplace and climbed quickly upward on bricks that suddenly extended themselves like rungs on a ladder. He faced a long climb, for the King slept on the fourth floor in a massive bedchamber with an abundance of side rooms and parlors, but eventually he reached his destination and stopped.

He placed his hand on the wall and listened for vibrations, and this time he felt them. One source came from within the room itself, while three others came from outside in the hallway. He smiled in satisfaction at the discovery, for the three guards meant that the sole occupant of the room was the King himself. He released his hold on his Earthborn ability and embraced his new Blood Magic ability. He instantly sensed the heat emanating from his target, and when he focused on it, he could actually feel the blood rushing through King Orem's veins. He watched in curiosity as the bright lines of his blood traveled through his system, and from the shape of the pattern, he could tell that the King was lying in his bed. He wasn't sure if the man was asleep or not, but at the very least, he wasn't moving.

He seized his Earthborn ability again, and repelled all of the soot that had gathered on his person, forcing it to fall to the ground. It would have been beyond stupid of him to come all this way and taken such careful precautions, only to leave a trail of footprints leading from the fireplace. So, he checked himself over thoroughly with his power until he was absolutely positive that not a speck remained. Once he was certain, he allowed himself to pass through the wall and into the bedroom.

A single lamp flickered from a side table, and by its light Morvandis could tell that the King was indeed asleep. He moved silently around the room until he found the King's accoutrements, and with a small smile he chose a gilded dagger from the glittering pile of jewelry. He drew the weapon and examined the blade, finding that, despite the gaudy appearance of the hilt, the blade itself was functional, and would serve quite well. Instrument selected, he walked back to the bed where the King was sleeping and pulled a vial from a hidden pocket in his robe. He opened the vial without checking the contents, and carefully poured two drops of liquid into the King's open mouth. The King stirred somewhat as the liquid trickled into his throat, but did not wake up. Morvandis resealed the vial, placed it on the table next to the bed and counted to himself.

Two minutes later, he reached out and snapped a finger above the King's face. The sharp sound woke Orem from his sleep, and he blinked several times in confusion trying to get his bearings. As sleep slipped away, a look of annoyance on his face changed to surprise, then quickly to fear as he realized that something was wrong. A slight movement was all that he could manage, and his eyes began to move back and forth in obvious panic.

"You can stop struggling," Morvandis said quietly. "The reason that you cannot move your body is that I have poisoned you."

He showed the vial to the paralyzed King.

"This is a common Illymari poison used by prostitutes and assassins. One drop of it will make you lose your muscle control and render you helpless for a few hours while still allowing you to speak. Used in that way, it is perfect for questioning a subject who would otherwise struggle. Two drops—the dosage I gave you—will paralyze you completely and removes your ability to speak. Three drops is a lethal dose and will paralyze your heart and lungs, killing you almost instantly."

A look of terror filled Orem's eyes at the sight of the vial, and his panic-filled gaze turned to look at the door of his room. Morvandis followed his gaze. "The guards are still stationed outside of the room, completely oblivious to what is going on inside. I'm afraid they won't be able to help you." Orem's eyes shot back to Morvandis, and tears of helpless rage filled them. Morvandis pulled back his hood to reveal his face, and Orem's eyes opened wide as he looked upon the face of his assassin for the first time. "I could have killed you in your sleep, of course, but King Madari did not want that. Instead, he bid me read you a letter before I kill you. Please bear with me."

He slid a folded message from his hidden pocket and opened it, reading just loudly enough for the King to hear.

To His Majesty, King Orem of Illymar,

Please allow me to thank you for the generous hospitality you extended to my family during our recent stay in your fine country. I enjoyed my time within your kingdom immensely, and I very much look forward to seeing it again—perhaps much sooner than you might expect. I am sorry you will not be there to greet me upon my return, but, alas, you made it quite clear at our last meeting that you would view my presence as unwelcome. A pity, really. We could have been such wonderful allies.

As you enter the next world, I want you to contemplate two things. The first is that you, yourself, chose this path the moment you decided to make yourself my enemy. Had you treated me with an ounce of the dignity and respect you showered upon Emperor Xan, instead of insulting me publicly at every turn, I might have been inclined to spare your life. It is a bad business, murdering Kings, but as you have no doubt noticed by now, I am not above it. The second is that during our stay I took a tremendous liking to your oldest daughter, the exquisite Princess Tais, and when I do return to your island and have broken it to my will, I will be certain to offer her whatever comfort I can at the tragic loss of her father when I take her to my bed.

Take heart in knowing that I do not intend to put your entire family to the sword, however. Your sons will have to die, of course, as will your brother, but it is my intention to wed the fair Princess Lyrahe to my son, Valeriad. It is a good match, and one you should have had the wisdom to consider for yourself. Nevertheless, your beautiful daughter will no doubt willingly bear many fine Dakkadian sons. You, of course, will not be around to see your future grandchildren, but I thought you should at least know about them.

Farewell, Orem. Know now that the manner of your death will lead directly to the subjugation of your kingdom at my hands. After all, civil war—just like the murder of kings—is a bad business.

Madari Dhaerhan

Message delivered, Morvandis folded up the note and placed it back inside his pocket, followed by the vial of poison. The tears of impotent rage which filled King Orem's eyes flowed freely down his face, but Morvandis wasn't moved.

"I will give you a moment to make your peace with the Archon, Your Majesty, and when you are ready, I promise you, I will make your death quick and painless."

A look of pathetic gratitude appeared in Orem's eyes, but though his lips trembled with terror, no sound emerged. Morvandis stood next to the bed waiting patiently until, after a few quiet moments, King Orem finally bowed to the inevitable. Morvandis could see the surrender in his eyes, and knew it was time. He gently placed his hand upon the King's forehead and said,

"May the Archon grant you peace, Your Majesty."

He slid his hand down to cover King Orem's eyes to keep him from seeing what he was doing, and picked up the knife he had selected from the King's belongings. He turned the blade downward in his clenched fist, and with a single powerful stroke, he drove the dagger into Orem's chest and straight through his heart. There *was* a sound then, a slight gasp as his victim breathed his final breath, and then nothing at all, as King Orem Illvanin, Third of his Name, died.

Morvandis waited for several minutes to be certain that the job was done, and then turned back to the fireplace to retrace his route back to the inn, leaving the King's own dagger buried to the hilt in his chest.

EPILOGUE

"Disciple"

Standing silently on the rear deck of the Ithram-flagged transport ship she had hired to take her and her companions to Dakkadia, Enaria watched the lights on the coast of Illymar shrink into the distance, and smiled to herself. She was over 300 years old now, and during her life she had seen more wars than she cared to remember. So, she knew what the future held for the island she had come to think of as her home. The murder of the King of Illymar in his own bed would send shockwaves throughout the Kingdom. Accusations would fly, arrests would be made, people would die . . . and war would begin—a bitter civil war with Crown Prince Ethan on one side, and his uncle, Duke Ascham Illvanin on the other.

There was still a slim chance for the Illymari Royal Family to stop the war before it began, but she judged the possibility to be highly unlikely. It would require one side, or the other, to possess the wisdom and the foresight to see what was going to happen beforehand, and to take immediate action by arresting and executing the leader of the other faction before their supporters were allowed to organize. Unfortunately, Enaria could not think of a single member of the Illvanin family who possessed such foresight, and once the first drop of blood was spilled, events would inevitably take on a life of their own.

The ensuing war, once begun, would not stop until one side, or the other, was completely wiped out. Far from being repulsed by the notion of a bloody civil conflict, Enaria found herself becoming strangely excited, for she knew that no matter how terrible the civil war might be, in reality, it would be nothing more than the prelude of a much greater conflict . . . a conflict that would eventually force Morvandis to leave the safety of the shadows and to take an active hand in the events that could culminate in his own Ascension. Her gaze hardened, and her fingers curled into claws at her sides as she watched Illymar shrink into the distance.

If Illymar itself must burn in the fires of the Archon for Morvandis to Ascend, then so be it. Let it burn. It would be an insignificant price to pay for the potential gain.

She stared into the darkness long after the lights of the coast of Illymar had faded away, and even the island's shadowy outline had, at last, disappeared from view. Then, she turned in place, and her eyes were instantly drawn to the only other visible landmark in sight. In the distance, she could just make out one of the Teeth of Amhar glowing faintly in the pale moonlight: a silvery sentinel which had stood for over 2,500 years as a warning to one and all that Il'Amhar belonged to the Archon. As she contemplated the colossal stone monument, she couldn't help but wonder what Zarryiosiad would have thought about the assassination of the King of Illymar.

The answer was as troubling to Enaria as it was obvious, for the Archon's own father had been assassinated in his bedchambers, and Zarryiosiad's wrath had been legendary. She had retaliated against her father's murderers by beginning a war that had lasted 400 years. It had finally ended with her death, as well as the total annihilation of every last one of her enemies. True, in the end Zarryiosiad's thirst for vengeance had destroyed her as well, but Enaria knew better than most that greatness requires sacrifice. For a moment, she spared a thought for the doomed Lyx—the Earthborn Fae destroyed in the Valley of Fire.

If they had known what would happen to them for ordering the murder of Zarus, would they still have done it? Probably. After all, the Lyx were completely mad.

The situations were not truly parallel, despite the striking similarities in the way both assassinations had been carried out. In the past, Zarryiosiad had been the most powerful Mage alive, and even knowing that, the Lyx, in their madness, had still foolishly decided to provoke her. They had completely underestimated her power—or more likely, had greatly overestimated their own—and they had paid for their ignorance—or their arrogance—with their lives. This time it was the assassin himself who held claim to the title of the most powerful Mage alive, and there was not a single person in Illymar who could stand against him.

Enaria still feared for Morvandis, for the greatest threat to him at this point was the combined power of the Mage Citadel. According to history, Zarryiosiad had won victory after victory against the Lyx because they refused to see her as the threat she truly was, and had let their own petty jealousies and rivalries keep them from uniting against her. Once the threat the Archon posed had finally become too obvious for them to ignore, the surviving Lyx had united at the Valley of Fire and had used their combined magical might to contain Zarryiosiad's power long enough for their army to destroy hers. Had Zarryiosiad not Ascended, they undoubtedly would have killed her as well. The same thing could happen to Morvandis. If the Mage High Council decided that he was a threat or, even worse, they somehow discovered that he was in fact an Earth Mage, the Citadel combined could destroy him. She could not—would not—allow that end to come to pass.

With no little effort, Enaria turned her thoughts away from the Citadel that had been her home for so very long, and back to the beautiful demigod-made-flesh who was resting below decks, waiting for her return. Enaria knew her own limitations better than anyone, and she had long ago accepted the fact that, despite her mastery of Blood Magic, she would never attain the heights of power that both the Archon and Morvandis could so effortlessly reach. But that fact no longer mattered to her. For most of her life she had mourned the fact that Zarryiosiad was dead and gone, and that all of her knowledge, her secrets, and her power had died with her. But Morvandis . . . Morvandis was gloriously alive, and she was earning his trust. It was a slow process, for a man who had been burdened for so long with so many secrets learned the hard way never to trust anyone, but she had plenty of time . . . and patience. And though he might not believe it now, one day he would learn for himself he could trust her, for she would never betray him. Standing at his side, she would witness new miracles firsthand. She would help him achieve the destiny he was meant to attain, and when histories were written about Morvandis, her name would be as synonymous with his as Kalindral was to Zarryiosiad.

Morvandis and Enaria.

The thought made her smile all the broader, and the smile remained, even as she finally turned from the railing and walked to the quarters that had been set aside for them. Before she had even reached the door, she began to undress, already eagerly anticipating what would come next. And as her fingertips caressed the handle of the door to their cabin, she had one final thought.

If I cannot become the Archon, then I will become his greatest disciple.

GLOSSARY

DRAGON WITCHES/LORDS

Asiria (ah-SEER-EE-uh): Known as the Queen of Knowledge or informally as "Halo", Asiria is the librarian of the Mage Citadel. Her dragon is bright metallic gold.

Astranaithes (ass-truh-NIGH-theez): Known alternately as the Queen of Fate, Oracle, or the Queen of Wisdom, Astranaithes is the oldest and most revered of the Dragon Witches. Her dragon is a deep emerald green.

Cassiramaithris (kuh-SEER-ruh-MAI-thrus): The Queen of Assassins. Cassiramaithris was the lover of Severius, the Lord of Time, prior to the events of the Valley of Fire. She is currently the personal assassin of Severeielle, the Queen of Shadows. Cassiramaithris' dragon is Red.

Furionchires (fury-ahn-KAI-reez): Known as the Queen of Battles or the Queen of Conflict, her original host was slain by Severius, the Lord of Time at the Valley of Fire. Furionchires has since recovered and is currently the personal bodyguard of Astranaithes, the Queen of Fate. Her dragon is red.

Kaizenerimakagi (KAI-ZEN-era-ma-KAH-gi): The Lord of Snows. He is the mysterious benefactor responsible for Dakkadia's sudden rise in military power. Kaizenerimakagi's dragon is white.

Myerasalomé (MY-year-uh-SALL-oh-may): The Queen of Havoc. She is the absolute ruler of a shadowy cabal of Blood Mages known as the Fallen. The color of her dragon is silver.

Severeielle (seh-VAIR-ee-ell): The Queen of Shadows. Twin sister to Severius the Lord of Time, Severeielle seeks the death of the Harbinger at any cost. Her dragon is black with red wings.

Severius (seh-VAIR-ee-us): Formerly known as the Lord of Time, now known as the Lord of Death or the Dragonslayer. He is the Champion responsible for the killing of the last Harbinger, Zarryiosiad. His dragon is black.

THE KINGDOM OF ILLYMAR

Alessandro Savonne (all-eh-SAHND-roh SAV-own): The Duke of Skye and father of Queen Althea Illvanna. Alessandro was a successful merchant of common blood before his daughter married King Orem Illvanin. He received his dukedom because of his relationship to the Queen. Currently 66 years of age.

Althea Illvanna (al-THAY-uh ill-VAHN-nah): Queen of Illymar. Althea is the daughter of Alessandro Savonne, a merchant commoner. Currently 42 years of age.

Ascham Illvanin (ASH-em ill-VAHN-in): The Duke of Saerce, a large area in the northern part of the island of Illymar. Brother of King Orem Illvanin. Currently 47 years of age.

Chesare Illvanna (chez-uh-RAY ill-VAHN-nah): Youngest daughter of King Orem of Illymar. Chesare is a princess, and is also a Fireborn of incredible talent, considered to be a prodigy. Currently 16-years-old, she is studying magic in the Mage Citadel.

Ethan Illvanin (EE-thun ill-VAHN-in): Son of King Orem and Queen Althea of Illymar, he is the Crown Prince of Illymar. Currently 23 years of age.

Lucas Savonne (LOO-kuss SAV-own): Lord High Admiral of the Illymari navy. He was selected for his post because of his family connections and his ability as an administrator rather than for his martial abilities. He is known as the "Bathtub Admiral", a name his subordinates gave him because the only ships he has ever commanded were toys in a bathtub. Currently 32 years of age.

Lyrahe Illvanna (LIE-ruh ill-VAHN-nah): Middle daughter of King Orem of Illymar, Lyrahe is a princess. Currently 17 years of age.

Orem Illvanin III (Or-rem ill-VAHN-in): King of Illymar. Currently 61 years of age.

Tais Illvanna (TAY-us ill-VAHN-nah): Oldest daughter of King Orem Illvanin, and Princess of Illymar, Tais was briefly married to Lord Marcus Danshire, the Earl of Danshire, before Marcus' death at the hands of Prince Ethan Illvanin at the orders of King Orem Illvanin. Her marriage was disavowed, and her title of

Princess restored after a year-long imprisonment in the Tower, an Illymari prison. Tais is currently 20 years of age.

Vitaly Saxe (vih-TAHL-ee SACKS): Earl of Saxe, and chief political advisor for Ascham Illvanin, the Duke of Saerce. Frequents a house of ill-repute called the Penitentiary. Currently 41 years of age.

THE KINGDOM OF DAKKADIA

Antonio Salazar (ANN-toe-knee-oh SAL-uh-ZAR): Master at Arms and sword master of the Dakkadian warship *Sovereign.* Salazar is currently 52 years of age.

Aveliad Dhaerhan (ah-VAIL-ee-add DARE-hahn): Queen of Dakkadia and wife of King Madari Dhaerhan. Aveliad is the widow of Lord Phaedril Daane, a minor Dakkadian lord. Considered to be the most beautiful woman in the world, she hides her beauty behind a porcelain mask. She is currently 62 years of age, though she is half-Fae and looks to be in her early 20's.

Brendenn DeVir (BREN-den da-VEER): The Prince of Palantine, a Dakkadian province, Brendenn is the half-brother of Queen Aveliad of Dakkadia. A lifelong soldier, Prince Brendenn currently holds the rank of Master of the Heavy Horse in the Dakkadian military, a rank equivalent to General. He is currently 52 years of age.

Cahrick Rantrefal (KARE-rick RAN-tref-fall): Water Mage in the service of Dakkadia. He is currently assigned to the *Sovereign,* the ship owned by Lady Prudence Daemira. He is 60 years of age.

Deirdre Dhaerhan (deer-DRUH DARE-hahn): Known as the "Jewel of Dakkadia", she is the youngest child of King Madari Dhaerhan and Queen Aveliad, Deirdre is betrothed to Prince Lain of Ferralin, the marriage to take place when she turns 17. She is a singer of exceptional talent, which brought her to the attention of Emperor Xan of Ferralin. She is currently 14 years of age.

Kirtland Frederick (KURT-land FRED-er-rik): First officer of the *Sovereign,* under the command of Lady Prudence Daemira.

Madari Dhaerhan (mah-DAR-ee DARE-hahn): King of Dakkadia. Youngest of three sons of the former king of Dakkadia, Dhaegus IX, Madari ascended to the throne of Dakkadia after the death of his father, by engineering the deaths of his older brothers. Currently 45 years of age.

Morvandis Dhaerhan (more-VAAN-dis DARE-hahn): Mage-Lord of Dakkadia and Duke of Cairengale, Morvandis is the bastard son of King Dhaegus IX, the former monarch of Dakkadia, and a courtesan of the Flower Court named Orchid. At the age of nine-years-old, Morvandis killed the former head of the Flower

Court by accident, and took his place as the Master of the Gardens. He is acknowledged as the most powerful Mage alive, and his abilities dwarf those of any other Mage save Chesare Illvanna, a novice at the Mage Citadel. He is also the Spymaster of Dakkadia, and King Madari's closest advisor. Currently 30 years of age.

Phaedron Daane (FAY-drun DANE): Earl of Daane and son of Queen Aveliad and her first husband, Lord Phaedril Daane. Phaedron is an expert horseman, swordsman, and marksman. He holds the rank of Master of the Light Horse in the Dakkadian army, roughly equivalent to a brigadier general. Phaedron is also a Waterborn of exceptional power, and holds the rank of Mage, granted after his successful Testing at the Mage Citadel. Currently 20 years old.

Prudence Daemira (PROO-dense DAY-MEER-uh): Also known as the "Corsair", Lady Prudence is the youngest sibling of Sethred Daemira, Prince of Rohm. Choosing military life over a life as a pampered princess, Prudence enlisted in the Dakkadian military where she chose service in the Navy. Through sheer merit, she progressed through the ranks very quickly until she reached the rank of Captain. When Dakkadia found itself in a covert war with Illymar and in need of privateers who could fight where the true military could not, Prudence volunteered for the duty and was "discharged" from service. As a private citizen, she then "purchased" a new-build warship of a previously unseen class from the Dakkadian navy named the *Sovereign*, and has since singlehandedly cut a swath through the Illymari navy, who consider her to be little more than a pirate. She is currently 25-years-old.

Rory Sornin (ROAR-ee SORE-nin): Air Mage in the service of Dakkadia. He is currently assigned to the *Sovereign,* the ship owned by Lady Prudence Daemira. He is 27-years-old.

Sethred Daemira (SETH-red DAY-MEER-uh): Prince of Rohm, he is the ruler of the Dakkadian province of Rohm. Prince Sethred is the older brother of Prudence Daemira, the Corsair and the younger brother of Duchess Danae DeVir, wife of Prince Brendenn DeVir. As a soldier in the Dakkadian military, he holds the rank of Master of the Halberdiers, a rank equivalent to Lieutenant General. He is currently 30 years of age.

Thanarilliad Demestira (than-uh-RILL-ee-add dem-mest-TEER-ah): Earl of Demestira, Thanarilliad is the bastard son of King Dhaegus IX, and half-brother of King Madari Dhaerhan and Mage-Lord Morvandis. As a reward for his mother's support for Madari in his bid for the Dakkadian crown, Madari legitimized Thanarilliad's birth and allowed him to inherit his mother's estates and titles. He is married to Thorn Demestira, a former courtesan from the Flower Court. Thanarilliad is currently 26 years of age.

Thorn Demestira (thorn dem-mest-TEER-ah) Countess Demestira and wife of Thanarilliad Demestira, Thorn is a former courtesan from the Dakkadian Flower Court. Specializing in sadomasochism, bondage, and domination, Thorn left the Flower Court to marry Thanarilliad, though she remains active in Dakkadian service as a spy. She is currently 25 years of age.

Valeriad Dhaerhan (vuh-LAIR-ee-add DARE-hahn): Oldest son of King Madari Dhaerhan and second son of Madari's wife, Queen Aveliad, Valeriad is the Crown Prince of Dakkadia, and holds the rank of Master of Artillery in the Dakkadian army, roughly equivalent to a Colonel. He is currently 17 years of age. Valeriad is also a Fireborn of exceptional power, and holds the rank of Mage, granted after his successful Testing at the Mage Citadel.

THE EMPIRE OF FERRALIN

Lain (LAYN): Crown Prince of Ferralin. Only son of Emperor Xan of Ferralin, and a young noblewoman named Tahani (deceased), he has been the ruler of Ferralin in all but name for over ten years. He was engaged to marry Princess Tais Illvanna of Illymar, and when that engagement ended due to scandal, he was in turn engaged to marry her sister, Princess Lyrahe Illvanna of Illymar. That engagement was broken off at his father's command, in favor of a marriage with Princess Deirdre Dhaerhan of Dakkadia in order to cement an alliance. He is currently 23 years of age.

Shar (SHAAR): Grand Vizier of Ferralin. Chief advisor to both Emperor Xan of Ferralin and his son, Prince Lain, he is an Air Mage of great power. Currently 45 years of age.

Tahani (tah-HAWN-ee): Wife of Emperor Xan, and mother of Crown Prince Lain. She was murdered by her husband four years after giving birth to Prince Lain.

Xan (ZAN): Emperor of Ferralin. He is currently 76-years-old, and has been the absolute ruler of Ferralin for 60 years. In his later years he has lost his hold on sanity and began to victimize and murder young children. Though quite mad, he is still an excellent ruler, and through his guidance Ferralin has had 60 unbroken years of peace and prosperity.

THE MAGE HIGH COUNCIL OF ITHRAM

Se-ir Windwhisper (SAY-year WIND-whispur): First Seat of the Mage High Council of Ithram, and holds the permanent rank of Archimagus. An Elf born in the Elvish capital city of Cyn'Lariath, he traveled to the city of Ithram for training when he learned that he was a Powerborn. He is both an Air Mage and a Fire Mage. Currently 850 years of age.

Tavian Two-Blade (TAV-EE-enn TWO-blade): Second Seat of the Mage High Council of Ithram. An elf born in the Elvish city of Cyn'Carath, Tavian is both an Air Mage and a Fire Mage. Currently 450-years-old, he holds the permanent rank of Archimagus. He is the older brother of Archimagus Enaria Wintersong.

Enaria Wintersong (EE-NAR-EE-uh WINTER-song): Third Seat of the Mage High Council of Ithram, and younger sister of Tavian Two-Blade, the Second Seat of the Mage High Council of Ithram, she is both an Air and Fire Mage, though she is also secretly a master of heretical Blood Magic. An Elf born in the Elvish city of Cyn'Carath, Enaria holds the permanent title of Archimagus, and is currently 300-years-old.

Kyaran (KEY-YAR-uhn): Fourth seat of the Mage High Council of Ithram Kyaran is a Faeborn. Her history and place of birth is unknown, though she is both a Water Mage and Air Mage. She holds the permanent title of Archimagus.

Etienne Giradon (ET-TEE-enn GEAR-uh-dawn): Fifth Seat of the Mage High Council of Ithram, Etienne is a human Fire Mage, born in the city of Karraldazaar, located on the eastern edge of the Badlands. Etienne holds the permanent title of Archimagus, and is currently 54 years of age.

Syad Bahr (SIGH-add BEAR): Sixth Seat of the Mage High Council of Ithram, Syad is a human Water Mage born in Ferralin. He holds the permanent title of Archimagus, and is currently 45 years of age.

Lirielle (LEER-EE-ell): Seventh Seat of the Mage High Council of Ithram, Lirielle is a Faeborn Air Mage. Her history and place of birth is unknown, although she is also a secret practitioner of heretical Blood Magic, which she is studying under the tutelage of Archimagus Enaria Wintersong. Lirielle holds the permanent title of Archimagus.

Cedric DeVir (SED-rick da-VEER): Eighth Seat of the Mage High Council of Ithram, Cedric is a Fire Mage born in the Principality of Palantine. Younger brother of Prince Brendenn DeVir of Palantine, he is also the half-brother of Queen Aveliad of Dakkadia. He holds the permanent title of Archimagus, and is currently 41-years-old.

THE ZARRYIOSTROM

Ephraim Semarill (EFF-fraime SEM-ma-ril): Archidraconus and High Inquisitor of the Zarryiostrom, Ephraim is the Patriarch's most trusted advisor. Trained to recognize deception no matter how well-disguised, he serves as an Investigator when crimes against the Zarryiostrom or their interests are committed. Born in the city of Shahalizaar in the Badlands, he is currently 55 years old.

Samuel Varic (SAM-myu-el VARE-ik): Patriarch of the Zarryiostrom and the head of the Church of Zarryiosiad, Samuel Varic is the most powerful member of the church. Currently 62 years of age.

Zarryiosiad (zarr-EE-ah-see-odd): Known to the general population as the Archon, and to the Dragon Witches as the Harbinger, Zarryiosiad is considered to be the savior and liberator of the human race, after she destroyed the evil race of Earthborn Fae known as the Lyx and freed humanity from their enslavement 2500 years ago. The Church of Zarryiosiad is one of the oldest and most influential human institutions, and its adherents consider Zarryiosiad to be a goddess. Zarryiosiad was the single most powerful Mage ever born until the birth of Mage-Lord Morvandis of Dakkadia. She was slain in what is now known as the Valley of Fire by the Dragon Lord Severius after she transformed herself into a silver dragon and destroyed the entire race of Lyx in a single instant.

Zarus (ZARR-us): Known as the "Liberator", Zarus was a Water Mage responsible for leading a successful uprising of slaves against their captors, the Lyx. He discovered the island of Il'Amhar (now Illymar) and relocated his freed slaves upon it. Father of Zarryiosiad, he was later murdered by assassins in the employ of the Lyx emissaries of the Lyx.

MISCELLANEOUS LOCATIONS AND ITEMS OF INTEREST

Black Ships: Secret Illymari treasure galleons that bring gold and precious gems from a hidden location once every three months. Only two Black Ships have ever been successfully captured, both by Lady Prudence Daemira, the Corsair.

Lyx: Literal translation, "Earth Demon" or "Demon of the Wind", Lyx is a name used by the Zarryiostrom to describe the Earthborn Fae who enslaved humanity before the birth of Zarus the Liberator and his daughter, Zarryiosiad the Archon. The Lyx were insane, and their insanity usually manifested itself in the form of megalomania and delusions of godhood. The entire race of Lyx was destroyed by Zarryiosiad at the Valley of Fire.

Fallen: Collective name for anyone who uses heretical Blood Magic.

Lexicon of Purifying Flame: The holiest book of the Zarryiostrom, it was written by Zarryiosiad's oldest son, Zaharrik, shortly after his mother's death. Responsible for the creation of both the Zarryiostrom and the Mage Citadel, Zaharrik is considered to be one of the most influential people in human history, behind only his mother and his grandfather.

Throne of Obsidian: Zarryiosiad's personal throne, it is a large black chair with a high back made of a single piece of obsidian, covered with carvings of animals. The armrests are carved to look like two roaring lion heads. To people born without the ability to use magic, or to Powerborn who can only use one, two, or three powers, the Throne is a normal chair with no special properties. To anyone who can wield all four powers as Zarryiosiad could, the chair becomes a weapon of surpassing power providing the Mage attempting to access the chair has the strength to empower it. Once activated, it grants the user the ability to not only see anywhere within the borders of the Teeth of Amhar, but to project Mage abilities as if he or she were physically present.

Teeth of Amhar: A ring of sharp monoliths made of flawless white stone hundreds of feet high that surround the island of Illymar, spaced dozens of miles apart in a perfect ring. Created by Zarryiosiad over 2500 years ago, the Teeth contain an interlocking series of spells of immense complexity that utilize all four Powers, which are capable of destroying any vessel trying to pass between the monoliths. This defensive shield has successfully prevented any invasion of Illymar from succeeding for over 2500 years.

Valley of Fire: Legendary site of the final battle of Zarryiosiad. It is in this place that the combined armies of the Lyx who had survived Zarryiosiad's 400 year campaign to destroy their kind fought their final battle against Zarryiosiad's army. It was during this battle that the Dragon Lord Severius slew Furionchires, the Queen of Battles, Zarryiosiad's lover, Kalindral, and finally Zarryiosiad herself after she had transformed herself into a dragon and destroyed both her own army and the army of the Lyx with a single blast of dragonfire. The location of the Valley of Fire is unknown, as is the location of Zarryiosiad's final resting place.

White Wall: A wall of unblemished white stone twenty feet high, 20 feet thick and hundreds of feet long that surrounds the Cathedral of Zarryiosiad. Originally created by Zarryiosiad using Earth Magic to surround her father's estate on Il'Amhar, it was meant to protect her aging father and allow him privacy. After the death of Zarryiosiad, her children donated the site to the newly created Church of Zarryiosiad as the location of the great Cathedral of Zarryiosiad. The wall has stood for over 2900 years, and is still perfect in every way.

Printed in Great Britain
by Amazon

46244219R00307